"He'll never get round that bunch," Amelia said.

"He doesn't have to," Leander cried. "There's a gap on the rails . . . you could drive a bus through it."

"I don't think Michael's seen it," Emma said, starting to twist her handkerchief into a tourniquet.

"Yes, he has!" Leander shouted. "Come on, Michael, it's easy!"

It was anything but: for twenty nerve-racking seconds, during which everyone stared at the screen in wide-eyed silence, it was touch and go. Not until the rising ground of the last fifty yards did Quartermaster get his nose in front.

"That will do!" Leander said, clapping her hands.

"We are going to have champagne," Leander went on. "And I shall stay up very late. So there!"

Laughing, Amelia did not attempt to contradict her.

As Bess prepared to leave, Leander beckoned to her. "Isn't it wonderful, my dear?" she said. "We've won the Derby on your sixteenth birthday!"

Bess knelt down at her feet and their hands clasped tightly. "That's what happened to you," Bess said.

"Yes, with Bellerophon . . . and there have been ten others." There was a fierce intensity in Leander's eyes as she spoke in a voice that none of the others could hear. "I shan't see any more, but you will, Bess. You will!"

**Also by the same author,
and available from Coronet:**

THE BLUE RIBAND
WITH MAGIC IN HER EYES

About the author

Derek Nicholls was born in Birmingham and educated there and at Durham University. His grandfather was a racehorse trainer in Co. Kildare, Ireland, and the author has been a racing enthusiast from an early age. His first novel, THE BLUE RIBAND, was published to acclaim and was shortlisted for the Boots Romantic Novel of the Year Award. WITH MAGIC IN HER EYES, is his second novel. HEIRS TO ADVENTURE is his third novel which carries the story of Latimer's Barn to the present day.

HEIRS TO ADVENTURE

DEREK NICHOLLS

CORONET BOOKS
Hodder and Stoughton

First published in Great Britain in
1992 by Hodder and Stoughton Ltd

Coronet edition 1993

British Library C.I.P.
Nicholls, Derek
  Heirs to adventure.
  I. Title
  823[F]

ISBN 0 340 58024 0

Printed and bound in Great Britain for
Hodder and Stoughton Paperbacks, a
division of Hodder and Stoughton Ltd,
Mill Road, Dunton Green, Sevenoaks,
Kent TN13 2YA (Editorial Office: 47
Bedford Square, London WC1B 3DP) by
Clays Ltd, St Ives plc. Typeset by Hewer
Text Composition Services, Edinburgh.

For
John Griffith

Who put the fear of God up me when he disappeared
into an alarmingly murky Wiltshire night in 1958.
Happily, he returned to be a splendid friend.

LATIMER'S BARN
1939–1990

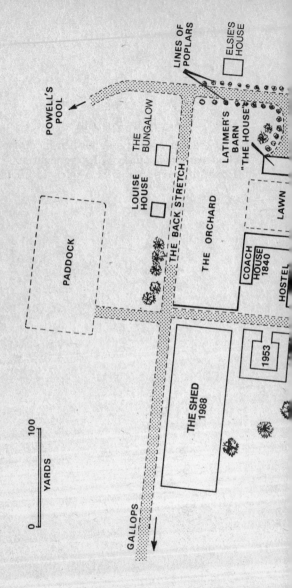

YARDS

0   100

N

POWELL'S POOL

PADDOCK

THE BUNGALOW

LOUISE HOUSE

THE BACK STRETCH

THE ORCHARD

LINES OF POPLARS

ELSIE'S HOUSE

LATIMER'S BARN "THE HOUSE"

LAWN

COACH HOUSE 1840

HOSTEL

1953

THE SHED 1988

GALLOPS

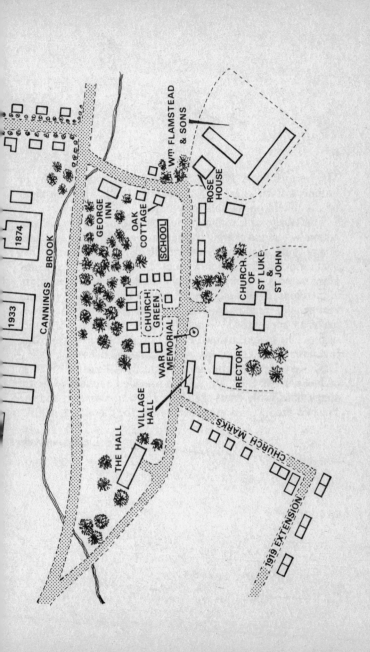

CANNINGS BROOK

1874

1933

Wᵐ FLAMSTEAD & SONS

ROSE HOUSE

GEORGE INN

OAK COTTAGE

SCHOOL

CHURCH GREEN

WAR MEMORIAL

CHURCH OF ST LUKE & ST JOHN

RECTORY

THE HALL

VILLAGE HALL

CHURCH MARKS

1919 EXTENSION

Author's Note

My previous book, *With Magic in Her Eyes*, took the story of Latimer's Barn as far as 3 September 1939. This one picks up the thread on the following day.

The village of Cannings Ambo is a figment of my imagination – but those who happen to pass that way will find a very good site for it a mile west of Marlborough on the south side of the A4 to Calne! The village's inhabitants, Hawksworths, Flamsteeds, their employees and friends are all fictitious. They do, however, have a habit of bumping into real people. In addition, one or two of Racing's great horses make an appearance. Generally happy to adjust the history of the Turf to suit my own ends, I drew the line at depriving my hero, Mill Reef, of his magnificent 1971 season.

My very special thanks go to Anna Powell and Bill Massey of Hodder and Stoughton. Anna provided a wealth of useful suggestions while I was sketching *Heirs to Adventure*, and the finished product is a great deal better for the efforts of Bill.

Derek Nicholls

CHAPTER 1

1939

'Hey, Mom, is that Queen Mary?'

Bess Collier arrived in Wiltshire on Monday, 4 September 1939, the day after war was supposed to have broken out. She was three months old and had no idea what was happening.

Bess's mother, Elsie, was jauntily cheerful about it. Unlike the desperately worried crowd around her, she was grateful to Hitler for driving them out of London's East End. The pompous functionaries with bowler hats, clip-boards and rigmaroles of jargon had saved her the trouble of making a decision, or of having to argue the toss with her in-laws. Ordered to Paddington station, already further west than Elsie's twenty-six years had ever taken her, they had been shoved on to a train with five hundred other evacuees, and here they were, at Chippenham.

It was pandemonium. As they all spilled out on the platform and struggled to get through the narrow exit, anxiety boiled up into panic. Unruffled, Elsie cradled the sleeping Bess in one arm and grabbed the enormous suitcase that was held together with an old clothes line. Determined not to let the responsibility get on top of him, six-year-old Joe staggered under the weight of a rucksack nearly as big as himself and took a carrier-bag in each hand. They tottered five yards to a massive oaken trolley and dumped everything, except Bess, on it.

Elsie stood back, checking. The big case, the rucksack and

1

two carriers contained all their worldly goods. What had been left behind was of no account because, come what may, they were never going back.

"Typical! It's Marjorie Featherstone-Dudley, you know! She's even worse than her blasted husband."

Clementine, Duchess of Laverstoke, surveyed the chaos in the station yard and drew several ominously deep breaths. Baines, her chauffeur, who had driven as close to the shambles as he dared, had the horrible feeling that it was going to be one of Her Grace's more alarming days. Slowly, he began to disappear from view. Despite his constant prayers, the earth had never opened to swallow Baines, but he had perfected a method of slithering into obscurity below the Rolls-Royce's high windows.

Mrs Featherstone-Dudley had turned confusion into mayhem by putting herself in charge of the evacuees, the thirty twittering members of the WVS who were supposed to be helping them, and the motley collection of charabancs, lorries and farm carts waiting to take the newcomers to their war-time billets.

The Duchess soon spotted that there was no plan. Most of the villages within a ten-mile radius had sent one or more vehicles. Evacuees were loaded as they emerged from the booking-hall: when the lorry, or whatever, was full, off it went. That was the theory. Mrs Featherstone-Dudley had other ideas.

Eventually, common sense began to break out. People got the hang of ignoring Mrs Featherstone-Dudley, the departures increased in frequency, the station yard began to empty and the Duchess decided that it was time to call up Jeremiah Barnfather, commandeered for the day, along with his bus, from Compton Bassett. To do so, she clambered on to a pile of crates and gesticulated flamboyantly. When this failed, she stuck two fingers into her mouth and produced a piercing whistle that galvanised half the town as well as the dozing Jeremiah.

About to return to pavement level, the Duchess was startled

to hear a bright voice say, "Cor, you ain't 'arf got the 'ang of that, Missis!" Turning, she found herself regarded incuriously by a vivacious pair of eyes. Clementine Prideaux and Elsie Collier, perched on the trolley to look over the wall, examined each other.

"Are you with this lot?" the Duchess asked.

"Yes."

"Well, you'd better hurry up! There's only my coach and Wilkinson's stinking old rattle-trap left."

"I'll be as quick as I can, but the case weighs a ton, Joe's on his knees, and I got this one." Elsie held up the shawl-wrapped bundle that was Bess.

At that moment, a churlishly officious voice came from behind Elsie. "Now then, you get off that trolley, there's a good woman. You're trespassing on company property!"

The Duchess recognised the voice. "Catchpole, I've got a job for you!" she bawled.

Scrambling up beside Elsie, the porter stuck his head over the wall, removed his cap, smiled sheepishly and said, "'Afternoon, Your Grace. Turned out nice again."

"Never mind that! Stop acting like a bloody Nazi and give these people a hand."

By the time Elsie came out of the booking-hall, she seemed a changed person. Joe was quite worried by the transformation that the brief, muttered conversation with the porter had produced in her. However, there was no time for worrying; they were bustled towards the charabanc, only to find Jeremiah Barnfather barring their way.

"We'm full up," he intoned with doleful glee.

The Duchess saw that the coach was indeed packed solid. "You have room for three more," she said defiantly.

"No, I haven't. You know the rules."

"This is a national emergency!"

"Rules is still rules."

"You always were an obstreperous bugger, Barnfather," the Duchess fumed. "Your father was the same. All right, be off with you. Make sure you report to the office when you get there – I don't want you blundering all over the place with those people." Without pausing for breath, she generated another ear-splitting whistle: a mortified Baines brought the Rolls alongside and Catchpole assisted with the loading.

They were almost out of the town before Elsie plucked up the courage to speak. "Begging your pardon, ma'am," she said. "That chap wot lugged the bags says you're a duchess."

"Yes, I am."

There might have been an awkward hiatus had not Bess chosen that moment to wake. Finding herself staring at the Duchess's finely chiselled features, she gurgled and smiled.

"What a beautiful child," Clementine Prideaux said.

"She is, ain't she?" Elsie replied proudly. "I have to say it, though it's mostly her dad. He was an 'andsome bleeder."

"*Was*?" the Duchess asked carefully, prepared to offer sympathy.

"Probably still is for all I know or care!" Elsie shrugged the question into oblivion and settled down to admire the scenery. Joe shared her wide-eyed astonishment.

"Look at all them trees, Mom," he whispered, and Elsie squeezed his hand, as if to say, "I know. Ain't it bleeding marvellous!"

She had never seen so much green. A few minutes later, they entered Eaton Mandeville through a pair of magnificent gates as high as a house, and they were in fairy-land. The estate consisted of three thousand acres of lush park with woods of oak and beech and one of the finest Tudor mansions in England, home of the Prideaux family for goodness knows how long and the seat of the Dukes of Laverstoke since 1716.

The charabanc had discharged its passengers at a Georgian building set apart from the main house. Argument and uproar already reigned supreme. "Step on it, Baines!" the Duchess ordered. "That lot wants sorting out."

As she sallied forth, Elsie sat back in the Rolls and grinned broadly at her children. Things were probably going to take a while to settle down, but if this was the countryside she'd heard so much about, London would be very lucky to see her again, even for a day trip.

*   *   *

There were many reasons why it took the Duchess of Laverstoke over a week to discover that she had more evacuees than Eaton Mandeville could handle.

Hubert, her husband, was away until nearly midnight on Friday, dealing with pressing matters in the House of Lords and at the War Office. On his return, he was dispirited.

"Chamberlain may have found the gumption to declare war, but the poor devil hasn't got a clue what to do now," he said.

"At least he's put Winston in charge at the Admiralty."

"It's something, I suppose," the Duke sighed. "Apparently Churchill wanted to drop mines in the Rhine, but Kingsley Wood refused. Said if he started that, there was no telling where it would end."

Where indeed, the Duchess wondered: it was a fearful worry.

And, on top of everything, she became a grandmother for the second time in the early hours of Friday, 8 September.

The birth was to Rachel, wife of the Duke and Duchess's eldest son, Charles, Marquess of Glastonbury. The infant Lord Edmund Prideaux appeared at a quarter past two in the morning, gave a token bawl, and promptly fell asleep in his mother's arms. The Duchess sat with her daughter-in-law in the west-wing bedroom until the first signs of dawn appeared, then went back to the ducal quarters in the main part of the house. She was well-pleased, and knew that the Duke would share the sense of security she felt at having two grandsons. The continuance of the title into the twenty-first century was important to both of them.

Thus it was that a mixture of stress and excitement clouded the issue of the evacuees until Sunday afternoon, when the Duchess's housekeeper insisted on presenting a report.

"We have thirty-eight children and three mothers on the premises, Your Grace. That's too many."

"How many ought we to send somewhere else?" the Duchess asked.

"Six children."

"Lady Milton will have them over at Malmesbury," the Duchess announced confidently.

"Then there are those people we had to put in the cottages at Baxter's Spinney," Mrs Travers went on.

"Mm. Yes." That *was* a problem. The cottages were isolated, without mains water or electricity and in poor repair. The Duchess suspected that Elsie Collier and her baby had ended up in one of them. "They're hovels, aren't they?" she asked.

"*I* think so, Your Grace."

After skilful preparation of the ground, the Duchess broached the topic with the Duke over tea. "Hubert, I don't suppose you'd care to have that pair of houses at Baxter's Spinney done up?" she asked in an offhand sort of voice.

"Oh, no, my dear. If it hadn't been for this blasted war, I was thinking of demolition." His bland gaze suddenly focused into amused suspicion. "Don't tell me you've got evacuees in *them*?"

"I'm afraid so."

"The roofs are unsound, you know. When it starts raining there'll be a shocking mess."

"What am I going to do with the poor souls?"

"Tell me, are we expecting a visit from Edmund's great-grandmother?" he asked.

"Tomorrow."

"She'll take them off your hands. She's always keen enough to pull her weight."

The Duchess beamed happily. "That's it, Hubert! You're absolutely right."

In all honesty, the Baxter's Spinney cottages were fairly dreadful, yet Elsie thought she was in paradise.

Although the conditions were spartan, the setting was idyllic. There was no traffic, no noise, no smell. Instead, there were birds, hundreds of the chirpy little bleeders, all shapes and sizes and different sorts. Joe was going to have a whale of a time finding out which was what: he'd already

6

decided that the funny furry things that scarpered up and down the trees must be squirrels. Genuine fresh air and a sun undimmed by clouds of filth were just the job for Bess. The only fly in the ointment was that the isolation seemed to make long-term prospects dodgy: Elsie wanted work.

On the Monday afternoon that began their second week in Wiltshire, Elsie was outside, belabouring the ancient water pump into life, when two Rolls-Royces came to rest in front of the cottage. The first, driven by Baines, contained the Duchess. The other, under the command of a man who looked formidably fit despite being nearly seventy, conveyed two ladies of obvious quality.

The elder of the two stepped down with nimble grace and a frank, calm stare at the scene confronting her. Her trim figure and upright stance somehow made complete sense of the fact that she appeared to be dressed for a Royal Ascot of fifty years ago.

Cor, blimey! Elsie thought to herself. *She definitely ain't no spring chicken, but she looks a treat.*

Joe was inspired to go further. "Hey, Mom, is that Queen Mary?" he asked in a hoarse whisper.

Hearing him, the old lady smiled, her blue eyes lighting as she did so. "Her Majesty would be most aggrieved at that, young man," she said. "Apart from everything else, she's seven years younger than me . . . that's a lot, you know." There was a slight pause before she said, "I'm Leander Hawksworth, and I'm taking you to Cannings Ambo."

For the first time in her life, Elsie was ashamed of her ignorance. "I felt a proper fool," she used to tell people in later years. "Imagine me not knowing who she was!"

The move took place the following day. Cyril Osgood, the chauffeur of the previous afternoon, came to fetch them with a lorry. Elsie was tickled pink. There were deck-chairs for them to sit on and the guarantee of a good view over the sideboards. Joe thought it was classy.

Skirting Chippenham, with Cyril keeping his promise not to exceed twenty miles an hour, they came to Calne, where,

7

to Elsie's vociferous amusement, signs proclaimed that bacon was produced from contented pigs in the Harris factory. Beyond Quemerford, they were climbing to the highest point on the London to Bath road, past the white horse at Cherhill, to the summit that gave Elsie her first sight of the Downs.

At West Overton, they saw workmen removing the boards from a sign-post. Elsie had read about it in her dad's *Daily Herald*: "That's to confuse the Jerries," she told Bess, now awake and taking an interest.

Another mile and they turned right through lush water-meadows. There was a village ahead; Elsie saw the church tower on one side and the outline of an imposing house, screened by poplar trees, was visible on the other. A little before the lane divided, with Cyril taking the left fork, Elsie had a view up a drive and saw that the poplars were in twin ranks, lining both sides. Beyond them, the roofs of two handsome structures were adorned with the distinctive ventilator cowlings that indicated stables. It was the famous Latimer's Barn.

Now, however, they were passing The George Inn and Oak Cottage. Then came Rose House, the headquarters of Wm Flamsteed & Sons, 'Makers of Fine Furniture', the sign said. Church Green, with its well-kept gardens, faced the fourteenth-century church of St Luke and St John, and they saw the War Memorial and Village Hall. Finally, after passing the entrance to Church Marks, the lorry eased into the gravelled drive of The Hall, where Leander Hawksworth herself was waiting to greet them.

She introduced her two companions. "These good folk are Ann and Sam Briggs who will be looking after you until you've settled in and learned to fend for yourselves." Sam, an old soldier of seventy-five, and Ann, a young-looking sixty, smiled up at Elsie and recognised a kindred spirit, albeit one not knowing what to do next.

Seeing Elsie's problem, Leander stepped forward, her arms extended. "Give her to me," she said quietly, but in a tone that expected instant obedience. Unhesitatingly, Elsie passed Bess down.

She and Leander gazed at each other with two pairs of very nearly identical blue eyes; Leander was struck by the most powerful sense of affinity.

"Isn't she gorgeous," she said to Elsie, who was rewarding Sam with a dazzling smile and a wink for helping her down. "How old is she?"

"Just over three months," Elsie replied. "June the first she turned up."

"*Really?*" Leander's face shone, creating the illusion that at least forty years had fallen away from her. "She was born on the first of June?"

"'Sright!"

"Well, well!" Leander shook her head, gazing at Bess in wonder. "That's my birthday, too. Eighteen-sixty!"

'Strewth, that makes her seventy-nine! Elsie thought to herself.

"Tell me . . ." Leander was baffled by how and why the question had occurred to her, but that wasn't going to stop her asking it. "Has this child been baptised?"

"Er . . . no, ma'am," Elsie admitted. Joe was taken aback; he'd never seen his mother look *that* uncomfortable before.

"We must attend to it," Leander said. "And what about a perambulator and cot? Do you have those?"

Elsie shook her head.

"Leave that to me," Leander said. Somewhat unwillingly, she handed Bess back.

An hour later, while Elsie was still taking in her palatial surroundings, Cyril returned, this time with a horse and cart because of the petrol shortage. The pram was of 1912 vintage and had, Cyril explained, been given by Mrs Emma Hawksworth, the lady accompanying *the* Mrs Hawksworth on yesterday's visit to Eaton Mandeville. It had been used for Rachel, now Marchioness of Glastonbury. Cyril knew nothing about the oak cradle: it was, in fact, the one in which Leander Hawksworth had slept as a child.

That evening, after Elsie had put Bess and Joe to bed, she went downstairs to help Ann and Sam in the kitchen. Glad of her assistance, they were happy to talk freely about the history of the village they loved so dearly.

By the time she went upstairs at half past eleven, Elsie had heard the whole story and absorbed most of it. The two families who mattered, Hawksworths and Flamsteeds, were descended from Giles Flamsteed, once the heir to a well-established wine-merchant's in Greenwich. In 1859, when the family received the two-thousand acre Cannings Ambo estate as a bequest to settle a debt, Giles had decided to turn himself into a racehorse trainer. His first winner had appeared on 1 June 1860, the day his daughter, Leander, was born. A little over a year later, Giles's wife had died giving birth to William. Elisabeth Flamsteed, Giles's sister, had come to look after the children, eventually marrying the vicar. The present incumbent, the Reverend John Shepherd, was their son.

Leander married Steven Hawksworth, the young man on a bicycle from Pewsey Wharf, while William took Ruth Burgoyne, also from Pewsey, as his wife. Leander and Steven ran the stable, William set up a furniture-making business in a shed at the back of Rose House and everything had flowed from the two families and their enterprises. Ann made it sound so easy and straightforward, but there were clearly troubles beneath the placid surface. Leander's eldest son, George, had been packed off to South Africa thirty years ago and William's daughter, Maude, went to live in Paris in circumstances that were obviously scandalous. And the Great War had treated the village particularly harshly: Sam reckoned that if the whole country had sustained the same proportion of losses as Cannings Ambo, there would have been ten million dead instead of one million, or whatever it was supposed to be. Now, it was starting all over again.

Elsie was as worried as anyone about this new war, but she was bright and breezy the following morning when she saw to her children, cleared up everybody's breakfast things, arranged for Ann to keep an eye on Bess and Joe, and set off for Latimer's Barn. Hurrying up the long drive, Elsie collected her thoughts, remembering the important facts. It was called 'The House' with very big capital letters, and no one *ever* went to the front door; that had been taboo since the dismal November night in 1917 when wreaths had been piled high in the porch as a tribute to Leander's other son, Giles, killed at Passchendaele and awarded the Victoria Cross.

There was a bustling crowd at the back door that might have fazed a lesser person than Elsie. War meant uncertainty for racing; for the moment, however, there was no viable alternative to carrying on with normal stable routine and hoping for the best. Elsie had arrived at the conclusion of breakfast and found herself in the midst of plans to get the second lot of horses out to the gallops on Cannings Down. As she hesitated, uncertain how to interrupt the half-dozen men who were far too preoccupied to take any notice of her, a friendly female voice said, "Good morning, Elsie. Can I help you?"

It was Mrs Emma Hawksworth, the widow of Major Giles.

"I was wondering if I could have a word with Mrs Hawksworth, please, Mrs Hawksworth," she said, feeling silly.

"Of course. Come along." Elsie found herself guided through a huge kitchen.

Leander was in the small sitting-room, breakfasting on tea and toast, frowning at yesterday's newspaper. She seemed glad of the interruption.

"Good morning, Elsie. What brings you here?"

"I want a job."

Elsie could have kicked herself. She was so tense that the request, rushed out in response to a direct question, sounded like a rather graceless demand. At first, Leander's appraising stare was alarming; then she nodded and said, "Sit down and tell me all about it."

"It's like this, ma'am," Elsie said, collapsing gratefully on to the sofa beside Leander. "I ain't never going back to London!"

"What does your husband think about that?" Leander asked, leaving Elsie in no doubt that she always went straight to the heart of the matter.

11

"I don't know and I couldn't care less. He cleared off again the week before I had Bess."

"*Again?*"

"'Sright." Thinking about it, Elsie realised that she had lost count. "Seven years we been married and I reckon we must have spent over five of 'em apart."

Leander and Emma exchanged a brief glance: now they knew why there was such a difference in ages between Joe and Bess.

"Where were you living?" Leander asked.

Elsie looked grim. "Two rooms in Stepney. We had damp and vermin."

"That won't do at all," Leander said. "Yes, I'm sure we can find you a job. What are you good at?"

"All sorts!" Elsie replied, made chirpy again by the realisation that everything was going to be all right. "I'm a dab hand at cooking."

"Are you, now?"

Seeing how keen Leander's interest was, Elsie decided that qualification was necessary. "I only do plain stuff and pastry," she said. "But I used to look after a gentleman in Southwark when he threw a dinner-party."

"We don't go in for *fancy* food," Leander said, implying that to do otherwise smacked of criminal decadence. "In any case, we're going to be on very short commons when rationing starts." She turned to Emma. "What do you think, my dear?"

"I think we can kill two birds with one stone," Emma said.

Leander nodded. "You see, Elsie, we've got ourselves into a pickle over the last few years. A lot of our devoted friends have died and now we're in a mess with the War. The upshot is that with one thing and another, we don't have a cook here, in The House. Would you like to do that for us?"

Elsie was stunned. She had thought that there might be some cleaning or washing, but this was very different. "I'm not sure I'd be up to it, ma'am," she confessed.

Leander bathed her in a warming smile. "I daresay that

a good many people have thought that over the years," she said. "But very, *very* few have ever failed. Perhaps the way we do things here encourages success."

"I'll do it!" Elsie declared confidently. "You won't regret this, Mrs Hawksworth, I promise you."

"Excellent!" Leander said. "The rooms that Ellie Goakes used to have will be ideal for you and the children."

The flat used by Ellie, Leander's maid for nearly half a century, was at the eastern end of the ground floor and consisted of a sitting-room, two bedrooms, a kitchen, and, most wonderful of all, a bathroom. All the carpets were taken out to be beaten, men materialised out of thin air to paint everything, and new furniture appeared from Wm Flamsteed & Sons. Emma apologised for the fact that all the pieces were rejects: Elsie, who had only seen such quality on rare trips to gaze into Oxford Street's shop windows, refused to take notice of the minor faults, even when they were pointed out to her.

During the three days that the work was in progress, Joe was enrolled at the Village School and Bess was baptised by John Shepherd, with Leander, Emma and Matthew Flamsteed acting as her godparents.

Then, on the afternoon of 16 September, Elsie took Joe and Bess to their new quarters at Latimer's Barn. Within an hour of arriving, Elsie was hard at work.

Shortly after establishing herself in the kitchen, Elsie realised that she was in a most privileged position. Cooking was only one of the activities carried out in the vast room. From early morning until the end of evening stables at about six o'clock, an endless procession of people came in for mugs of tea and meals. They discussed everything from a strained fetlock, or a horse that was off its feed, to the progress of the War. Sooner or later – and it was mostly sooner – anyone of importance in Cannings Ambo passed through the kitchen. Elsie and Polly Izzard, the young girl who fetched and carried for her, picked up an endless stream of information and gossip.

In that third week of September, there were three major

13

concerns. In order of importance they were: when was Mr Steven going to enlist in the Navy, how was the War going to affect racing, and when was Neville Chamberlain going to *do* something? It was accepted that only time would provide answers to the last two questions, so all attention was fixed on Steven Hawksworth, Emma's son, the man who held the licence to train and was thus the most important person at Latimer's Barn.

Elsie soon discovered that he was an odds-on certainty to volunteer rather than wait for conscription.

"That Hitler's really upset Mr Steven," Polly said. "He reckons we've got to sort him out, or our lives won't be worth a farthing. You see, he'll join the Navy."

Elsie learned that, as well as knowing all about horses, Steven had considerable experience of navigation. Norman Redmayne, a Marlborough architect, had an eighty-ton schooner, *Merry Dance*, at Lymington on the Solent. Norman was always grateful for help in taking his pride and joy to sea and Steven had become a regular weekend sailor when he was thirteen. At sixteen, on a three-week holiday, he had navigated to Gibraltar and back: thereafter, his skill was a by-word.

Only Emma, in whom Steven always confided, knew of the girl who nearly upset the apple-cart. Norman Redmayne had two children: Clive, the eldest, was Steven's exact contemporary and school-friend. Ann, three years younger, and once dismissed as a pestilential nuisance, grew into a beautiful girl who occasionally sailed on the *Merry Dance*, playing havoc with Steven's emotions, but also turning him into a tongue-tied twerp. Emma thought that it was all for the best when Ann Redmayne faded away to spend a year in Canada before joining her father's firm as a secretary. Steven, now twenty-six, was known to have been mildly involved with several girls since, though they had all been kept at arm's length. According to Polly Izzard, any Hawksworth or Flamsteed man was in much the same position as royalty when it came to marriage: they had to be very careful who they chose. Still resentful of the mess King Edward VIII had got himself into with the dreadful Mrs Simpson, Elsie understood perfectly.

She had already discovered that would-be gold-diggers stood no chance of success. Since 1886, ownership of land, houses and money had been vested in a board of Trustees, who, as individuals, did not have personal wealth. It was rumoured that Steven drew a salary of £600 a year, a bit more than the average bank manager, but nowhere near what most people would have imagined.

The speculation about his intentions came to an abrupt end much sooner than anyone had expected. On 18 September, leaving the head lad, Alfred Merriweather, to supervise the morning's work with the horses, Steven drove to the recruiting offices in Swindon. William and John Flamsteed, the sons of Matthew and Louise at Rose House, went with him.

The bare facts were common knowledge by lunch-time. John Flamsteed was joining the Army, William was going to the RAF, probably as a pilot, and the Royal Navy had accepted Steven. Apparently, the only delay in processing his application had been caused by the Senior Service's initial reluctance to accept the 'irregular' spelling of his name with a 'v' instead of 'ph'. The parish clerk who registered the birth of the original Steven Hawksworth, Leander's husband, had made a mistake that was now enshrined in family tradition. Eventually, the Royal Navy had condescended to accept this strange state of affairs and ordered its new recruit to report to Rosyth on the Firth of Forth by eighteen hundred hours on Saturday.

"How are we going to manage without him?" Elsie asked Polly. "This sounds dead serious."

"They'll cope," Polly said. "It'll be the same as last time . . . my dad says it was easy. Mrs Hawksworth will sort it all out."

In the event, there was no need for Leander to do anything.

When Matthew Flamsteed arrived at The House, he found everyone he wanted in the kitchen: Leander, Emma, Steven and Alfred Merriweather were in conference. Elsie, honoured that her table should be used for such important matters, was working happily in the background.

"I've come to give myself up," Matthew said. "You'll be looking for a muggins to hold the licence."

A look of intense relief swept across Leander's face. "You are a good boy," she said, holding out a hand that he clasped warmly. "I think we were just about reaching the stage where I was going to be detailed to *tell* you that you were doing the job!" Smiling mischievously, Steven nodded.

"Actually, it doesn't seem as though I shall have much to do, does it?" Matthew asked.

"Not at the moment." Steven was disapproving. The outbreak of war had caused the immediate cancellation of all racing, an unnecessary panic measure that had created an upsurge of ill-will against the authorities. "The feeling is that they'll *have* to allow some racing next year – even if it's only at Newmarket," Steven added.

"Don't worry," Leander told Matthew. "We'll find someone who can tell you how to go about things." In response to his questioning look, she shook her head. "No, we don't have the faintest idea who it will be. You might end up with me cracking the whip."

"That would be ideal," Matthew said.

"I'm afraid I was joking, my dear." Leander was wistful. "It will have to be someone who can ride out on the gallops. I do pretty well, but I can't manage *that*. What about *your* business? Will it be all right without you?"

Matthew grinned ruefully. "I can't see there being any business . . . if there is, Fred and Young Jim can cope."

Later, when she and Polly were alone in the kitchen, Elsie asked about the two new names.

Fred Cartwright had talked himself into a job with Wm Flamsteed & Sons in 1897 and married Tish Merriweather, daughter of the legendary Abraham, a year after moving to Cannings Ambo from his native Birmingham. Now sixty-five, and with his Brummie accent still defying all attempts at disguise, Fred could be relied upon to make a first-class fist of whatever he was given.

16

Young Jim Goakes seemed to have even more impressive credentials. He was the son of William Flamsteed's original partner and the grandson of Dan, the man who had ridden the stable's first winner on the very day Leander was born.

"I suppose it's a bit daft calling him 'young'," Polly said. "He must be forty-five if he's a day . . . only his dad's name is Jim as well, see."

"Seems all right to me," Elsie said, and turned to the corner where Bess spent most of the day in the pram that had once carried a marchioness. "She thinks so, too, look."

Later that afternoon, Leander and Emma went to the library and hoisted the Big Book on to the table. With its marbled covers and leather binding, it looked like an enormous, old-fashioned cash-book. In fact, the unruled pages, each measuring fourteen by twenty-three inches, contained a record of life at Latimer's Barn and in the village since 1859, the year Leander's father arrived from Greenwich. After his death, in 1891, all the entries were in her firm, generous hand.

There were nine hundred and sixty pages, all numbered by the printer who had constructed the great tome. On 3 September, Leander had written:

We are at war with Germany. Again!

at the top of page 336. The word 'again' with its angry exclamation mark was underlined, Leander's state of mind causing a fine spray of ink to fly from the nib.

"What on earth do I say now?" she asked. Emma, always allowed to witness her real emotions, saw that she was irritated and fearful.

"You must write about Steven joining the Navy and Matthew taking his place," Emma replied. "John and William, too."

"I hear there are others."

Emma nodded. "I'll go round and make up a list tomorrow. And don't forget your new great-grandson."

"That's something, isn't it?" Doing her best to cheer up, Leander reached for the pen.

*   *   *

17

The 'Phoney War', as it was later called, got on everyone's nerves. While London waited to be bombed and gassed, and the talk along the south coast was of invasion, nothing happened. Neville Chamberlain made speeches declaring that Germany would be defeated by economic pressures inside six months: it was, he said, very silly of Hitler and his henchmen not to have come to terms with this simple fact.

This patent nonsense was enlivened by elements of sheer farce. Early in October, a manically zealous ARP warden from Marlborough stole into Cannings Ambo one night to check the black-out precautions. Finding all four windows of The George's public bar showing chinks of light, he smashed them with the pickaxe handle that he regarded as his staff of office. Only the supreme diplomatic skills and wicked right hook of Jack Foxton, the formidable licensee, saved the officious lunatic from a lynching.

Mostly, however, everything that happened was devoid of any opportunity for humour. On 30 September, Parliament passed a Bill that imposed identity cards on people, an affront they had escaped in the Great War. Leander, whose photograph in a newspaper was immediately recognised by at least half the country, took it badly.

"I don't like the way things are going," she told Elsie one evening. "It was King and Country that mattered in nineteen-fourteen . . . it looks as though we're fighting this one for the benefit of the bureaucrats. That seems very unhealthy."

Elsie nodded wisely. Never a day passed without her learning something new, a constant reminder that she and her children were in a world that might have been ten million miles away from the East End.

As in 1914, a British Expeditionary Force had been dispatched to France soon after the declaration of war, but Leander's daughter, Amelia, was firmly of the opinion that the four divisions, commanded by Lord Gort, were no more than a token gesture.

"We all know what the Kaiser would have called it," she

said to Leander during a weekend in early November when she was home from Cambridge.

"A contemptible little army!" Leander echoed the notorious phrase and shifted uncomfortably. Discussion of the War with Amelia always made her uneasy.

Now middle-aged, Amelia was, according to her own harsh judgement, an intellectual has-been, fit only to give simple lectures to undergraduates. She claimed that she did nothing except trade on the international reputation as a mathematician she had acquired twenty-five years ago. At the height of her powers, she had been a frequent visitor to Germany and became aware of the Nazi menace as early as 1929. Resolutely unwilling to believe that there could possibly be another war, Leander had brushed Amelia's warnings aside.

"Not that this looks like being anything like the last time," Amelia continued. "Our boys were up to their necks in action from the minute they landed in 'fourteen. What are they doing now?"

"They're helping the French," Leander said, attempting to sound convinced by what she had heard on the wireless.

"Helping them to do *what*?" Amelia demanded, tilting her chin challengingly. The unconscious gesture emphasised her beauty: at fifty-two, with her blonde hair still resplendent, she looked as she had since she was ten, a younger replica of Leander. "They hardly need help to skulk behind the Maginot Line."

"Well, isn't that all for the best?" Leander asked. "We aren't ready for war, so this delay will give us a chance."

Amelia, a scathing critic of Chamberlain and his supporters, looked doubtful, although she knew that the men who had already gone from the village were providing evidence to support the idea in their letters home. While William Flamsteed was learning to fly a Tiger Moth in Gloucestershire, his brother, John, was at Bicester, suffering the trials and tribulations that were necessary to become a subaltern in an infantry regiment. He drew no comfort from the knowledge that many of his friends, called up as private

19

soldiers, were enduring what sounded like total purgatory at places like Aldershot and Catterick.

Keeping a watchful eye on her widely scattered 'family', Leander was fascinated by the metamorphosis of Ernest Cartwright, son of Fred and Tish. Ernest, a somewhat staid thirty-seven, had been the salesman for Wm Flamsteed & Sons for some years. A confirmed bachelor, he lived with his parents at Alma Cottage, and mostly affected the manners and style of a country gentleman. To the amused disbelief of Cannings Ambo, portly, pompous Ernest was somewhere on Salisbury Plain, finding out how to be a tank commander. Opinion in The George was unanimous: if the Army could pull *that* off, Hitler's hordes would be chicken-feed when the time came.

Only the Royal Navy was in action and a desperate business it was, giving rise to constant worry about Steven.

Germany wasted no time in deploying her formidable fleet of U-boats and they proved themselves to be lethal. As well as sinking over 200,000 tons of merchant shipping in the first three months of the War, they inflicted two grievous losses on the Navy. On 17 September the aircraft carrier *HMS Courageous* went down with the loss of five hundred men from a ship's company of twelve hundred. What followed a month later was far worse; during the night of 13/14 October, a U-boat sneaked through the defences of Scapa Flow and sank the battleship *Royal Oak* at her moorings. This time, the losses were too terrible to publish. Steven did not finish his training until the end of November, but once he was at sea in the destroyer *HMS Hunter*, Leander and Emma were prey to incessant fear.

As the end of the year approached, there was something to cheer about. After three months of unhindered pillaging in the South Atlantic, the German pocket battleship *Graf Spee* was brought to action by the cruisers *Ajax*, *Achilles* and *Exeter* on 13 December. The battle was fought off the coast of Uruguay, near the estuary of the River Plate. When the British and New Zealand ships broke off the struggle, the

Graf Spee sprang a surprise: instead of attempting an escape to the open sea, she put into the port of Montevideo.

With Uruguay's neutrality in question, three days of frenzied diplomatic activity followed while more ships raced to the assistance of the gallant trio who had engaged the vastly superior enemy. In the event, they were not needed; on the evening of 7 December, the *Graf Spee* sailed, only to be blown up in an act of deliberate immolation. After so much bad news, the end of the German battleship was greeted ecstatically in England.

But, on 19 December, the mild celebrations and preparations for Christmas in Cannings Ambo were cut short by the death of Rupert Timberlake.

After three months at The House, Elsie was making good progress with learning the detailed history of the past eighty years.

The picture gallery was the ideal schoolroom. It was located in the corridor that ran almost the full length of the ground floor from the entrance hall behind the sealed front door to Elsie's own quarters. Between the doors that gave access to the library, the small sitting-room, the dining-room and the big sitting-room that was only used for large gatherings on special occasions, the walls carried a priceless collection of photographs. In identical frames and strict chronological order, there was at least one for each year since 1876: the only break in the pictures, hung three deep, was the glass-fronted case that contained Giles Hawksworth's Victoria Cross. The pictures were there to be studied and Elsie did so. Polly Izzard was able to answer some of her questions, Emma dealt with the more difficult ones.

Herself the daughter of a famous trainer, Emma was fiercely proud of the Latimer's Barn traditions and responded to Elsie's curiosity with frankness. Elsie got to know all the members of the family, including George, the black sheep, and Maude Flamsteed.

"She looks a proper little madam," Elsie said bluntly. "Face like the back of a bus."

"It's said that she was never happy here," Emma replied. "I didn't really know her . . . she'd run off with a perfectly dreadful man before I married Giles. I don't think I missed very much."

This, from the scrupulously fair Emma, who detested speaking ill of anyone, was damning condemnation.

Next, Elsie studied the great horses in the photographs, especially the nine Derby winners, from the legendary Bellerophon of 1876 to Hyperborean in 1938. Without exception, the horses were accompanied by Leander: the progression from the over-confident sixteen-year-old in breeches and canvas jacket to the regal old lady in an unfashionably long dress and broad-brimmed straw hat was fascinating to follow. In one striking respect, Leander had not changed at all over the sixty-odd years: the benign confidence with which she stared at the camera, chin up, head slightly to the left, was immutable.

Elsie had learned a great deal, but she remained baffled by the Timberlakes. Clearly, they were special, very special indeed: how they fitted in was a puzzle. Several years were to pass before Elsie realised that she had created the mystery herself by refusing to believe the simple evidence of her own eyes and ears. She was not the first to make the mistake and there were to be plenty after her. The Timberlakes were immensely disparate, yet stuck together like nobody's business and had the arcane status of being a 'funny lot'.

"You can never be sure how many of them there are," Polly said. "Mr Claude lives in the house off Marlborough High Street and he's sort of 'in charge', if you see what I mean." Elsie pretended to. "But they're here, there and everywhere," Polly went on. "There's a good few of 'em supposed to live in Savernake." Elsie was impressed. She had yet to see the famous forest and regarded it as an awesome and romantic place. "And there's more up north . . . looking after factories and things."

Rupert, together with Silas, the illegitimate son of Rupert's cousin, Martha, lived at Louise House on the Back Stretch, built in 1919 for Matthew and Louise at the time of their

22

marriage. Now, it was Amelia's home when she was not in Cambridge.

Leander had insisted on Rupert moving from Marlborough to Latimer's Barn almost exactly a year ago after he had suffered a heart attack. Although his death at the age of eighty-four was not unexpected, or particularly tragic, Elsie could see that Leander was profoundly upset.

"Mother and Mr Timberlake were good friends for sixty years," Emma explained. Never having known her own mother, who had died when she was born, Emma had adopted Leander soon after marrying Giles. "Mr Timberlake did a great deal for us over the years."

As Emma left the kitchen, Polly was nodding vigorously. "I've heard that this place might have been ruined several times over if it hadn't been for Mr Rupert," she said.

Thinking that she understood, Elsie attributed the friendship of Amelia and Silas to gratitude for past help. If anyone had asserted that Leander Hawksworth and Rupert Timberlake had been lovers for most of her long widowhood, or that Amelia and Silas knew no lessening of the passion that had first exploded between them in 1919, Elsie would have told them not to be so bloody silly.

Elsie found the funeral, held on the morning of Christmas Eve, very enlightening.

"Please come to church . . . if you'd like to, that is," Emma said after lunch the previous day. Elsie sensed that this was tantamount to a command.

Sure enough, the entire village was present. They were joined by over forty Timberlakes, some from as far away as Carlisle and Newcastle, despite the difficulties of war-time travel.

Undeterred by rain, most of the congregation filed to the grave that had been prepared in the south-eastern corner of the churchyard, where, after the death of her father, Leander had decided that Hawksworths and Flamsteeds should be buried. Elsie began to appreciate something of Rupert Timberlake's importance when she saw that he was

23

to be laid to rest in a grave next to Steven Hawksworth. Much more significantly, however, for the first time in her life, she felt part of a community. After the interment, as she made her way back to The House with the seventy or so people who had accepted invitations to take refreshments, Elsie found herself in earnest conversation with total strangers. Some of them seemed tremendous toffs and swells, but they treated her as an equal because she worked at Latimer's Barn.

Once inside The House, there was a brief sign of possible friction. A formidable old woman by the name of Mathilda asked why Rupert had not been taken back to his native Yorkshire to be buried. It was, she said ominously, a custom.

Claude, the nephew whom Rupert had chosen as his successor, dealt with it quietly but firmly. "Uncle spent all his adult life in Wiltshire and he loved *this* place. When Mrs Hawksworth made the offer, I thought it was absolutely right and fitting."

And that was that. Although he was not much more than forty and could, if he put his mind to it, be self-effacing, Claude Timberlake was the undisputed leader of the far-flung tribe.

Leander did not allow the gathering to last for very long. "Rupert wouldn't want Christmas spoiled on his account," she told everyone, fully composed now that her dear friend's funeral was over. "Some of you have a long way to go, so you must be leaving soon. Thank you all for coming."

That evening, Leander came to Elsie's flat with presents for Joe and Bess. After they had chatted for a while, Elsie was emboldened to ask: "You're going to see Hitler off then, Mrs Hawksworth?"

"Most definitely!" For a moment, Leander looked alarmingly fierce. "We had all this in the Great War, you know. My brother was afraid that I would die and leave everybody in the lurch." She was gentle again. "How are you finding it here, Elsie? We're not too much for you, I hope?"

"Bless you, no, Mrs Hawksworth! I love it here, I really do. Me and the kids'll stay forever if we're allowed. No, the only

24

way you'll shift me is feet first, in a box." Realising that the remark was in poor taste on this, of all days, Elsie blushed. "Oh, I *am* sorry!"

"Don't worry." Leander laid a reassuring hand on her shoulder. "I was about eight when I came to exactly the same conclusion." She pulled a rueful face. "I must have been an *awful* child! Mind you, I was right!"

It was the first time Elsie had seen Leander's special smile at such close quarters. The way her eyes sparkled really was astounding.

CHAPTER 2

1940

'Oh, God, here we go again'

With the advent of a new year, the Government continued to dither, sidling into war with averted eyes. The Duke of Laverstoke, most conscientious in the performance of his duties in the House of Lords, told a fuming Leander that inactivity was making London complacent.

Food rationing was introduced and Elsie, with her ability to work wonders from nothing, became more popular than ever.

One morning, as she served a breakfast that was a fair imitation of scrambled egg made from powder, Leander dashed into the kitchen waving a circular from the Jockey Club.

"They've seen sense and reason," she shouted. "There's going to be a restricted programme of racing."

" 'Bout time, too!" Elsie said stoutly. She was, by now, an expert, of course.

"How 'restricted'?" Emma asked.

"I don't know," Leander replied. "Newmarket only, probably. Still, it's better than nothing."

The effect was instantaneous. Latimer's Barn began work the following morning. War had reduced the number of horses from ninety to sixty, while eighteen of the fifty lads had either volunteered or been called up. The numbers worked out well, allowing the principle of two lots to be continued, and Matthew soon had things reasonably organised.

26

Secretly, however, he worried. All that he was doing was to play the part of a very polite sergeant-major, putting men and horses through an undemanding routine. What happened when it was time to start working animals up to full fitness and entering them for races?

The answer was forthcoming inside a week. For as long as the War lasted, the guidance of the stable's affairs was to be in the hands of a marchioness. The news was greeted with quiet pleasure; it was, everyone agreed tacitly, no more than Latimer's Barn deserved.

Much as she had come to love Eaton Mandeville, Rachel jumped at the chance to return to Cannings Ambo. Charles had created a minor sensation by landing himself what sounded like a key job in military intelligence at the War Office and would be away for the duration.

"It's rather worrying," the Duchess told Leander over the telephone. "If they're letting an idiot like him loose on *intelligence*, it makes you wonder what the rest of the show is going to be like."

"Oh, come on, Clem!" Leander protested. A great fan of Charles, she was annoyed at hearing him belittled. "They gave him a thorough going-over before they offered him that job, and I expect they were impressed by his French and German."

"French and German? What *are* you blathering on about, Leander?"

"Charles is a fluent linguist!"

"Good God!" It sounded as though the Duchess was treating the discovery of her son's ability as a manifestation of utter depravity.

Rachel thought it was all a bit of a whizz. "They've had to make Charlie a major," she told Emma. "I mean, they couldn't very well have '*Private* the Marquess of Glastonbury', could they?"

She appreciated that her husband's work was going to be demanding, with a thirty-six-hour pass only every second weekend if they were lucky. Leander's offer of a chance to run Latimer's Barn, instead of twiddling her thumbs and getting involved with whatever war work the Duchess eventually dreamed up, came as a godsend. The sheer volume of luggage that accompanied Rachel was a clear indication that she had come to stay for as long as was necessary. Naturally, young Henry and baby Edmund came with her, providing joy for Emma and Leander, who made it clear that their grand- and great-grandsons were about to be spoiled rotten.

With milder weather conditions around the middle of February, Rachel set to with a will, always careful to explain everything to Matthew in private first, so that he could give the orders and put up a good show of being in charge. Joe Collier, who was fascinated by the stable and its workings, and was out with the first lot every morning before he went to school, was not fooled for an instant. His reports to Elsie invariably began with, "Lady Rachel says . . ."

On a morning of special excitement, he came out with: "Lady Rachel reckons we're going to show the buggers how to do it with Icy Socks in the Guineas!"

"Icy socks?" Elsie asked. "What are they when they're at home?"

"It's a 'orse!" Joe said confidently.

"That don't sound right to me, love," Elsie replied.

"It is! He's an Agamemory!"

Isocracy had raced only once as a two-year-old in 1939. After taking a long time to come to hand, he appeared at Newbury in August, where, with Sammy Thorn making his début as a jockey, he had disposed of a decent-class field with minimal effort. The subsequent abandonment of all racing prevented what might well have been a highly successful autumn campaign.

The handsome colt, owned by Claude Timberlake, was by the great Agamemnon, the 1929 Triple Crown hero, out of one of the Duke of Laverstoke's mares. He had wintered well and was eager for work; even Matthew could see that he was in a class of his own and Joe was merely retailing an open secret when he told Elsie of Rachel's intentions.

"What do you think?" Rachel asked Leander after Isocracy

28

had been cantering and galloping for three weeks and the early morning scrutiny with binoculars from the bedroom window that commanded a superb view of Cannings Down had become a standing joke among the lads.

"Nowhere near as good as his sire!"

Rachel studied her grandmother's desperately straight face. "Honestly, Leander, you are a scream," she said, copying Steven's habit of using her Christian name, a practice thoroughly welcomed by the recipient. "You of *all* people know that you only get a horse as good as Agamemnon every twenty years – if you're lucky!"

"That doesn't stop me hoping and wanting more," Leander replied.

Hitler acted with galvanic speed to signal the end of the Phoney War.

On the night of Monday 8 April, four days after Neville Chamberlain had assured the nation that 'Hitler had missed the bus', German forces occupied Denmark and launched the invasion of Norway. Someone, probably Winston Churchill, seemed to have anticipated the move because a strong Royal Navy force, including the destroyer *Hunter* with Steven on board, was engaged in mining Norwegian territorial waters that very night. Almost immediately, the British flotillas were engaged in a full-scale battle at Narvik, one hundred and fifty miles north of the Arctic Circle.

Charles Prideaux had one of his precious passes the following weekend. Using a borrowed Austin Seven to make the most of the petrol, Rachel drove out to Savernake station to meet him. Arriving at half past two, she was resigned to the prospect of a long wait: conditions were making it impossible for the Great Western Railway to operate anything like a predictable service and there was no telling which of the available trains Charles would be able to catch. Two weeks ago, a last-minute flap had trapped him in his office until six o'clock.

At three o'clock, shortly after a heavily laden non-stop express had blasted through on its way to London, the porter brought her a cup of tea and a morsel of hopeful news.

"There was a likely one left Paddington twenty minutes ago, My Lady. Let's hope his Lordship's on that 'un, eh?"

"That would be nice, Bill. What time's it due?"

The old man screwed up his eyes in concentration. "He should do it by four if they got a good engine for him at Newbury."

Smiling her thanks, Rachel addressed herself to the tea and enjoyment of the bird-song in the woods surrounding the station.

It proved to be one of those days when everything went well. The train, audible for five minutes as it tackled the climb up from Bedwyn, pulled in at ten minutes to four and Charles was on it. Before flinging herself into his arms, Rachel realised that he looked pretty good in his uniform.

Their first journey was of less than a mile to the forest cottage that had once been the haunt of Rupert Timberlake and Leander. They would stay there, enjoying each other, until the following morning when it was time to go to Latimer's Barn to spend an English Sunday with their children, relatives and friends. The War had made them look upon that as a great treasure and it put an even higher price on their Saturday evenings and nights in the forest.

Charles, ten years older than Rachel, had begun the process of falling in love with her when she was only fourteen. Six years later, unable to believe his good fortune, he had gone to their marriage bed a completely callow virgin. Although Rachel was similarly inexperienced, her natural flair for passion had made their first night together gloriously memorable. It was the basis for a relationship that bloomed as they discovered more and more about satisfying each other's needs. Now, although they had been married for five years, they found the hardship of separation unbearable.

That afternoon, they were making love ten minutes after reaching the cottage. Not until eight o'clock did they experience hunger of another kind. Together, they prepared a simple meal, enjoying it as though it was the most sumptuous banquet ever served.

30

"This Norwegian business sounds serious," Rachel said as they washed up.

"Bloody serious," Charles agreed. "Jerry's throwing everything in."

"Is Steven involved?" Rachel asked.

Charles smiled secretly at the over-casual question: she was probing, trying to find out how much he knew and thus assess his importance. "His ship was on the spot when the balloon went up," he replied. "So, I think we can assume that he's joining in the fun."

"Oh. I see." Rachel was impressed and asked no more questions, making Charles grateful. Avoiding the necessity of lying to her was, if anything, more important than guiding her back to the bedroom. By virtue of his position, the status of which his family had not begun to guess at, Charles knew that Steven's ship had been sunk on Thursday. However, he also knew that only eleven men had been lost and wished to remain silent until he was certain that his brother-in-law was not among them.

Not surprisingly, the news from Norway dominated the conversation over lunch at Latimer's Barn on Sunday. By then, the wireless had announced that the first British landings had taken place at Harstad in response to King Haakon's appeal for help.

Charles was glad that no one asked him any searching questions about the progress of the campaign. To have been forced into telling the truth, that the War Cabinet and Chiefs of Staff were spending most of their time arguing amongst themselves, would have lowered morale as well as betraying his position.

The day was longer than usual because Charles was getting a lift back to London with a friend from Bath, who was returning after a week's leave. When he said his goodbyes at dusk and set off to walk to the main road, he and Rachel had never spoken of the lives they led apart from one another: to have done so would have been a violation of their precious hours together.

* * *

31

The news from Norway became very bad indeed. The papers and the wireless put a brave face on things, dutifully promulgating what they were given, but Leander saw through the fog straightaway.

"It's turning into a complete shambles," she said. "We don't stand a hope in hell!"

"I wonder if Steven is in it," Emma said, voicing the fear that had been with her for over a week.

"I doubt it," Rachel declared confidently. "He's probably still stuck in a Scottish loch, wondering what sort of mess I'm making of Isocracy!"

The colt was in magnificent condition, so much so, that a surprisingly large crowd at Newmarket on Two Thousand Guineas day took one look at him and backed him into favouritism at five to four.

Leander's absence caused a stir. It was an established principle that she never missed a big race in which a Latimer's Barn horse was competing. Starting with New Invention when she was eight, she had seen all the subsequent thirty-one Classic winners do the business. Rachel and Matthew found themselves dealing with scores of anxious questions about Leander's health, trying to explain that she had stayed at home so as not to be a nuisance in travelling conditions that seemed to be worsening by the day. The idea that Leander Hawksworth could ever be a nuisance was greeted with such outright derision that Rachel decided that they should have made her come.

Leander would have enjoyed it hugely. Sammy Thorn, who was acting as jockey to Latimer's Barn until young Michael Pilgrim was old enough, claimed not to have seen another horse during his lightning progress from starting gate to winning post.

"He's making that up!" Leander scoffed when she heard about it the day after. "You know what a devil he is for gilding the lily."

"I think it's true," Rachel insisted. "Our boy made all and did them by five lengths."

"Will he get a mile and a half?" Leander asked.

"You tell me!" Rachel laughed. "You've forgotten more than I'll ever know."

"He's bred to stay forever," Leander pointed out.

"You'd better watch him work and tell me what you think," Rachel said. "And you're coming to the Derby! There's more than enough on our plates without having to tell all and sundry that you're *not* crocked up at death's door."

Using an ancient dogcart, Leander drove herself out to the gallops to watch preparations for the Derby. As Isocracy and his lead horse came pounding towards her on a wonderful May morning, Leander felt that she was, and always had been, the luckiest woman on earth. Her keen eye told her that the rapport between Sammy and the colt was increasing by the day. During her life, incessant change meant that virtually everything *looked* different; not the magical harmony of man and horse, however. That was changeless.

Returning from the gallop, Leander toured the two yards, chatting to the lads, joining in their banter. For the first time since the dreariness of war had fallen on everything, she felt the joy of what seemed very distant days.

But it all faded in an instant that evening. A grave-looking Duke of Laverstoke called in on his way home from London. "Hold on to your hats and knickers," he said. "All hell's broken out at Westminster."

"What is it, Hubert?" Leander asked, her face strained.

It seemed that the cat was well and truly out of the bag over the Norwegian business. Badly bungled by infirmity of purpose on the part of Government and service chiefs, it had become a terrible fiasco. The best to be hoped for was that British and Allied forces could be withdrawn without heavy casualties. In a brutal simplification of the crisis, the Commons decided that Chamberlain and most of his Cabinet had done nothing since entering the War against Germany. The prevailing sentiment was that any fool could *declare* war, *waging* it was a different matter.

The most damaging attack came from Chamberlain's own back-benches. At the end of a scathing speech, Leo Amery quoted Oliver Cromwell's words to the Rump Parliament:

"You have sat too long here for any good you have been doing. Depart, I say, and let us have done with you. In the name of God, go!"

"Will he?" Leander asked.

"He has no option."

"Who will take over? Lord Halifax?"

"Good heavens, no! He'd run a mile faster than Isocracy if he was offered the job. In any case, Labour wouldn't work with him – there's got to be a coalition, a 'National' Government, you see. No, it's going to be Churchill."

Leander nodded approvingly. She knew that there were many, notably within the Trade Union movement, who hated Winston's guts, but he was almost certainly the right man for the time.

Sure enough, less than seventy-two hours after the furore erupted, Winston Churchill became Prime Minister. His sixty-fifth birthday, the age for retirement, had passed the previous November.

That same day, 10 May, Nazi Germany invaded Holland and Belgium. The catastrophic series of events that would lead to Dunkirk was in train. When the evacuation from the beaches began on 27 May with the country trembling and praying, Rachel gritted her teeth over Isocracy's final preparations for the Derby and Leander wondered what she ought to do about her eightieth birthday. The matter was taken out of her hands.

The plan, hatched, refined and nurtured by Emma and Elsie for over a month, had to be revealed the day before, thus losing the element of *total* surprise. It was Steven who caused the trouble: just as lunch was finishing at The House on 31 May, he telephoned to say that he was in Marlborough and could someone possibly come and fetch him?

Laughing and crying simultaneously, Emma dashed off with Matthew in his car, while Leander scuttled upstairs to change into one of her newer, shorter dresses and high-heeled shoes.

Matthew was back inside fifteen minutes, alone.

34

"What's wrong? Where are they?" Leander demanded, looking anxiously for Emma and Steven.

"Don't worry," Matthew replied. "They asked to be dropped at the bottom of the drive so that they could have some time together."

Leander understood at once. Since the death of his father when he was only four, Steven had been the most devoted son that any mother ever had. Their relationship, usually more suggestive of brother and sister, was exceptionally close.

When they finally appeared at the back door, where Leander was waiting impatiently, Steven had his good arm round Emma's shoulders. "Hello, Leander," he grinned. "Showing off your legs again, I see."

Ridiculously vain about her superb physical condition, Leander came close to blushing. Her grandson's right arm, strapped in a sling, was her opportunity to change the subject.

"You're wounded. Is it bad?"

"It isn't a wound. I broke it falling down a companionway."

"You fell downstairs?" Leander was disapproving.

Steven nodded mournfully. "More or less inevitable when you're doing twenty knots and the whole caboodle stops dead."

"How did that happen?"

"The captain got so fed up with one of our German friends that he decided to ram him and have done with it."

"That sounds awfully dangerous!" Leander said.

"Oh, it is," Steven replied earnestly, keeping a straight face despite Elsie's laughter. "So much so, that Jerry sank."

"But your ship was all right?"

"Well, it stayed afloat, which is more than can be said for the other two I was on."

Leander and Emma exchanged worried glances.

Exhausted after the two-day journey from Scapa Flow, Steven sank into a chair in the kitchen, offered Elsie five pounds for a 'proper' cup of tea and turned expectantly to Leander.

"Are you ready for your great day?" he asked.

"I expect a few friends will be looking in," she replied. "There's no question of a big party, of course."

Shocked, Steven turned to Emma. "Is this true, Mother? What's gone wrong? You promised you'd organise a knees-up."

"Well . . . I . . ." Emma squirmed, her discomfort made worse by Leander's searching stare. "Yes, I have made arrangements."

"How many are coming?" Leander asked.

"About three hundred," Emma said sheepishly.

"Three hundred!"

Emma decided on a firm line. "I've had to turn over two hundred down to keep it as *low* as that," she said. "People from all over the country have been writing and telephoning, *begging* to come."

"Really?" Leander was taken aback.

"Yes, really, Mother! So, you're jolly well going to have to put on a good face and enjoy yourself."

"Hear, hear!" Steven said. "There has *got* to be a party and that's that."

"But, darling, what about this awful business at Dunkirk?" Leander asked.

"That is going miraculously well," Steven replied, suddenly serious. "It will carry on that way, or turn into a disaster whether you have a birthday party or not. People are very keen to enjoy themselves at a time like this, so you will put on a show for them. Understood?"

"Yes, my dear."

"Good!" Steven stood up. "I'm going to have a bath now that's settled."

After his departure, Leander said, "It was very bad in Norway, I take it?"

Emma, who had been told something of the truth during their walk up the drive, nodded. "Very."

"He's looking well on it, though," Leander said. "And he seems much more confident and relaxed. What a funny business war is!"

*   *   *

36

1 June was a day of sunshine and enough breeze to stir the tops of the poplars along the drive. Leander set the seal on the occasion by decreeing that tea could be served on the lawn. The edict forbidding anyone to set foot on the immaculate turf between The House and the original ten-box stable was nearly as old as Leander and had been relaxed only once previously, for her twenty-first birthday.

Once the tables from the workshops of Wm Flamsteed & Sons were set up, surprising quantities of food materialised. Edward Mallender, grandson of the man who had opened the first of what were now fourteen Mallender and Giffard grocery shops, made several journeys with a delivery van. In response to Leander's anxious queries about ration books, he winked and made himself scarce.

During the afternoon, Leander visited each of the tables in turn, having a word with everyone and accepting their good wishes. She stayed close to old Jim Goakes, often linking arms with him to move between tables. Apart from the Duke of Laverstoke, then a mere marquess of seventeen, Jim was the only person present who had attended her twenty-first birthday celebration in 1881, when Queen Victoria still had nearly twenty years of her reign left.

To the delight of everyone except Leander, the Duke climbed on to a stool to make a speech. While Leander muttered: "Silly old fool!" at frequent intervals, Hubert Prideaux's words were listened to with great respect.

"I don't have to tell you how much Leander has done for this village and the people in it," he said after spending ten minutes doing so. "There's one thing, though, that ought to be especially in our minds today: she brought Cannings Ambo through the last war and I'm damned sure she'll get us through this one." She was astonished at the strength of feeling in the widespread agreement to this notion. Not only were they convinced that she could work miracles, they believed she would go on forever.

The Duke turned towards Leander, smiling affectionately. "I believe there's the small matter of another Derby to be won first," he said, and she nodded vigorously. "Now, ladies and gentlemen, raise your glasses to Leander Hawksworth. A very happy birthday to you, my dear. And many more of them!"

As the toast was drunk, using generous measures of the eighty bottles of champagne that had been sent over from the Eaton Mandeville cellars, one for each year of Leander's life, Steven saw that she was not quite as unmoved and dry-eyed as she made herself appear.

Nevertheless, when she stood up to thank everyone for their presents and good wishes, her voice was as clear and steady as ever. At what seemed to be the end of her succinct bit of oratory, some had started to clap, only to find that she was extending a hand to command silence.

"I have something very important to tell you all," she said. "I'm not the only one having a birthday today." She reached out to Emma, who had been looking after Bess while Elsie was busy serving tea and cakes. "This lovely little soul is Bess Collier and she's one today."

Held up by Leander, Bess gurgled at the "Oohs" and "Ahs". Those with cameras were unable to resist the urge to take snapshots. "Isn't she gorgeous?" Leander smiled. "She's one of our evacuees and I'm adopting her as my great-grandaughter."

With only one exception, the announcement was greeted with indulgent approval. Briefly, Rachel was astounded; then she frowned; finally, she looked at Leander almost sorrowfully, as though forgiving her for the foolishness of old age. Steven, sitting directly opposite his sister, was the sole observer of her reaction.

He was puzzled. Within seconds, Rachel was back to normal, laughing gaily at something Emma had said: but while it lasted, her disapproval of what Leander had done was very strong indeed.

It was nothing remotely like Epsom, of course, but Newmarket did its best for the Derby. The prize-money was only half what Blue Peter had won for Lord Rosebery in 1939 and the crowd was a fraction of pre-war numbers, with the men wearing lounge suits or uniforms, rather than morning dress.

38

The efforts of the Jockey Club and course officials to make something of the day were boosted most handsomely by Isocracy. Half-way through the mile and a half, he had the other fifteen runners off the bit and struggling. At the two-furlong marker, Sammy Thorn forgot his orders and allowed the colt his head. Lengthening his stride with consummate ease, Isocracy strolled away to become the easiest of the nine Derby winners sent out from Latimer's Barn so far, giving the crowd exactly what they needed, a popular and impressive victory.

The ovation Isocracy received when Claude Timberlake led him into the winner's enclosure had much more to do with events at Dunkirk, rather than what had transpired at Newmarket. The morning's papers reported that the evacuation had been completed the previous evening, 4 June. In eight days, over 330,000 men had been brought back to England, nearly 140,000 of them members of the French forces. The Army was safe, the nightmare prospect of destruction or surrender averted. Churchill called it a miracle and no one felt like arguing with him. Casualties were minimal, although material losses were massive. The Army had been forced to abandon all its equipment, six destroyers were sunk with nineteen badly damaged, and four hundred and seventy-four RAF aircraft were lost. But the Hurricane flown five or more times a day by William Flamsteed from his base at Tangmere in Sussex was, like its pilot, completely unscathed.

The knowledge helped Matthew through the awesome task of being nominally responsible for training a Derby winner. Not that all that many people believed he had: the older hands, steeped in decades of racing folklore, were confident that Leander had been in charge of Isocracy. The theory became cast-iron fact in the space of a few minutes.

Resigned to being treated as a hero because of his broken arm, Steven congratulated Matthew, exchanged a few words with Claude and Lily Timberlake and went to the stables to inspect Isocracy. He found the colt being hosed down by his lad, Jimmy Farrant, the young genius from Chippenham who had been declared unfit for military service by virtue of problems with his eyesight, ears and feet.

One glance at the contentment with which Isocracy was receiving his sluicing told Steven that he had come through the race without difficulty. It was a different matter with Rachel, who seemed downright peevish as she watched Jimmy at work.

"What's up?" Steven asked.

"Nothing!" she snapped. "Nothing at all!"

Steven studied her. "Come along, Sister, spill the beans," he ordered.

"Well . . ." She kicked at a pebble, glowering. "Why should everyone want to think that it was Leander who trained the bloody animal?"

After what he had seen at the birthday party, Steven considered this ominous, but remained calm. "It's a natural enough assumption to make," he said mildly. "Mention Latimer's Barn to anyone and they always say 'Leander Hawksworth'. As a rule, they don't know anything else about the place, but by gum, they've heard of our grannie!"

"I think it's time the people who did the work started getting the credit," Rachel said angrily.

With a gentle hold on her elbow, Steven guided her to a point where he could be sure they were out of Jimmy's hearing, defective or not.

"Rachel, if you want to think and behave like that, I suggest you go back to Eaton Mandeville and take up being a marchioness again," he said. "Just give the word and I'll get it organised tomorrow. I'd drive you myself, but for this arm!"

Without further ado, he strode off, leaving Rachel open-mouthed and marvelling at how much the Navy was changing him.

When Steven rejoined Leander a few minutes later, there was nothing to show that his equable temperament had been badly disturbed. He found her deep in a most earnest conversation with Gideon Timberlake.

Gideon, the ten-year-old son of Claude and Lily, was

attending his first race meeting and was very smitten by what he had seen. With Lily's brown eyes and perfectly shaped nose, and his father's broad brow, he was going to be a very handsome young man. At the moment, not caring that excitement had made his hair a tousled mess, he was having his first lesson in basic principles from one of the Turf's greatest authorities.

"And the Derby really is a very important race?" he asked.

"It's the most important race in the whole world, Gideon."

The boy was still for a moment, taking it in. "They're saying that Father's horse isn't *all* that good. Epsom would have made a big difference."

"Epsom *is* very different, my dear. It does take an exceptional animal to win over a mile and a half there. I'm convinced that Isocracy would have been good enough."

"You're sure?" Gideon's eyes were intense.

"I'm absolutely certain," Leander promised him. For a moment or two, Gideon was satisfied. When his eager curiosity sparked itself off again, keeping a straight face was not easy. "Leander, how would I set about winning the Derby?"

Steven left them to it. All being well, he would be training horses for Gideon Timberlake one day. There was the small matter of a war to win first.

Elsie and Joe were in no doubt about what it meant to win the Derby. Anything that was capable of putting Cannings Ambo in such a good mood when the War news was so bad was obviously of the greatest importance. And Elsie soon cottoned on to the fact that prize-money and a few hours of fame were by no means the end of the story: Isocracy's potential at stud was considered to be enormous.

But the euphoria was short-lived. It was forty-eight hours before the colt was sufficiently rested from the tedious railway journey back home to pose for a photograph with Leander and, no sooner was that out of the way, than Matthew arrived with

41

the news that the Government had ordered the immediate cessation of all racing.

"Why?" a dismayed Leander asked.

"It's not consistent with the war effort," Matthew replied.

"Rubbish!" Rachel fumed. "We aren't interfering with whatever it is they want to do."

"I'm sure it's nothing but an excuse," Matthew said. "Remember that we've got Labourites in the Cabinet and you know what they're like! According to them, we aren't supposed to enjoy ourselves at the best of times, let alone when there's a war on."

This, like so many significant conversations, was taking place in the kitchen. Matthew's bitter remark, with which the others were obviously in full agreement, gave Elsie food for thought. One of the few things that her parents had taught her was that the Labour Party was the working man's only hope of a better life. However, at Latimer's Barn, where they definitely knew a thing or two about looking after people, it seemed that the Party's name was mud. She resolved to mull it over carefully, recalling that her dad had been wrong about most things.

In his quiet way, Steven was very annoyed. "That's sheer bloody-mindedness!" he said. "What are we supposed to do with the place, grow potatoes?"

Leander and Emma exchanged uncomfortable looks. According to the Duchess of Laverstoke, highly placed civil servants *were* casting covetous eyes on both Eaton Mandeville and Latimer's Barn as likely places for compulsory conversion to farming.

"This can't possibly last," Rachel said. "How on earth can the blood lines be maintained without racing?"

"The Jockey Club and others will be making that point," Leander replied.

"Well, I'm staying here," Rachel declared. "The stable *must* carry on as normal. You may as well concentrate on looking after things at Rose House, Matthew. Leave the horses to me until racing starts again."

Matthew thanked her, although there was precious little

for him to do at home. As foreseen, no one was buying furniture.

As gloom descended, Steven took himself off to Marlborough to see his old friend, Norman Redmayne. It was rumoured that Norman had made several trips to Dunkirk with the *Merry Dance* and Steven wanted to hear all about it. Given half a chance, he intended asking Norman Redmayne about Ann.

Matthew knew nothing of his French nephew. Nor did anyone else in Cannings Ambo have the faintest inkling that the unbelievably disastrous sequel to Dunkirk was witnessed at first hand by a young man who was half-Flamsteed.

When she went to Paris in 1912, Matthew's sister, Maude, was accompanied by a would-be artist called Donald Emmerson. Their unsatisfactory life together ended abruptly in August 1914 when Emmerson scuttled back to England at the outbreak of the Great War. Immediately, Maude made herself the mistress of Pierre Guillaume, a fashionable painter, going with him to Belle Ile, off the Breton coast, when a desire to avoid military service drove him into hiding.

The authorities eventually tracked Pierre down, causing him to flee the country rather than face the horrors of the Western Front. He left not knowing that Maude was pregnant. Unperturbed, she married Pierre's father, with whom she had slept during Pierre's long absences on painting expeditions. It was always a source of great amusement to Achille Guillaume that he could never be certain whether he was the father or the grandfather of Henri, born in 1917.

Maude's life was agreeable enough until Achille died. Then, the remnants of his family became grindingly unpleasant, willing her to go away, to leave them and the farm in peace. Unhinged by the failure of her affair with a young writer, Maude obliged them by hurling herself from the cliffs above Port Donnant during a furious Atlantic storm.

Henri stayed at the Guillaume farm until he felt sufficiently grown-up to have a chance of fending for himself. One summer's morning in 1933, when he was sixteen, he climbed out of his bedroom window at four o'clock and set off for Paris, carrying nothing more than a change of clothes and his mother's personal papers. It was a strange collection. There was her birth certificate, a prayer book to commemorate her confirmation, some faded photographs, and a page from a 1929 English newspaper which was devoted to singing the praises of Latimer's Barn and Cannings Ambo. The long article had been prompted by Agamemnon's capture of the Triple Crown.

Finding work and congenial lodgings at Café Rostand near L'Opéra, Henri put Maude's papers into a safe box at the bank where he began to save his money and set about building a career.

He did outstandingly well, finally receiving a bonus so wonderful that he had not dared to hope for it. Monsieur Rostand's daughter, Marie-Claire, three years his senior and thrillingly beautiful, told him that they were to be married. He had the good sense not to argue.

During the first few months of their marriage in the spring and summer of 1939, their happiness was overshadowed by the continual threat of war and the discovery that much of France's self-styled upper-class were Nazi sympathisers.

"They're shit-scared of the communists," Marie-Claire used to say. "They think the only way to save their necks and keep their privileges is to have Hitler running the country."

The advent of war was almost a relief. The French Army, wonderfully prepared and protected by the impenetrable Maginot Line, would soon put a stop to the Führer's megalomania. To Henri's chagrin, he was unable to take part: an arrogant young medical officer, recently qualified and pedantic, discovered the heart murmur that occasionally caused him to black out. Henri's protests were in vain. According to the sour-faced doctor, his condition made him a potentially lethal liability to his comrades-in-arms.

As with England, there was a need to change the Prime Minister. Edouard Daladier, a partner to the Munich agreement and the man widely perceived as the architect of the slump in France's moral courage, was replaced by Paul

Reynaud, an implacable opponent of Hitler and all his works.

To most people, everything seemed in order. Men such as General Charles de Gaulle, who spoke out against what they saw as France's defensive mentality, were regarded as defeatist eccentrics, besotted by the sound of their own unpalatable voices.

But the moment Germany unleashed the blitzkrieg on Belgium and Holland, supplementing it with a deadly rampage through the Ardennes, Henri Guillaume knew that the game was up.

"What a stroke!" he said to Marie-Claire, half-admiring Hitler's nerve. "He isn't even bothering to attack our magnificent Maginot Line – he's going *round* it!"

After Dunkirk, the French Army seemed to offer little resistance. Much worse, their retreat was panic-stricken; no bridges were blown up and vast supplies of food and petrol were left to fall into enemy hands. The men of the panzer brigades became exhausted, not by fighting, but from the sheer speed of their advance.

The Germans entered Paris on 14 June. In some minds there was the festering suspicion that they did so at the invitation of the Government. With the swastika flying from the top of the Eiffel Tower, Henri watched the *Boche* victory parade along the Champs Elysées to the Arc de Triomphe in livid, taut-faced silence. Not until he and Marie-Claire were safely back at Café Rostand did he give vent to his feelings.

"This country was beaten two years ago, not last week!"

Reynaud resigned as Prime Minister, refusing to have anything to do with the armistice negotiations. It was Marshal Pétain, the eighty-four-year-old hero of Verdun, who was the titular representative of France at the ignominious charade that took place on 22 June in the Forest of Compiègne, at exactly the place where Foch had dictated terms to the defeated Germans in 1918, in the very same railway carriage. The Marshal then removed himself to Vichy where he set up an administration that many felt was doomed to be a Nazi puppet, the more so since the cynical double-dealer

45

Pierre Laval was the power behind the geriatric Pétain's decrepit throne.

In London, de Gaulle formed the Free French movement to continue the fight against Germany. Two days before the armistice was signed, Gaston Lefèbre, one of Henri's few close friends, came to the Café during the quiet period of early evening. His demeanour gained him an immediate invitation to the private back room.

"There is to be a meeting at Boulanger's tomorrow," he said. "Ten o'clock. You must come, Henri."

"What is it about?"

"*Résistance*! De Gaulle is right, there is much we can do."

Henri wasted no time in thought or pointless questions. "I will be there," he said, shaking Gaston by the hand.

Marie-Claire looked on, approving and proud.

Amelia had been unsettled at Cambridge since the outbreak of the War, obsessed with the idea that she should be doing something *useful*. Conscription had deprived the University of all but a trickle of undergraduates as well as many of its youngest and best dons. Research was at a standstill and the atmosphere was dominated by incestuous political intrigue.

In vain, Amelia had applied for several posts on scientific development projects connected with the War. There was always some fault to be found with her experience. After a discussion with Leander and Emma had ended with the facetious suggestion that she might like to be a Land Girl, a member of the agricultural army who were 'digging for victory', Amelia surrendered to boredom while considering the possibility that she might abandon Cambridge, return to Wiltshire and force someone to give her a worthwhile job.

On 21 June, after a morning in her room at the Maths School, Amelia cycled out to Girton, her own college, to have tea with two old friends. Returning to her small house in Honey Hill, a quiet side-street above Magdalene Bridge, at about six o'clock, she found an official car and a young Royal Navy lieutenant waiting. He was out of the car in a flash, intercepting her before she could reach the front door.

"Beg pardon, ma'am, are you Doctor Hawksworth?" the young man asked, looking as though he might burst into tears if the answer were 'no'.

"Yes, I am."

"This is for you." He handed her a buff-coloured envelope. "It's urgent. *Very* urgent."

Baffled and slightly apprehensive, she tore open the envelope to pull out the single sheet of high-quality paper, almost falling over as the message registered. Below an embossed, single-line address, the note was hand-written.

10 Downing Street

My Dear Dr Hawksworth,
Pray come to see me at your earliest convenience on a matter of national importance. It is most desirable that you accompany the bearer of this message.

WSC

"He wants to see *me*?" Amelia gasped.

"And the sooner the better! I've been here since one o'clock. I'll take you."

She turned to look at her house. "I ought to change into something more respectable."

"You look all right to me, Doctor Hawksworth . . . if you don't mind me saying so, ma'am. *Please* can we go?"

Amelia made up her mind and turned towards the car. "Yes!"

The lieutenant introduced himself as Martin Browne. Driving quickly through Cherry Hinton to pick up the main road from Newmarket to London, he suggested that Amelia was about to be offered a job. "The old man has been pulling in specialists from all over the place these last three days . . . dreadful flap! I don't think he *ever* goes to bed!"

When they arrived in central London, Martin drove into the Mall from a strangely subdued Trafalgar Square, quickly turning into Horse Guards Road and then across Horse Guards itself, threading a path through a mass of brand new tanks and Army lorries. Once out of the car, Amelia was surprised to be guided to a door in a high wall, beyond which they were in a large and very pleasant garden.

"This is the tradesmen's entrance," Martin explained. "The workers come in this way."

The moment they were inside Number Ten, Amelia was swept into a whirlpool of activity that left no time for nervousness. An old gentleman, seeming very much like a butler in his frock coat and winged collar, stepped forward to meet her. When Martin Browne said, "This is Doctor Hawksworth," he nodded and guided her towards a dreadfully efficient-looking woman who would have been utterly forbidding but for the suggestion of a twinkle in her eyes.

"Goodness, you've taken some tracking down," she said. "Come along. As luck would have it, he's free at the moment."

Trance-like, Amelia found herself being escorted up the magnificent main stairs, past portraits of earlier prime ministers, every one of whom gave the impression of never having known a second's anxiety. They reached a corridor. Before Amelia had a chance to take stock of her surroundings, the woman came to an abrupt halt and knocked firmly on a door. Something akin to a rumble came from within, the woman opened the door and pushed Amelia inside. "Doctor Hawksworth, Prime Minister," she announced.

Churchill was sitting at a gigantic desk facing the door. To Amelia's horror, he appeared to be scowling at her until intuition suggested that this was part of his bulldog impersonation. When he rose to greet her, there was genuine, old-world gallantry in his manner.

"It is very good of you to come, Doctor Hawksworth," he said, his tone admitting that he had allowed her no choice. "Allow me to present Captain Vane of the Royal Navy."

Vane, emerging from the shadow of the desk, bowed as he shook Amelia's hand. "It is a great pleasure, Doctor Hawksworth," he said. He had the air of the scholar rather than the sea-going man of action, not quite at ease in the splendid uniform.

48

"Be seated, please," Churchill commanded. Amelia sank into an armchair alongside Vane.

"I want you to work for me," Churchill said. "Or, to be strictly accurate, for Captain Vane." There was a pause, during which Amelia sensed that she was meant to remain silent. "We are in grave difficulties with codes for the transmission of intelligence," the Prime Minister went on. "All the existing Admiralty code books are useless because the enemy captured at least two complete sets during the Norwegian campaign. I want us to have new codes *and* I want us to keep changing them – every day if necessary!" He scowled to emphasise the point. "Moreover, I have no intention of allowing the enemy the freedom of the air-waves for his transmissions. We *must* set about deciphering the codes he is using. Will you do it for me?"

Amelia was aghast. "Er . . . why me, Prime Minister?" was the only, completely stupid, thing that occurred to her.

"Because Professor Lindemann tells me that you are the ideal person for the job!"

"Oh. I see." Amelia struggled against light-headedness. Frederick Lindemann, born in Germany but brought up in Devon, was a brilliant physicist with tremendous advances in aircraft design to his credit. One of Churchill's first acts on becoming Prime Minister was to appoint Lindemann as his personal assistant. His task was to find the right people to solve all the scientific problems that the War was bound to throw up.

Conscious of his warmth and friendship, Amelia looked to Vane for guidance. "I think you should do it," he smiled.

"Of course I will!" she replied.

"Splendid!" Churchill was like a small boy given a treat. "Captain Vane will tell you all you need to know. I will attend to the people at Cambridge who might wonder where you've gone. Good luck and work hard!"

The interview was over. Amelia complied with the courtly gesture by which Vane implied that they should leave.

"By the way, Doctor Hawksworth," Churchill said, causing her to stop and turn in the doorway. "Pray tell your mother that when *Herr* Hitler . . ." he invested the name with a wonderful sneer ". . . gives me a moment, I shall see what's to be done about racing."

Amelia and Captain Vane exchanged eloquent looks as they hurried downstairs together.

"May I suggest that you and I go to the Admiralty mess for dinner," Vane suggested. "The food isn't bad and I can start putting you in the picture. Afterwards, Lieutenant Browne will drive you back to Cambridge."

"He's going to be out *awfully* late," Amelia said, realising that they would not be back at her house until one or two o'clock in the morning.

"Don't worry, he's quite grown-up," Vane replied gravely.

Three days later, Amelia put the thirty-five years at Cambridge behind her and began work in Room 39 at the Admiralty. The two friends with whom she had been having tea while Martin Browne was looking for her took over the house on Honey Hill, while Amelia moved into a surprisingly palatial flat in the attic of the Foreign Office. There were dormer windows that gave superb views across St James's Park; there was also Susie Bellchamber. Susie was a young Wren from Norfolk, whose myriad duties included spending two hours a day cleaning the flat and ensuring that the larder was kept stocked with food.

Amelia was rarely home before midnight and the work was the hardest she had ever done. The magnitude of the task was daunting, and it had to be carried out amidst the constant interruptions of endless crises. Yet, at the end of the first week, Amelia, Ambrose Vane, and their six assistants had provided the Navy with a new code book and established a mechanism for changing it at twelve hours' notice, a time they hoped to reduce sharply by the autumn.

In the early days of July, Amelia had first-hand experience of the harrowing decisions involved in modern war.

France's battle-fleet, a modern and well-equipped force, was giving grave cause for concern. At the time of the country's surrender, Admiral Darlan had taken most of the ships to Oran in North Africa. Fearful that this most valuable of prizes would inevitably fall into German hands, Churchill instigated vigorous diplomatic activity to have the fleet handed over to England, or sailed to a neutral port, far away from any possible theatre of war. Darlan, very able, worshipped by his crews, but politically ambitious, refused to cooperate.

Churchill, a frequent visitor to Room 39, made no secret of his intentions if all else failed and, on 1 July, Amelia was given the job of coding up a signal to Vice-Admiral Somerville at Gibraltar. With the formidable resources at his disposal, he was to prepare to destroy the French ships at Oran. Somerville replied that the action should be avoided at all costs. Churchill glowered at the signal and returned to Downing Street where he was assumed to be instigating further negotiations. Obviously they came to nothing for, at 10.45 p.m. on 2 July, Amelia coded the orders to sink the French.

The day after, she travelled to Wiltshire for a well-deserved three-day break. Meeting her at Savernake, Silas was struck by how strained and tired she looked.

"I think you ought to rest this afternoon, my love," he said when they had finished lunch. "It would do you good to put your feet up for a while."

"I can do *much* better than that," she replied. "I'm going to bed. And you're coming with me!"

Amelia was fifty-three, Silas fifty-six, but their relationship continued to be robustly satisfying. There was an extra spark that afternoon that Silas suspected lay hidden in the unhappiness that Amelia was carrying deep within her: whatever the reason, they made love four times with increasing intensity, almost without pausing.

"Pretty good going for a pair of old crocks," Amelia murmured, all her tension gone and tranquillity replacing weariness.

"Very good indeed," Silas said. "This job seems to be taking it out of you."

"It is quite demanding," she agreed, offhand.

He left it at that.

At breakfast on 4 July, they read the accounts of Somerville's success at Oran. Amelia was dismayed to find Silas gazing across the table at her in the very special way that usually heralded a tricky question.

"You knew this was going to happen," he said quietly.

Amelia was in a predicament. Mindful of the great secrecy of her work, she had invented the story that she was developing nutritional statistics for the Ministry of Food. On the other hand, she and Silas had always made a point of being totally honest with each other.

"Yes, I knew," she said at last.

"H'm. That doesn't sound like the Ministry of Food."

"It isn't."

Silas nodded. There would be no more questions, nor would he breathe a word to anyone else.

"I'm at the Admiralty," Amelia said.

"Talk to me about it any time you want."

She smiled gratefully.

When Silas drove Amelia to Savernake for a train to London at the end of her short break, Steven went with them. He had declared himself fit and been ordered to join a new ship at Devonport. With nearly an hour to wait for a train to Plymouth, he rather got in the way of Amelia's and Silas's parting, and, as she finally waved from a receding carriage window, he was unable to resist a droll remark.

"Keep your eye on the calories and protein, Auntie, you've got Hitler worried!"

Behind Steven's back, Silas winked and blew her a kiss.

The Battle of Britain began on 10 July.

Whether it was to allow unimpeded bombing of London and other major cities, or to pave the way for an invasion, the clear object of the exercise was to destroy the Royal Air Force. The first tactic was to attack the airfields of Kent and Sussex so as to wipe out Fighter Command on the ground. At the same time, every attempt was made to bomb the aircraft factories and engine plants in the Midlands to cut off supplies of new machines.

Allowance had to be made for the exuberant claims of the young fighter pilots; even so, the *Luftwaffe* seemed to be getting a bloody nose from the beginning. The early warning of attack provided by the south-coast radar stations was used to the full by Sir Hugh Dowding's superbly organised head-quarters, enabling rapid and precise interception of enemy formations. It soon became the practice to give what was tantamount to a score-sheet on the nine o'clock news each evening. By 17 August, for two hundred and twenty-eight British aircraft destroyed, the Germans were said to have lost well over six hundred.

In Cannings Ambo, there were times when the Battle of Britain seemed almost like a game. The skies of the south-eastern Downs and Weald might be full of scream-ing combat and death, but Wiltshire remained peaceful, eerily so. The village had to remind itself of its inter-est in the deadly struggle: William Flamsteed was a par-ticipant.

Busy though she was with naval matters, Amelia received daily reports on the progress of the battle from Winston Churchill, who spent ten minutes with her and Ambrose Vane at about eleven o'clock each night. And, after 7 September, she obtained a dismal new perspective on the War. That was the night when the air-raid sirens wailed out in anger after a year and four days of false alarms. Very soon, as the word 'blitz' entered the language, Amelia found that she was remaining at her desk, working calmly, while London quaked and burned.

The day after the first raid on London, Matthew came to The House in the middle of the morning with news from the Jockey Club.

"They're going to start racing again," he said.

"Marvellous! When?" Leander was overjoyed.

"Next week, as far as I can see."

"Next week!" Leander was outraged. Amelia had felt unable to pass on Churchill's promise: after all, close contact with him was not consistent with the tin-pot job she was supposed to be doing. "Is this a joke, Matthew?" Leander asked in the sort of voice she normally reserved for rogues and idiots.

"No. Look." Matthew handed over the official notification.

She saw at once that what was being proposed bore no resemblance to a worthwhile programme. "This is no good," she said after her first quick look. Matthew remained silent, waiting for her to discover the most bizarre feature of the plan: the St Leger was to be run on 23 November, ten weeks later than normal, at Thirsk, not Doncaster.

"Lunacy!" she said, tossing the two sheets of paper on to the table with dismissive contempt.

Rachel grabbed them. "Don't you think we ought to give Isocracy a go?" she asked.

"Definitely not! We've *never* worked or raced horses after the middle of October and we're not starting now."

"Oh, go on, Leander," Rachel urged. "Let me have a go with him. I'm sure he can win it."

"No, Rachel, I absolutely forbid it!" The frustration of having to forgo a Classic victory that was surely there for the taking made her sound harsh. "The animal has been roughed out for stud. You know as well as I do that it would take months to get him fit to race – even if we had the weather, which we shan't, of course!"

Angrily, Leander went to commit her feelings to the Big Book. Matthew, surprised to see how resentful Rachel was, exchanged looks with Elsie.

Although the nightly bombing of London continued, the Battle of Britain was as good as won by the end of September. Coming at a time when the oppressive tension of fear was easing, news of Cannings Ambo's first loss in the War was particularly shocking.

The village was already touched by sadness. At a few minutes to midnight on 14 October, old Jim Goakes died. As well as helping to found Wm Flamsteed & Sons, he left a thousand acts of kindness to ensure his fond remembrance.

The Reverend John Shepherd, accompanied by Cyril Osgood in his capacity as sexton, went up to The House soon after breakfast. They knew that Leander would be deeply concerned about the funeral arrangements and did not wait to be summoned. Fred Cartwright, anxious that his friend and mentor should be buried with due honour, rolled up a few minutes later.

It was a slow business, with frequent digressions to talk lovingly of Jim, and it was half past eleven when they were satisfied that everything was taken care of. Leander was gripping the arms of her chair, ready to stand up, when the door of the small sitting-room opened with sudden urgency.

After the brief burst of drama, Matthew stopped dead, so bewildered that he looked almost comical. Behind him, Emma's face was telling a vastly different story, one of shocked desolation. Leander felt sick with fear. *Oh, God, here we go again*, she thought.

"What is it, my dear?" she asked Matthew.

"Well . . . it's William. He's been shot down."

"When was this?" Leander asked steadily.

Matthew made no attempt to reply. Instead, he sank into a chair, his face vacant. It was left to Emma, who had been with him and Louise when William's commanding officer telephoned, to provide such details as were known.

It had happened the previous afternoon. A strong force of German bombers were heading towards Portsmouth and William's squadron was sent up to deal with them. The bombers turned away as soon as they saw the Hurricanes, but their escort of Messerschmitt 109s attacked. William, it seemed, had been lured out of the formation in which his squadron always fought and set upon by three of the 109s. "His aircraft went down in flames and no one saw him bale out," Emma concluded. "About a mile from St Catherine's Point off the Isle of Wight."

Leander was standing by Matthew's chair with an arm round his shoulders. "They may still find him," she said with a brave attempt at confidence.

"I doubt it." Matthew was submissive and Leander knew that he was right. For the second time in less than twenty-five years, war had taken the life of Rose House's eldest son.

CHAPTER 3

1941

'I'm nothing but a silly old woman . . .'

At about 2 p.m. on 28 May, Amelia felt about a hundred as she clambered off a train at Savernake station. The journey from London had relaxed her enough to feel all the strain and weariness of the past seven days. Bill Churchward, the porter, hurried to meet her with news and comment.

"'Afternoon, Miss Hawksworth," he said, taking her bag. "Mr Timberlake was on the blower a few minutes ago to say he'll be here as soon as maybe. He's fixing a puncture."

"Thank you, Bill." Drinking in the scene around her, Amelia began to feel better, but Bill insisted on dragging her back to the nightmare.

"Well, we done for that bugger *Bismarck* good and proper, didn't we!" he crowed gleefully.

"We did indeed, Bill," she replied.

"Ar! No messing! We showed 'em!"

At 10.40 the previous morning, the German battleship *Bismarck* had finally been sunk with, it was thought, very heavy loss of life. She and the heavy cruiser *Prinz Eugen* had been sighted fleetingly in the Kattegat during the early hours of 21 May, precipitating a tremendous crisis. The two warships were clearly intending to make their way into the Atlantic via the Denmark Strait. The prospect of the convoys bringing the life-blood of vital supplies from America being exposed to such dreadful fire-power could produce only one response: the *Bismarck* had to be sunk.

Far too remote in Room 39, Amelia and Ambrose Vane had moved into the main Operations Room at the Admiralty to handle the immense signal traffic that the hunt, spread over two million square miles of ocean, generated.

Amelia made no attempt to dampen Bill's patriotic excitement. There was no point in reminding him of *HMS Hood*, blasted out of existence with most of her crew in less time than it took to think about it; and he wouldn't appreciate being told what a close-run thing it had been, even with a third of the Royal Navy involved. The *Bismarck* was gone and that was all that mattered.

Arriving in the booking-hall, Amelia almost fell over a clutter of luggage. There were two cabin trunks and a wooden packing case.

"Watch your step with this lot," Bill said, taking her arm. "Sorry it's such a mess, but it come off the train in front of you and I ain't had time to sort it out yet. Matter of fact, it's to go to your place when I can get hold of a waggon."

"Really?" Amelia was barely interested.

"Belongs to a young gent who turned up the day before yesterday. Good-looking chap." Bill consulted a bundle of papers that were stapled to the crate. "Come from Lincoln, this lot has."

Much more important was the noise of Silas's car arriving. Amelia dug deep into her reserves for the energy to throw herself into his arms.

"*Bismarck*?" he asked as they drove away from the station.

"Yes."

"Bad?"

"Dreadful!"

"I have to say that you look rather washed-out, my love," he said apologetically.

"I can't imagine why," Amelia said. "I've had at least six hours' sleep."

"Since when?"

"Last Wednesday."

"Good God ! Never mind, I'll soon have you tucked up. You've got something very interesting first, though."

"What?"

There was a slight pause as Silas wondered how to phrase it. "Your nephew has turned up, all the way from South Africa," he said.

Suddenly wide awake and alert, Amelia gave him a long, very hard stare. The rest of the journey to Latimer's Barn passed in thoughtful silence.

Pieter Hawksworth's arrival in Cannings Ambo was attended by his usual good luck.

Reaching Marlborough by means of the branch line from Savernake, he decided to walk. Slinging the rucksack on to his back, he set out without bothering to ask for directions. His father had described it all so often that it did seem like coming home. He took the main Bath road, passing the College, a few large houses, and headed confidently into open country. Reaching the turning that was without a signpost to confuse German paratroops, he took it almost automatically.

Approaching the drive to Latimer's Barn, he saw a woman emerge from the lane that led to the village. She was old, but moved with supple energy. Very little imagination was needed to see the silver hair as blonde, and the bone structure of her face was familiar from the fifty-year-old photograph he was carrying in his pocket.

Leander, who had been at Rose House, always took notice of the rare strangers who turned up in the village. This one caused her to stop dead. Seeing her struggling with recognition, Pieter walked towards her.

"Can I help you?" she asked, a good deal less assured than she would have liked.

"I'm looking for this lady." Pieter produced the photograph. "I think I've found her." His natural charm was very much in evidence.

Recovering from the shock of seeing herself ready for Royal Ascot in 1890, Leander blurted out the thought that had come to her the instant she set eyes on him. "You're George's boy, aren't you?"

"That's right, I'm Pieter. Hello Grandmother!"

"My dear, how wonderful!" She kissed him with great warmth and he found that her face was as fresh and smooth as a young girl's. "Tell me . . . how is your father?"

"He died in 'thirty-eight. A heart attack . . . very sudden."

Leander's face clouded and there was desolation in her eyes. "What a shame," she whispered. "Only fifty-five. Not much older than his poor father."

"He often talked about you," Pieter said. "I always felt that he thought you were the most wonderful person on earth."

"Oh!" Leander stifled a nervous laugh and found herself blinking at tears. "And what about your mother? Her name's Gertrude, isn't it?"

"Yes. I'm afraid she's married again."

"And you don't approve?"

"I'm afraid not, Gran. She's married one of her own, a dreadful old Boer called Kruger."

"A famous name, at any rate," Leander said. "What brings you here, Pieter?" She did her best with the South African pronunciation, making him smile affectionately.

"Call me Peter . . . it's easier for you and I prefer it. Why am I here? Well, the old country's up against it, so I've come to lend a hand."

"Oh, how good and brave of you!" Leander's eyes shone. "What on earth are we standing in the middle of the road for?" She took him by the arm. "Come along, let's get you settled in. When did you land?"

"Four o'clock this morning. I'm starving!"

"We'll soon put a stop to that!"

Ushering her new-found grandson up the drive, Leander Hawksworth had already decided that he could do no wrong.

Amelia caught the atmosphere the instant she entered the kitchen. Emma and Elsie, both busy with pastry, looked

60

fed-up to the back teeth; even the effervescent Polly Izzard was sullen.

"Hello, Amelia, you look tired," Emma said. "Has Silas told you about the new arrival?"

"Yes. Where is he?"

"Closeted in the library with Mother. As usual."

"What's he like?"

"Go and see for yourself."

"Yes, I suppose I must." Amelia flashed an appealing glance at Silas, but he was sitting down at the big table, smiling ruefully and shaking his head.

Leander was startled when Amelia went in. "Oh, hello, darling. Are you home for a few days?" Her tone was distracted, lacking its normal warmth. As she spoke, the man sitting with his back to the door turned round, a smile already fixed on his handsome face. Amelia felt giddy; the resemblance to the George of thirty-odd years ago was unnerving.

"This is Peter," Leander said. "He's George's son, all the way from South Africa. Peter, meet your Aunt Amelia."

When he stood up, the smile widening, Amelia saw that he was very like the brother she had not seen since 1906. At twenty-eight, Peter Hawksworth was a good-looking devil, with George's attractively dark colouring.

"I'm delighted to meet you, Aunt Amelia," he said. "Father said you were the clever one. Cambridge and all that, eh?"

To forestall an embrace that she knew would have been repugnant, Amelia held out her hand to him. Taken aback, he shook it and looked at a momentary loss for words.

"George died two years ago," Leander told Amelia.

"Oh, I'm sorry." There was no question of her being genuinely upset by the news: however anxious his grandmother was to make amends, Peter realised that Amelia would never forget the past. She made an effort to be pleasant. "I'm afraid you catch us a good deal short of our best, Peter. The War is making everything very difficult."

He nodded earnestly. "That's why I'm here, to do my bit."

61

"You must have had a difficult journey," Amelia said.

He laughed. "Awful! I was on the *Caerphilly Castle*. We were stuck at Gibraltar for ten days while the captain and owners decided whether it was safe to go on. When we *did* get going, we went half-way to America to miss the U-boats. We finally fetched up at Southampton at four o'clock on Monday morning."

"Terrible, isn't it?" Leander said.

Amelia agreed, concealing her feelings. She had no doubt that if she asked Ambrose Vane to check up, he would find that the *Caerphilly Castle* had indeed arrived on Monday morning after a circuitous and troubled passage from Gibraltar. She was equally certain that her nephew had not been on it.

"Are you staying long, dear?" Leander asked Amelia. She sounded vague, scarcely interested.

"A week. The first thing I need is a day's sleep."

"Yes, you look as though you've been overdoing it." Leander turned to Peter. "Your aunt is doing very important work at the Ministry of Food."

Amelia could easily have imagined that it was made to sound derogatory. When she left the library after promising to have a long talk with Peter tomorrow, she felt that she was removing an interruption between two close friends.

"Well?" Emma asked when Amelia returned to the kitchen. "What do you think?"

"I don't like him," Amelia said bluntly.

"None of us do," Emma replied unhappily. "Except Mother. She's utterly besotted with him."

"Yes . . . well . . . there are reasons for that." Amelia was evasive, not wishing to be explicit about George in front of Elsie. "Anyway, I'm going home to bed. Come and see me tomorrow, Emma."

Silas said nothing as he walked Amelia up to Louise House. He was, as she imagined, pursuing his ingrained policy of staying out of family problems. There were, however, more powerful reasons for his silence. Silas knew things about Peter's father that were the village's darkest secret. Now that George himself and Rupert Timberlake were dead, Leander was the only other person privy to the story.

Indoors, Amelia went straight to the telephone and put through a call to an Admiralty office above a shop in Trafalgar Square. Silas heard her say: "Daphne, it's Amelia Hawksworth. Will you contact Captain Vane on the ATN and ask him to ring me at home, please? It's fairly urgent."

Replacing the receiver, she called out for Silas to come and sit beside her. "This is a long way round," she explained. "But I don't want the operator to know Ambrose's number. Those women in the exchange are fearful gossips!"

Vane's call took only ten minutes to come through and he was able to provide the information Amelia wanted from papers that were on his desk. "Oh yes, we know all about the *Caerphilly Castle*," he said. "We've been waiting to grab her to take troops out to Port Said. She eventually docked at Southampton on Monday morning from Cape Town."

"What time, Ambrose?"

"Er . . . hang on . . . good gracious! It was four o'clock. I'm surprised those blasted dockers let her in!"

Amelia thanked him, promised an explanation of her interest and terminated the call.

"Do you want to tell me?" Silas asked, seeing that she was deep in calculating thought.

"My nephew says that he arrived in Southampton on Monday morning on board a ship that was three weeks late. Captain Vane confirms his story about the voyage and the time of docking."

"So what's wrong?"

"Two things." Amelia paused to reconsider them. "There's a stack of luggage for him at Savernake that's come from Lincoln. And, if he wasn't on it, how does my *dear* nephew come to be so well-informed about the *Caerphilly Castle*?"

Despite the urgency of both questions, Amelia allowed Silas to put her to bed and was asleep even as he bent to kiss her.

Fifteen minutes later, he tip-toed back into the bedroom, checked that she was dead to the world, then set off to see Claude in Marlborough. There was, Silas thought, every chance that the Timberlakes would shortly be resuming their traditional role as the undertakers of dirty work for Latimer's Barn.

It was eight hours and nearly midnight before he returned. Amelia stirred and grumbled when he slipped into bed beside her, but stayed fast asleep. By that time, a Timberlake employee from Grimsby had been in Lincoln long enough to check that Peter Hawksworth's luggage had indeed been dispatched from St Mark's station on 25 May. He also knew the address at which Peter had lodged for the previous eight months.

When Emma invited herself to lunch at Louise House the following day, Amelia, now refreshed and alert, learned that Leander was not the only person to be entranced by the newcomer.

"Rachel thinks he's the bee's knees." Emma was obviously far from happy with her daughter.

Amelia shrugged. "I could see them getting on well together," she said. "From what I saw of Peter, they're very similar types." She frowned at a sudden thought. "By the way, where's he sleeping?"

"Oh, nothing but the best," Emma replied. "Mother's given him Steven's room." Although Amelia said nothing, her look was worth a great many words. "Tell me, does Mother *really* have this much reason to feel guilty about George?" Emma asked.

"*I* certainly don't think so," Amelia said. "George came very close to ruining the stable. Being packed off to South Africa was actually quite mild."

"Well, as I said, Mother is besotted with Peter," Emma repeated. "She's talking of making him a Trustee and letting him do something in the stable after the War."

"That's outrageous!" Silas, a passive observer, blinked at the uncharacteristic vehemence of Amelia's anger. "*That* will definitely have to be squashed." Sighing, she shook her head sadly. "Of course, we have to accept that Mother is getting very old."

Changing the subject deliberately, they talked about the progress of the War, especially in the new Mediterranean and North African theatres. Amelia's inquiry for news of Steven brought the information that he had been promoted to the rank of lieutenant and caused Emma to become animated about Ann Redmayne.

"Has there been a development?" Amelia asked.

"Definitely! Steven had a drink with Norman, her father, during his last leave. I don't know what they cooked up, but Steven asked Ann to go out with him a few days later."

"And?" Amelia asked impatiently.

"She jumped at it! They had a super time. He saw her every day after that *and* she came to dinner at The House on his last evening."

"Prospects?" Amelia wondered.

"I hope so! She's a lovely girl and they seem awfully taken with each other."

"What did Mother think of her?"

"She liked her a lot." Emma's spirits fell. "That was before the golden boy turned up, of course."

Peter Hawksworth appeared at a time when Rachel was at a very low ebb.

Very little was happening in the yard. With frequent racing at Newmarket, those who had stables near the course, and could walk their horses to a meeting, were able to maintain something closely resembling normal routine. To be constantly ferrying horses from Wiltshire to Suffolk by train was simply not a practical proposition, however, and, on Leander's insistence, they had virtually stopped doing it.

Money was not a problem since the War was precisely the sort of emergency for which the Fund had been built up. The interest on the two million pounds was more than enough to run the stable, especially with its sharply reduced outgoings, and the stud was making a handsome contribution. Most of its foals were now being sold into Newmarket stables instead of being 'home-trained'.

Matthew, the Fund's Treasurer, essayed a flippant comment at the April meeting of the Trustees to approve the annual accounts. "It's starting to look as though we might make more money if we didn't bother with *training* horses."

Leander gave him a look that guaranteed there would be no more attempts at humour along those lines.

More determined than ever not to return to Eaton Mandeville now that the Duchess had turned the place into a knitting factory for Army socks, Rachel sat tight and fumed.

Peter came as a great gale of invigorating fresh air.

"My God," he laughed when Leander introduced them. "Fancy having a cousin who's a real-live Marchioness."

"It's no better than finding you've got a cousin as good looking as you," she responded. Peter grinned and kissed her again.

While Emma was at Louise House, Rachel showed Peter over the two yards, doing her best to be cheerful about the lack of activity.

"Don't worry, I can imagine what it must be like," he assured her. Looking round the feed-store of the 1874 yard, he noticed the ladder that disappeared into the loft and asked, "What's up there?"

"Nothing, only a loft. It's absolutely out of bounds."

"Why?"

"We had a terrible fire four years ago . . . six horses and two lads killed." Peter looked suitably upset. "It was in the other yard, not this one, but it started in the loft."

"How?"

"One of the lads was up there with a girl. They were at it – you know."

"*That* never started a fire, surely?" he said with a straight face.

"No, don't be silly!" Rachel giggled in spite of the story's tragic seriousness. "The lad always liked a smoke afterwards and he was careless with the match. The lofts used to be full of straw and rubbish. It was *awful*!"

"So folks keep well away now?"

"On pain of instant dismissal, if not death," Rachel said.

"Let's go and have a look, eh?"

"All right."

They climbed up the ladder like two children sharing a forbidden adventure. "It isn't all that dark," Peter said, helping Rachel off the ladder.

"That's the ventilators," she explained. "Very necessary . . . the horses can produce a terrible fug, even in winter."

Peter looked round curiously as his eyes adjusted to the gloomy half-light. "You've got electricity up here," he said, spotting the line of bulbs hanging from the beam that supported the ridge of the roof.

"Oh, it's all mod cons," Rachel laughed. "You might get electrocuted, but at least it's clean. There's nothing to burn. Come on, let's go before we get shouted at."

Back at ground level, Peter said, "I suppose this is all locked up at night?"

Rachel found the idea hilarious. "You need keys for that. They got lost *years* ago."

"According to Dad, Grandmother never allowed things like that to happen," Peter said.

"Sorry, even Leander has to bow to the foibles of human nature. If we want security we can close the main gate." She pointed to the archway. "It's always left open these days in case we need to get at the horses in a hurry if some bastard starts dropping bombs. Where to now? Would you like to go to Rose House and see the workshops?"

"I don't think so." He smiled as though involving her in a conspiracy. "To be honest, it sounds boring."

"How right you are!" Rachel whispered, hugging one of his arms which he promptly put round her. "It's very good furniture, but they don't half go on about it. In any case, they aren't doing any now."

"No market?" Peter suggested.

"I think it had gone pretty dead, then they were taken over by the Ministry of Aircraft Production."

"They're surely not building aeroplanes?"

"Don't be silly! They're messing about with bits and pieces

for some daft bugger who thinks he can make a bomber out of wood . . . I know, ridiculous, isn't it?"

"I tell you what we could do," Peter said. "I don't think the railway company is ever going to deliver my luggage. Can we go and fetch it?"

"Definitely!" Rachel jumped at the prospect of something to relieve the boredom. "I'll get one of the vans." Glancing at her watch, she thought of a way to enhance the adventure. "I know a lovely little pub where we can get some decent sandwiches and a drink."

Bill Churchward, glad to be rid of the trunks and crate, went through the form-signing ritual without mentioning Lincoln. Afterwards, when they were in a cosy corner of a quaint bar, Peter enlisted Rachel's help with the disposition of the crate.

"It's full of books," he told her. "I shan't want them until the War's over."

"What sort of books?"

"Civil engineering."

"Golly, you don't *look* like an engineer!"

"What are they supposed to look like?"

"Not nearly as interesting as you, my dear!"

He smiled briefly before returning to the problem. "I can't see any point in taking that ugly great box into The House. Where can I put it until it's needed?"

Rachel frowned thoughtfully. "Would it be all right in the stable-loft?"

"That's ideal! What about Gran, though? You said no one and nothing was allowed up there."

"You leave her to me," Rachel promised.

A couple of hours later, Silas was in the 1874 yard. He was talking to Alfred Merriweather about the very vague possibility of three horses being allowed to go to Newmarket. If they did travel, he, and three men of a type Leander preferred not to know about, would be in charge of looking after them.

Leander herself turned up to supervise the hoisting of the box into the loft. With expressionless faces, Silas and Alfred

68

watched the straining and heaving of the five lads roped in for the job. When it was all over, surprisingly without injury, Alfred gave Peter Hawksworth a filthy look as he returned to The House with Leander.

"It's all right for some," Alfred growled.

"Is he making things difficult?" Silas asked.

Alfred teetered on the brink of an unusual burst of feeling, then thought better of it.

At ten o'clock the following morning, Silas was chatting to friends in Marlborough when he saw Peter emerging from a bank on the other side of the broad High Street. Patting the breast pocket of his jacket, he was looking smugly satisfied as he hurried towards the car he had borrowed from Rachel.

To the casual observer, it would have seemed perfectly innocent: either he had brought money with him from South Africa, or he was arranging for funds to be transferred from Bloemfontein, his erstwhile home town. Silas was convinced that it was anything but innocent.

On the day before Amelia's leave finished, Peter went to London, saying that there were people who wanted to talk to him about a job. Leander told everyone that after telephoning a man whose name Peter had been given on the boat from Cape Town, he had received an important-looking letter.

"Keep this under your hat," she said to Emma. "I think it's got something to do with the invasion of France. Oh, yes! Winston will be thinking about it. And they'll need engineers, you know, as well as guns and muscle."

Silas would have given anything to have Peter followed but, as yet, he had no one capable of doing the job.

That evening, while he and Amelia were adjusting to the unpalatable prospect of another long separation, she interrupted the deep peace that followed their love-making with an uneasy question.

"Can I ask you to do something for me while I'm stuck in London, darling?"

"Of course."

"It's pretty awful."

"It sounds worth doing!"

"I think it is. Will you keep an eye on Peter?"

"I already am doing."

She misunderstood him. "I mean be really nosy. Try to find out why he's here."

"I told you, I am."

"Are you?"

"Yes. I have a fair idea what he was up to for eight months in Lincolnshire."

"*Eight months*!" Amelia was staggered. "What was he doing?"

"Never mind, just leave it to me."

Reassured, and wanting to make the most of their ebbing time together, Amelia snuggled into his arms. "It's quite like old times," she said.

"In what way?"

"When the Timberlakes spent nearly all their time dealing with scoundrels."

On his first night alone, Silas did not bother going to bed. After clearing up his supper things, he listened to the wireless for an hour, after which he settled down to read Ernest Hemingway's latest novel, *For Whom the Bell Tolls*. At one o'clock, he picked up a torch and went outside into a still, warm night.

There was no need for furtive caution and Silas strode briskly along the Back Stretch and Roadway, straight into the 1874 yard. Treading more carefully to avoid disturbing the horses, he went to the feed-store and climbed the ladder to the loft.

The crate was within easy reach of the entrance. Settling down to examine it, Silas was immediately struck by the care that had been used in its construction: it was screwed together, not nailed, and the timber was of above-average quality. He had been peering at the box for well over a minute before making the truly significant discovery. The lid was hinged, and so was what he now realised must be the front. The two by three foot panel was divided horizontally. Silas took a great deal of time examining the screws, fixing them indelibly in his mind's eye.

Borrowing a screwdriver from Wm Flamsteed & Sons turned out to be much the worst part of this initial operation. Matthew wanted to know what it was wanted for and why couldn't he send a man up to fix it. At long last, Silas was taken to a workshop in which a group of carpenters were puzzling over an assembly of spars and struts and allowed to make his own selection from the two-hundred-odd screwdrivers available.

That night, after another session with Hemingway, Silas returned to the loft. There were a dozen screws to be removed, each three inches long. With the painstaking care that he hoped would leave no sign of tampering, it took a quarter of an hour. In the instant before he lifted the lid and eased the front flap down, Silas realised that he had no idea what he was expecting to find.

He stared at it for an eternity, resisting the temptation to fiddle. Silas did not put the screws back in until he had decided precisely what he was going to do next and that occupied him until the first light of a June dawn was stealing into the eastern sky.

Ignoring his sleepless night, Silas had a busy day, mostly fetching and carrying for Leander, all things that kept him near The House and Peter Hawksworth. Then he spent the evening looking for Solstice Jackson.

'Solstice' had always been something of a celebrity. His natural mother abandoned him on a doorstep in Jackson's Lane, off Marlborough High Street, on Midsummer's Day, 1920. The Parish took him in, calling him Jackson after the lane and Trevor for whimsical good measure. When found on 24 June he was no more than two days old, strongly suggesting that he had been born at the time of the summer solstice. The nickname stuck like glue.

At the age of fourteen, Solstice had removed himself from the care of the Parish and talked himself into a small stable at Ogbourne Maizey where he had developed into a

71

phenomenally talented rider. When the War began, there was talk of him becoming a jockey, but Solstice ended up being evacuated from Dunkirk with his right leg shattered and the certain knowledge that he would never be able to ride properly again. His guv'nor, far too old to be fooling around with such things, stopped three German bullets the day after Solstice was brought home and the stable's new owner could barely make a living for himself, let alone think of looking after a cripple. Solstice had been to Latimer's Barn for a job, only to be sent packing by Alfred Merriweather, albeit with a pound note to keep him going.

Silas found him in a pub at Alton Priors, one of the half-dozen villages strung out between Cannings St John and Devizes. Solstice, engaged in a game of crib, looked expectant when he saw Silas and hurried to his side in response to the nod that denoted a summons.

"How are you keeping, Solstice?" Silas asked.

"Mustn't grumble, Mr Timberlake."

Silas ordered two pints of beer and looked round the room. "Over there," he said, pointing to a table in a dingy corner. "How's the leg coming along?"

"Not too badly, thank you, sir." The way he winced as he sat down told a different story. "Er . . . we don't expect to see you down this way," Solstice said tentatively.

Silas was in no mood to waste time. "I've been looking for you," he said. "What are you up to these days?"

"I got nothing doing at the minute, Mr Timberlake."

"This assignment is unusual . . . what you might call definitely out of the ordinary," Silas said. "Make a decent show of it and I'll guarantee you a permanent billet at Latimer's Barn."

"And if I muck it up, you'll have my guts for garters?" Solstice asked.

Silas ignored the question. "I hear you're living rough," he said.

"Oh, no, Mr Timberlake! Tommy Weston's letting me use his shed in return for a bit of this and that."

"That's no good to me. I need you where I can get

hold of you quickly. How do you fancy the Castle and Ball?"

Solstice laughed. "Nice, if you can afford it!"

"I can, so that's where you're going."

"Blimey, Mr Timberlake, are you having me on?"

"No, Solstice, I am not. Be there with your kit at seven tomorrow evening. And only bring decent clothes with you . . . burn the rest." He looked suspiciously at the things Solstice was wearing.

"That won't leave me with much, Mr Timberlake."

"Never mind, I'll fix you up with new stuff."

Twenty-four hours later, Solstice was duly installed in the Castle and Ball hotel at Marlborough. Silas paid the astonished proprietor a month's full board in advance, plus a generous allowance for use of the telephone. In the privacy of a room about ten times better than anything he had ever known, Solstice was given his orders.

"Within the next two weeks, I shall want you to follow a man," Silas said. "It will be a long trip, lasting several days, and he'll probably wander all over the shop. There's unlikely to be much notice, so I want you ready to leave at the drop of a hat. Ring me up at eight o'clock *every* morning and again at ten o'clock at night. Don't go swanning off anywhere . . . stay within easy reach of this place. Here's your beer money."

Solstice was so surprised to find that the bundle thrown at him contained twenty-five one-pound notes that he forgot to ask who the man was.

Peter was away for eight days. Silas witnessed his return and saw how excited Rachel and Leander were. In an obscure way that Silas was unable to pin-point, there was something disturbing about Rachel's enthusiasm. Before Peter was whisked away to give a full account of his experiences, he told everyone in the kitchen that he had landed a job with the Air Ministry. It was concerned with the building of new airfields and very secret.

Silas left Louise House as soon as darkness fell at eleven

o'clock. Hurrying to the 1874 yard, he made himself comfortable in his prepared hiding place, an empty box next to the feed-store and directly under the crate. Closing the top half of the door fully, but leaving a one-inch gap in the lower half, Silas settled down for a long wait. If Peter were coming out, he would have to put up with Rachel's notorious late-night gossiping and then allow plenty of time for The House to settle down.

It was nearly three o'clock before Silas heard the light footfall coming towards him. Entering the feed-store, Peter was only six feet from the unobtrusive opening to which Silas had an eye fixed. The ladder creaked. Soon afterwards, there was the sound of a ratchet screwdriver. This was followed by a series of strange noises that puzzled Silas until he realised that Peter needed electricity. After a five-minute silence, the tapping of the Morse key, with the crate acting like a sounding box on the floor above Silas, was perfectly audible.

Later that morning, while Silas was fighting his tiredness and running errands for Leander, Peter slept until Rachel brought him a lunch-tray at half past twelve.

"What are you planning to do today?" she asked, sitting on his bed as he began to eat.

"As little as possible," he replied. "I've got half a ton of paperwork to get through, but that can wait until tomorrow."

"How about an afternoon out?" Rachel asked. "I need to get away from this place before I start screaming."

"What's the trouble?"

"Everything!"

Peter saw that she was thoroughly overwrought. "You could show me Savernake Forest," he said quietly.

Considerably more cheerful, Rachel hurried away to have lunch with her sons and Emma, a part of her daily routine that was turning into a chore. Rachel knew that Emma's delighted willingness to look after Henry and Edmund was masking a problem. By the normal standards of the nobility, Rachel was an adequate mother: in fact, her sons probably saw far more of her than did most aristocratic offspring who were still subjected to Victorian regimes of being seen only occasionally and *never* heard. But looking at the issue from a Latimer's Barn point of view gave a very different answer, one that suggested Rachel was the worst mother the family had known. She found that it required considerable effort to say, "I'm taking Peter out for a drive this afternoon," without sounding nervous or guilty.

"That's nice," Emma replied with a bland smile. "I expect you both need a rest. Peter seems to have been very busy."

"We might decide to have a meal out this evening," Rachel ventured.

"Well, good luck to you," Emma said. "I think we have a choice between toad-in-the-hole and spam fritters."

Rachel made a gruesome face that was faithfully copied by the children. "The horses eat better than we do," she said. "Not that it does us any good!"

Refusing to respond to the jibe against Leander's policy, Emma told Rachel to enjoy herself.

Leaving Cannings Ambo twenty minutes later, Rachel and Peter had their customary air of schoolchildren escaping for a treat. The mood persisted until they had been in the forest and bumping along its rutted tracks for half an hour.

"Let's stop and stretch our legs," Peter suggested. "Look, here's a good place."

Rachel swung the car into a grassy clearing. The silence was startling once the engine was turned off. For a while, neither of them wanted to break it. Rachel finally did so with a question that made Peter smile by its directness.

"Will you stay here after the War?"

"No, I don't think so," he said. "Nearly everyone seems to hate my guts."

"That's your father's fault," Rachel replied. "Latimer's Barn bears grudges for a *long* time. Do you know, Leander still goes on about a man who tried to do her down in eighteen-eighty-something . . . imagine that!"

"I can. Dad always said that she was a marvellous friend and a terrible enemy. I seem to be getting the best of her!"

75

"Will you go back to South Africa?" Rachel asked.

"Very likely . . . it's a good place so long as they keep the blacks down and Pretoria won't take chances over that. In any case, win or lose, England will be finished." Rachel did not challenge the opinion: she had heard others say the same thing. "What about you?" Peter asked.

"Oh, I'm going to be a Duchess when I grow up!" Rachel replied mockingly.

"Aren't you looking forward to it?"

"It will have to do, won't it? I shall keep reminding myself that most women would like to swap places with me." Rachel neither knew nor cared what drove her to say such a stupid thing. Later, she came to the conclusion that it was to hasten the inevitable.

Peter stared at her. They both moved together. Their kiss had nothing to do with being cousins. It was a flagrant expression of need between a man and a woman who had been powerfully attracted to each other from their first meeting.

"What about your bloody husband?" Peter asked, made frantic by the way she reacted to him. "Why doesn't he look after you?"

"He's busy," Rachel said. "Military intelligence. Very important work . . . he can't be bothered with me any more." She was angry and elated. For more than two months she had suspected that Charles was inventing excuses to stay in London. Travelling took up too much of his precious thirty-six hours; there had been tentative comments about invitations to spend weekends at Lord Dorchester's place near Esher; perhaps he was involved with a woman: it was being said that most men were finding war had its compensations.

"It would take more than military intelligence to make me neglect you," Peter muttered.

She dragged him from the car. Blundering into the trees, they found a suitable place at once. Finesse was out of the question. Rachel unbuttoned the front of her dress. "Now, Peter," she snapped as they sank to the ground. "Do it to me now!"

He lunged into her with blind disregard for her comfort. Even as she uttered it, her cry of pain turned to pleasure.

"Go on, go on!" she urged.

By invitation, Peter Hawksworth took his cousin savagely. Despite his inability to control the act, she climaxed before him, enjoying a second, lesser wave of pleasure when she felt his semen erupt.

"Bloody war!" she whispered as she drove herself against him to extract every last morsel of relief from their brutishness.

The bloody war!

At a pinch, it would have served as an excuse for a single reckless exploit. But as the minutes passed, there was no question of embarrassment or shock: on the contrary, they were proud of themselves. Having actively encouraged the resurgence of Peter's desire, Rachel urged him into her again. This time, fully conscious of what they were doing, they spun the pleasure out, teasing and savouring each other's bodies.

Later, after dinner at a hotel in Hungerford, Rachel stopped the car at the foot of the Latimer's Barn drive and set Peter's mind at rest.

"I'll come to your room when everyone's asleep," she promised.

She did so. And on each of the following eight nights before Peter went away again, Rachel was creeping back to her own bedroom at four o'clock in the morning.

In the event, there was plenty of time for Silas to give Solstice a thorough briefing over supper at the Castle and Ball on the evening before Peter's departure.

"Our man is going to London tomorrow morning on the eleven-twenty from Savernake," he said. "*You* will already be on the train. It stops at Pewsey about ten minutes earlier. If I pick you up at ten that will give us plenty of time. Now, you know Lady Glastonbury, Miss Rachel Hawksworth as was?"

"Yes, sir. Lovely young lady."

"You'd recognise her?"

77

"First time, Mr Timberlake."

"Good. Your man will be with her . . . at least, she's taking him to the station and I'm assuming that she'll stay with him until the train comes. Just in case, here's a photograph." Silas handed over a snapshot he had taken a few days previously on the pretext of keeping Amelia's album up-to-date. To the surprise of everyone except Silas, Peter had been reluctant to pose.

"And this chap's going to London?" Solstice asked, putting the picture into his smart new wallet.

"He *says* he is, Solstice, but I want you to be prepared for anything. Do your damnedest to stay with him for at least two days. Find out what he's up to."

Summoning up all the common sense and downright cunning he had acquired during his unusual life, Solstice seemed to age at least ten years. "I'll do my best, sir," he promised.

"Here's a hundred pounds for your expenses." Silas gave him an envelope. "Have a good think about it . . . try to work out where you might have problems and we'll talk about it on the way to Pewsey tomorrow morning."

Peter left on a Monday morning. That evening, Amelia arrived for a short visit.

"Have you discovered anything about Peter?" was the first thing she said to Silas when they were alone together.

Knowing that her job at the Admiralty would cause Amelia to take terrible fright if his theory was correct, Silas restricted himself to Peter's strange comings and goings. He made no mention of the crate in the stable-loft or of Solstice Jackson: absolute proof was needed before he risked exposing the woman he worshipped to such strain. It was the first time he had ever been less than frank with her and he vowed it would be the last.

"And you think he's lying about this job with the Air Ministry?" Amelia asked, frowning.

"I reckon so."

"I think we ought to talk to the police," Amelia said.

"All in good time, my dear. There are one or two things to be checked up on first."

Amelia came close to protesting, then thought better of it, remembering that her mild and loving Silas could be utterly ruthless when the need arose. He knew what he was doing.

The uncertainty was resolved far more quickly than Silas had anticipated. On Tuesday afternoon, while Amelia was over at The House, Solstice telephoned.

"Is that you, Mr Timberlake, sir?" he asked, circumstances and a poor connection making him sound uneasy.

"Yes. Are you in trouble?"

Solstice scorned the idea. " 'Course not! I've got our man, and very interesting it all is."

"Where are you?"

"Okehampton. It was like you said, he wasn't going to London. He was off that train at Reading. I had a bit of a ta-ta finding out where he was making for, but we eventually fetched up in Exeter about five o'clock. There was two blokes waiting for him . . . they were huddled in the buffet for ages. Then he left them and came to this place. I must say, it's very handy. He's got digs on one side of the main street and I'm slap-bang opposite."

"Has anything been happening today?" Silas asked, unable to work out what attractions a sleepy Devon town could possibly hold for Peter Hawksworth.

"You bet your socks it has!" Solstice chuckled. "There's an Army camp two miles down the road. It ain't much to look at, but they've got a bloody great artillery range . . . reaches all the way across Dartmoor to the prison. Our man was out there at six o'clock this morning with the funniest looking telescope you've ever seen."

"How do you know?"

"I was watching him," Solstice said, as though speaking to an idiot. "My old guv'nor's binoculars can see a gnat peeing at half a mile."

"Were they firing?" Silas asked eagerly.

"Started about eight o'clock and carried on until ten. They

were shooting at some old tanks . . . made a right mess of 'em!"

Silas was thinking. The silence was shattered by the noise of Solstice feeding more coins into the call-box telephone. "You can come back," Silas ordered.

"Oh, sir, I'm enjoying myself," Solstice protested. "Haven't had so much fun since I was a kid."

"You've done what I wanted and there's no point in hanging around. Get back here."

"Does this get me that job, Mr Timberlake?" Solstice was doing his best not to sound anxious.

"Yes. Definitely. Listen carefully. Stay in your digs tonight and catch the first train in the morning. Do *not* go near that man. Is that clear, Solstice?"

"Oh, yes, Mr Timberlake!" He had picked up the hint of danger.

"Get yourself into the Castle and Ball and I'll see you tomorrow evening."

Returning to Louise House half an hour later, Amelia saw at once that Silas was tense and excited. "Tell me!" she said.

"Do you think your friend Captain Vane could find out what the Army have been doing today at Okehampton?" he asked.

Room 39 was making her very resilient. She looked completely unruffled. "No, that would be awkward for him," she said calmly. "I can try Charles."

"Charles?" Silas was baffled.

"He's very highly placed and he knows about me. We turned up together at a Joint Services Planning Committee last week." She smiled. "We promised to keep quiet about each other."

"I should think so, too," Silas laughed. Most people were under the impression that Charles was even more insignificant than Amelia. "Will he help?"

"I can but try. In the interests of sparing my blushes and security, will you go for a walk while I do it, darling?"

Silas mooched round the orchard, his mind furiously busy.

80

He was so abstracted that Amelia was unable to gain his attention by waving and shouting from a window; eventually, she went out to fetch him. Linking an arm through his, she maintained silence for a few paces. When she did speak, it was in a matter-of-fact sort of way.

"A new anti-tank gun is being tested on the Okehampton range today and tomorrow. It was to have been last week, but there was a hold-up with the ammunition." She paused. "Charles wondered how you came to know about it."

"Because Peter has gone to watch the test."

"While telling all and sundry that he was with the Air Ministry in London!" Amelia was determined to give the impression that she was remaining calm. "Could I ask how you know?"

"I had him followed."

"Do you think he's spying for the Germans?"

"I'm damned sure he is!" Silas told her about the transmitter in the stable-loft and the way Peter had used it in the dead of night after his first absence. Amelia's calmness evaporated.

"That settles it! You *must* talk to the police."

"I have an appointment to see Superintendent Croft tomorrow morning."

"Is that soon enough?" Amelia asked doubtfully.

"I think so. Your nephew won't be back here until Thursday afternoon at the earliest."

"Don't you *dare* call him that again," Amelia seethed. "It's a pity his blasted father wasn't sterilised!"

Superintendent Croft, after listening to Silas's tale in gravely attentive silence, made an astounding statement.

"I've been wondering what to do about that scoundrel." Seeing the look on Silas's face, he hastened to explain. "This doesn't show the authorities in too good a light, I'm afraid, Mr Timberlake. The fact is, this chap got into the country six weeks before the War started."

"From South Africa?"

"No, from Berlin. The immigration people don't seem to

have been nearly as interested in him as they should have been. He gave them a cock-and-bull yarn and they swallowed it. He was in London until October of 'thirty-nine, then he cleared off to East Anglia. After that, it's *believed* he went to the Birmingham area . . . to be honest with you, no one's all that sure. Last autumn, he got lost altogether."

Silas shook his head. "That seems terribly sloppy, Mr Croft."

"It is, especially when you consider the number of perfectly innocent people who've been hounded from pillar to post. I have to admit that I didn't know he was on my patch until last week, then I smelt a rat."

"Why?" Silas asked.

"He's always coming into town to use a phone-box." Croft smiled. "I can't imagine Mrs Hawksworth getting cut off for not paying her bill. And he collects letters from the post office. Anyway, here was I, wondering what the hell to do, and you've sorted it all out for me."

"You're going to arrest him?"

"The moment I can get my hands on him, Mr Timberlake!"

They spent half an hour discussing the best way to do it. Silas went home to find that Amelia had been speaking to Captain Vane, obtaining permission to extend her stay at Latimer's Barn.

He understood at once. "Your mother, of course."

"She's going to get an awful shock!" Amelia said grimly.

"Oughtn't you to give her advance warning?"

"No!" Having come to terms with a distasteful truth, Amelia looked severe. "She's so ga-ga about the wretch that I wouldn't put it past her to try something stupid."

It was the first time that Silas had seen her display Leander's implacable toughness and it was not long before she provided another example of her resolve. During the afternoon, while The House was quiet, she searched Peter's room. Silas, not expecting her to find anything incriminating, was surprised when she returned with a small, linen-bound, grey book.

"That," she said, tossing it into his lap, "is a German

military intelligence code book. We believe it's about to be replaced. I wonder how he gets the new one?"

"Surely he didn't leave *this* lying about?" Silas said, flicking through the book without expectation of understanding a word.

"Of course not. Even he can't afford to be that arrogant. No, it was locked up in one of his trunks." Amelia had taken a shopping-bag with her. Now, with comical insouciance, she removed two kitchen knives, a pair of dressmaker's shears and a tyre lever. "I need more practice," she sighed. "I made a shocking mess of the locks."

When Silas went into Marlborough to see Solstice, Amelia accompanied him to thank the young man who had proved such a capable sleuth by standing him the best dinner that rationing allowed. Solstice, realising that the gesture from such an august member of the Cannings Ambo clan meant that he was home and dry, had only one worry.

"I've got seventy quid of that expense money left, Mr Timberlake. Do you want me to hang on to it for next time?"

"There isn't going to be a next time," Silas replied. "Keep it for your wages, Solstice."

"What, *all* of it?"

"Yes."

"And I carry on living it up at the Castle and Ball?"

"Unless you want to go back to Tommy Weston's shed before you move to Latimer's Barn."

Silas was all for going straight to bed when they were back home, but Amelia shook her head. "I'm sorry, you'll have to be patient for an hour or two," she said. "I want to look at that thing in the loft, so we shall have to wait for everything to settle down."

At long last, Amelia was holding the torch while Silas removed the screws from the crate. When the transmitter was exposed, she stared at it with utter loathing.

"I suppose you'd like to smash it up?" Silas said.

"No, I imagine we shall need it in working order," she replied. "I tell you what I would like to do, though."

"What?"

"Use it to send false information."

"You could soon find out how to do that."

"No, it wouldn't work. The way a person taps out Morse code is as distinctive as their voice, or handwriting. Peter's opposite number on the other side would recognise another operator within seconds."

Silas grinned. "You're learning some amazing things at the Ministry of Food, my dear." After a pause, he asked, "I wonder what made Peter do it?"

"That's easy enough," Amelia replied. "I expect his father brought him up to hate England and the Nazis will be paying him well. As an added bonus, he was probably hoping to get us into trouble . . . no, don't fasten it up, leave it as it is. Let's go to bed now."

Inadvertently, Rachel ensured that the arrangements were easy enough to make. Peter telephoned her on Thursday and she trumpeted the news to all and sundry.

"Peter's coming down on the five-fifteen from London and he wants *me* to meet him!"

Going back to Louise House, Amelia said, "They'll be here about ten to seven." Silas telephoned Superintendent Croft.

In the event, the train was late and it was nearly ten minutes past seven when Rachel turned into the drive: having missed Peter dreadfully, she was euphoric. After a very successful trip, he had only one worry: how did he get Rachel out of his bedroom so that he could go to the stable-loft and relay his findings to Berlin? He was confident that the near violence of his pent-up lust would exhaust her in time. Chatting gaily, and preoccupied with the delights that lay ahead, neither of them noticed the police car lurking in the village lane.

Leander, who was sitting in the library, looked up from the Big Book as she heard Rachel's car on the gravel in front of The House. She was at the window, waving to Peter, when the police car hurtled from the drive and skidded to a halt behind Rachel's bull-nosed Morris. Shocked into disbelief,

Leander found herself fuming at her own embargo on the use of the front door.

Rachel was trying to work out what on earth the police thought they were doing when she realised that Peter had wrenched a dull black object from the leather bag at his feet. The menace of the Luger automatic pistol terrified her, as did the look of hatred in his eyes.

"You bitch!" he snarled. "Clever, aren't you!"

"What do you mean?" Rachel stammered. "Peter . . . I don't . . . what's happening?"

Ignoring her, he leaped from the car, turning to face Superintendent Croft, a sergeant and two constables.

"Stay where you are," Peter said, his voice steady but unpleasant. "Don't move . . . any of you." He was starting to back away, the gun in his right hand marking the four policemen. Rachel was frozen in her car. "I suppose you thought this was going to be easy," Peter sneered. "What fools!"

"That gun isn't a very good idea, sir," Superintendent Croft said. If he was frightened, he was concealing it well.

"I think it's a brilliant idea," Peter replied. "It evens things up nicely."

At that moment, still edging backwards, he collided with someone.

"The officer is quite right," Amelia said, and, while he was rattled and off-balance, she disarmed him. Ludicrously, it was as easy as pie: while Peter was looking over his left shoulder, she reached round his blind side and took the gun from his slack grasp. Silas, who had inched silently across the gravel with Amelia, struck Peter on the jaw as he attempted to snatch the Luger back. It was not a damaging blow, but it knocked him down. The sergeant and the sharper of the two constables were on him. Yet instead of calm, pandemonium had erupted.

Out of her car, Rachel was screaming hysterically at the policemen: after scratching the sergeant's face, she began kicking the shins of the constable who was struggling with Peter. To cap it all, Leander appeared from the side of The House in a towering rage. "What the *hell* are you doing,

Mr Croft?" she demanded. Emma, following her, made a rapid assessment of Rachel's state of mind and gave her a resounding slap across the face that stunned her into silent immobility. Unobserved, Amelia became aware that she was still holding the Luger and passed it to Silas. More concerned with his knuckles, he shoved it absent-mindedly into a jacket pocket.

"Well, Mr Croft?" Leander demanded.

"I'm very sorry, Mrs Hawksworth, but I have to take this gentleman into custody," he said.

"Don't be ridiculous!" Leander's eyes spat fire. "I warn you, I shall speak to the Chief Constable about this outrage. I'll make sure you lose your pension!"

"Mother!" Amelia moved to her side. "Peter is a German spy."

Emma, alone, remained impassive; Rachel sank on to the running-board of her car and sobbed quietly; with every vestige of colour drained from her face, Leander looked like death. "Is this true?" she whispered.

Amelia nodded, turning to Silas.

"Peter has been in England since before the War, Mrs Hawksworth," he said. "When he turned up here, he'd just spent eight months snooping round Lincolnshire, looking at the new airfields that are being built for bombers. This week, he's been watching a new anti-tank gun being tested on Dartmoor." Turning sharply, Leander saw that Peter was looking at Silas with astonished respect. "And I'm afraid to have to tell you that the crate you let him put in the stable-loft has a radio transmitter inside it. I've examined it and I've heard him using it."

There was absolute silence as Leander struggled with her emotions. When she finally spoke to Peter, her voice was sorrowful. "Why?" she asked him. "Why did you do it, Peter?"

"Don't you know?" Suddenly he was defiant. "My God, Dad said you were an arrogant hell-cat! Are you really so wrapped up in your own conceit that you're incapable of seeing why I should want to get back at you and this country after what you did to my father?"

In the tense silence, there was a barely perceptible change. The two policemen holding Peter eased their grip on his arms: they were fascinated by this unexpected turn; one of them was worrying about the damage Rachel had done to his face.

"And nothing changes, does it?" Peter continued, glaring hate at Leander. "You're still using Silas Timberlake for the nasty stuff, I see. I suppose after he kept Dad a prisoner in that bloody forest, you have to make sure he stays sweet. Aha!" He was gloatingly triumphant when he saw the disbelieving look that Amelia flashed at Leander. "I see no one knows about that little episode!"

Everybody made the mistake of staring at Leander. In that instant, Peter broke free. Before the policemen had time to realise it, he was behind them and holding another gun, a wicked-looking Mannlicher revolver that he had whipped from a holster under his jacket.

Superintendent Croft, the only one of the onlookers not paralysed with fear, flung himself towards Peter, who, without the slightest hesitation, shot him in the stomach. Before anyone had a chance to register shock, the weapon was turned on Leander.

She swayed and winced as the bullet struck home. When Emma reached out to support her, there was no visible sign that she had been hurt. Not until she sank to her knees and slumped forward was the growing bloodstain on the shoulder of her dress visible. Only Silas saw Peter steady himself to take a second aim at the prostrate Leander. He reached for the Luger and shot Peter Hawksworth through the heart.

When Sergeant Mole visited Louise House three days later, he was perfectly content to drink tea and let the conversation take its inevitable course.

"And how's Mrs Hawksworth?" he asked, after reporting that Superintendent Croft was off the danger list and confidently expected to pull through.

"Awful!" Amelia laughed. "I defy you to imagine a worse patient. She was as good as gold while Kathleen Stanton was getting the bullet out and stitching her up, but it's been

87

moan, moan, moan, since she found she had to have her arm in a sling."

"Makes sleeping very difficult," the sergeant said.

"And don't we know it! Thank the Lord for Elsie Collier – she's the only one who can do anything with her. We shall *have* to get her up tomorrow for some peace and quiet."

"No permanent damage then?"

"She's lost a few splinters of the collar-bone . . . otherwise, she'll be as right as rain in a few weeks."

Sergeant Mole nodded appreciatively. He fiddled with his cup and saucer, making the silence awkward.

"Spit it out," Silas said. "Have you come to charge me?"

"No, sir, I haven't," the sergeant said, glad of that at least. "But I do have to warn you of the possibility. It depends on the inquest."

"I understand," Silas said. "If Peter Hawksworth is deemed to have been killed unlawfully, I'm in trouble."

"It don't seem right to me," Sergeant Mole grumbled. "They'd have hung the bugger as soon as look at him if he'd still been alive."

"Never mind," Silas said calmly. "You know where I am if you want me."

Amelia and Silas found Leander looking more her old self that afternoon. Elsie had washed and set her hair and she was feeling all the better for a lunch of ham and eggs, personally delivered by Edward Mallender in defiance of rationing.

"There's something you can do for me," she said straightaway. "I want the Big Book and a pair of scissors."

"I'll fetch it," Silas offered.

"Oh, thank you, my dear."

As soon as Silas had gone, Leander looked at Amelia and was suddenly on the verge of tears. "I'm nothing but a silly old woman, aren't I?" she said. "Imagine being taken in like that. *Me*, of all people!"

"Now, Mother . . ." Amelia climbed on to the huge old bed to lie beside Leander, taking a tight hold on her good hand. "Perhaps you *were* too quick to accept Peter, but I know why you did it."

"George," Leander said tonelessly. "I wanted to make amends."

"You didn't have to," Amelia said quietly. "Silas has told me all about George coming back and doping the horses in nineteen-twelve and what you did about it. I think you were absolutely right – and very brave."

"I had George beaten until he signed a confession, you know."

"Silas told me *everything*, Mother, and I don't think you have anything to reproach yourself for." She paused and smiled. "Fancy Silas keeping that to himself all these years . . . he never breathed a word and I'm sure he never would have but for Peter."

"He's a very good man," Leander said, then, when it seemed she might cheer up, her face clouded. "Imagine Peter doing that, though! There's bad blood somewhere."

"That doesn't say much for you and Father," Amelia replied, trying to be flippant.

"Oh, no, darling, it was my mother. I'm sure of it. William and I were carriers. It came out in Maude, as well as George. If she ever had any children, they'll be the same."

Amelia thought the idea fanciful in the extreme, but said nothing. They remained lost in silent thought until Silas returned with the Big Book. Obeying Leander's instructions, he rested it on her legs and passed over the scissors.

"This is something that's never happened before," she said. Grimly, she added, "And it had better not happen again." Opening the book at the latest entries which were marked by a sheet of blotting-paper, she set to work with the scissors. "I'm afraid I wrote nearly two pages about my blasted grandson." She smiled. "In fifty years, whoever has charge of this book will see the missing page numbers and wonder what went wrong."

"You could put a note in to say that you spilt ink all over them," Amelia suggested.

"Don't be so damned prosaic, Amelia!" Leander scolded.

"No, we'll leave a mystery. God knows, we deserve it after this affair."

Amelia was reminded that within two hours of being shot, Leander had been sufficiently in possession of herself to ask the police to take Peter's body away. "I wonder where they'll bury him?" she mused.

"As far away from here as possible, I hope," Leander said. "Thank you, Silas." She closed the Big Book and he relieved her of its bulk and weight. "Thank you for everything. I'm going to look on the bright side and believe that you stopped me making a *complete* fool of myself. You saved my life, too . . . Emma tells me he wanted to finish me off."

"I'd do anything for you, Mrs Hawksworth," Silas said, quite unnecessarily. "I'm afraid you owe me a favour, though."

"Go on." Leander assumed an expression of mock-woe.

"I roped Solstice Jackson in to help with Peter. I said you'd give him a job if it all worked out."

"Young Solstice!" Leander was delighted. "That's how I used Joe Symes, you know. He once . . ." She stopped, aware that Amelia and Silas were looking expectant. "Yes, of course Solstice can have a job. Get him moved in and fixed up. Now, what about the news? Elsie tells me that Hitler has invaded Russia."

"Yes. He's bitten off more than he can chew this time," Silas said.

"Is it going to help us?" Leander was curious, eager to know, starting to put Peter behind her.

"Eventually," Amelia said. She had already spoken to Captain Vane and knew Churchill's thinking. "But there aren't going to be any quick solutions."

Gradually, The House and village returned to normal, pushing the trauma of Peter Hawksworth further into the past with each day that went by. There were even opportunities to make light of the episode's terrible culmination. Three weeks afterwards, the man whom Rachel had described as 'the daft bugger who thinks he can make a bomber out of wood' visited Rose House to inspect the prototype wing that Wm Flamsteed & Sons had now finished.

"I hear you had a German spy in the village not so long ago," he said to Matthew as they enjoyed the lunch prepared by Louise.

"Yes, but we shot the swine before he could get anywhere near this place," Matthew replied.

Geoffrey de Havilland's eyebrows rose. "My word, that is the ticket," he said, vastly impressed.

It was Rachel who had the greatest difficulty. The nervous energy she expended in appearing normal reduced her to a prostrated wreck by the end of every interminable day. When, four weeks after Peter's violent end, Charles telephoned to say that at long last he was able to get away from London, *and* for a whole fortnight, Rachel's reaction left him licking his lips with anticipation. Nor was he disappointed. The time he spent in the forest cottage with a wife who appeared insatiable was a memory he thought he would cherish forever.

Rachel had hoped to find that Charles could make her forget Peter. Instead, she discovered that he was nowhere near such a good lover as her cousin. Once she had admitted this to herself, she found their love-making totally unsatisfactory, yet Charles, who had never so much as looked at another woman, was completely deceived by her simulated passion.

Disgusting though it was, there was a powerful force driving Rachel to repeated union with the husband she had betrayed: a visit to a doctor in London two days before Charles's leave began had confirmed that she was pregnant.

She was confident that she could get away with the deception. Charles was always vague about dates and no one at Latimer's Barn took the blindest notice of her, particularly after it was learned that Silas would not have to face charges for shooting Peter Hawksworth.

For a time, Elsie, who had never concealed her intense dislike of Peter, was a worry. She was, Rachel felt, the sort of woman who would instinctively *know* things and was nauseatingly close to Leander. But, when all was said and done, what on earth did a peeress have to fear from a mere cook?

CHAPTER 4

1944

'This isn't the Ministry of Food, Auntie!'

There was still an hour to go before the January dawn when a battered old Citroën car finally gave up the struggle with the steep mountain track. Henri Guillaume knew that the clutch was done for. The raw morning air was vicious with the threat of snow; somewhere to his right, a mountain stream was breaking up into a waterfall, the roar of its cascade sounding unearthly in the freezing darkness.

His two companions emerged from the back of the car. Despite the noise and discomfort, they had slept for several hours, but they showed the harsh training and experience of the last three years in immediate wakefulness: their eyes had a feral alertness.

"It's given up on us, Henri?" the man asked. He was Alain de Mourville, twenty-six, the only son of a once noble family. Pampered in childhood, fawned upon in adolescence and early manhood, he had been given half a fortune and a bed of roses for his twenty-first birthday. Two years later, the Germans took possession of the family estates at Fontainebleau and de Mourville joined the *Résistance*. Now, he was one of the most illustrious members, a close friend of the legendary Colonel Romans-Petit, and one of the three men the Gestapo was most anxious to capture.

"Yes, *Patron*." Even after the years of partnership and the shared danger of the last two weeks, Henri was respectful.

He considered it the greatest honour to be de Mourville's escort.

"Have we far to go?"

"I don't know. I've been lost since midnight!"

De Mourville grinned sympathetically. They were high in the Pyrenees, making for the Spanish border. The last few days had been easier, especially since Henri had 'borrowed' the car in Toulouse, but even in the unoccupied part of France there was evidence of pro-German activity. Laval, now in charge of the Vichy clique, was said to be collaborating with the *Boche*.

"It can't be far," de Mourville said. "Come on, let's start walking."

"Shall we get rid of the car?" his companion asked.

The shapeless dungarees, donkey jacket, and woollen hat concealed the most beautiful girl that Henri had ever seen, more beautiful even than his own Marie-Claire. Nadia Cresson-Joubert was only twenty; she had matured fast, killing her first German when she was seventeen. She was de Mourville's inseparable companion and he had refused to go to England without her.

"What do you think, Henri?" de Mourville asked. "Do we push it over the edge, or can you use it going back?"

"Leave it," Henri said. It might be good for the first thirty kilometres, all steeply downhill.

They took the rucksacks from the car and set off, Henri in the lead, Sten gun at the ready. The mountains had a bad reputation for bandits and smugglers and the prospect of falling prey to a Spanish thug after eluding the Germans was something Henri refused to contemplate.

As well as the bitter cold, altitude made breathing difficult. Adapting, they trudged on, all resources dedicated to negotiating the rocky track. They became hypnotised by the effort; even Henri's vigilance lapsed. He was startled when de Mourville called out.

"Hey! We're going *downhill*. We have been for some time."

Henri blinked. It was true. Without knowing it, they had

94

crossed the border. Somewhere ahead of them, through the mist that was reflecting the risen sun, lay Pamplona and freedom.

There was no time to waste. De Mourville embraced Henri.

"*Au revoir, mon ami*," he said. "We shall have dinner with you at Café Rostand on the night that Paris is liberated."

Henri nodded. "Take care, *Patron*," he urged. "Spain is full of Fascists."

"They're neutral Fascists, thank God!"

Henri turned to the girl. "*Au revoir, Mademoiselle*," he said, holding out his hand.

Instead, she kissed him, first on both cheeks, then on the lips, driving away the mountain chill for a few sweet moments. "*Merci*, Henri," she murmured. "God go with you. Give my love to Marie-Claire and your little boy." She used a finger to mark the Cross of Lorraine on his forehead, their talisman that had been Joan of Arc's emblem, and turned away.

Before the mist swallowed them, de Mourville stopped. "If you happen to bump into Laval on your way back, Henri, kill the bastard!" he shouted.

Henri raised a hand in acknowledgement and turned for home. It was, he thought with sardonic confidence, a mere seven hundred kilometres.

HMS Manxman had been lying at Devonport for nearly a week, awaiting orders. Amelia dealt with the signal at lunch-time on 10 February, coding it with an encryption machine that had been built by a scientific instrument-maker in Guildford to her own design. She smiled to herself. What took only a few minutes with her contraption would keep *Manxman's* captain, armed only with a code book, busy for at least half an hour; she had a fair idea what Commander Steven Hawksworth would think of the tedious chore.

Locked in his cabin to unravel the hieroglyphics that the W/T operator brought him, Steven did indeed do a great deal of muttering about the mentality of people who had nothing better to do than invent such convoluted twaddle.

After ten minutes, it was obvious that he was under orders to sail immediately, so he spoke to his First Lieutenant through the voice-pipe, instructing him to make ready. An hour later, they had weighed anchor and were passing Drake's Island on the way into Plymouth Sound.

HMS Manxman, a fleet mine-layer of three thousand tons displacement, was always either in passage between Plymouth and Gibraltar, or in constant readiness to do so. Although her incessant comings and goings were often described as the 'milk run' by cynics in other ships, she was a vital link between the Admiralty and C-in-C Mediterranean. Her qualification for this demanding task was quite simple; apart from a few motor torpedo launches, *Manxman* was the fastest vessel in the Royal Navy. Her huge turbines produced forty knots with ease, enabling a dash from Plymouth to Gibraltar in well under twenty-four hours. What was left of the German navy had nothing remotely capable of catching her; the only dangers were from the air, or a lucky shot from a U-boat torpedo. The newly promoted Steven had been in command of *Manxman* for two months.

Once all the formalities of leaving harbour were out of the way and the crew had been stood down, Steven moved across the bridge to brief Lieutenant Commander John Dyer, his second in command.

"We're going to fetch a couple of VIPs, John," he said. "Best possible speed *there*, as well as back, I'm afraid."

Dyer pulled a face. On anything other than a mill-pond, forty knots was a sore trial to all but the best of sailors. As to be expected at this time of year, the forecast for Biscay was not good.

"They must be ever-so-very-important VIPs," Dyer said, thinking of the fuel consumption. It was rare for them to make both trips absolutely flat-out.

"French Resistance people, I think," Steven said.

"Oh! I thought the RAF normally took care of them."

"It's a risky business, I believe, John. It looks as though they have to be certain with this pair. Churchill wants to see them."

"Does he, by God!" John Dyer was suitably impressed.

At two-thirty, they cleared the breakwater with its twin light-houses and Steven rang down for full speed. As *Manxman*'s bow came up and she settled to her task, he gave the sky a defiant look. It glowered back at him.

It was a good run, despite the weather, and they had the last four hundred miles, with a light sea and clear blue sky, to recover from the battering of the night. When *Manxman* came alongside at Gibraltar, there was much more than the usual activity on the dockside.

"Rear-Admiral's coming this way, sir!" the bridge look-out warned Steven. He hurried to be at the head of the gangplank as Arthur Bowyers was piped aboard.

"'Afternoon, Hawksworth," the Admiral said. "What kept you?"

Steven grinned: the passage had been one of their fastest. "It took me all day to unscramble my orders, sir."

"Do you mean to tell me that a bright young chap like you has trouble with this tripe, as well!" Bowyers exploded. "I thought it was only me and my idiot Flag Lieutenant. Well that settles it. I'm going to send them a stinker. We're supposed to be fighting a bloody war, not doing puzzles." Rear-Admiral Bowyers looked round conspiratorially, lowering his voice. "I heard an incredible story last week. Mountbatten flew in for a conference and he told 'Porky' Hawkins that they've got a *woman* making all these codes up at the Admiralty!"

Knowing that it was expected of him, Steven looked appalled. "That's very strange, sir," he said before turning to business. "Where's my cargo?"

"They're at the Residency. You're dining there tonight, by the way."

"It's not a formal do, is it, sir?" Steven asked, worried.

"Good God, man, of course it is! We're keeping standards up, you know."

"My mess dress is likely to be in a bit of a state," Steven said. "Even if I can find it."

"I can arrange a loan if you want," Bowyers said. "The brown jobs always need a lesson in style." He become roguish. "In any case, you'll want to look your best . . . one of these Frenchies is a gal and she's a real whackeroo!"

Because it once had been one, the Governor's Residence was known as 'The Convent'. At eight o'clock, when the dockyard car dropped him off, Steven was the last of the ten dinner-guests to arrive.

The Governor's ADC presented him to the eight of his fellow-guests assembled in the ante-room, explaining that the other one was taking an important telephone call.

Alain de Mourville and Nadia Cresson-Joubert stood out on two counts. The corduroy trousers and sweaters they had worn for the greater part of their ten-day journey through Spain might have received the best laundering that Gibraltar could provide, but they still looked bizarrely out of place in surroundings where the stiff upper lip of the British had been given at least two extra doses of starch. What most struck Steven, however, was their beauty. They were one of the most good-looking and well-matched couples he had ever seen, sharing the same light-brown hair and hazel eyes. Nadia had a 'peaches-and-cream' look, Alain was pale, with an air of almost medieval haughtiness about him, an impression that was dispelled the moment he spoke.

"We are very pleased to meet you, Commander. Now that the Royal Navy has charge of us, we know that we are finally safe." His English was perfect, his sincerity as firm and genuine as his handshake.

Not even the autocratic determination of the Governor's wife could part Alain and Nadia when it was time to sit down for dinner. They insisted on being together, directly opposite Steven, as though, having found him, they were unwilling to let him out of their sight. Steven talked to them, ignoring the empty place to his right.

The soup plates were being cleared away before the missing diner finished his phone call and came to sit beside Steven. It was General Alexander.

"How do you do, sir," Steven said, doing his best not to fall off his chair. "My name is Hawksworth."

Alexander waved away the waiter who was trying to offer him soup and stared hard at Steven. "Are you the little blighter who sat on my knee and thought I was too young to be a colonel?" he asked.

In 1917, when he was the youngest colonel in the British Army, Harold Rupert Leofric George Alexander had been the commanding officer of Steven's father at Passchendaele. On his way to visit friends in the West Country, he had called at Latimer's Barn to offer his condolences on Giles Hawksworth's death, and had ended up staying the night.

"Yes, sir," Steven replied.

"Bless my soul!" Alexander chuckled and slapped Steven on the back. "Tell me, how's that incredible grandmother of yours? Still going strong, I hope?"

"She is, sir. She'll be eighty-four in June."

"Good! Do you know what she said to me? 'One day, you will make a marvellous general, but I hope to God we never need you.' How about that, eh?"

Steven nodded. It had cropped up in the dark days of 1940 when it became known that Alexander was the last British officer to be evacuated from the beaches at Dunkirk.

"She'll be delighted to hear that I met you, sir," Steven said. "I expect she'll want to know what you're doing here."

"On my way to Italy," Alexander replied. "We're going to finish Mussolini and his gang off. Give her my best regards, won't you? What's that unusual name of hers . . . Leander, isn't it?"

"Yes, sir. She would wish to be remembered to you."

After that, Steven ensured that Alain and Nadia were included in the conversation with Alexander. Soon, everyone round the table was listening to their coolly unemotional account of French life under the Nazis.

When the party broke up, Alain and Nadia, who were spending a last night at The Convent, walked with Steven to the car waiting to take him back to the dockyard.

"What time do we sail tomorrow, Commander?" Alain asked.

"Nine o'clock," Steven replied. "I like to do the leg from Finisterre to Ushant in darkness ... it makes things more difficult for the *Luftwaffe*."

"And you'll have us in Plymouth in less than twenty-four hours?"

Steven nodded. "I'm afraid that you'll find it uncomfortable unless you're better sailors than most of my crew."

Nadia shrugged. "It will be nothing compared to other things."

She was probably right, Steven thought.

They sailed promptly.

From the bridge, Steven saw the three Spanish dockyard workers hurry away with a furtive sense of purpose as *Manxman* eased clear of the quay. Alain and Nadia gave them an ironic wave from the quarter-deck.

"Enemy agents!" Nadia scoffed.

"They are off to notify the *Boche* that de Mourville and Cresson-Joubert are on the way to tell Churchill how to conduct the invasion of France," Alain said, causing Nadia to laugh. In this fifth year of the War, with the Allies tightening their grip remorselessly, the once invincible German machine was developing serious defects: many of its network of spies and informers were known to be totally incompetent.

No sooner had the crew been dismissed from their stations for leaving harbour, some obviously disenchanted at being deprived of the chance to goggle at Nadia, than the engine noise changed. Before long, the sea was tearing past them and a broad, foaming wake hung behind their stern.

"Commander Hawksworth means business," Nadia said, bracing herself against the rail.

"I never doubted it," Alain replied.

Nadia smiled. Unlike many Frenchmen, her companion was an ardent Anglophile: he had rejoiced at the destruction of the fleet at Oran, saying, "This is good. It means that Churchill is a strong man who knows what he is doing. Hitler will be beaten."

Once he was sure that the ship was running itself, Steven left the bridge to join them.

"Nothing much doing until nightfall," he said. Glancing across to the starboard beam, he pointed out a massive headland. "Cape Trafalgar," he announced with an apologetic smile. Alain bowed solemnly and they shook hands.

"How has your war been, Commander?" Alain asked.

"Oh, average, I suppose." Steven made himself more comfortable, his back against the rail. "I started off on the Norwegian thing . . . bit of a mess really."

De Mourville shook his head vigorously. "Not at all! You did terrible damage to the German Navy."

"The *surface* Navy," Steven corrected. "Don't forget the U-boats! Yes, we didn't do all that badly . . . but we didn't know that at the time."

"And after Norway?" Alain prompted.

"The Atlantic. Convoy escort."

"I see you kept busy." Alain reached out to touch the DSO ribbon on Steven's left breast.

"There *were* one or two interesting bits."

Alain's eyes twinkled; he realised that he was going to get nothing more. "You are the proof that the English have the sea in their blood, Commander," he said. "Look at you! You have the air of a man who has been a sailor all his life, yet you are a trainer of racehorses."

Steven was startled. "How do you know that?"

"I was listening to what you and General Alexander were saying last night. If *the* Leander Hawksworth is your grandmother, you are a trainer!" He saw that more explanation was called for. "Like my father, I am a keen *turfiste*. We used to own horses . . . we shall again when we repossess our house and lands. Your Latimer's Barn is very famous."

"Is it?" Steven was pleased.

"Definitely. We were told that the filly Hyperborean was outstanding."

"Ah, yes!" Steven's face softened and there was a faraway

101

fondness in his eyes. "She was marvellous. We're going to breed from her when all this nonsense is over and done with."

"Why didn't they think you were important enough to be exempted from military duty?" Alain asked.

"The matter never arose," Steven replied firmly. "It occurred to me that Hitler was the biggest menace ever to afflict mankind, so I volunteered." He changed the subject quickly. "Look, this wind's getting nasty, do you want to go and put your feet up? It's going to be a long day."

Entering his cabin, Nadia immediately spotted the framed photograph on the shelf above Steven's bunk. Clapping her hands delightedly, she went to look closely at it.

"Your wedding day?" she asked.

"Yes." Steven reached up for the picture of him and Ann outside the Church of St Luke and St John.

"When was this?" Alain asked.

"November, nineteen forty-one."

"Nearly two and a half years. Have you a child yet?"

Steven looked pleased with himself. "We have a son . . . he was born nine months and a few days after that!" He tapped the photograph.

"Bravo!"

"Your wife's dress . . . it is beautiful," Nadia said. "How was this possible with the *rationnement*?"

"That was the wedding dress my mother wore," Steven replied. "They altered it quite a lot, but it had kept wonderfully well."

"*Mais oui!* It is obvious!" Nadia agreed enthusiastically.

They talked for an hour about what the War had meant to them personally, Alain hinting that Europe might find the problems of peace rather more than it was bargaining for. Steven, familiar with the idea, became rather despondent and was eventually glad to excuse himself when he felt it was time to return to the bridge.

Alain and Nadia stayed in Steven's cabin for the remainder of the day. The wardroom steward brought them lunch and dinner, both meals carefully prepared from fresh food taken on board at Gibraltar; thanks to Rear-Admiral Bowyers, there were two bottles of a very good Beaujolais.

At ten o'clock, Steven looked in to see them and was pleased to find that they were coping well with the vessel's unsettling motion. "We're making forty-four knots with this wind behind us," he said, adding, "That's about eighty kilometres an hour." Nadia, especially, looked impressed. "We passed Finisterre half an hour ago, so we're entering a possible danger zone. In case there's the odd Heinkel swanning around, I'm going to anti-aircraft action stations. There'll be an uproar in about ten minutes, but there's no need to worry."

Soon after he left them, the urgent ringing of bells was followed by the pounding of several hundred feet on ladders and decks. Then, resonating bedlam as guns were swung into position and the ammunition lifts groaned into life. Afterwards, the normal sea noises seemed soothing.

Alain and Nadia talked until nearly midnight, then, as *Manxman* continued her unimpeded dash towards England, they made themselves comfortable and slept.

Steven found them still fast asleep in each other's arms when he went down to shave at six o'clock. His stealthy entry to the bathroom did not wake them; that happened a few minutes later when coffee and croissants, both a fair imitation of the genuine article, arrived from the wardroom. Hearing their bleary mutterings and the chink of cups, Steven stuck his head round the door, inspiring Nadia to a fit of giggles; half his face was smothered in lather, the other half shiny smooth.

"I shan't be long," Steven said. "Then you two can have a rinse, or whatever."

"Where are we?" Alain asked.

"Passing the Lizard. We shall be in by eight. The weather's pretty miserable."

Expecting a reception committee of big-wigs, Steven donned his best uniform, and it was as well that he did. A captain from

HQ Plymouth came down the Sound in a cutter to meet them. Alain and Nadia watched from the vantage point of a Bofors gun turret as the ticklish job of getting him on board was accomplished.

"Sorry about this, Hawksworth," he said, wasting no time on preliminaries. "You haven't finished with these French people yet . . . you've got to escort them to London. The Foreign Office were supposed to be sending someone down, but they've fouled it up as usual!"

"Isn't there anyone more suitable, sir?" Steven asked, automatically looking for an excuse.

"I'm sure there is!" the captain said bluntly. "However, this is the PM's idea . . . he thinks you'll have built up a rapport with them and they'd appreciate that on the way up to London. So, tell your First Lieutenant to take over and we'll get cracking."

"You want us to come ashore with you now, sir?"

"That's the idea. We're holding a train for you."

The best thing about the hectic minutes that followed was Nadia's athletically trouble-free descent into the cutter, complete with rucksack and spurning all help. Steven, still telling John Dyer what was happening, missed it.

"When will you be back?" an anxious-looking Dyer asked.

"As soon as bloody possible, John. Tomorrow morning, I hope! Now, whatever you do, don't bump this thing when you park it." As he was meant to, John Dyer saw the funny side of a problem that could easily lead to a court martial.

The cutter dashed away from *Manxman* on a north-westerly course towards the Citadel, virtually in the centre of Plymouth. As they rounded the bend into Sutton Harbour, Steven looked back; his ship was ploughing doggedly upstream in the murk of the wet February morning, still two miles from Devonport.

At the quay, two Royal Navy policemen bundled Steven and his charges into a car, and the Wren driver set off for the station. When they got there, she had to chase after Steven, waving an envelope and shouting, "Sir, your tickets!"

On the platform, a senior railway official and a Navy RTO were standing at an open carriage door. Hurrying towards it,

Steven was conscious of passengers leaning out of windows, all with impatiently hostile frowns. Whistles were blowing while the RTO was shoving them in through the door.

Catching his breath, Steven found himself confronted by a massive Royal Marine warrant officer who contrived to execute an impeccable salute even in the confines of the narrow corridor. "Anywhere you like in here, sir," he said. "The whole coach is reserved and there won't be anybody else."

Nadia chose a compartment in the middle of the carriage. As Steven followed her and Alain into it, with the train gathering speed past Laira, he saw that the other end of the coach was guarded by a Marine sergeant who was bigger than the warrant officer.

Somewhere between Exeter and Taunton, they began to use each other's Christian names.

"My God, Alain, you must be important," Steven said after a visit to the toilet had led to an informative chat with one of their escorts. "I've just found out that this train was held for over an hour on the Prime Minister's orders."

"Surely you'd realised that already, Steven," Alain replied. "Why else would someone like you be sent to fetch us?"

"I'm no great shakes!" Steven protested.

"You underestimate yourself, my friend. As the captain of the Navy's fastest ship, you are very significant." Alain leaned forward. "I am wanted to provide information for the invasion. I have the disposition of all the German forces in France."

Automatically, Steven looked up at the rucksacks on the luggage rack, causing Nadia to laugh. "No, Steven, it is in a much safer place," she said, and pointed at Alain's head.

After speculating about the date of the invasion, they fell silent. While Alain and Nadia looked out of the window at the passing countryside, Steven found himself studying them. Sometimes they affected indifference towards one another, but the bond forged by a thousand shared and conquered dangers was never out of sight for long.

"You'll be getting married when all this is over?" Steven asked.

"Of course!" Nadia was stating a self-evident truth.

"It will be soon after we return to France," Alain added. He smiled at the look on Steven's face. "Don't worry, you will not have to take us back. We shall go after the invasion, through the front door, with our heads high!"

After the stop at Taunton, the warrant officer put his head into the compartment to say that they were now running non-stop to London. "We got two new engines on now, sir, and they're going to see what they can do for you."

They were treated to a run of pre-war standard. Steven realised that the train was travelling fast, nevertheless he was surprised when they roared past Pewsey, seventy miles from Taunton, in an hour.

"That's where my grandfather came from," he told Alain and Nadia. "We're only a few miles from Latimer's Barn."

"And they have no idea that you are so close?" Alain asked.

"No." He looked out, trying to persuade himself that he could see the ridge of Cannings Down. Suddenly, an idea occurred to him. "Look here, Alain, what will you be doing until the invasion?"

"I have no idea. General de Gaulle will want to see us when we finish with Churchill. After that, we sit and wait."

"Why don't you come and stay with us?" Steven asked eagerly. "I'm due for two weeks' leave in April. Come down then."

"That is wonderful!" Nadia said. "London is supposed to be very dreary these days."

"I'm afraid it is," Steven said, rummaging in his wallet, finally finding a dog-eared business card of 1937 vintage. "There's the telephone number."

"Thank you, Steven." Alain put the card away carefully. "We shall look forward to seeing your stable . . . and the famous Leander Hawksworth!"

At Paddington station, they were spirited through the crowds towards a waiting car. Nadia had time to respond to the admiring glances of the men on the footplates of the two locomotives that had given them such a good run, the two Royal Marines produced extravagant salutes, for the benefit of the gawping onlookers as much as Steven, and they were away.

There was hardly any traffic to impede their progress and they were soon in Trafalgar Square.

"My orders are to take you to the Admiralty Ops Room, sir," the Wren said to Steven, who was sitting beside her. "The PM has been there since six o'clock this morning."

"Trouble?" Steven asked.

"Looks like it, sir. There's been a lot of running about."

At the inconspicuous entrance on Horse Guards, a military policeman checked Steven's identity and asked him to sign a form to vouch for Alain and Nadia. The duty officer, a young-looking lieutenant commander, hurried from his office and waved them to a door that opened to reveal a steep flight of stone steps. After a descent of some thirty feet, they were in a long corridor, whose brick walls were covered in dark green gloss paint, a feature that emphasised the subterranean nature of this secret world.

Turning round to look at Alain and Nadia as they hurried along the passage, Steven saw that they were infinitely more composed than him. Seeing his discomfort, the duty officer became chatty.

"There's been one hell of a flap on, but it seems as though it's over."

"What's the problem?" Steven asked.

"They got the idea that *Tirpitz* was trying to break out of Alten Fiord."

The seriousness of such a threat needed no elaboration. *Tirpitz*, more formidable even than *Bismarck*, had been penned up for over two years and was supposed to have been incapacitated by an audacious midget submarine attack the previous autumn.

"False alarm?" Steven asked.

"It looks like it. One of the old man's pet boffins has come to the conclusion that the signals were bogus. The current theory is that Jerry captured a Norwegian resistance unit and decided to have some fun with their wireless."

Steven's relief was curtailed abruptly by their entry into the main Operations Room. The huge, brightly lit cavern was a scene of quietly intense activity, with well over a hundred officers and ratings busy at desks and plotting tables. In a far corner, three people were in deep conversation in front of a huge wall-map of the North Atlantic. Winston Churchill, in striped trousers and black jacket, was listening to Admiral Cunningham, the First Sea Lord, who was explaining something and pointing to the coast of Norway. Sandwiched between them, a handsome, middle-aged woman was poring over a sheaf of notes and nodding. The sight of her convinced Steven that he was suffering from hallucinations.

Churchill looked up, saw them and beckoned. The duty officer moved swiftly towards him. Trance-like, Steven followed.

As Churchill took several paces to meet them, Amelia turned away from the wall-map. Steven, busy shaking hands with the Prime Minister and accepting his thanks, missed the look of exasperation on his aunt's face.

Steven introduced Alain and Nadia to Churchill, who kissed Nadia's hand in a great show of gallantry and then insisted on trying to talk to her in execrable French. Seeing that Nadia was on the brink of one of her giggling fits, Steven began to sidle away from the group. Amelia worked her way round a cluster of desks to intercept him.

"This isn't the Ministry of Food, Auntie!" Steven whispered.

"You're right!" she retorted. "And I'll thank you to keep quiet about it." Although she sounded cross, there was a sparkle in her eye. Taking his arm, she guided him to the door. "I knew you were coming, of course," she said when they were out in the corridor. "But I was hoping to be back in my hidey-hole by the time you got here."

"Did you know that there's a story going the rounds about

a woman who makes up all these impossible new codes?" Steven asked, absolutely po-faced.

"Nothing would surprise me. Where did you hear that?"

"Rear-Admiral Bowyers in Gib. Mind you, he claimed that he got it from Admiral Hawkins, who was told by Mountbatten!"

It emerged that Bowyers had been a perpetual source of irritation to Amelia: her tirade on the subject was not cut short until the door of the Operations Room flew open and Churchill burst out, followed by Alain and Nadia.

"We must go," Alain said, hardly pausing. "Thank you, my friend. I will be in touch."

"*Au revoir*, Steven." Nadia planted a kiss on his cheek without interrupting her pursuit of the Prime Minister.

Amelia's face was a picture as she watched Nadia disappear down the long corridor, a rucksack bobbing up and down on her back.

"I'll strike a bargain with you," she said to Steven. "You don't breathe a word about seeing me here, and I won't tell Ann that a delightful young Frenchwoman could hardly keep her hands off you."

"Done!" Steven laughed.

"How soon do you have to be back with your ship?"

"Tomorrow morning will do."

"You can take me out to dinner this evening. Until then, you can put your feet up in my flat. Come on."

On the day she married Steven, in November 1941, Ann Redmayne found that she had acquired much more than a new home and name. Leander and Emma decided that she must start preparing for the responsibilities that peace-time would bring.

"When the War is over and Steven comes home, *you'll* be the lady of the house," Leander told her. "Don't look like that . . . I know what you're thinking and it isn't true!"

At twenty-five, Ann had the wisdom and poise of a much older woman: she also knew how to put her beautiful face, with its high cheek-bones and expressive blue eyes, to good use. Her look of quizzical scepticism was a masterpiece.

"I'm far too old to be interfering in what happens here," Leander said. "Damn it, I was supposed to be taking a back seat twenty years ago! Once Hitler's been finished off, it's all up to you."

"And I shan't be getting in your way," Emma promised. "It's going to be a time for new ideas. In any case . . ." she gave a rather sad smile ". . . *three* Mrs Hawksworths will make it very confusing unless two of them keep out of the way!"

Ann set to with a will. Her standing in the village was established when, in July 1942, she gave Latimer's Barn a son and heir, Giles. Before that happy event, Elsie had been busy telling everyone that the new Mrs Hawksworth was 'all right'.

The War had brought an upsurge in the social life of Cannings Ambo as people felt the need to place their worries in the hands of the communal pool of courage and determination. Either The George or the Memorial Hall hosted some sort of event on at least four evenings every week and Ann was a tireless organiser.

When Alain de Mourville and Nadia Cresson-Joubert spent five days at Latimer's Barn during Steven's April leave, Ann shone. It was the first time she had been able to entertain real guests in nearly two and a half years of marriage, and she made the most of it. The preparations for the visit caused her to pose Steven a question that tied him in knots.

"How many bedrooms will they want?"

Steven was flummoxed, unable to understand her difficulty. "Well . . . two, of course."

"Are you sure, darling?" Ann asked. "From what you've said about them, they're very close. And they are French!"

The penny dropped, making Steven squirm with embarrassment. "I don't know . . . I . . . er . . . I'm sure you can cope with that, my dear."

Ann did. When Alain and Nadia arrived, she spoke unobtrusively to Nadia in fluent, idiomatic French. Without anyone else being aware of what had happened, the double bedroom at the west end of The House, already prepared, was accepted as ideal.

Alain spent each morning with Steven. They looked at every part of the estate, with Alain, a competent horseman, very much at home on a hack. A few horses were now going out to race, so there was some work on the gallops which Alain watched avidly. Both the stable and the stud, at Cannings St John, impressed him, although the levels of activity were low.

"You will be able to make this one of the finest establishments in Europe when the War is over," he told Steven.

"I intend to." Steven seemed almost offhand about it, but his companion noticed the steely determination behind the screen of apparent indifference. Having seen them both together, Alain was of the opinion that Steven Hawksworth and his legendary grandmother were birds of a feather, far more alike than many of the locals seemed to think.

"It isn't going to be easy, though," Steven added. "The country's in a terrible mess. I'm afraid I can see things getting a damned sight worse before they improve."

Alain had heard as much from de Gaulle and his aides, who believed that Britain might become worthless once the war was won. "It will be the same everywhere," he said tactfully. "France will be torn apart." He veered away from the subject. "I think that your sister has worked miracles with the stable."

"We're still in business," Steven agreed. "We're not doing all that much, but we shall be ready when the time comes."

There was nothing in Steven's tone to indicate anything other than confidence. During his visits on leave, he made it a strict rule not to interfere in the stable. "The last thing you want is to have me sticking my oar in," he told Rachel, and she was profoundly grateful.

In truth, Steven thought that his sister had become difficult, if not downright impossible. Ann, who usually kept well away from the stable, was aware of it, and Nadia's highly tuned sensitivities wasted no time in detecting that Rachel was not at ease with herself or the world.

An incident during their tour of the stable stuck in Nadia's mind. Entering the 1874 yard they had discovered a small girl taking an avid interest in all that was going on. As pretty as a picture in a print frock and with her blonde hair in plaits, she obviously had no fear of the horses.

"What a lovely child!" Alain said, glancing at Nadia in a way that suggested they would soon be hoping for such a daughter.

Steven smiled. "That's Bess Collier," he said. "Elsie's little girl."

"Ah!" Nadia nodded vigorously. "The woman who does the miracles with the cooking."

"She looks very much at home," Alain said.

"She'd live out here, given the chance," Steven replied. "She adores horses and see how careful they are with her . . . that thing she's standing next to doesn't have the best of tempers as a rule . . . now look at him."

"Will she work for you?" Alain asked.

"Oh, it's far too early to tell," Steven said. "She isn't quite five yet and we haven't tried to teach her to ride . . . but, yes, I wouldn't be surprised if there wasn't talent there."

Nadia was about to say that it would be a good thing to get girls into the male-dominated world of racing when she saw the look of sheer hatred that Rachel was giving the child. What on earth could young Bess Collier possibly have done to deserve that? The answer, of course, had to be nothing.

The Marchioness of Glastonbury was most definitely a bitterly unhappy woman.

Lady Helen Prideaux, born in March 1942, was the apple of Charles's eye. He had doted on her from the first and the prettier she grew, the greater his infatuation became. Helen's two brothers were afforded every opportunity for jealousy: Edmund, the younger, always rose to the bait, Henry, terribly grown-up at seven, and already looking forward to prep school, was philosophical enough to find it amusing. Helen was capable of charming the stoniest of hearts when the fancy took her; at other times, she displayed a vile temper. She was invariably on her best behaviour for Charles's visits, but was such a handful when he was away that Emma, tiring of her role as nanny, insisted that Rachel should take charge.

There had never been the slightest doubt in Rachel's mind that Charles was *not* Helen's father. She resented his fondness for the child and despised his stupidity in not questioning the 'premature' birth: nor had anyone else ever mentioned the subject. Yet Rachel was not entirely sure that her secret was safe.

When it came to be told, the full story of how Silas had trapped Peter Hawksworth contained an element that horrified her. It concerned the day on which Solstice Jackson followed Peter to Okehampton. Solstice was already on the London-bound train at Savernake in order to identify Peter. Thinking about it afterwards, Rachel remembered that there was a man hanging out of a window as the train drew in. At the same time as he was spotting and marking Peter, he could hardly have failed to notice the passionate farewell in which his quarry was engaged. That morning, after a frenziedly satisfying night, Rachel had made a complete fool of herself on the station platform.

Nor was that all. Some days after Peter's terrible return from that trip, Rachel had discovered the loss of a pair of lace-trimmed French knickers: they were a pre-war present from Charles that she saved for special occasions. Almost certainly, she had worn them on her last visit to Peter's room, at the end of which they had been carelessly left in his bed. Who had found them? Most probably, it was one of the maids.

Now, Solstice was a permanent feature of Cannings Ambo. He lived in the converted loft of the original 1840 stable-block and looked after the gallops, as well as busying himself with the odd-jobs that Cyril Osgood delegated to him. However, until Rachel began to draw attention to herself by her arrogance, Solstice had much better things to do than indulge in speculative tittle-tattle.

It began with the yard staff and was a defence mechanism against poor results. From 1942 onwards, racing was allowed at Salisbury and Windsor, as well as Newmarket. Since Salisbury had witnessed the stable's first winner, Rachel felt honour-bound to contest every suitable race that was held there. The results were abysmal. From over seventy runners in 1942 and 1943, she obtained one winner, a second and two third places. Finding it necessary to bite his tongue more and more, Alfred Merriweather watched Rachel turn into an imperious harridan. With Matthew working night and day at Rose House on the production of wings for the phenomenally successful Mosquito bomber, there was no one to check Rachel's destruction of the yard's morale.

On an evening a week before the visit of Alain and Nadia, Solstice trudged into the kitchen for a bite of bread and cheese at nine o'clock, two hours later than his normal time.

"Where the devil you been 'til now?" Elsie asked as he collapsed wearily into a chair.

"Her Ladyship's been at me again," Solstice muttered. "Said I was letting the gallop go to rack and ruin. She won't be satisfied until I'm on my hands and knees with scissors!"

"I see his Lordship's looking as miserable as sin," Polly said. She had just returned from taking after-dinner coffee into the dining-room: Charles was at Latimer's Barn for a short leave.

"Can you wonder?" Elsie asked. "I reckon he's had his conjugal rights stopped."

Polly was horrified. "What makes you think that, Elsie?"

"When did they last go to that place in the forest?"

After a visible search of her memory, Polly said, "Not since Lady Helen was born."

"Exactly!" Elsie produced a knowing look. "And do you know, I've always wondered if there wasn't something *very* funny about that."

The inevitable drawing together of the isolated snippets began. They would not, of course, mention their suspicions to anyone else: it was not their place to do so.

* * *

114

Alain and Nadia felt a great sadness when it was time to go back to London.

"I do hope we shall meet again," Ann said.

"Oh, we must!" Nadia agreed.

Steven and Alain were gravely tense as they shook hands, both sensing the upheaval that would probably convulse Europe before their paths crossed again. "Be assured of one thing," Alain said. "When I am able, I will send you some horses to train."

That night, as they lay in bed in their London hotel, Alain asked, "And what did you think of the famous Latimer's Barn?"

"It was very good."

Alain studied her closely, knowing that there was something else. "But?" he prompted.

"It will only be good if Milady Rachel goes away."

"She will," Alain replied. "One day soon she will be a Duchess with a very grand place called Eaton Mandeville to worry about." He paused. "You didn't like her, did you?"

"I didn't *dislike* her," Nadia said. "I simply think that such an unhappy woman shouldn't go near horses. They are so easily upset!"

"I thought it was her husband who was unhappy."

"Well, of course he is! She is refusing him sex. I heard them arguing about it!"

"That's bad. He needs to assert himself."

"Lord Charles is too weak," Nadia said.

"Or too nice," Alain suggested.

The long-awaited invasion of France took place in the early hours of 6 June. By the evening, 156,000 men were ashore on the Normandy beaches and the greatest feat of arms in all military history was underway. When, three days later, the bridgehead had been consolidated and the Allies were landing men and supplies at will, many people in England believed that the war was over. On 13 June, the first of Hitler's flying bombs landed on London. There was a new evacuation; by the end of July, one and a half million badly unnerved people had fled the capital.

There were set-backs for the Allies as they fought their way across France, but nothing to delay them by more than a day at a time. General de Gaulle and the greater part of his Free French retinue began to trickle away from London on 19 August, and, when Paris was liberated seven days later, de Gaulle strode down the Champs Elysées at the head of the first troops to reach the city. Immediately behind him, with a dozen or so other *Résistance* fighters, were Alain and Nadia.

That evening, ignoring the celebrations at the Palais De L'Elysée, they went to the Café Rostand. Turning the corner, they received an unpleasant surprise: the place was lifeless, with drawn curtains and the sign gone. When Alain reached it, he found the door locked. He hammered with his fist, the noise reverberating through emptiness.

"Now what?" he asked Nadia.

"Try again," she insisted. While he banged, she crouched down to shout through the letter-box. "Henri! Marie-Claire! Monsieur Rostand! It's Alain and Nadia! Henri, where are you?" Suddenly, she looked up. "All right, someone is coming."

The drawing of the bolts, slow and dispirited, conveyed an air of hopelessness. Finally, the door swung open to reveal a Marie-Claire so changed that Nadia stepped back in horror. The once beautiful young woman was gaunt and haggard, her listless eyes seemed blind. A flash of recognition brought a pathetic life to her face. "Alain!" she gasped, and fell forward into his arms. She weighed next to nothing.

Alain carried Marie-Claire inside and Nadia followed them, closing and bolting the door.

"I'm all right, now. You can put me down," Marie-Claire said. Nadia gazed round the dining-room, taking in the disarray – chairs piled haphazardly on tables, cloths and cutlery in random piles, empty wine bottles on the floor.

"What is all this?" Nadia asked.

"Come." Marie-Claire led them into the back room, where Jacques, her two-year-old son, was cowering in the arms

116

of Monsieur Rostand. She took the boy into her arms, murmuring reassurances; when the old man stood up to greet Alain and Nadia, they were shocked at his condition. The bruising on his face and the gash across one cheek were healing, but still disfiguring.

"Where is Henri?" Alain asked softly.

Marie-Claire waved them to seats, her father fetched a bottle of Calvados and glasses from a cupboard.

"The Gestapo took him," Marie-Claire said.

"When? How?"

"They were waiting when he returned from escorting you to the border." Marie-Claire was obviously exerting great self-control. "After a week, when I went to find out if I could see him, they told me that he had committed suicide."

"How did they know about him?" Nadia asked.

"We heard that he was betrayed by a man called André Dumont from Esternay."

Alain nodded slowly and thoughtfully, Nadia sensing that the name was familiar to him. "And you, M'sieur." Alain said. "What happened to your face?"

"I have sold the Café, Alain." The statement was accompanied by an ironic smile. "The Gestapo suggested that one of their friends wanted it."

"We shall get it back!" Alain declared. "Everything is changed, France is free! Who is this 'friend' of the Gestapo?"

Monsieur Rostand shook his head. "Don't worry, Alain, he paid a good price . . . the money is in the bank."

"We couldn't have carried on here, anyway," Marie-Claire added.

"So, what will you do?" Alain asked.

"We are leaving the day after tomorrow."

"Where are you going?"

Marie-Claire and her father exchanged questioning looks. "We are thinking of going back to Lyon," the old man said. "It will be difficult, but we've had a bellyful of Paris."

"Come with us!" Alain urged. "I shall need all the help I can get with the estate. My father has already taken the first

117

steps to regain possession. We shall have to live rough for a while, but it will be worth it."

There was no argument.

Alain drove to Esternay the following day, only to be disappointed. André Dumont had been buried two months ago. Interpreting what neighbours were able to tell him, Alain came to the conclusion that Dumont's violent end had been the handiwork of Henri's great friend, Jean-Louis from Magny-en-Vexin. He returned to Paris to pick up Marie-Claire, her father, and young Jacques.

Marie-Claire set out for a new life at Fontainebleau with Henri's gold watch and crucifix as the only mementos of the brave man she continued to adore. Unworried about money, she left Henri's savings in the bank to accumulate for Jacques. Reduced to chaos by the demands being made on it in the euphoria of the Liberation, the bank eventually posted a terse acknowledgement of Marie-Claire's wishes to her new address. There was no mention of the packet of papers in the safe box, papers that would have fascinated Alain de Mourville by their mention of Cannings Ambo and Latimer's Barn.

CHAPTER 5

1945

'I don't believe in austerity!'

In 1918, Leander had thought it strange that not a single foreign soldier stood on German soil at the time of the Armistice; Germany sued for peace with its defences on the Western Front more or less intact. Any hope that there was to be an equally rapid end to this conflict were soon dashed. By some evil miracle, Hitler persuaded his people to believe that the Fatherland should be defended to the death. A continuous battle of appalling attrition followed.

Throughout the winter of 1944–45, the eastern advance of the Allies was frustrated by the great natural barrier of the Rhine, but in March the river was conquered and the final push to Berlin began. Simultaneously, the Russians were moving through Poland into East Prussia, with, it subsequently emerged, far greater ambitions than mere victory.

And, as if there had not been enough abominations already, the armies advancing into German territory discovered the horrors of the concentration camps, Belsen and Dachau in the west, the unspeakable Auschwitz in Poland.

In the midst of all this threatening turmoil, on 26 March, Hubert Charles Prideaux, seventh Duke of Laverstoke, died.

A week later, after the burial in the family vault of the twelfth-century church on the edge of the Eaton Mandeville estate, Clementine, making a brave show of being the Dowager

Duchess, drove back to the house that had been her home for forty-six years. Her only companion was Leander. The other mourners followed in a long procession of cars that defied petrol rationing.

Clementine Prideaux found cause for gentle amusement in that it was she who had to do the comforting.

"You need to pull yourself together, my girl," she told Leander. "Hubert *was* eighty-one, you know, and he was going like a good 'un to the end. I'm damned if he would have approved of your performance."

"I'm sorry, Clem." Leander dabbed at her eyes for what she hoped was the last time. "Hubert was *such* a wonderful friend . . . and I do seem to be turning into a silly old woman."

"Yes, you are," Clementine said in a brutally matter-of-fact way. "You must stop it!"

Leander gave a determined nod. "What happens now?" she asked.

"Charles takes up his inheritance, of course. Oh, some good news. The Army are letting him out early! It seems they can just about tolerate a marquess, but a duke is too much! In any case, there doesn't seem to be all that much for chaps like him to do . . . everyone knows where the Germans are and what they're up to."

"How soon will he be able to come here?" Leander asked.

"The end of next week, I think."

"I don't imagine Rachel will be joining him for a while," Leander said. "She wants to run the stable until Steven is back."

"So I believe. As a matter of fact, I'm half-surprised to see her here today. I heard her telling Sibley's frightful wife that it was all a bit of a nuisance because she's running a full programme of work."

"Oh, I say!" Leander was mortified. "She might be a duchess, but my granddaughter needs her backside tanning."

"Don't worry about it." Clementine produced one of her owlish looks that always seemed so disconcertingly penetrating. "It might be all for the best if Charles is here on his own for a while. Mind you, I don't think the children should stay with you, now. Eaton Mandeville is their home and I know of an ideal woman to be their governess."

"We shan't be sorry to see the back of Helen," Leander admitted.

"Isn't she an absolute stinker, eh!" It was not easy to tell whether Clementine's warmth of expression was anger or admiration. "I'm sure she's got bad blood."

"George and Maude," Leander murmured.

"And my lot," the Dowager Duchess said with feeling. "I had an uncle who went to the bad and Cousin Algie got himself locked up."

"I never knew that, Clem!" Leander was agog. "I thought your family was as pure as the driven snow."

The only response was an eloquent sniff.

For some reason, the other cars all discharged their passengers at what was meant to be a respectful distance from Clementine and Leander when they reached the front of the house. Both ramrod straight, the two old women seemed like relics of a previous age in their veils and long black coats that reached almost to their ankles. Fifty yards away, the new Duke regarded them gravely, while his two sons stood on either side of him, the eight-year-old Henry trying to work out what it felt like to be a marquess. Slightly apart, Rachel and Helen seemed to be doing their best not to belong to each other.

"There's one thing I'd like," Clementine said, confident that the movement of her lips was invisible behind the veil.

"Yes?" Leander asked.

"I shall have to have come back here to be buried with Hubert, but until the good Lord decides my time has come, I'd love to come and live in Cannings Ambo."

"Really?" For the benefit of the scores of onlookers, Leander tried to contain her surprise.

"I've always loved it."

"It's a marvellous idea, Clem, but I've no idea where we could put you. The Hall isn't in very good shape."

"Oh, I don't want anything that grand! Do you think Amelia and her young man would have me at Louise House?"

"I'll ask," Leander said, amused by her friend's description of Silas. "He may be in awe of you."

"Stuff and nonsense! I can be as nice as pie . . . sometimes."

"That doesn't alter the fact that you've been a duchess for an awfully long time, Clem."

"See what you can do, Leander. If I clear off away from here, it might give the new regime a chance to settle down and find its feet." Clementine sighed. "I suppose we'd better make a move, or those idiots will stand there all day. Give me your arm. Now look at Steven's Ann . . . isn't she marvellous? She's a real credit to you." Her final remark was very nearly inaudible. "This place could do with someone like her."

The rumours began to circulate on 5 May. The War was over. Or as good as.

It was a Sunday. Amelia went to Morning Service at St Martin-in-the-Fields, then walked back to the Admiralty through nearly deserted streets. Finding herself alone in Room 39, she settled down to finish writing the instruction manual that had eaten up all her spare time over the last eighteen months. No one disturbed her and no telephones rang. When Ambrose Vane came in from a meeting in Downing Street, she was astounded to discover that it was nearly six o'clock.

"Is that masterpiece finished?" he asked, weary after the day's discussion.

"Yes!" Briefly, Amelia looked very pleased with herself. "If the Navy adopts that, it need never have trouble with codes again."

"I'll do my best to see they take notice of it," he said with something less than his usual conviction. Amelia put it down to tiredness. "How about dinner?" Ambrose suggested. "I'm pretty confident I could wangle you into the Army and Navy Club."

"A fitting finale!" Amelia said, impressed. "For that, I'll put my best frock on."

There were no problems. Indeed, after Ambrose Vane had spoken to the club secretary, Amelia was received as an honoured guest. With very few people dining that night and the air full of expectation, the menu proved lavishly pre-war: there was soup, fish, and a choice of beef or chicken. When they were settled, Ambrose dispensed with small-talk.

"The War's over," he said. "Well, in Europe at any rate. The Japs are carrying on. They're going to call it 'VE Day' – Victory in Europe – when they proclaim it."

Amelia gave him a long, appraising stare. "What do you mean, Ambrose, 'When they proclaim it'?"

"There appears to be some difficulty in agreeing things."

"What things?" Amelia demanded. "Did Admiral von Friedenburg surrender to Montgomery yesterday, or didn't he?"

"Yes, he did. But it now seems that only involves German forces in north-west Europe. It's still going on in the east."

"So the Russians are determined to smash Berlin to smithereens?" Amelia asked.

"You must bear in mind that they've suffered appallingly," Ambrose said. "Dickie Webster is convinced that the Ruskies lost well over a million at Leningrad alone."

Although she failed to see what purpose could be served by vengeance, Amelia signalled her acceptance of yet another terrible statistic. "What do you think the Russians are trying to do?" she asked.

"Quite a few of us think that they want to split Germany and take over a fair slice of it."

"Along with Poland?"

"I'm afraid so."

"As if they haven't suffered enough," Amelia muttered. "What does Winston think about all this?"

"Well, to be honest, I don't think he has much say on it. Marshal Zhukov is running everything east of the Brandenburg Gate, and he's obviously under strict orders from Stalin."

Monday dragged by in tedium, relieved only by rumours that refused to materialise. On Tuesday, there were persistent stories that Germany had surrendered totally and unconditionally at Eisenhower's headquarters, but there was no official statement. News that the fighting really had stopped was eventually leaked by an American reporter in Berlin: without bothering to question the decidedly sinister implications of the embargo on the information, London erupted into celebration.

As she lay in bed on 8 May, Amelia could hear the pandemonium of the thousands of revellers in Trafalgar Square and The Mall. The sky was awash with a garish brilliance as every available floodlight put an end to the black-out.

At two o'clock, abandoning the attempt to sleep, Amelia got up, made herself a pot of tea, and reached a decision. Before going to the House of Commons to announce victory, Churchill had toured the Admiralty, thanking everyone for their efforts and wishing them luck for the future: he obviously did not expect to see many of them again. The drunken racket from the streets finally made Amelia realise how much she had missed the peace of Wiltshire and her loved ones. If London was going to be like this, drastic action was called for. She began to pack.

Ambrose Vane, not in the least surprised by her decision, went with her to Paddington station, and it was as well that he did. Even with his help, it took over two hours to buy a ticket and find a suitable train; without him, she could have been stuck in the uproar all day. At the last minute, Ambrose abandoned his stilted speech of farewell and planted a warm kiss full on her lips. Afterwards, as the heavily laden train struggled to pick up speed, Amelia was unable to decide whether the oh-so-proper Captain Vane had been infected with VE fever, or whether the poor man had been wanting to do it for nearly five years. It did not, of course, matter one iota, and *that* was the epitaph for the whole sorry business.

At Savernake, she flung herself at Silas like an overjoyed

eighteen-year-old. "Have you really finished?" he asked when he finally extricated himself.

"Yes. I've demobbed myself."

"You're very lucky," Silas told her. A report in that morning's paper suggested that it might be months before the process of returning men and women to civilian life from the armed forces could even begin. "What now, a good rest and back to Cambridge?"

"Not on your life!" Amelia retorted. "I sent them my resignation in January and sold the house. I shall probably never go there again. I'm fifty-eight and it's time I took life a little easier. I've come home for good, Silas."

With a particularly nasty war involving many thousands of Britons continuing against Japan in the Far East, it was felt inappropriate to resume a full programme of racing. The Derby was still to be run at Newmarket, although there were expectations of an abbreviated Royal Ascot and the St Leger was announced for 5 September at York, at least returning to the right county.

There was, however, no upsurge in activity at Latimer's Barn. The number of horses was down to thirty, the lads to nineteen, the stable's lowest ebb for seventy years. Inevitably, as the war had dragged on, some of the lads had left, attracted to Ireland by the prospect of more frequent racing. Or so most of them claimed. In fact, the exodus had at least as much to do with Rachel's temper as expectations across the Irish Sea. Steven was unconcerned: he had always known that his first post-war task would be a major reconstitution, and he saw distinct advantages in being able to start from scratch.

At Rose House, Matthew, young Jim Goakes and Fred Cartwright set about clearing away the paraphernalia of aircraft production, and, ignoring the empty order-book, prepared to make furniture again. Like so many in the village, they were awaiting the return of soldiers: John Flamsteed and Ernest Cartwright had gone over to France on D-Day and were now at Cologne and Dortmund respectively.

Optimism was greatly tempered by uncertainty. Boredom

was a real danger until, on 25 May, England was plunged into a General Election campaign. On that day, Amelia was alone in suspecting that the weeks ahead would produce a momentous and lasting change in the way Cannings Ambo viewed the outside world.

It seemed that Churchill had suggested to his coalition colleagues that they should continue with the National Government until the defeat of Japan. At first, Attlee, the Labour Party leader, was in agreement; however, the overwhelming mass of the party rank and file thought very differently.

Having resigned, Churchill formed a caretaker Government and advanced on the hustings with relish. The orotund vituperation with which he had belittled Hitler at every turn was now directed at his erstwhile partners.

After the campaign had been in progress for two weeks, Silas sat and listened as four women, all called Hawksworth, discussed it on an evening when Rachel had driven over to Eaton Mandeville for dinner with Charles.

"Do you know, I'd forgotten all about politics," Leander said, vastly entertained by it all. "What are we supposed to think?"

Emma, who loathed the topic, and Ann, unsure of how acceptable her opinions would be, looked at Amelia.

"This election is about houses, jobs and social security," she said. "As far as the people are concerned, nothing else matters. There doesn't seem to be the slightest interest in foreign affairs . . . not even the Empire. The one thing the electorate won't tolerate is a repeat of what happened after the last war. Lloyd George promised them a land fit for heroes, but he never looked like getting started. The twenties and thirties were a soul-destroying time for millions."

"Aren't both parties pledging more or less the same things?" Leander asked.

Amelia pulled a face. "Yes . . . sort of. The trouble is, the Tories are giving the impression that they don't really believe what they're saying. The Labour people sound much more convincing *and* they're offering something that looks complete."

"The Welfare State," Ann said. Her tone caught Leander's attention.

"You don't approve, my dear?"

"It isn't a question of approving or disapproving," Ann replied. "I think we're at a very dangerous crossroads."

Leander looked startled. "How do you make that out?"

"When Germany was still in a mess in the thirties, I'm told that one of the Nazi leaders asked the people what they wanted, guns or butter." Silas grunted and nodded. "They said 'guns' – and we know what happened. My feeling is that the British want jam and expect the Government to spoon it into their mouths."

"Is that so very wrong?" Leander asked.

"In principle, no," Ann said. "But it does imply an awful lot of Government interference. We've *had* to put up with that during the War, but it would be a very different matter during peace-time. Look at Rose House . . . nobody minds being ordered to make aeroplanes to beat Hitler . . . what about if the Government were to say that we could only make chairs of a certain type?"

"Surely, that's ridiculous," Leander said, only to find Silas shaking his head. "Do you agree?" she asked him.

"I'm afraid I do, Mrs Hawksworth. They might even tell you to employ twenty men instead of ten."

"Oh, no!" That was too much for Emma. She found the idea laughable. Leander was becoming uneasy, thinking of the nation's growing obsession with bureaucracy.

She was relieved when the conversation drifted into less uncomfortable territory. However, when Amelia and Silas returned to Louise House, Leander strolled through the orchard with them, ostensibly to discover what they were thinking about providing a home for Clementine Prideaux.

"Ann seems to have some very strong views," Leander said, doing her best to sound inconsequential.

"You'll find that Steven agrees with her," Amelia said. "So do I."

127

"Oh dear!" Leander's spirits sank. "You, too, Silas?"

He thought carefully before answering. "I don't believe there's anywhere in the country with a better record on jobs, houses and welfare than this village," he said. "And how was it all achieved?"

"Well . . . we just did it," Leander said, at something of a loss to understand the significance of the question.

"Whose money and effort did you use?"

"Our own, of course!"

"People have always known that and respected it, Mrs Hawksworth. Frankly, I can't see this Welfare State business being the same . . . not with outsiders trying to tell us how to do things."

With a feeling that he might be right, Leander forgot all about the Dowager Duchess's problem.

Two days later, Leander shut herself in the library to deal with a harrowing duty. William Flamsteed, lost in the Battle of Britain, was not the only son of Cannings Ambo who would not be coming home. Polly Izzard's brother, Peter, died at Anzio; Mark Dundas, son of Jeremy and Josie at the stud, had been lost in the frightful mess of Arnhem; Jim Goakes's boy, Jeffrey, had burned to death on a destroyer in the North Atlantic, and there were eight others, including three of the stable's most talented lads. Checking carefully against the entries she had made in the Big Book at the time their relatives were notified, Leander compiled the list of names in alphabetical order.

"Twelve," she murmured to herself. "Two less than last time. I wonder if we're meant to be grateful."

When Hezekiah Dangerfield had provided the Portland stone War Memorial for the village in 1919, he had, on his own subsequent admission, made a mistake. The inscription:

IN LOVING MEMORY OF THE MEN
OF CANNINGS AMBO
WHO FELL IN THE GREAT WAR
1914 – 1918

THEIR NAMES WILL LIVE FOREVER

followed by the list of fourteen names, was at the top rather than in the centre of the plinth. The lack of symmetry had bothered old Hezekiah to the day he died in 1936. Now, Leander reflected, he might almost deserve congratulations for his anticipation of terrible events.

She said as much to his son, Daniel, who came over from Compton Bassett at once in response to her telephone call.

"Dad wouldn't have got no consolation from that, Mrs Hawksworth," Daniel said. "He always maintained there couldn't be another war, you know." He shook his head sadly. "Still, you'm right, it does make it easier for me." He pulled out his notebook and licked the tip of his pencil. "What can I do for you, ma'am?"

"I thought we'd have 'And in 1939 – 1945' as a sort of heading, then the names." She gave him the list.

"Yes, that seems right enough." Daniel paused awkwardly. "Forgive me asking, but are any of your chaps out East, fighting the Japs?"

"No, thank God!" She recognised the point he was trying to make. "Don't worry, Daniel, we know where they all are. There aren't going to be any more names."

"I'll get started next week, Mrs Hawksworth."

To Leander's relief, there was something that promised to be much more pleasant awaiting her attention.

The frail health of the Reverend John Shepherd had been worrying her since before the War. Now, nearing seventy-two, his retirement was a pressing necessity. Happily, a letter had come from the diocesan authorities in Salisbury to suggest that, at long last, they had found a replacement. The language of the letter amused Leander. In 1900, following the retirement of John Shepherd's father because of ill-health, an insufferable individual called Tompkins had been foisted on to the village. Much put out, Leander went to Salisbury and threatened the Dean with the direst consequences if young John were not rescued from a parish in Sheffield and installed in his father's place. There were new faces in The Close at Salisbury, but the incident was obviously recorded: the letter was littered with such phrases as, 'Respectfully beg to propose', and 'Always dependent upon approval by your good self'.

But there was also substantial hedging of bets. The Reverend Frobisher, an Army chaplain for nearly five years, had been invalided out with severe wounds, he was a widower and he had an eleven-year-old son. "Don't blame us if he's not up to par," the letter seemed to be saying. "At the moment, he's all we've got!" In conclusion, the information was provided that Frobisher was staying with his sister at Lower Woodford, a village near Salisbury.

Anxious for progress, Leander rang the telephone number provided. Frobisher was at home and very willing to come to Cannings Ambo for an interview. "The trouble is, I don't have a car, Mrs Hawksworth," he said. "Do you think I could scout round to find out about buses, or trains, and give you a call back?"

Leander, who had reached the conclusion that she had never heard a more robustly cheerful character, was having none of this. "I'll send a car for you, Mr Frobisher," she replied. "How about ten o'clock tomorrow morning?"

"I'm looking forward to it already!" he replied.

Using the momentous occasion of VE Day as an excuse, Leander had finally persuaded Cyril Osgood to accept honourable retirement after fifty-one years' service. Now aged seventy-five, he was busily engaged in bringing the gardens of the Church Green cottages up to standard, but he found the time to give Solstice Jackson advice on the best way to tackle his new responsibilities.

"Don't you go getting all familiar with this gentleman. I hear he's got enough problems without having to put up with your gabbing. And watch the third gear on that old Morris . . . you'll never find it if you're heavy with the clutch."

Three hours later, Solstice was back at Latimer's Barn with Malcolm Frobisher and his son, Robert. Leander, who was at the front of The House watching a group of lads weeding the garden to relieve the tedium of the almost non-existent stable routine, knew at once that she had found the man for the job.

Malcolm Frobisher was a strongly built, no-nonsense man of forty-six. His amiably rugged face reflected harsh experience, but not self-pity. The stick he still needed to back up his right leg seemed an object of fun rather than a nuisance.

"How do you do, Mrs Hawksworth?" he smiled. "I'm afraid I was totally ignorant of Cannings Ambo until I set out this morning. Solstice has rectified that, though."

Leander succeeded in giving the culprit a suitable look before he was able to make himself scarce. "It's good of you to come, Mr Frobisher," she said. "This is your son?"

"It is. His name is Robert."

"Hello, Robert," Leander said.

"I'm very pleased to meet you, madam," the boy replied respectfully. He was a good-looking lad, tough, like his father.

"Do please come inside," Leander said. "I've asked John Shepherd . . . he's our retiring vicar . . . and his wife to have lunch with us. After that, you will want to look at the church and the Rectory."

It was apparent that John and Mary warmed to Malcolm Frobisher at once, and the conversation before lunch was easy.

"Where were you wounded, Mr Frobisher?" Leander asked, intending to use this as a way into a much more difficult topic.

"At Caen, a week after D-Day. It was one of the few places where the Germans were able to make a fight of it."

"And your wife . . . she died in the War?" Leander asked gently.

"Yes, I'm afraid so." Briefly, there was pain. "It was in one of the air-raids on Plymouth." Malcolm Frobisher appeared to make his mind up about something. "Look, let me put my cards on the table. Strictly speaking, I ought to be trying to find a living in my old diocese of Truro, but Robert and I decided that we could face up to more or less anything *except* living in the area where Lorna was killed. So, I stuck a pin in the map and came up with Salisbury

131

. . . and with my sister having a house nearby, that was very convenient. I have to admit that the powers that be in Sarum seem to find me a bit of an embarrassment. Theologically, I'm a dyed-in-the-wool traditionalist, whereas they seem to be getting some very fancy new ideas. And they obviously don't like a man on his own with a young son. If you could force them to be honest about it, Mrs Hawksworth, I wouldn't be in the least surprised if they told you I was a misfit."

Having smiled throughout his explanation, Leander burst into laughter. "Well said, Mr Frobisher! It looks as if you've come to the right place. You see, this village has a long history of taking in misfits. I, and my father before me, have been doing it for over eighty years, and our results have been absolutely first-class."

"Do you mean . . . ?" He bit back his optimism.

"Let's have our lunch, Mr Frobisher. Then John and Mary can show you round and we'll make up our minds."

It was well past five o'clock when the tour finished and they were back at Latimer's Barn. The most cursory of glances was enough to tell Leander how people felt.

"I shall be in touch with Salisbury first thing in the morning," she told Malcolm Frobisher. "The sooner you start, the better. My only problem is working out where you're going to live until I've got a house good enough for John and Mary's retirement."

"We've already decided that," Mary announced. "Malcolm and Robert will stay with us in the Rectory. It's about time the old place had some young life in it."

It was the first time for many years that Mary had made any sort of reference to the one unhappy aspect of her marriage, its lack of children. Leander saw that young Robert was very taken with the idea; the vast, rambling Rectory must seem like a wonderland to a boy who had forgotten what a proper home was like.

"It's ideal," Malcolm Frobisher said, bewildered by his good fortune. "I haven't got any furniture left after the bombing, so this gets me off to a marvellous start."

After Leander had made a thorough nuisance of herself with the people at Salisbury, everything moved with magical speed. The Reverend Malcolm Frobisher took up residence in Cannings Ambo on 5 July, the day that voting took place in the General Election.

The results were not announced until 26 July, after a three-week delay imposed by the complexities of giving servicemen and women all over the world the chance to vote. The outcome was sensational. With three hundred and ninety-three seats, Labour had a majority of one hundred and eighty over the Conservatives and one hundred and forty-six over all parties.

Amelia, who had half-expected the result, was stunned by its magnitude. The man who had stood on the balcony of Buckingham Palace between the King and Queen on the evening of 8 May, receiving a prolonged and thunderous ovation that was audible at Euston station, two miles away, had been rejected. The people had cheered Churchill, but they had refused to vote for him. Leander's face was a study in shock, followed by anger. Amelia saw that she had made her mind up about something.

Ann took it outstandingly badly. Steven, kicking his heels in Portsmouth, waiting for demob, had warned her that the greater part of the service vote would go to Labour. Eventually, after three days of morose brooding, Ann confined herself to one comment. "I expect Attlee's people will do *some* good, but I don't relish the idea of being fleeced to subsidise the feckless."

There was an uncomfortable silence in the dining-room: it was the first time that anyone had brought fears about penal levels of taxation into the open. After a worrying few moments, an authoritative voice came from the head of the table.

"I have no intention of allowing a bunch of socialists to succeed where the Kaiser and Hitler failed." Having been slow to appreciate what most of those around her perceived as a danger, Leander was now at her most implacable.

Amelia glanced at Silas and saw that he was thinking the

133

same as her: in response to the new spirit in the country, Cannings Ambo was going to change. At the age of eighty-five, having faltered and almost given up in the face of the War and the problems caused by her lamentable grandson, Leander Hawksworth was about to fight a new battle. There was no doubt that she would have the unstinting and formidable support of Ann.

For the moment, however, other matters were dominant. America took Draconian action to bring the War with Japan to a rapid end by dropping atomic bombs on the cities of Hiroshima and Nagasaki. Ten days after the obliteration of Nagasaki, on 19 August, the first of the demobbed servicemen came home to Cannings Ambo. To the delight of everyone except Rachel, it was Steven.

He was barely in The House before Leander took him to the library, pointed to a form lying on the writing-table and said, "Sign that!" in a way that brooked no argument.

"What is it?" Steven asked. He was bemused by the reception committee he had found at the end of the drive and suspected that their exuberance was only a taste of what was to come.

"It's the application for your licence, you fool! I've filled in all the details, so sign it and I'll get someone to take it to the post."

He did so, smiling at her organising forcefulness, then headed for the door.

"Where do you think you're going?" Leander demanded.

"Clearing off with Ann. We've arranged to spend a few days in Silas's old lodge. Don't worry, Mother has promised to take care of Giles."

"You're not going anywhere today, my lad!"

"Why not?" Steven looked so disappointed that she laughed.

"Because there is going to be a big knees-up at The George in your honour tonight and you will be there!"

"H'm. Yes. I suppose so." He was still despondent.

"If I were you, I'd talk to Ann," Leander said. "She seems to have a very good understanding of these things."

Ann was firmly of the opinion that they needed the privacy of their bedroom for the discussion, but when they arrived, she spent a long time over her own uniquely delectable welcome.

"That will have to do to be going on with," she said afterwards. "We'll start making a proper job of it tomorrow. The only thing you have to do until then, darling, is to make sure that you enjoy yourself this evening."

"They're really set on a party?" Steven asked, still looking for a way out.

"Of course they are. There hasn't been a celebration of the War ending yet. Now they've got you back, there's something to shout about. You're the most important person in the village, darling." She paused for emphasis. "So was your father, but he didn't come back."

Steven took the point.

Returning to The House at nearly midnight after a riotously entertaining four hours at The George, he was suddenly stone-cold sober and pensive as he walked up the drive with an arm round Ann's shoulders.

"I'd forgotten what a huge responsibility this place is," he said. "By comparison, running a warship is child's play."

"You've done it before," Ann reminded him. "It won't take you long to get back into the swing of things. I intend helping you!"

They spent four days at the forest lodge. Two things were strikingly obvious when they returned to Latimer's Barn. First, their relationship had flowered marvellously: Leander thought they were probably closer than any couple she had ever seen.

"Am I to have another great-grandchild?" she whispered to Ann.

"If you aren't, it won't be for want of trying," was the happy reply.

Secondly, Steven was in the mood for business. He spent the afternoon at Alfred Merriweather's house, re-emerging at

135

six o'clock with the air of a man who has been confronting and solving problems. Before a somewhat resentful Rachel had a chance to ask him what was going on, he told her.

"I'm back in the saddle from tomorrow, so you can make tracks for home." Anxious to have done with it, he was rather more brusque than he intended to be.

"Oh! This is all rather sudden." It was a half-hearted protest that gave her the option of an argument if Steven said the wrong thing.

"Not really. I'm here, so I may as well start. There's a lot to be done. In any case, you must be dying to get back to Charles and the kids."

There was a great deal that Rachel wanted to say, but with Leander and Emma present, she decided to feign pleasure.

Two days later, Charles came to fetch her. Convinced that they were about to make a new beginning, he was in an unusually cheerful mood. Despite Rachel's frosty silence during the journey, he contrived to be light-hearted when they reached Eaton Mandeville. In under two minutes, Rachel destroyed his hopes.

To mark her official homecoming as the Duchess, all the staff were assembled in the hall. Ignoring them completely, she strode towards the stairs and ran up to the galleried landing, disappearing towards the west wing. When Charles eventually caught up with her, she was inspecting bedrooms.

"What's going on, old girl?" he asked fearfully.

"I am looking for a room that's vaguely fit to make my own!" she snapped. "What the devil's been going on here? It doesn't look as though the place has been touched since those dreadful evacuees left."

Charles took his time coming to terms with the enormity of what she was saying. "Look, my dear, at least sleep in our room." The attempt at conciliation was, he knew, taking him dangerously close to grovelling. "I'll shake down in the dressing-room . . . or I could use the Blue Room."

"No, Charles, I want to be *here*!"

He saw that it was useless. As he walked to the suite that Dukes and Duchesses of Laverstoke had occupied for at least four generations, Charles counted the paces he took. There were three hundred and eleven. The only way in which Rachel could get further away from him was to move into the servants' quarters or the gardens.

As August came to an end, Leander began what she devoutly hoped was the final stage of a long-running battle with Elsie.

Joe was eleven and posing a problem. Mary Shepherd, who ran the village school, was convinced that he had a bright future, provided he moved to a school with the best facilities and teaching staff. Kathleen Stanton, who combined part-time teaching with her medical practice, was in complete agreement.

Leander's answer was direct and simple: Joe must go to the Grammar School in Marlborough. With fees of twelve guineas a term, Elsie had some excuse to throw up her hands in horror, saying that she couldn't afford it. Leander's immediate counter that the fees would be paid by the Fund, and that there would also be money for uniform and sports kit, set Elsie back until she was able to get into her stride about not accepting charity.

"No, Mrs Hawksworth, it's ever so kind of you, but it won't do. I was brought up to believe that you can't have what you can't afford, and charity's no answer!"

Leander, suspecting that the truth was an ingrained prejudice against an education that might make Joe too big for his boots, tried everything short of threatening Elsie. It all failed. Now, with time running out if a place were to be secured for Joe in the new school year, Leander prepared for a last attempt.

"Elsie, I expect you'll curse me for dragging it up yet again, but I really would like you to have another think about letting Joe go to the Grammar School."

"I have done," Elsie said brightly. "I'd like to take you up on the offer, and thank you very much, Mrs Hawksworth."

"I'm very pleased to hear it." Leander peered at her with something approaching suspicion. "What made you change your mind?"

"Well, Joe's chummed up with the Reverend Frobisher's boy," Elsie replied. "*He's* going to the Grammar School and I don't see why my Joe should be left out. Besides . . ." Elsie grinned ". . . Joe wants to be a doctor, and he can't do that without decent schooling, can he?"

"You'll never regret this decision, Elsie," Leander said. "And I very much hope that we don't have the same trouble when it's Bess's turn." It was worth making the point, even though the assumption that Bess would work in the stable was gaining ground.

"Education don't matter for girls, does it?" Elsie said, without thinking. Quick as a flash, she changed the subject when she saw Leander's face. "Here, talking of doctors, I hear that Miss Stanton and Mr Frobisher seem to be getting on like a house on fire."

"Oh?" Leander, never one for gossip, was dismissive. In any case, she was turning her attention to what promised to be another tricky problem: so that Mary Shepherd could share her husband's retirement, Amelia had to be persuaded to take over the village school.

To Leander's surprise, when she went to the Rectory that evening to report Amelia's capitulation, Mary mentioned Kathleen and Mr Frobisher in what was undoubtedly a significant manner.

"Mary, are you trying to tell me that there's something *going on*?" Leander asked.

"Good gracious, no!" Mary said. "It's far too early for that." Smiling roguishly, she added, "But it isn't going to be long. He's going round for supper at Kathleen's again this evening."

Ernest Cartwright came home on 5 September, lean, fit and tanned. In 1939, he had gone to war as a tubby, pompous old man of thirty-seven. Six years later and three stones lighter, he was an incisive young man of forty-three, having been

138

through Montgomery's desert campaigns and all the way from Normandy to the Rhine with the 7th Armoured Division. In the process, he had achieved the rank of Lieutenant-Colonel and won a Military Cross. Fred and Tish were stupendously proud of him, Fred being so overcome that he sat patiently through Ernest's carefully prepared theory on a new way to sell furniture without having the heart to tell him that no one yet saw the faintest hope of making any.

On the evening after his return, Ernest put his foot in it over dinner at Rose House. Louise, complaining about not having heard from John for two weeks, wondered when it would be his turn for demob.

"Oh, he's out, Mrs Flamsteed," Ernest said. "We came across to Harwich together." He made matters worse by stopping dead and looking foolish; momentarily, he forgot his new man-of-action style and was in confusion.

"Well, where is he?" Matthew asked.

"I . . . er . . . I think he was staying in London to look up a friend," Ernest replied.

Matthew grunted. "Must be a very special friend!"

"Well . . . yes . . . I did get that impression." Ernest was beginning to wish there was a hole to crawl into.

"I do think he might have let us know," Louise grumbled.

"No doubt all will be revealed to us 'ere long," Matthew said, becoming altogether happier as a strange thought occurred to him. It was completely illogical, but had a power that rendered it convincing. "Lou, we must make sure that we don't tell John that Ernest let the cat out of the bag."

"Very well, dear," Louise said dubiously and was given a grateful smile by Ernest.

Although he made no attempt to explain his presentiment to Louise, and was thus deprived of the chance to say, "What did I tell you?" Matthew gained great satisfaction from being proved right. He rather enjoyed the chaos it caused, too. They were about to start lunch the following day when it happened.

There was never a shortage of beautiful women in Cannings

Ambo. Someone – it was probably Rupert Timberlake – had once suggested that a strictly enforced law forbade ladies who were less than exquisite to set foot in the place. The girl whom John Flamsteed helped out of the taxi was a most worthy addition to the scenery. She was a stunner. As Matthew scrambled out of the front door to greet her, Solstice was rooted to the spot in the lane, goggling like a lunatic.

"Why didn't you ask me to meet you?" Matthew asked John as they embraced.

"I didn't want to put you to any trouble." John laughed at his pathetic attempt at deception. "Actually, Dad, I wanted to spring a surprise on you."

"You've succeeded!" Matthew said, and turned to the wondrous girl. "Hello, my dear, I'm Matthew Flamsteed. I'm this idiot's father."

As if fearing that her strawberry-blonde hair and cornflower-blue eyes were inadequate, the girl produced a dazzling smile. "I'm Julia Turner, Mr Flamsteed. I'm afraid I've been told all about you."

Shaking hands with her, Matthew prayed that John had retained the sense he was born with and intended marrying the girl. That would justify a celebration that might finally help them start to forget the loss of William. Julia Turner was powerfully evocative of the Louise of twenty-six years ago, completely unaffected about her looks, warm and with a delicious sense of humour. Not prepared to be kept on tenterhooks, Matthew came straight out with it.

"Are you two getting married?"

John and Julia exchanged looks of mock anguish. They were able to use the appearance of Louise to avoid an immediate answer. After being introduced to Julia, Louise gave her son a quizzical look.

"John, how on earth did you manage to find such a gorgeous girl?"

"Actually, Mother, she was in the middle of the New Forest." John's seriousness baffled Louise until Julia came to her rescue.

"I was a supply officer with the ATS, Mrs Flamsteed.

My unit was at Brockenhurst issuing new kit to the troops before they went over on D-Day. I drew the short straw and got lumbered with part of the Wiltshire regiment." Matthew didn't know whether to look sympathetic, or offended: that was *his* old outfit. "I'm afraid that Major Flamsteed's contingent was a complete pain in the neck," Julia concluded.

"Steady on, darling!" John said, much aggrieved. "It wasn't my fault you'd got nothing but odd socks and left boots by the time we turned up."

"Rubbish! In any case, who was a day late because he took a wrong turn in Southampton?"

While John was attempting to gloss over his map-reading, they moved indoors. Julia and John, still arguing, were shoved into the big all-purpose room, while Matthew went to the kitchen with Louise as she set about stretching their lunch into four servings.

"Someone will be down from The House soon," Matthew said.

"What for?" Louise was puzzled.

"Solstice was passing when they arrived. His eyes nearly popped out when he saw Julia, then he went off to spread the message. I wouldn't be surprised if Leander doesn't come."

After careful consideration of the news, Leander decided that Ann was the best person for the job. She arrived after a decent interval to find Louise and Julia gossiping like old friends as they washed up.

"Don't tell me," Louise said, as Ann marched in through the ever-open back door. "You've come to borrow some margarine!"

"Of course I haven't!" Ann laughed. "I've been sent to inspect John's fantastic girlfriend." She smiled at Julia. "Hello, I'm Ann Hawksworth. Blimey! We thought Solstice was exaggerating, but he wasn't!"

While Ann was explaining, Matthew and John wandered into the kitchen, John moving to Julia's side.

"Come on, John, spill the beans," Matthew said, but no one took any notice of him. Ann had spotted that the home-made frocks she and Julia were wearing had been based on the same pattern. Louise joined in the enthusiastic exchange of cutting and sewing hints. When it seemed that they were never going to stop, John cleared his throat portentously.

"Yesterday, I asked Julia to marry me," he announced in what was very nearly a shout.

It was most gratifying: Louise and Ann gaped at him expectantly, Julia did her best not to blush.

"Well?" Louise demanded, maddened by John's unwillingness to go further. "What did she say?"

"I said, 'Yes, please'," Julia replied.

"How wonderful!" Ann shrieked, starting to hop about with joy. "I say, you don't believe in wasting time, do you?"

"It's exactly what Lou and I did after the last war," Matthew said. "If they're as happy as us, they'll be all right!"

Louise, suddenly a good deal less composed than she would have liked, found the ideal excuse for tears of joy in the arms of her daughter-in-law-to-be.

"Hey, where are you going?" Matthew asked as Ann made for the door.

"To tell Leander, of course! She'd skin me alive if she found out I hadn't told her at once!"

In 1919, Louise had insisted on marrying Matthew in Cannings Ambo, rather than her native Birmingham. To everyone's delight, Julia repeated the compliment. Her mother and father and an array of uncles and aunts, all pillars of Wimbledon middle-class society, had misgivings about the venue, but were mostly won over by the village and its inhabitants. And, as the least refined of the aunts whispered to her embarrassing 'gentleman friend', "Julia's done very well for herself and no mistake!"

Leander, who had taken to Julia at once, was especially pleased by her decision because of the opportunity it gave Malcolm Frobisher. "He'll have done nothing but funerals in the Army," she told Emma.

She was perfectly right and the new vicar enjoyed himself tremendously, conducting the service with a joyous gusto that was ideally suited to the happy couple. Afterwards

142

the reception was held in the Rectory gardens and had the atmosphere of a church fête in beautifully mellow, late-September sunshine. Leander and Emma, who were anxious to be in a good position to see the bride and groom off as they restored the old family tradition of going to Torquay for their honeymoon, sat slightly apart from the main crowd, sipping their tea and reminiscing about Emma's wedding in 1912.

Leander's attention had been hovering on something near the rose garden for several minutes before she murmured, "That's interesting, don't you think?"

"What is?" Emma asked, searching in vain for the source of Leander's curiosity.

"Elsie and that Polish chap," Leander replied.

Elsie was in animated conversation with a dark, lean man of about thirty, her own age. When she went to the nearest makeshift table in search of more food, Bess said something to the man: he crouched down to listen to her. After a few moments of intense concentration, he laughed and his saturnine features were transformed into something akin to radiance. When Elsie returned with a laden plate, she sat down on the grass to join in the mirth.

"Yes, it *is* interesting," Emma agreed.

Stanislaus Bogisiewicz had escaped from Warsaw in 1939 and somehow got himself to England where, like so many of his compatriots, he joined the Royal Air Force. He started off with an all-Polish unit as a member of the ground staff, but in 1943 he was transferred to an English Lancaster squadron as a rear gunner. Demob brought no desire to return to the Russian-occupied shambles of Poland, so Bogisiewicz had accepted the invitation of his mate, Flight Sergeant Bill Izzard, to try his luck in Cannings Ambo.

The day after they got back to the village, Bill took Stanislaus up to The House so that he could ask Steven for a job. After listening to what the Pole had to tell him, Steven put him up on the stable's most difficult horse, a four-year-old colt of such a vile disposition that no one had ever succeeded in breaking him properly. The results were astounding: after half an hour that taught him a very great deal, the colt was angelic. There was a perfectly simple explanation: from the age of twelve, Stanislaus Bogisiewicz had been a rider in a touring circus.

"Well, there you are," Steven said to an open-mouthed Alfred Merriweather. "It may be unusual, but the man's a genius. I've set him on."

That night, Bill Izzard took Stanislaus to The George, where he proved an instant popular success. Before the evening was out, the transformation of his difficult name to Stan Boggysevick signalled his full acceptance into the community.

Now, a few weeks later, here he was, getting along like a house on fire with Elsie and Bess. When Joe turned up, accompanied, as ever, by Robert Frobisher, it was apparent that he, too, thought Boggysevick was the cat's whiskers.

"Do you know, Elsie seems totally bewitched by him," Emma said.

Leander shook her head and smiled. An ex-circus performer, who was virtually a gypsy before the RAF had taught him the necessity of belonging to a well-disciplined group, and a woman who had never seen a green field in her life until driven out of London by bombing: what was the world coming to? But then, looking again at the enchanted pair in the light of her vast experience, Leander saw that they were a continuation of all the remarkable people who had made the village what it was.

On Armistice Day, 11 November, Malcolm Frobisher had a solemn duty that he insisted John Shepherd must share with him. Every man, woman and child in Cannings Ambo was at the War Memorial at twenty past ten for the service of rededication, to honour the twelve new names, before the two minutes' silence at eleven o'clock. After the silence, Leander laid the wreath of poppies that symbolised the feelings of the whole village. Steven, on behalf of Latimer's Barn, and Matthew, for Wm Flamsteed & Sons, followed her. This year, there was an innovation: Amelia had decided that there

144

should be a tribute from the school, and Bess Collier had been chosen to place the small wreath at the foot of the Memorial. Leander watched intently as the child performed the task with a presence and gravity that transcended her tender years.

At the traditional gathering in the Rectory that followed, Ann noticed that Kathleen Stanton, sticking close to Malcolm Frobisher, looked nervous and excited. Holding her hand, Robert appeared to be exerting a calming influence. While Ann was working her way across the packed room to ask Leander what she thought of it, Malcolm made his announcement.

"Ladies and gentlemen, I know you were all glad to see John Shepherd on parade this morning, so you'll be delighted to know that he has consented to come out of retirement again to perform a function that is beyond my powers." In the expectant silence, Ann saw that Leander had finally cottoned on: the realisation that the stories she had steadfastly ignored were true brought a happy smile to her face. "Kathleen and I are to be married," Malcolm went on. "You will see why we need John's help!"

In the midst of laughter and applause, Kathleen, forty-seven years of age, did her best to convey the impression that she was perfectly calm. Leander was the first to get to her with congratulations.

"My dear, I'm thrilled! I'm sure you'll be very happy."

Kathleen, with Robert still holding her hand, was supremely confident. "It proves it's never too late," she said, showing the first dissatisfaction with the long years of spinsterhood that everyone had always assumed she did not mind.

Five minutes later, Leander had solved the problem of where John and Mary Shepherd should live. Mary had always admired Oak Cottage, the house restored for Kathleen's grandparents in 1863. It was agreed that Kathleen should keep her surgery there after she married Malcolm and moved to the Rectory, while John and Mary lived in the rest of the lovely old house.

"It's like musical chairs," Ann said. "Everyone's happy and we don't have to do any building."

"I intend starting soon," Leander said. "We need new houses badly."

"Will that be possible?" Emma asked.

Leander knew what she meant. Inasmuch as the Government had yet made any policy statements other than those concerned with a massive nationalisation programme, austerity even greater than that needed in the War seemed to figure prominently in their plans.

"I don't believe in austerity!" Leander said firmly.

Kathleen and Malcolm were married on the first Saturday of December. The Dowager Duchess of Laverstoke sat in the front pew, flanked by Leander and Emma. Having arrived at Louise House only two days previously, she was still concealing her intense relief at escaping from the poisonous atmosphere that was marring life at Eaton Mandeville.

CHAPTER 6

1947

'Isn't this a criminal offence, Mother?'

In 1946, Ann gave birth to the child that she and Steven had conceived immediately after his return from the War. Leander's fourth great-grandson, delivered by Kathleen Frobisher, baptised by Malcolm, was named Oliver in memory of Emma's father. Four months later, the font was in use again for John and Julia's son. To universal acclaim, the village gained a third William Flamsteed. There was a minor sadness, however; Kathleen was fairly sure that Julia would not be able to bear any more children.

Quietly and patiently, Steven laid the foundations for a new beginning at Latimer's Barn. By the late summer of 1946, the stable was working to seventy-five per cent capacity and the winners were coming. Some were ridden by Sammy Thorn, others by Michael Pilgrim, now old enough to hold a licence.

The list of owners had a much regretted absentee. For the first time since 1874, a Duke of Laverstoke had no horses in training. No one was more bitterly disappointed than Charles himself.

"I simply can't afford it," he said privately to Steven. "The estate's in a shocking mess."

Dismayed, Steven offered tentative help. "I wonder if the Fund could do anything?"

"Forget it!" Charles said resolutely. "You'd be throwing

147

good money after bad the way things are at the moment. The Government still haven't made up their mind how much they want in death duties for the poor old governor and it's going to cost a fortune to put everything right after the War."

Glumly, Steven accepted the position, delicately avoiding the question of how things stood between Charles and his duchess.

There were compensations. In 1909, Guy Mallender and Harry Giffard, the two grocers, became joint-owners, a custom carried on by their sons. Now, their grandsons, Edward and Leslie, decided to become individual owners. When Steven commented on their ability to contemplate this in such difficult times, they looked almost furtive.

"The fact is, we did rather well out of the War," Leslie Giffard admitted, rather shamefaced. "Nothing to do with us – it was rationing and the way the Government ran it."

"It might even get worse for a few years," Edward Mallender said.

"Or *better*," Steven smiled.

"God forbid! We want to get back to normal commercial operation, offering people a good choice of food at fair prices," Edward replied and his sincerity was beyond question. "We're planning for expansion, of course, but we thought we might as well spend a bit more on enjoying ourselves." It was a common enough aspiration: post-war Britain looked set to remain a cheerless place for a long time.

"And you never know," Leslie Giffard chipped in. "We might find a good 'un that would do well at stud. We could clear up a packet on that!"

It was the first time that Steven had heard the sentiment expressed so blatantly.

The greatest support came from Claude Timberlake. He put twenty two-year-olds into the stable, and, as the season drew to a close, one of them sent Leander hurrying to the Big Book.

The Dewhurst Stakes, run at the mid-October Newmarket meeting, was a well-established test for the best juveniles. Latimer's Barn had won the first running in 1875 with the great Bellerophon, repeating the achievement with such regularity that Leander had come to regard the race as her own personal property.

Royal Wessex, one of Isocracy's offspring, had already won his début at Newbury in June and shown great *élan* at Sandown Park in August. After working hard to tone down Jimmy Farrant's extravagant optimism, Steven decided that the colt had a fair chance in the Dewhurst.

The grin on Jimmy's face as he watched his latest pride and joy setting a new course record, reducing the opposition to mediocrity, was something to cherish. And two days later, after the leading lights of the bookmaking fraternity had mulled matters over, the news from the Victoria Club indicated that things were getting back to normal: Latimer's Barn had the ante-post favourite for next year's Two Thousand Guineas.

The winter of 1947 was the worst since 1881.

England, like much of Europe, was reduced to weeks of freezing paralysis. All transport ground to a halt, food supplies were in jeopardy and power stations either broke down or ran out of fuel. In addition to the discomfort of the weather's unmitigated ferocity, there was the fear that the dreadful conditions would finally push the country over the precipice of economic ruin. Nothing – short of another war – could have been more damaging.

The fierce and prolonged blizzard that began the difficulties precipitated a crisis that led to carelessness. This, in turn, led to tragedy.

When Cannings Ambo was cut off by the snow drifts supplies of feed for the horses were perilously low. A scheduled delivery had been delayed due to a strike by the hauliers who carried stocks from the mill to the merchant in Marlborough. However, late on the afternoon before the snow came, Steven received a telephone call to say that all was now well and that a lorry would be out the following morning. In the event, with the blizzard still raging, conditions were so bad that an attempt to get through to the main road had to be deferred until first light on the day after.

The task looked impossible. The half-mile of lane to the main London to Bath road was blocked by at least ten feet of snow. In places, the drifts were twenty feet deep. As digging began, they had no idea what was at the other end because, by now, the snow had cut off every telephone in the village. There was nothing for it but to dig and hope for the best. With men and women slaving in relays, the work carried on until three hours past darkness when all those involved were in a state of near-collapse.

Steven, looking and feeling totally exhausted, said that he thought they might be half-way through when he returned to The House.

"I take it that we're sure everyone in the village is safe and provided for?" Leander asked.

"Yes. I saw Louise a couple of hours ago. She's had search parties out."

But at dawn on yet another bitter day, both Louise and Kathleen realised that a proper check had not been made on The Hall. A party of men were detached from the main group in the lane to dig their way in. When hammering repeatedly on the massive front door produced no response, a further ten minutes was wasted on a futile debate as to whether to break a window. When someone finally had the idea of digging a path round to the back, the bodies of Sam and Ann Briggs, lying midway between the scullery door and one of the outbuildings, were frozen solid and partially covered in snow.

Leander was horrified that such a terrible thing could happen, virtually under everyone's noses. So badly shaken was she, that she indulged in overwrought recriminations, accusing anyone who came near her of incompetence. With Steven busy in the lane and unaware of the tragedy, it was left to Ann to take command of the situation.

"That's enough, Leander!" she said angrily. "It looks very much as though they'd been dead for at least two days. I don't suppose we shall ever know what happened and carrying on like that won't help! What we *must* do is open the lane as quickly as possible so that Kathleen can get the bodies to hospital."

To the amazement of those onlookers who were unaware of Ann's influence, Leander shut up. Leaving Emma to soothe ruffled feathers, Ann went to help in the lane. Once news of the deaths had circulated, there was no question of giving up until the job was done.

Finally, at one o'clock in the morning, by the cold light of a full moon, they found that the last seventy-five yards to the main road had been swept by a freak of the wind. The main road itself seemed to be clear of any substantial amounts of snow. There was only one thing to do and Steven did it unhesitatingly, setting out to walk to the police station in Marlborough. He returned three hours later with the ambulance that was to take poor old Sam and Ann Briggs to the mortuary at Savernake Hospital.

The feed arrived during the afternoon. Although the horses would have been on miserably low rations without it, the success was greeted with listless indifference: everyone was stunned by the calamity at The Hall.

After the post-mortems, there was an inquest. The facts were simple. Sam had perished from a massive heart attack, Ann had frozen to death after breaking a leg. The coroner was inclined to accept Kathleen's view of what must have taken place: one of the outbuildings was stacked with logs. Sam had collapsed and died on the way to fetch some. Rushing to him, Ann had slipped on the treacherous surface and broken a leg, leaving her immobile, probably fainting with pain, and at the mercy of the evil temperature.

While a small group of men began using crowbars on the frozen ground of the churchyard, the coffins were made in the workshops of Wm Flamsteed & Sons.

Leander had The Hall locked up and swore that it would remain empty forever. She even spoke of having it razed.

Slowly, the weather improved, but it was a painfully drawn-out affair. Realising that he was probably being over-cautious, Steven refused to do anything with the horses until the end of the first week in April. At that stage, the chances of being able to get Royal Wessex fit for the Two Thousand Guineas were negligible, so he was scratched.

That same day, Leander decided that action was needed and sent for Sid Irons.

The Irons family had built The House from the ruins of Hugh Latimer's tithe barn in 1839 and had been adding to and improving the stable and village ever since. Sid, a representative of the fifth generation, knew that Mrs Hawksworth never wasted time with idle talk and drove the ten miles from Calne an hour after receiving the summons.

"What's business like, Sidney?" Leander asked him.

"Terrible, Mrs Hawksworth, ma'am. You can't get planning permission for love nor money with all these new busybodies and bewricrats."

"And yet there's a desperate need for houses?"

"It's wicked," Sid said.

"Can you build me two to be going on with while I work out what else we need?"

"We've got the men and materials," he replied. "Have you got the permission?"

Leander smiled triumphantly. "I don't need it, Sidney. This is a private estate and I can do what I like. Don't worry, the lawyers have been over it with a toothcomb and we're all right. Even that new Housing Act doesn't affect us . . . look!" She brandished a letter. "I've made the County Council admit it!"

Sid rubbed his hands and reached for his notebook. "Fire away, Mrs Hawksworth," he said.

"I want a bungalow on the Back Stretch – something a little bit out of the ordinary."

"We did a very nice one for Captain Laybourne over at Bremhill just before the War," Sid said. "I've still got a set of drawings for that."

"Perhaps you could let me see them. The other thing is a house on the drive . . . well away from the others, so that it's nice and private."

"Up towards the Back Stretch?" Sid suggested.

"Lovely! That doesn't need to be so grand, but I don't

want a chicken-coop, Sidney. It must have three decent-sized bedrooms."

Sid returned the next day with drawings and a photograph of the bungalow at Bremhill. They agreed a price, Leander gave him a down payment in cash, then they went outside and she showed him exactly where the two buildings were to be sited. Work began within the week.

The Bungalow – and it acquired its capital B immediately – was a belated wedding present for John and Julia Flamsteed, who were comfortable enough with Matthew and Louise at Rose House, but longed for their own place. The intentions for the house on the drive were a secret, and no one asked any questions until building was well advanced.

Elsie's curiosity finally got the better of her in early May, after Leander had spoken to her about Bess's forthcoming eighth birthday.

"I want her to have a couple of pairs of breeches," Leander said. "Can you measure her up, please?"

For well over a year, Bess had been visiting the yards every day, admiring the horses, making friends with them and talking incessantly of learning to ride. Elsie saw a possible stumbling-block. "What about coupons?" she asked. Two years after the end of the War, rationing was still in force.

"You ought to know us better than that," Leander said, mildly reproving. "We've always made things like that for ourselves. There's enough best-quality, pre-war twill to keep us going for years, and Mrs Flamsteed can run up a pair of breeches in no time."

Elsie understood that Leander was referring to Julia, whose dress-making abilities were being used for all manner of jobs. "I know it will be difficult with having to measure Bess, but I'll try and keep it secret," Elsie vowed. After a momentary pause, she decided to make the most of having Leander to herself. "Do you mind if I ask you something, Mrs Hawksworth?"

"Ask away."

"Everybody's wondering what that new house is for . . . the one on the drive."

"That's a big secret, Elsie," Leander said.

"I won't breathe a word. Honest! Cross my heart!"

After thinking about it very carefully, Leander gave in. "It's for you, Elsie," she said.

"Me?" Elsie was flabbergasted. "Blimey! But that's going to be *ever* such a nice place."

"It better had be!" Leander said with the air of one who was spending good money to achieve that end.

"Well . . . I mean . . . I never thought I'd ever have anything like that."

"Don't be ridiculous, Elsie," Leander replied. "You deserve it. Joe needs more space for his homework and it will be nice for Bess to have her own room instead of sharing with you." There was a slight pause. "I think it will be good for you, as well, Elsie. You'll have a better chance of leading your own life."

"I . . ." Elsie thought better of it. Leander was looking at her in a way that suggested she knew everything. For a moment, Elsie prayed for the floor to open up and swallow her, then she realised that she had no cause for shame: by giving her the house, Leander was showing that she understood and approved.

Soon after the wedding of John and Julia, Elsie and Boggysevick had become lovers, but the comfort they derived from each other was severely constrained by the lack of an appropriate place for their encounters.

"That's very good of you, ma'am," Elsie said, touched by what she knew Leander was thinking. "I won't let you down."

"You said that nearly eight years ago," Leander reminded her. "As you can see, I believe you!"

Royal Wessex made rapid progress in his work. After two weeks, he went to Newbury for what was no more than a training gallop over a mile and a half. The opposition was undemanding and he won in a canter. Three weeks later, at Lingfield in the Derby trial, Michael Pilgrim had to give him a shake-up against a much tougher bunch of horses, but the result was the same: he won it as he pleased. It was a very public demonstration of Steven's intentions, yet few people outside Cannings Ambo took any notice of it because they were preoccupied with Tudor Minstrel, the hottest Derby favourite for over a hundred years.

Royal Wessex's lad, Jimmy Farrant and his two cronies, Solstice and Boggysevick, debated the issue at great and earnest length. Most evenings, between seven and eight, they were huddled in a corner of the bar at The George, glaring antisocially at anyone who ventured within earshot of them.

"Mind you, I can see what they mean about Tudor Minstrel," Solstice admitted one evening. "He's supposed to have won the Guineas like a champion."

"The best ever," Boggysevick agreed, repeating the perceived wisdom after the colt's stunning eight-length victory in the Newmarket Classic.

Jimmy Farrant would have none of it. "I keep telling you, it don't matter. He won't get the trip at Epsom. Our boy will eat him!"

"Are you sure?" Boggysevick, hunched over his pint, looked very intense.

"Dead certain. He's too fast to get a mile and a half. Alec Dawson saw the Guineas and he reckons that Tudor Minstrel was *fading* at the end. Alec swears that another half furlong and he'd have got beat."

And so it went on, night after night, until Solstice and Boggysevick were convinced. Eventually, they each put fifty pounds into a kitty and Solstice was given the job of getting it on Royal Wessex without causing any tremors among the local bookmakers. Patiently, placing no more than ten pounds at a time, he completed the ticklish task, obtaining odds of ten to one about their colt.

Steven looked forward to the race. In public, he tended to accept the theory that Tudor Minstrel was invincible; privately, he had reservations about the favourite's stamina which led him to believe that Royal Wessex had a good chance. And the occasion of his first post-war attempt at the Derby was to be made more special by the presence of Alain and Nadia de Mourville, who, spending a month in England to renew their war-time friendships, were to be guests at Latimer's Barn for several days.

They arrived looking splendid and wonderfully happy. Having married soon after the Liberation of France, they had a twelve-month-old daughter, Lisette, who had stayed with Alain's parents at Fontainebleau. The only sign of their hard life during the War was the tremendous affinity between them although, on reflection, Steven thought it unfair to give the Nazis credit for such a beautiful thing.

Alain was pleased to see the stable working normally. "You have done well, my friend," he said, pausing outside Royal Wessex's box to admire the colt. "You will soon be able to forget that Hitler ever existed."

"How are things with you in France?" Steven asked.

Alain pulled a face and made an eloquent gesture. "Some things are good. We have all our property back and we're making progress. The winter hurt us, but you will have had the same trouble. As to the country . . . well, it is not so good yet. We lack stable government."

Steven knew that having set up a provisional administration in 1944, de Gaulle had been forced out of office in 1946 because it was suspected that his views were too authoritarian.

"We have too many factions," Alain explained. "No one can hold any sort of coalition together. There is no discipline."

"Borrow some of ours!" Steven urged. "We have a Government that wants to tax all the things it doesn't ban."

As a relief from austerity, Nadia had brought a huge bottle of Chanel perfume and three pairs of silk stockings for Ann, whose reaction to the precious gifts was stupefaction.

"Can you buy things like this in France?" she asked.

"Not in the shops," Nadia replied. "But anything is possible in the black market."

"And what about customs?" Ann asked.

Nadia glowered. "There was a *cochon* at Dover who wanted to search me. Alain had to give him a special look!"

"He was only doing his job, *chérie*," Alain said, winking at Steven.

"Pooh! Gestapo filth!" Nadia fumed.

On Epsom Downs, austerity was set aside for Derby Day when half a million people set out to enjoy themselves. Alain and Nadia, he immaculate in morning suit, she wearing an emerald-green dress of deceptively good imitation silk, gazed around and were clearly at a loss for words.

"Not so *chic* as Longchamp or Chantilly?" Steven asked.

"Well . . ." Alain struggled. "I wouldn't want to condemn it for that. Maybe the French avoid giving the impression that they are so *determined* to have a good time."

Steven grinned, knowing exactly what he meant: the English had an unfortunate talent for crassness on such occasions.

Eventually, however, the tomfoolery stopped and the horses came into the paddock for the main event. Ann stayed on the rails with Alain and Nadia while Steven stood at the centre of the ring with Claude and Lily Timberlake. As so often for a big race, their eldest son, Gideon, had wangled a day off school to be with them. Now seventeen and handsome enough to turn the heads of thirty-year-old women, he was becoming a shrewd judge of a horse.

"Don't worry, Mr Hawksworth," he said, seeing Steven casting anxious glances at Tudor Minstrel. "He won't stay."

"He looks well, though," Steven muttered, unable to resist another look at the big, strapping bay.

"So does ours," Gideon replied. "He also looks very businesslike and settled. If I had anything to do with Tudor Minstrel, I wouldn't be too happy about his temperament."

Never having heard the doubt expressed before, Steven dismissed the remark as the work of a young man trying to show off. However, no sooner was Gordon Richards mounted on Tudor Minstrel than the colt starting acting up alarmingly, and he gave the famous jockey a terrible ride down to the bridle-path by which the runners had to cross the horseshoe-shaped course to reach the start.

Once the race was underway, after being badly delayed by Tudor Minstrel's antics, the big colt resolutely refused to settle. Head high, he surged to the head of the field and built up what looked like a formidable lead. Two or three of the more nervous jockeys, unwilling to fall too far behind so early on, went after him: Michael Pilgrim sat still on Royal Wessex, who bowled along at little more than a canter.

On the hill down to Tattenham Corner, the wayward Tudor Minstrel lost interest. As he slowed, a jostling, bumping group formed on his heels. To Steven's relief, he saw Royal Wessex, still cruising, taking a wide line round the scrimmage. Out of the bend, Tudor Minstrel retained the lead and gave the impression that he had finally settled: Royal Wessex was fourth. Michael Pilgrim made up his mind to go sooner rather than later and set about discovering what his horse was really capable of.

It was all over in a few strides. The only thing that put Michael off momentarily was the sepulchral groan of the crowd when they realised that the hottest favourite since God knows when was done for. They had backed Tudor Minstrel down to seven to four *on* and with two furlongs still to run, he was left without a hope in hell. Against opposition widely thought to be unbeatable, the tenth Derby winner to emerge from Latimer's Barn came home in a trot. Steven nodded to Gideon, acknowledging his astute reading of the race, and went to collect his horse.

"I am impressed," Alain said to Steven, gladly accepting the invitation to join the group in the winner's enclosure. "My first time on an English racecourse and look what happens!"

"You've brought me luck," Steven smiled.

"That wasn't luck, my friend." Alain glanced round at the sea of faces. Very few of them had backed Royal Wessex, yet, as the winner of the world's greatest race, he deserved and received their admiration. "I think I would like to be here with my own horse one day," Alain added.

"We shall have to see what we can do," Steven replied, not taking him all that seriously.

After listening to the commentary on the wireless, Leander behaved as though Royal Wessex were the first winner

Latimer's Barn had ever produced. Sending for Solstice, she gave him a shopping list.

"We're going to have a party," she explained. "I know some of these things will be difficult to find, but do your best."

Running his eye down the list, Solstice was taken aback. "This is all under-the-counter stuff," he said.

"I know. I've already spoken to Mr Mallender and he can help out with some of it." She smiled archly. "I have an idea that he may be able to make suggestions where you might find the rest. And possibly you know one or two people, Solstice?"

"Well . . . yes . . . strictly between you and me, ma'am . . ."

Leander stopped him. "Never mind the sordid details, just get on with it. You'll need this." She gave him one hundred pounds in five-pound notes.

"I shall have to go all over the place," Solstice said, informing, not complaining.

"I imagine that might be handy for you," Leander said. "*Should* you run into Mr Sykes at Hungerford, or Mr Barrowclough in Salisbury, give them my regards."

Elsie stared at Solstice as he passed through the kitchen on his way out. "What you grinning at?" she asked.

"Mrs Hawksworth," he replied.

"What about her?"

"Oh, nothing special," Solstice said and passed on his way. Sykes and Barrowclough were two of the bookmakers with whom he had placed the syndicate's investment on Royal Wessex.

At lunch on the day after the Derby, Alain proved that he was serious. "Can you take four or five horses for me, Steven?"

"Really?"

"Yes!"

"I'd be delighted. What had you in mind?"

"Next season's two-year-olds."

"Where are they now?"

Alain laughed. "I don't know. I haven't bought them yet."

"I see." Steven was thoughtful. "So, you want some decent yearlings. Will you buy them in France and send them over?"

"No! Our own stock is badly run-down. The Aga Khan and Boussac are struggling to get going again, so they won't sell me anything and I wouldn't trust anyone else. Tell me, do you have any yearlings at your stud?"

"Yes, there are a few we were thinking of sending to the autumn sales."

"Could I see them?"

"Yes, I suppose so."

Alain guffawed at Steven's reticence. "My friend, you are a brilliant trainer, but I don't think you would ever succeed as a salesman!"

Steven grinned sheepishly. "I didn't want you to feel that you were being forced to buy."

"Arrange for me to take a look and I'll do the rest."

They went to Cannings St John for lunch. Jeremy and Josie Dundas, given hectic last-minute warning of the visit, laid on a good meal and were delighted by Alain. He saw the photograph of their son, Mark, on the sideboard, asked about him, and was sympathetic when told of his death at Arnhem.

"He did not die in vain," Alain said. "Believe me, there will never be another war like that."

"Do you *really* think so?" Jeremy asked. The dreadful conflict that had nearly done for him in 1916 was supposed to be the last.

"I do," Alain replied with total conviction. "Europe has frightened itself to death with this one. From now on, they will do *anything* to avoid war."

"Including giving in to the Russians?"

"I think so, yes." He smiled reassuringly. "But let us hope that the new treaties and alliances stop it ever coming to that, eh?"

There were six yearlings at the stud. Alain spent all afternoon inspecting them, discovering their breeding, making copious notes about the blood lines that went back seventy

160

years to Bellerophon and New Invention. When he returned to Latimer's Barn with Steven, who had evening stables at six o'clock, there was no sign of a decision and the subject was not mentioned during the remainder of the day.

The next day, Alain returned to Cannings St John, taking Nadia with him. Jeremy left them to wander round as they pleased and saw no more of them until they came to say goodbye three hours later. Anxious not to appear pushy, he refrained from asking if they had come to a conclusion. Steven, whom they met outside The House, threw caution to the winds.

"Is there anything you like?" he asked.

"We cannot make up our minds!" Nadia wailed. "Some I like, some he likes." She spread her hands in Gallic despair.

"The answer is perfectly simple," Alain said. "I'll buy all six!"

Whooping with glee at the prospect of getting the filly that had so taken her fancy, Nadia dashed off in search of lunch, leaving Steven and Alain to disappear into the library to talk about money. They soon found a bone of contention: Alain insisted that the prices Steven was asking were far too low.

As they argued the toss, three other men were involved with finance. Each armed with five hundred pounds' winnings from Royal Wessex, Solstice, Jimmy Farrant and Boggysevick were in Marlborough High Street, resolved to be sensible. Intending to buy a house for his mother and father, Jimmy put the money in his bank account; Solstice and Boggysevick made tracks for a building society and slightly better interest.

Eventually, Alain persuaded Steven that the six yearlings were worth four thousand pounds apiece and they shook hands on the deal.

"And how am I to pay you?" Alain asked. "Our foreign currency restrictions aren't as bad as yours, but we have a problem, I think."

"Oh, Lord!" Steven was perplexed. "I hadn't thought of that." He tried to think constructively instead of cursing the

Government. "I say, do you have any financial links with Switzerland?" he asked.

"But of course! All my family's money went there before the War. I have three companies registered in Zurich."

"In that case, we don't have a problem," Steven said.

Amelia had been wondering about the Fund for eighteen months or so. Because of the challenge and fascination of running the village school and the sublime way of life that she and Silas enjoyed, her thoughts on the subject were sporadic and lacked concentration. She was far from sure what she was trying to discover. Had there been subtle changes, or was she imagining things? Once, she had almost convinced herself that Matthew, the treasurer, was being deliberately evasive: the idea was so absurd that she laughed at herself and gave the matter no further thought for some time.

Two days before the July meeting of Trustees, Sir Miles Christopherson visited Cannings Ambo. Ostensibly, he was looking at his horses: Sir Miles was one of the new post-war owners. He was a merchant banker who, Amelia suspected, did business with and for the Timberlakes. There was no doubt that he radiated the calm, magisterial authority so essential in a top-flight financier, but beneath the veneer Amelia felt that there was something reprehensible about Sir Miles.

The Dowager Duchess was outspoken when she discovered he was in the village.

"I understand that frightful tick Christopherson is here again," she told Amelia when she returned to Louise House from school one afternoon.

"Oh!" Amelia blinked. "Don't you like him, either?"

"Like him!" Clementine looked to be on the verge of apoplexy. "He's the most disgusting old lecher!"

"He doesn't seem all that old," Amelia said, glad that she could say something vaguely good about him.

"He's fifty-eight, with a wife young enough to be his daughter and at least two mistresses."

"Surely not!" Although the allegation would explain the

162

unease that Amelia always felt in Christopherson's company, she was unwilling to believe it.

"It's perfectly true. He married Patricia Spalding in 1940 – she was what they call a 'film-star'. Lady Milton swears that he keeps a doxy in Leatherhead and another in Knightsbridge – just round the corner from Harrods, if you please!"

"I don't suppose his proclivities stop him being a good banker," Amelia said.

"I hope not! It seems that he's looking after the Fund nowadays. Ah . . . didn't you know that?"

"No, Clementine, I did not." Amelia was shocked.

"Oh dear, I've put my foot in it again. Look, this is all hush-hush, so if you let on that I've told you, I'll skin you alive, right?" Amelia nodded. "Your mother got me some money from the Fund to keep Eaton Mandeville going while Charles was sorting out those bloody death duties – I passed it over as savings which I didn't need. Anyway, when I received it, it was a draft from Christopherson's, not a Western Counties cheque."

Amelia was angry. The Fund had been with Western Counties Bank since Giles Flamsteed had set it up in 1886: to have moved it without the consent of the Trustees seemed astoundingly high-handed. After brooding on it for a couple of hours, Amelia went to Rose House, determined to extract an explanation from Matthew.

She discovered that she would have to wait. "I don't think I can disturb him," Louise said. "He's shut himself in the study with that awful Christopherson man."

"Oh . . . so I'm not the only person that can't stand him?" Amelia asked, feeling better, in spite of her frustration.

"Good God, no! He gives me the creeps."

"What are they doing?"

"Going over the balance sheet, I expect. Shall I ask Matthew to telephone you when they've finished?"

"No, don't bother, Louise, I'll see him tomorrow."

On the way back, Amelia found that she was not prepared to wait and went into The House, finding her mother alone in the library.

"What's wrong, darling?" Leander asked. "You look pretty aerated."

Amelia sat down, collected her thoughts and came straight out with it. "Has the Fund been moved from Western Counties?"

"Yes." Leander was unruffled by the question.

"When?"

"Let me see . . . between August nineteen forty-five and May of last year. Western Counties still have about seventy-five thousand in case we need a substantial sum in a hurry."

This had puzzling aspects, but Amelia ignored them to ask: "No doubt there were good reasons for the move?"

"*I* thought so," Leander said confidently.

"And you satisfied yourself that Christopherson was the right man?"

"Of course! Claude Timberlake vouched for him. It all worked very well."

The past tense bothered Amelia. "What do you mean, Mother? Why do you say 'worked'? Is it all over?"

"In a way, yes. Sir Miles's main function was simply to handle the transfer."

"Transfer? You mean he *isn't* looking after the Fund?"

"Good gracious, no. That would have left us no better off than having it with Western Counties."

Amelia was certain that Leander was being deliberately obtuse. "Mother, where is the Fund?" she asked.

"In a Swiss bank. Our links are through Sir Miles via a system I don't pretend to understand. He makes a charge, of course, but we're getting an extra one and a quarter per cent a year which leaves us in pocket."

"How on earth did the money get to Switzerland?" asked. "With the controls they've got on currency, you can't move a shilling without three lots of permission."

"It was taken to Jersey in notes – a hundred thousand at a time."

"Who by?"

"Silas."

"Silas!" Amelia was stupefied.

Leander chuckled wickedly. "He said you never bothered to ask him where he went."

"I assumed he was doing things for you," Amelia spluttered, recalling Silas's two- and three-day absences.

"He was," Leander laughed. "About a million and a half pounds-worth – and every last penny of it got there safely."

"Isn't this a criminal offence, Mother?" Amelia asked weakly.

"Probably." So far, Leander had been treating it almost as a joke: suddenly she was stern. "The interest on invested capital is now taxed at nineteen shillings in the pound. Can you imagine anything more destructively *vindictive* than that? At Western Counties, we should have earned about forty-five thousand interest and paid forty-three thousand in tax." She paused, glaring to drive the point home. "And that isn't the end of it. They're still talking about taxing *capital* at ten shillings in the pound *every* year! You're a mathematician, so I don't have to tell you what that leaves us with after three or four years. They'll *never* get their hands on it now, but if sending me to prison gives them any satisfaction, let them get on with it! The answer to your next question is that we kept it secret so that people don't worry and the risk is minimised."

"Matthew knows?" Amelia asked.

"Of course he does!" Leander snapped. "And Steven."

"No one else?"

"There's you, now."

"Won't they catch up with us eventually?" Amelia asked.

Leander was contemptuous. "You don't seriously suppose that Attlee and his mob will be in power after the next election, do you?" she asked. "I know we don't have a very high opinion of the electorate after 'forty-five, but even they won't put up with this misery any longer than they have to. Now, promise me that you will keep the secret."

Amelia looked at the old woman of eighty-seven, who was defending Latimer's Barn against the British Government with the same vigorous inventiveness that she had always used against scoundrels, and gave in. "Yes, Mother, I promise," she said.

"Good! And don't nag Silas. He was carrying out orders." Her mood changed as she saw what was in Amelia's mind. "As to Christopherson, my dear, I'm aware that he isn't the sort of man we would have entertained in the old days, but he's very good at his job."

In the end, after she had thought about it, Amelia found that she was saddened. Times were undoubtedly difficult and changing, but did they really need the help of such an odious individual as Sir Miles Christopherson?

After Royal Wessex's Derby, the winners came thick and fast as Latimer's Barn regained its pre-war touch. It was common knowledge that Royal Wessex was going for the St Leger and the bookmakers made him the firm ante-post favourite for the Doncaster Classic.

Regardless of the excitement on racecourses, the major talking point in the village that summer was of Bess Collier learning to ride.

Never had a youngster so looked the part. In the breeches made by Julia and with her attitude of calm single-mindedness, Bess was clearly destined to be an instinctively good rider. From the outset, her progress confirmed that belief: within a week it was being said that she would be riding work by the time she was fourteen.

What no one could fail to notice was the interest Leander took in it all.

It began with the choice of a teacher. Not surprisingly, Boggysevick volunteered. He was disappointed when Leander squashed the idea: she did it as gently as possible over a cup of tea in the parlour of Elsie's new house.

"No, Stan, I'm afraid I don't think that's a very good idea. You and Bess are far too much alike to do well together on this job. You'd end up screaming abuse at one another."

Boggysevick, who thought the world of Bess, nodded gloomily. "This is true," he said. "Maybe we kill each other."

"Oh, I can't see it coming to that," Leander laughed. "But I do think it might get out of hand. In any case, she must be taught properly . . . I wouldn't want to see her charging round the paddock standing on the saddle after you'd shown her your circus tricks."

"Who is the right person?" Elsie asked.

"Solstice Jackson," Leander replied. "He hasn't done any riding for ages, so there's a lot for him to rediscover. While he's doing it, he can pass it on to Bess."

It worked beautifully. Glad of the chance to get on a horse again, albeit daunted by the responsibility given to him by Leander herself, Solstice treated Bess like a princess. She responded by abandoning her strong will, doing precisely as she was told, and showing constant concern for Solstice's right leg which played up until muscles and tendons learned to accept the exercise. After two afternoons in the paddock with Bess on a pony controlled by a lunging rein, they went on to the gallop where Leander, driving herself in the dogcart, looked on.

Almost immediately, Solstice suggested that Bess might find the pony too small and childish. "There's old Freemantle that Lady Rachel used to ride," he said. "I reckon he'd be ideal for you."

Bess considered it carefully. Freemantle was a fourteen-year-old gelding who had once belonged to the Mallender and Giffard partnership and won a number of good-class handicaps in the years immediately before the War. Completely devoid of vices, nothing pleased him more than an outing to the gallops and Steven often used him as a lead horse to show the two-year-olds what was expected of them. Tempting though the prospect was, Bess turned it down.

"No, I'm not ready yet, Solstice," she said. "They say he can take a fierce grip when he wants to."

"Fair enough. You let me know when you feel up to it and we'll have a go."

From the corner of his eye, Solstice was aware of Leander's approving smile.

When they returned their horses to their quarters in the

167

original 1840 stable, usually at about half past three, Bess spent up to an hour grooming and feeding the pony, always asking about the correct way to do things and wanting to know more. Afterwards, she went to The House for tea with Leander, frequently staying for two hours. Comfortable in the library, the room that was Leander's special preserve, they talked of horses, with Bess always displaying the one sure sign of talent and dedication. On the rare occasions when she mentioned her friends at school, or matters of general village interest, her views betrayed all the immaturity and prejudices of her age. But when Bess spoke of horses, Leander felt that she was conversing with an adult. It did not seem all that fanciful to see herself as she must have been, eighty years ago. And behind all they said was the tacit assumption that Bess would go to work in the stable on the day after she was legally free to leave school.

There was less than a week of the summer holiday left when Bess told Solstice that she was ready for Freemantle. Waiting on the gallop, Leander felt nervous, a condition worsened by the eternity that Bess and Solstice took to prepare themselves. At last they appeared and Leander experienced a thrill of pride that took her to the brink of tears.

But for the War, Bess would have grown up in London's East End. Once or twice, she might have been lucky enough to ride a donkey on the beach at Southend: there would be a photograph of her, no doubt looking as ungainly and slightly frightened as children always did in such circumstances. Now, she and the old racehorse seemed to have been made for each other. When they broke into a gallop, Leander was reminded of what her father used to say about her when she was Bess's age: "She's very together."

Throughout that August, Charles began to derive pleasure from Eaton Mandeville. Two great difficulties had confronted him on his succession to the title: he was learning to live with one of them and had beaten the other.

For six months after her return from Cannings Ambo, Rachel's temper had been persistently vile. Charles reached the stage of amusing himself by trying to forecast the point at which she would move from waspishness to downright venom. Eventually, in time for the Christmas of 1945, Rachel became grand and condescending, apparently as a result of realising that she was a duchess. She continued to enjoy upsetting people, especially the long-suffering servants, but once it was accepted that there would always be crises to clear up, life became more bearable. There were even times when she was pleasant, although there was never the remotest chance of an invitation to her bedroom.

Against this, Charles was able to draw comfort from his children. Appropriately enough, since the second of his five Christian names was Hubert, Lord Henry, now ten, was showing every sign of being a replica of his grandfather, and, like the seventh Duke, loved his visits to Latimer's Barn. By contrast, Edmund was decidedly short on grey matter, but was loyal, instantly likeable, and immensely strong for his age. He would play a solid game of rugby and be able to thrash a cricket ball out of sight. And there was Helen! She had already put two governesses into decline and offended those servants untouched by Rachel. To her credit, however, she was the only person capable of provoking and winning a blazing row with her mother. That would have been remarkable at any age; in a five-year-old, Charles thought that it displayed immense spirit and talent. He was sure that it must be the genetic influence of his mother, the redoubtable Clementine.

The problem Charles had overcome was money. In addition to the £20,000 that his mother had convinced him was her own personal savings, over £60,000 had come from the sale of pictures that had been in one of the attics for so long that no one knew the first thing about them. Having quite literally stumbled across them during a roof inspection, Charles sent for his war-time chum, Benedict Lambert.

Lambert, a few years older than Charles, had returned to the family business after his stint in military intelligence. Following the death of his father, he was now head of Lambert's, fine-art dealers since 1806. Obligingly, he travelled to Eaton Mandeville two days after Charles's call and examined the

169

fourteen pictures. After two hours, he had sorted them into three groups, leaning against the wall of the lumber-room in which they had been dumped after rescue from the attic.

"I haven't the faintest idea what they are," he said, pointing to three placed well apart from the others. "They're obviously awful." He smiled at the look on Charles's face. "Hold on, old chap, things are going to get better! That bunch over there are almost certainly by George Stubbs."

"I say!" Charles was much more cheerful.

"You really should have suspected that," Lambert said, wagging a reproving finger. "A glance at those horses should have been enough. Now, unless I am very much mistaken — and I never am — the rest are by dear old John Constable."

"Ah . . . now I *was* wondering about that," Charles claimed.

Lambert bestowed a smile of kindly scepticism on him. "You want to sell them?"

"How much do you think they might fetch?"

"Well . . . one doesn't want to raise false hopes . . . however, you might look forward to forty thousand."

"By Jove!" Charles was elated. That was more or less what he wanted to get the estate back into shape. "I'll sell!"

In fact, after Lambert's commission had been paid, Charles was left with £61,250, a sum that made him feel light-headed for a few days. And the contact with Benedict Lambert brought other benefits. When Charles went to the Bond Street offices and sale-rooms, Lambert admitted that the place was in need of a face-lift.

"A lick of paint is easy enough to organise, but I can't find anyone who's interested in letting us have any good-quality furniture and woodwork," Lambert grumbled. "All I get is excuses, or the offer of rubbish."

"I'm sure Flamsteed's could do it for you," Charles said.

"Are they still in business? I thought the War would have done for them."

When Ernest Cartwright called on Benedict Lambert in response to Charles's tip-off, the size of the order he took was big enough to justify re-opening the main workshop at the back of Rose House and set Matthew scouring the country for additional supplies of timber.

Charles was able to put heart back into Eaton Mandeville's existing farms and bring another eight hundred acres into cultivation. By the autumn of 1947, a bumper harvest was making the future look healthier than had ever seemed possible in the months following his father's death. As the evenings began to draw in, Charles's only worry was the prospect of spending the winter cooped up at Eaton Mandeville. Despite its size, he had discovered the house could be claustrophobic.

The answer came out of the blue. On his way back to London after sifting through the contents of a manor house near Bath, Benedict Lambert called in to see Charles on a miserable October afternoon.

"Look here, I've got a proposition for you," he said as soon as the opening formalities were out of the way. "I'm expanding Lambert's. The blunt fact of the matter is that this blasted Government is good for business and I can see it carrying on that way." Charles nodded: he had never supposed that he was the only peer or landowner forced to dispose of family treasures. "We've opened an office in France, I'm looking at Portugal and I'll be into New York the minute I get the chance. How would you like to join the board?"

"Me?" Charles laughed at the idea. "I don't know the first thing about your business."

"You don't need to, old boy. Look, I'll be straight with you. Lambert's has a pretty good reputation, but I want to jack it up a few notches. There's nothing like a duke for doing that. Come to board meetings once a month, get yourself seen in the sale-rooms occasionally and I'll pay you fifteen hundred a year plus expenses."

Charles did not need to think it over. It was the perfect opportunity to escape from Rachel and earn a substantial slice of pocket-money. The arrangement was sealed on the spot.

Three weeks later, Charles went up to London feeling apprehensive at the prospect of his first board meeting, only to find that the respectful yet cordial welcome he received was very much to his taste. Moreover, towards the end of the formal proceedings, it emerged that there was a real job for him to do.

"I'm sorry to say that the Lisbon connection isn't going as smoothly as I'd expected," Benedict reported. He smiled ruefully. "The fact is, we're having trouble with the language. We don't stand a chance with the native lingo, of course. Our man, Vasco da Silva, can manage French, but I'm ashamed to say that we're stuck at the 'esker-vous-away' stage. I think we might have to . . ." He stopped, looking at Charles. "I say, you're virtually bilingual, aren't you, Charles?"

It started as nothing more than translating the flow of letters between Bond Street and da Silva, but Charles hoped that his duties would expand.

As the year of the terrible winter drew to its end, there was hope and signs of change. For Amelia, not all the changes were for the best.

On a dark, miserable mid-December day, she went to London to window-shop and have lunch with her friend from Room 39, Ambrose Vane, now a Rear-Admiral, sailing a desk in Whitehall, and counting the days to retirement.

Later, making her way down the platform at Paddington in search of an empty first-class compartment, Amelia realised that this was destined to be her last journey on the Great Western Railway. In two weeks' time, on 1 January 1948, the organisation that had served Wiltshire so well for over a century was to become part of something called 'British Railways'. She knew that the arguments in favour of nationalisation were powerful; Amelia's emotions nevertheless insisted that it was a bad thing, like *having* to use men such as Sir Miles Christopherson. By the time Silas met her at Savernake, she was muttering about the end of an era and might have wept, given the flimsiest excuse.

Steven spent most of that day at Claude Timberlake's house in Marlborough, discussing racing plans for 1948. Their talks began with Claude giving Steven a most surprising piece of news.

"I was offered a hundred thousand for Royal Wessex the other day."

"Who by?"

"Two chaps from Newmarket that I'd never heard of. They're trying to set up an American system called a syndicate. Apparently a stallion has forty shareholders."

"I've read about this," Steven muttered. "What did you say?"

"I told them to go away, of course. We have our own stud arrangements."

Steven felt immense relief. During the year, Agamemnon, the 1929 Triple Crown winner, had been put down after developing a bad heart condition. Royal Wessex, who had turned the St Leger into a ragged procession spread out over two furlongs, was desperately needed to take his place alongside Isocracy at Cannings St John.

"I believe you've made a very important decision, Claude," Steven said.

"That's what I thought. Presumably he's capable of earning forty thousand a year?"

"Oh, at least," Steven replied. "Nearer fifty, more like."

"So, by sacrificing our established practices, we would have lost out within two or three years – *and* we wouldn't have had Royal Wessex's services for our own mares." Claude was silent for a few moments. "Mind you, Steven, we shall have to keep an eye on this quick-buck mentality . . . it's catching on everywhere."

CHAPTER 7

1951

'Does this mean I'm a snob?'

It was the year of the Festival of Britain and the fall from grace of socialism; it was also the year in which Amelia had to own up to what she really did during the War.

It began with a wedding that was as popular as it was surprising; only two months before it happened, not even the participants considered it possible.

Early in November 1950, Elsie received a letter from her mother that made her ill with worry for several days. Leander finally got the truth out of her after nearly a week: Ray Collier, Elsie's husband, had turned up in the old family stamping grounds round Green Lane and Borneo Street and was making a total nuisance of himself. It seemed that he had spent the War working his way round Canada as a labourer, then joined the merchant navy.

"What does he want?" Leander asked.

"Me!" Elsie replied bitterly. "And Joe, of course. He doesn't know about Bess. My old ma ain't telling him where I am . . . trouble is, that rat-bag Hilda Messenger might."

"Look on the bright side, Elsie, At least we know where he is. We might be able to do something about him," Leander said.

"Please, Mrs Hawksworth," Elsie begged. "Do your best to find a way out!"

The highlight of the previous year had been Leander's

ninetieth birthday, a two-day celebration that had involved a reception in Marlborough Town Hall. Everyone *knew* how old she was, even though she looked nowhere near her age, but they still came asking for miracles.

This time, however, she was spared the effort. While Elsie was still agonising over what to say to her mother, a second letter came with the news that Ray Collier was dead.

"Good heavens above!" Leander cried. "That's incredible. What happened?"

Unsure of whether to be sad or happy, Elsie resorted to a brutal-sounding factuality. "Came out of the Duke of Wellington blind drunk, started carrying on and fell under a bus. Lunch-time, if you please! I wouldn't be surprised if somebody didn't give him a push."

"Well . . ." Leander collected her thoughts. "This changes things, doesn't it?"

"For the better!" Elsie said bluntly. "Not 'arf!"

"You'll go to the funeral?"

"Have to, won't I? I'd better make sure the sod gets treated proper."

"What about Bess and Joe?"

"Oh, no, Mrs Hawksworth. There's no need for that!"

"I think they should go," Leander said with quiet insistence. "They've never been to that part of the world and it might do them good."

Elsie protested, but she knew that she had to agree, if only for the sake of appearances: in any case, she was proud of her kids and decided to show them off. They were away for three days, returning late in the evening. Next morning, Leander made a point of going into the kitchen after breakfast to hear Elsie's account of events. On the whole, it seemed to have passed off satisfactorily. Ray Collier's mother had become thoroughly odious on a skinful of brown ale and there had been some caustic comments about Joe's school uniform, but such minor incidents were only to be expected, it seemed. Obviously anxious to put the whole business behind her, Elsie said as little as possible and shut up. Rather than press her, Leander decided to

175

wait for Bess's opinion when she came for tea at four o'clock.

Bess shuddered when the question was put to her.

"It was awful, Mrs Hawksworth. I shall never go there again. *Never!*"

"What was wrong?"

"Everything! The place was ugly and filthy and the people were so . . ." she took a while to pluck up the courage ". . . common. It's terrible to think that I was born there." She stopped. Something was worrying her. "Does this mean I'm a snob?"

"Most people would say so, my dear," Leander sighed. "But you're bound to be. You're surrounded by them in this place . . . look at me!"

Bess grinned. "That's all right, then! But I shan't go back . . . in fact I don't want to leave the village ever again. Joseph feels the same. He didn't say so, but I can always tell what he's thinking." Bess was the only person who never abbreviated her brother's name. "There is one good thing, I suppose," Bess added more cheerfully. "Mother will be able to marry Boggysevick now."

Leander pretended surprise. "Gracious me, is that a possibility?"

"Oh, yes." Bess leaned forward to ensure the confidentiality of her revelation. "But don't mention this to anyone, Mrs Hawksworth. It's a tremendous secret."

Gravely, Leander promised.

The wedding took place on 6 January 1951. The groom, who might once have been a Roman Catholic, was perfectly content with an Anglican ceremony administered by Malcolm Frobisher. Solstice was best man and Elsie arrived on Matthew's arm to be turned into Mrs Smith.

For most of 1950, in the time not taken up by looking after Redgauntlet, Sir Miles Christopherson's Two Thousand Guineas and Eclipse Stakes winner, Boggysevick had been embroiled in changing his name by deed poll. Amidst constant hilarity, he was fighting to be known as Stanley Smith. Victory came in time for the wedding. So it was that Elsie became Mrs

176

Smith, Joe and Bess stayed as Collier and everyone, except the building society manager who was guarding Mr Smith's nest-egg, carried on calling him Boggysevick.

Gideon Timberlake was the first member of the family to go to university. His choice was Cambridge and he read modern history. Everything went well until that January when, instead of turning his thoughts to final examinations, he had a brief fling with one of the college servants. After two weeks, the affair petered out, but the girl showed that she was keenly aware of the Timberlake wealth by threatening to create a scandal unless £1,000 was forthcoming. Gideon kept his head and contacted Claude, who immediately recognised a job for Silas. As he set off for Cambridge, he expected to be away for a week. At the same time, Clementine Prideaux, with all the enthusiasm of someone on the way to have teeth dragged out by a blacksmith, went for a visit to Eaton Mandeville.

Amelia was thus alone at Louise House when the letter arrived.

The contents of the stiff, embossed envelope were stunning. For two hours, she felt panic and indecision. Then she realised that she must discuss it with her mother and went to The House.

"What's wrong, darling?" Leander asked, alarmed by Amelia's demeanour. "It's not Silas, is it?"

Shaking her head, Amelia passed the letter across. Leander stiffened with excitement. "What have you been up to?" she asked. "Why is the Lord Chamberlain writing to you?" When she began to absorb the letter's contents, her eyes widened.

"Well?" Amelia asked.

"Well, what?" Leander retorted.

"Do I accept it?"

"Accept it!" Leander seemed about to explode. "They offer to make you a Dame Commander of the British Empire and you come asking if you should accept it? You silly girl!" She smiled, opened her arms wide and Amelia knelt down to nestle in them. "I say," Leander chortled. "*Dame* Amelia Hawksworth . . . what a hoot!" Still holding the letter, she peered at it over Amelia's shoulder. "It says that this is in recognition of your work during the War," she said, sounding rather bemused.

"Er . . . yes . . . it would have to be, wouldn't it? I've never done anything else that was at all important."

"Don't be silly, darling, you've always been important. Mind you, I'm surprised that messing about in the Ministry of Food warrants *quite* such a high honour." There was no getting away from the fact that Leander thought the honours system might be slightly awry. Amelia drew away from their embrace and prepared to set her mind at rest.

"Well, actually, Mother, I wasn't really with the Ministry of Food."

"I see." Leander sounded as though she was preparing to deal with an errant child. "Where were you?"

"The Admiralty."

"Doing what?"

"It was to do with codes and things."

"And things?"

"Yes, Mother."

"That sounds more like it! And it was all so vital and secret that you couldn't even tell anyone where you worked?"

"I'm afraid so. As a matter of fact, I saw quite a lot of the Prime Minister."

"Aha! So this is his doing. Good old Winston!"

"Probably not . . . I don't think he has much influence these days. I hear he spends all his time writing books."

Leander was derisive. "He's going to be Prime Minister again before very much longer and everyone but you knows it. Of course he has influence!" She smiled radiantly. "This is marvellous, darling . . . I'm so proud of you. I can't wait to tell everyone."

"No, Mother!" Amelia said firmly. "This has *got* to be kept quiet until the official announcement in the Birthday Honours List. No one must know. It's very bad form to go round blabbing."

178

Although disappointed, Leander was forced to admit the point. "Aren't you even going to tell Silas?" she asked.

"I expect he ought to know," Amelia admitted. "But he can be trusted to keep quiet – as you well know, Mother!" Leander smiled weakly at the reference to all the things she entrusted to him. "In any case, Silas had a fair idea of what I was doing during the War. I had to use certain channels when we started to suspect Peter."

"Ah . . . I see." It seemed that Leander now understood something that had always mystified her. "Very well, my dear, I'll keep my mouth shut."

With great relief, Amelia saw that the reference to her awful grandson had caused Leander no pain.

No one was sure whose bright idea the Festival of Britain was. Ann alleged that Attlee, dismayed by the way the country was turning against him, had organised a year-long jamboree in order to cheer people up for what would have to be the second General Election in two years. In February 1950, Labour's majority of one hundred and eighty-six had been cut to a mere eight; the people were not yet ready to trust the Conservatives, but they were sick to the back teeth with the joyless hardship that socialist policies seemed to be prolonging.

A great deal of what was done in the name of the Festival was of a dismayingly poor quality; however, a new spirit of confidence did seem to be running through the country. At Latimer's Barn, every box in the yard was occupied by a good horse and Steven found himself turning would-be owners away. At Wm Flamsteed & Sons, a growing order-book caused Matthew to reinstate the apprenticeship scheme as a means of ensuring a secure supply of craftsmen into the foreseeable future. Edward Mallender said that he and Leslie Giffard were looking for big expansion in their chain of grocery shops.

He gave the information during the small-talk that punctuated lunch after a Trustees' meeting. His appointment, a year previously, had been carried with one abstention: Amelia thought it odd that an outsider, with no financial interest

179

in Cannings Ambo, should join them, despite the long-established precedent of the Timberlakes. It was Steven's idea, a display of gratitude for the way Edward had helped get Latimer's Barn back on its feet by means of a plentiful supply of horses to train. Amelia had a quiet word with Steven ahead of the vote.

"Are you sure you want to do this? Strictly speaking, the rules say that a Trustee must live and work in Cannings Ambo."

"I think we ought to turn a blind eye to that. These days, we need the skill and experience of chaps like Edward. We're running a big business in a changing world."

Here we go again! Amelia thought.

For a reason that she freely admitted was unworthy, Leander was all in favour of Edward Mallender's nomination. "He kept us awfully well-supplied with food during the War," she chuckled.

Amelia shut up and kept out of it. Presumably, it was only a matter of time before Leslie Giffard joined them.

Lambert's made a great social occasion of their mid-April board meeting. On the evening before, the directors and their wives had dinner at the Dorchester Hotel, at which suites were reserved for them. Then, while business was being dealt with, the wives spent a morning shopping. The party regrouped for lunch aboard a Thames cruiser as it made its way to Hampton Court where arrangements had been made to take over a riverside hotel for two days.

Rather to Charles's surprise, Rachel jumped at the chance to accompany him. At the Dorchester, she was pleasantly relaxed, basking in the respectful admiration of the other wives. By the time they met up on board the cruiser, Her Grace, the Duchess of Laverstoke was a popular heroine, having cut a swathe through several department stores, putting uppity sales assistants well and truly in their place.

Over cocktails before they went into dinner at Hampton Court, Rachel made herself the centre of an admiring group of men. Her patronage, mixed with the drinks, encouraged them to vie with each other in making stupid statements. Unhappy at this, Benedict Lambert took a firm grip to restore order.

"We're all very thrilled at the prospect of having some of our sales at Eaton Mandeville," he told Rachel. "Our American cousins will love it. I always knew that Charles would be an asset, and that's a brilliant idea he's come up with."

The conversation stopped in response to an obvious call to order. After favouring her husband with a brief look of disbelief, Rachel smiled superciliously. "I suppose there has to be a first time for everything," she said.

Charles dived in valiantly to pass it off as a joke, pointing out that after centuries of inbreeding, the aristocracy were pushed to have intelligent thoughts. Nearly everyone laughed, but the atmosphere was strained and Rachel made sure it was beyond redemption. Over dinner, she told a series of less than kind stories about Charles's family, pausing only to create what nearly became a nasty scene when a nervous waitress forgot to offer her the full range of vegetables.

The ebb and flow of the fraught evening was observed impassively by Lambert's only woman director. Laura Waterman, one of the world's leading authorities on the French Impressionists, was without an escort. As a consequence of her striking beauty, she remained virtually isolated: with their wives watching like hawks, none of the men dared exchange more than cursory snatches of dialogue with her.

Later, when the party had broken up and people were drifting off to bed, or going outside for a breath of air, Laura, concealed in an alcove with a last cup of coffee, accidentally overheard a revealing exchange.

"God, Charles, that was sticky," Lambert said as the two men met outside the cloakroom.

"I'm sorry about that, Ben."

"My dear fellow, think nothing of it. Not your fault . . . I have heard stories."

"They are to be believed," Charles replied stoically. "Not to worry, I expect Rachel will clear off home tomorrow."

"Ah . . . probably for the best. Look, one or two of the

chaps are thinking of going over to Hairy Metcalfe's place tomorrow . . . you might find it amusing."

"No, thanks, Ben. I'll go down to Eton to see my boys. The beaks should let them out for a few hours if I put on a dog."

"Follow the example of your good lady and you can't go wrong!" Lambert said grimly.

Giles Hawksworth was nine and knew that he would take over the stable one day. The matter had never been formally discussed, but there was no need to. He had been given a pony for his sixth birthday and was soon charging round the paddock with a style all his own, always leaning backwards with his feet pushed forwards. Ann called it the 'gung-ho method' of riding and an amused Steven saw what she meant. Especially with the furious scowl of concentration that accompanied his efforts, Giles was suggestive of a crusty old cavalry colonel at the head of a punitive expedition against a bunch of intransigent frontiersmen.

Three years later, he knew how comical he looked and was learning to live with it. Only on Saturday mornings, when Steven tended to concentrate on the two-year-olds, was there any difficulty with this. As often as not, the juveniles were led by Bess on old Freemantle and Giles was treated to a brilliant display of what was possible from someone only three years older than himself – and a *girl* at that!

"I wish I could ride like Bess," Giles said on a perfect morning in May. There was no envy in his voice; if anything, he sounded wistful.

"She's exceptional," Steven replied. "She's so good that she got out of being packed off to boarding-school."

"Is she as good as Great-grandmother used to be?" Giles asked.

"I've no idea!" Steven laughed. "I'm not *quite* old enough to have seen her when she was riding work every day." It suddenly occurred to him that Leander probably thought Bess *was* that good. "You don't have to worry about it, Giles. No one will expect you to be a brilliant horseman.

As long as you can get round the gallop on a hack, you'll do. Your job will be to know everything so that you can tell people what to do."

"How long will it take me to learn?"

"If I ever get there, I'll let you know!"

The year was teaching Steven new aspects of patience and disappointment.

Alain de Mourville's colt, Apollinaire, was by Royal Wessex out of Leander's great mare, Hyperborean. The temptation to have the highest hopes of him were so great that Steven decided to assume he was a complete duffer with no chance of winning anything. As predicted by his lad, Boggysevick, Apollinaire turned in the most brilliant two-year-old career that anyone could remember. After winning his debut at Salisbury, he triumphed in the Coventry Stakes at Royal Ascot, the Gimcrack at York, the Royal Lodge Stakes at Ascot in September, and, as a rousing finale, the Dewhurst Stakes at Newmarket. As 1950 ended, Apollinaire was favourite for the Two Thousand Guineas and Derby.

The spring and early summer of 1951 would have driven a lesser man than Steven to distraction. Striding eagerly down to the start of the Craven Stakes, his warm-up race for the Guineas, Apollinaire pulled a muscle in his loins. Withdrawn from the race, the colt was out of action for over a fortnight, unable to canter, let alone gallop, until two days after he should have run in the Two Thousand Guineas.

His progress back to full fitness was rapid and Steven had no qualms about sending him to Lingfield for the Derby Trial. The day was significant for several reasons. Apollinaire was taken to Lingfield on the morning of the race in a brand-new horse-van, purpose-built to Steven's specifications on a lorry chassis. After the race, the return journey to Wiltshire was to be made at once: Steven had never liked having a horse in racecourse stables overnight and intended abolishing the practice whenever possible.

Solstice was the proud driver of the new vehicle, while Boggysevick travelled in the back to comfort his pride and joy throughout the journey. Beside Solstice in the cab, Bess was making her first visit to a race meeting.

Apollinaire gave her a memorable baptism. He took the lead a hundred yards from the start and never had another horse anywhere near him. His winning margin was restricted to five lengths by the seemingly casual way Michael Pilgrim let him stroll the last two furlongs.

Steven allowed himself a rare show of optimism. "I never imagined he'd get a mile and a half that easily," he said to Ann, who made a point of accompanying him to races whenever she could. "It looks as though we've got a good 'un."

"It's a shame Alain didn't see that," she replied.

"He's a very busy man. But he'll be at Epsom and *that* should be worth a celebration!" He actually went so far as to rub his hands with excitement.

Three days later, Apollinaire took fright at something on the gallops: neither Boggysevick, nor the other riders in the group had any idea what it was. There were horses that had the second sight and previous incidents suggested that Apollinaire was one of them. This time, he veered sharply into his galloping companion, receiving a glancing kick on the knee of his off foreleg. An hour later, the swelling was like a balloon. The vet was confident that no permanent damage had been done, but Steven did not need telling that it would be at least two weeks before the colt was fit for work.

Steven made two of the most difficult telephone calls of his life that afternoon. First, he contacted Wetherby's and took Apollinaire out of the Derby; then he spoke to Alain.

Publication of the Birthday Honours List produced the uproar of celebration that Cannings Ambo had felt disinclined to unleash at the end of the War.

Amelia's worst moment came at breakfast in Louise House when the Dowager Duchess glowered at her over *The Times* and said, "I am perfectly well aware that one has to observe the utmost discretion in these matters, my dear, but I do think you might have given *me* a little warning."

"Oh, Clem, I *am* sorry," Amelia said, squirming. "I meant to tell you yesterday."

"But you forgot?"

"No, I couldn't pluck up the courage!"

Clementine laughed. "I understand. My warmest congratulations, Amelia. Your mother will be pleased."

"She is . . . I *had* to tell her."

"This is recognition of your work in the War, I take it?"

"Yes. I'm afraid I didn't tell people the truth about that."

"I know," the Dowager Duchess said smugly.

"How?" Forgetting that it no longer mattered, Amelia was alarmed.

"Well, I don't know *exactly* what you were doing, but Charles told me that you'd turned up at a meeting that only the most top-secret big-wigs were allowed into. It didn't sound like the Ministry of Food to me."

Amelia was clearing the breakfast things away when Leander arrived with the first of the well-wishers from the village. By half past ten, she decided to go down to Church Green herself in order to save the older folk the walk up to the Back Stretch. Later, at Rose House, Matthew took her down to the workshops where the eighteen craftsmen queued up to shake Amelia's hand. After that, it was on to The George; the lunch-time drinkers very nearly came to blows over the privilege of buying Dame Amelia Hawksworth a tiny glass of sherry. It was at The George that Steven finally caught up with the celebration after finishing the morning's work in the stable. He arrived whistling 'There is nothing like a dame' from the tremendously popular Rodgers and Hammerstein musical *South Pacific* which he and Ann had seen three times in London. The catchy tune soon developed into a chorus, with Leander insisting that everyone did their bit to kick up a joyous rumpus.

It was well past two o'clock when Amelia, rather overcome by it all, extricated herself and set off back to Latimer's Barn, with Leander and Steven. In the drive, they found a harassed-looking Silas.

"Buckingham Palace have been on the phone," he said.

"You're to ring back, darling. It's something to do with your investiture. There's the number." Trance-like, Amelia took the piece of paper from him.

"This sounds interesting," Leander said. "Come on, let's go into The House and do it from the library."

Amelia was shaking as she waited for the operator to put the call through. She announced her name and received a warm greeting from a man with an urbanely well-modulated voice.

"Thank you for calling, Dame Amelia," he said. "His Majesty wonders if we could make slightly special arrangements for you to receive your honour."

Amelia sat and listened. She said, "Yes," and, "Of course," several times, doing her best to avoid looking at Leander and Steven who were bulging with impatience. At last, when everything had been fully explained to her, Amelia said, "That sounds very nice, Sir Victor. I accept. Would you thank His Majesty for such a kind thought. I would like my mother to come with me."

Leander, ears pricked, heard the throaty chuckle at the other end of the line before the concluding remarks. Amelia replaced the receiver and sat back with a beatific expression on her face.

"For heaven's sake," Leander exploded. "What did he say?"

"In view of my 'family connections'. . ." Amelia smiled at the phrase ". . . the King has suggested that it would be rather nice if he gave me my damehood at Windsor Castle during Ascot week. On Thursday to be precise."

"That's Ladies' Day," Leander said.

"Furthermore," Amelia went on, "my guest and I are then invited to lunch with the King and Queen. That means you, Mother!"

"Oh, I say!" Leander glowed.

"After which, we shall drive down the racecourse with them in their carriage."

Steven thought that Leander was going to weep: for a few moments it was touch and go. It was panic that saved her. For the first time in her long life, she went to pieces.

"Do you realise that this is *next* Thursday? What are we going to wear? Steven, don't just sit there grinning like an imbecile, go and fetch Julia. Tell her it's a matter of life or death. Go on, get on with it!"

As Steven shot through the kitchen, Amelia was in pursuit shouting, "And tell her to bring the pattern-book. We must have that!"

The cheering began as the first of the five carriages drew level with Tattersall's. It struck Leander that it was louder than she remembered, but then she had never been here before, riding up the centre of the course.

Smuggled into the Silver Ring by Solstice, Bess watched and marvelled, aware that she was watching a piece of Cannings Ambo history in the making. In recognition of the incalculable contribution she had made to racing over the years, Leander was with the King and Queen, rather than in one of the following carriages, the normal place for distinguished commoners.

Bess smiled at her secret knowledge of what Leander was wearing. The simple cream dress had been part of Ann's Royal Ascot wardrobe until Julia made the suggestion that it was ideal for Leander. Hardly any alteration had been necessary. The broad-brimmed straw hat was incredibly old: one story suggested that it belonged to the famous Derby of 1905, won by The Atheling for Mrs Fandine-Browne. It was certainly totally unfashionable, yet, given the panache of the magnificent old woman underneath it, it looked wonderful. Beside her, Dame Amelia was in pink, her dress and hat created by Norman Hartnell during an incredible forty-eight hours. Mother and daughter were obviously enjoying themselves.

Queen Elizabeth leaned forward to speak to Leander.

"A good deal of this noise is for you, Mrs Hawksworth," she said. "Give them a wave to thank them."

Leander did so and the crescendo of cheering proved Her Majesty's point. Bess, who sometimes shuddered at the thought of how her life might have turned out but for the luck of the draw, felt tremendous pride. She watched the carriage procession until it had turned out of sight into the Royal Enclosure, then hurried to the stables to watch the preparation of the first of their three runners for the day.

Her disappointment at the failure of Edward Mallender's filly to make any sort of showing was cut short by Solstice's arrival with sensational news.

"Come on, Bess, you're going up in the world," he said, taking her hand to guide her through the crowd.

"What's happening, Solstice?" she asked.

"Mrs Hawksworth has found out you're here and wants you in the family box."

At the entrance to the Royal Enclosure, Bess was taken over by a uniformed attendant who looked frighteningly grand, but proved to be very friendly.

"This way, young lady. There's no need to worry, you're expected."

Once inside the grandstand, Bess was escorted into a rickety old lift that took ages to clank itself to the top. A woman, who was clearly in charge of everything, was waiting. She and Bess had to pick their way along a corridor crowded with food trolleys. In response to the efficient woman's knock at the last but one of the doors, Silas appeared, smiling broadly when he saw Bess.

"Oh, good, you managed it," he said. "Come on in."

The room, with French windows leading on to a balcony, was full of people, twenty-five of them, most of whom Bess knew, at least by sight. The only strangers were three friends of the Dowager Duchess of Laverstoke: the Earl and Countess of Milton, who lived near Malmesbury on an estate nearly as grand as Eaton Mandeville, were accompanied by their beautiful daughter, Lady Amaryllis Drax-Templeton.

Ann hurried to greet Bess. "It's so nice to have you here. Make yourself at home. There's plenty of trifle and ice-cream left if you'd like some."

"No, thank you, Mrs Hawksworth," Bess said, glancing round guardedly.

Ann understood her unease. "Leander and Dame Amelia

are in the Royal Box . . . I expect they'll come back to us after the Gold Cup. Go and talk to Giles."

He was always glad to see Bess: unlike the other youngsters of Cannings Ambo, who regarded him with wary respect, she treated him as an equal. They fell into easy conversation, exchanging their own views on the great events of the day. Neither was so absorbed, however, as to miss Rachel's comment as she came in from the balcony.

"What the *hell* is that child doing here?"

Bess felt the disdainful stare.

"Leander wanted her," Emma said quietly, moving swiftly to forestall a scene. "Shall we go down to the terrace and show ourselves off?"

"Uncle Charles isn't here," Giles told Bess after Rachel had gone. "Nobody blames him. Aunt Rachel can be so rotten, you see." He indicated a man on the balcony. "That chap has been with Aunt Rachel all week. Mother and Grandma Emma aren't very pleased."

Bess sneaked a look out of the window, discovering another stranger. The man had his back to them and was affecting an air of breezy indifference.

As the time for the Gold Cup drew near, Bess and Giles found themselves alone. Claude Timberlake's mare, Rejoicing, was a strongly fancied contender and everyone went down to the paddock to watch her parade. With no adults to worry about, Bess and Giles enjoyed a superb view of the two-and-a-half-mile race, the first two-thirds of which were run fairly slowly. There was a slight quickening up the hill towards the home turn, but it was only in the final straight that battle was well and truly joined.

"Ours is beaten," Giles said as two French-trained horses surged into what appeared to be a commanding lead.

"Don't you believe it!" Bess retorted. Michael Pilgrim had brought Rejoicing very wide round the bend and had a clear run down the centre of the course. The six-year-old mare had immense courage and would run as straight as an arrow under pressure. In a finish that had the crowd on its toes, she got up to win it by a neck.

When Bess finally calmed down, she saw that Giles looked miserable. "What's wrong?" she asked.

"I wish I knew how Father did it," Giles said. "It must be awfully difficult. I bet I'll make a hash of it."

"Don't be daft!" Bess said. "By the time it's your turn, you'll be brilliant. Look!" She was craning over the balcony to get a good view. Joining her, Giles saw that there was uproar round the winner's enclosure: while Steven and Claude Timberlake stood back with broad grins on their faces, Leander was walking the gallant Rejoicing round and posing for an army of photographers. The crowd loved it.

Later, after a deluge of merrymaking, Bess got to hear Leander's impressions of the day. Told that it was out of the question for her to go back to Latimer's Barn with the horses, she sat between Leander and Dame Amelia in the back of Steven's magnificent new Series S Bentley. Ann was in the front passenger seat, while Giles travelled with Emma in Claude Timberlake's Rolls.

The very first thing that Leander wanted to tell them was of the wonderful chat she had enjoyed with dear old Queen Mary over lunch at Windsor Castle.

"We met in nineteen-eighteen when your mother and I went to Buckingham Palace for your father's Victoria Cross, Steven," Leander said, tapping him on the shoulder with her parasol to ensure that he was not wasting too much concentration on driving. "She's a jolly old soul, nothing like as forbidding as she looks."

"What about the King?" Amelia asked.

"Ah, yes!" Leander shook her head. "That poor man is not well! He needs to take things easier."

"By the way," Ann said, "did anyone else see Claude's boy, Gideon, getting bowled over by Amaryllis Drax-Templeton?"

"It was mutual," Amelia said. "They were in one of the tea-tents, acting as though they were the only people on earth."

"They'll make a marvellous couple," Ann said. "What's all this business with Rachel and Hetherington?"

Bess was aware of the sudden change of atmosphere in

the car. For a few moments, Steven's hands gripped the steering wheel very tightly; Amelia shifted uneasily. It was left to Leander to guide the conversation into safer waters.

"It's been such a wonderful day – and we had an extra treat thanks to Steven and that lovely mare. Fancy me ending up in the winner's enclosure again! I made the most of it, I don't mind telling you. It won't happen again."

"Mother!" Amelia was shocked.

Leander gave her daughter a look of mock-pity over Bess's head. "Being a Dame hasn't given you any more sense, has it? I'm *ninety-one*, darling . . . you can't expect me to go capering round racecourses all the time."

Steven was determined that his grandmother would be proved wrong: Leander Hawksworth was going to pay at least one more visit to the races.

On the last Saturday in July, Ascot was staging a new event. Initially called the King George VI and Queen Elizabeth Festival of Britain Stakes, it was over a mile and a half for three-year-olds and upwards. At £25,000, the prize-money was £6,000 more than the Derby and was, as far as Steven could ascertain, the highest ever offered in England. Apollinaire was entered.

The knee injury that had kept him out of the Derby was cleared up by the middle of June and a careful programme was worked out to bring the colt up to peak fitness in time for the race. All those involved crossed their fingers, held their breath and hoped that the jinx would not strike again. Bess, thrilled to find herself unexpectedly involved, said prayers.

At first, Apollinaire showed a strong disinclination to take part in any serious exercise. He was an extremely intelligent individual, and Steven felt that he might have become fed up with doing all the right things, only to be denied a chance to show what he could do. After a week of trying everything, Steven was prepared to consider any proposal, no matter how outlandish. So, when Boggysevick suggested that they put Bess up on him, Steven shrugged and said, "Why not? It can't do any harm."

Clearly smitten by the novelty, the colt thought he would give it a try and found it to his taste. After two weeks, he was going for Boggysevick and Michael Pilgrim, as well as Bess, but always delivered his best when he knew that she was nearby. Keeping him company on Freemantle, Bess joined in his twice-weekly work sessions on Wednesdays and Saturdays, granted leave of absence for two hours from school for the mid-week gallop.

Nothing went wrong. Two days before the race, Alain and Nadia arrived from France and helped with what proved to be the most difficult part of the operation, persuading Leander to get into a car and allow herself to be driven to Ascot.

France and Ireland had sent runners for the nineteen-strong field, a clear indication that the race would gain the prestige its originators hoped for. Among the horses who shared the paddock with Apollinaire were the winners of both English and French Derbys.

For the first time, Apollinaire failed to jump off boldly to dominate from the start. To Steven's dismay, he took an age to settle, then seemed content to amble along in the rear: at least, that was the story of the first six furlongs. At the half-way stage, he lengthened his stride, passing the other eighteen before their jockeys realised that they were now participating in a six-furlong sprint. Turning for home, no one doubted that Alain de Mourville's royal-blue silks with a gold Cross of Lorraine on Michael Pilgrim's chest and back were on their way to their first big-race triumph in England.

It was a popular win. Alain's war record had made him well-liked in England and most of the crowd had picked up the whisper that Leander was present. Positioning herself in the winner's enclosure to wait for Alain and Nadia to lead their champion in, she glowered up at Michael Pilgrim when they arrived. "What was wrong with him at first?" she asked.

"I don't know, ma'am. He didn't seem to be in the mood."

"What did you do to make him go?"

"I told him Bess would be waiting with a treat."

Queen Elizabeth came to talk to them. Ominously, the

King was unable to be present that day. Whatever reasons were given, Leander knew that he was too tired and ill. However, she pointed out to Alain that the race was bound to live on.

"And we won the first one!" Nadia said happily.

"We always do," Leander replied airily. "The only reason we didn't win the first Derby was that my family were still selling wine at the time."

"Don't think she's joking," Steven told Alain, who laughed. "She isn't!"

Ignoring the remark, Leander gave Steven a piece of advice. "With the scheme you're cooking up, you'll need a passport for Bess!"

He gaped at her. "Are you clairvoyant?" he asked.

"Don't be silly!" she replied, leaving the question unanswered.

Four days after the race, Charles Prideaux travelled up to London for a Lambert's sale that he had organised. A fellow-peer was disposing of his London house in order to have money to spend on the family seat in Norfolk and Charles wanted to do his best to ensure that some rather nice pictures fetched a good price. After that, he intended taking up a long-standing invitation to visit an old friend in Sussex. It was a decision reached on the spur of the moment after Rachel had shown signs of entering an outstandingly difficult phase.

Benedict Lambert himself conducted the sale, wasting no time in raising over £110,000 as against the £80,000 that Charles had hoped for. At the end of the proceedings, Lambert accepted Lord Aldridge's thanks in his customary self-deprecatory way, passed him over to an assistant and took Charles to his office.

"Look here, this is bloody difficult, so I won't beat about the bush," Lambert said. "The fact is, Charles, there's a hell of a lot of talk going round about you and your wife. We don't mind . . . it doesn't hurt Lambert's, but I thought I'd better let you know. You're the sort of dull bugger that might not have heard."

193

Charles smiled at his friend's all too accurate assessment. "It's all right, Ben, I think I know. Is it Hetherington?"

Lambert nodded. "He was in tow when she went to Badminton for the christening last weekend."

"She was parading him round Ascot, too," Charles said.

"Who the devil is he?"

"My estate manager."

Lambert was astounded and annoyed. "Of all the cheek! How long has this been going on?"

"Not all that long," Charles replied. "He's been with me for eighteen months, but they've only been sleeping together since May." He might have been talking about a matter of passing academic interest.

"Well, for God's sake, Charles, get rid of him!"

"Oh, no, I couldn't do that. He's doing a jolly good job, actually. The estate's in better shape than it has been since I was a kid. In any case, if I booted him out, I could see Rachel going off the rails and causing a terrible scandal." The expression on Lambert's face suggested that there might already be one. "I don't want divorce, or anything squalid, you see, Ben. Mother wouldn't like that. I think Hetherington works wonders for Rachel. He's only thirty-four."

"How old are you?" Lambert asked weakly.

"Forty-six," Charles said solemnly. "Getting rather long in the tooth for all that sort of thing."

Lambert was at something of a loss for words. "I simply wanted to make sure that you knew the score, Charles," he said.

"Don't worry, old man, I do."

As Charles was leaving the building, he encountered Laura Waterman, also on her way out.

"Hello, Charles, what are you up to?" she asked.

"I came up for the Aldridge sale."

"I hear that went very well." She eyed his suitcase. "Where are you going?"

"I thought I'd drop in on some friends in Sussex."

"Whereabouts?"

"Petworth."

"I'm driving to a place four miles away. Is that any good to you? You could telephone and ask them to come and fetch you."

Despite her beauty, a quality he often found intimidating in women, Charles always felt at ease with Laura and accepted her offer gratefully.

"Are you going to friends?" he asked as she drove them across Vauxhall Bridge.

"No, I'm having a peaceful weekend at my place in the country," Laura replied. "I bought it last year and I've decided it's time I started using it instead of stewing in a London flat."

After a quick journey whose only discomfort was the heat of the afternoon, they reached Laura's house at four o'clock. A mile from a village called Broomer's Green, it was a delightful pantiled building in an acre of garden and shrubbery. While Charles removed his case from the boot of the car, Laura unlocked the front door and dashed round opening windows to dispel the stuffiness.

"Help yourself to the telephone," she said, waving at the instrument on the hall table. "I'll melt if I don't change into something more comfortable." She was already half-way up the stairs.

Returning ten minutes later, she found Charles looking decidedly embarrassed.

"What's wrong?" she asked.

He shook his head. "I feel a bit of a fool. I hadn't actually let these people know I was coming . . . the fact is, they've gone to the South of France for a month. Their butler gave me a lecture on 'the advisability of proper arrangements'! He's quite right, of course. Oh dear!" He seemed to pull himself together. "Er . . . where's the nearest railway station?"

As he stared helplessly at Laura, he realised with the suddenness of shock that, in a plain cotton blouse and skirt, with no shoes or stockings, and her normally immaculate auburn hair in disarray, she looked more attractive than ever.

When she spoke, it was evident that she was weighing her words very carefully. "If you were looking forward to a few days in Sussex with good company, Charles, there's no reason for you to be disappointed. Stay here."

"You mean . . . er . . . with you?"

His ingenuousness was such that she almost laughed. "Yes, Charles, with me." She walked to within a foot of him. "I'm a very successful woman of forty-four . . ." His look of surprise was flattering, but she refused to be diverted. "Everyone thinks that I'm completely self-sufficient and slightly dangerous. The truth is that I'm a lonely war-widow and that you're quite the nicest and most handsome man I know." She paused. "Is there any need to talk about your dreadful wife?"

Charles stuck his shoulders back in a gesture of defiance. "No, there isn't," he said. "You're abso-bloody-lutely right!" To Laura's dismay, he turned on his heel and marched out through the still-open front door.

"Hey! Where are you going?" she called.

"To fetch my suitcase. I left it out here for a quick get-away."

When he came back, he took her in his arms and kissed her with a passion he thought had gone forever.

"This feels as though it's going to be good," Laura said, stretching out to kick the door shut.

"I say, aren't we going to wait until after dinner?" Charles said as she began to shuffle towards the stairs, dragging him with her.

"Are you insane?" she cried. "That's *hours* away!"

Feigning resistance, Charles allowed himself to be led to Laura Waterman's bedroom.

Steven was the leading trainer for the 1951 season, a position firmly established before the great expedition that set off at the end of September. As Leander had suspected, Latimer's Barn was to make its first attempt on a big foreign event, the Prix de l'Arc de Triomphe at Longchamp.

They went five days before the race, leaving Latimer's Barn at five o'clock in the morning, Steven and Ann in the Bentley, Solstice, Boggysevick and Bess in the horse-van with Apollinaire. Elsie turned out to wave them off, bursting with pride that her husband and daughter should be involved in the greatest step forward that the stable had attempted since Leander and her father took Bellerophon to Epsom in 1876. Joe and Robert Frobisher were there, too. They had started their last year at school, were thinking of university and were not without self-importance: but they were both overawed by Bess. With her passport and all the papers for Apollinaire in a leather brief-case that she had bought for the trip, she had the air of a seasoned professional going out to do a routine job. When Elsie turned back towards The House, she saw Leander at her bedroom window. Even as they waved cheerfully at each other, Leander was sad: nowadays, there was nothing for her to do except sit and wait.

The little convoy went to Newhaven for the ten o'clock car ferry to Dieppe. Throughout the four-hour voyage the sea was light, and Apollinaire, fascinated by Bess's endless stream of advice, information and tactics for Longchamp, was unaware that he was crossing to a foreign land.

Alain and Nadia were waiting for them at Dieppe and once the formalities had been completed they set off to lead the way in their Alfa Romeo, acting as a constant reminder to Solstice that they were driving on the 'wrong' side of the road. They stopped for a late lunch as soon as they were clear of Dieppe and into the open country of Seine-Maritime. Nadia had brought two hampers packed with food; while she and Ann prepared the picnic, Bess took Apollinaire out of the van to walk him round. He seemed unimpressed by the grass at the roadside, but, to Alain's amusement, showed a great liking for French bread.

"You see, my friend, he knows he is a French horse," Alain said to Steven.

"I hope that means he's going to be at home here," Steven said, smiling ruefully at Bess. She knew that Monsieur de Mourville needed a good stallion in France and that the decision had already been taken to retire him to stud somewhere in Normandy when he finished racing. She was putting a brave face on it.

They drove on, passing Beauvais, Senlis and Melun, a

route that took them to the east of Paris. Finally, they entered the great Forest of Fontainebleau at Barbizon on its north-western edge.

"My word, this puts Savernake in the shade," Ann said.

Chuckling at her unconscious joke, Steven agreed with her. Even more impressive things lay in store for them: after four miles they approached a sign telling them that they were entering the village of Mourville.

"Goodness, we'd better not tell Leander about this," Ann said. "Can't you imagine her wanting to call Cannings Ambo 'Hawksworth'?"

"I think even she might understand that you have to be around for seven or eight hundred years before you do that," Steven replied. "Look at this!"

One end of what might have been thought of as the village square in England was dominated by an enormous pair of gates: and it soon became obvious that they were not a grandiosely empty gesture. At ten thousand acres, the de Mourville estate was five times the size of Cannings Ambo, and, following the death of his father in 1949, belonged to Alain. The first view of the seventeenth-century château was unforgettable. Although almost half of the great building was clad in scaffolding as work progressed to repair pre-war neglect, as well as the ravages of the Nazi occupation, its high-pitched roofs and conical turrets, with an octagonal staircase slightly off-centre of the main structure, made it a delight.

Like so many of his countrymen, Boggysevick spoke French: he also rolled his eyes and waved his hands. He had been wonderful at Dieppe before Alain and Nadia could get to them, now he was able to converse with the château's most senior *domestique*. To ensure that Bess, the stepfather she always called 'Dad', and Solstice were looked after superbly well, Nadia had sent her housekeeper to supervise their accommodation and food.

Marie-Claire, gradually recovering from the loss of Henri, reduced Boggysevick to near-speechless admiration with her beauty and serenity. Monsieur and Madame de Mourville were, she explained, the finest people in the world. "When we came here after the Liberation, the place was in a terrible state," she said. "Madame and I cried for days over it. Do you know what they did first? They rebuilt the servants' quarters! What do you think of that?"

Seeing the result in the rooms that he, Bess, and Solstice had been given, Boggysevick replied that the de Mourvilles were very good indeed, not unlike the people he was lucky enough to have found after the War.

"*Mais oui!*" Marie-Claire said. "I have heard all about Mr and Mrs Hawksworth and their famous old grandmother!"

Early the following morning, well over two hundred people turned out to watch Apollinaire exercise over part of the park that bore a strong resemblance to Cannings Down. All the servants and most of the villagers, complete with children, were there to inspect the horse responsible for such great hopes. As usual, Jacques Guillaume, Marie-Claire's son, was nowhere to be seen. It was being said that Monsieur de Mourville was going to pay for him to be sent to a special school in Paris next year, when he was ten. The establishment had a reputation for straightening difficult children out: whether they could do anything with this spiteful malcontent remained to be seen.

Given an audience, Boggysevick rode Apollinaire for all he was worth, but it was Bess who stole the show. Mounted on a huge chestnut from Alain's stables, she displayed skills that drew applause from the onlookers.

"She really is going to be awfully good," Ann said to Steven.

"She already is!" he replied.

Alain and Nadia's six-year-old daughter, Lisette, was beside herself at the sight of Bess and demanded to start riding lessons immediately. Later, she came to watch Bess grooming the horse she had borrowed: ignoring the differences of age and social position, and with Boggysevick acting as translator, the two girls struck up a friendship that was to be longer-lasting than either of them could foresee.

*　　*　　*

Apollinaire and his entourage left Mourville for the journey to Paris and the Bois de Boulogne at eight o'clock on the morning of the race. Leander had already been fretting for an hour.

"I hate not knowing what's going on," she told Emma, who did her best to be sympathetic. In truth, Emma had more than enough to be getting on with. She was looking after her three grandchildren, Giles, Oliver and Rebecca, while Ann and Steven were away. Rebecca might be only three and normally well-behaved, but she had kicked up a terrible fuss over not being allowed to go to France.

As the morning wore on, Leander speculated endlessly about what would be happening at Longchamp, what Steven might be thinking and doing, whether Apollinaire was sound, how Bess was getting on with the food. Elsie joined in, thinking that the *chic* Parisiennes were bound to turn Boggysevick's head. Not until the race was due to be run, at half past three, did a tense silence fall. Twenty minutes later, while Emma was wondering what on earth was supposed to happen next, Matthew arrived in a lather of excitement.

"He's won it!" he gasped. "Apollinaire has won the Arc!"

"How do you know?" Leander asked, rocketing out of her chair.

"Jim Goakes tuned into Radio France on that posh ten-valve set he bought last month. He heard the commentary."

"I didn't know he spoke French," Leander said, anxious to squash false hopes.

"He can't," Matthew replied. "But you don't need to be a genius to know who won it."

"Let's wait," Leander said firmly.

Steven was under siege by several hundred journalists. Once the questions degenerated into irrelevant impertinence, Alain helped him to escape, leading him to an office belonging to a friend who was a course official.

"They will be waiting anxiously at Latimer's Barn," Alain said, picking up the telephone. "I will talk to the operator for you."

200

The call, which went through very quickly, was answered by Emma. Curbing her excitement, she did as Steven asked and fetched Leander. Everyone gathered round as she stood with the receiver to her ear. She said very little, but her look was enough. "Thank you, darling," she said at the end. "Have a safe journey back."

They could all see the tears glittering in her eyes and did not press her for information. "Apollinaire won it," she announced in her own good time. "Steven said he made all the running, like he did at Lingfield."

When the first surge of excitement had died down, Leander turned to Elsie. "That husband and daughter of yours are in fine fettle," she said. "They did very, very well. Isn't it wonderful?"

She let Elsie help her back to the chair. She was drained, but triumphant. It was indeed the biggest step forward since 1876, the start of a new era. Latimer's Barn was now an international force to be reckoned with.

At a little after four o'clock on a blustery November afternoon, Leander and Bess were having their regular chat in the library. They had been studying what the Big Book had to say about the years around the turn of the century, but had strayed into politics. Bess was listening attentively to Leander's summing-up of the position following the previous month's General Election.

"So, you see, my dear, although Winston and his friends are back in power, I'm not all that happy. I think the country is developing some very bad habits." She paused reflectively. "I've always been very interested in what was going on, but I can't help feeling that the time has come to wash our hands of it. After all . . ."

The door opened abruptly and Rachel came in. Leander smiled at her. "Hello, my dear. What brings you here?"

"I'm on my way back from Reading and the car's on the blink. I thought I'd drop in and get it looked at by one of your chaps." She stared at Bess with unconcealed hostility. Unperturbed, the girl looked back boldly, with a hint of

201

friendliness. "You can go," Rachel said. "I wish to talk to Mrs Hawksworth."

"Yes, Your Grace." Bess stood up, bent to kiss Leander's cheek and was gone. Immediately, Rachel exploded.

"*Really*, Grandmother, I wish you wouldn't fraternise with that wretched girl!"

Leander hated that word 'grandmother'; Rachel had been using it for three or four years. "I think that 'fraternise' is a very strange way of expressing yourself," she said. "You make it sound as if I'm associating with an undesirable."

"She's the cook's daughter, for heaven's sake," Rachel retorted angrily and pointed accusingly at the Big Book. "Have you been telling her family secrets?"

"I have been explaining our history to her," Leander said patiently. "With any luck, she will stay here all her life, so I think it's important that she understands certain things."

"I'm aware that you think she's some sort of good-luck charm, especially after that performance in France, but you must be going wrong in the head to make such a pet of her."

In the dreadful silence that ensued, Rachel toyed with the idea of apologising. Leander, her voice simmering with anger, decided the matter for her. "To the extent that I have stood by and allowed you to get away with *the* most disgraceful things, I probably am going ga-ga."

"What do you mean?" Rachel asked, by no means as assured as she pretended.

"Rachel, you really should give the most serious thought to putting your own house in order before you have the unmitigated gall to criticise me – or anyone else, for that matter. Since you have taken it upon yourself to be thoroughly unpleasant, let me tell you something. If you intend persisting in your liaison with that ghastly man Hetherington, I'd rather you kept away from Cannings Ambo. We all disapprove very strongly of what you are doing and I do *not* want to give anyone the idea that matters are otherwise."

Those in the kitchen, including Emma, watched in dismay as Rachel stormed out of The House in a black rage.

Emma realised that something awful had happened and part of her died. A mixture of embarrassment and lack of will prevented her from asking Leander for an explanation, nor was one ever offered. From that day, people found it easier to ignore Rachel; some went so far as to pretend that she no longer existed.

CHAPTER 8

1955

'I'm leaving a very precious legacy'

Gideon Timberlake and Lady Amaryllis Drax-Templeton did not announce their engagement until November 1954, well over three years after their first meeting at Royal Ascot. It was Gideon who exercised the caution: having been given a demanding job by his father, he wanted to make his mark in the rapidly expanding Timberlake business empire before asking Amaryllis to be his wife. The wedding, arranged for May 1955, triggered off a chain of events that kept the builders busy in Cannings Ambo for most of the year.

It began at the January Trustees' meeting. Steven mentioned that Gideon and Amaryllis had expressed a desire to live in the village. "I was wondering if they'd like The Hall," he said.

All eyes turned to Leander. Eight years after the deaths of Sam and Ann Briggs, The Hall was still empty, in accordance with her decree. To everyone's relief, she smiled and nodded. "That sounds like a good idea," she said. "I have to admit that it is a liability in its present state . . . if it isn't lived in, we ought to knock it down and I wouldn't want to see that." She paused to remember the associations with the Beresford brothers, great supporters of her father, and Alexandra Fandine-Browne who had given him such love and comfort. "*Would* Gideon and Lady Amaryllis like to live there?"

204

"I can't see them refusing," Steven said, and looked to Gideon's father for an opinion.

"My guess is that they'd jump at it," Claude said.

A week later, Steven told Leander that Gideon and his bride-to-be were bowled over by the idea. "They're coming to see you on Saturday to talk about a price," he added.

"I want to *give* it to them as a wedding present," Leander said. "I presume I can do that?"

"I'd be very surprised if anyone voted against it."

"I'd be *disgusted*!" Leander said sharply. "I also want to pay for it to be done up."

Steven was far from certain about this. "That's going to cost a few thousand. The Trustees may well feel that Gideon should attend to that himself."

"You weren't paying attention," Leander scolded. "I said I will pay . . . with my own money. It's time I gave the Timberlakes something to show my appreciation of all they've done for us."

As Steven suspected, but did not say, Gideon and Amaryllis objected to the idea.

"It's immensely kind of you, Mrs Hawksworth, but we couldn't possibly accept a gift of that magnitude," was Gideon's immediate reaction.

"Why not?" Leander asked pugnaciously.

"Well . . ." Gideon looked to his fiancée for support.

"We couldn't," was the best she could do. Thereafter, although they struggled valiantly, they were bound to lose.

"In any case, it's beautifully convenient for the builders," Leander said when she knew they were weakening. "They're coming here in March to do some big jobs and Sidney Irons wants to start early. If you two put your heads together to decide what you would like doing, it will all fit in nicely."

"Father tells me that you're having another yard built," Gideon said.

"Yes, isn't it exciting!" The walking stick that had become necessary two years ago was at her side, but the enthusiasm scintillated with girlish zest. "We've been badly pushed for space since Apollinaire won the Arc the *first* time . . . when

205

he did it again in 'fifty-two . . . well! As I expect you know, Gideon, we've been turning owners away."

"Someone was telling us that this will make Latimer's Barn the biggest stable in England," Amaryllis said.

"I shouldn't be at all surprised," Leander replied. "And when the new yard is finished, we shall be doing an enormous amount in the village . . . nearly everybody is going to have a new bathroom and we're putting some more houses on Church Marks . . . oh, yes, we're improving the stud, too. So it's perfectly logical to get The Hall set to rights first."

It was, of course, nothing of the sort: however, Gideon and Amaryllis were so bamboozled that they were unable to argue. "I hope I shall be able to put a few horses in the new yard, Mrs Hawksworth," Gideon said.

Leander smiled graciously. "If I speak to Steven, I'm sure he'll put your name at the top of the list. Now, you must have a good look round The Hall and decide on the changes you'd like. Sidney Irons is coming to see me next Tuesday and he's bound to want to get cracking straightaway . . . you know what he's like."

"Yes, Mrs Hawksworth," Gideon said, even though he had never heard of Sid Irons before today.

The wedding took place at Malmesbury on 21 May. Leander and the Dowager Duchess headed a strong Cannings Ambo contingent. Driven by Solstice in the pre-war Rolls Royce, they proudly paraded themselves as survivors of a bygone era and had a whale of a time.

The bride was magnificent in a dazzling dress by Pierre Cardin, a new designer in Paris whom Nadia de Mourville claimed to have discovered. Gideon, totally in awe of the occasion, contrived to look strong as well as handsome.

There were the inevitable incidents. Amaryllis's great-uncle Fulke, not seen in public for years, was taken suddenly drunk at the wedding breakfast and began ranting on about family skeletons. Mortification was transformed into high farce when a bevy of dowagers, ably led by Clementine Prideaux, set about him with handbags that appeared to be laden with bricks.

The old reprobate disappeared into the nether regions of the ancestral home and comparative calmness reigned until the newly-weds had departed for their honeymoon aboard a cruise liner.

The following day, a Sunday, Malcolm Frobisher's Morning Service at Cannings Ambo was extended for a christening. In 1952, Michael Pilgrim had married Molly, a pretty girl from Devizes. Their son, Jonathan, was born the following year; now it was time to baptise Ursula, their daughter. Leander, who had not missed a christening for over seventy-five years, was present, but asked to be excused standing as godmother.

"You want someone who's going to be around for rather longer than me," she told Michael and Molly. They had to see her point; Ursula Pilgrim became Ann's first godchild.

That evening, Leander complained of feeling slightly unwell; she had a sore throat and was light-headed. Ann and Emma packed her off to bed at seven o'clock with a hot lemon drink. After a restless night, she awoke with a streaming head cold.

"This is ridiculous!" she complained to Amelia. "It's summer for God's sake!"

"That doesn't stop you getting a chill. Kathleen was saying that there are some nasty things going round."

"Pah!" Leander was disgusted. "Go away and leave me alone. I don't want idiots goggling at me when I'm in this state."

Amelia did as she was told, but returned an hour later with Kathleen, who silenced Leander's protests by sticking a thermometer in her mouth. While she was waiting she was busy with her stethoscope and checked Leander's pulse.

"You'll do," was her eventual opinion. "Your temperature's a bit hectic, but that should be easier by this evening."

"I've only caught a cold!" Leander fumed, very displeased at being stared at while she had a red nose and running eyes.

"I know that, Leander," Kathleen smiled. "We do, however, have to be careful. You're quite an old lady, you know."

"At last! Somebody's noticed." Leander looked pleased.

"Plenty of fluids," Kathleen said to Amelia. "Keep her warm and let her eat what and when she likes. I'll send some medicine round to help it clear up."

Four days later, Leander was up and about. From her bedroom window, she watched Edward Mallender's big bay colt, Quartermaster, do his last piece of serious work before the Derby.

"What do you think?" she asked Steven at lunch.

"I really don't know about this chap," he said. "My fear is that he's too brilliant over a mile to get this trip." Leander nodded understandingly. Quartermaster had taken the Two Thousand Guineas by a street, but there were many at Latimer's Barn who agreed with the press pundits that a mile and a half would be beyond him.

As in 1876, and on nine occasions since, the Derby was run on Leander's birthday, her ninety-fifth. She watched it on the television set that had been installed in the small sitting-room for nearly a year. With her were Amelia, Emma, Clementine Prideaux, Elsie and Bess, also having a birthday, her sixteenth.

At Tattenham Corner, it seemed that the theorists were to be proved right: Quartermaster was going badly, with most of the other twenty-two runners in front of him.

"Oh, well, not this year!" Emma sighed.

Leander leaned forward eagerly. "This race hasn't started yet," she said. "Our boy hasn't blown up, he's been held back. There you are, look, he's quickening now."

"He'll never get round that bunch," Amelia said.

"He doesn't have to," Leander cried. "There's a gap on the rails . . . you could drive a bus through it."

"I don't think Michael's seen it," Emma said, starting to twist her handkerchief into a tourniquet.

"Yes, he has!" Leander shouted. "Come on, Michael, it's easy!"

It was anything but: for twenty nerve-racking seconds, during which everyone stared at the screen in wide-eyed silence, it was touch and go. Not until the rising ground of the last fifty yards did Quartermaster get his nose in front.

"That will do!" Leander said, clapping her hands.

When the shrieking and laughing subsided, they caught their first glimpse of Steven as he helped Edward Mallender lead his colt in. "I say, doesn't he look a toff!" Clementine chuckled.

"Ann looks jolly nice," Emma added.

Amelia was bemused. "Isn't it weird seeing people on television when you know them very well?"

"You'd better get used to it," Leander told her. "Your nephew is going to be a regular performer on that thing." She gesticulated at the set, then scowled truculently at Amelia. "I don't know whether you've got any daft ideas about wrapping me in cotton-wool for the rest of the day, but you can forget them! I'm going to see Quartermaster come home and Elsie is going to cook a marvellous birthday and Derby dinner."

"That's dead right!" Elsie said fervently.

"We are going to have champagne," Leander went on. "And I shall stay up very late. So there!"

Laughing, Amelia did not attempt to contradict her.

As Bess prepared to leave, Leander beckoned to her. "Isn't it wonderful, my dear?" she said. "We've won the Derby on your sixteenth birthday!"

Bess knelt down at her feet and their hands clasped tightly. "That's what happened to you," Bess said.

"Yes, with Bellerophon . . . and there have been ten others." There was a fierce intensity in Leander's eyes as she spoke in a voice that none of the others could hear. "I shan't see any more, but you will, Bess. You will!"

Next morning, Leander watched the last slates being put on the roof of the new yard. An exact replica of the other two, even down to the materials used, the forty-box quadrangle was sited on the Roadway between the 1933 yard and the Back Stretch, its archway entrance facing the rear of the original stable of 1840.

Leander, supporting herself on Steven's arm, looked round

209

proudly. "This place is something like, now, isn't it?" she said. "Tell me, when do you think you'll have to expand again?"

"Steady on," Steven laughed. "Give me a few years to get used to this. Seriously, I can't see us ever wanting more."

"You're quite wrong," Leander assured him. "One of these days . . ." She was cut short by a violent fit of coughing. Doubled up and with Steven rubbing her back, it was fully two minutes before she was able to bring it under control. Weak and breathless, she was incapable of speech.

"All right," Steven said to an anxious-looking group of builders and lads who had gathered round them. "I can manage." He picked Leander up tenderly and began to carry her towards The House. The temptation to cut across the lawn was very great, but she saw what was in his mind and shook her head. "Your great-grandfather would never forgive you," she whispered. Smiling in an attempt to cheer them both up, Steven plodded round the path.

Elsie, who had seen them from the kitchen window, came rushing out to meet them, followed closely by Emma and Ann.

"What is it?" Emma asked, quiet but panic-stricken.

"Nothing at all," Steven said. "She had a coughing fit and it knocked her about."

"I'm much better now, thank you," Leander said when they were inside and Steven had set her in one of the chairs at the big table. "Wasn't that silly of me. Elsie, if I could have . . ."

The coughing began again, much worse. Leander's distress was terrible to watch. Ann hurried after Steven as he went to the library. "Are you telephoning Kathleen?" she asked.

"Yes. Make sure she doesn't choke while I'm doing it!"

They had got her into bed by the time Kathleen arrived. The coughing had stopped and Leander was reasonably composed, but she looked very ill. Kathleen's examination lasted for well over ten minutes during which Leander made no attempt to argue or bluster. "You've got bronchitis," Kathleen said. "It's developed amazingly quickly and it's bad."

"You aren't going to suggest that I go to hospital, are you, Kathleen?" Leander asked.

"I wouldn't dream of it." Kathleen smoothed her hands over Leander's shoulders and arms in a gesture of loving reassurance, intent on dispelling something she had never expected to see: briefly, Leander had shown fear. "I can get you all the medicines you need and you'll receive the best care in the world here."

Leander was cheerful again. "I expect it would help if I were to get up and move about from time to time?"

"That would be very good," Kathleen replied, knowing that Leander understood the dangers ahead. She had seen it often enough in others.

As Kathleen left, Amelia arrived from Louise House, flustered and worried sick. "Oh, Mother, what have you been up to?" she asked, almost in tears.

"Settle yourself down, or you'll be ill," Leander told her. "There's something I must do. I want writing paper, an envelope and my fountain pen, please, my dear. Will you fetch them from my desk in the library?"

Amelia returned, carrying a large atlas to use as a working-surface, to find Leander businesslike. "I want to be on my own, darling," she said. "Don't let anyone in here. Come back in an hour."

It was difficult, but Amelia obeyed the instructions, fending off a barrage of questions. At the end of the hour, she went back to be greeted with a broad smile. "Come and sit here," Leander said, patting the bed.

"Don't interrupt, just listen," she said. "Some very great things have been achieved in this village because everyone has always worked together in harmony. We've been lucky . . . mind you, we've had to be very strong. It would be nice to believe that we could carry on like that." She closed her eyes and sighed. "But I mistrust the times, Amelia . . .

211

there's change and it may not be for the best. I want you to look after this." She took a sealed envelope from under her pillow. "Keep that in a safe place. If the stable is ever in bad trouble, you are to show that letter to the Trustees. It's up to you to decide if and when the situation is serious enough and you must *not* open it before then. Do you understand?"

"Yes, Mother."

"And when *you* go, if you haven't used it, pass it on to Ann. She'll do the right thing. Will you promise to do that for me, my darling?"

"Yes, Mother, I promise."

Amelia took the envelope, unsure of whether she was humouring a fanciful old woman, or taking part in something of the utmost importance.

"There's something else," Leander went on. "My personal savings are still with the Western Counties. I signed the papers for you to have them a few years ago. This is what you must do . . ."

Four days later, on 6 June, Kathleen's morning examination confirmed that, despite everyone's best efforts, especially Leander's own, she had pneumonia.

"It's her poor old lungs, you see," Kathleen explained. "They're too tired to cope."

"What ought we to do?" Steven asked.

"Love her," Kathleen replied. "I'd recommend that some-one stays with her at night."

Steven went upstairs to talk to Leander. He was smiling when he came back. "She intends carrying on as normal to the end," he said. "What a surprise! Yes, she wants company through the night. She says it's a job for young women and she'd like Ann, Julia and Bess."

"I'll go and see Julia," Ann said. "You tell Bess."

After finishing school the previous year, Bess was a stable-lad. It was widely believed that she was the first girl in England to do the job. Her initial appearance on a race-course, to lead one of her two charges round the paddock at

Newbury in early May, had caused something of a sensation. To Steven's amazement, several of his fellow-trainers had marched up to him to protest. They accused him of letting the side down and endangering the established order by employing a girl in his stable. Thanking them for their contribution to what was strictly his own business, Steven had taken quiet delight in watching Bess's horse, a two-year-old filly called Wessex Princess, win her début race in fine style.

Bess was with the filly, preparing her for work with the second lot. She looked up as she heard Steven's footsteps on the cobbles of the 1874 yard, moving to the door of the box when she saw that he wanted her.

"Mrs Hawksworth is quite poorly, Bess," Steven said. "Doctor Kathleen says it's pneumonia."

"I'm very sorry, sir." Bess's privileged position with Leander never interfered with her strict observance of the rules. Some people said that Steven was too free and easy away from the stable; inside it, everyone treated him as a demi-god.

"It's best if someone sits with her every night," Steven said. "She's asked for my wife, young Mrs Flamsteed from the Bungalow, and you. How do you feel about that?"

"It's a great honour," Bess replied.

Steven was touched that she saw it that way. "I'd like you to do every third night from, say, ten o'clock until six. I expect your mother, my mother and Dame Amelia will be looking after her during the day. I'll arrange for you to be excused from evening stables so that you can sleep in the afternoons and evenings."

"No, please don't do that, sir!" Bess was suddenly worried. "I wouldn't want her groomed and fed by anyone else." She ran a hand down the filly's neck.

Steven smiled. "Won't you even trust your father?" No one ever thought of Boggysevick as her stepfather.

"Well . . . yes . . . I suppose he'd be all right."

"I'll talk to Mr Merriweather," Steven promised.

"When do you want me to start, sir?" Bess asked.

"My wife will work out a roster and let you know." In the instant of hesitation before he hurried away, Bess saw how dreadfully upset he was.

Bess went to The House for her third night of duty on an evening of torrential rain and cold wind, dreadful weather that had lasted for three days. Leaving her dripping riding-cape in the porch, she made her way through the deserted kitchen, into the entrance hall and along the corridor to the small sitting-room. Only Ann and Amelia were there tonight, both looking tired and drawn.

"Hello, Bess. Have you had something to eat?" Ann asked.

"Yes, thank you, ma'am. How is Mrs Hawksworth?"

Ann and Amelia exchanged sad looks and shook their heads. "I'm afraid it's pretty bad," Ann said. "She hasn't really been conscious all day. Doctor Kathleen is with her now. We'll take you up when she comes down."

They sat and waited, Bess on the edge of her chair, Ann and Amelia listlessly resigned. However, when they heard the light steps on the stairs, they moved swiftly to intercept Kathleen; very little was said before Ann returned. She nodded to Bess and they went upstairs.

Steven was on the point of leaving his grandmother, who, to Bess's relief, seemed to be sleeping peacefully.

"At least her breathing is more normal," he whispered. "It's been terrible all day." The distress in his eyes caused Ann to reach out to him.

There was no need for instructions or advice. The routine, in progress for eight days, was firmly established. Ann and Steven slipped away to their room, Bess settled into the armchair that put her within reach of Leander, in the ambit of the twenty-watt night-lamp on the bedside table. It was nearly half past ten.

Bess never took her eyes off Leander's face. The concentration of her unblinking gaze was phenomenal, yet she was perfectly relaxed, experiencing no discomfort as minutes imperceptibly turned into hours.

The fierce power of Bess's vigil gave her warning of Leander's awakening: for some time before her eyes opened, there was a delicate, rosy flush on her face and, even before she recognised Bess, she was smiling.

"I was having a lovely dream," she said. Although her voice was weak, it had a timbre that went back to her youth. She gazed at the ceiling, savouring the images that had flickered through her mind, but showing no inclination to talk about them. Glancing unobtrusively at her wrist-watch, Bess saw that it was nearly a quarter past three.

"Is it still raining?" Leander asked.

"I don't think so," Bess replied. "And that awful wind has gone away at last."

"Everyone has been coming in with long faces about the weather," Leander said. "They were forgetting that we *needed* that rain. The ground at Ascot would have been very bad after the dry spring."

They fell into a companionable silence, both preoccupied with identical thoughts. At last, Leander put some of them into words. "I'm one of the luckiest women who ever lived."

"I've always thought that you must have had an absolutely wonderful life," Bess said, continuing the blithe tone.

"Oh, I have, Bess, I have!" The old eyes closed to assist the recall of memories. "Do you know, the day before Bellerophon won the Derby, I walked the course with my father . . . we'd never been there before. They'd been racing and the place was still full of nobs and swells. I was wearing boots, breeches and a terrible old canvas jacket . . . what a sight I must have looked! When we got to the grandstand, we heard someone say, 'Look at that girl. She must be Leander Flamsteed, the one they're all talking about.'"

"And they never stopped," Bess murmured.

"I sometimes wished they had!" Leander said, briefly irascible. "Never mind . . . I was very lucky. And I think I've made a reasonable job of it . . . I'm leaving a very precious legacy."

Bess forgot herself and looked surprised. She had known the rules governing the estate since she was a little girl: personal wealth and property did not exist. Seeing what she was thinking, Leander shook her head.

"No, I don't mean money . . . it's something *much* more valuable. You see, Bess, I'm afraid most people lead such dreadfully *dull* lives. For me, it's been one big adventure . . . very exciting! I think it's easy for everyone here to carry on like that, so that's my legacy. You're all heirs to adventure."

"What a lovely idea!" There were a million other things that Bess wanted to say, but the words refused to assemble themselves. Instead, she was content with silence. It lasted for fifteen minutes until Leander stirred, apparently searching for something.

"Could you hand me my Bible?" she said to Bess. "It's on the lower shelf, I think."

Bess reached down to the bottom of the bedside table for the leather-bound volume. To her surprise, Leander took a letter from it. Unfolding it, Leander mused over it for several minutes before returning it to its place of concealment. Closing the Bible, she let it rest on the counterpane.

"I'm ready to keep the very last part of the bargain," Leander said quietly. Bess made no response to the mysterious statement; she merely clasped the hand that was offered to her.

The eastern sky was showing the first pale glow of dawn when Bess felt her go. Leander Hawksworth died as she had lived, with dignity, grace and cheerful thankfulness. It was eight minutes past four on the morning of 15 June 1955, two weeks into her ninety-sixth year.

Bess sat motionless for a long time, still holding the lifeless hand. She felt strong and at peace, as though some great force had passed into her during the last moment of Leander's long life. Finally, she stood up and went to the window to draw the curtains back. The weather had changed completely: now, the sky was the clearest blue except where the first rays of the sun made it colourless. Turning, Bess noticed the Bible and took it from the bed. Placing the book on the deep window-sill, she opened it and took out the letter. She held it in her hand for an age before deciding to read it. Written in the same bold hand as much of the Big Book, the letter was dated 15 June 1881.

Dear Steven,
What on earth are you doing? Have you taken fright? There is no need to. See Ruth 1, verses 16 & 17.
> *Your very good friend,*
> *Leander Flamsteed.*

Bess gasped. This was the famous letter that Leander had written to Steven Hawksworth after he had failed to turn up at her twenty-first birthday party because he thought he wasn't good enough. The date astounded her: seventy-four years ago to the very day.

There was no need to hunt for the reference; the letter was positioned in the Bible so as to mark the first chapter of Ruth. Bess soon found the words.

. . . for whither thou goest, I will go; and where thou lodgest, I will lodge: thy people shall be my people, and thy God my God: where thou diest, will I die, and there will I be buried . . .

With the understanding of Leander's statement about keeping the last part of the bargain, Bess's tears came. Returning to the bed, she knelt down to pray over Leander, weeping in heart-broken grief.

Gradually, the misery faded. When Bess raised her head, she was greeted by a sight that took her breath away. Death was already bringing the appearance of fine porcelain to Leander's face as all the signs of age faded. The morning sun caught her white hair, causing it to gleam like burnished gold and, for a few moments, Bess had a clear vision of what had fired the first Steven Hawksworth's admiration and love when he bicycled along the Devizes Lane all those years ago.

217

For nearly an hour, Bess had Leander all to herself, and she cherished every second. Then, at a quarter to six, she heard Steven getting up. She closed the curtains to shut out the sun, plunging the room back into the gloom that people thought was appropriate for death, and waited for Ann to come.

Ann was gentle. She was also very firm.

"This is where you really have to show what you're made of, darling," she said to Steven. "Leander hasn't played much of a part in running Latimer's Barn since before the War, but you know what people might think?"

They had spent a few minutes of quiet prayer at Leander's side and were now back in their own bedroom.

"The legend is dead and things will never be the same again," Steven replied. "It's easy enough to understand."

"Oh, I agree. You have to make sure it doesn't happen. Show people how well she taught you and we shall win through."

Steven smiled sadly. "By God, I'll miss her, though. This place is going to seem empty without her."

"*That* is precisely the attitude we have to avoid," Ann said. "It's ruinous and you know what Leander would have thought of it."

"What do we do?" Steven asked, needing guidance.

"We go down to breakfast, you get the first lot out as normal and I'll start making arrangements for the funeral. Monday afternoon seems best."

Steven thought about it. "Get it out of the way before Ascot, you think?" He thought again and smiled wistfully. "I know . . . it's what she would have wanted."

"Absolutely! Come on, shoulders back and chin up! Let's get on with it."

Leander had not been snatched from them in a sudden tragedy and her life had been rich as well as long. Nevertheless, a great hush fell over the village as the news spread. The chatter of children in the playground stopped when Amelia made the announcement; at the stable, the lads gathered in the 1874 yard, the cradle of Leander's greatest triumphs, to observe a full five minutes' silence before the first lot went out, and the horses, the beautiful creatures who had been Leander's greatest love after her family, curbed their restiveness, waiting with sad-eyed patience. The workshops of Wm Flamsteed & Sons fell silent. In the shop behind The George and by the War Memorial, folk shook their heads and looked desolate. No one attempted to describe what they had lost.

At about ten o'clock, Solstice slipped into the churchyard with the Reverend Frobisher and Ann. They made their way to the Hawksworth and Flamsteed family plot in the south-eastern corner and began a careful examination of Steven Hawksworth's grave, untouched since 1908. Solstice had taken over the duties of sexton after the death of Cyril Osgood in 1952. Now, he had to prepare for what everyone knew was the most important burial of the century. As they examined the headstone and supporting masonry, a lone craftsman began using a saw behind Rose House. Wm Flamsteed & Sons were making the coffin.

Elsie found herself very busy at lunch-time. Matthew and Louise came, as did John and Julia, and Amelia, Silas and Clementine Prideaux from the Back Stretch. Lady Amaryllis arrived from The Hall with the Timberlake family condolences, saying that Claude and Gideon were cancelling business appointments in order to return from London as quickly as possible.

Ann told them of an aspect of Leander's death that no one had foreseen.

"I thought I should put an announcement in *The Times*," she said. "About half an hour after I'd telephoned, they rang back to say that it was actually *news* and that they're doing a few paragraphs on page four or five. They're also doing an obituary so I gave them a few details." Steven nodded his approval. "The story must have gone the rounds," Ann went on. "Several other papers have been on. The *Telegraph* is going to print a picture of Leander with Mrs Fandine-Browne and The Atheling."

219

Everyone was pleased, yet it was of no great significance. Whatever interest the world might take in Leander now that she was dead, she had belonged to Cannings Ambo. Every single one of the village's two hundred and seventeen inhabitants was indebted to her, often to the extent of home and livelihood. During the afternoon, they began to bring flowers up to The House, piling them in the front porch as they had done for her son, Giles, in 1917. The earlier tribute had taken place in winter when flowers were in short supply: now, with every garden and greenhouse in mid-summer profusion, the results were unbelievably beautiful and moving. By six o'clock, the blossoms covered the semi-circular steps up to the front door and several square yards of the drive. When Steven went to look on his way back from evening stables, he could see a dozen people coming up the drive with more wreaths. Later, two of Edward Mallender's delivery vans brought the first flowers from Marlborough.

Latimer's Barn now had five telephone lines and they handled a never-ending stream of calls the following morning. There were requests from all over the country for permission to attend the funeral. Between them, Ann, Emma, Amelia and Julia answered over two hundred calls before lunch. When the flood showed no sign of abating, Elsie scrapped the idea of a sit-down meal and began making sandwiches.

In the midst of a renewed burst of activity at two o'clock, Rachel arrived, making her first visit to Latimer's Barn since Leander had effectively banished her in 1951. She found Steven was at the front of The House with the Duke and Duchess of Dorchester. Ardent supporters of racing, with horses at Saxon Court, the stable that had once belonged to Emma's father, the young Duke and Duchess had driven over from their home at Hungerford to offer their sympathies.

Rachel's sudden appearance gave rise to an unexpectedly nasty moment. Arabella de Vere Lawson-Grey, although only twenty-four and a duchess for barely six months, knew Rachel by sight and reputation, and displayed only minimal civility to her before deciding that it was time to go. Unconcerned,

Rachel, who had seen Steven two or three times a year at Eaton Mandeville during her long absence from Cannings Ambo, scowled at the flowers.

"I presume you're going to move that lot and open the front door," she said.

Steven was baffled. "Why on earth should I?" he asked.

"To bring Grandmother out. Presumably she's worth that honour." There was a slight emphasis on the last word that was not entirely pleasant.

"Leander made the rule about the front door," Steven said. "She wouldn't regard herself as an exception."

"It's a very silly rule!" Rachel snapped.

"It came about because of Father," Steven reminded her.

"I know that!" Rachel resented the lesson she imagined her brother was attempting to teach her. "You've obviously no idea how inconvenient and humiliating it is."

"Humiliating?" Steven looked at her in disbelief.

"The only way into this place is through the kitchen with the servants staring at one."

"I see." Steven was justly famous for not losing his temper: for a moment or two, the strain of maintaining his reputation showed. "Have you come here to chuck your weight around, Rachel?" he asked.

The question sent Rachel towards the detested back door in a huff.

Later, the visitors were more agreeable. Gideon Timberlake, full of unnecessary apologies for being late, brought more flowers, as did Ernest Cartwright, who had returned from sales calls in Scotland. Steven had a soft spot for Ernest and took him outside for a stroll along the Roadway.

"Much as I admire the ladies, there are times when you need to escape from a house full of them," Steven joked.

Ernest nodded sagaciously. "I'm very sorry about your grandmother, Steven," he said. "I know she'd had a damned good innings, but it's still a blow, isn't it? Dad would have been very upset." Fred had died three years ago. "Mother's taking it badly."

It was inevitable that Tish would. Born a year after her

father had been given the job of head lad at Latimer's Barn, she had always worshipped Leander. Shortly before the new generation of Timberlakes had moved to The Hall, someone had said that things were really looking up now that the village had a dame and someone entitled to call herself 'Lady'.

"That's no improvement," Tish had snorted. "We've had a queen for as long as I can remember."

At a quarter to two on the afternoon of Monday, 20 June, Leander left Latimer's Barn for the last time. The six most senior stable-lads carried the coffin out through the back door. Waiting for them, on the gravel path between The House and the lawn, was the old feed cart.

Steven had spent two sleepless nights wondering how they should take her to church. On the point of abandoning the desire to find something original and opt in favour of a Rolls-Royce hearse, he suddenly remembered the flat, four-wheeled cart in the corner of the coach-house. There was a mass of evidence to suggest that Leander's father had bought it in 1859, the year he took the momentous step from Greenwich to Wiltshire. It was certainly the vehicle that Leander's brother, William, and Jim Goakes had used when they went to fetch a load of timber from Pewsey Wharf in 1881, taking the famous letter with them and returning with Steven Hawksworth. Amelia, Emma and Ann were consulted and thought it ideal. Teams of men worked on the cart non-stop for two days and nights, stripping ancient paint and burnishing the metalwork. It was painted black and a professional was brought in to apply gold lining. The boards were covered with a lush bed of flowers on which the coffin was laid.

There was no horse between the shafts. Instead, six young people were to draw the cart to church. They were Joe Collier, home from London University Medical School, Robert Frobisher, waiting to go to a theological college after Oxford, an apprentice at Wm Flamsteed & Sons who had come to the village from one of Dr Barnardo's homes, two stable-lads who were making a new start to their lives after

222

juvenile court appearances in Swindon, and Bess. When they set off, the six pallbearers, with Steven at their head, followed behind.

The Devizes Lane and village street were lined with the cars of those who had travelled from far and wide to pay their last respects to the most remarkable woman that British racing had ever known. There was not a sign of life, however: apart from Malcolm Frobisher waiting at the lychgate, the village seemed uninhabited. The illusion that they were alone in an eerily empty world vanished abruptly as they entered the porch of the church. The congregation numbered well over five hundred, with every pew jammed tight and about fifty people standing at the back. As he walked with the coffin to the purple-shrouded table at the foot of the chancel steps, Steven saw that Ann had indeed arranged matters according to her plan; the residents of Cannings Ambo were at the front, the guests, whatever their rank or status, were behind them. It was a family occasion with distinguished spectators. Steven sat down in the empty seat beside Ann; the pallbearers and those who had drawn the cart slipped in behind him. Malcolm Frobisher began.

"Rest eternal grant them, O Lord: and let light perpetual shine upon them."

The service proceeded. Amelia read a lesson from St Paul's First Epistle to the Corinthians; after the choir, augmented by boys from Marlborough, had sung the *De Profundis*, Steven read the second lesson from the Revelation of St John the Divine.

Malcolm stood up to announce the hymn.

"I spoke to Leander on the day before she died," he said. "None of you will be surprised to learn that she told me which hymn she wanted at this service." Many of those present smiled and nodded. "It isn't a hymn that we normally associate with funerals, but that needn't worry us . . . as a matter of fact, it must have been even more unusual at her wedding seventy-four years ago. Four hundred and thirty-seven in Ancient and Modern – 'For all the Saints'."

With Solstice working the bellows for all he was worth,

Matthew's distinctly robust style of organ-playing soon had the great gathering singing joyfully, for all they were worth, exactly as Leander had wanted. At the end, there was a pause that allowed the last echoes to die away, then the six lads moved into position and hoisted her on to their shoulders for the last time.

Steven and Ann, now the leaders of Cannings Ambo, took their place at the head of the procession. As they neared the door, he saw that Alain and Nadia de Mourville, who had arrived the previous evening, were accompanied by two famous French trainers; he made a note to speak to them afterwards.

At the grave-side, Steven looked down quickly to check that Solstice and his helpers had carried out their instructions: they had, to the letter. Despite the camouflage of planks and sheeting, Steven could see his grandfather's coffin, as sound as the day William Flamsteed and Jim Goakes had made it. Leander and her husband were to lie side by side.

The final prayers were said and the coffin was lowered. Steven threw down the first handful of earth, then Amelia stepped forward. After that, Leander's six great-grandchildren made their contributions. Following the example of Henry, Marquess of Glastonbury, they all acquitted themselves well. Giles and his cousin, Lady Helen Prideaux, were holding hands as they stepped forward: Steven had noticed their curious friendship growing over the past two years, often wondering whether he should do anything to discourage it. On balance, he thought not. Although he never displayed much strength of character, Giles was one of the few people capable of exerting a calming influence on the persistently wilful and wayward Helen.

It was done and the group of forty people who had gone to the grave turned away. Unobtrusively, Solstice moved forward with his spade. Those who had travelled long distances drifted towards Latimer's Barn, the villagers coalesced into their habitual groups. As they did so, the pallbearers, together with Bess and the others who had drawn the cart, began to transfer the mass of newly arrived wreaths to the grave.

Entering the drive from the Devizes Lane, Ann was at the centre of a bunch of more than a dozen people. As they went towards The House, the conversation fragmented and individuals went with it, forming new clusters until, much to her annoyance, Ann found herself alone with Rachel.

Initially, the Duchess of Laverstoke seemed to be going out of her way to be pleasant, complimenting Ann fulsomely on the success of her organisation. When she did switch tack, it was with an effortless ease that took Ann by surprise.

"You'll find that you're the lady of the manor now," Rachel said. "Mother won't interfere – I don't think she's ever wanted to be influential – so you can do things your way. You can put that wretched girl in her place."

"Which 'wretched girl'?" a baffled Ann asked.

"Bess what's-her-name . . . the cook's daughter. She's been leading a charmed life, well above her station."

Ann bristled with anger. "Don't you dare come the *grande dame* with me, Rachel!" she said. Her voice was kept low to prevent anyone else hearing, but the force of her words made Rachel flinch. "Leander and Bess were devoted to each other. It so happens that Bess was with her when she died." Rachel looked appalled. "Quite apart from personal feelings, Bess is a very talented girl and Steven has high hopes for her. I shall do everything I possibly can to help her."

"Really, Ann, I was only trying to . . ."

Ann cut her sister-in-law brutally short. "Unless we can find a better way of doing things – and that doesn't seem very likely – we intend running Latimer's Barn exactly as it has been for the last ninety-five years. If you remember that, it might help to avoid arguments . . . not that you have any right to come here trying to start them."

Astoundingly, Rachel was contrite. "Yes, you're right, Ann, I'm sorry, I really am." She paused, staring at the ground, biting her lower lip in anguish. "God, aren't I a bitch sometimes? Please forgive me, Ann. I wish Charles would help me. I know I haven't been all that brilliant to him, but we could try to start again."

Following Rachel's gaze, Ann saw Charles ahead of them.

She frowned, suddenly realising how he had changed. He was standing in front of The House, talking to two attractive women whom Ann did not know. What was so surprising was Charles's debonair manner: Ann had always found him painfully diffident with women. Had working for Lambert's given him so much confidence? And he looked awfully young: what was going on?

Irrationally, possibly as a result of the strain of the last few days and the harshness of her words, Ann felt a wave of pity for Rachel. "Let's go and hide in the library," she said. "We'll put our feet up and have a stiff drink."

Late that evening, when all the visitors were long since gone and the village was settling down, Amelia went to the house on the drive.

"I'm so sorry to bother you," she told Elsie. "I have something to tell Bess."

"Oh! Come in, Dame Amelia."

Elsie was alarmed. "There's no need to worry," Amelia hastened to assure her. "I think you'll find that this is good news."

There were a few moments of awkwardness as Boggysevick and Joe shuffled round the parlour, wondering whether they ought to stay, arguing over the best seat for Amelia, generally getting in the way. It was Bess who eventually told them to sit down and shut up.

"As I expect you know," Amelia began, "Mother didn't leave a will. That is because all the important things belong to the Trustees, so there's no need to bother. It saves family squabbles and death duties." Boggysevick nodded approvingly. "However, she did have a little money of her own in a private account and I am her executor. She paid for The Hall to be done up and she gave me very strict instructions that you were to have what was left, Bess."

"Oh!" Bess was taken aback, as were Boggysevick and Joe. Elsie smiled and said, "That's nice."

"I settled Sid Irons's bill for The Hall the other day," Amelia continued. "As soon as you have the time, Bess,

226

we can go into Marlborough and arrange for the transfer of the residue to you. It's a little over seventeen thousand pounds."

Afterwards, Amelia realised that the only reason they had taken the news so calmly in the first place was that they were thinking in terms of a couple of hundred. There was an uproar of protest. Amelia had to be firm.

"No, Bess, you *must* have it. My mother was adamant." She gave a sad little smile. "We can hardly start defying her now, can we?"

"I don't know what to say," Bess muttered, shaking herself like someone recovering from a physical blow.

"You'll be set up for life, love," a dazed Elsie said.

"That is precisely what Mother intended." Amelia was brisk. "Now, my dear, shall we go into Marlborough at lunch-time tomorrow?"

"Yes . . . no . . . I can't." Bess was struggling to collect her thoughts. "I'm going to Ascot with Wessex Princess."

"Ah. Of course. We're carrying on as normal, aren't we?" Amelia stood up, preparing to leave. "Come up to Louise House when you're ready, Bess. And don't worry . . . it's a very simple business."

After she had gone, there was silence until Joe saw the look on Elsie's face. "What's wrong, Mum?" he asked.

"Nothing, Joe, nothing. But this place don't half take some getting used to. Look at Dame Amelia . . . she needn't have said a word about this, you know. There's nothing in writing. She could have put that money in her own pocket and nobody would have been any the wiser." Boggysevick and Joe, both keen students of human nature as practised outside Cannings Ambo, nodded. "You can't credit it, can you? And but for that bastard Hitler, we'd none of us be here."

Boggysevick put an affectionate arm round his wife's shoulders. "I think of him often," he said. "He gets extra pain as he burns in hell because of the happiness he brought to me, a lump of rubbish from Poland!"

Bess suddenly sat up very straight and looked fierce. "We

shall have to share this out," she said. "You must have some, Joseph. You need it far more than me."

"Oh, no!" Joe was going to scotch this one straight away. "What do I want money for? All my education is being paid for by the Fund; they buy all my books and equipment *and* give me money so that I don't have to work in the holidays. On top of that, I'm guaranteed a good job at the end of it." As soon as Joe was qualified, he was taking over from Kathleen as the village doctor. "Things are different for you, Bessie. Your job is risky . . . you could be badly injured and crocked up any time. Mrs Hawksworth wanted you to have that money and have it you shall!"

Bess looked at her mother and father. The expressions on their faces told her that the matter was closed: they agreed with her brother, the only person allowed to call her 'Bessie'.

In Louise House, Amelia told Silas and Clementine Prideaux all about it. "By the way, this is secret," she concluded.

"I can well imagine!" Clementine said grimly, thinking of Rachel's probable reaction to the bequest.

After a period of deep thought, Silas, very unusually, indulged in speculation. "If I were a betting man, I'd put a tidy sum on that letter being something to do with Bess," he said.

"Well, we shall never know," Amelia replied. "Mother said that it was only to be opened in the event of a serious crisis – and there isn't going to be one!"

The scepticism of Clementine, Dowager Duchess of Laverstoke, went unnoticed.

For Bess, Steven's 'business as usual' policy seemed utterly wrong, although she knew that her alternative of at least one month's 'official' mourning was totally impractical. Once she arrived at Ascot with Wessex Princess, she became too busy to fret. She groomed the filly to perfection, earned praise from Steven and Claude Timberlake in the paddock, then slipped away to watch the race from the tiny enclosure reserved for stable-lads.

That, she discovered almost at once, was a mistake. Two of the lads, an unpleasant pair of youngsters from Newmarket, decided that the time had come to show the celebrated Bess Collier that she was in the wrong job.

"Do you reckon tarts are gonna catch on, Bill?"

"Shouldn't think so, Ivor, me old son. It's only the Latimer's Barn crowd being clever again."

"'Specially with the old crow dropping off her perch at last, eh?"

"Fair dos, though, Bill, she's got good tits."

"True enough. And did you see her in them breeches this morning? Lovely arse!"

"Oh, she's not totally useless . . . Harry Perkins fancies her rotten. Mind you, that's sheer spite!"

This conversation, taking place immediately behind her, was a tactic that nearly worked. Quivering with rage, Bess told herself that she must not rise to the bait: words were one thing, but if they touched her, she knew she would create a terrible scene.

The strain of keeping calm rendered her blind to most of the race: the runners were at the furlong marker before the noise of the crowd silenced her persecutors and forced Bess to take an interest. She did so just as Michael Pilgrim decided that it was time to ask Wessex Princess the big question. He gave her a mild back-hander and off she went, winning the Queen Mary Stakes in four electrifying strides. They still had half a furlong to run when Bess slipped away, not bothering to look at the two youths.

Once she had caught the filly, Bess had no qualms about handing her over to Claude Timberlake, who was very good with his horses and knew how to lead them up.

She walked by his side, conscious of the atmosphere. As they neared the winner's enclosure, the men began to remove their hats and the filly was greeted with restrained clapping that fell away into almost total silence. From the tautness of their faces, Bess knew that Steven and Claude shared her thoughts: Wessex Princess was a daughter of Hyperborean, Leander's celebrated Derby and St Leger winner and this was

Ascot's tribute to the woman laid to rest deep in the earth of her beloved Wiltshire almost exactly twenty-four hours ago.

The five minutes in the enclosure were an ordeal that Bess escaped from only in the nick of time. The tears were in her eyes as she trotted Wessex Princess back to the stables: once inside the yard, she broke down completely. Her tormentors were there and one of them responded gleefully.

"Oh, Christ, look at this, Bill. Miss Smart-Arse has got her knickers in a right bloody twist. What's wrong, darling, can't you take it? It's like everybody's been saying, this is a man's job!"

Jimmy Farrant emerged from a nearby box with the air of a man on his way to scrounge the loan of a dandy-brush and his demeanour did not change until the fraction of a second before he launched the punch. It was a beauty that landed squarely on the jaw of Bess's abuser. He came close to turning a somersault before landing badly on a pile of buckets and shovels. While he groaned and writhed in half-senseless agony, Jimmy grabbed his mate by the throat and shook him until his eyes bulged. Then, relaxing his grip, he imparted certain things to him. Bess did not hear what Jimmy said; however, on all her subsequent visits to racecourses she was treated with great respect by lads from every stable in the country.

Charles was in Portugal with Laura Waterman for most of August.

There were good business reasons for the trip. Vasco da Silva had found a treasure-trove of possible French Impressionist canvases and Laura needed to spend several days authenticating them. There were one or two calls for Charles to make, but the main part of their stay was an idyllic three weeks in a villa by the sea at Cascais. Not until the afternoon of their last day was any mention made of problems back home.

"How is Her Grace?" Laura asked quietly.

"She's the same as ever . . . more or less."

"Still enjoying herself with Hetherington and not giving a damn?"

"She's trying to be more discreet," Charles said. "During the Easter hols, it emerged that young Lord Glastonbury wasn't awfully struck on Mama's shenanigans."

Laura was always amused by the way Charles talked about his eldest son. "He can be awfully snooty, can't he?"

"Very much so, my word! Henry has a taste for high moral principles and does a mean line in haughty stares. I got another lecture on what I should do about Hetherington." Charles sighed. "The boy is going up to Oxford in October . . . that *might* turn him into a human being." He sounded less than optimistic. "No, Rachel's developed a new thing for making life a pain in the neck. She's got raving paranoia over Bess Collier."

"Who's Bess Collier?"

"She's a stable-lad at Latimer's Barn. Despite being the cook's daughter, she was very close to Leander Hawksworth – she was with her the night she died, in fact."

"And?" Laura was mystified.

"Well, I don't really know," Charles confessed. "It's all rather bizarre . . . I think that Rachel imagines that Bess has picked up some sort of mystical power from Leander."

"Oh, dear!"

"It's a very rum business," Charles said. "Rachel didn't have too good a time at the stable during the War . . . I believe she thinks they weren't grateful enough for what she did and she's after some sort of revenge."

Laura's attention was drifting to more agreeable things. They were both naked after an earlier session of love-making and Charles was becoming aware of her breasts again. She decided to put a stop to his theorising.

Giles Hawksworth, like Steven before him, was attending the Grammar School in Marlborough. As the summer holidays approached, he had pestered Ann to be allowed to spend them at Eaton Mandeville.

"I don't know, darling," Steven said when she brought the matter up yet again as they prepared for bed one night. "What do you think?"

She smiled at him with affectionate exasperation. "Steven, I've been telling you what I think for the last month!"

"H'm!" Steven took refuge in brushing his teeth. "Rachel's very keen to have him," he said eventually.

"I should jolly well think so!" Ann hooted. "Poor Giles is the only person who can do anything with Helen . . . apart from Charles, of course, and he's hardly ever there."

Steven had noticed Rachel's attempt to improve relations and wished to encourage them. Their childhood together had been so happy, despite the loss of their father, and the long-standing link with Eaton Mandeville was precious. "I think he should go," was the final verdict.

The decision worried Amelia. The eldest son of Latimer's Barn should devote all his spare time to learning the basic principles of the immensely difficult job that would be his one day. The last time this fundamental had been ignored was in the case of her brother, George, producing consequences that people preferred to ignore.

There was no point in saying anything. Everyone knew that Dame Amelia detested Helen Prideaux. Up to a point it was understandable: the wretched girl had been expelled from two schools before she was thirteen. But since one of them was the revered Godolphin School, of which Amelia was proud to be a Governor, the old dear was regarded as prejudiced.

Summer passed into autumn and people in high places talked of a memorial service for Leander. In the event, there were two.

Amelia, Steven and Ann were the only representatives of the village to attend the one organised by the Jockey Club in London at the end of October.

Two weeks later, Wiltshire paid its own tribute with a service in Salisbury Cathedral. This time, Cannings Ambo and Marlborough turned out in force, as did hundreds of others from the county.

It was Bess's second visit to the great church of Sarum: the Bishop had confirmed her when she was ten. For most of the service, she gazed into the magnificent vaulted roof, feeling

232

perfectly at one with her companions and surroundings. Yet again, she thanked God for the twists of fate that had brought her to this lovely corner of England and given her the friendship of such a marvellous woman.

The six hired buses got home with enough daylight left for a simple ceremony at the entrance to the 1874 yard. Amelia unveiled a slab of Portland stone that Sid Irons himself had inserted into the brickwork five feet above the ground on the left-hand side of the arch. Daniel Dangerfield had carved the inscription, inlaying it with gold.

IN LOVING AND THANKFUL MEMORY
OF
LEANDER HAWKSWORTH
WHO LIVED AT
LATIMER'S BARN
ALL HER LIFE
1 June 1860 – 15 June 1955

CHAPTER 9

1960

'What a smashing name for a horse!'

The talk had been gathering momentum for months and the expectations were enormous. On New Year's Day, Steven told Ann that he was already a nervous wreck at what was being forecast for 1960, the Centenary. It went without saying that it had a capital letter.

The first thoughts of making the year special were floated in The George on a Friday evening when above-average consumption of special bitter gave rise to inventive eloquence. To Steven's horror, the bar-room exuberance soon evolved into a Centenary Committee with Dame Amelia as Chairman.

Steven's January pessimism was profound. Not for a second did he imagine that he would have no difficulty in eclipsing almost every event the Committee staged, ending the season as the most successful trainer in the history of racing.

The ebb and flow of evolutionary change, so familiar to Leander, had continued since her death. As Jim Goakes, now of an age to retire and beginning to lose the prefix 'young', said: "Parson and builders have been busy."

Among the deaths were Clementine, Dowager Duchess of Laverstoke, who was duly taken back to Eaton Mandeville for burial in 1957, and Mary, widow of the old vicar, John Shepherd, in 1958. Perhaps the worst loss was that of Silas in 1958. A few hours before he died, he thanked Amelia for all the happiness she had given him after he thought himself done for in the horror of Passchendaele, over forty years ago. Shutting herself away, Amelia had wept for three days. Then, after his burial in the Hawksworth and Flamsteed family plot, she acquired a new serenity that was never to leave her. Now that Amelia was alone, Emma moved from The House to live with her and the two women, one the sister, the other the widow of the man who *had* died at Passchendaele, found that they were perfect companions.

Included in the christenings that Malcolm Frobisher carried out were the first Timberlakes to be born in the village, Noel in 1956, then Desmond the following year, sons of Gideon and Lady Amaryllis. Poring over the Big Book, Steven was surprised to discover how long it had taken to bring the happy event about: the Timberlakes had been deeply involved with Cannings Ambo for nearly seventy years.

The enlargement of the stable to one hundred and twenty boxes, together with expansion at Wm Flamsteed & Sons, brought an influx of new people that caused Steven and Sid Irons a headache in finding room for new houses. It was Ann who suggested that, rather than risk spoiling the appearance of the village by squeezing houses into odd corners, they should go for new ground. The chosen site was two hundred yards to the north of the drive and work began in the summer of 1956, providing a far greater talking-point than the Suez crisis. A sewer, water and electricity were provided, on top of which a road surface was laid. The facilities provided gave ample scope for expansion beyond the original batch of twenty cottages.

Appalled by the quality of many of the houses that were springing up around the country, Steven laid the law down to Sid Irons.

"I don't want any of these awful boxes that look as though they've come off a production line, Sid. Get me a new design that's up-to-date *inside*, but looks decent *outside*. We've got to have something that belongs to the village, not one of these blasted housing estates!"

Sid Irons, who was incapable of building an ugly house, treated Steven to a pained look.

There were several suggestions as to what to call this new part of the village. 'Brook View', 'Downs Avenue' and 'Cannings Mead' were the most popular; the others, Steven told Ann, were even worse. He decided on 'The Extension', certain that it had the right ring about it. Leander would have approved; it was of a piece with 'Back Stretch' and 'Roadway'. By the summer of 1959, the twenty new cottages had been constructed, their front windows looking towards the poplars along the drive, their backs facing a new tree screen.

The final part of what Steven called 'Phase One' was a major rebuilding of the stud at Cannings St John, supplementing the work done in 1955. It was a far bigger and more costly job than the new yard. When completed, there were boxes for five stallions, twenty resident mares and fifteen visitors, modernised accommodation for the staff and an operating theatre.

Phase One cost £200,000. Steven was bluntly outspoken to the Trustees' meeting that approved the expenditure. "I think we should be looking to move into a position where we can pull the ladder up and let the rest of the country get on with it," he said. "We need to be insulated from whatever lunacy the Government or Trade Unions come up with next."

With £3.5 million in the Fund, there was no argument. Matthew and Claude Timberlake, the most influential of the Trustees, backed Steven to the hilt, believing that whatever Government had power, the result was likely to be an unholy mess. Amelia was never sure whether their lack of faith stemmed from a low opinion of politicians, or the electorate.

At the start of 1960, there was a new manager at the stud. Jeremy and Josie Dundas, who had run the place since 1919, went into well-deserved retirement at Oak Cottage, left empty by the death of Mary Shepherd. Lady Amaryllis Timberlake became the non-resident manager of the stud, with her staff supplemented by the transfer of two of the senior lads from Latimer's Barn. While she worked, her sons were looked after in the nursery that Amelia had started as an adjunct to the school.

But, as Jeremy and Josie never tired of reminding folk, *they* had been in charge at the stud when *the* colt was born.

Faithful old Hyperborean produced him at the end of February 1957. She was now twenty-two and the bay colt was her last before she was put out to enjoy the sun and grass. The foal was her third by Royal Wessex and was thus a full brother to Apollinaire and Wessex Princess.

From the start, the colt had a jaunty look about him. Many horses were born worriers, but not this one. As Steven got to know him, he thought that if he had a fault in his temperament, it was an excessive sense of fun. Of one thing there was no doubt: he was going to make a first-class athlete once he learned to use himself correctly. As a yearling, he was much admired by all the visitors to Cannings St John and Steven had him marked down for Alain de Mourville. Then, quite out of the blue, Charles turned up.

"It's about time I had a horse now the finances are on the mend," he said. "I've been neglecting family traditions."

"Just one?" Steven asked quizzically.

"To start with . . . but I'd like a good one, Steven."

"We don't have any other sort, Charles!"

They drove down to the stud where Charles carried out a cursory inspection of the five yearlings on offer, at the end of which he pointed to Hyperborean's foal. "That one," he said. "Why are you laughing?"

"If even *you* can pick him out like that, he must be good."

"Steady on!" Charles laughed. "The governor had a good eye for a nag . . . I could have inherited it, you know. How much do you want for him?"

"I'm afraid you've chosen a very expensive one, Charles," Steven said, and went on to explain the colt's breeding. "I know that doesn't guarantee anything, but he's certainly got the right look about him."

"How much?" Charles persisted.

"Ten thousand guineas," Steven replied.

After studying current bloodstock prices and speaking to a

number of owners, Charles knew that this was a more than fair price and did not haggle. "I suspect you're robbing yourself, Steven, but ten thousand it is and I'll give you twenty per cent of everything he wins."

They went back to Latimer's Barn to finalise the deal. Enjoying a gin and tonic before lunch, Charles suddenly shot off at a tangent to avoid a question about Rachel. "I say, I was thinking about the other half of your family . . . Flamsteed . . . that's a very unusual name. You don't come across many."

"Matthew looked into this a few years back," Steven said. "He couldn't find *any* – although someone said there might be a few in Yorkshire. The famous one was John Flamsteed, who got himself made Astronomer Royal in sixteen seventy-five. His observatory was in Greenwich, so my great-grandfather *could* have been a descendant."

Ann was about to add something when she saw that Charles was miles away. "What is it?" she asked as a satisfied smile spread across his face.

"Astronomer Royal," he said, savouring it like a good wine. "What a smashing name for a horse!"

Steven and Ann thought about it and nodded approvingly.

"Very good indeed," Steven said. "Do you want him registered as that?"

"Yes please. And I'll use the governor's colours. There's a good few keen to see them out again."

Bess was nineteen when Astronomer Royal came into the yard for schooling at the back end of 1958.

It had been a foregone conclusion for at least ten years that she would develop into an extraordinarily attractive young woman and she had fulfilled the promise. Not that she was entirely to everyone's taste: her broad forehead, strong jaw-line and the severely practical style that she favoured for her blonde hair caused some to describe her as 'handsome', rather than pretty. Men who liked their women to be flashily glamorous went so far as to say that she was almost masculine, although they had to admit that the tight sweaters and breeches she wore for work promised a lithely exciting body. Well and truly one of the lads, Bess was always ready for a joke and joined in the regular Saturday-night revelry at The George, but her blue eyes always held the hint of seriousness and could quickly become disconcertingly grey when she was annoyed or suspicious.

She was not pestered for dates these days. Nearly all the lads claimed that they had a mate who had tried, only to be turned down with resolute politeness. Her popularity was such that there were no carping suggestions that she was 'saving herself' for a toff, and it was accepted that horses were her life. Certainly there was no one, not even Jimmy Farrant, better than Bess at the job.

Knowing that she still missed Apollinaire and would be disappointed not to have charge of his brother, Steven allocated Astronomer Royal to Bess.

The big, precocious bay and Bess were so well-suited to each other that Steven found himself repeatedly shaking his head in disbelief. Ann was with him on the gallops one morning to witness an astonishing incident while Astronomer Royal was being prepared for his first race. Cantering towards them alongside Boggysevick on a colt belonging to Edward Mallender, Astronomer Royal was playing the fool, using his potentially superb action in wasteful extravagance. A few yards away from Ann and Steven, Bess began to lecture him.

"Honestly, Bert, you are an idiot! Will you stop arsing around and concentrate. You're supposed to be a finely tuned thoroughbred, not a bloody liberty horse."

Grinning broadly at the reference to his circus activities, Boggysevick made a satanic-sounding pronouncement in Polish. Ann turned to Steven, her face a picture. "*Bert?*" she asked.

"The lads nearly always have a pet name for the horses," he said. "It's like pedigree dogs. An animal called 'Montague Everard of Budleigh Salterton the Third' will usually be called 'Fido' or 'Rex' at home."

Ann shook her head. "I've seen everything!" she laughed.

239

"No you haven't. Look at *that*!"

Half a furlong away, Astronomer Royal was settling into the most effective and elegant stride that Ann could recall seeing.

Steven's high hopes for the colt gave rise to extreme caution during his 1959 two-year-old career, when he raced only three times. After the Dewhurst Stakes, in which another horse had finished a mere three lengths behind him, Michael Pilgrim apologised to Charles for what he considered a lack-lustre performance.

"He could have done a lot better if I'd tickled him up, Your Grace, but it's more than my life's worth to lay a finger on that horse."

Charles nodded appreciatively, only to find that Steven was disassociating himself from the policy. "That's nothing to do with me – it's Bess who's putting the frighteners on. I agree with her, of course."

On the way home from Newmarket, riding in the cab of the van with Solstice, Bess was lost in thought until they reached Marlborough.

"What odds are they laying on him for the Guineas next year?" she asked.

"I heard eight to one as we were leaving."

"They're fools!" Bess paused slightly, changing from contempt to calculation. "I hear that you're the man to get bets on, Solstice."

He grinned. "That's supposed to be a secret. I expect your dad told you, so that's all right."

"Can you get me a thousand on?"

"A thousand!" The van swerved as both the sum and Bess's coolness shocked Solstice.

"He'll never be worth backing again," she replied.

"But a thousand, Bess! Blimey, girl, it's over six months away. He could go wrong ten times over and you know where that would leave you if you took ante-post."

"It's an acceptable risk."

Solstice wondered how she could possibly have so much money: then he remembered Claude Timberlake. Bess had done at least a dozen good winners for him and Mr Timberlake was rumoured to be very generous.

"All right," Solstice said, deciding that Bess knew how much she could afford to lose. "I'll probably have a bit on myself."

"I'll get you the money on Monday," she told him.

When the two hundred five-pound notes were handed over, Bess had already amended her punctiliously maintained account book. The thousand pounds was half what Claude Timberlake had given her in tips: Leander's legacy, together with the interest it was earning, remained inviolate.

Giles Hawksworth spent the Easter holidays of 1960 in concentrated revision for the GCE A-level examinations he was to take in early summer. With half a mind to go to university, an idea of which Steven approved, he needed good results.

Lady Helen Prideaux was under no such constraints. For the past five years she had been at a hideously expensive boarding school in Worcestershire that prided itself on its handling of 'difficult' girls. A curious mixture of harsh discipline and pandering to a pupil's every whim did produce some near-miraculous transformations, but there was no pretence at academic excellence. When they left, girls were either expected to go abroad for 'finishing', or to enter a two-year engagement with a preordained marriage partner. Unsure of which was to be her lot Helen went to spend Easter with her friend Amanda Fenton.

The brashly renovated early Victorian house in a village midway between Nottingham and Leicester was a proclamation of Amanda's father's success in knitwear. Ron Fenton, tiresomely proud of his humble origins, employed three hundred workers and flaunted the resultant wealth with a vulgarity that was almost engaging. His wife, originally a solicitor's daughter, was not nearly so convincing, largely because she still insisted on telling all and sundry that she had married beneath herself. Roger, Amanda's twenty-one-year-old brother, was in his father's business and squeezing every last ounce of prestige and opportunity out of it.

The Fentons rarely came together as a family, so Helen and Amanda were left very much to themselves.

"I like it here, but it's a strange set-up," Helen said to her friend after the first two days.

"It's all to do with sex," Amanda replied.

"Really?" This was exactly what Helen had hoped to hear. She had decided that, in all probability, sex was the one thing she could both enjoy and be good at: the hope of turning this notion into practical reality had been her prime reason in accepting Amanda's invitation.

"Father runs at least two women," Amanda said. "The one in Leicester is a scrubber, I think. The Nottingham one is more classy. Mother has a young artist three villages away."

"That's obscene!" Helen shrieked. "She's far too old."

"She's about the same age as your dear mama," Amanda pointed out. "Is she still having it off with the gardener?"

"Actually, he's the estate manager," Helen said stiffly, as though this changed everything. "What about you?"

Amanda rolled her eyes. "I'm hoping to carry on where I left off at half-term. I found myself this *incredible* bloke who works in a garage at Loughborough. He's *very* uncouth, but he's terrific in bed. Have you had it properly yet?"

"Of course!" Although Helen was eager enough to claim the loss of her virginity, she did not look back on the episode with any pleasure. "I managed to get Giles to take an interest in me last summer."

"What, your Latimer's Barn cousin?" Amanda was impressed. "What was he like?"

"Not very good," Helen admitted.

"How many times did you do it?"

"Lots. And I made him try again at Christmas. It was still hopeless. He comes as soon as you look at him."

"He's too young and inexperienced," Amanda said. "You want someone older who knows what it's all about."

"Like your brother, for instance?" Helen asked.

"Could be," Amanda replied. "I think he spends most of his time delving into the knickers of the local peasantry, but you should see them off if you put your mind to it."

Helen did. When Roger Fenton went up to his room that night, she was in his bed. He made no bones about accepting the offer and they both found the consequences enjoyable. Thereafter, they spent every night of Helen's holiday together.

While Helen was indulging herself in Leicestershire, Astronomer Royal went to Newmarket for the Craven Stakes, giving devastating proof that he had wintered well and turned into a most formidable racing machine. His size was the only thing that worried Steven, who could not remember having seen such a big horse before. "If all else fails, we can geld him and put him in the Cheltenham Gold Cup," Steven joked, making sure that Bess was well out of the way.

Two days before the Two Thousand Guineas, there was a surprise. No one had seriously thought that Alain de Mourville's filly, Madame Bovary, was good enough to win the One Thousand Guineas, yet her victory was utterly convincing, and she won it in a way that suggested she would stay well beyond a mile.

Steven was pleased, but confessed to Ann that the unexpected good fortune bothered him. "I'd wanted that slice of luck for Astronomer Royal on Saturday," he grumbled.

"Don't start getting superstitious," Ann ordered. "In any case, if that colt needs luck to win a race, we'd better start looking for alternative employment."

On the day itself, Solstice watched Bess watching the race that made her richer by £8,000 and gave the Prideaux family their first Classic winner since Agamemnon in 1929. Her face remained devoid of expression until she went to the course to bring her Bert back for Charles to lead into the winner's enclosure: then, she permitted herself a brief smile.

Ann, who had made herself into the statistical guru of Latimer's Barn, was quick to point out that this was the first time they had won both the Guineas races in the same year, although the feat was not quite as rare as she would have liked: other trainers had done it at least eight times.

"Still, it's a good start to our Centenary," she conceded.

"What else are you expecting?" Steven asked.

"Quite a lot, actually, but I won't bother you with it yet."

On the way home, Solstice sensed that Bess did not want to talk about her stupendous winning bet. At last, he said, "He won it well," deeming it to be a suitably harmless remark.

"Didn't he though!" Suddenly Bess was all smiles and girlish enthusiasm. "The way he came up from the Bushes!" She whistled. "What price are they laying him for the Derby?"

"The big boys are down to six to four."

"A bit mean . . . but it's not surprising."

Michael Pilgrim had held Astronomer Royal up at the back until the two-furlong marker: he said afterwards that he wanted to keep the colt secret until it was time for him to do the business. As soon as he was sent on, he worked up a murderous pace that left the opposition in tatters.

"Will he get the distance at Epsom?" Solstice asked.

"With plenty to spare," Bess said confidently.

"They're saying he's too big to act round the corners."

Bess laughed. "Don't you ever wish that you could earn a fancy wage for spouting rubbish, Solstice?"

It took him three days to collect all her winnings. When the last wad of notes had been handed over, she insisted that he have five hundred pounds.

"Come on, Solstice," she urged. "You put a fair bit of time into that for me."

"I don't deserve that much."

"Take it and shut up!"

He did. Although he never breathed a word of the bet to anyone, not even his close friends Elsie and Boggysevick, Solstice thought about it a great deal. He came to the conclusion that Bess was going for a clearly defined objective. He wondered if she'd set herself the target of having her own stable by the time she was, say, thirty. It was common knowledge that the Jockey Club would have to surrender over the question of licences to women before too long.

Yes, that was definitely it, Solstice decided. Bess was after her own place. Nothing as grand as Latimer's Barn, of course, but there were several small yards to the north of Marlborough, any one of which would be ideal. Bloody good luck to her! If she asked him, he'd probably go and work for her.

Amelia and her helpers were forced to laugh ruefully when their greatest plan came unstuck. It was the consequence of a breakdown in communication that beggared belief.

The Centenary Committee had earmarked 1 June for the biggest celebration. That was the day in 1860 when The Beresford Lathe had won the first race for Latimer's Barn: as if to ensure that the date would be remembered, fate delivered Leander at ten o'clock that morning.

The plans were phenomenally ambitious. There was to be a Grand Centenary Fair on Church Green and the Rectory lawn, with a sack race, egg and spoon, thirty- and fifty-yard dashes, bran tubs galore, bowling for a pig and goodness knows what else. The Marlborough silver band would play a selection of music popular in 1860, the stables were to be open for conducted tours, and high tea would be served in the workshops of Wm Flamsteed & Sons. The evening began with a dance in the Memorial Hall, speeches outside The George and, the grand finale, a Victorian fancy-dress parade by torchlight to a bonfire on the ridge of Cannings Down.

There was only one thing wrong with the plan: 1 June was Derby Day.

The discovery made Amelia feel an utter fool.

"I don't understand it," she wailed. "How could I possibly have overlooked *that*?"

"Don't worry," Steven said, struggling not to laugh. "This is what we'll do . . . on June the first we'll take *everybody* to Epsom and your wing-ding can be the following day."

Unconvinced, Amelia asked the question that demonstrated

how dreadfully out of touch the endless committee work had left her.

"Is it worth going? Do we have a decent runner?"

Patiently, Steven told her about Astronomer Royal, explaining how he had got his name and his performances to date, the most recent of which was a victory in the Derby Trial at Lingfield that had left the pundits bereft of superlatives.

Amelia agreed to change the date on the posters.

Steven went to Epsom so determined not to have hopes that his mind was blank. Arriving at midday, five hours after Bess, Solstice and Astronomer Royal, he found it impossible to adjust to what was happening. He was vaguely aware that Bess and the colt were probably the two calmest individuals on Epsom Downs: beyond that, nothing registered. It was Ann who guided him through the afternoon and she did it splendidly.

The Latimer's Barn owners and their guests had taken over a corner of the members' dining-room: while Steven was glad of a congenial gathering in which to lose himself, Ann found herself sitting back to appraise them.

She settled first on the Mallender and Giffard partnership. Edward Mallender, Leslie Giffard and their associates were basking in the general air of merriment, enjoying themselves. But there were persistent whispers of trouble between them, apparently over the direction in which their company should go. One story had it that they could barely stand the sight of each other: there were also rumours about Edward Mallender's sons, both involved in the business, yet constantly falling out with their father.

Sir Miles Christopherson, whom Ann had never cared for, was the centre of a group that made her uneasy. The ex-film star had divorced Sir Miles long ago. At seventy he was still the subject of scandal; it was entirely possible that at least one of the flashy young women who appeared to be accompanying his twenty-year-old son, Freddie, was for Sir Miles's consumption. Much as she approved of having the Fund safe in Switzerland, Ann felt that they really ought to find someone more wholesome than Christopherson and the already notorious Freddie to administer it for them.

As expected, Astronomer Royal's proud owner had brought a large party. Rachel, looking lovely in a dress that Ann thought was probably by Christian Dior, seemed to be in a good mood and her two sons were devoting most of their energies to maintaining that happy state of affairs. Helen had not bothered to come.

At Charles's insistence, the entire board of Lambert's had joined him. The younger wives both fascinated and repelled Ann; like the girls with the Christophersons, they were exponents of the 'if you've got it, flaunt it' approach that was sweeping the country. Their strident enjoyment of privilege was quite distasteful. But despite the attention they claimed for themselves, Ann spotted Laura Waterman, quietly and with much understatement, the best looking and most elegantly turned out of all the women. It really was incredible, Ann thought, that everyone else was so busy 'enjoying' themselves that she was the only one to notice the glances that passed between Charles and Laura, or the way that Laura studied Rachel.

Ann discovered later that she was wrong. Nadia de Mourville had also seen the affinity between the two lovers; however, she was preoccupied with stopping her daughter making too much of a nuisance of herself.

It was Lisette's first visit to England and she was enjoying herself enormously. She was especially taken with Lord Henry, Marquess of Glastonbury. After her father, he was the most handsome man she had ever seen and he spoke French beautifully. Unfortunately, he seemed terribly pompous. For his part, Henry thought that Lisette was very pretty, but found her boisterous fourteen-year-old attentions a sore trial.

Lunch seemed to go on forever and most people drank far too much. Steven came out of a reverie with a jolt when he realised that the first race was being run.

"I'd better go and see how things are," he said to Ann.

"I'll come with you," she whispered. "I could do with some fresh air."

"You mean you've had enough of this lot?"

She smiled enigmatically.

The seventeen runners for the Derby were already in the pre-parade ring at the back of the stables. Bess, smiling and relaxed, waved at Ann and Steven and carried on her way, talking incessantly to Astronomer Royal.

"He's very composed," Ann said.

Steven found that he was too nervous to think of a sensible reply.

Although the horse in front of him played up badly, Astronomer Royal remained placid when they went into the paddock. There was a long delay at the start caused by another horse getting rid of his jockey and bolting. Unable to look, Steven waited for Ann to tell him that he had nothing to worry about. By the time she did so, the race was in progress.

Trusting his experiences of doing ride-work on the colt and with absolute faith in what Bess had told him, Michael Pilgrim pushed Astronomer Royal into the lead at the end of the first half mile.

"God, I hope he knows what he's doing!" Steven muttered, now taking an interest.

"Of course he does," Ann replied. "He's got the rail all the way round that wretched bend and he doesn't have to worry about the others tripping up."

Steven knew she was right: for a bold horse with plenty of stamina, the safest way round the interminable bend that plunged downhill to Tattenham Corner was in front. Astronomer Royal handled it superbly: entering the straight, he was a length up on the rest. Immediately, four horses had a go at him, one of them very nearly getting his nose in front. Michael Pilgrim had been given permission to use the whip once: he did so, put his head down and started to ride as though this was the most important race of his life. It was, of course.

There was a moment of complete silence as the vast crowd

realised that Astronomer Royal was in total command. The popular newspapers had spelt out exactly what his win would mean today and half a million people gave vent to their approval in the most almighty uproar.

"Golly!" Ann was jumping up and down like a schoolgirl. "Look at him . . . he's going like a train!"

"I had no idea he was *this* good," Steven said. He kept on repeating it.

"What a shame, Michael's pulling him up," Ann complained. "It's only going to be five lengths."

Pandemonium broke out. Steven was bombarded with questions he could not hear because of the din the crowd was making. Charles was red in the face with excitement and Rachel seemed genuinely pleased. There was real warmth in the kiss she gave Steven. "Well done," she said. "This must be the most brilliant *coup* that even Latimer's Barn has ever pulled off."

Down on the rails, a young freelance photographer got the picture that the following day's papers fought for: he caught Bess at the moment in which she and Astronomer Royal were reunited. The expression of pure joy on her face summed the occasion up to perfection. When Ann saw the picture the following morning, she immediately ordered two big, glossy copies, one for Bess, the other for the portrait gallery in The House.

It was fully half an hour before the enormity of it all caught up with Steven. Finally escaping from well-wishers and journalists, he made his way to the stables. Bess and Solstice had finished sluicing Astronomer Royal down and were watching him tucking into a good feed. As he tugged affectionately at the colt's ears, Steven realised that they had won the Derby on what would have been Leander's hundredth birthday with a horse whose name had been suggested by the work of a man called Flamsteed.

Bess, studying him across her Bert's gracefully bowed neck, was compelled to advise him of an imminent danger. "I'm sorry, sir, but if you start crying, you'll have me at it as well and that could put you off your food for a week."

Snapping out of it, Steven grinned broadly. "We mustn't have that, not with all the celebrations coming up." He looked at her, trying to remember something. "It's your birthday, isn't it, Bess?"

"Yes, sir. I'm twenty-one!"

"You won't forget this in a hurry! Have you got anything planned for this evening?"

"No, sir. I think Mother's organising a party for the weekend."

"Come to supper at The House. Ask your mother and father to come, too. There'll only be my wife and I. Monsieur and Madame de Mourville are off to see some people in Newbury." Although there was no need to, he lowered his voice conspiratorially. "All the hangers-on were blotto *before* the race, so I don't suppose they'll notice us dumping them."

"Thank you, sir, I'll look forward to it."

"Good." Steven pointed at Solstice, who was preparing the van to take their twelfth and most wonderful Derby winner home. "And bring that character with you, this evening."

With the day's delay yielding a priceless dividend, the Centenary Fair was a colossal success, untouched by even the minor disasters generally considered an inevitable part of such functions. And from mid-afternoon, a tremendous celebrity was ambling round the village, affably aware of the adulation being heaped on him.

Astronomer Royal was allowed to sleep late that morning and had no work to do. Steven had a good look at him after lunch and decided that he was completely unaffected by his exertions at Epsom. On the contrary, he seemed slightly restive, eager for a little gentle exercise.

"Take him into the village," Steven suggested to Bess. "That will give Dame Amelia a star attraction she didn't expect."

Bess agreed, but dashed home to change first. This was an ideal opportunity to show off the birthday presents that Elsie and Boggysevick had given her. The expertly tailored breeches were in navy-blue instead of the conventional beige and the full-length riding boots were made of leather as soft and supple as velvet. With a bright yellow sweater to complete the outfit, she earned an admiring glance from Steven as she hurried back into the yard.

"That should make them sit up and take notice," he said.

He was right. Bess and Astronomer Royal were a study in quality that excited intense admiration in the onlookers. In a world where the facile and tawdry results of mediocre talents were being promoted with dismaying success, Cannings Ambo had the genuine, top-class article. It was something to be proud of and they were grateful for it. There were scores of less than dry eyes as people told each other what Leander would have thought of it all.

The bun-fight, dance and bonfire were rousing successes, so much so that Friday was a quiet day, with a good many hangovers being nursed. Early on Saturday morning, Solstice was on his way to Epsom again, this time with Jimmy Farrant and Madame Bovary for the Oaks. All hell was let loose at Latimer's Barn when those who had been listening to the radio commentary began dashing round to spread the news that she had won it.

"Four out of four Classics," Boggysevick said happily. "That is good."

"It's *very* good," Elsie said, concerned to have it right.

"Five out of five will be better," Bess murmured.

When they returned to Latimer's Barn that evening, Ann stood over Steven while he wrote in the Big Book. "Don't be shy," she commanded. "It's a wonderful achievement, so be a bit bombastic about it. There'll be plenty more times when everything goes against us, so enjoy this."

She was so pleased that she had forgotten the misgivings that had begun to worry her in the members' dining-room on Derby Day.

There was much soul-searching over what Astronomer Royal should do for the remainder of his three-year-old campaign.

An attempt on the Triple Crown obviously *had* to be made, but Steven was chary about risking the colt again before the St Leger. Eventually, Charles talked him into having a go at the King George VI and Queen Elizabeth Stakes at the end of July.

The opposition was formidable. Unlike the Classics, the race was open to horses of all ages and Astronomer Royal was up against some very good four-year-olds. Among them were three from France that included one of Alain de Mourville's Chantilly-trained horses.

"We cannot allow you to have everything your own way, my friend," Alain said to Steven.

"Fair enough," Steven smiled. "Don't expect any favours from my boy."

Alain was horrified by the suggestion. "We must have a good, fair race!"

Astronomer Royal provided that in full measure. In what was certainly his finest performance so far, he made all the running, leaving the best of the others to argue over the very respectable prize-money for second place.

It was the same in the St Leger at Doncaster where he had to prove that he could go an extra two furlongs. He did it with an ease that seemed languid, his ears pricked to the admiring roar of the crowd. Yorkshiremen, with their great respect for out-and-out excellence, cheered the Triple Crown winner to the echo, then gave a great ovation to Steven, the first man to train the winners of all five Classics. Knowing that he would never have another season like it as long as he lived, Steven settled down to relax and enjoy himself for a few days.

Astronomer Royal had rewritten the record books. His winnings of £103,630 made Charles the leading owner in only his first season. Prince Aly Khan had broken through the £100,000 barrier for owners the previous year, but he had needed considerably more than one horse to do it. When Madame Bovary's prize-money was taken into account, plus the little matter of eighty-two other winners, Steven required only two or three more moderate victories to become the first trainer to bring in more than £200,000 in a season.

The euphoria lasted for two weeks. Then the delayed news of Charles Prideaux's death reached Latimer's Barn.

Charles and Laura travelled to her house near Broomer's Green on a Thursday evening. They spent Friday, a lovely September day, by the sea at Pevensey, then went to dinner with friends at Lewes. On Saturday, they took a leisurely walk after breakfast, calling in at The King's Head in Broomer's Green for a snack lunch. It was while he was ordering sandwiches at the bar that Charles suffered the massive heart attack that killed him in fifteen seconds.

Shocked into a state of clear-headedness, Laura telephoned Margot Trubshawe, her doctor and a friend of long-standing. She arrived quickly, examined Charles, professed herself fully satisfied as to cause of death and sent for an ambulance.

"Who is he?" Margot asked Laura while they waited, alone in the bar with Charles's body.

"The Duke of Laverstoke."

"Bloody hell! Is there a duchess?"

"Yes. She won't know where he is."

"I'd better stay with you and sort it out."

Once they were following the ambulance to Brighton, Laura began to shake as the ghastliness of the loss of Charles hit her. Margot Trubshawe, herself no stranger to traumatic tragedy, decided on a brisk, no-nonsense antidote.

"It could have been much worse," she said. "It isn't unknown for that to happen in bed during intercourse."

"Good God!" Laura's face was ashen. "That must be horrific."

"It is!" Margot replied grimly. "I had it four years ago. He was a lovely man . . . married to a complete bitch."

"Same as Charles," Laura replied sadly.

"How long had you known him?" Margot asked.

"Ten years. We'd been lovers for nine."

"Oh dear!" Dr Trubshawe squared herself resolutely over the steering-wheel. "Let's see what we can do about it!"

Margot completed the hospital formalities in half an hour. "I'm going to borrow Fred Hopkins's office to make a phone call," she said. "You stay here. Do you have a number for this Eaton Mandeville place?"

Laura handed over her address book.

Instead of Rachel, who was away, Margot found herself talking to a young man who was devastated to learn that he had become the ninth Duke of Laverstoke about two hours ago. Nevertheless, his mind functioned with astonishing clarity.

"I must arrange for Father to be brought home. I know it's Sunday tomorrow, but could our undertaker collect him?"

"Yes, that's no problem. Will you be coming with them?"

"I think so."

"If you could call me back when you've made the arrangements and have some idea of time, I'll meet you and let you have the death certificate." She gave him her home telephone number.

"That's very kind of you, Doctor Trubshawe. I'm very grateful for the trouble you've taken." Although badly shaken and upset, his manners were impeccable: and no awkward questions, Margot thought as she replaced the instrument. She went to rescue and comfort Laura; eighty miles away, the young Duke of Laverstoke wondered how to get hold of his mother.

Charles Prideaux's body was taken from the mortuary and began its journey back to Eaton Mandeville at midday on Sunday. Margot Trubshawe was surprised by his son's invitation to lunch, but accepted without hesitation. He was a gorgeous young man behind the stuffy façade with which he concealed his shyness: if she were twenty, or even ten years younger . . .

Once they had found a restaurant and ordered, Henry wasted no time in asking his question. "Do you, by any chance, know what my father was doing in this part of the world, Doctor Trubshawe?"

Hesitation and the look she gave him showed that she did. "Were you on your father's side?" she asked.

"You mean as opposed to my mother's?" He leaned back, raising his eyebrows ironically. "Yes, I was."

"Your father had a lady friend in the area."

"I see." It was obvious that he was very pleased. "Do you know if they were happy?"

"I understand that they were very happy indeed over several years."

"Good! One last question: I know it sounds rather quaint, but does the lady want for anything?"

"No, she's very well provided for, thank you. She's dreadfully upset, but I'm looking after her."

And that was that, the subject was closed. For the next hour, confiding in Margot as though she were an old and trusted friend, Henry told her about the trepidation his future as a high-ranking peer of the realm gave him. At the end of the meal, they shook hands with the absolute certainty that they would never meet again.

The funeral was a dire affair, crushed under an atmosphere of unmitigated poison.

No sooner had Ann, Steven, Giles, Oliver and Rebecca arrived, than Rachel commandeered Giles to be her companion and supporter for the ordeal that lay ahead of her. It was a gesture of spite against Henry, who, immaculate in morning dress, made it clear that he was unconcerned.

There had, of course, been a fearful bust-up. Lord Edmund, who had grown up precisely as his father had envisaged, strong, bluff, likeable, but not wildly bright, had developed a strong affinity with Emma, and driven over to Latimer's Barn two days before the funeral to warn her of possible ructions.

After recounting how Henry had received the call from a lady doctor in Brighton and organised the collection of the late Duke's body, he approached the crux of the story in such a way that Emma found herself perched on the edge of her chair.

"Henry had an idea that Mother and that blighter Hetherington were having a revolting weekend at a hotel in Salisbury, so off he goes! It was a terrible shock to

Mother, of course, but Henry was pretty good and strong – you know what he's like, Gran. They packed up in Salisbury and went home. As far as I can see, they made the best of a pretty lousy job."

"So, when did the fireworks start?" Emma asked.

"First thing on Monday morning!" Edmund rubbed his hands. "Henry sent for Hetherington and sacked him. Mother went up in sheets of flame and said that if lover-boy went, so did she. 'Fine,' says Henry, 'but I shall cut you off without a penny.'"

"Can he do that?" Emma asked, goggling.

"Oh yes, Gran. You see, the aristocracy is run on feudal lines. As head of the family, Henry owns absolutely everything and can do what he likes with it. Most dukes and earls look after the scroungers, but they don't *have* to. If Henry wants to go throwing his weight around, he's perfectly entitled."

"How did all this end up?" Emma asked weakly.

"Hetherington's gone and Mother is still trying to work out what to do. Oh yes . . . she wanted to know what the poor old governor was doing in Sussex."

"I was wondering that."

"Another woman," Edmund said gleefully.

"Really?" Emma was aghast.

"Definitely! Henry was pretty cryptic about it, but he knows something. Oh, the other thing, there's every chance that he's going to boot Helen out if she doesn't mend her ways."

Emma thought the forcefulness of the new Duke was going to raise a few eyebrows. There had been times when Henry had seemed a weak character who was uninterested in his family's status: having looked after him as a child, Emma knew these views of him were misguided. She found that she was looking forward to seeing him exert his authority.

Apart from the dreadful atmosphere at the funeral, very little was on show, however. Very much on her best behaviour, Helen was showing signs of strain, and Rachel, miserably aware that the formal widow's weeds demanded by convention did not suit her, flashed a few venomous looks at her elder son.

For Ann, the worst moment was provided by Oliver, now fourteen and passing through a phase in which his cleverness was frequently odious, especially when he chose to lace it with a worldly cynicism that came from goodness only knew where. After the interment in the family vault, Ann saw Oliver holding forth to a group of youngsters that included Rebecca and the sons of a marquess. Ann edged closer, finding that she was eavesdropping on his best effort yet.

". . . all the money and property goes to Henry, you see. It's called 'primogeniture'. That's nearly as bad as the system we have in Cannings Ambo where nobody ever gets anything. When my great-grandmother Leander died, no one got a bean, which was a bit of a cheek. *Theoretically* she must have been absolutely filthy rich!"

Ann was outraged. Catching Oliver's eye, she indicated that it was time to be going and that a good talking-to awaited him when they did get home.

It was while the Hawksworth family were trying to escape that Rachel came closest to making a scene. She asked that Giles should be allowed to stay with her for a few days to help her recover from the shock of bereavement. When the request was met with evasion, she turned it into a demand. Embarrassed, and seeing that Giles sympathised with his aunt, Ann and Steven capitulated and fled.

It was nearly four weeks before the Duke of Laverstoke was able to get over to Latimer's Barn and he met Steven's opening greeting with a request that would have been priggish but for its sincerity.

"I want to be called 'Hubert', Uncle Steven. It *is* my second name and I want people to remember Grandfather . . . he was an awfully nice bloke."

Steven found such a reminder of the seventh Duke rather touching and agreed at once. "I'll do that if you drop the

'Uncle' . . . apart from making me feel ancient, we've never bothered much with handles round here."

"It's a bargain!"

"Now, *Hubert*, what can I do for you?"

"Once I've sorted out the finances, I'd like to be one of your owners, hopefully in a fairly big way."

"I'd be very pleased to be of assistance," Steven said. "Between you and me, I like having a duke on the books . . . it adds a touch of class. Tell me to mind my own business if you want to, but how are you fixed for money?"

"Pretty well," Hubert replied. "Father seems to have worked miracles in that department."

"There are death duties, of course?"

"Don't remind me! According to my calculations, I shall have to pay out something like three hundred thousand."

"Astronomer Royal will earn that for you in two years."

"Good God!" Hubert's resolve never to show emotion deserted him.

"Your father and I never discussed whether he would stay in training for another year, or go down the road to stud," Steven said. "With things as they are, I'd advise the stud. However, you do have a problem to solve first. That animal is worth about half a million pounds."

"Which increases my tax load even more," Hubert said.

"Unless you give him away." Steven smiled at the quizzical look the suggestion produced. "We can charge three thousand five hundred a go for his services as a stallion. Fifty mares a year makes a hundred and seventy-five thousand, of which only twenty-five thousand would be expenses. If you give the horse to three nominated Trustees of the Cannings Ambo estate, I'll pay your tax bill."

"And when Astronomer Royal has cleared the debt?" Hubert asked.

"We give eighty per cent of him back to you. On an animal of that quality, I would want to see the Fund making thirty-five thousand a year."

Hubert nodded. "Good! Let's do that." He laughed. "So,

Steven, on top of everything else, you act as a de luxe pawnbroker!"

"Only for the select few," Steven assured him.

Hubert showed his mettle by launching into a new and difficult topic with barely a pause. "What do you think I should do about my mother?" he asked.

"Why ask me?" Steven protested.

"You're her brother."

"That doesn't mean I'm an expert. You're her son and it obviously hasn't helped you. Is she still seeing Hetherington?"

"I imagine so." Hubert did not seem unduly concerned. "He's got himself a job with the Forestry Commission in Gloucestershire. It isn't all that far away and I can see it having a nicely isolated cottage for a love-nest! I don't suppose you'd consider having her to live here, like Grandmother Clem did when she was dowager?"

Steven shook his head firmly. "Out of the question, I'm afraid. Apart from the fact that she's such a disruptive force these days, she's suspected of wanting to run the stable."

"Oh, well, I thought I'd ask," Hubert said, perfectly philosophical about it. "I'm thinking of demolishing the old Dower House and putting a new one up – that might make her happy."

"And Helen?" Steven asked.

"I've sent her to be finished," Hubert said. "I doubt if it will improve her, but it gets her out of the way for a couple of years."

Giles elected to spend three years at Exeter University, studying modern history. Secretly, Amelia was disturbed, not only by his going, but by the fact that everyone thought it was a good thing. She was at a loss to imagine why Giles and his supporters imagined that a degree would help him to train racehorses when his time came. Amelia also had the uncomfortable feeling that Giles would have been better served by the discipline of Cannings Ambo than the liberal environment of a new university.

259

Another eighteen-year-old was making an important move that autumn.

Jacques Guillaume left the special school in Paris with some of his shortcomings smoothed out. Marie-Claire gave him two months at the château, then asked Alain de Mourville for a favour: could a job be found for her son that would take him away, preferably for good?

When he had begun to rebuild the family fortunes after the War, Alain had bought a number of run-down companies very cheaply. All were now doing well, particularly the haulage firm based at Epinal in the Vosges. With prosperity bringing an ever-increasing movement of goods between countries, the much-enlarged depot at Epinal was the centre of a network that extended from Milan to Calais and used over one hundred of the most modern lorries.

Taken to see for himself, Jacques was impressed and jumped at the offer of a job as a trainee mechanic. Hoping that the good Lord would forgive her, Marie-Claire heaved a great sigh of relief.

When Astronomer Royal went to Cannings St John in October to be prepared for stud duties, it was a happy experience for Bess that finally made up for the loss of his brother, Apollinaire.

Finding the idea of using the van to take him ridiculous, Bess rode the Triple Crown winner across Cannings Down to his new home, unaware that she was following in the footsteps of Leander on Bellerophon in 1876. At a sedate canter, the journey took five minutes instead of the two minutes thirty-six seconds in which he had covered the same distance at Epsom on 1 June.

Lady Amaryllis Timberlake hurried from her office at the noise of hoofs on cobbles.

"Gracious!" she laughed. "It's obvious when you think about it, but one doesn't expect a new stallion to arrive under his own steam!" She moved forward to hold the colt's head while Bess dismounted. Noel Timberlake, who insisted on spending part of each day with his mother at work, came running out to see what all the fuss was about. Aware of the potential danger of horses, he stood at a respectful distance, stricken with wonder.

"Do you think Noel could sit on him?" Lady Amaryllis asked.

"Of course, ma'am," Bess replied. Crouching down, she opened her arms invitingly. The little boy ran to her, squeaking with delight as she swung him into the saddle. Astronomer Royal, turning his head to find out what was going on, gave Bess a look that reduced Lady Amaryllis to hysterics. "I'm blessed if I know," it seemed to say. "Here am I, the first Triple Crown winner for thirty-one years, and I'm giving rides to kids!"

Noel's treat took him all the way round the stud's new perimeter track to the palatial stallion boxes. As they went, Lady Amaryllis commented on her son's shining eyes and enraptured expression. "I can't work out whether it's you or the horse he's besotted with," she whispered to Bess.

After Astronomer Royal had been handed over to the groom who was to look after him, Lady Amaryllis gave Bess the final reassurance that she had hoped for.

"You will feel free to come and see your boy whenever you like, won't you, Bess?"

"Thank you, ma'am. Yes, I will."

"I've still got millions of things to learn about horses, but I know he'll be all the better for seeing you. Mr Hawksworth goes on *endlessly* about how incredibly close you are to him . . . he swears that the results wouldn't have been half as good without you."

Bess, always ill at ease with praise, smiled bashfully. "I'll come and see him twice a week."

There were times when she felt half-guilty about what the colt had earned her. Between them, Steven and Charles had given her over £6,000 for her part in the miraculous year; there was also the prodigious winning bet on the Two Thousand Guineas.

Bess's savings now stood at £41,760, a seemingly indecent

amount of money to have made from a job that was its own reward. Yet Bess was certain it was what Leander had intended.

Her purpose remained a mystery.

CHAPTER 10

1962

'I'll cope with this my way'

In 1860, Laidlaw's veterinary practice had dealt with pigs, sheep and poultry. Perched on a ridge between Cannings St John and the next village towards Devizes, there was no call for any other skills until Giles Flamsteed arrived at Latimer's Barn. Thereafter, continuous association with the stable had ensured at least two horse specialists in every subsequent generation of the family.

Outsiders were never allowed into the business, especially after the Hawksworths, with their steady flow of work and wonderfully prompt payment, put the enterprise on a sound footing. However, in 1961, after nearly ten years of coping by the skin of their teeth, the brothers Dennis and Cecil finally admitted that a combination of war losses, infertility, feuds, and downright bad judgement had landed them with a crisis: they had only one son between them. Since Dennis was systematically drinking himself to death, there was no alternative to changing the rules and taking on an assistant from outside.

Richard Morton came from a big practice in Newmarket, where, although he dealt single-handedly with one of the town's biggest stables, he was treated like an office boy by the senior partners. Sensing the frailty of the Laidlaws' grip on their business, Morton saw that a move to Wiltshire could bring rapid advancement. At twenty-nine, he envisaged himself in control of a practice that attended to Latimer's Barn and the smaller stables to the north of Marlborough by the time he was thirty-five. All that he needed was a worthwhile slice of capital to buy himself in.

Cecil Laidlaw, the one who did not drink, did his best to keep Latimer's Barn to himself, only allowing Dennis's son to carry out follow-up treatment for minor ailments. It was a punitive strategy that allowed few weekends off and no holidays. Richard Morton was told to look after some of the small stables near Ogbourne. Before long, Cecil was receiving good reports of his new assistant: Morton had a first-class eye for diagnosis, and treatment techniques that were an effective blend of traditional and modern methods. After three months, he was allowed a crack at Latimer's Barn, albeit under the strictest supervision.

The results were gratifying. The two most influential members of the yard staff, Alfred Merriweather and Bess, were impressed.

"Your new man, Morton, seems to have found favour, Cecil," Steven said after the trial had been going on for several weeks. "Why don't you let him get on with it? You could even go away for a few days!"

Embarrassed that the strains under which he had been working were so apparent, Cecil Laidlaw complied.

Richard Morton was tall, had the sort of classic, clean-cut features that Bess had always admired, and carried himself with the air of the natural athlete. And, as they worked together, she discovered that he could talk amusingly and informatively on an astounding range of topics, providing insights into the world beyond Cannings Ambo.

Sensing the way the wind was blowing, Elsie was relieved. She was proud of the way Bess had made herself a force to be reckoned with in the stable, but feared that something might have been lost in the process. Although Boggysevick laughed at the idea that Bess had turned herself into a bit of a tomboy in order to compete on equal terms in the yard, Elsie worried. When Richard Morton began to put a new, softer tone into Bess's voice, Elsie grabbed every chance to nudge and encourage her daughter towards closer friendship with the handsome vet. Eventually, Bess was asked out to dinner and Elsie was overjoyed.

That first evening together was pleasantly relaxed. Bess told Richard of how she came to be at Latimer's Barn, he recounted his struggle to become a vet against the wishes of his family. The Mortons, it seemed, owned a chain of garages in Kent and East Sussex. "They're an avaricious mob," Richard said, pulling a face.

"And they wanted you in with them?" Bess asked.

"Naturally. I was the golden boy that was going to raise the tone. My father and two uncles started on a bomb-site after the War and they've never shaken off the slightly shady image. They spent a fortune on my education so that I could pull them out of it."

"Were they upset when you refused?"

"Upset! It was the end of the world! I was disowned. If it hadn't been for a maiden aunt in Essex, I'd never have got through university."

On their next evening together, Bess discovered how truly appalling the brothers Morton were: Richard's mother was in a mental asylum. "The poor love went off the rails five years ago when the old man started an affair with one of the bloody office girls," Richard said bitterly. "It wasn't all that serious, but they managed to get her put away."

"Wouldn't divorce have been simpler?" Bess asked.

"Mother wouldn't agree to it. In any case, this doesn't cost Father a penny."

"She's surely not shut up and ignored, is she?" Bess asked.

"Not on your life! I make damned sure I see her most weekends. It's a bit of a chore going all the way to Canterbury, but I have some good friends there who look after me and the nurses say it's the only thing that keeps her going."

After expressing horror, Bess was happy to let the disturbing topic slip away into the background.

They fell into the habit of dining in Chippenham or Bath on

Mondays and Thursdays. Bess was sure that Richard's choice of venue was designed to protect her from gossip. Instead of parading her round Marlborough as if to say: "Look, you lot, the inaccessible Bess Collier is my girlfriend," he was at pains to preserve her privacy. He also conducted their courtship with a decorum that was at once old-fashioned and mildly irritating. They invariably stopped for a kiss and cuddle on the way back: although Bess was grateful that Richard showed no desire to maul her, she soon wished for more enthusiasm to enhance the agreeable sensations induced by their kissing.

When he did eventually suggest that she might like to see his cottage, Bess agreed with an eagerness that made them both laugh.

"I hope you understand that there's every chance I shall want to seduce you once I get you there," he said, doing his best to make a joke of it.

"I shall be disappointed if you don't," she replied, not quite matching his levity.

For as long as she could remember, Bess had been aware of the richly fulfilling sexual bond between her mother and Boggysevick: she wanted to experience the wonder for herself and was not disappointed. Everything, from Richard's admiration of her body, to his careful entry into her, their increasingly wild motion, and the harmonious climaxes seemed perfect.

For a while, love-making occupied the role of an agreeable addition to the mainstream of the relationship. The change came on a Saturday night in November. Instead of spending the whole of that weekend with his mother in Canterbury, Richard was on call for the practice and Bess stayed all night at his cottage. What began as an almost routine act of affection suddenly caught fire, becoming nearly six hours of incandescent passion.

There was no turning back. As 1962 began, Bess revelled in the insatiable appetite she had for Richard Morton.

It was to be Kathleen Frobisher's last year as doctor of Cannings Ambo and Joe Collier, with an eighteen-month stint as a houseman at St George's Hospital in London behind him, was acting as her understudy, preparing to take over. When he returned to the village, Joe brought a wife with him. Eileen Collier, a pretty brunette who came originally from Devon, was a teacher and an absolute godsend. At seventy-five, Amelia was beginning to think of retirement and Eileen was the ideal replacement.

Once Eileen was secure in her new job, Emma was Amelia's greatest worry. For weeks, she had been experiencing headaches, the severity of which she struggled to conceal. Amelia suspected that there were other symptoms, such as wildly erratic vision and spells of giddiness, although they were never mentioned. On Easter Monday 1962, it all became very bad; Emma was in a state of collapse and Amelia sent for Kathleen. She brought Joe with her. After they had examined Emma and conferred in hushed tones, Kathleen asked Amelia's permission to use the telephone: she wanted an ambulance.

"What is it?" Amelia asked, desperately worried.

"We aren't sure," Kathleen replied. "That's why we want to take her to hospital for X-ray."

"I'll see that Steven knows," Amelia said.

It was 23 April, St George's Day, and the latest that Easter could fall. Steven had gone to Newbury with three horses and was not expected home until six o'clock at the earliest. In fact, much to Ann's relief, he arrived at five-thirty.

"What's up?" he asked when he saw the look on her face.

"Your mother has been taken ill," she said, acutely conscious that she was not as calm as she would have liked. "Kathleen and Joe took her for an X-ray, now she's gone to the Princess Margaret at Swindon. Kathleen hopes they'll operate this evening."

"What's the trouble?" Steven asked.

"It's a brain tumour, darling."

"Oh. I see." Ann had never seen him so cast down. For a few moments, she thought he was going to cave in. The effort with which he pulled himself together was painfully evident. "Can we go over there?" he asked.

"Yes, I"m ready now."

"What about Rachel?"

"I telephoned her an hour ago. She was going straight to the hospital."

Before setting out, Steven told Alfred Merriweather where he was going and why. "You never know, Alfred, it might be a long night. If I'm not back in the morning, make sure everything goes smoothly. You've got the latest work schedules, haven't you?"

"I have, sir. Good luck. I hope she's all right."

Then, pointing the way to a decision that would surprise people in two years' time, Steven also told Bess.

Rachel was at the hospital, greeting them with the news that Emma had been in the operating theatre for nearly an hour.

"I'm sorry I'm so late." Overawed by circumstances and the surroundings, Steven whispered. "I was at Newbury."

"Don't worry, dear." Rachel moved to sit at his side. "Everything possible is being done." For a while, she seemed completely composed until she said, "Oh, Steven, I don't want our mother to die," in a small, frightened voice.

Steven reached out to grasp her hand. He was still holding it nearly three hours later when a staff nurse came to tell them that the operation was over.

"How is she?" Rachel and Steven asked simultaneously.

"We think she's going to be all right," the nurse replied. "I'm afraid there isn't much point in you waiting . . . it's going to be a very long time before she wakes up. You could come and see her tomorrow afternoon."

"You will let us know if anything . . . er . . . develops?" Steven asked urgently.

"Of course, Mr Hawksworth."

"Rachel, would you like to come and stay with us until we know how things are going to work out?" Ann said.

The gratitude was instantaneous and sincere. Now settled into the new Dower House, accompanied by a maid who could put up with her, Rachel saw Hubert once a week and Edmund, who was proving to be an excellent estate manager, more frequently. Even allowing for her still regular, albeit much more discreet, encounters with Hetherington, it was not an ideal situation in which to face a bereavement that Ann saw was going to be a heavy blow.

"Rachel is very upset about your mother," Ann said to Steven as they were getting ready for bed.

"Well, of course she is! She's not a monster." For the first time in their twenty-year marriage, Steven snapped at her. His contrition came at once. "I say, I'm awfully sorry, darling. This is making me very edgy."

Ann understood.

The following afternoon, they found Emma, her head swathed in bandages, very drowsy and not entirely of this world. But she soon demonstrated that she was in possession of some faculties.

"They've shaved my head!" she said. "I shall look a terrible mess."

"You can have a wig, Mother." Relief at finding Emma so chirpy made Rachel inclined to giggle.

"A wig! I shall look a fearful old freak!"

"Only if it's a bright red one," Steven said. After ten minutes of banter, he slipped away to have a word with the sister.

During the ensuing weeks, Bess and Richard Morton shared the general anxiety for Emma.

"She's making some progress, I think," Bess said one evening. "It's a slow business, though."

"Bound to be. The operation must be nearly as bad as the illness. How old is she?"

"About seventy."

Richard shook his head. "She's one of the last of the old school . . . she was Ollie Derwent's daughter, you know."

"Yes. Mrs Hawksworth – Leander, that is – told me all about it. He used to have Saxon Court up at Compton Norris in Berkshire."

"He was a damned good trainer, by all accounts," Richard said. "Not in the Latimer's Barn league, of course."

There was a hint of irritation in Bess's brief smile. For all his easy-going gentleness, she had discovered that Richard admired success to a degree that sometimes made her uneasy. He was always singing the stable's praises, yet Bess was starting to see that his eulogies often had a hidden meaning: by drawing attention to Steven's achievements, Richard was inviting praise for himself, the man whose talents kept the horses in the sound health vital for their racecourse triumphs.

She also knew of his ambitions towards Laidlaw's business. For six months, the sum needed to procure a partnership had been drifting inexorably upwards from fifteen to twenty thousand pounds. Bess thought about it a great deal. Ought she to give, or lend, Richard the money? No, it was best if that were governed by his proposal of marriage, a subject Elsie was raising with unwelcome regularity. In any case, if Richard did ask, what was her response to be?

Richard interrupted her thoughts. "By the way, has any decision been taken about sending that filly to Longchamp?"

"Oh, yes!" The mention of an important race galvanised Bess. "She's going for the Prix Saint-Alary on the twenty-first."

"Leaving on the twentieth?"

"Yes."

Richard reached for his appointments diary. "I'll be down to give her the once-over at nine o'clock."

It had become a standard routine. Steven and Alain de Mourville had been flying horses between England and France for two years.

"Is she going to win?" Richard asked.

"She's very good," Bess said. "One of mine's been working alongside her for three weeks. Mind you, Jimmy's doubtful."

"Aha, the omniscient Farrant!" Richard's smile did not make up for his sarcastic tone.

"Jimmy knows what he's talking about," Bess said hotly. "He thinks Monsieur de Mourville is running her a class too high." She began to clear away the remains of the meal.

Nowadays, they hardly ever ate out, agreeing that it wasted too much time. Richard enjoyed cooking and had excelled himself that evening with salmon steaks.

"Leave those dishes," he said, jumping up to embrace her. "I'll do them later."

Guiding her upstairs, he sensed a slight reluctance. Unconcerned, he proceeded at his usual unhurried pace, removing her clothes with devout care. Proud of her body and relishing his admiration of it, Bess began to relax. When he bent to kiss her inner thighs, she quivered with anticipation: as his tongue went higher, she consciously waved a temporary farewell to sense and reason.

Emma was allowed out of hospital after five weeks, returning to live with Steven and Ann at The House. Everyone, including Emma herself, accepted this as a practical necessity. Although her life had been saved, the brutal truth was that the deliverance was tenuous, leaving her in need of constant attention and care.

While Kathleen and Joe took it in turns to look in on her twice a day, Rachel withdrew to Eaton Mandeville. There was a widespread understanding that her retreat stemmed not from indifference, but an inability to accept the state to which her mother had been reduced.

The Duke of Laverstoke did not need reminding that he had a problem. Having inherited the title at least ten years sooner than the earliest estimate that had ever crossed his mind, it was his duty to provide an heir.

First, there was the far from trivial task of finding a duchess.

Carefully avoiding the heavy-handedness that she knew would be counter-productive, Rachel arranged for a procession of suitable girls to be placed in her elder son's path. He treated them all with unfailing courtesy, always concealing his dismay at their *un*suitability. Sooner or later, they all cottoned on to the fact that they were not required and faded away. All, that is, except one.

Lady Leonie Pryce-Renshawe was boisterously attractive in a tomboyish sort of way and thought that a handsome young duke touting for a wife was a hell of a hoot. A year older than Hubert, she was the owner of an exclusive travel agency for the wealthy, discerning and eccentric. "If you fancy a month in Timbuktu or a yak trek to Kathmandu, you need me!" was her slogan.

They became friends to the extent that Hubert bought her lunch or dinner whenever he happened to be in London and not engaged in a business meeting. Politely declining the offer to follow in his father's footsteps at Lambert's, he used his old-Etonian contacts to obtain places on the board of Stewart's, a merchant bank, and a number of Government advisory bodies.

In February 1962, Hubert had invited Leonie to Eaton Mandeville for a weekend.

"Why?" she demanded, making a meal of the mock-suspicion.

"I'm having a bit of a shindig for my twenty-fifth birthday and I thought your presence might shut Mother up."

"Give her the idea that we're actively pursuing negotiations?" Leonie suggested.

"Precisely . . . although it beats me why she ever thought you were 'suitable'," Hubert said.

"Do you keep anything decent in the stables?" Leonie asked.

"Naturally."

"And am I to be the only fabulously beautiful young woman at this séance?"

"Yes."

"All right. I'll be down on Friday evening, but I've no idea what time, so don't hang around with dinner."

She arrived at eight-thirty to find him eating soup and sandwiches while poring over papers in his study.

"You poor old sod!" she chortled.

"I don't bother much when I'm on my own," he said. "You can have something more exotic. Let Mrs Angell show you to your room and I'll organise it."

"Hubert, do you think I could be an absolute pig and have an omelette in bed?" Leonie asked. "A bunch of Americans have just given me the worst two days ever known to man or beast and I'm utterly knackered."

"Of course, anything you want."

"Gawd bless you, Your Grace!" Leonie bowed and scraped, tugging at a lock of her hair. "I'll be as fresh as a daisy tomorrow, honest, O most stupendous importance!"

Before his housekeeper's astonished gaze, Hubert waved a hand dismissively. "Go away, you wretch, I must get on with this work."

Leonie was as good as her word, appearing at breakfast ready for a day's riding. There were only a handful of things that could stop her acting the fool for any length of time: one was her work, another was getting on a horse. During her teens she had been horse-mad, getting as far as a couple of Badminton trials. She sat on a horse wonderfully well and was aware that Hubert had noticed how good she looked.

The bitingly cold day curtailed their excursion to only three hours; even so, they were still able to look over the greater part of the estate.

"This is pretty decent, isn't it?" Leonie said, surveying the woodland, all of it in good heart. "It's nice to see land being looked after so well. Some girl is going to be lucky . . . any idea who?"

"Not a clue." Disquiet clouded his reply. "I don't want to marry simply to get a son."

"Why not? Isn't it what our class have always done? Ma and Pa are frightfully keen on each other, but they're exceptional."

"My lot have a tradition of love-matches," Hubert said.

"What about your parents?"

"They were happy enough at first. Something went wrong in the War, I think."

Sceptical about the overworked excuse, Leonie shivered. "Can we go back, Hubert? This wind's getting beyond a joke."

After a lunch consisting of whisky, hot soup and two

immense slices of fruit-cake, Leonie announced that she was going up to her room for a hot bath and a rest to prepare for the ordeal of dinner. During their ride, Hubert had informed her that he had felt honour-bound to add a bunch of local worthies to the guest-list. After checking with his butler, Mr Angell, that everything was proceeding smoothly towards dinner and that the extra servants were sure to arrive, Hubert decided to follow Leonie's example. After his bath, he found that he was in no mood to rest. Instead, he came to a momentous decision. Pulling on a towelling robe, he hurried along two corridors to Leonie's room.

"Come in!" Her answer to his knock was distant, but clarion clear.

Framed by the door to the bathroom, Leonie was brushing her hair. She was quite naked.

"Have you come for your birthday present?" she asked. Hubert's purposeful advance was answer enough. "Good! I was hoping you would."

Leonie Pryce-Renshawe was one of the few people who had not, on meeting Hubert, made the mistake of thinking him pleasant, but somewhat ineffectual. The ninth Duke of Laverstoke was, she had decided, a young man who knew exactly what he wanted and how to get it. The way he embraced her, his hands roving over her body with expert firmness, proved her intuition.

"Let's have one thing straight," he said. "This does *not* mean that I want to marry you."

"I'd be off like a bloody flash if you did," she retorted. "I've seen what being a duchess did to Aunt Victoria." Her tone changed. "However, that doesn't stop us enjoying ourselves."

"It doesn't!" Hubert agreed. "I must say, Leo, you're rather smashing! You feel absolutely lovely."

"Thank you!" She unfastened his robe and pushed it from his shoulders. "You're rather gorgeous yourself, young sir! And I see you do believe in getting things straight . . . very straight indeed!"

After that, she stopped joking: sex was another of the topics that Lady Leonie treated seriously.

Rachel detected the change between Hubert and Leonie the moment she arrived from the Dower House. As the forty dinner-guests gathered, Hubert was here, there and everywhere, acting the perfect host. Leonie remained firmly anchored in front of a blazing fire, letting people come to her, and they all did, drawn by her sheer good spirits and down-to-earth beauty. Although Hubert stayed away from her, the occasional look that passed between them was enough for Rachel.

It was the same over dinner itself. Leonie and Hubert were seated well apart, yet the looks were still there, especially when County Councillor Sir Bernard Morrison made several attempts to become tedious on the subject of planning permission.

Satisfied that she was witnessing the genesis of a process that would transform Lady Leonie into a duchess before the year was out, Rachel led a comparatively early departure at ten o'clock. Half an hour later, even the stragglers had gone, finally shifted by the first flakes of snow and the prospect of blocked roads. One of Hubert's banking friends was staying overnight, but since he had turned up with a wanton-looking girl who was a photographic model and would-be actress, Hubert and Leonie were soon alone.

"That wasn't too bad," he said.

"I've known worse. Tell you one thing, though." Despite the fact that they were completely isolated in the huge house, she leaned forward confidentially. "Your mother needs watching."

Hubert smiled wryly. "She spent the whole evening jumping to conclusions about us."

"No, no, I don't mean that," Leonie said hurriedly. "It's difficult to explain . . . she strikes me as a woman eaten up by some sort of hatred . . . or ambition, perhaps. I think she's bloody dangerous."

Hubert stirred uneasily. "I know what you mean," he muttered. "I don't think it's got anything to do with us."

"No, but you need to bear it in mind. Now, are you up to a spot more exercise?"

"Yes, please!"

This time, they spread themselves on an eiderdown in front of the log fire in Leonie's bedroom, stretching out the preliminaries in an act of hedonistic mutual admiration.

"You're pretty damned good at this," she said, writhing voluptuously under his caresses. "Quite unusual in one so young!"

"I had an expert tutor at Oxford."

"Not the dreaded all-purpose landlady?"

"No, as I said, my tutor . . . an attractive lady of a certain age who thought there was much more to life than essays about the growth of nationalism in the nineteenth century."

"God bless her! Come on, I want it."

When she finally recovered from the splendid piece of indulgence that followed, Leonie had a suggestion.

"Look, you get up to London a fair bit, so we can do this regularly. Let's face it, Hubert, it's bloody nearly impossible for people like us to get a good screw."

"Very, very true," he said.

"The newspapers are getting to be a complete pain in the bum," Leonie went on. "You probably haven't noticed, but some imbecile has decided that London is 'swinging' and they're continually grubbing for dirt."

"They had a go at Honoria, didn't they?"

Leonie's younger sister had suffered a brief period of lurid notoriety the previous autumn as a result of her affair with a taxi-driver. "Earl's daughter in romp with cabbie!" screamed a new type of headline. Honoria had been frog-marched off to the family's estate in Sutherland, and was now engaged to the son of the local laird, a callow individual of surpassing ordinariness.

"Well, what do you think?" Leonie asked. "I'm only ten

minutes from Paddington, so we could be hard at it by seven if you caught the five-ten from Chippenham."

"Leo, I think that's the best idea I've heard for a long time," Hubert grinned.

As they began to spend one night a week together, Hubert soon discovered that Leonie had other assets besides her sensuous virtuosity: she was well-established on the periphery of London's social life and knew a great deal about what the so-called 'top people' were up to. Twice, she was able to provide information that was of value to Stewart's bank, and it was Leonie who acquired early news of Helen after her return from Switzerland in June.

"That charming sister of yours has got herself a job as PA to Harrison Delaney," she said as they tucked into a Chinese meal one evening.

"Really?" Hubert laughed. "That pair deserve one another." Delaney, a property developer, was responsible for an ever-increasing number of office blocks that were disfiguring the skyline of London and a number of provincial cities. Both his private life and business methods were dubious.

"She is also," Leonie added, "seeing a great deal of Freddie Christopherson."

For nearly a year, Freddie, now twenty-two, had been nominally at the helm of the family-owned bank, Sir Miles having been laid low by a stroke. The assumption was that he was held in check by the senior staff, but at least in name and salary, Freddie was enjoying exalted status.

"Do we know how serious that is?" Hubert asked.

"It looks downright frenzied at the moment," Leonie replied. "They were at 'Rasher' Bacon's place for dinner last week and disappeared between courses. Gertie found them in the conservatory, hard at it!"

Hubert glowered. "You mean . . . ?"

"Yes, Your Grace, indulging in sexual intercourse! Dashed bad form, eh? And Young Lochinvar hadn't even bothered to take his dinner jacket off."

277

Hubert looked sourly disapproving. He must, he told himself, step up his efforts not to discuss business in front of Helen. Niggling away at the back of his mind was the feeling that there was another reason why a liaison between Helen and Freddie was a bad thing.

That summer, Giles Hawksworth spent the whole of the long university vacation at Latimer's Barn. The parlous state of Emma's health was a major factor in his decision to forsake the large circle of friends to whom he had committed himself for the past two years. He was also aware that it was time to show more interest in the stable. The pressure on him to do so was increased by Oliver, who finally made it plain that he wanted nothing to do with horses.

"I hope I'm not too much of a disappointment," he said. "But I've never thought I had the talent – or whatever it is – to do anything here."

"Have you any idea what you *would* like to do?" Ann asked.

"Not a clue!" Oliver responded, terrifyingly cheerful. "There's a lot of talk about television – it's supposed to be a brilliant career. Old Wilkins suggested I should have a go at law, but it sounds too much like hard work." He pulled a gruesome face, making Ann wonder where she, poor Mr Wilkins and several others had gone wrong.

Oliver's indifference, openly declared and accepted, put Giles on the spot: he *had* to accept his destined role. Rebecca added to the strain by her competence and enthusiasm. Fourteen, enjoying life to the full at the Godolphin School in Salisbury where, like Amelia sixty years before her, she played a fiendish game of cricket, Rebecca had made herself completely at home in the stable. By contrast, Giles had set himself apart: it was time to make up for lost time.

He rode out with Steven for both lots each morning and dutifully trailed round in his father's wake at evening stables. It took Giles two days to realise that he was a fairly useless appendage in a world that was frighteningly arcane.

The lads were ill at ease in Giles's presence, not knowing

278

what to make of him. His ignorance of the job was common knowledge and taken for granted. Giles was treated with respect, but it was formal and starchy, lacking the affection normally given to members of his family.

He found a friend in Bess and decided to put his cards on the table. "Look, Bess, I've neglected my education as far as this place is concerned. To be perfectly honest with you, I haven't got the first idea what goes on." He paused, frowning thoughtfully. "No, that's not strictly right . . . I know what happens, but how it fits together is beyond me."

"Afternoons are a good time," Bess said briskly. "Unless one of my horses is racing, I'm free from half past one until five."

At Giles's suggestion most of the lessons took place on Cannings Down, where he and Bess rode out on hacks. If it was wet, they sat in the tack-room of the 1874 yard. As she laid bare the mysteries of her craft, Giles learned and became happier. He also marvelled at the depth of her knowledge and dedication.

"Are all the lads as good as you?" he asked.

"Of course!" Bess's loyalty was total.

"They all know as much as you?"

"Well . . ." She smiled hesitantly. "Perhaps I know a bit more than *some* of them. Now, come on, it'll soon be time for me to go back to work and I want to make sure you understand how we grade the two-year-olds."

At the end of the second week of lessons, Elsie became nervous.

"Bess, you aren't getting involved with Mr Giles, are you?" she asked over supper one evening.

"Don't be silly, Mom!" Bess found the idea absurd. "He's out of my league . . . in any case, he's too young for me. He's still growing up and he must have dozens of girlfriends at university."

"Just you make sure that Richard's nose doesn't get put out of joint," Elsie insisted. "He'll be getting round to popping the question soon."

Always sensitive to Bess's moods, Boggysevick detected her discomfort and changed the subject.

"How is the education of the young master proceeding, my dear?" he asked. Over the years, he had diminished his Polish accent by making his use of English more stilted.

Bess shrugged. "He's all right. I'll make something of him."

Solstice, who often looked in for supper with Elsie and Boggysevick, shook his head. "Do your best, my love," he said. "Any improvement will be much appreciated by one and all."

"Why? What are they saying in the yard?" Bess demanded. "Come on, Solstice, spit it out!"

He looked tense. You had to be brave when Bess was in this mood: either that, or run away. "They're hoping it won't be too much longer before women are allowed to have a licence. That would give Miss Rebecca a chance and she's the best option by thirty lengths."

"Don't be ridiculous!" Bess snapped. "A woman couldn't run this place."

"What the hell do you think Leander did for the best part of seventy years?" Elsie asked.

"That was different," Bess said. "There'll never be another one like her. And in any case, she never actually ran it . . . there was always a man up front."

"Jim Goakes wouldn't agree," Solstice said.

"What do you mean?" Bess asked sharply.

"He said his piece in The George the other night. He reckons Miss Rebecca *could* do it. All right, she's no Leander, but she's got her head screwed on. You can see Dame Amelia in her."

The discovery that the topic was being openly discussed appalled Bess. She was determined that the dissension and wrangling that was permeating every aspect of British life must not be allowed to take root in Cannings Ambo. "Solstice, you tell your boozing pals that Mr Giles will be up to the job, right?" she said forcefully. "And what are we talking about, anyway? I don't think Mr Steven is fifty yet . . . he's got *years* ahead of him."

In October, Giles returned to Exeter with mixed feelings. For the first time in his life, he had begun to feel something for Latimer's Barn: on the other hand, he was relieved to have escaped from Bess's training. Once she had found out what people were saying about him, her redoubled efforts made Giles wonder if there was a fearsome examination at the end of it all.

Three weeks into the autumn term of his final year, he was back home for his grandmother's funeral.

The end was mercifully quick.

As he did every night, Steven sat with Emma between ten o'clock and eleven on 19 October. At first, their conversation was desultory and disjointed as her mind wandered more than usual, unable to fix on anything for more than a few seconds. It was a distressing business that always made Steven feel that part of him was dying with her.

Tonight, however, after a five-minute silence, he found her gazing at him in a way that recalled the years of her prime.

"Today is my golden wedding anniversary," she said.

Steven stared back at her, incapable of framing a response. For forty-five of those fifty years, his mother had been a widow. She saw what he was thinking and reached out for his hand.

"I've been much luckier than most of the women who lost husbands in that war . . . I had Leander and you. You stopped me from going mad, Steven." She closed her eyes. "The best son a mother ever had. Everyone said so." Opening her eyes wide, she smiled at him. "For once, 'everyone' was right!"

"And Rachel," Steven murmured. "You can be very proud of her."

After a few moments, he realised that Emma's silence was deliberate, not an accidental product of her mental state. One of her guiding principles had always been: "If you can't speak well of someone, don't speak at all." He was sure that she was applying it now.

"Fifty years ago today," Emma said, and her face lit up, "we went to Torquay for our honeymoon and Hubert's grandfather drove us to Reading to get the train. The station-master gave me a bouquet. We were *so* happy, Steven . . . like you are with Ann. Look after her and take notice of what she says . . . she's strong . . ." Her concentration went and she appeared to lapse into semi-consciousness. "Fifty years ago today," she repeated dreamily. "I shall be with him again tonight. How lovely!"

Emma Hawksworth achieved her last wish: she died at a few minutes to midnight.

At first, everyone thought it natural that Steven should take his mother's death so badly and sympathised. He had, after all, been devoted to Emma. It was two days after the funeral when Rachel, the last of the guests to leave, had returned to Eaton Mandeville that Ann saw that he was seriously disturbed.

"Tell me about it," she said, when a long and difficult day was over and she had him in bed.

He shook his head, in bewilderment, not refusal. "I can't understand it, darling," he said. "If anything was going to be the end of an era, you'd have thought it would be Leander going, wouldn't you?"

"I told you *not* to think that," Ann reminded him.

"Yes, you did. This is different. It's something to do with the way the world is changing and what Mother stood for."

"We've still got Amelia," Ann pointed out.

"She's seventy-five," Steven said.

"And look at her! She's as sprightly as anything. Did you hear that she's a leading light on yet another committee?"

"What is it this time?"

"The Kennet and Avon Trust."

"What are they up to?"

"They're going to re-open the canal," Ann said with deliberately child-like simplicity, as though the job was expected to be finished next Thursday.

Steven spluttered. The Kennet and Avon Canal, neglected

since long before the War, was falling into dereliction. Bringing it back into use was not merely a question of dredging out weeds and silt, there were major engineering obstacles to be overcome. "They'll never do it," he said. "Have you seen the state of those locks at Devizes?"

"They think it might take them fifteen years," Ann replied. "A lot of people have promised to help and Amelia is one of the whippers-in."

"Good luck to her!" Steven said. He was tremendously proud of his aunt and news of her latest exploit seemed to buck him up. Ann hoped that the worst of his introspection was over.

Two weeks after Emma's funeral, Leonie had some news that Hubert found unpalatable and disturbing.

"My mother came across yours at one of Frieda Dickens's ghastly soirées."

"Oh?" Hubert raised an eyebrow, attempting to look interested. They were lying on Leonie's bed, drifting in the aftermath of love-making.

"They talked about us," Leonie went on.

"Naturally."

"Then your mama seems to have gone on blind about Latimer's Barn."

"Really?" Hubert's interest was genuine now. "What was she saying?"

"I was afraid you'd ask that," Leonie groaned. "The trouble is, Mother doesn't know the first thing about racing, and she gets bored frightfully easily. Anyway, as far as I can see, your mama thinks that the stable isn't being run properly. It's gone to the dogs – if you'll pardon the expression – since she was in charge of it."

Hubert sniffed sardonically. "You won't find anyone queuing up to agree with that nonsense! Steven Hawksworth has been in the top three of the trainers' list for the last fifteen years. And he's winning some damned good races in France."

"Have you got interests there?"

"I'm starting off with some two-year-olds next year. Father had a horse called Astronomer Royal who's well on the way to paying the death duties, so I'm all in favour of the way Steven does things."

Leonie was puzzled. "I know all this is pretty poor second-hand stuff, but I'm sure your mother feels she ought to have a hand in running the place."

"There aren't any vacancies," Hubert said. "Never likely to be, either . . . it's a job for highly trained professionals."

"Isn't she a shareholder – or whatever it's called?"

"She's a Trustee."

"That's it! And she wants Freddie Christopherson to be one, too. Surely that's weird?"

"No, it isn't," Hubert said. Suddenly, he saw why the news of Helen's relationship with Christopherson had bothered him. He recalled being told by his father that most of the Cannings Ambo money was in Switzerland, with Christopherson's acting as the go-between. "Are Helen and Freddie still at it?" he asked.

"Goodness, yes. There's even the faint tintinnabulation of nuptial chimes floating round. Your mother's very keen." Leonie frowned. "Funny, isn't it? Most women lock their daughters up when Freddie appears, yet she thinks he's marvellous."

"In many ways it would be an ideal marriage," Hubert pointed out. "It packs Helen off to a rich family and the Christophersons get the cachet of a duke's daughter. I'd say that was good value all round."

"You're a cynical bastard!" Leonie laughed.

"I'm a cynical bastard who makes a hell of a lot of accurate assessments," the Duke of Laverstoke said.

Hubert waited a week, using much of the time to make inquiries among his close-knit circle of banking friends, before calling in at Latimer's Barn. Ann invited him to stay for dinner and began pulling his leg about the possibility of his engagement.

"You mother expects great things of Leonie," she said.

284

"I can't imagine why, Aunt Ann," Hubert replied. "We've never given her any encouragement to think that we're getting wed. Leo and I are simply friends with interests in common."

"That's what I thought," Ann said, smiling in a way that told him she had a shrewd idea of what those interests were.

Sensing that Hubert had something on his mind, Steven took him into the privacy of the library for a drink before dinner.

"So, that's the famous Big Book, is it?" Hubert said, seeing it open on a side table.

"I'm still trying to think what I can put in about your grandmother," Steven admitted. "It's difficult."

Hubert nodded understandingly. "You could say that she was a lovely lady who spread charm and grace without ever knowing she was doing it."

"That's not bad!" Steven said admiringly.

"It's certainly true. That's how I always saw her. Those five years she spent looking after me in the War were delightful."

Greatly moved, Steven scribbled a few notes on a scrap of paper, then looked up expectantly. "What can I do for you?" he asked.

"I know it's a dreadful cheek, Steven, but I think it might be to the estate's advantage if I became a Trustee." In his usual calm way, Hubert came straight out with it.

"I'd vote for that," Steven replied. "What shall I tell the others – assuming they need convincing?"

"I'm acquiring quite a few good directorships. My major interest is with Stewart's, the bankers, but that probably isn't any use to you. I know you're with Christopherson's and I wouldn't attempt to change your mind, but I could promise Stewart's support if ever you needed it. I do have other contacts that might prove helpful and I intend becoming one of your major owners. I also care very much about Cannings Ambo and want to help protect it."

Over dinner, Ann listened carefully to what Hubert had to

say. "You give the impression that you think we need help of some sort," she said.

"I'm afraid I do."

"Why?"

"The threats of modern life," Hubert replied.

Ann stared at him. He was, she knew, being deliberately vague: pressing him would get her nowhere. "How would you help us?" she asked.

"I can find out things and make sure that I attend all meetings and vote with you."

Steven could see that Ann, though satisfied, was thinking very deeply about something. There was a point he felt bound to make. "Trustees are supposed to live and work in Cannings Ambo."

Ann snapped out of her reverie. "That went by the board ages ago, darling. Look at Mallender and Giffard."

When he felt it was time to be on his way after the meal, Hubert found Steven accompanying him to his car.

"That strikes me as a good idea," Steven said. "I think you can assume that you'll be elected."

"Aunt Ann approves."

"Looks like it!" Steven grinned, but it was a tired and slightly forced gesture, Hubert noticed, lacking the old sense of fun that had gone with Emma.

Back inside The House, Steven found Ann frowning in fierce concentration. "Wasn't that interesting?" she said. "He was quite adamant about it: 'Make sure I attend all meetings and vote with you'," she quoted.

"We were meant to take notice of that, I think," Steven said.

"I jolly well did!" Ann replied. "I think the sooner we make our noble nephew a Trustee, the better."

On 16 November, after devoting over forty-eight hours to ensuring that Bess would have a host of passionate memories to sustain her during his absence, Richard Morton went on holiday for three weeks. He was, he said, intending to remove his mother from the institution to which his father had committed her. Once free, she was to be installed in the house of a long-time friend in Broadstairs.

"How do you go about getting her free?" Bess asked.

"Psychiatrists and solicitors," Richard replied. "It's a dreadful business . . . I've been setting it up for months."

Bess, relieved at an explanation for his occasional abstraction, saw a big bonus to set against the three weeks of separation. "Perhaps you won't have to spend so many weekends with her after this?"

"Right! Once a month should be enough to keep her going."

A week after his departure, one of the yearlings that Bess was schooling for 1963 developed a nasty hoof infection. Cecil Laidlaw came to attend to the filly. A quick worker, he had finished cleansing the hoof and was preparing to administer cream and an injection when Steven turned up to see what was going on.

"What's this, Cecil?" he asked. "I haven't seen you for ages. To what do we owe the honour?"

"That slacker Morton has cleared off on holiday," Cecil grumbled, his head remaining bent to his work. A few moments later, he straightened up with a mischievous grin. "I mustn't be too hard on him . . . he's acquiring the wherewithal to buy into the practice. Between you and me, Steven, I'm going to rob him blind!"

"Where's he gone?" Steven asked. "To hold up a bank?"

"Oh, nothing as easy!" Cecil laughed. "He got himself married last Saturday."

Bess, holding the yearling's head, leaned against the door-post to support herself.

"The lady has money, does she?" Steven asked.

"She does! Needs it, mind." Cecil put a wealth of meaning into the statement. "She's the sourest-faced bitch I've ever come across. Her father's one of them high-speed jerry-builders . . . Crabtree, down Andover way. You've probably heard of him." Steven shook his head. "You've got to admire young Morton's planning," Cecil went on. "As I understand it, he found the fair Jean pretty soon

287

after he got here and he's been working on her ever since. Went over to butter her and the old man up nearly every weekend, I think."

Bess could think only of the extraordinary secrecy in which she and Richard must have shrouded their association. It was utterly bizarre: Cecil Laidlaw and Steven, listening avidly, clearly had no idea. She was so engrossed with the outlandishness of it all that she thought the reverberation in her ears and swimming vision were all part of the hallucinatory scene to which she was a spectator.

When Steven called out, his voice sounded miles away and she was unwilling to believe that it was her name he was shouting.

"Bess . . . what's the matter? Quickly! Sit down." She was guided to a bale of straw. She collapsed on to it and Cecil Laidlaw shoved her head between her knees. Gradually, the noise like roaring water faded and she began to focus her eyes.

"Her colour's coming back," Cecil said.

"I thought you were going to pass out," Steven said. Bess saw that he was badly shaken and worried.

"I'm all right," she said, and was glad when the next lie came more easily. "I haven't been feeling too good for a couple of days."

"You must go home," Steven said earnestly. "Go home and don't let me see you again until you're better. Ah . . . . good!" He ran to the door of the box and waved to Boggysevick who was walking into the yard with a load of hay.

After Steven had given him his instructions, Boggysevick helped Bess through the orchard towards their house. She was horrified to discover how badly she was shaking. Supporting her, Boggysevick respected her desperate need for silence.

"She nearly fainted," Boggysevick told Elsie when they were indoors and Bess, ashen again, had sunk into an armchair. Elsie was always good in a crisis; after what appeared to be only a cursory glance at Bess, she went to the kitchen to make a pot of tea. The cup she brought

288

a few minutes later was laced with whisky, causing Bess to wrinkle her nose in distaste.

"Drink it!" Elsie said firmly.

Bess did and felt better.

"Now, what's all this about?" Elsie asked.

"You know I told you that Richard was going on holiday to see if he could get his mother out of the mental hospital?" Bess said. Elsie nodded, her face sharpening with anticipation. "Well, it seems he lied to me. He went away to get married."

"Married!" After speaking in unison, Elsie and Boggysevick exchanged looks of amazement into which anger was creeping.

"When did he fix this up?" Elsie demanded.

"I've no idea. Cecil Laidlaw says he's known the girl since he came here from Newmarket."

"I am buggered!" Boggysevick said with the strange dignity that always heralded his worst tempers.

"And you had no inkling of this?" Elsie asked. After Bess had shaken her head, Elsie paused before diving in. "You're in love with him, aren't you? And you've been sleeping with him?"

"Yes, Mother," Bess said wearily.

Elsie's answer was to sit on the arm of Bess's chair so that she could comfort her. Boggysevick, thinking that Bess was about to relieve her feelings with a good cry, slipped away.

"What a bastard!" Elsie said.

Bess nodded agreement, not sure whether sorrow or anger was dominating her. For a year, Richard Morton had carried out a cynical deception that was breathtaking in its scope.

A terrible thought struck Elsie. "I as good as pushed you into this, didn't I?" she muttered.

Bess was having none of it. "No, Mother, it *wasn't* your fault! I wanted him badly enough."

Returning about an hour after dark, Boggysevick told them that Richard's cottage was up for sale.

"How do you know?" Elsie asked.

"I drove down in the van to have a look. Solstice went with me. We are going to kill Mr-bloody-Morton."

"No you aren't, Stan," Elsie said mildly. "You might get into trouble." She turned to Bess. "What are you going to do, love? Do you fancy working somewhere else? Tommy O'Neill up at Ogbourne would give anything to have you."

"In more ways than one!" Bess replied grimly. "No, I expect I'll stay." She smiled at Boggysevick's look of deep concern. "Don't worry, Dad, I'll cope with this my way."

Three weeks later, Bess was on tenterhooks as she worked in the yard: Solstice had warned her that Richard Morton was making his first visit to Latimer's Barn since returning from honeymoon. She still felt unable to trust her feelings: the only good thing about the time since the discovery of her lover's treachery had been the gradual realisation that no one, apart from her tight circle of intimate friends, knew anything of the passionate affair into which she had been lured.

She worked slowly, making each task last several times longer than normal, keeping well out of sight as she did so. All the horses in the 1874 yard were bursting with health, so there was no reason why he should come anywhere near her.

At twelve-thirty, as she was beginning to think that he must have gone, she heard hurried footsteps and there he was, in the centre of the cobbled area, looking round, searching. Dignity, and the knowledge that it had to be faced sooner or later, stopped her ducking out of sight behind the lower half of the box door. He ran towards her.

"Bess! How are you?" he asked. At least he was different; on top of his immediate anxiety, there was an underlying tension that made him seem furtive.

"I'm very well, thank you, Richard." She was pleased with her steadiness. "What about *you*?"

"I got married."

"I heard."

He grimaced and shuffled. "I'm sorry about that, Bess. The fact is, I didn't have the guts to tell you."

"How's your mother?" Bess asked pointedly.

Unwilling to admit the full extent of his deception, he remained silent.

"According to Cecil Laidlaw, you've married for money," Bess said.

He laughed nervously. "Well . . . yes . . . that's about the size of it." He pushed at the door. "Let me in, Bess. I *must* talk to you."

"You can do it from there." The forced neutrality of her voice was losing ground to hostility.

"Look here, Bess, this marriage is very much a business arrangement," he said.

"How very old-fashioned of you, Richard!"

"We can still see each other. I'll find a way."

"Tea at the Ailesbury Arms?"

"No, for God's sake! You know what I mean. We're marvellous together." He assumed a tragic expression. "Jean doesn't believe in too much of that sort of thing."

Bess was unable to believe what he was suggesting. "You mean we should carry on going to bed?"

"Yes!"

"As if nothing had happened?"

"Of course!"

Later, Bess realised that it was a good thing she didn't have a whip handy. Whatever else he was, Morton was a bloody good vet: at the very least, Steven Hawksworth would have been extremely embarrassed if she had struck Richard across the face.

"I think you'd better go," she said, white with fury. "Stick to your rich wife and leave me to get on with being a *stable-girl*!"

Ann saw Morton leaving in a state of confusion, but had too much on her mind to give it any thought. There had been yet another row over Freddie Christopherson at that morning's meeting of Trustees. Rachel, determined not to be beaten, had raised his nomination for the sixth time in as many months. As usual, Matthew had spoken strongly against it. There was, he

291

said, little point in having a Trustee whose only connection with Cannings Ambo was a minor business link that should not be regarded as permanent. "At this rate, someone will be suggesting that my timber merchants ought to be Trustees," he concluded in a remarkably outspoken rebuff.

Matthew's opinions carried substantial weight and no one supported Rachel's motion, not even, she noticed bitterly, her own son, Hubert. Unwilling to accept defeat with anything other than bad grace, Rachel treated the meeting to a diatribe, telling them that they seemed hell-bent on ignoring modern developments. When Ann asked which particular developments Freddie Christopherson represented, Rachel stormed off in a huff.

As the year turned and the severe winter of 1963 covered the gallops in deep snow for six weeks, Bess did consider leaving Cannings Ambo. Somehow, the story of her and Richard Morton finally became public knowledge, almost certainly as a result of deliberately loose talk from Morton himself. She went so far as to attend interviews at two stables in Newmarket. In the end, she decided to stay at Latimer's Barn because of an overwhelming feeling that Leander wanted her to.

However, in her twenty-fourth year, Bess saw herself as anything but one of her benefactor's heirs to adventure.

CHAPTER 11

1964

'. . . upstarts in positions of authority'

"This is all set to be a triumph of arrogance and avarice over common sense," Lady Leonie said to Hubert as they prepared to leave for the wedding of Freddie Christopherson and Lady Helen in April.

"You are almost certainly right, my dear," he replied in a tone that was a conscious parody of his usual gravity. "What a pity we didn't have a prior engagement!"

Hubert and Leonie had maintained a close watch on a relationship that seemed to have come to grief twelve months previously.

"The story is that Freddie is somewhat weird between the sheets," Leonie said. "He has proclivities! Informed opinion suggests that your sister has gone in search of a more straightforward approach."

"Has she found someone?"

"It seems so . . . but no one has any idea who he is."

Cavalier with personal relationships unless it suited her to be otherwise, Helen had re-established contact with her school-friend, Amanda Fenton. They met regularly for a drink or a meal, and it was during one of these encounters in the spring of 1963 that Helen asked after Amanda's brother, Roger.

"He's fine," Amanda replied. "Father hasn't been too well so Roger's been taking on more responsibility with the good old family firm." She frowned reflectively. "Actually, he sometimes mentions you. I think you made an impression on him."

"The feeling is mutual," Helen replied. "I wouldn't mind a few days alone with your brother."

"Give him a call," Amanda suggested.

After his recovery from the initial shock of the bolt from the blue, Roger Fenton made sure that Helen knew he was delighted to hear from her.

"How are you?" he asked warmly.

"Find out for yourself . . . what are you doing this weekend?"

"Nothing that can't be cancelled!"

After that first skirmish in Helen's London flat, they met regularly. It was a satisfying, uncomplicated arrangement with no mention of marriage. While they enjoyed themselves, Freddie Christopherson worked hard, pursued a number of girls, and came to the conclusion that he wanted Helen to be his wife. The attractions were her title and beauty; he had no expectations that the union would be remotely conventional. His proposal, made over a mid-week dinner, was accompanied by a statement that made this a compulsory feature.

"What do you think?" Helen asked Roger Fenton a few days later. "He wants a son to inherit his precious bank, then we more or less do what we like."

"He's stinking rich, isn't he?" was the first thing that Roger Fenton wanted to know.

"Rolling in it!"

"I'd do it."

"It's his obsession with an heir that pisses me off," Helen grumbled. "Hubert's the same . . . at least, Mother is on his behalf."

"Dukedoms and merchant banks are important things, my sweet. Your failure to grasp such fundamentals makes you a traitor to your class."

"Balls!" Helen retorted. "And look here, clever-clogs, what happens if I start churning daughters out?"

Fenton laughed immoderately. "He'll chop your head off!"

Helen took the next available opportunity to strike a hard bargain with Freddie. "What's my allowance going to be?" she asked, making no attempt to soften the mercenary brutality of the question.

"Will you keep the pressure on your mother to get me elected as a Cannings Ambo Trustee?" he countered.

"Yes. Although I don't see what good it will do you. As far as I can see, Matthew Flamsteed is dead against you and he pulls a lot of weight."

"Just keep trying. And you promise not to interfere with my 'friendships'?" Freddie himself invested the word with a sneer.

"I wouldn't touch them with a barge-pole," Helen snapped.

"In that case, you can have five thousand a year."

It was generous. Helen knew that her brothers lived very well indeed on half that amount. She accepted and they went shopping for a diamond ring.

It only remained for Helen to spend the week before the wedding with Roger Fenton, while Freddie had several last flings, to make Lady Leonie's assessment of the happy couple stunningly accurate.

The ceremony, which took place in a fashionable London church, and the subsequent function at Claridge's were near-disasters.

Freddie was suffering from a wicked hangover; his best man was the worse for drink consumed that morning. And Sir Miles Christopherson, hanging on to life with malevolent glee, managed to upset an inordinate number of people from the confines of his wheel-chair.

At what passed for a wedding breakfast, the guests split into two factions, those who looked thoroughly disgusted by the whole business, and those who gave them ample justification. Encouraged by a speech from the best man that was mostly smutty innuendo, a group of young people in their early twenties began to pair off in a blatant manner.

"Who on earth are they?" Hubert whispered to Leonie.

"They are the up-and-coming chaps, my dear old geriatric. Our future is in their hands."

"No, I mean what are they *doing* here? Who invited them?"

"I imagine they're friends of the happy couple."

"Are you sure they're not gate-crashers?"

"'Fraid not, Your Grace, they're all bona fide."

"They most certainly are *not*!" Hubert replied angrily. "I've never seen such a rabble. Is it nearly over?" He was looking round. "How soon can we get out of here?"

As they were slipping away, intent on going to Eaton Mandeville for a few quiet days together, they discovered the one good thing to have come out of the fiasco. In the cool sanity of the hotel foyer, Lord Edmund was in earnest conversation with a serenely beautiful girl. Seeing Hubert and Leonie, he hurried over to them.

"Are you leaving?" he asked.

"At once!" Hubert told him.

"Will you give us a lift? I don't want to let Judy out of my sight until I've fixed up to see her again."

Judy le Marchant, immensely relieved to be escaping from the madhouse, treated Hubert and Leonie like saviours.

"I was only invited because I was in Helen's address book," she said. "I met her a couple of years ago, but I'm afraid I don't know her."

"She was probably making up numbers," Leonie replied. "Damn it all, you'd have to do *something* to compete with Freddie's mob, wouldn't you?"

Judy shuddered. "Wasn't it awful! I think I'd have run away and hidden if it hadn't been for Edmund."

Under gentle cross-examination from Leonie, it emerged that Judy worked as a receptionist for her father, a dental surgeon in Bath. Badly unnerved by the experience of Helen's wedding, she vowed never to set foot outside her family circle and elegant home city again. With Hubert concentrating on driving, Leonie and Judy chatted happily throughout the two-hour journey, with very occasional contributions from the tongue-tied Edmund.

Appreciating that Edmund would wish to collect his own car to take Judy on to Bath, Hubert drove straight into the park at Eaton Mandeville, swept round the front of the house, and deposited his passengers outside the old outbuilding in which cars and an array of farm machinery were kept. Edmund, eager to be away, and Judy, overawed by her surroundings, were on the point of departure when Hubert made his contribution.

"It's been a very great pleasure meeting you, Miss le Marchant. Do you ride at all?"

"Well, yes . . . sort of. I'm not very good."

Hubert laughed. "None of us are! You must come and have a go. As you can see, there's plenty of space and the horses are very docile. Arrange it with Edmund."

After they had waved them off, Leonie dug an elbow into Hubert's ribs. "You old softie!" she said.

"What *do* you mean?" he asked, all innocence.

"You've saved Edmund at least two hours of buggering about and soul-searching. He's your friend for life!"

"He always has been," Hubert replied. "He's a bloody good chap. It's time I did something to help him."

Talented and hard-working though she was, Liz Challenor never seemed to be the sort of person to make a radical improvement to the operation of Latimer's Barn.

She came to the village in January 1963 to do a year's teaching at the school while Eileen Collier gave birth to the baby that was due in March and spent nine months looking after the infant before Elsie took over.

Liz was twenty-seven, recently divorced and unwilling to talk about it. She had a degree from London University, was a good, workmanlike teacher, and settled into Cannings Ambo with the ease of one who was glad to be safely hidden in surroundings that were miraculously isolated and unspoilt. Less than a mile away, a continual stream of traffic roared along the main trunk-road from London to Bristol, yet the

Devizes Lane remained as quiet as ever, protected now by signs declaring everything in sight to be private property.

Oak Cottage was big enough for Liz to have both a bedroom and a study, while sharing her meals with Joe and Eileen. There was a tough casing of reserve surrounding Liz that few people were able to break through: Eileen was the first in Cannings Ambo and the two women became firm friends. During the critical forty-eight hours after Eileen gave birth, Liz was a tower of strength, earning Joe's undying gratitude by the way she helped Eileen come to terms with the fact that her son, James, was the only child she would ever be able to bear. Once the worst of the crisis was past, Joe noticed how Liz drew back into her normal routine, anxious that Eileen should do the rest for herself, thus avoiding dependence on an outsider.

Not until the summer holidays, when she had been within two hundred yards of the place for over seven months, did Liz visit Latimer's Barn. "I really think you ought to say, 'Hello'," Eileen suggested. "Mrs Hawksworth must be thinking it awfully odd that you haven't been to see them."

They arrived at a bad time. Lunch was over, and Elsie and Polly Izzard were taking their afternoon break. The kitchen should have been deserted and peaceful; instead, the table was piled high with papers, notebooks and ledgers. Ann and Steven looked decidedly harassed.

"I'm afraid we're trying to catch up on some of the paperwork, Miss Challenor," Steven said after Eileen had made the introductions. "It's the only thing we aren't very good at."

"Most of this often gets left until we stop racing in the autumn," Ann added. "I insisted that we ought to make an early start this year."

Eileen was startled by the transformation in Liz, who prowled round the table, inspecting its shambolic load, looking for all the world like a wild animal surveying a tasty prey.

"Don't you have better things to do than be messing about with this lot, Mr Hawksworth?" she asked in a way that could easily have been construed as offensive.

"Definitely! There are a hundred and twenty horses out there." Steven pointed. "The trouble is, we've grown bigger and bigger without ever making proper arrangements to deal with this lot."

"That was remiss of you," Liz said, implying that a severe penalty might be attached to such a heinous crime. She began picking up pieces of paper, her disapproval mounting as she did so. "All invoices should be arranged in date order and have a unique number," she said. "What's this? Race entries?"

"Yes," Steven said weakly.

"And this?"

"Er . . . prize-money in May."

"Hm. I see." Liz reached across for the cash-book. "Oh, good, you are using a double entry system . . . that's something, I suppose." Steven, who had no idea what she was talking about, kept quiet. Liz took a deep breath and sailed in. "Can I suggest that you leave this lot with me for a couple of hours, Mr Hawksworth?"

It was, of course, sheer effrontery, but instead of telling her to mind her own business, Steven looked helplessly at Ann.

"Yes, Miss Challenor, feel free," was Steven's final, rather involuntary decision. "Could I explain how . . ."

"That won't be necessary, Mr Hawksworth. Leave it to me."

Ann and Steven found themselves shooed out of the kitchen. "What on earth do we do now?" Steven asked.

"Come to Oak Cottage for tea," Eileen said.

"Your Miss Challenor is a formidable lady," Steven said as they went down the drive.

"This is a new one on me," Eileen confessed.

"*Is* she any good with clerical work?" Ann asked.

They spent the next two hours debating the matter and agonising over when it was safe for them to return: only the fear of being late for evening stables gave Steven the courage to face Liz. He found that the mess on the table had been resolved into neat piles, but she was into her stride before he had time to be complimentary.

"These bills are quite badly overdue, Mr Hawksworth," she said, handing him a list in beautifully neat handwriting. "I know that your reputation is high, so you probably enjoy considerable goodwill. Nevertheless, I do think that these poor people deserve paying. I will make out the cheques for your signature when I come tomorrow."

"You're coming back tomorrow?" Steven asked, not knowing whether to be pleased or panic-stricken.

"Yes, and I'd like to spend ten minutes with you before I start. I have some questions." She looked stern.

"I think you ought to have somewhere more comfortable and private to work," Steven said, doing his best to seem in control of the situation. "Let me show you where the library is."

When Liz returned to Oak Cottage, Eileen did not dare ask how she had got on. Over dinner, Liz announced that she was returning to Latimer's Barn the following afternoon, then made it plain that she had nothing further to say on the topic.

Four days later, all Steven's clerical and administrative problems had vanished. Eventually softened by his fulsome praise, Liz agreed to work regularly in return for a wage. When the children went back to school, she promised to do Saturday mornings and two evenings a week.

With the approach of Christmas 1963, and the expiry of Liz's contract at the school, Steven began to fret. After talking it over with Ann, he went to Oak Cottage one evening.

"Look, Liz, I won't beat about the bush," he said. "Have you got another job to go to?"

"No, I haven't, Mr Hawksworth. The agency has offered me several posts, but they're all in big cities. Very unpleasant, especially after being here. I shall have to start looking for myself." She paused, uncharacteristically diffident. "I was wondering if you could find me a job."

"What about teaching?" Steven asked.

"It wouldn't worry me to give it up."

"You're sure?"

"Certain."

Steven smiled. "I came here to offer you a job," he said.

"I shall need a proper office," Liz warned, regaining her composure.

"I think we have an answer to that."

"And I must have some filing cabinets and a decent typewriter – we cannot carry on as we are."

"Leave it with me," Steven said.

After they had agreed on a salary and arranged for Liz to carry on boarding at Oak Cottage until new accommodation could be found, Steven hurried back to The House to telephone Sid Irons.

The opening move in the conversion was two days of fearsome hammering as a hole was knocked in the wall at the western end of The House. The new door gave access to space that had never been put to good use, in which two offices were built.

"I may as well have one for myself while I'm at it," Steven said.

Between the offices, a short corridor led to the main entrance hall and staircase. Thus, the side door that faced towards the 1874 yard was effectively a new front door.

"We could have killed several birds with one stone," Steven told Ann. "This might even satisfy Rachel."

"Don't bank on it!" Ann replied.

Although Elsie missed the flow of people and information through the kitchen, it so happened that the new door *did* please Rachel. However, 1964 was not very old before Steven took a step that infuriated her beyond all reason.

With the administration running like clockwork in Liz's capable hands, it was time to return to a topic that Ann had been attempting to discuss since the 1955 yard had given Steven a workload she considered excessive.

"You need an assistant," she said. "I've been telling you that for years and it's time we did something about it."

"What would this assistant do?" Steven asked. He was

not arguing, or attempting to stall, merely seeking to obtain a clear idea of what the job would entail.

"Look after the routine work on the gallops, take a share of evening stables and do some of the race meetings."

Steven nodded. "That sounds fair enough. It would give me time to concentrate on the really talented horses." He was silent for a moment or two. "All right, who do you suggest?"

"Giles?" Ann said tentatively.

"I don't think so." Steven sounded as though he might not be fully convinced. "It isn't a good idea to make him appear as second-best or a factotum. Everybody knows that Giles will take over when I retire, so there's no need to prove the point. It's best if he stays on the sidelines, keeping his hands clean instead of falling out with me!"

"What about the Merriweathers?" Ann asked.

Steven shook his head decisively. "They're dyed-in-the-wool head lads now. They wouldn't thank you for the chance of trying something new and why should we ask them to? They've always been the best in the business."

It was perfectly true. In three years, when Alfred reached retiring age, his son, Arthur, would assume the mantle of sergeant-major of Latimer's Barn and the transition was guaranteed to be smooth.

"Who, then?" Ann asked. "Jimmy Farrant?"

"I've given him a lot of thought. At one stage, I almost persuaded myself that he was the man. The trouble is, he'd have difficulty putting distance between himself and his mates; he's very much one of the lads, a bit of an institution and he likes it that way."

"If you want someone who can stand a little bit aloof and be respected, you only have one choice," Ann said.

"Exactly!" Steven replied, looking rather smug. "I intend talking to her tomorrow after we've found out what Giles thinks."

Giles, having been to Salisbury with two horses, both of whom won, returned in good time for dinner. They were joined by Oliver, who rarely bothered with the meal. He

302

was working ruthlessly hard for the examinations that would decide his place at university. Although his dedication was impressive, Ann found herself unable to admire it, since she understood the motive: Oliver was ensuring his escape-route from Cannings Ambo.

Taking great care, Steven outlined his plan to Giles. He had expected a favourable reaction and was not disappointed.

"That strikes me as a pretty good idea," Giles said.

"You don't feel slighted?" Steven asked.

"Good heavens, no! As you say, I'm the heir-apparent. It's a step towards continuity, as well."

"How?"

"Bess will still be doing the job when I take over. I can't see her getting married after that business with Richard Morton."

Ignoring the reference to Morton, which he considered irrelevant and in questionable taste, Steven agreed with the idea. "I've more or less decided to retire when I'm sixty." Steven smiled across the table at Ann. "Your mother and I are going on a three-month world cruise, then we'll decide what to do with the rest of our lives." Seeing that Ann was very pleasantly surprised, he offered an explanation. "We went without a decent honeymoon, darling, and I seem to have been on the go ever since."

"So, that's in nine years?" Giles said.

"Yes. What do you think?"

"Fine!" Giles was undoubtedly satisfied.

Suddenly, despite the unexpectedly good news about Steven's retirement, Ann was apprehensive. There was something not at all right with Giles's attitude; he was, she suspected, looking forward to nine years of playing the dilettante. The disturbing thought was pushed aside, however, by Oliver's sardonic comment.

"Aunt Rachel isn't going to like this."

Steven looked at him blankly. "Why not?" he asked.

"She's got a real thing against Bess Collier." Seeing that Giles was nodding, Oliver felt entitled to say more. "She's always thought that Bess got preferential treatment. I can hear her now: 'Good God, he's made the cook's daughter his assistant. He must be mad!' I tell you, Dad, she'll blow a gasket."

"You may well be right," Steven said, recalling his sister's antipathy to Bess. "But it won't get her anywhere. I run this place, not her."

"I bet she creates hell with the Trustees," Oliver persisted.

"No, she won't," Giles said. "I'll sort her out. I can twist Aunt Rachel round my little finger."

After that, Giles was in a hurry to finish his meal and go out: he was seeing a girl in Hungerford. As he left, Ann wondered whether it would be him or Rachel who would be doing the manipulating.

Steven and Alfred Merriweather were in their usual positions when Bess rode out at the head of the first lot the following morning. Leaving five minutes before the main body, they were a furlong down the main gallop, watching the sixty horses walk towards them, ready to spot the slightest defect. Without appearing to interrupt his hawk-eyed scrutiny, Steven leaned forward in the saddle of his hack as she passed close to him.

"Come to breakfast afterwards, Bess," he said. She nodded and the lad alongside her pulled a face: breakfast in The House between first and second lots was a great honour.

Several days later, when she was able to start adjusting to her new status, Bess wondered whether Steven had been slightly unfair in making his astounding offer in the kitchen so that Elsie was there to hear it. He almost certainly had no ulterior motive, but the fact remained that the urge to refuse died when she caught her mother's eye.

"That's a very great honour, sir," she said. "Thank you. I'll do my best."

Steven made the announcement to the sixty-odd lads at the end of work for the second lot. Bess was petrified by the fear that her erstwhile mates would feel resentful at her promotion, but it was obvious immediately that Steven had made a wise and popular decision. She found that lads were queuing up to congratulate her and stake their claims to the two horses she had been doing, both of whom were top-class animals with substantial prize-money potential.

"I shall do them, as well as my own pair," Boggysevick said, shoving bodies out of the way so that he could get to his daughter to kiss her. "We must keep all this good stuff in the family!"

Amid the hoots of friendly derision, Bess tried to say that Alfred Merriweather was looking into the matter, but no one took any notice.

When he discovered that Steven intended spending the afternoon with Bess to work out a plan of campaign, Giles decided to take himself off to visit an old Exeter University friend. He did not bother returning for evening stables.

After two weeks, Bess admitted to Elsie that she found her new job very much to her liking; she also enjoyed the modicum of status that went with it. She remained mercifully level-headed about it all, but breakfast and lunch at The House every day and being called 'ma'am' for most of the time was not something that embarrassed her. Elsie, who never missed an opportunity of reminding Bess that she had damned nearly turned the job down, was very proud of her.

Without a shadow of a doubt, the highlight of those early days was her first encounter with Richard Morton in her new role.

Morton had moved swiftly to establish his grip on the practice after marriage had enabled him to become a partner. The brothers, Dennis and Cecil, had needed little persuasion to retire; then, it was simply a matter of being odious to Dennis's son until he agreed to sell his share and clear off to Devon to start up on his own. Morton acquired two newly qualified dogsbodies and changed the name of the practice.

Making what he thought was a routine call to Latimer's Barn two days after Bess's promotion, Morton found himself directed to the office Bess now shared with Liz.

Clearly fazed by events, he offered awkward congratulations.

"Thank you," Bess said briskly. "If you come with me, I'll show you what needs doing."

Glad to be away from Liz's searching gaze, Morton accompanied Bess to the 1933 yard, wondering what, if anything, he should say, knowing that she was watching the workings of his mind. After letting him stew for several painful minutes, Bess showed him how they stood.

"As you can see, Richard, we're making changes, getting ourselves better organised. Liz Challenor is in charge of all financial and administration matters, so will you liaise with her in future, please? I shall be keeping an eye on treatments and costs. I don't need to remind you how much we spend with you, so we shall be looking for service and value." She smiled in what seemed a more friendly manner. "How's your wife?" Before he had time to think of a suitable answer, she showed that she was fully aware of the stories. "And Pamela Anderson . . . you're seeing a lot of her, aren't you?"

The only thing that stood between Richard Morton and a great deal of worry was the knowledge that no vet within thirty miles was good enough to be considered a serious rival.

A meeting of Trustees took place at The House that morning. There was no major business. Matthew floated the idea of an expansion of the furniture workshops. After half an hour's general discussion, he was satisfied that he would be allowed at least £100,000 when the necessity arose.

Purely as a courtesy, Steven then told his fellow-Trustees about the changes he had made at the stable.

"I find all this extraordinary," Rachel said.

"Oh. Why?" Steven looked at her blandly.

"First of all, you put a failed teacher in charge of your accounts . . ."

Ann was having none of this. "Liz Challoner is not a failed teacher, Rachel. She chose to give it up when we offered her a job."

"And she makes my life very much easier," Matthew said,

speaking as Treasurer. "I get proper financial reports the day after the month ends. It's wonderful!" He grinned at Steven to show that he hadn't minded the previous hit-and-miss system.

"Be that as it may," Rachel persisted, "what about the Collier girl?"

"What about her?" Steven asked mildly. He could see that Rachel wanted a row, but he wasn't going to make it easy for her.

"Why have you made her your assistant?"

"Because I needed one and she was the best person."

"Absolute stuff and nonsense! You've taken up with this ludicrous idea that Grandmother had. I can assure you, Steven, that there isn't anything special about her. Far from it, in fact. She's a money-grubbing tart without breeding."

There was a stunned silence round the table. Only Edward Mallender, who seemed to have developed a taste for mischief since he passed sixty, showed anything other than abhorrence for Rachel's outburst. It was Hubert who attempted to take her to task.

"I think you should withdraw those offensive and wildly ill-informed remarks, Mother," he said.

Ignoring him, Rachel attacked Steven again. "And what about Giles? Isn't this rather insulting to him? Come to that, why isn't he here to speak for himself? He was twenty-one a year ago, yet you've never proposed him as a Trustee . . . I believe you're trying to exclude him."

"Giles is perfectly happy with the situation," Steven said.

"I think you should rescind the girl's appointment," Rachel said as though giving an order.

"I think not," Steven said calmly.

"I insist!" Rachel was losing control of herself. "You shouldn't be allowed to put upstarts in positions of authority. Our family has worked hard for over a century to see that Latimer's Barn is properly run by the *right* people."

It was time for Amelia to have her say, and she did so with a taut anger that came close to frightening even Rachel.

307

"I have attended every one of these meetings for the last fifty-six years, and I have *never* heard the like of this," she said. "Rachel, as Trustees, our function is to care for the village and the people in it. We are not here to dictate to Steven, or Matthew, how they run their businesses, nor is it our function to cast arrogant aspersions on *anyone*, let alone a young woman who has proved herself to be a very talented and loyal servant. Will you remember that, please, Rachel, and be so kind as to shut up!"

Hubert saw that he was not the only one who felt like cheering. Rachel, however, was in a terrible all-or-nothing mood.

"I insist on having that girl removed!"

"Fair enough," Steven said. "Let's vote on it."

"One moment!" Hubert said. "If this is a formal motion, we need someone to second it."

"True." Steven looked round the table. Total silence reigned and no one moved a muscle. Edward Mallender's eyes showed that he considered it, then thought again.

"I'm sorry, Rachel, no one agrees with you," Steven pointed out.

She remained for a few moments, her face frozen, the knuckles of her hands white. To everyone's relief, she stood up and stalked out. In the fraught silence that followed her departure, Steven declared the meeting closed.

Sensing the extent to which Steven had been upset by Rachel's disgraceful performance, Ann steered the conversation to more congenial topics over lunch. But when he went to the office to spend the afternoon on race entries with Liz, she set off to Louise House.

"Are we of the same mind?" Amelia asked the moment she saw Ann.

"I imagine so. There's a battle to be fought and the sooner it's done, the better."

When they had made themselves comfortable in the sitting-room, Amelia sighed, gave Ann a hard look and said, "I'm very much afraid that we must find a way of removing Rachel's Trusteeship."

308

It was the right decision. Unfortunately, events conspired to prevent its prosecution.

On the day after the meeting, Matthew and Louise left Cannings Ambo early to go to London. They had to drive to Swindon to catch a train. Savernake station and the branch line to Marlborough, a lifeline to Latimer's Barn for nearly ninety years, had closed the previous month. A man called Beeching, an industrial chemist of all things, had been put in charge of British Railways and told to run them at a profit, rather than worry about providing a service.

They parted when they reached London at nine-thirty. Matthew went to Chancery Lane to talk to the general manager of an insurance company about what promised to be a huge order for office furniture, Louise headed for Knightsbridge and at least five idyllic hours in Harrods.

As arranged, they met at four o'clock in the buffet at Paddington station, both fairly tired, but happy. Louise had ordered new curtains for every window in Rose House, Matthew had done enough business to pay for them fifty times over. After a cup of tea, they went to look for their train, the four-forty to Cardiff, first stop Swindon. While walking along the platform, they bumped into Claude Timberlake, who had travelled up to London even earlier than them for his day's work. They found an empty first-class compartment at the front of the train and Claude raised the unavoidable topic.

"What did you think of the Dowager Duchess's performance yesterday?"

"We don't know whether to laugh or cry," Louise replied. "I can't imagine why she has to be so awful."

"I'm afraid it strikes me as all rather personal and unpleasant," Matthew said. "I think Rachel came to regret marrying Charles. It might have made her a duchess, but it took her away from Latimer's Barn. She was terribly fond of the place, you know."

They became absorbed in conversation. Half an hour after starting from Paddington, the train ran through Reading and headed for Goring, following the sweep of the River

309

Thames. About fifteen minutes later, approaching Didcot, there was a substantial reduction in speed and they crossed on to another track.

"Hello, we're being switched to the slow line," Claude said; he took an interest in railways and was suspected of collecting engine numbers. For a while, he peered out of the window, satisfied when he saw several groups of men working on the fast line. He turned his attention back to the conversation which was poised at a critical issue: Matthew had stated that Rachel was not fit to be a Trustee.

"What do we do about it?" Claude asked. "I don't know what the rules say about this sort of thing."

Matthew, who had spent the previous evening studying the articles of association that Giles Flamsteed had drawn up in 1886, began to explain. Claude was attentive until he realised that the train was travelling very fast again.

"That's odd. I must have missed us changing lines," Claude said.

As he spoke, there was a violent application of brakes. They had time to exchange frightened looks before the carriage lurched to the right with a sickening jolt and all hell was let loose on them.

The subsequent official inquiry into the accident found that the driver, who was uninjured, had forgotten he was on the slow line. The layout and appearance of all four tracks along that stretch suggested and invited speed, so he pushed the diesel locomotive up to eighty miles an hour. His mate did not advise him of the error, nor was any notice taken of the three railway officials on Didcot station who tried to signal their alarm as the train roared through.

The track was perfectly capable of handling the speed; the problem arose a mile further on, where a set of points to switch the train back to the fast line was restricted to twenty miles an hour. It was when he saw the points and realised his mistake that the driver slammed on the brakes.

The locomotive negotiated the junction, but was turned over by the second and third coaches toppling on to their sides. When the whole mess finally came to rest, the train, originally two hundred yards long, was spread out over half a mile and all four tracks.

Of the nine who died, all but one were in the first coach which was crushed when the locomotive rolled over it. Louise was killed almost instantly; Matthew and Claude were still alive when rescue teams reached them two hours later. Matthew died on the way to hospital, Claude in the operating theatre.

It ranked with the Great War and the stable fire of 1937 as the worst tragedy ever to afflict Cannings Ambo and the village was in a state of deep shock for days. Both Matthew and Claude were seventy-two years old; Louise was sixty-six. But all three were full of life and had so much to offer. Claude's widow, Lily, a youthful fifty-six, was devastated. Gideon and Lady Amaryllis took her to live with them at The Hall; it was a foregone conclusion that she would never return to the Timberlake house in Marlborough.

Alone in the shocked desolation, Amelia was angry. "This is what comes of closing things down!" she raged. "They should never have been on that train in the first place . . . Savernake has always been our station, not Swindon!" Jim Goakes, who had worshipped Matthew and Louise, was inclined to agree with her, but everyone else was stunned into mental torpor. Amelia caused a flutter in the higher echelons of the British Railways Board and Ministry of Transport with an outspoken letter to *The Times*; officialdom issued a series of mealy-mouthed denials and the issue faded.

Six days after the accident, Matthew and Louise Flamsteed and Claude Timberlake shared a funeral, an occasion that proved utterly wretched, with none of the sense of thanksgiving that had illuminated Leander's going. It was followed immediately by an emergency meeting of Trustees at The House.

"We've lost three very valuable members," Steven said. "Between them, they had one hundred and thirty years' experience. I'm afraid they aren't going to be easy to

311

replace." He paused uneasily. "To be frank, we should have recruited new blood some ages ago."

"Who are you proposing?" Rachel asked. Although her manner seemed normal, Steven had the uncomfortable premonition that she had no intention of making concessions to the circumstances that had made the gathering necessary.

"Perhaps we should consider Giles," Steven said, unhappy at yielding to exigency.

Ann watched the reactions; they were very interesting.

Amelia disapproved. Unaware that she had such strong feelings, Ann was surprised. Hubert Prideaux seemed not to care one way or the other. Edward Mallender and Leslie Giffard, the two men whose presence increasingly worried Ann, showed lukewarm approval. However, they did it in the strangest way. Separately, ignoring each other, they both nodded at Rachel.

"You know my views on Giles," Rachel said. "Who else?"

"Obviously John and Julia must replace poor Matthew and Louise," Steven replied. "Gideon should follow Claude and I'd rather like to see Lady Amaryllis joining us."

"Do we need a Timberlake?" Leslie Giffard asked. For Ann, at least, there was the stench of collusion between him and Rachel.

"Yes!" Amelia's reply, like a gun-shot, was reinforced by a daunting look.

"You're sure?" Rachel asked.

"I've just said so!"

"Very well." Rachel bowed her head graciously. "I do wonder about wives though. For example, John is now in charge of William Flamsteed and Sons and must be one of us, but what contribution could Julia make?"

"She could vote with her husband," Edward Mallender declared unpleasantly.

Ann, deeply annoyed, was drawing breath to propose a formal motion that Rachel cease to be a Trustee when Steven made a fearful blunder.

"I think there's a strong case for Lady Amaryllis," he said.

312

"She's in charge of the stud and responsible for a great deal of income – nearly a quarter of a million last year."

Ann felt like screaming: Steven had conceded the point on Julia. Still upset by the funeral, she lacked the stomach to kick up a fuss: it was a moment of weakness that was to haunt her.

Aware that she had achieved much of what she wanted, Rachel did not object to Lady Amaryllis, nor did she raise the question of her son-in-law, Freddie Christopherson.

The meeting ended a few minutes later in an atmosphere of formal frigidity: the Trustees seemed anxious to leave, avoiding each other as they did so. Hubert hid in the kitchen, waiting for Ann.

"It looks very much as though Mother is forming a pretty unholy alliance with Mallender and Giffard," he said.

"I wasn't imagining it?"

"Definitely not! I don't take kindly to being caught napping like that. You can rely on me to find out what's going on."

"Thank you very much, Hubert."

Bess got to hear about the meeting from Liz Challoner, who had helped Steven prepare the minutes.

"It isn't serious, is it?" Bess asked nervously.

"I doubt it." Liz was dismissive. "As far as I can make out, political intrigue and backbiting has reared its ugly head in Cannings Ambo. They've done well to keep it at bay for so long. I don't think it amounts to much."

Hubert told Ann the same two weeks later over a drink in the members' bar at Newbury where one of his two-year-olds was making a début.

"It looks like some silly game that Mallender and Giffard are playing," he said.

"Why?" Ann asked.

Hubert shrugged. "They can't stand the sight of each other."

"And your mother?" Ann asked.

"She's using them to put Uncle Steven in his place. By the

313

way, now the dust has settled, I have to say that he dropped a fearful clanger over Julia."

"Don't I know it!"

"There is one interesting thing," Hubert went on. "Things look sticky with Mallender and Giffard Foods. It's difficult to be sure of what's going on because they aren't a publicly quoted company, but all the educated guesses suggested that they've over-extended themselves with expansion. It seems that Freddie Christopherson is giving them a loan."

"Hence their sucking-up to your mother?"

"Probably."

"That's all right, then." Ann liked simple explanations. "Incidentally, Gideon is going to be the new Treasurer."

"He's a tough nut," Hubert said admiringly.

"Very much so. He's already taken a strong dislike to Freddie, so I can't see his chances of becoming a Trustee have been improved."

"Good!"

"How are Freddie and Helen getting on?" Ann asked.

"They seem to be behaving themselves – or keeping it all behind wraps," Hubert replied. "They've bought a plush place down in Surrey and are pretending to be respectable. It won't last, of course. By the way, Edmund's getting married to a girl he met at their wedding."

"Quick work," Ann said.

"Oh, Edmund can move when the fancy takes him and Judy's a sweetie."

"What about you?" Ann asked. "Still no plans?"

"No. Come on, let's go and see how this horse gets on."

Gradually, the shock of the Didcot tragedy faded.

Three months after the funeral, Rose House, empty since the deaths of Matthew and Louise, became a home again. John and Julia, with their son, William, moved from the Bungalow on the Back Stretch to live in the Flamsteeds' traditional residence. William, eighteen that summer, left school and began full-time work at Wm Flamsteed & Sons the following

314

day. It was, Amelia thought, the correct, old-fashioned way to do things, unlike what was happening at Latimer's Barn. Being a Trustee was making no difference to Giles's offhand attitude to the stable.

Steven asked Bess and Liz if they would consider sharing the Bungalow. "It's big enough to stop you falling over one another," he said. "And you both deserve some sort of status symbol."

The arrangement worked very well, soon producing the solution to a problem that had been threatening to derange Bess. "It's clothes," she told Liz. "I'm hopeless. The only time I've ever bothered was when I started buying decent breeches and sweaters. That's fine for work, but what happens when I go racing?"

"I know of a place in Bath that could fix you up a treat," Liz said. "The only trouble is, it costs an arm and a leg."

"That doesn't matter. Take me to it."

When they both had a full Saturday off, they went to Bath in Liz's battered old jalopy and Bess was absorbed into Farquharson's of Milsom Street. Established in 1842, the shop looked after gentlemen on the ground floor, while ladies were taken care of upstairs. The atmosphere belonged to a bygone age that might, Bess suspected, never actually have existed. It was, however, very pleasant and all the clothes had a strong appeal. Farquharson's *métier* was understated elegance, superbly executed in the best quality materials. Assisted by Liz, Bess chose two suits, one dark blue, the other tweed, and three dresses, two in pastel colours, the other a rather daring Paisley. Amazed to discover what she could look like when she put her mind to it, Bess handed over a phenomenal sum of money and did her best to treat the saleswoman's parting remark with the gravitas that was clearly expected. "You will find, madam, that our branches in Fort William and Singapore stock the same clothes with the same high standard of service."

"Thank you, I'm pleased to hear it," Bess replied with due solemnity.

It was not one of Liz's Saturday nights away, so they treated

315

themselves to an orgy of shopping for bits and pieces and a meal before setting off back to Cannings Ambo. Every other weekend, Liz disappeared for twenty-four hours, generally returning in a state of relaxed exhaustion.

"I have a man," she explained. "It's therapeutic."

"I know," Bess said.

"You should get fixed up. It would do you good."

"I think it's probably more trouble than it's worth," Bess replied, trying to forget that there were times when she could cheerfully sell her soul for a few hours with a man capable of exciting and satisfying her as well as Richard Morton had done.

CHAPTER 12

1967

'The son's a washout'

After three years as a curate in Bristol, the Reverend Robert Frobisher took over from his father as vicar of Cannings Ambo on 1 January 1967. It was a Sunday and the two services he conducted, both well-attended, earned him the approval of his flock of reactionary traditionalists. He had been warned by Dame Amelia that his appointment was conditional upon him having nothing to do with new-fangled prayer books or silly versions of the Bible.

At the end of the same week, Robert carried out his first major duty when he married Giles Hawksworth and Gillian Foley. Even as a newcomer to the village, Robert Frobisher sensed that all was not as it should be, although he was not aware that the bride viewed the prospect of living in Cannings Ambo with such dismay that she intended to avoid it if possible. But no one, not even the groom, knew that.

And there was much worse in store. Several people noticed how unwell Steven looked that day: they went so far as to comment on it afterwards. Naturally, there was no inkling of the nightmare ahead.

When it came, Steven's courage became a beacon: the only thing that worried him, he said, was dying before Ptolemy won the Derby.

Giles had been aware of Gillian Foley for three years before they became lovers and engaged to be married on the same day in 1966. She was the sister of Simon Foley, a close friend from Giles's time at Exeter University.

The Foleys lived in considerable style at a huge house in ten acres of gardens on the outskirts of a village a few miles west of Reading. Ralph Foley, Simon and Gillian's father, was a third-generation partner in Foley, Nettles and Mayo, arguably the south of England's most grandiose estate agents, whose brochures and fees were legendary.

From their first meeting, Giles had been mesmerised by Gillian's beauty and physical attraction. Over a three-year period, during which he saw her a dozen times, the effect she had on him prompted some robust leg-pulling from Simon. Her copper-coloured hair, green eyes and sensual lips were complemented by a body that begged for lustful attention.

Yet Giles found her daunting. Despite his sexual adventures at university, which exceeded the scope of any other member of his family, apart from the infamous George, Giles remained conscious of the Cannings Ambo perception of a 'suitable' girl. Gillian would have failed all the tests. Well-aware of her endowments, she did everything in her power to make the most of them; every movement, gesture and look were calculated. Her taste in clothes was strident, pleasing the eye only inasmuch as it displayed her to advantage. Although she spent a fortune on her wardrobe, she frequently came within an ace of looking cheaply garish.

Gillian was never particularly civil to Giles and he knew she was 'wrong' for the Hawksworths and Flamsteeds: nevertheless, she always reduced him to speechless excitement.

It was left to Gillian's mother to feel irritation at his inability to start any form of relationship.

"Why hasn't Giles Hawksworth asked you to go out with him?" Janet Foley inquired as she and Gillian sunbathed together one afternoon in July 1966.

"Are you thinking of grabbing him?"

It was a perfectly serious question. Gillian knew that the body that made a nonsense of her mother's forty-five years

318

had been used to enslave at least two young men whose original intentions had been very firmly directed towards herself.

"No, he's not my type. He's far too serious and sincere. He's bloody dishy, though!"

"He is rather." Gillian sighed. "I'm pretty certain he fancies me like mad. He doesn't seem to have the guts to do anything about it."

"Don't you think it's time you rectified that?" Janet asked.

"I thought you wanted me to carry on being nice to Gordon!" Gillian protested. There was something of an understanding gaining ground between her and Gordon Mayo, the son of another of the partners in the estate agency.

Janet Foley displayed her talent for going straight to what she saw as the heart of the matter. "Giles Hawksworth is much better off than Gordon. I believe that young Mr Hawksworth could buy the whole of Foley, Nettles and Mayo tomorrow morning without noticing that he'd spent anything."

"Really?" Gillian was interested.

"I think we are talking of *millions*, my love, not mere hundreds of thousands. You ought to have a look at that Cannings Ambo place . . . you'd find it enlightening."

"Aren't they up to their necks in horses?" Gillian asked.

"That's where the money comes from, silly! I'm sure you wouldn't be expected to go anywhere near them." She paused to rub more suntan oil on her legs, momentarily diverted by the thought that they were still nearly as good as Gillian's. "Why don't you give him a call?"

When she telephoned Giles, Gillian made no attempt to be ingratiating. She told him that she had been let down by someone and was bored: would he like to take her out to dinner? Not in the least deterred, Giles rushed to oblige her. Once she had him to herself in a secluded corner of a specially selected restaurant, Gillian set about convincing him that he was the most important person in the world.

Giles never bothered to question her motives, and, from that evening, was incapable of viewing Gillian objectively.

Gillian's first visit to Latimer's Barn, a week after that first dinner, confirmed what her mother had said. Giles was keen to show her everything: it was the flying visit to the stud, revealing the full extent of the estate, that finally tipped the balance.

"And you own all this lot?" Gillian said, waving an arm that sought to encompass most of Wiltshire. For once, she was genuinely impressed.

"*I* don't," Giles laughed. "The family does."

Having taken a mental photograph of the estate, Gillian discussed it with her father when she returned home that evening.

"It's *very* difficult to put a price on that sort of place," he said. "A lot depends on the use a buyer would put it to."

"How about as it stands?"

"At least two million." Ralph Foley sounded confident and Gillian knew that his professional judgement was good. "Given planning permission, you could name any figure you liked, of course. But, there's more to it than that. The Hawksworths are believed to have a great deal of money in Switzerland."

"How much?" Gillian asked eagerly.

"Three million."

Again, she believed him. While his wife amused herself with young men, Ralph Foley indulged in his own escapades, most of which seemed to add to his fund of knowledge about other people's confidential affairs. Unaware that she was getting only a misleading fraction of the truth, Gillian felt better: she had enjoyed looking at Cannings Ambo, but some of the people were a different matter.

Giles's parents seemed nice enough. There was a simple explanation for their pleasant indifference: Ann and Steven had decided within minutes that their son would have far more sense than to become involved with a flashy girl who knew nothing about horses. Dame Amelia, gimlet-eyed and astute, had given Gillian the uncomfortable feeling that she was

320

being taken apart and found wanting, while Lady Amaryllis Timberlake, proud of the fact that she had never heard of Foley, Nettles and Mayo, was amused by the way Gillian's stiletto heels caused her to flounder on the cobbles of the stallion yard.

Things were much better at Eaton Mandeville, or the small part of it covered by the Dower House. Seeking Rachel's approval, Giles took Gillian to meet her soon after the inspection of Cannings Ambo. Overawed by the prospect of meeting a dowager duchess, Gillian both dressed and behaved with demure restraint. In spite of this, Rachel saw through her at once and was quietly jubilant. She made up her mind to do everything in her power to foster the romance.

Two months later, it was Rachel who suggested to Giles that he should ask Gillian to marry him.

Once in possession of a diamond ring, Gillian took Giles back home. She had arranged for the house to be empty so that she could seduce him.

By now genuinely fond of Giles, and aroused by the discovery that his naked body was alluring, she approached the task with greedy anticipation. Unfortunately, Giles climaxed far too quickly to be of any use to her. Accustomed to the effect she had on men, Gillian remained patient, expecting that Giles would soon be ready to make a much better job of it, only to find that she was wrong. If anything, the rampant enthusiasm she cultivated gave him even less endurance than the first time. Dismally, the next three hours saw several repetitions of the unsatisfactory performance. The final insult was that Giles thought he had done magnificently well. While he was driving the forty miles back to Latimer's Barn, Gillian complained bitterly to her mother, who had returned from an arranged absence.

"He's lousy!" Gillian moaned. "Futile! Pathetic! He's got no more idea how to please a woman than fly to the moon."

Janet Foley was disturbed. She knew that Gillian, like

321

herself, set great store by sexual gratification and found frustration impossible to bear: Giles's ineptitude could easily prove an insurmountable barrier to marrying Gillian into a gold-mine. There was one possible explanation, and Janet advanced it firmly, as though she believed it to be right. "He may be very inexperienced, dear. You know how shy he is. You'll have to educate him."

"I suppose so," Gillian replied sulkily.

Giles's announcement of his engagement caught Steven and Ann on the hop. They were relieved when he left them alone soon after breaking the news.

"Well, what do we make of *that*?" Steven asked.

"So far, I think we're coping damned well," Ann replied.

"We've only known for two or three minutes," Steven said.

"True, but we didn't make the mistake of flying off the handle and telling him that he couldn't have found a more unsuitable woman to marry if he'd spent months scouring the entire country!"

"Is that what you think?" Steven asked.

"Yes. What about you?"

He rubbed his chin. Steven had now seen Gillian a dozen times and most of what she had done and said had caused him concern. "I very much doubt whether she's right for Giles," he said, careful to keep his sentiments within reasonable bounds.

"She's definitely not right for Cannings Ambo," Ann declared. "What do we do about it?"

Unable to decide anything that night, they went to Louise House the following afternoon to consult Amelia.

"Yes, I'm afraid to say that I agree with you," was Amelia's reaction to the news. "She's no good."

"What should we do, or say?"

Amelia shook her head. "I don't see how you can stop him . . . if you try, you'll make it worse. You must hope he comes to his senses in time."

"It's a shame Oliver was never interested in the stable,"

Steven muttered. Ann glanced at him sharply, realising what he was implying: if the worst happened, he would like the option of booting Giles out.

"We have Rebecca," she said.

"Of course!" Steven looked much more cheerful. "Women can hold a licence now." Some months previously, the Jockey Club had finally caved in. "She'll be eligible in three or four years."

Amelia nodded. "Given that escape-route, you can sit back and let Giles get on with it," she said. "Keep your heads and there's every chance that he'll come to his senses."

Grabbing the initiative, Ann telephoned Janet Foley. "It's *such* good news about Giles and Gillian," she gushed. "I can't tell you how pleased we all are. You must all come and stay with us for a weekend so that we can get to know one another."

The meeting took place two weeks later, in early October. The Foleys, including Simon as well as Gillian, arrived in time for dinner on Friday and stayed until after lunch on Sunday. Ann detected that they were uneasy at pretending to be content with each other for such a long time, but knew it was an affliction suffered by many families. Although Gillian was in an uncertain mood, there was only one incident.

It came on Saturday morning, when Giles was giving her a comprehensive tour of the yard. The second lot had just returned and all was bustle. Gillian was bored, fretting to go back indoors. Just as she felt that the moment had come, they bumped into Bess. Giles's introduction was fulsome.

"This is Bess Collier, darling. She's Father's assistant. She's brilliant. If she isn't still here when I come to do the job, I don't think I'll bother!"

There was never any question of friendship as the two women eyed each other. Bess, in navy-blue breeches, crimson sweater and highly polished boots, was immaculate and svelte; Gillian was obviously displeased by what she saw. For her part, Bess reflected the underlying disapproval of all the staff. Saturday was an important work morning and there were better things for Giles to be doing than parade his fancy woman around, especially in those ludicrous heels and a dress that might have looked right at a cocktail party.

"I thought all horsey women were supposed to be ugly freaks," Gillian said to Giles on the way back to The House.

He laughed. "Most of them are."

"Well that one bloody isn't!" Gillian spat the words out and her eyes flashed with sheer bad temper. Before Giles had a chance to ask her what she meant, she stormed off, leaving him standing.

The return visit to the Foleys, which did not take place until the end of November, was restricted to a single day, a Sunday. After a great deal of patient explaining to Janet Foley over the telephone, Ann succeeded in getting the message across that their absence overnight was undesirable because of the yearlings that were coming into Latimer's Barn.

Initially, the signs were good. Ralph Foley's *bonhomie* was judged to a nicety, Janet was poised and at ease and Gillian, after spending most of the previous night with one of her mother's young men, was so calm that she appeared sedated.

At one o'clock, a magnificent lunch was served and Janet Foley rose in Ann's estimation by stating that she had not been involved in its preparation.

"There are two girls in the village who cook meals for special occasions," she said. "As you can see, they're treasures."

The meal progressed with unforced affability on all sides. At one point, Gillian began to ask Giles questions about horses; some of them were sensible and seemed carefully thought-out. It was after the main course had been cleared away and they had agreed on a respite before tackling apple pie and cream that Ralph Foley ruined the day for Ann and Steven.

"I bought you two love-birds a wedding present the other day," he said to Giles and Gillian. "I know these things are supposed to be secret, but you need to know about this so that you don't go shooting off and making your own arrangements."

"This sounds exciting," Ann said. "What is it?"

In the fraction of a second before the answer came, Steven saw that Gillian was smug: she knew.

"What else would you expect from an estate agent?" Foley chuckled. "I've got them a house."

Ann froze. "A house?" she echoed in a strange voice that made Giles look alarmed.

"That's right. Nice place . . . only five bedrooms, but there wasn't as much choice as I would have liked."

"Where is it?" Ann asked.

"Marlborough."

"Mr Foley, Giles doesn't *need* a house," Steven said. "His work is at Latimer's Barn and we have plenty of accommodation." Ann marvelled at his control; he was, she knew, very angry.

"Don't you think it's very restricting to live over the shop, as it were?" Janet Foley asked.

"It would be if we were talking about a corner grocery," Ann replied. "We happen to be the country's leading racing stable."

"I think young people need a little more elbow-room in this day and age," Ralph Foley said soothingly. "It's not fair to expect them to be cooped up with the job all the time."

That phrase, 'in this day and age', always annoyed Steven. He had no sympathy with the idea that everything, including standards, had somehow changed during the last twenty years.

Giles saw that an attempt at peace-making was necessary. "Gillian and I have talked about this, Father. I think we came to the conclusion that it would be best if we tried to live away from the stable."

"Giles, the Hawksworths have always been at Latimer's Barn," Steven said. "And there's more to it than the stable, as you well know. The village will expect you to play a leading role in its affairs."

Gillian shook her head. "No, that's not for me!"

"Well . . . there are a few years to go yet before I take over," Giles said, a note of desperation creeping into his voice. "We may have changed our minds by then."

"A lot of things may have changed," Steven said. To Janet Foley's dismay, he stood up. "You will excuse us if we leave, now. Ann and I want to think about this surprising and very unwelcome turn of events."

Janet Foley and Giles, who was staying until Monday morning, flew into a twittering panic, trying to persuade them to stay. Nothing had any effect and, with stiffly polite farewells, Ann and Steven left.

They travelled most of the way home in silence, each half-afraid that anything they said would make things worse.

"I had no idea that Giles was so weak," Steven said at last.

"He's a very *nice* person," Ann replied. "He wouldn't hurt a fly if he could help it."

"I don't consider myself to be nasty, exactly," Steven muttered, neatly highlighting the irrelevance of Ann's loyal remark. "Thank God for Rebecca."

The afternoon was blustery, with masses of cloud driving up from the south-west to bring rain. When they reached Latimer's Barn, Steven looked into the three yards, found them quiet, as they should be on a late-November Sunday afternoon, and hurried back to The House.

"Are we all alone?" he asked Ann as she finished making a pot of tea.

"Yes. I imagine Rebecca is at Rose House."

Steven placed cups, saucers and milk on a tray and waited expectantly for the teapot. "Let's take this upstairs," he said.

Ann smiled. "I thought you were getting old and past it."

"The cheek of the woman! I'm fifty-three and as good as ever."

There was no such mood in the Foley household. After the sudden departure of Ann and Steven, Gillian decided to go to her room to rest, leaving a deeply worried Giles

326

to wander off for a walk. The prospect of an afternoon and evening devoid of interest caused Ralph Foley to remember that he had promised to see friends at Henley: his wife knew what this meant and was glad to see the back of him.

Janet Foley was alarmed. She knew now that she had underestimated the Hawksworths. The ruse of the house in Marlborough, essential to placate Gillian, had misfired badly. Belatedly, it occurred to Janet that the Latimer's Barn clan had not achieved their present position by allowing themselves to be pushed around and outmanoeuvred by the likes of jumped-up estate agents.

That evening, Janet Foley came close to instructing Gillian to break her engagement. Later, she used the excuse that she was unable to find her daughter; in reality, she lacked the courage to drag Gillian out of Giles's bedroom.

Ann and Steven were also guilty of neglect. When Rebecca came back from Rose House at eight o'clock, they did not discuss the problem with her. It was a conscious decision.

"What would we say to her?" Steven asked. "'Your brother is hell-bent on a marriage that will ruin his chances here. There's damn all we can do to stop him and Oliver isn't interested, so stand by to pick up the pieces, there's a good girl.' How does *that* sound?"

"Awful," Ann agreed.

"So, let's leave it, eh? We can rely on Rebecca; she's steady and she loves this place as much as we do."

When Giles came back the following morning, circumstances made it easy for him to avoid his parents. A full-scale crisis was raging over three yearlings who were thought to be suffering from a lethal form of equine influenza. Ann was dashing round doing what she could to help, Bess was being nice to Richard Morton to ensure his best efforts and Liz was driving to Bristol to collect drugs from the University Veterinary School. Until he went out soon after dusk, Giles was able to use the sheer size of Latimer's Barn to shirk contact with anyone.

Next day, relief at the recovery of the yearlings obliterated all else: the one chance that Steven might have taken to talk to Giles about Gillian was gone.

By the time of the wedding on 7 January 1967, Steven had been concealing the fact that he was unwell for over three weeks. Those who noticed his strained demeanour, both in church and at the reception, attributed it to the whispers of trouble over the arrangements that had inevitably circulated.

The bride was unhappy at marrying in Cannings Ambo, rather than her own village. In a successful attempt to distract attention from the more serious problems, Ann had told Elsie to spread the story. As a quid pro quo for the house in Marlborough, Ann had insisted on having the wedding at the church of St Luke and St John. Anxious to mend fences, Janet Foley had told Gillian that she would do as she was told and look cheerful about it.

She did not make much of a job of complying with the second part of this requirement, and, although the photographers from the glossy magazines were over the moon about it, her extravagant wedding dress did not go down well in the village.

"Is that supposed to be 'fashion'?" one jaundiced onlooker asked.

"Ar! Looks a right mess to me."

"Cost a bit, that did."

"She's just a clothes-horse. You mark my words, that's all there is to her."

Sensing the atmosphere, the Reverend Robert Frobisher gave the ceremony his best endeavours and turned it into something close to a success. Contrary to the separate fears of Ann and Janet Foley, the reception passed without any awkward incidents. It was done, Janet noticed, with a massive closing of ranks by the leading lights of Cannings Ambo. Seeing them all in action for the first time, Janet felt fearful; all courtesy and smiles on the surface, they were as hard as nails underneath. Giles was the obvious exception and Rachel behaved oddly, creating a stream of opportunities to be outstandingly nice to Gillian. This, from a dowager duchess, was pleasing; unfortunately, her son, the devastatingly eligible Duke of Laverstoke, plainly thought that she was stepping out of line.

Whether they showed it or not, everyone was glad when it was over and they could go their separate ways. Gillian's brother provided a last-minute threat to unity. As the numbers dwindled, Janet saw him talking to Rebecca. The girl's attitude said that he was making a nuisance of himself. With a beautifully executed swoop, Janet removed him. Once they were in their car, Simon protested.

"You are a killjoy, Mother. I was making terrific progress there."

She laughed derisively. "Simon, if you can't see when a girl is on the verge of telling you to shut your face and go away, I despair of you."

"Don't be silly, she was lapping it up! I say, fancy not knowing that Giles's sister was like that! Isn't she a corker?"

"Simon, forget it!" Janet snapped. "We're in enough trouble with the Hawksworths already, without you making an idiot of yourself over someone they *really* care about."

That night, Giles and Gillian flew to the island of Grand Bahama for a three-week honeymoon. After two idyllic days in a superb hotel, Gillian began to question Giles about the financial arrangements of Latimer's Barn. Glad of what sounded like innocent interest, he explained the Fund and how it was administered by the Trustees. Unwilling to believe what she was hearing, Gillian finally interrupted to ask: "Does this mean you haven't got any money of your own?"

"I get an allowance of fifteen hundred a year."

"Fifteen hundred!" Gillian screamed.

"Steady on, darling, I think Father only draws two thousand."

Having appeared to be teetering on the brink of a manic outburst, Gillian subsided pathetically. "My father pays his *secretary* more than that," she said.

329

For all the good that the remaining seventeen days of the honeymoon were going to do them, they might as well have caught that afternoon's direct flight to London.

On the Saturday following the wedding, Bess was struck by Steven's obvious discomfort as he moved round the yards, inspecting each horse in turn. At first, realising that his heart was not in the job, Bess thought he had something on his mind: Liz had told her that Giles's marriage was enough to worry ten men to death. But, as they went from box to box in the 1933 yard, she began to understand that he was distressed. She was on the point of asking him whether he was fit to be working when every last vestige of colour drained from his face and he sank to his knees, crucified with pain.

"Run to The House and fetch Mrs Hawksworth," Bess said to the lad who was in the box with them. "Go on, jump to it!"

Kneeling down beside Steven, she helped him into a more comfortable position, lying on his side, his knees drawn up towards his chest. "Pain!" he grunted through clenched teeth. "Bloody bad, actually."

"Where?" Bess asked. "Stomach?"

He nodded grimly. Looking closely at him, Bess saw beads of perspiration on his forehead and tears in his eyes. A shadow fell across her and she found Jimmy Farrant, his face tense with concern.

"What's up?" he asked.

"The guv'nor's bad," Bess said quietly. "I've sent Tommy for Mrs Hawksworth. I think we should have my brother, as well."

"I'm on my way," Jimmy said and set off at a run.

Ann was not long arriving. Bess noticed how calm she appeared despite what she must be thinking. It was as Boggysevick had always said: "Mrs Hawksworth has class. If you don't know what I mean, watch her when things are going wrong."

By now, Steven was feeling better and had struggled into a sitting position, his back against a wall.

"What's all this?" Ann asked, taking his hand as she sat down beside him.

"A bit of a pain," he muttered.

Ann looked inquiringly at Bess. There was no question of evasion.

"I'm afraid he was very poorly, ma'am. I think he was in pain all the time we were out here, then it suddenly got very bad. He nearly passed out."

"Is this true, Steven?" Ann asked. When he nodded miserably, she went on. "Did this start today?" His failure to reply was answer enough. "How long?" she demanded.

"Four weeks."

Ann turned to Bess. "I think we need Joe," she said.

"Jimmy Farrant's gone for him."

"Thank you." Without any warning, Ann found herself possessed by the most amazing thought: why the devil couldn't Giles have fallen in love with Bess? She was jolted back to reality by Steven falling prey to another searing attack.

He was still doubled up in agony when Joe Collier arrived.

As Ann and Bess had feared, Joe did not bother with examination, or an attempt at diagnosis, and made the only sensible response to pain of such terrible intensity. "I'm taking him to hospital. Can you get him into The House while we're waiting for the ambulance?"

Between them, Bess and Jimmy Farrant, each with one of Steven's arms round their shoulders, helped him into the kitchen while Joe used the telephone. Afterwards, he whispered to Ann and she hurried away purposefully, returning with a small suitcase in which she had packed Steven's pyjamas and sponge-bag.

"Joe's taking me up to the hospital," Ann told Bess. "Will you look after things while I'm away? And Rebecca's gone shopping in Swindon. If she gets back before I do, let her know what's happened."

Bess walked down to Alfred Merriweather's house, told him all there was to know and asked him to supervise the evening

331

feeds. As she was leaving, Rebecca was turning into the drive in her little car.

She took it badly. Panic-stricken, she wanted to dash off to the hospital. Elsie, in whom Rebecca had always had complete faith, settled her, but only for a few minutes.

"Do they know at Rose House?" Rebecca asked.

"I'm not sure," Bess replied.

"I must go!" Rebecca was on her feet, trying to walk in two different directions at once. "If you hear anything, will you give me a ring?" She dashed off, not waiting for confirmation.

"It's best for her to have something to do," Elsie said. After a pause during which she was obviously weighing her words with great care, she said, "And young William will be good for her."

Bess looked surprised. "Are they fond of each other?"

"Very close." Elsie tapped the side of her nose to signify that the information was confidential; Bess thought it probable that only Rebecca, William Flamsteed and Elsie were in on the secret.

The afternoon dragged on interminably. With a clear sky that threatened frost, dusk started to close in at four-thirty, late for mid-January. Ten minutes later, Elsie put the lights on and pulled the simmering kettle to the centre of the biggest hob on the Aga. Rebecca returned as the teapot was being scalded.

"No news?" she asked.

Bess shook her head. They drank the tea and waited, doing their best not to look at each other. At a few minutes to six, Rebecca shot out of her seat like a rocket when one of the telephones in the office began to ring. She returned quickly, looking dejected. "Lady Amaryllis," she said. "She'd heard from Kathleen Frobisher . . . Joe rang her up."

The news that Joe had been talking to his retired predecessor did not sound good. "Does Kathleen know anything?" Bess asked.

"She wouldn't tell Amaryllis," Rebecca said. "I wonder

if . . ." She froze at the sound of footsteps coming towards them from the side door.

Elsie was reminded of pictures she had seen during the War. Like the Londoners who had been bombed out of their homes, Ann and Joe had a dazed, sightless look to their eyes while the rest of their faces tried to be defiant. Rebecca opened her mouth, but remained silent, giving them time to sit down. In response to Ann's nod, Elsie set about reviving the teapot. As Joe cleared his throat, Ann put a hand on his arm.

"I'll do it," she said. She looked steadily at Rebecca, Elsie and Bess in turn. "Steven has cancer."

Elsie let out a gasp, smothering it by clapping a hand over her mouth. "I'm sorry, ma'am," she said.

Ann nodded. "It's in the lower intestine and very advanced, according to the X-rays. Mr Mayhew, who Joe tells me is a remarkably good surgeon, says that something may be gained by operating and he's going to do it as soon as possible . . . tomorrow we hope."

"How successful could an operation be?" Rebecca asked, trying to emulate Ann's calm.

Joe knew that it was up to him to answer. "It may give him another year."

With that as the best option, Rebecca was disinclined to ask the other question. Seeing the look on Bess's face, Ann said, "Three months," very quietly.

Joe stood up, moving towards the entrance hall beyond the kitchen door, signalling with his eyes for Bess to follow him.

"Mrs Hawksworth isn't showing it yet, but she's had the most terrible shock," he said when they were in the office with the door shut. "Do what you can to help her, Bessie."

"Of course I will, Joseph." She hesitated. "Tell me, is Mr Hawksworth done for?"

"As good as. To be frank, this operation could kill him."
"Christ!"

Joe saw that there was much more to her distress than the plight of a man for whom she had the greatest affection and respect, but made no comment. "Look, Bessie, Mrs

Hawksworth would like you to move into The House while all this is going on. She needs you."

"All right. Joseph, you will see that Mr Hawksworth is looked after, won't you?"

"Of course." He made a move to return to Ann, but saw that Bess, lost in desperate thought, was not ready. "This is terrible," she whispered.

He took her hand. "Come on, you're wanted."

As they slipped back into the kitchen, Rebecca's voice was taking on an urgency that pointed to hysteria. "Honestly, Mother, I think you ought. Giles would want to be here . . . you should let him know."

"It isn't necessary, darling." Ann's patience was cracking. "In any case, I don't know where they are."

"Gillian's mother is bound to have their address – or a phone number. You could send a cable!"

"No, darling!" Ann paused, then let it out. "What use would Giles be? And as for *her*!" Turning to Bess, she was suddenly calm again, unnaturally so. "Obviously you're in charge of the stable until further notice, Bess," she said. "That was Steven's express wish."

Although the responsibility would have scared most people witless, Bess knew that looking after a racing stable during the winter was not particularly difficult. It was that word 'obviously' that staggered her.

Ann, Rebecca and Amelia visited Steven every day. He had survived the operation but was very weak, and, to judge from looks and fragments of muttered conversation, extremely poorly.

"I want you to come with me to see Steven this afternoon," Ann said to Bess as they had breakfast together on the seventh day.

Nothing more was said until they were entering the small hospital six hours later: after a week of living together, they had become very close. "He isn't looking particularly well," Ann said and Bess knew that it was a warning. She braced herself.

334

Steven looked frightful. Everyone now realised that he had been losing weight before his collapse, but in the last week he had wasted. The brave smile he attempted for Bess resembled a death's head grimace, yet his sunken eyes had fight in them.

"It's very good of you to come, Bess," he said, reaching out a shockingly emaciated hand.

"No, it isn't," she replied cheerfully. "It was the least I could do. How are you, sir?"

He reacted to her mood. "Not all that bad, really. I feel like a limp rag, but that chap Mayhew seems to think I'm doing all right. They're going to let me start eating properly soon, so I might look a bit better. How is everything?"

"There's nothing at all for you to worry about," Bess assured him. "Sean Daly's done his collar-bone in."

"That filly of Giffard's?"

"That's the one!"

Steven shook his head. "Perhaps he'll learn now."

"You've been saying that for three years, sir," Bess reminded him.

"I have, haven't I? Is he all right?"

"Oh, yes, Joseph fixed him up in no time."

"Good. Listen, Bess." Steven became intense, tightening his grip on her hand. "If the frost holds off, you'll have to start working them in two weeks."

"Yes, sir." Ann felt like kissing Bess for the confidence she displayed.

"If there's anything you aren't quite sure about, you'll find a blue notebook in the drawer of the old writing-table in the library . . . that will tell you how I worked out what to do last year."

Bess nodded.

"One special thing," Steven went on. "I'm sure you don't need telling, but I will anyway. Look after Ptolemy."

"You're quite right," Bess smiled. "I didn't need telling."

They chatted about minor matters for a few minutes, then Bess excused herself to leave Ann and Steven alone

335

in the small private ward while she went back to the car. When she emerged half an hour later, Ann was in control of herself until she was sitting beside Bess and their eyes met. Momentarily, they were both on the brink of tears.

"Remember what he told you," Ann said brusquely. "Take care of that colt!"

Ptolemy belonged to Alain de Mourville. He was a diminutive chestnut named after the man credited with being the father of astronomy. His sire was Astronomer Royal and his dam one of Alain's French mares who had done well at Longchamp and Chantilly as a three- and four-year-old. The high hopes associated with Ptolemy began on the day he was born.

Unfortunately, he saw his mission in life as being the stable's jester. After Rebecca had given up in despair, Steven allocated the colt to a succession of lads, all of whom found themselves incapable of getting sense and reason out of him. He raced in May, June and July of 1966, recording a trio of impressive-looking fifth places behind opposition that ranged from mediocre to bad. Ptolemy's idea was that he was being taken to racecourses for an agreeable change of scenery and the chance to play the fool with a new bunch of horses.

In sheer desperation, without any hope of success, Steven gave the wayward clown to Jimmy Farrant.

"There you are," Steven had said to Bess as Ptolemy started working like a champion in the making. "That's the finest example of stupidity you'll ever see. Who's the best lad to make difficult horses go?"

"Jimmy Farrant," Bess laughed.

"Right. He's been at it for over thirty years. And who's the last person I think of trying?"

"Jimmy Farrant!"

"Let that be a lesson to you," Steven said with mock-solemnity. "Never forget what's staring you in the face."

Most of the pundits thought that Ptolemy was lucky to win the Dewhurst Stakes. His late run after an indifferent five furlongs gave Bess a few moments of stress, even though she regarded the thousand pounds she had put on him as expendable. His victory at odds of twelve to one allowed her to contemplate heavy investment on his future.

"You can get eight to one about him for the Guineas," Solstice said. "Do you want a go?"

"I'll have five thousand pounds-worth," Bess said.

The legalisation of betting shops in 1961, and their subsequent mushroom growth into every high street, made Solstice's task a great deal easier. As he zig-zagged across Wiltshire, dropping twenty-pound bets here, there and everywhere, he thought that if this one came off, Bess would definitely be poised to buy her own place.

Although Steven was improving rapidly when Giles and Gillian returned from the Bahamas, he still looked what he was, a very sick man.

Gillian was stupefied by the news that met them at Latimer's Barn. The shock of learning that her husband was likely to be a racehorse trainer in months, not years, left her numb.

Devastated by Steven's condition, Giles lost his temper with Ann. "Why didn't you send for me?" he shouted. "Whatever were you thinking of? It's too bad!"

"There was nothing you could have done." Ann's reaction to his anger was deliberately mild.

"What's that got to do with it? Good God, Mother, I should have been told!"

"I didn't want to spoil your honeymoon," Ann said sharply, giving Gillian a far from pleasant look. "Now, *do* shut up, Giles, and let's get down to business, shall we?" She took him to the library, making it plain that Gillian was not required.

It was one of Rachel's days for visiting Steven and she took it upon herself to comfort the newest Mrs Hawksworth.

"I'm very sorry about this, my dear," she said. "You'll have to do your best to bear with us for a while. As you can imagine, this has come as a frightful shock. My brother is only fifty-three, you know."

Gillian nodded miserably. She was completely lost and dispirited. With an enviable tan, three expensive suitcases festooned with exotic labels, and a husband who had every right to hate the sight of her after the way she had behaved for most of their honeymoon, she had walked into a disaster.

"On top of everything else, our house in Marlborough isn't ready," she told Rachel. "I rang Mother from Heathrow and there's been a foul-up with the furniture and electricity."

Rachel knew what advice she ought to have given Gillian: it was time to get into sensible clothes and start making a future for herself and Giles. Instead, she assumed a tone of syrupy sympathy. "That sounds *awful*! I suppose you *could* stay here, but I can't pretend that it's going to be very nice. The best thing may be to go to your parents until things are sorted out."

"Do you think so?" Gillian had been wondering how she could pluck up the courage to make the suggestion herself.

"Don't worry, I'll tell Giles," Rachel said. "If there are any brickbats flying I can deal with them."

Stupefied after an hour with his mother, Giles seemed not to comprehend what Rachel was telling him until she said, "So, will you drive the poor girl to her parents' house?"

"Er . . . yes . . . right." Giles rumpled a hand through his hair and stared round in bewilderment.

"Don't be all day about it," Ann ordered. "There are hundreds of things waiting to be done."

Steven left hospital at the end of February, on the same day that Giles and Gillian finally began living together as man and wife at their house in Marlborough. Throughout March, blessed by favourable weather, Bess got all the horses fit. She also made sure that Giles rode out with her on the gallops and played a positive part in running the yard. At the start of April, when Ann began taking Steven in a Land-Rover to watch the horses work, a casual observer might have thought that Giles was in complete control.

"He doesn't appear to be doing too badly," Ann said after a few days.

"She's not letting him anywhere near Ptolemy, though," Steven muttered. There was an amused glint in his eyes.

Not only was Bess keeping the colt very much under her own control, she was riding him that morning in order to get an accurate measure of his progress. Afterwards, she went to Steven for advice. "Do you think he needs a prep race before the Guineas?" she asked.

"How should I know?" Steven smiled. "I've only seen him work a few times. You and Jimmy Farrant are the experts."

"He can go straight for the Guineas," Bess said decisively.

Giles had fallen into the habit of accompanying horses to race meetings. He liked the opportunity for socialising and appreciated that his absence from Latimer's Barn enabled Bess to get on with running the stable without having him under her feet. However, at Steven's specific request, Bess herself took Ptolemy to Newmarket.

"Monsieur de Mourville is too busy to come over for the race," Steven told her. "I can't even pretend that I'm up to going, but I do want us to put on a bit of a show."

Donning her latest tweed suit from Farquharson's of Bath, together with a burgundy-coloured Fedora hat that Liz had forced her to buy, Bess went through the formalities with confidence, saddling Ptolemy herself, indulging in polite paddock talk during the parade, giving Michael Pilgrim a leg up, and looking coolly unconcerned as the horses went down to the start. The worst part was watching Michael execute the radical orders she had given him.

"He's capable of winning it from the front," she said. "I'm backing him to have speed *and* stamina – let him rip."

"Some of the others will want to go at a hell of a pace," Michael said doubtfully.

"I know that. Let's see if they can go faster than ours!"

It was a glory-or-bust tactic and it worked. For the first time, starting stalls were being used for the Two Thousand Guineas and Ptolemy, well-schooled to the new contraption, came out like a rocket and had a three-length lead before the others knew what was happening.

That was how they went past the winning post, with Michael

Pilgrim giving Bess a thumbs-up sign before settling to the serious task of stopping the colt.

Back at Latimer's Barn, with his feet up in front of the television set, Steven watched Bess lead Ptolemy up to the winner's enclosure. "Isn't she a credit to us," he said with a catch in his voice.

"She's done wonderfully well," Ann agreed.

As if by unspoken consent, they made no mention of Giles.

Solstice was also impressed by Bess's performance, albeit for very different reasons. Ahead of him lay the task of collecting her prodigious winnings of £40,000. He hoped to God she would start up on her own. With poor Mr Steven at death's door and the stories that were circulating about Mr Giles, Solstice was able to envisage the unhappy state of affairs in which he would be nearly as glad to leave Latimer's Barn as he had been to arrive.

Ptolemy's handsome victory, the twenty-first in a Classic against Steven's name, acted like a miraculous tonic on him. He gained valuable weight, his colour and strength improved, and, in six wonderful weeks from the middle of May, he rode out on the gallops every day, went to Epsom for the Derby and made seven visits to the winner's enclosure at Royal Ascot.

Ann scarcely let him out of her sight and Bess, still living in The House, was at his side whenever possible. Giles took horses racing and was rarely seen in Cannings Ambo. Steven, clearly unhappy with his son's behaviour, was moved to be outspoken to Bess. "He's trying to get his wife straight. I don't envy him the job!"

No one had ever had the remotest cause to say that about a Hawksworth or Flamsteed wife before.

During those six weeks, Steven did his best to tell Bess everything he knew about horses. He never mentioned his affliction: once a week he had to go to Savernake Hospital for tests, and Joe visited him each evening, yet Steven carried on as though these reminders of his vulnerable mortality were nothing.

On one occasion, while talking about the best way to bring a horse back after illness or injury, he paused in mid-stream to say, "You will look after Rebecca, won't you, Bess? Make sure that you train *her*." His meaning was so plain that Bess was profoundly upset.

That apart, they found much to joke and laugh about and Oliver, whom Bess hardly knew, proved a great help. Taking what seemed to be a cavalier view of his final examinations at university, Oliver was in and out of The House like a jack-in-the-box, invariably generating laughter and good humour. When Steven told him that he should be concentrating on getting a good degree, Oliver found the idea laughable.

"I've got a job all fixed up, Dad. And do you know what? It's true what you always said . . . television *is* run by a gang of idiots. I think they'd be unhappy if I turned out to be *too* clever!"

When Alain and Nadia de Mourville came to stay for the whole of Derby week, the light-hearted atmosphere was assured. Nadia wasted no time in unleashing her bizarre sense of humour, reducing perfectly ordinary events and conversations to hilarious chaos. Alain, always serious-minded and devastated by Steven's illness, made a big effort to follow his wife's example.

This time, Alain and Nadia had brought their son and daughter with them. Laurent, nineteen and very like Alain, was already involved in his father's increasing business interests. Nowhere near as dull as he liked to appear, and with Alain's saturnine good looks, he had already broken a few hearts in France. Lisette, now twenty-one, had turned into a young woman of exceptional beauty and poise. She seemed to have acquired a slightly forbidding regal air, although Bess knew that Lisette was charming and lively.

And she knocked the Duke of Laverstoke sideways.

Hubert looked into Latimer's Barn at least three times a week. He liked to give the impression that he was simply popping in on his way to or from London: Ann, with whom he always spent time privately, knew better and was grateful for his concern.

Their conversations, usually in the small sitting-room while Steven and Bess were ensconced in the library, revolved around a ruthless realism that would have shocked those who were too upset by Steven's condition to think of the future.

"The fact is, Hubert, we're going to have the devil's own job with the Trustees when Steven dies," Ann said at the first of their discussions. "We have problems that should have been sorted out years ago."

"I know," he said. "But don't worry too much . . . I'm looking into it."

For a time, Ann was troubled, then, in the week before the Derby, Hubert was bubbling with something close to excitement when he arrived.

"There's nothing to concern us," he said. "At least not in the immediate future. Mother, Edward Mallender and Leslie Giffard would be incapable of agreeing on *anything* if you paid them."

"This sounds interesting!" Ann said eagerly.

Hubert smiled. "It is, although I'd prefer not to give you any details yet. They are definitely at daggers-drawn and likely to stay that way, so we can grasp the nettle."

"You mean Giles as chairman of the Trustees?" Ann asked.

"Yes. Mother wants it, of course. I know that it's a break with tradition, assuming that he ends up with the licence, but he won't do. Setting aside other considerations, Mother would manipulate him."

"Who do you suggest we put up as chairman?" Ann asked.

"I thought of you," Hubert replied.

"Your mother wouldn't wear that," Ann said.

"I know. She might get Mallender and Giffard together on that one. What about Amelia? Who could possibly object to her?"

"No one!" Ann found the idea perfect. "She'll do it."

342

"Make sure she will," Hubert warned. "I'll propose her, Gideon will second it and we should be home and dry."

On a further visit, three days later, Hubert found himself being introduced to Lisette de Mourville.

Their last encounter had been seven years ago on Astronomer Royal's Derby Day. Then, Lisette had thought Hubert pompous, while he found her a nuisance: now, they came as a revelation to each other, an event that did not escape the onlookers.

"*Mon Dieu*! Look at that," Nadia whispered to Ann. "Is he married?"

"Not yet," Ann replied. "Dozens of mothers and daughters have given up in despair."

Nadia took another look and nodded. "Alain, your daughter is going to be a duchess," she said.

Gillian went to Epsom, determined to play her part in what she thought was a social occasion. She had a vague idea that she might help Giles while she was about it. Having finally realised that the name of Hawksworth was revered in racing circles, and with Ptolemy as favourite for the Derby, she confidently expected a good day in which she was near the centre of attraction. For once, her plain cream dress and broad-brimmed hat were suitable; she had even toned down her make-up.

She subsequently blamed Giles for the lack of attention she received, convinced that things would have been different if he had been prepared to push himself to the forefront. Giles agreed with those who thought that the day belonged to his father, and Steven, as unassuming as ever, gave Bess as much of the limelight as possible. Gillian became jealous of Bess, thinking that no woman had the right to look *that* good and be able to handle horses so expertly.

The race was the most exciting Derby seen for some years. Against tough opposition from France and Ireland, Michael Pilgrim always knew he had a job on, but would never forgive himself if he lost it. After a careful study of the other contenders' strengths and weaknesses, Bess had come up with new instructions: Ptolemy was to be kept covered up until the final three furlongs, then, with his speed and stamina unsapped, let rip.

It worked brilliantly, providing the crowd with that most stirring of all racing spectacles, a top-class horse tearing past his rivals as though they were standing still. Alain was nowhere to be found when it was time to lead the colt in; he was hiding, so that Steven had to do the honours with Bess alongside him. When Michael dismounted as dozens of cameras went to work, Steven drew him into a huddle with himself and Bess. For a few precious moments, they were the only three people in the world.

"Thank you both very much," Steven said. "The only thing that frightened me was that I wouldn't last long enough to see him win today."

The moment passed and all was smiles and celebration. Gillian, separated from Giles, found herself in the middle of a crowd, unable to see what was going on, listening to the conversation of the two men in morning suits who were blocking her view.

"It's a damned shame about Hawksworth," one said. "I suppose you've heard the doctors are giving him six months at the most."

"Hellish bad luck," the other agreed. "They say that Bess Collier has been running the stable this season."

"So I believe. One hears glowing reports of her."

"Not going to win an ugliness competition, either, is she? I wonder if they'll have the sense to let her take over when poor Hawksworth does go."

"Oh? Why should they?" The younger of the two men sounded surprised by the suggestion.

"The son's a washout! My chap, Brookes-Smith, was talking to him at Newbury a few weeks ago and came to the conclusion that he has no idea. To make matters worse, he admits it! What do you think of that?"

Even without knowing that the Brookes-Smith referred to was a successful trainer, Gillian felt humiliated.

* * *

Expecting four days of miserable tedium at Royal Ascot, Gillian toyed with the idea of trying to get out of it, realised that she *had* to go, and was soon glad that she had done so. She never doubted that Hugo Richardson was going to make life a good deal more pleasant.

He was a close friend of Hubert Prideaux, with links going back to Eton and Oxford, and had thus come to Latimer's Barn as a would-be owner with impeccable credentials. He had inherited wealth and lived the life of a country gentleman on a small estate near Newbury.

The first of the deluge of seven winners that Latimer's Barn produced for the meeting was in the very first race to be run and belonged to Hugo Richardson. As soon as he was free from the attentions due to a winning owner, Richardson made an unhurried beeline for Gillian. His opening remark showed that he understood a great deal.

"The all-highest of the Cannings Ambo mafia have lost interest in me now, so shall we have a bottle of champagne and become acquainted?"

This unusual introduction supplemented Richardson's physical magnetism and there was no question of Gillian rejecting the offer. They were inseparable for the rest of the meeting. On the third day, when Bess led in the Gold Cup winner, standing in for the absent Duke of Laverstoke, their conversation took a new turn.

"It's a great pity Hubert isn't here," Richardson said. "He would approve of this."

"I thought that racing fanatics would do *anything* rather than miss Ascot," Gillian said. "Where is he?"

"With the de Mourvilles, in France. Between you and me, there are very important things afoot."

"Their daughter?" Gillian asked. She had kept her eyes and ears open during Derby week.

Richardson smiled knowingly. "It's meant to be a secret," he said, unobtrusively tightening the bond between them. "I hope it works: Hubert's a good bloke." He leaned closer. "He tells me that you aren't having too good a time of it."

With no way of knowing that this was a gross distortion of what the Duke had said in a rare unguarded moment, Gillian took it as an expression of sympathy. "It's awful," she said. "I don't know what to do. They all hate me."

"Perhaps you need to give them time," Richardson suggested, pleasantly surprised by her reaction to his tentative exploration. "They're a pretty remarkable bunch, you know, and Steven's illness can't be doing them any good."

Gillian was disappointed: she had expected a far better response to her cry for help. It came the following day, before the final race of the meeting.

"When shall we get together?" Richardson asked. He made it sound like a casual request to join him for a perfectly innocent lunch, but as Gillian stared at him, the atmosphere became charged.

"Monday," she replied firmly. Giles was taking two horses to Thirsk and was likely to be away for at least fifteen hours.

"Where?" Richardson asked.

"Your place. Marlborough's too small and nosy."

"Shall we make a day of it?"

"That sounds marvellous!"

He drew a map of how to find his house on the back of her racecard.

On the day that Gillian Hawksworth and Hugo Richardson embarked enthusiastically on a passionate affair, Hubert Prideaux made a special journey to London to see Lady Leonie Pryce-Renshawe. From the tone of his telephone call to arrange the lunch, she expected something important and was not disappointed.

"It's a long way from being official, but there's something you need to know," Hubert began. "I've found the lady I want to marry."

"How absolutely super!" Leonie was delighted. "Who is this astounding paragon?"

He told her all about Lisette, ending with the fly in

346

the ointment. "She isn't all that keen on leaving France or becoming a duchess."

"But she loves you?"

"Yes." He looked abashed.

"This is terrific! I'm sure you'll soon win her over." She rubbed her hands. "This means I can flog the business and clear off to Northumberland."

"What for?" Hubert was baffled.

"Sheep farming. I'm going to marry Hector Dalziel."

"Who's he?"

"A friend of Alaric's." Alaric was Leonie's eldest brother, an unpopular individual who was widely known to be tired of being a mere viscount and wanted his father's earldom.

"I see." Hubert kept a straight face. "When did he pop the question?"

Leonie shrieked with mirth, attracting filthy looks from some of the other diners. "He hasn't yet. The poor dim-wit is still trying to pluck up the courage to do something about his putrid bitch of a wife. She cleared off to Australia three years ago."

"It sounds as though it's high time you put him right," Hubert said.

"Don't worry, my lad, I will, and eftsoons right speedily." Her mood became more serious. "Presumably, you see this as being the death knell of our bedroom gymnastics?"

"Er . . . well . . ." Hubert paused until a waiter had finished refilling their coffee-cups. "It's the only honourable course of action."

"Oh, quite!" Leonie's agreement was crisp and po-faced. "You don't think it might be worth our while to carry on until everything is all fixed and official?"

"I must confess that I hadn't thought of it," Hubert replied, starting to show what Leonie thought was a promising lack of moral fibre.

"Heaven forbid that I should divert you from the paths of righteousness," Leonie said. "I would, nonetheless, ask you to bear in mind that we're fearfully good at it. We have no

347

idea, I suppose, how our intended spouses will measure up in this respect?"

"I haven't!" Hubert said hurriedly.

"There you are, then," Leonie said, as if an important truth had been established. "You ought to think jolly carefully before invoking principles that might be to one's disadvantage."

"I will," he assured her.

Leonie grinned. There would undoubtedly be prevarication and soul-searching, but they both knew what his decision was going to be.

Steven's period of respite and reasonable health ended on 26 June. Ann saw him wince and knew that the pain was returning. For nearly two months, it was intermittent and controllable with the sort of pain-killers that Joe kept in the surgery at Oak Cottage. Steven rode out with the horses until the end of July. After that, he appeared every day with Ann in the Land-Rover. At Bess's insistence, Giles changed his working habits: he looked after the yards and gallop work while she took the horses racing. Steven approved of the change, knowing what she was trying to do. No one could see that when repeated later, the tactic was to prove disastrous.

Staying in Sussex for the five-day 'Glorious' Goodwood meeting at the end of July, Bess was approached by two Newmarket trainers; she agreed to have dinner with one of them in Chichester.

"Let's not beat about the bush," Ryan Jarvis said when they were settled. "I want you to come and work for me. As I expect you know, I've got eighty boxes and I'm going up to a hundred and twenty over the next three years."

"What makes you think I'm looking for a job?" Bess asked.

"Look, it's a bloody shame about Steven Hawksworth – I don't know anyone who isn't cut up about it. He's definitely been the best of the post-war generation. But

348

how are you going to feel about working for that idiot son of his?"

Bess indulged in a piece of play-acting, greatly embellishing her surprise at his brutal frankness. "It's true that Giles has some growing up to do," she said. "But these comments about him are getting totally ridiculous. You're all in for a shock when he starts."

"You're perfectly happy at Latimer's Barn then?"

"Most definitely."

"Really?" Jarvis didn't want to believe it.

"*Really*!"

They relaxed and enjoyed a pleasant evening, exchanging scurrilous gossip about some of the more colourful mavericks of racing. Later, Bess found that, much to Ryan Jarvis's credit, he had spread the word that she was happy and optimistic.

At the September meeting of Trustees, Steven stepped down as chairman and suggested Amelia as his successor. "I don't want anyone to attach a sinister significance to this," he said. "I hope it won't be long before Giles can take over, but I'd like him to have a little more experience before he does."

A vote was not necessary. Rachel was visibly upset by her brother's condition and neither Edward Mallender nor Leslie Giffard was present: their notes of apology spoke of urgent business matters.

Shortly afterwards, Steven's pain became so intolerable that Joe began giving him injections of something a friend at the hospital let him have. Thereafter, deterioration was rapid. Steven knew that Ptolemy flew to France on 30 September for the Prix de l'Arc de Triomphe, but Ann was certain that he never appreciated his last big victory. After lying in a coma for thirty-six hours, Steven Hawksworth died on 2 October.

His funeral, nearly as well-attended as Leander's, was a far sadder affair. Whereas his grandmother had been blessed with an immensely long life, Steven's death at the age of fifty-four was a tragic curtailment of a talent that still had much to give.

Noel Timberlake, the eldest son of Gideon and Lady Amaryllis, was not the only one to be in tears in the churchyard. At eleven, he was ashamed of letting his mother and father see him in that state; instead, he stuck close to Bess who had always been his heroine. She never imagined the circumstances in which, years later, she would tell him how difficult he made it for her to contain her own grief on that dank October afternoon.

A week after Steven's burial, when Ann had cleared everything up, including the harrowing task of completing the Big Book, she invited Giles and Gillian to dinner.

For over three months, Gillian seemed to have been making an effort, spending time at Latimer's Barn and keeping Giles in a good mood. Although she was half-ashamed of herself for thinking it, Ann wondered what ulterior motives lay behind the attempts to be pleasant.

The reasons were Gillian's sexual fulfilment and the consequent twinges of remorse. Hugo Richardson was a phenomenal lover, the best she had ever known. Twice a week, they copulated like mad things for hours on end, both always wanting more when the clock drove Gillian home. She salved her conscience by making sure that Giles's demands were met, especially after a day with Richardson, when she was able to give a very convincing imitation of enjoying herself.

Obeying the summons to dinner, Giles and Gillian found that it was a small gathering of only four. As well as Ann, Amelia was waiting in the small sitting-room, looking as though she had no intention of moving until a vital question had been resolved to her complete satisfaction.

Her opening words confirmed that impression. Without waiting for Ann to finish pouring the drinks, Amelia fixed Giles with a hard stare and said, "This evening, we are going to decide who takes up the licence to train at Latimer's Barn."

Facing what she thought was the worst crisis the stable had ever known, Amelia was forbidding.

CHAPTER 13

1968

'You never know, we might have a winner or two!'

1968 was the least successful and most vexatious racing season ever experienced at Latimer's Barn. Nothing went right. Many of the failures were embarrassing and most of the shambles took place without the benefit of any form of excuse. Worse still, everyone knew it. For the first time, the lads' hostels buzzed with discontent. Tempers frayed, fights broke out and five very promising youngsters left to find work in other stables.

Several of the lads had used their share of the handsome prize-money kitty that had been commonplace under Steven to buy cars. The principal change brought about by mobility was that about a dozen of them now did their drinking in Marlborough, rather than The George. During their taproom discussions, Bess was the person most frequently blamed for the difficulties. Instead of standing aside and letting 'them' foul everything up, she should have got stuck in and sorted it all out.

It was Alfred Merriweather who started the rot.

On New Year's Day, when Giles's licence became effective, Alfred marched into the office and demanded the retirement to which he had become entitled two months previously. No one, not even Margaret, his wife, or Arthur, his successor, knew of his intention. Completely unperturbed at finding himself confronted by Amelia, who was taking her duties as chairman very seriously, Alfred stated his case.

"Oh. I see." Amelia knew what this was all about, but was careful not to show it. "I know you're eligible, Alfred . . . we were assuming that you'd carry on for another year." She smiled. "Continuity, you know."

Alfred's determination not to be put off, not even by the village's most respected inhabitant, made him truculent. "There's no need for that, ma'am. Arthur knows what's what."

"I don't doubt it for an instant," Amelia replied. "I'd prefer you to stay on for a while."

"No, ma'am. I want to go."

"You're quite sure about this, Alfred?"

"That's what I'm saying!"

"Very well. When would you like to begin your retirement?"

"Today!"

While Amelia was trying not to look shocked, the lad who had been in the other office talking to Liz Challoner about a pay query, suddenly decided he was satisfied. Once out of The House, he sprinted to the hostel to spread the news. Within minutes, everyone knew that Alfred Merriweather, head lad for thirty-two years, was packing it in. The implications were glaringly obvious.

"What did I tell you, eh? I knew old Merriweather didn't rate that Giles. He won't have anything to do with him."

"Bloody marvellous! Where does that leave us?"

It was two hours before Bess found out. She had been to visit Astronomer Royal at the stud and got the story from Liz when she looked into the office.

"Hell's teeth and stomach pills!" Bess said. "How's that gone down?"

"What do you think?" Liz replied, rolling her eyes. "Total panic. Arthur nearly fell down when the Dame told him he was head lad."

"Didn't he know?" Bess gasped.

"No!" Liz pulled a gruesome face to emphasise the point. "Two more developments," she went on. "Giles is getting another assistant."

"Rebecca?" Bess asked.

"Correct. The other thing is that they're cancelling this month's meeting of Trustees."

Bess frowned. "That's unusual, isn't it?"

"According to Dame Amelia – who's bloody unhappy about it – it's the first time it's happened. Ever!"

"I'm going to talk to Alfred Merriweather," Bess said.

Stepping into the corridor, she found that Amelia, Ann and Giles had just come through the interconnecting door from the main part of The House. Bess paused, certain that they would want to speak to her. Only Ann, deeply worried and attempting to listen to the muttered conversation in progress between Amelia and Giles, saw Bess. But Ann's abstraction was so great that she looked straight through Bess, unaware of what she was doing. From Bess's point of view, Ann's stare gave the impression of hostility. As Bess turned on her heel and made off, the anger in her movement communicated itself to Ann. Too late, she realised what had happened; she should have run after her to apologise. Instead, she found herself listening to a badly rattled Giles digging up more complications.

On the way down the drive to see Alfred, Bess reviewed what she knew of the agreement Giles had reached with Amelia and his mother about taking over the licence. The two women, formidably determined, had been intent on browbeating him into surrender over the house in Marlborough: unless he gave it up and lived at Latimer's Barn, someone else would be put in charge of the stable.

They had reckoned without Gillian. She reacted explosively. There was, she said, no question of anyone dictating where she should live. If that was to be the case, the charade could end, she would go back to her parents and start divorce proceedings as soon as possible. Giles told Bess the story, idiotically proud of his wife's performance,

353

apparently incapable of seeing what a thoroughgoing bitch she had shown herself to be.

To Bess's disgust, Amelia and Ann settled for a compromise. During the week, Giles would live in The House while Gillian amused herself elsewhere. At weekends, they would be firmly resident in Marlborough. Although she had every sympathy with the demoralising consequences of Steven's untimely death, Bess was unable to understand why such ludicrous terms had been acceptable, especially to Amelia.

"Gillian threatened to kick up a stink," Giles explained. "You know, spread the dirt."

"What dirt?" Bess demanded.

"About how arrogant and unfeeling the Hawksworths are." Giles found his wife's antics mildly amusing.

"All this because she's supposed to live with you in the home that your family have occupied for over a hundred years?" Bess sneered. "You're all mad!"

Margaret Merriweather almost wept with relief when she saw Bess. "Oh, Miss Collier, do you think you can get him to see sense?" she asked earnestly.

"I don't think it matters now, Margaret," Bess said. "They've appointed Arthur and they can't change their minds."

"Talk to him, though."

"I will, don't you worry!"

Alfred, in the parlour with Arthur, got to his feet when he saw Bess. "Hello, Miss," he said. "What brings you here?"

"Don't be daft, Alfred!" Bess retorted. "You know damned well that the place is in an uproar over you."

"Can't help that," he replied stolidly. "I was due for retirement."

"You realise what all the lads are saying?"

"I've told him that," Arthur said. "He won't listen."

"Is there anything I can say, or do, to make you reconsider?" Bess asked Alfred.

"No point, is there?" Alfred said. "It's like you told Margaret, they've given Arthur the job. Anyway, I'm happy enough."

They argued the toss for two hours, getting nowhere. Not until Bess was leaving and Alfred walked to the front gate with her did he give an indication of his true feelings.

"We might have stood a chance if it hadn't been for that wife of his," he said. "It's her that'll ruin everything."

"I think she's poison," Bess admitted.

Alfred merely touched the peak of his cap and turned away.

At nearly five o'clock, the early January night had closed in. The front of The House was in darkness apart from a glimmer of light behind the heavily curtained windows of the library. In the offices, however, all was fluorescent brightness as Liz continued to work on the accounts.

"Any joy?" she asked.

"No, he's a stubborn old bugger," Bess grumbled.

"He's also been head lad during thirty-odd of the most successful years that any British racing stable has ever had," Liz said.

Bess regarded her through suspicious eyes. "You didn't make that up on your own," she said accusingly.

"No, I didn't. That's my version of the latest whispers from the yard. The afternoon's other snippet is that the young lord and master is bringing a management consultant in to tell us how to do things properly."

"You're making this up!"

"Oh, no I'm not, sweetie. It's some big cheese that his father-in-law has recommended."

"Happy New Year!" Bess said sardonically. The only thing that gave her any comfort was the thought that her savings now exceeded £100,000.

One of the main conclusions reached by the management consultant was that running Latimer's Barn would be much easier if horses did not have to be taken racing: it was, the report said, a labour-intensive activity that ate manpower and money. Bess was openly derisory when Giles told her about it.

"I've heard similar things said about the railways."

"Eh?" Giles was thrown by her remark.

"They could run a marvellous service if it weren't for all the passengers. It's a well-known fact." She took advantage of Giles being struck dumb to ask the obvious question. "What the hell does this idiot think we run the stable *for*?"

"Oh, he understands all about that," Giles said hurriedly. "What he's suggesting is that we need formal routines for getting horses to racecourses. In my experience, it's always been rather a hit-and-miss affair." The expression on Bess's face stopped him. She forbore to point out what she thought of his experience, or to remind him of the results achieved by the method he was criticising. Giles battled on. "You know the ropes, Bess, so how would you like to look after the racing side of things while Rebecca and I run the yard?"

"Permanently?"

"Yes, there'd be no point in doing it, otherwise. I know it means a lot of travelling, but there must be compensations."

Bess noticed that he was unable to think of any. It would, she thought, keep her away from the stable. No sooner had she said it to herself, than she was stunned: two months after Giles had taken over, she was looking favourably on a scheme that would take her away from Latimer's Barn for much of the time.

"Won't you be going racing at all?" she asked.

"I *was* intending to go to the big ones, but we doubt whether even they are worth the time and effort . . . Ascot, perhaps? I don't really know."

Bess wondered who he meant by 'we'. "I'll do it," she said.

She travelled with Solstice in the latest transporter van which had a much-improved cab. A lad accompanied them to look after the one or two horses they were taking. For Newmarket and courses in the Midlands, they left at six in the morning and were away until ten at night; the courses around London were easier and Bath, Salisbury and Newbury were no more than an afternoon out. York and the occasional visit to Thirsk meant a night in a hotel. Being with her old friend, Solstice, was always a pleasure, as was making the acquaintance of the lunatics and scoundrels on the circuit. The lads who accompanied them in the van were a different matter: nine times out of ten, they wanted to moan about what was happening in the yard.

Bess needed no telling that the job was not being done correctly. The results on the racecourse spoke for themselves. An incident at Salisbury in April was typical.

A two-year-old filly was making her début. This in itself was wrong. Steven had never raced youngsters as early as this, and the poor status of the race was an insult to the filly's breeding. By Quartermaster, the 1955 Derby winner, out of a mare who had finished second in the Oaks and St Leger, she should have been aiming for a race with at least £2,000 in prize-money, not the miserable £450 on offer in this case. However, both in the paddock and going down to the start, she looked a picture.

Then the trouble started. Watching through binoculars, Bess saw that the filly gave the starting stalls a terrified look and refused to go near them during the few minutes that were allowed for the roll-call and settling down. As soon as the other horses began going in, she was backing away, showing the whites of her eyes. When the handlers came to her, she flew into a blind panic. Everything was tried, all to no avail. Finally, she reared up and threw Michael Pilgrim. Fortunately, someone had a good hold on her reins and she was unable to make a dash for freedom. Michael, although badly shaken, was back on his feet quickly and able to take charge of her. The inevitable happened; the starter ordered the filly's withdrawal.

"That's going to get me on the carpet," a furious Bess told Solstice.

Sure enough, when he returned to his office behind the grandstand, the starter asked to see her.

"If I didn't know Latimer's Barn better, Miss Collier, I'd

say that filly hadn't been schooled on the stalls," he said, very pleasant about it.

"We have had trouble with her, but we thought she'd got over it," Bess lied.

"A word to Mr Hawksworth is in order, I think," the starter said. "*Unofficially*, I happen to know that you had trouble with two at Nottingham last week. Remember that it is incumbent upon trainers to ensure that their animals can cope with the stalls. A horse like yours can make things dangerous for the others."

"Yes, Captain Ayres," Bess said humbly.

After checking that Michael and the filly were none the worse for the experience, Bess turned to the lad.

"How many times have you been through the practice stalls with her?" she asked.

"I haven't, ma'am. She plays blue murder at them."

"Why the hell didn't you tell me?" Bess raged.

"I knew you'd shout at me!"

"What did you expect me to do after the poor thing had played up and made fools of us?"

The lad looked sheepish. "Mr Hawksworth thought there was a chance we'd get away with it."

"Let's go home, Solstice," Bess said. "This needs putting straight." Seeing the look on the lad's face, she hastened to reassure him. "Don't worry, Ken, I'll fix this without dropping you in it."

They were back at six and Bess went straight to the offices where she found Giles, and, since she was actually in residence for a few days and wished to advertise the fact, Gillian. Later, Liz said that she was pretending to help Giles when the fancy took her and getting everything in a frightful mess.

"Hello, Bess," Giles said. "How did we do?"

"We didn't even get a run. The starter pulled her out because she couldn't cope with the stalls."

"Oh, Lord!" Giles looked dismayed.

"That's the third in two weeks," Bess continued. "The starter had a go at me. I think we should regard that as an official warning."

"We don't seem to be able to deal with the difficult cases," Giles said. Bess thought he sounded pathetic.

"Jimmy Farrant knows how to do it," she replied forcefully. "Get rid of that damn-fool job he's doing and have him out on the gallops where he belongs."

At the suggestion of the management consultant, Jimmy was messing about in the yards as some sort of foreman, probably, Bess suspected, doing nothing except get in Arthur Merriweather's way.

"I'll give it a try," Giles said, far from happy.

"Please do," Bess replied. "It will help my nerves." She added a final sarcastic dig. "You never know, we might even have a winner or two!"

Bess delayed her departure for a few moments in order to return Gillian's filthy look with a bland smile.

As April turned into May, Bess found that Gillian's hostility to her was mounting. It started to show in the unlikely surroundings of racecourse paddocks.

The first time Gillian appeared, at Salisbury, Bess nearly fell over with surprise. Solstice solved the mystery by pointing out that she was accompanying Hugo Richardson, who had a runner in the third race.

"Supporting our owners, eh?" Bess said. "I suppose that's better than being totally useless."

Muttering incomprehensibly, Solstice turned away.

Richardson had twelve horses in training that year and they were out at frequent intervals, usually on the southern courses within easy reach of Cannings Ambo. When Richardson did turn up to watch, Gillian was always with him. Amused by how long it was taking Bess to cotton on, Solstice said nothing.

It was August before she said: "I've just realised what that pair are up to. The cheek of it!" She was incensed.

"It's been going on for twelve months to my certain knowledge," Solstice replied.

"Why didn't you tell me?"

"You don't like scandal."

359

Bess had to admit that this was true. Those who sidled up to her with defamatory stories received rough treatment. Solstice understood that Leander had been the same.

"Well, I'm damned!" Bess muttered. "And look at them . . . as blatant as hell!"

Fifty yards away, although Gillian was unmoved by Bess's glare, Hugo Richardson looked uncomfortable.

A week later, at Newbury, while Gillian and Hugo were inspecting his entrant for the second race, Gideon Timberlake turned up. Later in the afternoon, his colt, Brunswick, was running in an event widely regarded as a St Leger trial, so his appearance was not a complete surprise. He had, however, brought Dame Amelia with him.

She gave Gillian and her escort a caustically appraising stare and sniffed disdainfully. "I believe you've been seeing a good deal of that pair," she said to Bess.

"Yes, Dame Amelia."

Another sniff and Amelia went away to confer with Gideon.

Richardson's horse won and he joined Bess in the winner's enclosure, Gillian having made herself scarce after seeing Amelia.

"This makes a pleasant change," Richardson said with overdone affability. "We don't seem to be winning all that much."

"I've known better seasons," Bess said curtly.

It was a minor race and no one was much interested in the outcome. Bess was able to get herself and the horse away fairly quickly, terminating an encounter she found disagreeable. On the way back from the stables, she saw Gillian and Richardson hurrying towards the car park.

When Bess went into the paddock with Amelia and Gideon to watch Brunswick parade for his race, she was on edge, waiting. It duly came after she had given Michael a leg up and the horses were going towards the course.

"I'm going to ask you a very difficult question, Bess," Gideon said, his face grave. "Is that horse of mine fit? Is he ready for this race?"

360

Amelia saw Bess's discomfort. "Come along, my dear, we need to know," she said.

"I'd say he was short of work," Bess replied.

"Like he was at Epsom?" Gideon asked. Brunswick's performance in the Derby had been lack-lustre, contradicting his pedigree and leaving him tailed off with the also-rans.

"I'm afraid so," Bess said.

"What about Richardson's horse in that second race?" Amelia wanted to know. "How was he?"

"Over the top," Bess answered. "He looked as though he'd peaked a week ago. It didn't matter because all the others were no-hopers."

"He should have been in a better class?" Amelia asked.

"Definitely." Bess took a deep breath and went the whole hog. "Any fool can win the odd race by running a quality animal against rubbish."

Amelia and Gideon went away, but Gideon returned to look at Brunswick after he had trailed in last. Momentarily distressed, the colt was blowing like a grampus.

"He needed the race," Bess said. "At least, that's the polite way of putting it."

Gideon nodded. "Thank you very much, Bess. I'm grateful."

"What was all that about?" Solstice asked after Gideon had gone away.

"It seems that questions are being asked about whether young Mr Giles has got the faintest idea what he's doing."

Solstice shook his head sadly. "What a pickle! Mind you, it's about time someone sat up and took notice."

When Gillian and Hugo Richardson arrived at his house after their hurried departure from Newbury racecourse, she led the way straight to his bedroom. He watched, fascinated and bemused as she flung her clothes off.

"Don't stand there like a wet weekend," she commanded. "I'm bloody randy!"

Obeying, he found that she was even more frantically voracious than normal. Matching her savagery, Richardson thought that Gillian was undoubtedly the finest sexual instrument that good luck had ever given him. Afterwards, when other considerations were able to enter his mind, he was less happy.

"What's wrong?" she asked.

"There's nothing actually *wrong*," he replied thoughtfully. "Tell me, what did you make of the Cannings Ambo presence this afternoon?"

"Timberlake and the old crone? Nothing much . . . why?"

"I wonder what they were looking for."

Gillian shrugged. "How should I know? What do you think?"

"There are two possibilities," Hugo replied. "You probably aren't aware of it, or don't care, but your husband isn't making a terribly good job of running that stable. Only twenty-one winners by the middle of August – and not one of them in a decent race – isn't good. As a matter of fact, it's abysmal."

"So?" Gillian asked, not particularly interested.

"Gideon Timberlake is unhappy."

"How do you know?"

"My friend, the Duke, told me," Hugo replied. "He's not over the moon about things, either."

"What are they going to do about it?"

"Nothing, at the moment. It's difficult to be sure of facts. As it happens, I'm coming to the conclusion that your husband couldn't train a cat to eat cream, but I can't prove it and I imagine they're in the same position."

"So what do they hope to gain by watching a race or two?" Gillian asked.

"Not much," Hugo said. "It's a chance for them to talk to Bess Collier. That could be important."

"Don't be silly!" Gillian was contemptuous.

"Your hatred of the lady is blinding you to her abilities," Hugo said. "A lot of people are saying that Giles and the fair Rebecca must be out of their tiny minds to keep Bess Collier on a wild-goose chase all over the country while they make a mess of running the yard."

"What was the other reason they might have been there today?" Gillian asked, hoping that it would be more interesting.

"They'd come to snoop on us."

"A fat lot of good that will do them!"

"We have been piling it on a bit," Hugo said.

There was a note of warning in his voice. "Are you getting cold feet?" she asked.

"No . . . not really." For the moment, the only thing that bothered Hugo Richardson was the trouble and expense of moving his horses to another stable when the inevitable happened. "Perhaps we should be more careful . . . there's no need to flaunt it. Bess Collier must have known for ages."

Gillian broke away from his embrace and eased herself into a sitting position. It was a device to add emphasis to what she was about to say. "Look, Hugo, it doesn't matter a toss who knows about us. If the Collier woman did go running to Giles with tales, he wouldn't believe her. Even if he did, he wouldn't do anything about it. He'll put up with me for as long as I want him to."

"You sound very sure of that."

"I am! Believe me, darling, he wouldn't want to be without the treats I provide. Now, shut up and let's get on with something useful."

Like those that had preceded it throughout the year, the October Trustees' meeting was not fully attended: this time, it was Rachel and Leslie Giffard who were missing. In neither case did the formal written apologies give reasons for the absence.

The agenda contained nothing of any importance, so Edward Mallender had over half an hour in which to belabour the point he was impatient to raise.

"I want to know what the devil's going on round here," he said. His customary bluntness was elevated to a positively offensive level.

"Perhaps you could be more specific," Amelia suggested.

363

Since everyone round the table was only too aware of what Mallender was referring to, it was a valiant effort.

"Riotous disorder, that's what!" was the pugnacious retort. "High spirits is one thing, last Friday night was criminal."

He was alluding to a fight that had broken out in a Marlborough public house shortly before closing time. The landlord, whom Amelia regarded as level-headed and reliable, swore that the argument was originally between a dozen Latimer's Barn lads. However, once the fists started flying, everyone in the crowded bar was dragged in. They were a pretty rough lot who had been drinking heavily for three hours. Having wrought havoc inside the pub, they spilled outside in search of more room. Before three resolute policemen broke the affray up, the windscreens of several cars had been smashed, and, worst of all, one of the windows of Mallender's original 1875 shop, something of a shrine in the Mallender and Giffard Foods organisation, was pushed in.

John Flamsteed and Gideon Timberlake moved swiftly to heal the rift between town and stable. They spent all day Saturday soothing those who had suffered damage, paying at least twice as much compensation as was necessary and issuing promises that it would never happen again. Their efforts were so successful that it was early evening before anyone realised that Giles had played no part in the fence-mending exercise.

"That was a most lamentable and regrettable incident," Amelia said in a way that somehow evoked the nineteenth century. "As you are aware, Mr Mallender, we have paid for the damage – even though our people cannot have caused it all – and steps have been taken to ensure that it doesn't happen again."

"How?"

"The lads have been forbidden to drink in Marlborough."

"What about your own disciplinary measures? I know you're trying to persuade the police to go easy on them, but are any being sacked?"

Somewhat unkindly, Ann thought, Amelia turned to Giles.

"I'd rather not get rid of anyone," he said uneasily.

"Why not?" Mallender demanded.

"I'm already short-handed," Giles admitted.

Ann cringed and saw that Hubert Prideaux was also suffering. If Giles dared not dismiss people, how was he to enforce the ban on drinking?

"I heard you'd been losing lads," Mallender said. "Seven, isn't it? Why haven't you fixed yourself up with replacements?"

"We couldn't get anyone," Giles said.

Edward Mallender looked at him with something strangely akin to pity. "I can't help finding this very funny," he said. "Until last year, Latimer's Barn was the best stable in the country. Whenever there was a vacancy, lads came from far and wide to queue up for it. Now, all of a sudden, nobody's interested. Shall I tell you why? It's because the performance this season has been pathetic! There are people down in that churchyard turning in their graves at what's been going on."

"I'll admit we've had problems," Giles said. "But . . ."

"Problems!" Edward Mallender laughed mirthlessly. "You call it 'problems'? Do you know that there's a scruffy thirty-box yard up at Ogbourne that's turned out more winners than you – and they've collared twice as much prize-money. You never go to races, do you?"

"I've been too busy here," Giles said, badly rattled.

"God knows what you think you've been doing! It might have done you some good to go to Newmarket and listen to what folk were saying about the way you've been sending them out. Look at that colt of mine at the July meeting . . ."

Gideon Timberlake had heard enough. "We are aware of the difficulties, Edward, and I assure you that they are being looked into as a matter of urgency. In the circumstances, your comments aren't helpful."

Mallender gaped at him. Until recently, he had looked on Gideon as the ineffectually la-di-dah son of the much respected Claude. Now, here he was, speaking with the sort of authority that was expected from the Hawksworths. "Well . . . that's all right, then," he said huffily and shut up.

Amelia closed the meeting.

"That was all very uncomfortable," Hubert said as he drove Ann into Marlborough for lunch after the meeting.

"You don't know the half of it," she replied. "To be honest, I can't understand how Giles has done so *well*."

"Mallender's right, you know, Aunt Ann," Hubert said, thinking that she was trying to extract humour from the situation. "This season has been catastrophic."

"It could have been worse. Gillian is having an affair with Hugo Richardson, so it's a wonder Giles hasn't gone to pieces. He's idiotically fond of her."

"Hugo!" Hubert was appalled. "When did that start?"

"Last summer, apparently."

"Bloody hell!" Ann had never heard him swear before. "I'll have words with him." Apologetically, he added: "He's a good friend of mine."

"No, don't do that, Hubert," Ann said. "It's a shocking business, but it may be a good thing."

He thought carefully before answering. "I think I see what you mean. It's damned risky, though."

"Amelia is racking her brains to come up with something better . . . perhaps you'd do the same."

When they were settled in the dining-room of the Ailesbury Arms, Ann changed the subject. "How are things in France?" she asked gently.

Hubert, who had returned the previous evening from yet another visit to the de Mourvilles at Fontainebleau, progressed through a range of facial expressions before settling for one that was meant to represent qualified optimism. "Lisette is coming over to spend a week at Eaton Mandeville in November," he said.

"That must be a good sign," Ann suggested.

"It is. All that I have to do is make sure the place isn't too much of a beargarden when she arrives." Ann decided not to ask what he meant. "We've got as far as arguing about wedding arrangements."

"Lisette is a Catholic, presumably?"

"Sort of," Hubert replied. "Her parents are bending over backwards not to make an issue of it."

"I'll keep my fingers crossed for you," Ann promised.

"Incidentally, Alain isn't bothered by the way his horses are performing," Hubert said, glad to have news that could be regarded as good. "He takes the view that you're bound to have problems after last year. He's still very upset about Uncle Steven."

"Yes, I thought he might be." For a moment or two, it seemed that the iron self-control Ann had exercised since Steven's death was about to snap. Hubert suspected that there must have been times when she felt like screaming and running away as the loss of the husband she had adored was followed by Giles's inability to cope with the stable. "Alain thought the world of him," she said. "It started with that business during the War, of course." She made a conscious change of mood. "Tell me, do you see anything of your friend, Lady Leonie, these days?"

Hubert knew that the inquiry was based solely on sincere concern for his well-being. "No, she's been up in Northumberland since February."

"Doing what, for heaven's sake?"

"Motivating a chap called Hector Dalziel. He's a splendid fellow, by the way . . . I had lunch with Leo and him just before she cleared off. They're getting wed once his divorce is fixed."

"What about her business?"

"She sold that. It fetched a small fortune, most of which is going into Hector's farm."

"Isn't life amazing!" Ann said. "Leonie must be one of the best duchesses that never was."

"So everyone has always told me," Hubert replied. "She'll be even better as a sheep farmer's wife."

"Northumberland will never know what's hit it," Ann smiled.

"Indeed!"

As they came to the end of the meal, Ann broached the subject that had intrigued her for well over a year. "Hubert, you told me that there was no need to worry about your mother, Mallender and Giffard hatching a conspiracy because they were incapable of agreeing."

"I did."

"You were absolutely right. They hardly bother attending meetings – at least not together. Look at today."

Hubert waited, his face a blank mask.

"Do you think you could explain it to me?" Ann asked.

It seemed a difficult decision. "Yes, it would help you if you knew," Hubert said at last. "Not here, though." He glanced round the dining-room, obviously unhappy at the number of people within earshot of them.

"I know," Ann said when they were outside. "It's years since I've been up to the Savernake Forest. Is that private enough for you?"

On an afternoon of mellow October sunshine, the tints in the elms and beeches lining the Grand Avenue were breathtaking. Hubert dawdled along at ten miles an hour to give Ann a chance to stare and admire. Eventually, he drew off the road to park in a clearing. They made no attempt to leave the car, but wound the windows down to enjoy the wistful scents of autumn.

"Lovely," Ann said. "Quite lovely. All right, my dear, get on with it!"

"The only way to deal with this is for me to give you the facts," Hubert said. "Do your best to remember that I am *not* making this up."

"Very well, Hubert," Ann replied dutifully.

"Item one is that Mother is, and has been for nearly two years, having an affair with Leslie Giffard."

After a long silence, during which she gazed into the trees, Ann said, "I'm doing my best to obey your advice."

"Good!" Hubert smiled.

"Might one ask what the devil they think they're playing at?" Ann asked, deliberately flippant.

Hubert shrugged. "They're two lonely people who get on well together. Giffard's been a widower for over ten years and Mother's been fed up since Hetherington faded away. Amongst other things, Leslie's doing his best to turn her into an opera buff. I imagine there's also a good deal of old-fashioned lust in the air."

"At their ages!" Ann was horrified.

"Mother's only fifty-three," Hubert said mildly. "She's also wearing very well."

"Yes, she is," Ann admitted.

"As are you," Hubert hastened to point out, making her smile. "Giffard's fifty-five, I think, and perfectly sound in wind and limb."

"Is this why they weren't at the meeting?"

"Yes. They went to Covent Garden last night and they have tickets for *Der Rosenkavalier* in Paris this evening."

"Very nice," Ann said drily. Something was bothering her. "Doesn't Giffard have any ulterior motives?"

"He didn't originally," Hubert said. "Of late, he's been making sure that I like him. I assume he'll want me to put in a good word for him at Stewart's – you know, the bank I help out. It's probably only a matter of time before he asks for a hefty loan to finance all-out war against Mallender."

Ann thought it over. "This is all very interesting, Hubert, but I don't know that it explains very much."

"No, you need item number two for that," he agreed. "This concerns Helen." Ann groaned. "She and Freddie Christopherson aren't breaking up, but they're wide apart, conducting a most weird sort of marriage. It was all pre-arranged, I gather. Freddie knew what he was taking on and said that she could do what she liked once she'd given him a son. Miles, named after his *wonderful* grandfather, of course, is nearly three, Freddie has a firm grip on him, and Helen is doing as she pleases. Her preferred companion is Adrian Mallender, eldest son of the increasingly obnoxious Edward!"

"Good God!" Ann lapsed into stunned silence.

"I avoid him like the plague," Hubert said. "He's one of these dreadfully pushy, 'dynamic' individuals."

Ann shuddered. "What does this mean to the Mallender-Giffard relationship?" she asked.

"It makes it several times worse as far as I can make out. Adrian and his brother, Richard, were at each other's throats before romance reared its ugly head. Adrian appears to be leader of the group that wants to split up into two separate companies, Richard wants everything kept together. For a variety of reasons, Edward hates the sight of both of them, but is dead against Adrian on the grounds of moral turpitude and fouling the Christopherson nest. Leslie thinks that Adrian has insinuated himself into Mother's family circle to dredge up dirt on him and isn't pleased."

Ann shook her head. "It sounds a shocking mess." A new thought occurred to her. "Who's following in Leslie Giffard's footsteps?"

"Good question!" Hubert said. "He has a son and a daughter, both still at school."

"Tell me, Hubert, does any of this *really* matter to us?" Ann asked.

"No, I don't think it does," he replied. "At least, not in any positive way. As long as it carries on, I can't see Mallender and Giffard being all that interested in Cannings Ambo."

"We ought to get rid of them," Ann said thoughtfully.

"I agree, but it can wait. There are more pressing problems to be tackled."

"Don't I know it!" Ann said grimly.

Bess's arduous working year finished on 29 October. The season came to a fitting end when she and Solstice arrived at Salisbury with a horse that was unable to run because it had not been declared at the four-day stage.

Having telephoned Liz from the Clerk of the Course's office, Bess knew the answer before she broke the dismal news of the foul-up to Solstice.

"This is *not* Miss Challoner's fault," Bess said. "The declaration was due to be made last Friday, right? Liz had the day off to go to the dentist and do some shopping. Mr Hawksworth and his blasted wife were in charge!"

After gazing philosophically at the sky for a few moments, Solstice grinned. "Look on the bright side," he said. "This might have happened to us at Newmarket. As it is, we're only an hour from home."

Giles was apologetic, but not all that concerned when Bess gave him the stark facts. He had been studying the year's results. Out of four hundred and ninety-six runners, only thirty-two had won. Steven's lowest total was seventy, and that was before 1955, when there had been far fewer horses in the yard; thereafter, his average had been ninety. The prize-money was even more telling: during his last ten years, Steven had looked on £100,000 as being the minimum that was acceptable. Giles had produced £26,000. Bess, who knew the figures by heart, could have added that she and Solstice had travelled 60,000 miles to achieve the wretched results. Leaving Giles to his thoughts, Bess went home to the Bungalow to begin work on obliterating all memory of an ignominious season.

Three days later, Liz drove Bess to Southampton to board the Cunard liner *Carmania*. She was treating herself to a three-week Mediterranean cruise in one of the four most expensive suites on the ship. Liz went on board to inspect the accommodation and was mightily impressed.

"If you can't enjoy yourself in *this*, there's something wrong with you," she said.

Lying in the bath before dinner, as the vessel nosed down the Solent, Bess came to the same conclusion. She very much hoped that all the stories about cruises were true: if not, she would make them so. The first good-looking man to take an interest in her, who was presentable, free from vices and capable of intelligent conversation, could do what he liked with her for the next three weeks. If he was very good and made a convincing job of taking her mind off Latimer's Barn, they might be thinking of something permanent by the time they were back in Southampton.

CHAPTER 14

1969

'If the day ever dawns . . .'

It was no secret that the Inner Cabinet of Amelia, Ann, Giles, and Gideon Timberlake spent most of the winter agonising over what they were going to do for 1969.

Rumour ran riot with Gillian as the obvious focal point. Not seen in the village after the end of October, she was variously supposed to have returned to her parents, have gone abroad, or be living with a man in Cheltenham. An even wilder group of stories said that divorce proceedings were starting, but not before she had slunk off to London for an abortion.

All this was completely wrong. Gillian visited her mother on two afternoons each week, spending the rest of the time at the house in Marlborough. For six weeks spanning Christmas 1968, she was without the consolation of Hugo Richardson. For reasons he did not explain, he went to America and Canada. Confident that his sexual appetites would not go unsatisfied, Gillian fumed.

The next most popular topic of speculation was the identity of the trainer for 1969. Everyone agreed on one thing: it would not be Giles.

"I think he'd be happy to get the sack," Rebecca told the Flamsteeds one evening over dinner at Rose House. "The job terrifies him. I've seen him literally sick with worry."

"I've noticed," Julia said. "I feel sorry for him. On top of everything else, there's Gillian, of course."

"She isn't a great deal of help," Rebecca said with a simple earnestness that often reminded the older inhabitants of Cannings Ambo of the young Amelia. William Flamsteed, who loved her dearly, smiled at the understatement.

Rebecca did not know that some of the rumour-mongers, ignoring the fact that she would not reach the required age for another eighteen months, were suggesting that she would take over the licence. After weeks of fencing around with a rag-bag of half-baked ideas, the majority agreed that the job would be given to a distinguished outsider. Major Bruce MacDonald, who had recently handed over his Newmarket yard to a nephew, was believed to have tenuous links with the Timberlakes. Another, much younger, contender was Nigel Derwent of Malton in Yorkshire, a distant connection of the family from which Emma had come. Finally, a much-ridiculed minority put their money on Ann.

"I'll tell you what I think," Liz said to Bess as they finished supper on a January evening. "I don't believe they're going to change a thing."

Bess sat back to consider this, listening to the wind outside the Bungalow. There was talk of heavy snow by morning: that was all they needed!

"Yes, I could see that happening," she said.

"What will you do?" Liz asked.

"I don't know!"

Since returning from the cruise, Bess had tried to be objective about her surroundings. At first, the memory of David Brandon eased the task.

David was on *Carmania* for what he hoped would be the final stage of recovery from the two-year-old trauma of having his wife and baby daughter killed by a drunk in a stolen car. He had moved from his own modest cabin into Bess's suite on the second day of the voyage; what followed did them both immeasurable good. After his early shyness was disposed of, David proved to be a far better lover than Richard Morton, largely, Bess realised, because of his assiduous concern for her. So captivating was their love-making that they were happy to miss several of the shore excursions. At Palermo, Bess ordered both lunch and dinner to be served in her suite to avoid the waste of time entailed in getting dressed.

They devoted an evening to discussion of a possible future together. It fizzled out quickly because of David's career and preoccupation with suburbia. Not surprisingly, in view of his devastating loss, he was determined to hang on to his lectureship in the Faculty of Engineering at London University, and the house he was buying in Middlesex seemed almost as sacrosanct. Bess was fairly sure that he disapproved of her vocation. They had exchanged two rather disappointing letters since their return to the routine of an English winter.

During Christmas, when Bess spent a great deal of time with Elsie and Boggysevick, they unsettled her with a surprising idea.

"We've been wondering about retiring," Elsie said. Although the statement lacked her usual confidence, Bess was instinctively certain that much thought and discussion had taken place.

"Retire? Why? You're both only fifty-four."

"There's ever such a nice cottage for sale at Overton," Elsie replied. "And we've got a fair bit put by."

"Is that a good enough reason to pack it in?" Bess asked.

Boggysevick, looking uncomfortable, came out with the truth. "We are not happy with the stable's prospects. Things have looked very bad since poor Mr Steven went and we find it difficult to believe that certain people know what they are doing."

His stiltedly correct language and pronunciation made the situation he was describing seem even worse.

Once it was out in the open, they talked about it over several successive evenings. The nearest they came to a definite conclusion was Bess's insistence that an establishment like Latimer's Barn was bound to regain its successful touch. Gradually, the subject petered out: Elsie and Boggysevick did nothing. Like everyone else, they were drifting.

* * *

374

There was no announcement. In the middle of March, people began to wake up to the fact that serious work had been going on for three weeks to the same pattern as that employed the previous year.

"Never in the history of racing have so many debated for so long and come up with such bugger-all!" Bess said to Liz. "They must have spent *weeks* arguing the toss, yet they've nothing to show for it."

"If it's any consolation to you, all the important people have been looking pretty sick lately," Liz said.

"Rebecca's frightened of her own shadow," Bess added.

The assumption that there had been a fearful row was perfectly correct. After months of debate, both Amelia and Gideon Timberlake had run out of patience with Giles. Not only was he still dithering about how he should run the yard, he refused to recognise that his marriage was a menace. Since taking over from his father, Giles had been consistently weak; he now demonstrated that he was also stubborn.

"Giles, if you persist with this attitude, we shall have to find someone else to hold the licence," Amelia said, finally goaded into the bluntness that Gideon thought should have been employed months ago. "I am not prepared to sit by and see our reputation ruined. If you don't pull your socks up, we shall give the job to Rebecca."

Unbelievably, in all the time that this idea had existed, no one had seen fit to mention it to Rebecca herself. Ann was the first to spot that, after looking as though she was going to faint, Rebecca was staring at Amelia in utter horror. "I couldn't do that if my life depended on it," she said, her voice quavering.

"What?" Inadvertently, Amelia sounded severe.

"I can't run the stable!" Rebecca was becoming hysterical. "I wouldn't have the first idea what to do . . . I couldn't give orders . . . I'd be worse than Giles."

Amelia was on the verge of a forceful response when she saw the look on Ann's face and thought better of it. Eventually, Giles broke the uncomfortable silence.

"And we know Oliver's not interested."

"This needs thinking about," Gideon said grimly. That was the nearest anyone was prepared to go towards admitting the full enormity of the problem. The attempt to carry on as before, without saying anything to the staff, was an inevitable consequence.

3 April was a day that belonged more to February. As Bess and Solstice passed Netheravon on the way to Salisbury, snow was gusting in the unpleasant wind. Huddled in the cab of the van, they remained silent. Solstice had sounded cheerful enough when his: "Here we go again!" as they pulled out of Latimer's Barn heralded the start of a new season. Two miles down the road, there seemed no reason for anything other than pessimism. Brunswick, the biggest disappointment of 1968, had been kept in training as a four-year-old simply because there was no alternative. As a son of Astronomer Royal, he might have been a candidate for stud duties had his three-year-old career not been miserable. His lack of enthusiasm at being the first runner of a new season was almost laughable.

However, when Michael Pilgrim appeared in the paddock, ready for the race, things took a dramatic turn for the better.

"This one could be good," he told Bess. "I rode him at work on Saturday and he went well."

"I was thinking he was in pretty good nick," Bess said, taking another look at Brunswick as the lad walked him round. "He's going to be pretty decent when he comes into his coat." Aware that Michael, who had ridden over one thousand two hundred winners for Steven, was also disgusted at the way the stable was being run, she asked a blunt question. "Is this a fluke, or is common sense getting a grip?"

"Too early to tell," Michael replied. "Arthur Merriweather's been putting his foot down."

"About time!" Bess said.

"He's getting confident," Michael said. "Being new to the job, he didn't like to push himself last year."

"I'll have a word with him!" Bess realised it was wrong of her not to have done so already. It was a measure of how badly the Latimer's Barn machine had split into disillusioned factions.

The race was over a mile and a half, Brunswick's ideal distance, and the opposition was respectable: one of them had won last year's Dante Stakes at York, another had been a close second at Royal Ascot. The first mile was run at a casual pace, none of the jockeys keen to be the first to chance their arms. When the action did start, it was a scrappy set-to with a lot of bumping and boring. With a furlong to run, Brunswick strolled effortlessly round the ruckus and put four lengths between himself and the rest. Tactfully, Solstice turned away when he saw the tears shining in Bess's eyes: it did indeed seem an eternity since one of their horses had looked that good.

Going to Arthur Merriweather's house to tell him all about it that evening, Bess found that Michael was right.

"The way I see it, Miss, somebody's got to do something," Arthur said. "At least Mr Giles is prepared to listen this year."

"Make sure he does!" Bess insisted. "And don't be afraid of upsetting him. If you produce the winners, Dame Amelia, Mrs Hawksworth and Gideon Timberlake won't care how you do it."

Arthur looked uncomfortable. "There's a fair few of the lads asking why you aren't running the show, Miss Collier," he said, half-afraid that he was speaking out of turn.

Bess chuckled. "Listen, Arthur . . . and this is *strictly* between ourselves . . . the Dowager Duchess hates my guts. Always has done."

"I thought she didn't have all that much say in things nowadays."

"Don't you believe it, Arthur! I think she terrifies them. Anyway, there's no need for you to worry about that. Just put your head down and do your best."

He did. As April unfolded, Bess and Solstice became

almost euphoric. Of the twenty-eight horses they transported to racecourses, twelve of them won and seven came second or third. One of the winners was Edward Mallender's colt, Ivanhoe, whose victory in the Craven Stakes at Newmarket was the first success in a quality race since Steven's death. A fortnight later, the colt was a very creditable second in the Two Thousand Guineas: moreover, Giles Hawksworth was on the course to see him do it.

But, at the very moment when many at Latimer's Barn thought the worst was over, the initiative was snatched out of their hands.

Taking advantage of Giles's absence at Newmarket, Gillian spent Two Thousand Guineas day with Hugo Richardson.

As with all their meetings since his return from America three months ago, there was tension between them. A number of disconnected events had combined to produce a fundamental change in Richardson's attitude. The happy domesticity of friends with whom he had stayed in Vermont, the announcement of Hubert Prideaux's engagement to Lisette de Mourville, and a severe lecture from a respected aunt led him to the conclusion that he should settle down and raise a family. Whatever her other talents, it was difficult to imagine a more unsuitable candidate for motherhood than Gillian, and their relationship was an obstacle to the quest for the right woman.

Gillian suspected that something was in the wind. They had lunch at Newbury's most popular hotel and the elaborate meal that Hugo insisted on ordering was subjected to constant interruptions as a stream of acquaintances paused to chat to him. In between intrusions, he talked incessantly of the success Giles was enjoying. When he finally called for the bill, Gillian's nerves were at breaking point.

Taking a circuitous route back to his home, he stopped in a gateway in a little-used lane.

"Are you going to have me in that field?" Gillian asked. "It's rather cold, but if that's what you want, darling, who am I to argue?"

"No, Gillian, that is not why we're here," he said gravely. "I want to tell you something."

"What's wrong with your house?" she asked, panic edging into her voice.

He made no attempt to answer the question. Without preamble, he gave her the hard, unvarnished truth. "Our friendship isn't going anywhere and it has to end."

Richardson was surprised. He had expected a violent reaction: instead, she was quietly bitter. "Is 'friendship' all it means to you?" she asked.

"Well . . . I . . ." Momentarily, he was at a loss.

"You've got the wind up, haven't you?" Gillian seethed with accusation.

"To be honest, yes!" Richardson grasped the opening she had given him. "Everyone's talking about us. Frankly, Gillian, I'm at a loss to understand why the Hawksworths are tolerating it."

"Because they haven't got any bloody choice in the matter!" Gillian shouted. "I know the experts don't rate Giles, but he's all they've got."

Richardson shook his head. "If you carry on underestimating them, you could be in for a nasty shock."

A crafty look came into Gillian's beautiful eyes. "I know what's happened," she said slowly. "They've put their old mate the Duke of Laverstoke on to you, haven't they? He's been leaning on you!"

"I'm afraid so." Richardson reinforced the lie with a convincingly abject look.

"And you let him?" She was contemptuous. "My God, I thought you'd got more about you than that! All right, you've made your point. Let's get on with it."

They drove back to Richardson's house, where Gillian had left her car, in silence. As he expected, however, she had not finished. Drawing up in the forecourt, she was seductively wheedling.

"Hugo, darling, I don't want you to regret this. Why don't you think about it? Let's go to bed . . . you'll feel better."

It was what he had anticipated and the reply was ready.

"Gillian, I've been thinking about it for the last three months, so that's the end of it."

Even in the confined space of his car, she took an almighty swing to land a resounding blow across his face. "You bastard!" she spat.

Dazed, but satisfied, Richardson watched her drive off.

She was still boiling with rage when she arrived at her parents' house nearly an hour later. Her mother was at home and alone.

"Hugo Richardson's chucked me!" Gillian announced. "The swine's been cooking it up since he came back from the States."

Janet Foley took the measure of her daughter's mood. "Have the Hawksworths been getting at him?" she asked.

"Exactly! They've stopped the only pleasure I had," Gillian exploded. "Well, I know what I'm going to do."

"And what's that?" Janet asked.

"Get a divorce, of course!"

"Oh? On what grounds?"

"I hate their precious Latimer's Barn and Giles is no good in bed!"

"I'm sorry to be a wet-blanket, darling, but that won't do," Janet said. "Not even your father's slightly bent solicitor could do anything with that."

"All right, I'll do him for cruelty," Gillian snapped.

"That's a *beast* to prove," Janet replied. "And while you're trying it, they'll throw Hugo Richardson at you."

"I don't care!" Gillian was frantic.

"Yes, you do," Janet said with laboured patience. "You do *not* want to be involved in a mud-slinging end of a marriage to which you have contributed so little. I take it you'll want to marry again?"

"Of course I shall."

"In that case, you need to consider your reputation. We can't afford to have it said that you're an over-sexed, avaricious bitch who's wasted no time in making a mess of marriage into one of the best families in England."

"Don't be ridiculous!" Gillian flared.

"Audrey Pilkington is already making noises to that effect," Janet said.

Gillian blenched. The formidably well-informed Mrs Pilkington dominated society over a twenty-mile radius from Reading: when she put the word out, a person was as good as dead.

"All right, Mother, you got me into this mess, how do I escape?" Gillian asked through clenched teeth.

"The first thing is to accept the idea that you're going to need patience. I suggest that you wait for these new divorce laws to come into operation."

"When's that likely to be?"

"Everyone thinks it will be next year. It's going to make life *so* much easier."

"And what do I do while I'm waiting?" Gillian asked.

"You have to go through the motions of making it work. You're quite sure you can't stand the Latimer's Barn thing any more?"

"Another week and I'll be screaming."

Janet Foley looked thoughtful. "Haven't I picked up the impression that Giles himself isn't all that keen?"

"That's what makes it all so ridiculous!" Gillian wailed. "He hates it . . . it makes him ill!"

"Good. Let me talk to your father."

Giles reached Latimer's Barn at eight-fifteen on the Saturday evening of the Two Thousand Guineas to find himself something of a hero. Everyone was in high spirits: when Ann told him to ring Gillian, she sounded pleasant. "She's been after you for three hours, my dear. She's at her parents'."

Gillian answered the telephone with a speed that suggested she had been sitting by it, waiting. "Is anything wrong, darling?" Giles asked anxiously.

"No . . . not really. Things got a bit too much for me again, so I came here. Actually, I'm staying the night."

"You're well out of it," Giles grumbled.

"Why, what's happened?"

"We came second in the Guineas. Anyone would think we'd won a million pounds!"

"Can you get away tomorrow?"

After a worrying delay, Gillian received a reply that delighted her. "What's wrong with tonight?"

"Nothing at all, darling!"

"I'll be as quick as I can."

No one was much bothered when Giles said he had to leave at once because his wife was unwell. Without any contribution from him, they had come within a short head of winning a Classic race and would not miss him at the celebration.

Originally dismayed by his simmering anger, Gillian was subsequently startled to find herself enjoying the best night she had ever had with Giles. She did not have to feign orgasm and whatever fury was possessing him gave a new endurance to his efforts that wiped out much of the humiliation of Hugo Richardson's rejection.

Waking at seven o'clock on Sunday morning, Giles slipped out of bed. Half an hour later, when he had shaved and dressed, Gillian was still fast asleep and he decided to go for a walk to marshal his thoughts into some sort of order. Half-way down the stairs, he encountered the smell of fresh coffee; following it, he found Janet Foley in the breakfast-room.

"Hello. How are you this morning?" she asked, getting up to fetch him a cup.

"Marvellous!" he smiled.

"You're certainly bright and early."

"Habit," he replied. "At least, being early is. It's a long time since I felt this good." After a slight pause, he added: "I think it might be some time before Gillian appears. We had quite a night."

He felt perfectly comfortable making the statement and Janet's reply put their relationship on a new footing. "I know, I heard you." Seeing that he was in the process of deciding that she was probably naked under the tightly wound silk wrap, she went several steps further. "I was all alone . . . Ralph went to a business dinner in London and stayed the night. I had to . . ." A rueful smile left Giles in no doubt that, aroused by the noises coming from her daughter's bedroom, Janet Foley had been forced to look after her own sexual needs. Her mood changed. "You did jolly well at Newmarket yesterday!"

"Janet, don't mention it!" Giles said.

"Why not? What's wrong?" The transformation that swept over him was alarming.

"I had nothing to do with it. Arthur Merriweather – he's the head lad – did *everything* with that horse . . . and all the others that have done well."

Janet Foley sat back, assessing the depth of his emotions. There was rancour, as well as the threat of tears. "I had no idea you were so unhappy," she said softly. "Oh, Giles, I *am* sorry."

"They don't care about me as long as they get results!"

She knew that he was almost certainly wallowing in self-pity and talking rubbish, nevertheless, failure to exploit his state of mind would be criminal folly. "Giles, this is getting out of hand," she said, leaning forward to lay a hand on his knee. "Poor Gillian was in a terrible state when she got here yesterday. You know she hates Latimer's Barn and Marlborough is driving her mad."

"I know," Giles replied abjectly.

"She can't go on any more. I'm afraid she may be on the verge of leaving you."

He gaped at her in disbelief. "Oh, no, she mustn't do that," he said. "That would finish me."

"It's no consolation to you, but I think she's being totally unreasonable," Janet said.

"I don't!" A resurgence of anger made Giles pull himself together. "I think she's had a terrible time of it. My family have made no attempt to like her. And last winter was unbelievable, Janet . . . they messed me around as though I was a bloody servant. The only reason I'm still there is that I didn't have the guts to leave."

"Why not?"

"Apart from pretending to train horses, I'm next to useless. I can't do anything else."

"That's twaddle," Janet said, introducing a carefully controlled note of annoyance into her voice. "Ralph and I talked about this before he left for London. He's always thought you would be a great asset to Foley, Nettles and Mayo."

"Surely not!" Giles was astounded.

"As I understand it, there's a job waiting for you tomorrow," Janet said. "You may not realise it, Giles, but you have some very good connections. Ralph and his colleagues are prepared to place a high value on your services."

She saw that the prospect of freedom from a responsibility he could not handle was alluring.

"Ralph will be back for lunch," Janet said quietly. "I'm sure you'll believe *him*."

They talked for over an hour until Janet decided that it was time she bathed and dressed. "The sleeping beauty will think it's far too early, but you'd better take her a cup of coffee up," Janet said. She gave him a smile that was luminous with suggestion. "Or, you could scrub my back."

They both laughed.

After she had gone, Giles realised that there had been an element of seriousness in Janet's proposition. It had always suited his purpose to affect a naïve innocence of the lives that Janet and her husband led. Now, the prospect of being involved excited him.

Ralph Foley took Giles into his study before lunch. When they sat down to eat, Ralph gave Janet and Gillian the important news. "Giles has agreed to start work for us as soon as possible."

"That's absolutely splendid!" Janet said warmly. "When do you think you could begin?"

"Next Monday," Giles said. "I intend letting my people know today."

"Isn't that going to give them a problem?" Janet asked, pretending to be concerned.

"I don't see why it should. Whoever's been running

the show behind my back can come out into the open and do it."

His truculent manner added to Gillian's delight. "What's Giles going to be doing?" she asked Ralph.

"He's the very man we've been looking for to run that office in Wantage we keep talking about. With Giles on the team, I can have it open inside a month."

"That sounds ideal," Janet enthused. "All those stables around Lambourn!"

"Exactly," Ralph said. "And some of them change hands pretty frequently."

At the conclusion of the meal, Giles and Gillian strolled round the garden. After an excited discussion of their new life, he agreed to let her start looking for a house in north Berkshire and gave her an order.

"You must stop seeing that bloody man Richardson!"

It was the first time he had ever mentioned her ex-lover and Giles did it with an authority that demanded obedience.

"Darling, I sacked him the other day," Gillian replied happily.

"Good! Make sure it stays that way. I'd better make a phone call before I go."

"Who to?"

"Aunt Rachel. We might need an ally and she's bound to be on my side."

"What do you want an ally for?" Gillian asked, suddenly worried. "They can't stop you doing what you want, can they?"

"Certainly not." Giles hesitated, then decided to tell her. "Look, darling, don't build up too many hopes, but I'm going to have a bash at getting some money from the Fund. They might think it's worth it to be rid of me and we could find a use for it."

"That would be lovely," Gillian agreed, and took him to her father's study where he could speak to Rachel in privacy.

The conversation lasted nearly thirty minutes. Eager to be on his way to Cannings Ambo, Giles did not give any details, but was obviously well-pleased. At the moment of his departure, Gillian was uneasy.

"Will you ring to let me know what happens?" she asked.

"Of course I will. Don't worry."

When his car was out of sight, Gillian and her mother turned to each other with faces that were a riot of expression.

"Well?" Janet asked.

"I can't believe the change in him." Gillian laughed nervously. "This *could* have a happy ending."

Smiling brightly, Janet doubted it very much.

Leslie Giffard was spending the weekend with Rachel at the Dower House in its remote, private corner of the Eaton Mandeville estate. Throughout her telephone conversation with Giles, he did his best to remain immersed in the business section of a newspaper. At the end of the call, he waited, watching her digest what she had been told and evaluating the consequences. At last, when it was apparent that Rachel was in no hurry to share her thoughts, he spoke.

"That was Giles with some pretty earth-shattering news," he said. "You're looking pleased."

Rachel nodded. "Giles is on his way to Latimer's Barn to tell my *dear* sister-in-law that he's had enough. He's packing it in with immediate effect."

"Bloody hell!" Giffard was shaken. "What's caused this?"

"His appalling wife has duped him into starting a new life. As a gesture of goodwill, she's given up Hugo Richardson."

"What's he going to do?"

"He's turning into an estate agent." Rachel was monumentally disdainful. "He'll be working for that shyster Ralph Foley."

"What the hell happens at Cannings Ambo?"

"Chaos!" Rachel replied. "They haven't got anyone to take his place."

Giffard thought that her assumption was premature: he

also found her malicious glee unattractive. "What about John Flamsteed?" he asked.

"No!"

"His grandfather did the job for a good many years."

"Things have changed," Rachel said. "These days, trainers are expected to do the job full-time and be absolutely competent. I'm prepared to lodge an objection with the Jockey Club if they give the licence to a figurehead."

"Is there anyone *you* would recommend?" Giffard asked.

"Oh, Leslie, you are silly!" Rachel said fondly. "Edmund, of course! He's wasted messing around doing odd jobs for Hubert. He and Judy would be marvellous at Latimer's Barn and we can have things done properly – *our* way!"

Leslie Giffard disliked being included in the statement. "What are you going to do?" he asked.

"I don't have to do anything," Rachel said. "Give them two or three days to thrash around and they'll come to me." She looked at her watch. "I wonder what time the balloon will go up?"

Giles reached Latimer's Barn at twenty minutes to four. He found his mother in the library.

Half an hour later, Bess and Liz were nearing the end of a gardening stint at the front of the Bungalow when Ann drove past to stop outside Louise House. Amelia hurried out and got into the car which set off immediately, turning into the Roadway. Both Ann and Amelia ignored the waving from the pair in front of the Bungalow. Although the car was lost to sight behind the spring lushness of the orchard, the engine noise and slamming of doors indicated that it went no further than The House.

At five o'clock, Bess and Liz were walking down the drive to have tea with Joe and Eileen at Oak Cottage. First John and Julia, then Gideon and Lady Amaryllis went past on their way to The House. They all looked grim.

"Curious," Bess said.

"Serious," Liz replied.

There was a hint of facetiousness in their opinions; by the

387

time they reached Oak Cottage, they had forgotten about the unusual burst of activity.

Joe was out, checking on a patient who lived on the Extension. "There's nothing much wrong with Billy Patterson," Eileen said. "But you know what Joe's like – even on a Sunday. If he's not back in fifteen minutes, we'll start tea without him."

When he turned up, soon after Eileen's deadline, Joe immediately asked a question. "Is there some sort of flap on, Bessie?"

She looked up sharply. "Why?"

"The Duke of Laverstoke has just gone up to The House in that big sports car of his. I never thought he'd get into the drive at the speed he was going."

"Definitely serious," Liz said.

"What's happening?" Eileen asked.

"They're in a state of shock over coming second in the Guineas," Bess replied, smiling guiltily when her sarcasm earned one of Joe's pained, reproving looks.

They settled down to tea and small-talk. At a few minutes past six, when Liz was helping Eileen clear away, they heard a car accelerating furiously towards the main road. At six-twenty, Bess and her nephew, James, set out for church.

After the service, Bess found Arthur Merriweather loitering at the door, desperately trying to pretend that he was there by chance.

"Any idea what's going on at The House, Miss Collier?" he asked nervously.

"No, Arthur. Something is, though."

"Oh, there's no doubt about it," he said. "Mr Giles was away last night. He came back about four and it's been all go ever since."

"Is he still there?" Bess asked.

"No, he cleared off about six. Didn't look too pleased. The back of his car was full of clothes."

"It'll be the same as that malarkey that went on all winter," Bess said. "Doesn't mean a thing." With James at her side, she set off back to Oak Cottage.

Joe and Liz were playing their regular Sunday-evening game of chess; Eileen was sewing; James volunteered to get ready for bed on condition that Bess read him a story. They were settling down comfortably when car wheels crunched on the gravel and the doorbell rang. Eileen went, intending to tell whoever it was to come to morning surgery. To her surprise, it was Ann.

Upstairs, James saw Bess stiffen and cock her head as Eileen said, "Hello, Mrs Hawksworth."

"I'm terribly sorry to bother you, Eileen," Ann said. "We're trying to find Bess. Elsie says she's probably with you."

"Yes, I'll call her." As Eileen turned, she saw that Bess was already on her way down. Ann stepped across the threshold and walked to meet her.

"Could you come to The House with me?" she said. "I know I've a cheek dragging you out on a Sunday evening, but it's very, *very* important."

"Of course." Nodding a brief farewell to Eileen, Bess caught the urgency and hurried out to the car. As Ann reversed into the village lane, Bess was conscious of Liz and Joe, doing their best to remain invisible as they peered through the window.

They were across the Devizes Lane and up the drive in a flash, Ann having to brake hard for the turning to the front of The House. "We're all in the small sitting-room," she said, guiding Bess through the interconnecting door from the offices and across the entrance hall.

Bess's composure was solidly intact until Ann took her hand to lead her in. All three men, John Flamsteed, Gideon Timberlake and the Duke of Laverstoke, stood up: in that instant, Bess knew that something desperately serious was afoot. Lady Amaryllis, alone on a sofa, held out a hand to Bess, an invitation to sit beside her.

"Would you care for some refreshment, my dear?" Amelia asked. "There are three sorts of sherry, whisky, gin, or tea." She tested the pot with her hand. "Yes, it's still hot."

"No thank you, Dame Amelia."

"We have a crisis of unprecedented severity," Amelia said to Bess. "Gideon will tell you all about it."

Gideon spoke as though addressing an old and trusted friend. "Giles Hawksworth is giving up the licence, Bess. He wishes to pursue another career with the prime objective of improving his marriage. This has fallen on us this afternoon, without warning, and comes into effect almost immediately." He paused, nodding sympathetically at her shocked expression. "Obviously, there are some short-term problems, but we hope to solve those with the aid of a friend of Hubert's at the Jockey Club. After that, we have to find someone to run the stable, and, to be blunt about it, put the place back on the map. We would be very pleased indeed, Bess, if you were to take the job on. Apart from your outstanding ability, we believe that you could revive the stable's old tradition of being first with innovation. Although women are allowed to hold licences now, there's no sign of one getting her hands on a major training establishment."

Bess was flabbergasted. Looking round, she saw earnest faces, all willing her to say 'yes'. Her mind refused to function.

Amelia intervened. "Bess, a little while before my mother died, she gave me a letter with instructions that it was not to be opened unless we were in serious difficulty. I'm afraid to say that we didn't open it until two hours ago, despite all the trouble we've been experiencing for over a year." She drew two sheets of notepaper from her handbag. "This is my mother's view of the future – and I must say, we were astounded by its accuracy." She passed it across to Bess, who felt a thrill as the familiar bold writing leapt off the page at her.

Leander began by stressing that the great strength of Hawksworths and Flamsteeds had always been their unity: if this were broken and personal ambitions or greed surfaced, the consequences might be ruinous.

The second great danger she saw was the time when there was no one with both the talent and the will to carry on training horses. She was pessimistic about Giles and Oliver, and unsure of Rebecca. Her assessments of them, written when they were thirteen, nine and seven respectively, were outspoken and devastatingly perceptive. As Bess paused to look quizzically at her, Rebecca squirmed and turned slightly pink.

At the end of the letter, Leander gave her advice.

If the day ever dawns when there is no member of the family who can take charge of the stable, it should be entrusted to Bess Collier. Unless I am very much mistaken, she will grow into a strong, fair-minded person who will earn respect from every quarter. Her affinity with horses is remarkable and will, I am sure, become even stronger as she gains more experience. In recommending Bess, I believe that she will do the the best possible job.

So that was it, Bess thought. At last, Leander's purpose was made clear.

She handed the letter back to Amelia, aware of the silence surrounding her.

"I can't very well refuse, can I?" Bess said shakily.

"You'll do it?" several people said at once.

"Rebecca must be my assistant," Bess insisted.

"And anything else you want," Amelia promised.

"That will do to be going on with." Bess eyed the whisky decanter longingly.

"Would you like a drink now?" Hubert asked, jumping to his feet.

"Yes, please, Your Grace."

"No, no, none of that," he said. "You're one of the family. Call me Hubert like everyone else does." After giving her a tumbler containing a huge measure, he excused himself and went to the library to use the telephone. For several minutes, everyone wanted to talk to Bess, then Ann drew her away from the babble of relieved conversation.

"I owe you an apology, my dear," Ann said.

"Oh?" Bess was at a loss to know what she meant.

"We should have come to you *ages* ago. To be honest, Gideon thought you should have been put in charge when Steven died and Hubert's been pretty much on your side,

391

but we did so want to keep it in the family, you see. Very silly of us."

"Perfectly understandable," Bess assured her. "It's a shame it had to happen like this. It's so *sudden*!"

"Don't mention that, whatever you do," Ann pleaded. "I never imagined that Amelia could get so annoyed. God, she really tore into Giles!"

"What's happened to him?" Bess asked.

"He's going to be an estate agent," Ann said, plainly having difficulty in coming to terms with it all.

"No, I mean *now*," Bess said. "Where is he?"

"He's gone back to his wife."

"Ah . . . Gillian." The way she spoke, making it sound like a condemnation, caught Gideon's attention. He moved closer. "Isn't it strange that no one ever called her 'Mrs Hawksworth'?" Bess said. "Even the lads always referred to her as 'Gillian'."

"I didn't know that!" Ann was shocked.

"Doesn't surprise me," Gideon growled.

"I wonder why?" Ann asked.

"Think of the Mrs Hawksworths there have been," Bess said. "Leander, Emma and you." She paused to allow the point to sink in. "You wouldn't give the title to a creature like Gillian, would you?"

It was obvious that Gideon felt that she had given a perfect description of his views. He changed the subject to spare Ann's feelings.

"Tell me, Bess, now that you've had plenty of time to think about it, what are your plans?"

She treated the deliberately facetious question seriously. "Tomorrow, I'll get a grip on the lads: there are some bad habits that need exterminating. I shall put Rebecca in charge of the two-year-olds with instructions to bring them on for July. I'll take on the older horses and straighten them out. Jimmy Farrant will be travelling head lad . . ."

Gideon interrupted her. "Isn't Jimmy the chap who works the oracle with difficult horses on the gallops?"

"Yes. He's also fifty this year," Bess said. "So it's time

he was given something easier. There's a boy called Jerry Middleton working for George Tucker at Ogbourne. He's a genius. I'll have him here by the end of the week."

"Doesn't he like Tucker's outfit?" Gideon asked.

"I've no idea." Bess regarded the question as irrelevant. "He's coming here, though!" She paused, thinking of other things that needed doing. "Oh, yes! I'm going to have a go at winning the King George the Sixth and Queen Elizabeth with your Brunswick."

"That sounds like enough to be going on with," Gideon said, and made way for Hubert, who had re-entered the room, clearly the bearer of important news.

"The Jockey Club are sending a chap to see you about the licence, Bess," he said. "He'll be here tomorrow afternoon." She looked surprised. "Friends in high places," Hubert explained. "This fellow will help you with all the forms and give you the once-over to make sure that you're a fit person to be in charge of horses."

"When will everything be settled?" Ann asked.

"By the end of the week at the latest."

"Thank God for that!" Ann replied.

The universally shared sentiment was a signal for the break-up of the gathering. While Bess found herself drawn to Amelia, Hubert took Ann to one side.

"I ought to stay here for a few days," he said. "I've come prepared."

"That would be nice."

"You might need me," Hubert said. "Mother is likely to go up in flames when she hears about this."

Ann was horrified. "I hadn't thought about that," she whispered. "What do you think will happen?"

"Let's wait and see," Hubert advised. "There's no point in trying to cross bridges before we have to. If you were to twist my arm, I'd say she'd have a go at getting Edmund in."

"Heavens!" Ann said, still more worried.

"But she'll have made the same mistake that we did with Rebecca: she won't have asked him."

"And you think he wouldn't be interested?"

"Not at any price!" Hubert said confidently. "In any case, there isn't a vacancy, so the question doesn't arise."

It was perfectly natural that Amelia and Bess should walk to the Back Stretch together.

"A big surprise for you," Amelia said after they had covered most of the hundred yards up the drive in silence.

"Yes!" Belatedly, Bess was finding herself suffering from shock. A month short of her thirtieth birthday, she had been given control of the most celebrated racing stable in England. Her nerves had started playing up as they walked past Elsie and Boggysevick's house, hidden away behind the poplars. What were they going to think? Ought she to have stopped to tell them?

"My mother was terribly keen that you should spend the whole of your life here," Amelia said.

"Is that why she gave me that money?" Bess asked.

"Of course!" Amelia's eyes twinkled. "I suppose you could call it a bribe."

"What if I'd taken it and left?" Bess asked.

"She knew you wouldn't. She hardly ever made a mistake with people." Amelia smiled in a way that was almost cheeky. "She wasn't *quite* infallible, but she was sure about you."

"When I was with her the night she died, she told me that all her family were heirs to adventure," Bess said.

"Imagine that!" Amelia stopped, her face lit by a sublime smile. "How wonderful! And so true . . . especially for you, my dear." They stood in rapt silence until Amelia's mood changed. "If I can ever give you help or advice, come and ask," she said. "Don't be shy and don't be too long. I'm very old!"

Looking up after she had inclined her head in thanks, Bess saw a dim figure hopping round agitatedly outside the Bungalow.

"There's something you can do straightaway," she said. "Be an angel and help me explain this to Liz."

Gillian was not sure if she was pleased to see Giles back so quickly. "You promised to ring," she said. Her tone, verging on peevish complaint, caused Janet Foley a few moments of irritation. Giles, on the other hand, was too full of himself to notice.

"There was no point," he said. "I did what needed doing and cleared off."

"How did they take it?"

"Badly!"

"What are they going to do without you?"

"My cousin Edmund will take over." Giles was busy unscrambling the pile of clothes in the back of his car. "Probably a good thing . . . a lord will add tone. Don't just stand there, darling, give me a hand with this lot."

Later, Gillian asked: "Did you ask them about money?"

"Yes. They've promised to let me know."

She was disinclined to pursue the matter, even though she suspected that he was lying. Having spent several minutes parading naked round the bedroom, Gillian recognised a duty to satisfy what she had incited.

After three days without word from Latimer's Barn, Rachel was ill at ease. Nor did she care for Hubert's absence from Eaton Mandeville.

At nine o'clock each morning, her housekeeper brought Rachel *The Times* and *The Sporting Life*. The front page of Thursday's *Life* was sensational.

EX-STABLE GIRL TAKES OVER
AT LATIMER'S BARN

the main headline proclaimed. Below it was a photograph of an austerely attractive Bess, together with a report of the previous afternoon's press conference, organised by Gideon Timberlake.

When she drove into Cannings Ambo an hour later, one mystery was solved at once: the first person she saw was Hubert. Standing at the bottom of the drive, he was chatting to Robert Frobisher, who took one look at Rachel and remembered a meeting in the Memorial Hall.

Moving towards her with his customary languid grace, Hubert spotted *The Sporting Life* on the seat beside Rachel. "Good morning, Mother," he said. "Have you, by any chance, come to create a scene?"

"Are you mixed up in this disgraceful business?" Rachel countered.

"Up to my neck," Hubert replied.

"What has become of Giles?" Rachel asked.

Starting to look a good deal less affable, Hubert walked round the front of the car and got into the passenger seat. "We mustn't block the road," he said. "Drive up to the front of The House."

Rather to her own surprise, Rachel did as she was told. "This seems to have been done with indecent haste," she said.

"On the contrary, it was done with the decisive speed necessary to avert a disaster," Hubert replied. "As I suspect you know, Giles turned up on Sunday afternoon with the news that he wanted to clear off at once to rescue his so-called marriage. A majority of Trustees were present to approve Bess's appointment, which was, I might say, suggested in a letter from Leander."

"A letter? What letter?" Rachel was suspicious.

"She wrote it about ten days before she died and left it with Amelia for use in an emergency. You'll see for yourself when you read it."

Rachel was subdued by the discovery that death had not stopped Leander exerting an influence. As they approached the side door of The House, Bess was coming out. Dressed in maroon breeches, Tattersall check shirt and gleaming boots, she was immaculate. She smiled at Hubert, then directed a frank stare at Rachel. "Good morning, Your Grace," she said in confident tones.

"Good morning, Miss Collier. Er . . . congratulations on your new appointment."

"Thank you. I must go, the second lot is waiting."

They turned to watch her easy stride towards the 1874 yard where the horses were forming up.

"I have to confess that those breeches do a great deal for her," Rachel said wistfully.

"I've been told that you used to look that good," Hubert said. "I can remember you when we were here in the War."

"But I never had togs like that." She smiled sadly. Briefly, Hubert saw the real woman that was hidden behind the shell his mother had chosen to construct around herself; yet again, he wondered what had driven her into the devious, tormented world she had occupied for so long.

Rachel's mood remained downcast for the whole of what turned out to be a three-day stay at Latimer's Barn. Over lunch, Ann eventually realised that there was not going to be a flare-up and, for the first time in over fifteen years, found herself relaxing with her sister-in-law. Rachel lingered over the meal, recalling memories of her early days at Latimer's Barn. To Hubert's astonishment, she talked about her schoolgirl crush on Charles, the handsome Marquess of Glastonbury. Afterwards, Ann took her to the library and let her read Leander's letter, now pressed between the pages of the Big Book.

"There's no arguing with that, is there," Rachel said after studying it carefully. Secretly, she was relieved that the letter made no mention of her: she was half-convinced that during the last five years of her life, Leander had guessed at Helen's true parentage. At long last, it seemed that the dreadful facts were safely buried.

Gideon Timberlake pulled Bess's leg mercilessly about how badly she came unstuck over Jerry Middleton. She had vowed to have him working for her within a week: it took three.

By the time he arrived, attitudes in the yard had been transformed. Bess had decided that the way to success lay in setting herself up as an out-and-out martinet. It was wickedly hard work, full of stress, but she stuck at it, knowing that life would be easier for everyone once her reputation was established. She was backed to the hilt by Arthur Merriweather and was able to draw strength from the knowledge that, within hours of her appointment being made public, lads from all over the country were ringing up to ask for jobs.

The first onslaught was directed against the lads' working dress. Many had slipped into the habit of riding out in jeans and a variety of ugly, unsuitable shoes. "You'll dress properly, or go somewhere else," she told them when she called them all together in the games-room of the hostel after evening stables on her first day. "Anyone late for work will forfeit half a day's pay, a horse or a box below standard will cost you a day's pay. Tonight, you can clean this place up." She had inspected the hostel from top to bottom and was displeased. "I shall have another look at six o'clock tomorrow morning."

Bess saw that most of the sixty lads looked relieved and cheerful after her harangue: the others, four set on by Giles, knew that they were marked and would probably leave of their own accord. Her parting shot pushed the spirits of the majority even higher. "In case you think I'm nothing but a bullshit merchant, understand that I've been given this job to win races and that's what I intend doing. This stable is going back to the top of the league and both the horses and you lot are going to be a credit to it!"

Bess gave careful thought to the question of her first runner. Twelve horses had been entered by Giles for races that week and she scratched all except one, Big Ben, a five-year-old belonging to Edward Mallender. After riding him herself, Bess decided that he could take his chance in a respectable handicap at Newbury on the Monday after she took over.

"He's as right as he ever will be," she told Michael Pilgrim in the paddock before the race. "See what you can do with him. He's pretty tough."

Michael understood. In the event, every ounce of Big Ben's gritty stamina was needed, but he did it. Not only was Bess's first runner a winner, she arrived a mere ten minutes before the race and was away the moment her brief appearance in the winner's enclosure was over. Absent from Latimer's Barn for less than two hours, she showed that she intended doing the business with minimal fuss and bother.

Two more winners came that week and three in the week that followed. When Jerry Middleton arrived, he was joining an establishment that was starting to believe it could achieve anything.

Arthur Merriweather took him into the hostel to get him settled during the afternoon stand-down, when most of the lads were dozing or cleaning their kit. Deliberately po-faced and taciturn, Jerry found his new quarters palatial after the squalor of his previous billet. In addition to all the scrubbing and polishing done by the lads themselves, the decorators had been at work, fresh curtains adorned the windows, and, that very afternoon, brand new bedspreads had appeared.

Picking up the one that had been thrown, still-folded, on the bed he was to occupy, Jerry Middleton looked at it in bewilderment. Opening it out to reveal that the sheet of cream-coloured linen was edged with a scarlet Greek key pattern border did nothing to cure his bemusement. Finally, in desperation it seemed, he draped it over his shoulders, winding the surplus round his body. The watching lads erupted into laughter.

"Julius-bloody-Caesar!" one of them called out, seeing how the bedspread had been turned into a toga.

In years to come, the uninitiated often asked why Jerry Middleton was invariably known as 'Caesar'. Privileged to be present at the moment it happened, Arthur Merriweather knew that the nickname could never have come into existence without the *esprit de corps* generated by Bess.

And after she had discharged her promise to win the King George VI and Queen Elizabeth Stakes with Brunswick, bringing in £31,000 of prize-money in one swoop, morale went through the roof.

By the middle of September, Rachel was sick to the back teeth of hearing tales of Bess's success. At the same time, she knew that her bitterness was antagonising her only two friends.

"What *do* you want?" Leslie Giffard asked. "You're constantly going on as though you wished Latimer's Barn would fail. What sort of sense is that supposed to make?"

Rachel could find no answer. Later, she became painfully aware that Giffard was reducing the frequency of their meetings.

The message from Giles was similar. "I don't see anything to complain about," he said. "Bess is working wonders and I wish her luck . . . I want to see the place back on top. And I'm doing very nicely, thank you, so everyone's happy."

He had made a good start to his career with Foley, Nettles and Mayo, and claimed that he and Gillian were very happy in a magnificent new house on the outskirts of Wantage. However, when Rachel angled for an invitation to visit them, Giles was evasive. He had willingly resigned his Trusteeship and had no hope of getting money from the Fund: Rachel guessed that he was scared of Gillian finding out, and was keeping her away from anyone who might let the information slip.

To add to her misery, Rachel disapproved strongly of the arrangements for Hubert's wedding. The tradition that Dukes of Laverstoke should marry at Bath Abbey was being broken to please the bride. The ceremony was to be a Catholic nuptial mass in the church on the de Mourville estate and Hubert refused to say what religion his children would have.

And it seemed that Cannings Ambo might be playing a part in the wedding. Six months ago, Hubert and Lisette had fixed the first Saturday in October as their wedding day. At the time, the fact that the Prix de l'Arc de Triomphe was being run at Longchamp the following day was irrelevant; no one's wildest dreams suggested that Latimer's Barn would have the second favourite for the race. Yet that was the status enjoyed by Brunswick, and half of Wiltshire invited itself to the wedding as an aperitif for a day out in the Bois de Boulogne.

Rachel's attempts to put a good face on her visit to France were variable. Bess, who had flown over with Brunswick on Wednesday, was disgusted by the sourness of the Dowager Duchess's demeanour when she arrived at Mourville on Friday evening: no one who went near her could fail to detect her profound wish to be at least a thousand miles

400

away. Mercifully, she acted with serene dignity during the wedding itself.

Entering the church, Bess fell in with her old friend Marie-Claire Guillaume and they kept each other company for the rest of the day. Marie-Claire, who looked upon Lisette as a daughter, began to weep when her darling appeared on Alain's arm and continued to do so throughout the service. In a dazzling dress by Yves Saint-Laurent, the man who had assumed the mantle of Dior, and a veil made up of yards of Chantilly lace, Lisette did indeed look a picture, but Bess knew that Marie-Claire's tears stemmed from a sense of loss.

"You mustn't worry," she said. "The Duke is a very good man. He will look after her and make her happy."

"He is very handsome," Marie-Claire replied. It was totally illogical, but it cheered her up.

The wedding breakfast in the great hall of the château ended only when the photographer climbed on to a chair to announce that it was necessary to go outside to make use of the last half hour of the soft, October daylight. When Bess and Marie-Claire had taken part in the huge set-piece that included all four hundred guests, they moved to the rose garden bordering the terrace to watch the smaller groups being photographed. After a while, Bess's attention wandered and she found herself watching a man in a cluster of people on the opposite side of the terrace. Aged about twenty-seven or so, he spoiled his good looks with an ill-humour that could easily have been a permanent dissatisfaction with life. His reaction to a chic girl who was clearly rejecting his advances showed a foul temper.

"My son, Jacques," Marie-Claire said with quiet melancholy.

"Oh." Bess was embarrassed at having her thoughts read.

"He is no good," Marie-Claire said with damning finality. "His father was a brave, wonderful man, but he is rotten. He has a good job with Monsieur's transport company, yet he is always causing trouble."

401

"Oh, dear!"

Jacques Guillaume, finally leaving the girl in peace, turned to face his mother. Evidently on the point of departure, he bowed mockingly. Briefly, he examined Bess, caught her hostility and turned away. She found that there was something about his eyes that intrigued and disturbed her. Somehow they were familiar. When she woke the following morning, Bess had the answer: the striking spacing of Guillaume's eyes and the way they were set in his face was strongly suggestive of both Leander and Matthew Flamsteed. Although it was no more than a freak coincidence, the idea nagged at her disconcertingly.

At least, it did until Brunswick won the Arc, when the pandemonium that was let loose round Bess would have made anyone forget anything. For the first time since she was given her licence, Bess allowed her joy to show. Dozens of cameras captured her delight, particularly at the moment when Gideon and Lady Amaryllis tried to embrace her simultaneously.

Much later, when she was supervising Brunswick's departure to Orly airport, Noel Timberlake came up to her.

"I wish I could work for you, Miss Collier," he said. "It must be smashing! The trouble is, I'm going to be far too big to be a lad."

There was no arguing with him. At thirteen, Noel was obviously set to be a strapping young man.

"There'll be other things for you to do," Bess said. "I expect they'll be *better* than being a lad."

"I'm not sure about that," he replied. "They're going to send me to Oxford and make me work in London. It'll be rotten!"

"Go away and annoy the natives!" laughed Lady Amaryllis. She had been following him and sent him on his way with a robust shove. "Unless I'm going blind, the poor little toad has got a crush on you," she said when Noel had shambled out of earshot.

"I know!" Bess heaved a sigh of mock-despair. "*Another* responsibility."

* * *

402

At the end of October, Bess applied herself to tidying things up. The first item on her list was Hugo Richardson. Having taken him out to lunch and thanked him for his patronage, she told him that she no longer wanted to train his horses.

"I quite understand," he said. "I'm grateful to you for letting me carry on until the end of the season. There's a chap at Lambourn who promised to look after me when you chucked me out."

"Be careful what you get up to in that part of the world," Bess cautioned. "They tell me there are dangerous women at large."

"One in particular," he smiled. "Apart from my instinct for self-preservation, I don't want to upset my fiancée."

The encounter with Richard Morton was very different.

After living on tenterhooks since her appointment, he responded to her summons with great trepidation. As he was meant to, he found her newly equipped office intimidating. Bess had refused all attempts to make her a Trustee and declined Ann's invitations to live in The House; her one concession to the trappings of authority had been to set up an office of impressive grandeur in the room adjoining Liz. The carpet, the paintings that embellished the walls, and the purpose-built furniture from Wm Flamsteed & Sons were all calculated to overawe. They were an essential part of the armoury of a woman carving her way through a male-dominated world. As a rule, Bess sat with visitors on an L-shaped arrangement of easy chairs in a corner, but for Richard Morton she was entrenched behind the desk and she allowed no time for preliminaries.

"We, that is the Trustees and I, have reached a decision that I thought I should tell you about personally," Bess said. "After December, we shan't be needing your services, Richard."

White with shock, he jumped to the obvious conclusion. "You're surely not thinking of going to Bannister and Jones? They might be a shade cheaper than us, but they're awful quacks!"

"They are indeed and I wouldn't let them within a mile of one of my horses."

403

"Who, then?" Morton asked frantically.

"We're having our own resident vet."

He was stupefied. Such a thing had never occurred to him. "Well . . . yes . . . I can see that the idea could be attractive to you . . . but you couldn't possibly get the breadth of expertise that my partners and I provide."

"Oh? Not even with Eleanor Murdoch?"

"*The* Eleanor Murdoch?" Richard asked shakily.

"If you mean the principal lecturer in equine pathology at the Bristol Vet School, yes!"

Morton shook his head. "You'll never get her!"

"She's been here for two weeks. We're giving her fifty per cent more than she was getting at Bristol, a house and all the facilities she needs, and I expect to be showing a profit within eighteen months."

It had, he appreciated, taken a long time to organise: Bess must have started work on it soon after she took over in May. "This will ruin me," he said furiously. "You know the practice relies heavily on Latimer's Barn."

"In that case, you've been very stupid, Richard. You shouldn't have put so many eggs in one basket."

"I know why you're doing this," he seethed.

"I'm doing it for purely financial reasons with the full backing of the Trustees. Last year, you charged us forty thousand pounds, this year it's looking like fifty. That's daylight robbery and we've had enough of it."

He stayed for several minutes, blustering and arguing. Then, realising that there was nothing he could do, he stormed out.

"So help me, I enjoyed that!" Bess said as Liz poked her head round the door.

"Serve the bastard right!" Liz declared. "Will that really finish him?"

"Unless he changes to farm work," Bess replied. "And I doubt he's capable of it."

"I've heard that the great Leander was like this when she was in one of her moods," Liz said.

Bess rounded on her, a forefinger wagging in rebuke.

"Don't you dare let anyone else hear you say stupid things like that!" she said. "This job's hard enough without silly sods spreading the word that I'm a reincarnation. Got it?"

"Got it, Bess," Liz said meekly.

CHAPTER 15

1971

'. . . *an addition to the independence* . . .'

Amelia had never taken much interest in racing. "I was too busy," she would tell those who questioned her apparent indifference. "In any case, Mathematics was far easier and Mother always had everything under control."

In 1970, however, she changed completely. Appointing herself Bess's guardian angel, she began turning out on the gallops each morning and tearing off to race meetings as an excited passenger in Bess's fearsome old sports car, a battered and virulently noisy Triumph Spitfire, known among the lads as the 'Projectile'.

Without a shadow of a doubt, the horse of the year was Charlie Engelhard's magnificent colt, Nijinsky, trained in Ireland by Vincent O'Brien. At Newmarket for the Two Thousand Guineas, his appearance in the paddock was so overwhelming that Amelia wondered why the other thirteen runners were bothering.

"Take a good look at that boy," Bess told Amelia. "If Vincent can keep him right, nothing will touch him this season."

The Irish magician handled Nijinsky superbly well and he swept all before him, capturing the Two Thousand Guineas, Derby, King George VI and Queen Elizabeth Stakes, and the St Leger. He also won the Irish Derby. Only at the end of his arduous season did the great colt seem to falter, finishing second in both the Prix de l'Arc de Triomphe and Champion Stakes.

With winnings in England of £160,000, it seemed certain that Vincent O'Brien must be the year's leading trainer. However, as the season came to an end, the eighty-six Latimer's Barn winners had brought in very nearly £200,000 to give Bess the title in her first complete year. Unaffected by success, she found grounds for pessimism as she and Amelia watched their entry in the Dewhurst Stakes get soundly beaten by a colt called Mill Reef.

"We're going to have the very devil of a job with that one next year," she said gloomily.

"He doesn't look anywhere near as impressive as Nijinsky," Amelia pointed out.

"Handsome is as handsome does," Bess replied. "And I tell you, Mill Reef is good!" As an afterthought, she added, "And what he doesn't win, Brigadier Gerard will. Other stables have good horses, too, you know!" Amelia looked as though she might be about to protest at this scandalous suggestion when Bess produced another afterthought. "Giles wants me to have dinner with him."

"*Does* he, now?" Amelia's eyes narrowed.

"He telephoned the other evening."

"What's he up to, I wonder?"

"He said he was very pleased at the way things have gone this year and wanted to congratulate me."

Amelia nodded. "What are you going to do?"

"There's no reason to avoid him," Bess said. "And he did promise me a slap-up feed. In any case, Ann would be grateful for a report." These days, Bess was on Christian-name terms with all members of the family.

The meeting took place at a newly opened restaurant near Newbury. Bess was perfectly content to answer Giles's incessant questions about the stable and her plans for the future, since it absolved her from the responsibility of making conversation. But he did eventually dry up and the only way out of an uncomfortable silence was for her to ask: "How are things with you?"

407

"Oh, you know, pretty good, really," Giles replied. "I'm getting to be a dab hand at flogging property. It's fun."

To Bess's ears, there was enough brittle edge in the way he spoke to make it sound false. As the evening wore on, his laboured jollity, an unwitting caricature of his father-in-law, began to grate and Bess was heartily glad when she was able to go home.

As promised, she saw Ann the following morning and made her report. Alerted more by Bess's reluctance to go into details than anything she said, Ann jumped to the conclusion that was almost certainly right. "Things aren't at all as they should be."

In January 1971, the village warmed to a piece of wonderfully good news. After an immense amount of heart-searching Rebecca and William announced their engagement. With the betrothal of a Hawksworth to a Flamsteed, the wheel that had begun to turn ninety years ago seemed to have come full circle.

William and Rebecca had spent hours agonising over whether they might be too closely related to marry. The Reverend Robert Frobisher and Joe said that it was perfectly in order and, in any case, no one could work out what their relationship was. William's father, John, thought they were probably second cousins twice removed, but had no idea what it meant.

Wishing to revive the old family custom of a honeymoon in Torquay, William and Rebecca went to see Bess.

"Blimey, this looks serious!" she said, nervousness having made them tense.

"Well, you see, we'd like to get married at Easter," Rebecca spluttered, while William nodded furiously in support.

"Good idea!" Bess agreed.

There was a pause while they stared at her. "After that, we want to go away together," William blurted out. Bess almost collapsed into laughter at his deadly earnestness. With their sincerely held traditional beliefs, she was willing to bet that they would not consummate their love until they were married.

"That is allowed, William," Bess said with a very straight face.

"But we want to go for *three* weeks," Rebecca said.

"Another good idea," Bess smiled. "Look, what exactly is your problem?"

"You'll be without Rebecca for three of the busiest weeks of the season," William said.

Bess made a show of gritting her teeth. "In that case, I shall have to stop messing about and cope," she said.

"Don't you mind?" Rebecca asked, starting to look happy.

"Of course I don't mind!" Bess told her. "It would be a different matter if you wanted to go swanning off on something ridiculous, but getting married *is* quite important."

"We thought you'd hit the roof," William said.

"Twaddle!" Bess retorted. "Go away and let me carry on with this lot . . . oh, by the way, my best wishes to you both!"

She reached for more of the off-season paperwork that Liz had dumped on her desk, then found herself thinking about the way they had crept into her office. If her assistant and William Flamsteed were afraid of her, it was time to think of easing up on the reign of terror.

From the very start, the union of William and Rebecca was seen as a good omen: everyone was supremely confident that Easter Saturday would be a joyous occasion to obliterate the memory of Giles's wedding, an event that still had the malign power to evoke shudders and long faces.

Sure enough, good things did begin to happen, although Ann and Lady Amaryllis were suitably shamefaced at finding Edward Mallender's great misfortune a cause for private rejoicing. He suffered a stroke on New Year's Day. By the time the news reached Cannings Ambo two weeks later, on the same day that the engagement became public knowledge, it was apparent that the after-effects were likely to be long-lasting and debilitating. At sixty-nine, Edward was finally forced to relinquish his joint-chairmanship of Mallender and Giffard Foods, handing over to Adrian, his eldest son.

Adrian it was who wrote to Amelia, well in time for the

February meeting of Trustees, to say that his father wished to resign. However, because Trusteeship of the Cannings Ambo estate was an honour the family valued, they would very much like to carry on into another generation. Since he saw himself being fully occupied with company business, Adrian asked that his brother, Richard, should be considered.

"The cheek of the man!" Ann fumed when she, Amelia and Gideon met to discuss the letter.

"What do you suggest we do?" Amelia asked. "Say, 'No, we've had enough of the Mallenders and we're going to take advantage of your father's illness to get rid of you'?"

"I shan't lose any sleep over not having to put up with that dreadful Edward!" Ann said stoutly.

"Richard's all right," Gideon said. "And he cares about racing. He's always the one that turns out to watch when they've got a horse running and I'm fairly confident that he's been the influence behind the reinvestment of Quartermaster's earnings."

Edward Mallender's 1955 Two Thousand Guineas and Derby winner had proved a very popular and successful stallion at stud. Most of his fees, something like £350,000, had come back to Latimer's Barn in one way or another.

"And I suppose you're going to remind me that we have twenty-five Mallender horses under training this year?" Ann said, exasperated at her imminent surrender.

"Twenty-eight, actually," Gideon smiled. "It might help you to know that Adrian and your niece, Helen, are no longer . . . er . . . involved. *She* chucked him and appears to be turning towards respectability." Ann's surprise made him look pleased with himself. "Hubert isn't the only one with his eye on the ball, you see."

"How do you know?" Ann asked.

"There is, I believe, a long tradition that says the Hawksworths don't ask the Timberlakes about their sources," Gideon said with deliberately overdone urbanity.

"Right, Richard Mallender becomes a Trustee," Amelia concluded briskly.

* * *

In the strangest, most unexpected way, it was John Flamsteed who received the first tangible proof that Helen was mending her ways. On a morning towards the end of February, he received an unexpected telephone call from the owner of a famous luxury hotel in Henley.

"I'm organising a refurbishment, Mr Flamsteed. I want someone who can provide good, solid, traditional furniture. Would you like to come and talk to me about it?"

Two days later, after John had taken one of the biggest orders in his company's history, he asked: "Tell me, what made you think of us?"

"I wouldn't say I thought of you," the man replied affably. "You were more or less rammed down my throat."

"Oh? Who by?"

"Lady Helen Christopherson. I do business with Freddie and we had him and Helen over to dinner a few weeks ago. I was daft enough to mention this job – and the problems finding anyone who was interested in meeting our specification – and off she went! I got an hour of white-hot sales-pitch!"

John was still mulling this over a week later when he was contacted by the managing director of a group of furniture shops in Bristol and the west.

"Lady Helen Christopherson tells me that I'm an idiot for not stocking your stuff, Flamsteed. Can I come and have a look at your outfit?"

"Yes, with pleasure," John replied. "Have you known Lady Helen long?"

"Only since she barged into my office yesterday!"

The prospect of getting his merchandise back into good shops thrilled John. A great deal used to be sold through the Fletcher department stores in Birmingham and Coventry, owned by his mother's family, but they had chosen to go down-market and had not taken Flamsteed furniture for over ten years.

On a more practical level, the two new contacts were manna from heaven. For longer than he cared to admit, John had known that his sales effort was sub-standard. Ernest Cartwright, now nearly seventy, still worked part-time, but he was not interested in breaking new ground and John had fought shy of trying to find a replacement.

Helen made no attempt to contact John and he was wary of getting in touch with her. The opportunity finally came at the wedding.

Easter Saturday saw a continuation of the fine weather that had ushered in April, ten days ago. As Rebecca was taken to church in the same carriage used by Leander in 1881, the first blossom was in evidence along the village lane. At her side, Gideon, who had won the honour of giving her away, looked stupendously pleased with himself, doffing his top-hat to the well-wishers outside The George with all the assured condescension of royalty.

There was no question of Rebecca being nervous today: everyone saw how happily at ease she was and her confident declaration of her vows was audible in every corner of the church. Ann felt certain that her daughter was embarking upon a marriage that would be blessed and happy. Giles, without Gillian, seemed much more his old self. Oliver, determined to be the life and soul of the occasion, was accompanied by a girl who seemed positively suitable and was, therefore, not expected to last long. It was very nearly one of the happiest days in Ann's life, marred only by the absence of her Steven, who would have been so proud of Rebecca.

After the service, there was a beano in the biggest of the workshops behind Rose House. Ann noticed that Rachel, perfectly comfortable in the formality of the church, was inclined to retreat and stand on her dignity when surrounded by conviviality, whereas Hubert's beautiful young duchess was enchanted by the proceedings and went out of her way to meet people.

Ann also saw what happened when Bess arrived at twelve-thirty.

Because it was an important work morning with nearly a dozen horses being put through their final paces before racing, Bess had been forced to miss the wedding itself. Now, still wearing riding-boots and breeches, she hurried into the workshop to make up for her enforced absence. She went straight to William and Rebecca, greeting them warmly and raising a glass of champagne to their future happiness. After spending five minutes with them, she spoke to other guests, exchanged kisses and a wildly enthusiastic burst of conversation with Lisette Prideaux, and finally looked round to take stock.

Her gaze settled on Giles, all alone, but apparently happy. Moving purposefully through the crowd towards him, she refused his offer to fetch her food from the buffet and they chatted easily.

Once again, Ann found herself indulging in wishful thinking: if only Giles could have been attracted to Bess instead of the awful Gillian.

Rebecca and William drove off to Torquay at three o'clock. After waving them out of sight, John Flamsteed turned to find Helen standing within yards of him.

Helen had been the big surprise of the occasion. Punctiliously polite, she had telephoned Ann to ask for an invitation to stay at Latimer's Barn. Arriving two days before the wedding, she was relaxed, charming and alone.

"Freddie's in Australia sizing up a big property deal," she explained. "Goodness only knows why they can't finance their own eyesores!"

"What about your son?" Ann asked.

"He's at home with Mrs Brotherton. She is regarded as a good influence on the heir to the Christopherson empire." Seeing the look on Ann's face, she smiled. "It's all right, I don't mind. Miles and I think the world of one another, but I'm not really the right person to raise him to be a pompous, self-opinionated prig."

Astonished and strangely touched by Helen's frankness, Ann accepted Gideon's assessment of her niece. On the two days before the wedding, Helen borrowed a hack from Bess and rode out on Cannings Down to watch work. In the afternoons, she visited Lady Amaryllis at the stud.

"What do you think she's up to?" Ann asked Amaryllis.

"I don't think she's 'up to' anything," was the considered reply. "At least, not in any devious sense. I wouldn't be surprised if she isn't trying to get into our good books . . . a job perhaps?"

"That doesn't sound a very good idea," Ann said.

"I think she's knuckling down to behaving herself, which is more than can be said for that louse Freddie . . . you should hear Gideon's views on the subject! She wants something to take her mind off things and she's awfully fond of the village."

"I didn't realise that," Ann admitted.

Finding John staring at her as they stood in the lane outside Rose House, Helen smiled and moved towards him. She was, he realised, a very attractive woman with a tangible aura of class, nearly thirty now, but none the worse for that.

"I'd like to talk to you," John said. "You've done me two big favours."

"The first one was sort of accidental," Helen replied.

"I could use a few more accidents like that. What are you doing, now?"

"Nothing."

"Come inside."

Julia, bravely putting the vision of Helen the scarlet woman on one side, did her best to be welcoming as Helen and John paused briefly before going into the study.

"I won't beat about the bush," John began. "You got me two damned good orders and they were very welcome. The truth is, Helen, our sales and marketing isn't very good."

Helen remained politely silent.

"What you did will take most of our existing capacity for the rest of this year," John went on. "But I'd be a fool to say, 'Thank you very much' and get complacent. For those with gumption and guts, this isn't a bad time to be thinking of expansion. So, let me ask you this . . . would you consider working for us?"

"Do you think I'd be any good to you?" Helen asked.

"On the evidence so far, you'd be brilliant!"

"Are you *sure* about this, John? I may not be all that popular round here."

414

"Leave that to me," he said, respecting her realism.

"All right. As it happens, I would appreciate gainful employment. Until Miles is, say, fourteen or fifteen, I want to go through the motions of being Freddie's wife. That would be a lot easier if I had the interest and discipline of a job."

"Fair enough," John said, grateful for her honesty. "You certainly seem to have the flair for what I want."

"I also have a bit of a title," Helen pointed out. "That can be used to open doors."

"How much time would you like to give me?"

"Could we see how we got on with ten days a month?"

John grinned. "Bearing in mind what you did without trying, I'd say we couldn't keep up with any more!"

They settled down to discuss terms.

Although they were guarded in their talk, not everyone in racing was happy at the prospect of being shown how to do things by a woman; some of the sport's less successful practitioners resented Bess being champion trainer at her first attempt. Jim Sellars, based in Yorkshire and already embittered by the growing reluctance of owners to send the best horses to northern stables, was scathing when in the company of trusted friends, and his filly, Malton Princess, made things worse. Her two-year-old form was not absolutely impeccable, but most were happy to accept her as favourite for the One Thousand Guineas. She was certainly the best horse that Sellars had ever had in his yard and her early-season work was impressive.

Ron Cox, a jockey who rarely had a ride south of Nottingham, knew that Malton Princess was his best chance of a Classic victory after twenty years of partnering no-hopers and mediocrities. They could forget the honour: that was no good for keeping the roof over his head and running two women. His share of the prize-money, perhaps as much as £3,000 if the owner was generous, was what mattered.

Jim Sellars stopped short of saying that the race was to be won at any price, by fair means or foul, but Cox understood

415

him. When the cards were down, no nonsense was to be tolerated from the southerners, *especially* that lot from Wiltshire.

As they jumped off at the start, Ron Cox was tense and uneasy. Alain de Mourville's entry, Coriander, looked good, justifying the whispers of the previous two days. There was ample evidence of the much-vaunted 'Latimer's Barn condition' and Michael Pilgrim was definitely confident.

However, he made one of his rare errors of judgement. Charging into the final furlong with Malton Princess and Coriander the only serious contenders, Michael decided to make his run on the rails, inside his rival, rather than go round to the wide gap on the outside. Acting swiftly, with all his hard-bitten skill and cunning, Ron Cox pulled his whip through to his left hand, striking Coriander across the nose as he did so. Her reaction to the shock very nearly had Michael over the rails. Using every last ounce of his strength, he kept her running well enough to finish last but one.

While Jim Sellars swaggered and gloated his way into the winner's enclosure, Bess and Alain were unsure what to do. With a less than perfect view of the incident, they had to rely on Michael's opinion.

"I *think* it was an accident," he said, still badly rattled. "Cox had to change his whip and I was too close to him."

Bess, anxious about Coriander's distress, lacking confidence in such a fraught situation, and chary of crying wolf too readily, let the matter drop. No objection was lodged and the Stewards had seen nothing to cause them to mount their own inquiry.

Solstice Jackson had other ideas. Having watched the race from his favourite spot near the furlong pole, he was perfectly clear about what had happened. He made his way back to the Silver Ring where he fell, casually as it seemed, into conversation with two men who gave the impression of astonished saintliness at what he had to say. They met again the following evening at a pub on the outskirts of Reading. Their huddled conversation ended with Solstice handing over a substantial number of five-pound notes.

During the following week, Ron Cox ran into a terrible

stream of bad luck. His car was stolen, causing him to miss three races at Carlisle, all of them for a harshly unforgiving trainer; his wife stormed off to her mother after receiving a tip-off about the woman in Doncaster; no sooner was she gone, than the remote cottage in the hills above Kirbymoorside, the one thing in which Cox had genuine pride and joy, was broken into and wrecked. And, while he raged over the mess, information concerning his illegal gambling activities was laid before the Jockey Club. Jim Sellars, terrified of investigation into his own affairs and painfully aware of how the tongues were wagging, sacked Cox immediately.

The stories were legion. Collecting them in racecourse bars and the transport-cafés used by the fraternity, Solstice took them back to Bess.

"They're saying that doing us down has ruined Ron Cox."

"Oh?" Bess pretended ignorance. "How is he supposed to have done us down?"

"Interfering with Coriander . . . it was deliberate."

"That's what 'they' are saying?"

"Josh Taylor saw it all," Solstice replied, naming the jockey who had ridden the filly that finished third in the Guineas.

Bess nodded. Two days after the race, Michael Pilgrim had begun to have second thoughts about the 'accident'. "Tell me, Solstice, how much did Cox's bad luck cost?"

"Never you mind!" he retorted gruffly. "But it won't half make the buggers think before they try anything else!"

Three weeks later, Bess and Giles had dinner together again. In the absence of Liz, who was spending the night with her gentleman friend, Bess cooked and they ate in the Bungalow.

"How is everything?" she asked.

After a struggle, he decided to tell her something reasonably close to the truth. "Not brilliant," he confessed.

"What, work, or the marriage?"

"Work doesn't look too good," Giles said. "We lost a big piece of business last month – allegedly because of me."

"That would be Warren Grenville's place," Bess said, showing that she knew what was happening on the north

Berkshire Downs. The sixty-box National Hunt yard was on the market with Foley, Nettles and Mayo's most virulent rivals. "What went wrong there?"

"Father-in-law sent me along to work the old-boy act, but Warren wouldn't even give me the time of day." Giles grinned ruefully at the memory of his brush with the notorious tyrant. "He reckoned that if I knew as much about selling property as training horses, he might as well get the vicar's wife to act for him."

"He's a bastard!" Bess said, trying to provide comfort, although she knew that Grenville had merely said what a lot of people were thinking. "And the marriage?" she prompted.

Giles shook his head grimly. "Bad!"

"Is there any hope?"

"No!" Giles regretted the decisive answer as soon as he had uttered it. Watching him struggle for an explanation, Bess was irritated, then, much to her surprise, found that she felt sorry for him. "The trouble is, she's involved with a chap she thinks she wants to marry," Giles went on. "He does a lot of legal work for Foley, Nettles and Mayo, so it makes things very awkward."

"Who for?"

"Everybody," Giles replied, failing to respond to the irony that Bess had injected into her question. "This chap and I aren't on the best of terms."

"You surprise me!"

"No, there's been trouble at work, as well as the arguments over Gillian. We managed a fearful cock-up about two months ago . . . I got blamed for it."

"What will you do if it all folds up?" Bess asked.

"I shan't be coming back here!" Giles said firmly.

"Why not? Don't worry about me."

"It's not you, Bess. The Trustees are hardly going to welcome me back with open arms, are they? Both Dame Amelia and Gideon told me exactly what they thought of me when I went off with Gillian." He shuddered at the memory. "No, I'm keeping an eye on one or two possibilities."

Since Giles was spending the night at The House, there

was no compulsion on him to go and they talked until well past midnight. Bess saw that Giles's weakness had become a terrible enemy; he still entertained the forlorn hope that a miracle might be hidden somewhere in the maze confronting him. So, rather than cutting his losses and pulling out while there was a chance of salvaging some dignity, he intended waiting until the bitter end was forced on him.

When he did finally leave, Giles made an urgent request.

"I'd be grateful if you watered this down when Mother asks you what's going on."

"She's very worried about you," Bess pointed out.

"I know. She daren't ask me too many questions, of course, but I'll bet she cross-examines you."

Bess's smile confirmed his supposition. "I'll do my best," she promised.

"Thanks." He turned back in the doorway, grinning cheekily. "Very interesting about Coriander and what happened to Cox."

"Surely *estate agents* don't get to hear stories like that!" Bess protested.

"You'd be surprised," Giles chuckled. "I must say, things have become much tamer since Leander's heyday . . . from what one gathers, she'd have had Cox roughed up. I suppose you knew nothing about it?"

"Absolutely!" Bess insisted.

"Good. Now, remember what I said about Mother . . . tell her the tale." Almost as an afterthought, he gave her a brotherly kiss on the cheek and went.

Exasperated, Bess went to bed to worry about him.

As the season unfolded, Amelia's interest in racing was kept at fever pitch by the accuracy of Bess's predictions about Mill Reef and Brigadier Gerard. They raced against each other for the Two Thousand Guineas; in one of the most thrilling contests for years, the Brigadier came out on top by a convincing three lengths. Thereafter, whether by accident or design, they never met again. While Brigadier Gerard established himself as Europe's top miler, Mill Reef tackled middle distances, sweeping all before him. After the Derby, he won the Eclipse, the King George VI and Queen Elizabeth, and his year would end with victory in the Arc at Longchamp.

As if to emphasise the achievements of the two colts who elevated public interest in racing to new levels, the year saw the introduction of the European Pattern classification into British racing. Designed to offer a balanced programme of high-class, non-handicap events for horses in all age-groups over all distances, the intention was to provide a yardstick by which the best horses of each generation could be identified. Within the Pattern there were three Groups: the twenty races of Group One, which included the five Classics, were international championship events; Group Two had thirty races of a lower standard, while Group Three contained fifty-five races regarded as stepping-stones to higher things.

It was obvious that the cachet of a Group One win was likely to enhance an animal's attractiveness at stud: to make sure of his place in the annals, Mill Reef's four consecutive victories were all at Group One standard.

Having studied the Pattern and its implications, Bess made a firm statement of future policy. "We're going to win Group races . . . the more the merrier!"

Gideon Timberlake's filly, Spontaneous, notched up the first Group One victory in the Oaks; later, she did it again in the St Leger. In between, Royal Ascot, Goodwood, York and Newmarket provided a good crop of successes at the lower levels. On Bess's instructions, Liz began to compile a record of Pattern-race wins in a new notebook: Bess wanted nothing to do with the Big Book, which she assumed was being looked after by Ann.

Amelia found the excitement a valuable antidote to the persistent headaches that were often accompanied by spells of dizziness. Concealing it well, she saw no reason to consult Joe Collier: she was eighty-four and wearing out. On an evening at the end of August, alone in Louise House, she had a particularly bad attack. After recovering from a faint, she got herself into bed. Reviewing her life, she found that she had no regrets and decided that there was nothing left for her to accomplish.

At the next meeting of Trustees, she tendered her resignation as Chairman.

"I'm too old for this sort of thing," she said. "I'd better tell you, before you find out for yourselves, that my mind is wandering. I had the greatest difficulty in understanding this report that John has produced."

"That isn't one of my best efforts," John Flamsteed said.

"Stuff and nonsense!" Amelia replied. "I'm stepping down and that's the end of it. I suggest that you, John, take over at once."

"I agree," Ann said, darting in before John had a chance to suggest that she was more suited to the job.

If Hubert Prideaux had been present at the meeting, the unanimous vote in favour of John would not have been affected. He was, however, in France, struggling with the worst crisis of his life.

In July 1970, six months into her first pregnancy, Lisette had miscarried. Badly upsetting though it was, there was nothing to suggest that it was anything more than a misfortune that was unlikely to be repeated. By January 1971, with all misgivings cast aside, Lisette was happy to be with child again. She lived a normal life until May, then, fussed over by a nurse who had been brought to Eaton Mandeville to watch her every move, she was wrapped in cotton-wool.

Lisette bore it stoically, doing what she was told. Her upbringing, in a family conscious of its long history and prestige, had imbued her with an instinctive grasp of the importance of producing an heir to a dukedom, even though Hubert would never have dreamed of mentioning the matter, and Rachel had the good sense to keep quiet. In fact, the politely formal relationship between dowager and duchess precluded the discussion of all but the most commonplace of topics.

Despite all the precautions, disaster struck again in the sixth month. This time, Lisette was demoralised and distraught. As

421

soon as she had recovered from the physical trauma of the miscarriage, she fled to her mother at Château Mourville, hysterically refusing all suggestions of consultation with the best gynaecologists. For once paralysed by indecision, Hubert drove to Latimer's Barn to consult Ann.

"How long has she been away?" Ann asked.

"Ten days."

"Any news?"

"Alain is keeping me posted. She's still in a bad way."

Ann nodded. "I'm afraid that may go on for some time. There are women who never get over a thing like that."

"I know." Hubert was grim. "What do you think I should be doing?"

"You ought to be with her," Ann replied firmly.

"That's what I'd more or less decided," Hubert said. "What about you? Will you be all right if I'm away for a while?"

"Of course I will, my dear. Everything is under control these days. Your mother is behaving herself and Helen's working wonders."

"Amazing," Hubert agreed. "What's the latest news about Giles?"

"Fairly awful, I think. He and Bess are seeing quite a bit of each other, but she's not telling me the *whole* truth."

Hubert frowned. "There's nothing between them, is there?"

"Good gracious, no! I have an idea that Bess only meets him because she feels sorry for him."

The pretence of Giles's marriage finally ended on a Thursday afternoon in mid-October.

At lunch-time, he told his secretary that he was taking work home. Having been worried about him for several days, the girl asked if there was anything wrong: uncharacteristically, Giles snapped at her and rushed off in a temper.

The real crisis had occurred the previous weekend with a virulent row over Keith Rawlinson, the man with whom Gillian was obsessed. Rawlinson, a year younger than Giles, was supposed to be a solicitor. He undoubtedly had legal qualifications, but his piratical attitude to business would, Giles thought, either make him a millionaire or a gaolbird by the time he was thirty-five. Gillian had reacted to Giles's criticism of him with an outburst that was heard by several neighbours. After reiterating her intention of marrying Rawlinson, come hell or high water, she had stormed out of the house, not returning until Tuesday morning.

Giles took that Thursday afternoon off in order to talk to Gillian. It was his intention to produce a plan that would enable the break-up to take place as amicably as possible.

There was no sign of Gillian's, or any other car outside the house and he assumed the place to be deserted. Going to the kitchen for a glass of milk, Giles found the dishes from breakfast and several dirty coffee cups waiting to be tidied up. Irritably, he piled them in the sink and wandered into the lounge.

Gillian and Rawlinson, both proudly naked, were engaged in intercourse on the sofa. Although Rawlinson stopped ramming at her, they made no attempt to move apart.

"Well?" Gillian demanded, glaring defiantly over the shoulder of the man buried deep within her. "What are you going to do, watch and learn, or sulk?"

"I came home to talk to you," Giles said in a voice he hardly recognised as his own. "Perhaps you could spare me a moment when you're free!"

The bitter sarcasm was wasted. Rawlinson began to move again and Gillian appeared convulsed with pleasure. "All right," she gasped. "Meanwhile, piss off! This is serious."

Back in the kitchen, Giles found that he was shaking. What upset him most was their brazen exhibitionism. They must have known that he was in the house, yet had made no attempt to stop what had obviously been in progress for some time. To steady his nerves, he tackled the washing-up, not quite drowning Gillian's exaggerated cries of ecstasy with the noise he made.

Silence, unreal, somehow menacing, followed. It was some time before Giles realised that a muttered conversation was taking place in the lounge. He sat at the table, waiting, pretending that he had no interest in the rise and fall of voices, for

423

over half an hour before Gillian finally appeared. In an ultimate gesture of taunting contempt, she was still naked.

"This has got to stop!" Giles said, acutely conscious that he sounded petulant, not strong.

"You're absolutely right," Gillian replied. "I'm leaving you. Now. This afternoon."

"For Keith?"

"It seems the best idea I've had for a long time."

"Where are you going?"

"He's got a perfectly good house."

"Where?"

"Mind your own bloody business!"

"Are we getting divorced?" Giles asked.

She gave a nasty laugh. "Congratulations!"

"What do you want me to do?"

"Nothing. I'm going to petition on the grounds of your unreasonable behaviour."

"*My* unreasonable behaviour!" It was so absurd that Giles felt like laughing.

"That's right. If you've got any sense, you won't object."

"I haven't had any sense for a long time," Giles retorted bitterly.

"Oh!" Gillian made a great show of being disappointed by the appearance of Rawlinson, now dressed. "Does that mean we're finished, darling? What a shame, I fancied another!"

"I think it would be best if you put some clothes on," Rawlinson told her.

She took her time over making her mind up, not slipping away until she was satisfied that goading Giles further might be counter-productive.

"Look, Giles, I'm very sorry about this," Rawlinson said when they were alone. "But it's how things are. I hope you won't feel the need to cause trouble."

"Why on earth would I want to do a silly thing like that?" Giles asked. "It seems to me that you're going to have enough bother without me sticking my oar in."

He stayed in the kitchen while Gillian and Rawlinson tramped round the house, removing the more valuable of her possessions. When the front door finally slammed shut, Giles knew that he was waiting for Gillian's father to sack him.

It was to take much longer than he expected. And before it happened, something quite astounding lay in store.

On the same afternoon that Gillian left Giles, Bess and Amelia were settling into The Blue Boar hotel in Cambridge. Taking advantage of a trip to Newmarket for the Dewhurst Stakes, Amelia persuaded Bess to leave Rebecca in charge of the morning's work so that they could make an early start from Cannings Ambo.

They reached Cambridge in time for lunch and spent the afternoon in gentle sightseeing, strolling along the Backs. Bess was struck dumb by the view of King's College and its magnificent chapel; very little that she encountered away from Latimer's Barn impressed her, but this was uniquely beautiful and stirring.

"What was it like coming here as a young girl all those years ago?" Bess asked.

"Wonderful! Quite wonderful." Amelia smiled, then shook her head sadly. "Every boy and girl should have the chance to spend three years in a place like this, you know. But look at the mess they've made of education . . . they've levelled *down* instead of *up*. It beggars belief!"

Having delivered her verdict on a vital aspect of England's post-war record, Amelia's spirits rose and they wandered back to the hotel for tea and toast, a rest before dinner and a string of gentle reminiscences before an early night.

With Bess inclined to be more than usually optimistic about her horse's chance in the Dewhurst, they set out for Newmarket after breakfast, like a pair of young girls out for a treat. On the racecourse, Amelia took particular notice of the friendly respect extended to Bess by the officials and other trainers. It was a measure both of the success she had achieved in a short time, and the way she had gone about it. Bess Collier was very hard and firm, so much so that poseurs and parasites were apt to take avoiding action when they saw her coming. However, she was as straight as a die, her horses always looked a picture, and stories were beginning to circulate about the help she gave to several small stables.

Today's colt was an outstandingly fine example of the 'Latimer's Barn look'. Lindisfarne was a bay by Astronomer Royal out of a very good mare that Lady Amaryllis had bought at auction in Deauville. Full of condition, yet imperturbably calm, Lindisfarne walked round the paddock with an air of almost threatening authority.

"Well, Bess, he's in tremendous fettle – even by your standards," his owner, Richard Mallender, said. "Is this where we see the action?"

"He won't let us down," Bess replied, mocking her own caution with a smile. It was impossible to lose sight of the fact that Richard had paid 35,000 guineas for the colt and that so far, at her insistence, Lindisfarne had raced only twice, beating very moderate competition without coming off the bit and amassing the princely sum of £4,780 in the process. "Michael Pilgrim did the ride-work on him the other day and thought he was ready to have a go."

Michael Pilgrim's instructions were to win it if he could. "But no fireworks," Bess ordered. "He's a good sort, he knows what it's all about, so leave him alone."

Emerging from the dip as the last of the ten runners, Lindisfarne made his own mind up. After giving Michael a few strides in which to adjust to the new pace, he set about shredding the opposition. To Amelia's amusement, he did it in a way that struck her as affable and slightly apologetic. "Sorry, chaps," she imagined him saying to the other runners. "I'm afraid that with my breeding and price-tag, this sort of thing is rather expected of me."

Curiously, Bess received the same fanciful impression and giggled as she and Amelia exchanged looks.

"My goodness, Mother would have enjoyed that," Amelia said. "She always looked on the Dewhurst as *her* race, you know."

"And it's Group One!" Bess said, allowing a trace of her satisfaction to show. As well as pleasing Richard Mallender, it was another line in Liz's special notebook.

"What's your opinion of Richard Mallender?" Amelia asked when they were on the way home in the Projectile.

"He's very good," Bess replied. "Most trainers that I talk to would sell their souls to have such a knowledgeable owner who doesn't interfere. How is he as a Trustee?"

"He seems to understand the requirements of the estate and the way we like to work," Amelia said judiciously. "I . . . er . . . he isn't married, or anything, is he?"

Bess chuckled. "He's not my type," she replied. "And I'm certainly not his." Looking as though nothing had been further from her mind, Amelia fell silent, while Bess thought of the interesting girl that Richard had been doing his best to conceal at Newmarket. Richard and the girl had avoided each other with studied indifference while Richard was on show, but Bess had seen them closely huddled in a corner of the bar before the first race, and they left together soon after Lindisfarne was taken from the winner's enclosure to be prepared for his journey back to Wiltshire.

At Amelia's instigation, Bess stopped at a transport-café near Dunstable, where they enjoyed a fry-up, huge mugs of tea, and a good deal of curious attention from the indigenous lorry drivers, one of whom eventually summoned the courage to leave his mates and come to their table.

"I hope you don't mind me asking," he said. "Are you Bess Collier?"

"I am."

He grinned. "I had a tenner on that nag of yours. What was he returned at?"

"You should get nine to two," Bess replied.

"Blimey! That was generous for one of yours."

"He hadn't done all that much before today."

"Well, the bugger has now! Are you running him in the Derby?"

"All being well." Bess held up both hands with fingers firmly crossed.

"Keep up the good work, darling!"

"I will," Bess replied with one of her best smiles.

"There you are," Amelia said as the man returned proudly

to his seat. "The price of fame. Not even Mother got herself waylaid in a transport-café."

"That was probably because she had the good sense to keep out of them!" Bess laughed.

It was nearly nine o'clock when they reached Latimer's Barn. As the car drew up outside Louise House, Liz dashed out of the Bungalow to crow about Lindisfarne's performance. For a few moments, Bess was so preoccupied with listening to Liz that she did not see Amelia's discomfort. After getting out of the car, she had found herself in the grip of a dizzy spell, a bad one.

"Hey, steady on," Bess said urgently, hurrying to get hold of her. "Don't fall down on us!"

"Rather too much excitement in one day," Amelia said weakly. Rallying, she added, "Silly old fool!"

Bess and Liz got her indoors and sat her down. Instead of recovering, Amelia's face betrayed that she felt worse and Bess saw that she looked dreadful. "I'm going to call Joseph," she said and Amelia did not argue.

After telephoning her brother and receiving his promise to come at once, Bess rang The House. Rebecca, living there with William until it was decided where they should make a permanent home, answered. It was necessary to cut her enthusiasm for Lindisfarne short.

"Amelia came over funny just as we got back from Newmarket," Bess said, urgency making her brusque. "I don't think she's at all well. Joseph's on his way up, I think your mother ought to be here, too."

As good as his word, Joe arrived five minutes later. His face remained expressionless as he took Amelia's blood pressure and pulse and he was careful not to sound annoyed when he spoke. "I think you should have come to see me some time ago."

"No, I shouldn't," she replied pleasantly.

"Headaches?" Joe asked.

"One or two." Very grudging.

"I'd like you to go into hospital, Dame Amelia." Joe sounded as though he was already resigned to the answer.

"It's a point of view, I suppose," Amelia said. "I'm not going, though."

Joe nodded. "Fair enough. You must go to bed and you need medicine." He looked at Bess. "Will you see to things here while I go to the surgery?"

"Of course, Joseph. Come along, Amelia!" Bess extended her arms, the old lady struggled to her feet and they made their way into the hall. Hesitating at the foot of the stairs, Amelia swayed as another wave of vertigo swept over her: Joe and Liz watched anxiously as Bess provided support. Steady again, Amelia began to tackle the stairs. She had managed four steps when there was a flurry of activity outside the front door, still slightly ajar. Stopping to look, Amelia saw Ann, Rebecca and William being ushered in by Joe. They all looked worried.

"Oh! What's wrong?" Amelia asked. Before anyone had a chance to answer, Bess felt her stiffen. Amelia grunted, more in surprise than pain, quivered and was inert.

"Quickly! Get her down here . . . on the floor!" Joe ordered. He helped manhandle her down, flung off his jacket and tried every resuscitation technique he knew. None of them had any effect and the awful truth horrified the onlookers.

Amelia Hawksworth, conceived by Powell's Pool on an idyllic afternoon in the summer of 1886, one of the first women to become a distinguished mathematician, had suffered a massive heart attack and died in Bess's arms.

Bess remained visibly upset six days later at Amelia's funeral. She had lost a very dear friend and staunch supporter. Her shock and desolation were made unbearable by her closeness to that terrible moment of annihilation: she had actually *felt* death. And there was the additional burden that lay on everyone over the age of thirty who had known Leander. With Amelia, their last tangible link to the woman who had made Latimer's Barn and Cannings Ambo had gone.

In accordance with her wishes, Amelia was laid to rest between the grave of her mother and father and the plot occupied by her beloved Silas. As the mourners turned away, Ann, Rachel and John Flamsteed, now the most senior members of the family, formed the leading group. They were followed by Julia with William and Rebecca, then came Giles with Bess. On this most special and sad occasion, Bess linked arms with Giles. Briefly, for as long as it took to walk to the lychgate where the cars were waiting, Bess felt part of the family, drawn to them in shared grief. By the time they reached The House, however, the affinity was gone, finally demolished by a filthy look from Rachel. Using the need to look at two sick horses as an excuse, Bess soon extricated herself from the sombre gathering in the large sitting-room, putting herself back in the position she preferred, at arm's length from the family and Trustees.

Giles made an oblique reference to her attitude over dinner that evening. "You were close to Amelia, weren't you?"

"Very much so," Bess replied. "She loved going racing."

"I think Mother would appreciate your friendship," Giles said carefully.

"She's got it!" Stung by the suggestion of back-door complaint, Bess was angry.

"That isn't my impression," Giles replied. "And it *is* only an impression . . . Mother hasn't said anything. She wouldn't, would she, not to me!"

"I see." Bess made an effort to calm down. "And what is your *impression?*"

Bracing himself, Giles dived in. "I think you see yourself as nothing more than hired help. Very high-quality, of course!"

"What's wrong with that?"

"Absolutely nothing, Bess! But you've been here all your life and you're one of us." After a moment's thought, he made a rueful correction. "One of *them*, actually."

"And your aunt Rachel agrees?" Bess asked sharply.

"I'm sure she does."

"Giles, if you believe that, you really are the fool some people take you for! I don't know what she – and one or two others – are up to, but I'm having no part of it. All I want to do is train horses, which is what this place is here for!"

Telling himself that he had asked for it, Giles adopted a

430

bland, conciliatory tone. The rest of the evening was devoted to what was little more than small-talk. Bess, deep in thought about Amelia and her own standing in Cannings Ambo, was unworried by the shallowness of their conversation.

Giles was positively glad of it. There was never any danger of a question that might trap him into betraying the lunacy that had enveloped his existence.

Ten days later, Bess obeyed what sounded very much like a summons to dinner at The Hall with Gideon and Lady Amaryllis. The two boys, Noel and Desmond, were away at Eton, so the meal proved to be a relaxed, intimate occasion. Lady Amaryllis was smitten by the elegantly simple pale-blue dress that Bess was wearing and Farquharson's of Bath came in for much comment.

"Don't bother going on about it, darling," Gideon said to Amaryllis when they made themselves comfortable over coffee. "We'll go into Bath next week and get you signed up with these rag-merchants!"

"It's probably worth mentioning my name," Bess said. "For some reason, they regard me as one of their gems!"

"So I should think," Gideon laughed. "Now, a spot of business. Amelia made me her executor, Bess."

"Oh dear! She had a fair idea of what was coming."

Gideon pressed on. "I have to give you this letter," he said, passing over the envelope he took from the inside pocket of his jacket.

Opening it, Bess found that the note was dated 15 September, a month before Amelia's death.

My dear Bess,
I am asking Gideon to ensure that you receive my savings as a bequest. I thought of raising the matter a year ago, but decided it was best to wait until you were unable to argue with me! Please regard this gift as an addition to the independence with which you would be able to face any future crisis.
God bless you,

Amelia Hawksworth

431

A bigger shock came when she had finished reading.

"She seems to have been very careful," Gideon said. "The two deposit accounts total fifty-four thousand pounds."

All that Bess was able to do was gasp and look stunned. Apart from the munificence of the gift, she knew that the phrase ". . . as an addition to the independence with which you would be able to face any future crisis" was destined to haunt her. Amelia had perceived risks and troubles ahead and wanted Bess to be immune from them.

CHAPTER 16

1972

'What the hell do we make of this?'

Although it had been the scene of Amelia's sudden death, Louise House was too good to leave empty for long. Ann suggested that Rebecca and William might care to set up home there, and, seeing it as an ideal place to bring up the children they were looking forward to, they agreed. The move took place during two days of fitful snow showers in the middle of January.

Left all alone in the vastness of The House, Ann did not repeat her invitation to Bess to join her, but expressive looks and hints were always present during the lunches they often shared in the kitchen. Elsie spotted it and made her feelings plain.

"Why don't you move in?" she asked Bess. "Poor Mrs Hawksworth's lonely . . . anybody can see it. And she's got Mr Giles's divorce to worry about, now."

"Oh, it's happening, is it?"

"End of the month! Scandalous how they can rush things under this new law. She's *ever* so upset. Mind you, I'm buggered if I can see why . . . we ought to have a celebration when Mr Giles is rid of that Gillian!"

News of Eleanor Murdoch's forthcoming marriage, together with the background gossip provided by Liz, had a surprising effect on Bess: she was unnerved and jealous.

Eleanor, whom Bess had persuaded to leave Bristol University, had settled quickly into Cannings Ambo and made an immediate impact on the stable. The advantages of a resident vet, who was devoted to her work and treated each horse as a much-loved pet, were greater than anyone could have imagined. It was widely believed that Eleanor put a stop to ailments before the horse itself realised that anything was wrong: the fact that substantial sums of money were being saved hardly mattered, and Bess derived no satisfaction from the whispers suggesting that Richard Morton was experiencing hard times.

Eleanor's husband-to-be was Brian Davidson, a craftsman who had come to Wm Flamsteed & Sons from London in 1967. Bess was intrigued by the news; Brian was two years younger than the thirty-six-year-old Eleanor and a sophisticated professional woman might have been expected to show more discernment in choosing a husband.

Liz fell about laughing when Bess advanced this point of view. "Don't be daft! Eleanor doesn't give a damn about that sort of thing. She and Brian have been at it since the week after she arrived here."

"At what?" Bess asked, baffled into childlike innocence.

"*It!*" Liz hooted. "Sex! They're demon lovers."

"Never!" Bess's initial reaction, partly a defence mechanism, was shocked disapproval.

"Now, now, don't start getting on your puritanical high horse," Liz scolded. "Haven't you ever noticed Eleanor skipping round with a glint in her eyes?" Bess pretended that she had not. "When she's in that mood, it's a pound to a pinch of whatnot that Brian's absolutely knackered, but looking very pleased with himself."

"Surely not!" Bess said.

"Eleanor's *told* me," Liz insisted. "She's not all brain and dedication. Our lady vet has lived a bit and she reckons that Brian is the cat's whiskers in the sack."

"Well, I'm damned!" Bess said weakly.

"You will be, my girl, if *you* don't get yourself fixed up with a man," Liz retorted, suddenly serious. "How long is it since David Brandon?"

Bess made no attempt to answer.

Obsessed by the idea that she ought to do something useful instead of worrying about her own frustrations, Bess asked Ann if she could move into The House. The response was rapturous.

Giles received advance warning of the Divorce Court proceedings from Janet Foley when she visited him on 2 January, two days before the formal notification arrived.

Not that she was in any hurry to tell him: they had been together for a long time before she bothered.

She had first come to the miserable house in Wantage on the day following Gillian's departure with Rawlinson. After a few pious expressions of sympathy for the loss of his wife, she made her true purpose clear. "Now that she's cleared off, we can go to bed with a clear conscience."

Giles had, of course, been staggered.

"I've always fancied you," she said calmly, starting to remove her clothes. "And I've seen you looking at me. I haven't imagined that, have I?"

"No," he admitted. "You haven't!"

Janet Foley proved to be a revelation. At first sight, her body seemed little different from Gillian's, yet Giles soon discovered that it was somehow both corrupted and enhanced by the aura of her extraordinary promiscuity. A wealth of sexual experience was shamelessly deployed to one end, furthering her own pleasure. Unlike the younger women who had been Giles's previous partners, Janet Foley made no special attempts to please him, nor did she attach any sort of hidden price to her favours: as she was to prove several times a week after that first incredible encounter, she simply wanted to make love until they were both exhausted.

It was intensely exciting for Giles. The psychological aspects of the relationship proved to be the most arousing. He knew that there was impropriety in a sexual liaison with his mother-in-law; it felt downright wrong. But he enjoyed a triumph of grotesque revenge against Gillian

435

in the frenzied union with her mother. After the rapid establishment of the bond of brute sensuality between them, Giles became a far more effective lover than ever before and a type of insanity took possession of him. Often, as he sat in his office, waiting for Ralph Foley to pluck up the courage to sack him, Giles thought of nothing but Janet and what he would do to her when next they met.

Although the Christmas and New Year holiday had not interfered with their arrangements, Janet and Giles were frantic for each other on 2 January. Not until fatigue eventually took over did she give him the news.

"Gillian tells me that your divorce will be in court next month. It's the fourteenth . . . St Valentine's Day!"

Giles shrugged. "I'm surprised it's taken so long. Presumably your husband would like me to clear off?"

"If you resigned tomorrow and promised not to create any problems over this house, he'd give you six months' salary."

"Anything to oblige!" Giles said sardonically. "By the way, how is Gillian?"

"Nursing a black eye at the moment," Janet replied. "Rawlinson isn't as easy-going as you!"

"Bloody hell!" Giles muttered.

"What will you do?" Janet asked.

"I think I can get a job in Bath."

"You're not going back to Cannings Ambo?"

"Oh, no! My name's mud with most of the village and the rest think I'm an idiot."

"What a mess!" Janet seemed deeply sorry. "I suppose the truth is, you couldn't hope to compete with that Collier woman?"

"She's awfully good," Giles said, enthusiasm breaking through his despondency. "She can see into a horse's mind . . . there aren't many who can do that."

It was not a talent that Janet rated highly. "Will you be keeping in touch with me?" she asked.

"I'd like to. What do you think?"

"Why not? We get on well."

It was a patently insincere reply. Giles's spirits sank. Belatedly, and in the most bizarre way, marriage to Gillian had yielded something good, even though he now had the feeling that he would never again find such a satisfying woman as her mother.

Everyone commented on Bess's exuberant relief at the start of the 1972 racing season.

"Between you and me, she hasn't had a very good winter," Liz told Arthur Merriweather.

"She seems to have got over it," he said, touching wood. "We aren't half getting the run-around."

"Remember that we're going to be without Rebecca for most of the year. Perhaps that's why Bess is getting so wound up."

"Don't worry, she'll cope," Arthur said. "When's Mrs Flamsteed's baby due?"

"August," Liz replied.

"I'd have thought it was a bit soon for her to have stopped riding out," Arthur said, careful not to sound critical.

"It might be," Liz agreed. "But you only have to whisper the word 'miscarriage' round here and everybody has ten blue fits. The Duchess of Laverstoke, you see."

"Ah, yes." Arthur looked sombre. "How are things in that department?"

"Not so good, I imagine," Liz said. "His Grace came to see Mrs Hawksworth the other day – first time for months – and neither of them looked too pleased afterwards."

Shaking his head, Arthur went back to the yard, where he knew Bess would be raring to go with the second lot.

All eyes were on Lindisfarne, preparing for a Classic campaign. He duly went to Newmarket for the Craven Stakes in mid-April, but both Bess and Caesar, his lad, were not optimistic about his chances. During his winter transition from two- to three-year-old, the colt had grown substantially, turning into a most formidable individual with a long, ranging stride and an appetite for work. Bess's view was that at ten furlongs and above, he was capable of galloping all the known opposition into the ground: shorter distances, however, were likely to be too sharp for him.

So it proved in the Craven. Michael Pilgrim did well to get him as close as fourth and Bess scratched him from the Two Thousand Guineas the next day. Having previously praised Lindisfarne to the skies, the newspapers now damned him as a has-been. Completely indifferent to the criticism, Bess told Solstice to put £5,000 on the colt for the Derby. When he came back to report that most of it had attracted odds of ten to one, she decided that the idiots were multiplying and taking over.

Giles, now living in a furnished flat in Bath, became a regular visitor to Latimer's Barn. He freely admitted that his new firm was not in the same league as Foley, Nettles and Mayo, but experienced little difficulty in persuading Ann that this was all to the good. "Believe it or not, I'm selling quite a few properties," he said. "And there's no one trying to stick a knife in my back."

Now that she was living in The House, Bess saw a great deal of him, especially when he stayed for weekends, which, to Ann's delight, he did quite frequently.

"Apart from the fact that I like it here, I'm keeping out of Aunt Rachel's way," he told Bess.

"I don't understand," she replied. "I thought you and she got on well together."

He shook his head. "That's history. I went to Eaton Mandeville a couple of times when I started in Bath and got a hell of an ear-bashing about coming back here and demanding my 'inheritance' now that I'm a free man."

"And that doesn't appeal?"

"What, with you doing so well? In any case, can you see Gideon and Hubert standing for it? I wasn't much good when I had the chance, was I?"

It suddenly dawned on Bess that it was probably far from easy being a fourth-generation Hawksworth. The assumption that you would be able to start where all the others had left off and go on to achieve even greater things must impose awful pressure. It was much easier being a first-generation Collier! Giles seemed to be growing up: if nothing else, marriage to Gillian had brought him down to earth. Bess stopped feeling sorry for him and took the first steps towards positively liking him.

After several Saturdays on which he had ridden out with her to watch work on Cannings Down, Giles asked Bess if he could accompany her to Lingfield for the Derby Trial. "It will be a nice day out and I'd like to see what you've got up your sleeve," he said.

"*Me?*" She was all innocence. "Are you suggesting that I'm planning something?"

"Blimey, Bess, even *I* can see you are!" he laughed.

Their arrival together was noticed and, as they stood in the paddock with Richard Mallender before the race, Bess saw eyebrows raised in curiosity and speculation. Although there had been no publicity, Giles's divorce was common knowledge. Gillian's subsequent antics, which had found their way into the gossip columns of two Sunday newspapers, were generating sympathy for her ex-husband.

After Bess had given Michael Pilgrim a leg up and he was making himself comfortable on Lindisfarne's broad back, they nodded knowingly at each other. Richard Mallender disappeared, presumably to make contact with the mysterious girl, and Giles asked: "Tell me, Bess, what are Michael's orders?"

To preserve the secret, Bess leaned close to him and whispered. "I want him to win it, so that no one can say they weren't warned, but we're going to keep quiet about what he's *really* capable of."

Michael Pilgrim was forty-five and nearing the end of his race-riding career. Jonathan, his son, was already bringing winners home in apprentice events and would be taking over in two or three years. For the time being, however, Bess was more than happy to rely on Michael's twenty-seven years of experience, and he put it to superb use that afternoon.

A member of a not very distinguished field of eleven, Lindisfarne ambled along with the crowd until the two-furlong marker, when several of the jockeys decided to make a race of it. Lindisfarne did not seem all that interested: he needed three resounding back-handers before he exerted himself and even then, the resultant victory by a neck looked unconvincing. Only one of the 'experts' who watched the race, a hard-bitten cynic who freelanced for a gaggle of papers in the Midlands, saw through it all. Latimer's Barn horses *never* got hit like that, so it was little wonder that Michael Pilgrim had a spot of bother with his left leg when he got off Lindisfarne. That was the side away from the stands on which Michael's boot had taken the full force of the savage blows. In reality, the colt had toyed with the opposition, expending far less energy than he would when next he worked.

That evening, well-pleased with Lindisfarne, Bess took Ann and Giles out to dinner in Marlborough and told them what was going to happen at Epsom in two weeks. It was a light-hearted occasion: in the car park afterwards, Giles kissed Bess. Deciding that she rather liked it, she returned the compliment.

First and foremost, Derby Day was a great triumph. But it was also uproariously funny for supporters of Latimer's Barn. The village was given its best, most prolonged laugh for over ten years and the effect was a rallying and unifying of spirit.

The comic villain of the day was Humphrey Danvers-Jones, a Newmarket trainer responsible for the favourite, Gunboat. The more unkind of racing's observers were wont to remark that Danvers-Jones had, five years previously, given up a promising career as a first-class nonentity to become a fourth-rate trainer. The generally accepted view was that he had more money than sense, an allusion to the huge legacy that had enabled him to get started and launch an ostentatious life-style. His brash, ill-informed owners seemed to encourage his stupidity.

Danvers-Jones was a great theorist and liked the sound of his own voice. In search of the 1972 Derby, he excelled himself, going so far as to call a press conference three days before the race. As all the newspapers faithfully reported, the only other contender he worried about was Côte d'Azure, one of

Alain de Mourville's French-trained horses. Apart from that, the biggest menace was that the race might be run at an erratic pace, depriving Gunboat of the chance to show his mettle. Accordingly, Gunboat's owner, the handsome and witty property tycoon, Harry Barlow, had consented to run not one, but two other horses as pacemakers. The brilliant pair would take it in turns to see that Gunboat got a good, strong gallop to launch him into the final victorious assault.

Not content with this, Humphrey appeared in an eve-of-race television preview, where, with the aid of a model of the course, he explained how the master-plan was going to work. Giles, taking a day's holiday for the race and already at Latimer's Barn, found it difficult to keep a straight face as Bess watched the programme on a new twenty-six-inch colour set.

"Well, Miss Collier, what do you think of that?" he asked when it came to an end.

"Isn't he a silly sod!" was her considered opinion.

Believing that Epsom Downs belonged to them, Humphrey Danvers-Jones, together with Harry Barlow and his entourage, made enough noise in the paddock to startle some of the horses and elicit a barrage of black looks from the traditionalists. The fact that one of the pacemakers played merry hell at the start, unsettling the great Gunboat, went unnoticed by the Danvers-Jones clique as they began to celebrate.

None the worse for the rumpus at the stalls, both pacemakers took a firm grip on the race after fifty yards. At the end of the second fifty yards, Lindisfarne passed them. Quite casually, Richard Mallender's colt went up the hill with a two-length lead with Michael Pilgrim looking as though he was admiring the scenery. At the beginning of the long turn that extended all the way to Tattenham Corner, the first signs of panic came from the main body of the field, five lengths behind Lindisfarne's immediate followers. As they attempted to close up, Michael Pilgrim started to ride.

"Lindisfarne isn't going to get caught," Bess heard someone say uneasily.

"He's pulling away even more," his companion replied.

Both were obviously heavy backers of the favourite, currently last but one of the twenty-two runners.

Bess was sure that Lindisfarne lost ground between Tattenham Corner, where she judged him to be nine lengths clear, and the winning post, at which the official verdict was seven lengths. Happily, Alain's Côte d'Azure was second: Gunboat was followed home only by one of his pacemakers and a horse who had cast a plate.

"There you are, Mr Mallender," Bess said as she pretended to let Richard lead his horse into the winner's enclosure. "One Derby winner! Tell me, aren't you going to bring your lady-friend out of hiding for *this*?"

"Not with all these photographers around," he replied, smiling acknowledgement of her sharp-eyed observation. "The grocery business is getting very nasty, Miss Collier . . . I don't want to give the enemy a gift!"

And with that, Bess had to be content.

The only minor cloud over Ann's day was that Alain and Nadia de Mourville were paying nothing more than a flying visit. This was supposedly because of pressing business commitments, but the truth undoubtedly involved Lisette, who continued to isolate herself at the château. Although it was impossible to extract information from the tight-lipped Hubert, it was clear that Lisette's worsening mental state was placing the marriage in jeopardy.

Shamelessly, with an entranced half-smile on her face, Bess stood outside the weighing-room to watch Danvers-Jones, beside himself with rage, berate the three jockeys who had taken part in his grand strategy. Embarrassed into silence by her interest, he found his baleful scowl greeted with an impudent wink.

"Did you know your horse was going to do that?" he demanded.

Bess shook her head vigorously. "Good God, no! We only brought him for the outing . . . he likes crowds. Mind you, be fair, Humphrey, you wanted a good gallop. You said so on the telly!"

Leaving him pop-eyed and speechless, she bumped into

Giles, bursting to congratulate her. "That was marvellous, Bess," he said. "The first woman to train a Derby winner."

In the satisfaction of seeing her planning and hard work with Lindisfarne come to fruition, *that* aspect of the afternoon's work had eluded Bess. She tried to imagine what Leander would have said.

All in all, it was such a happy occasion that the thought of what Solstice would be doing over the next few days seemed almost unclean: there was, of course, the little matter of nearly £50,000 to be collected. Rather than dwell on such sordid matters, she was content to let Giles kiss her.

Two weeks later, Giles was bitterly disappointed to be faced with a workload that made him miss the whole of Royal Ascot, where Bess saddled six winners. However, by spending each weekend at Latimer's Barn, Giles was able to keep in touch with Lindisfarne's preparation for the King George VI and Queen Elizabeth Stakes, due to be run on the last Saturday of July.

It was the day in which Giles saw Bess in a new light.

Up and about at six o'clock, he found that it was Bess herself who gave Lindisfarne his pre-race exercise consisting of a walk, a two-furlong trot, then a gentle canter. Afterwards, she helped Caesar groom him, quietly explaining to the colt where he was going and what was expected of him.

While Solstice and Caesar were loading Lindisfarne into the van for the journey to Ascot, Bess took the first lot out to the gallops. Her concentration never lapsed for a moment, not even over breakfast, when Arthur Merriweather and Michael Pilgrim had to answer a barrage of questions, with Liz scribbling in a shorthand notebook as the orders flew thick and fast. The only thing that flustered Bess was being three minutes late for the second lot. As if to make up for her slackness, they got a going-over that was pitiless in its attention to detail.

At ten minutes to one, Giles was looking anxiously at his watch: having been ready for over an hour, he thought Bess was in danger of cutting it too fine.

"Relax!" she said, finally leaving the office to go upstairs to change. "There's plenty of time."

She was right. They were on the course by twenty past two, with time to kill before the race.

It proceeded very much the same as the Derby, the only difference being that Lindisfarne was the odds-on favourite. In a shade under two minutes thirty-nine seconds, he earned £60,000 for Richard Mallender and made it seem certain that Bess would be leading trainer that season.

To Giles's amazement, Bess was unable to contain her impatience to be away. After exchanging pleasantries with Richard Mallender and a few others whom she regarded as worthy or important, they were heading for home.

"It's like shelling peas the way you do it," he laughed as she hurled the Projectile round a maze of back lanes to avoid the traffic jams on the major roads near the course.

"There's no other way for professionals," she said firmly. "You saw Danvers-Jones?"

"Yes! What the hell was he doing there? He wasn't running a horse in *anything*."

"That's his idea of showing the flag," Bess replied. "He and his cronies will be in the bar until they're thrown out. Then they'll clear off to one of Harry Barlow's rural retreats to have a go at his latest harem."

On the verge of making a facetious remark, Giles realised the full measure of her contempt and kept quiet. He had, in any case, a great deal to think about. In the midst of providing the most comprehensive display of her effectiveness as a trainer, Bess had made him aware of what a singularly attractive woman she was. Somehow, the combination of her authority and the way she used it, her unerring skills, and her lithe physical beauty had come together in a way that left him wondering why it had taken him so long to see it all.

But what the hell was he to do about it? He had fouled Latimer's Barn up once: making a nuisance of himself with Bess could produce an even worse shambles.

Ann was very tired that evening. It had been one of the bad

weeks when she had hardly slept for thinking about Steven. After five or six nights, she would give in, seeking oblivion with one of the sleeping pills that Joe insisted she kept handy. Bess knew the signs: Ann could hardly keep her eyes open as they ate supper, yet it was certain that she would be awake within two hours of falling asleep now that she was prey to the vicious circle of grief and exhaustion.

"Come on," Bess said, guiding her upstairs. "It's a pill and a good twelve hours for you, my girl."

She stayed with Ann until the tablet was starting to take effect, returning to the kitchen to find Giles looking worried.

"What's wrong with her?" he asked.

"She's worn out. She still misses your father dreadfully and it sometimes gets her into this state. There's no need to worry, she'll be as right as rain in the morning."

Giles was silent for a few moments. "I haven't helped," he said morosely. "I don't think I ever considered what a terrible blow Dad's death must have been to her."

"Not very good," Bess said bluntly. In a gentler tone, she added: "Still, I suppose you had enough problems of your own."

A strange, disturbed expression came over Giles's face. Afraid that she was forcing him into self-recrimination, Bess moved to comfort him with a kiss.

They both knew that the habit had ceased to be an automatic, sibling-like gesture shortly after the Derby. Perhaps, subconsciously, they had been waiting expectantly for something else. In the event, they were astounded at the energy that was unleashed between them. When she finally drew back, Bess saw that Giles was tense and wild-eyed.

"What the hell do we make of this?" he asked shakily.

Bess shook her head, shocked to find that she was running her hands through his hair.

"It's ridiculous!" Giles muttered.

"Is it?" Moving away from him, she tilted her chin challengingly. "I don't think I agree with you. Why don't you come to my bedroom in half an hour and we'll see which of us is right?"

Before Giles had a chance to open his mouth, she fled.

"I'm mad!" she said to herself in the safety of her room. "Raving!" She thought of piling furniture against the door so that Giles could not take advantage of her demented invitation, even if he wanted to – and she doubted that he did. She drove the idea away by flinging off her clothes and getting into the shower, where, far from calming her madness, the jets of water twisted her senses up to the point at which she felt she would become deranged without sexual gratification.

When Giles came in after a gentle tap on the door, her clothes had been put away and Bess was composed. Flat on her back in bed, she was covered only by a sheet. He sat on the edge of the bed, saying nothing. Staring into Bess's eyes he saw that they gave the lie to her superficial serenity; although paler and greyer than normal, they burned.

Giles found that it required considerable courage to reach out and draw the sheet from her, but an exquisite prize awaited him. Bess's firm, shapely breasts stood proud, despite her prone position, and the nipples cried out for his tongue: she sighed as he bowed his head, and placed an arm round his neck. Soon, Giles supplemented the efforts of his mouth with a hand that slid over her taut stomach to caress her labia and Bess moaned with pleasure. Her free hand stole inside his dressing-gown to discover an erection so hard that she thought it must be causing him discomfort.

When their patience with exploration and minor delights ran out, Giles found that her reaction to his penetration was almost alarming.

"Go on!" she moaned, sensing his hesitation.

"Are you all right?"

"Yes, yes, of course I am!"

Her lissom body, acting in response to the turmoil within her, did all that was necessary for both of them. As Bess approached the peak of her climax, Giles, desperately eager to be a good lover for her, found his resolve taken from him and joined the oblivion of the woman beneath him.

Immediately, Bess wanted to begin again. First, she got rid of Giles's dressing-gown.

"Yes," she said, inspecting his body with eyes and hands. "You'll do!"

"You're not so bad yourself," Giles smiled. "Is this what riding and dashing about like a mad thing does for you?"

"I wouldn't be surprised."

At three o'clock, Bess kicked him out. "Your mother *may* wake early," she said. "We don't want to give her anything else to worry about."

He agreed. After opening the door, Giles hurried back to kneel at the side of the bed. "That was wonderful, Bess," he whispered.

"It wasn't bad, was it?" she smiled.

It was true; they both meant it. Bess knew that the time had been exactly right for them.

On Sunday morning, while Ann enjoyed a late breakfast in her room, Bess and Giles strolled up to Powell's Pool. They remained silent until reaching the trees, then Bess wanted an explanation of his mood.

"Come on, spit it out."

"It's probably a bloody stupid thing to say, but I think I'm in love with you." Giles shuffled uneasily, dreading her response.

It took a long time. At last, Bess gave up the struggle with pros and cons, sense and reason, and plunged. Her face cracked into the broad, oblong grin that was a great rarity; usually, it was associated only with the performances of the very best horses.

"I think the feeling is mutual," she replied. "And believe me, Giles, *no one* could be more surprised than me."

"Oh!" he seemed pole-axed. "This is none too clever."

"I was wondering if it didn't cure everything," Bess said in an offhand, mildly speculative sort of way.

"How?"

"We get married, of course!"

Had it not been such a fearsomely serious business, Bess would have laughed at the emotions that paraded themselves across Giles's face.

447

"You'd want to live here and carry on with the stable?" he asked eventually.

"Giles, try to think of something *sensible* to say," she pleaded.

"Well . . ." he was struggling for coherence. "I'd do very well out of it, wouldn't I . . . and Mother would be over the moon. What about you?"

"I'd have the man I love, who's a bit of an idiot, but very nice, and the privilege of being the mother of the next generation."

Deeply affected, Giles turned to look at the village and Latimer's Barn, spread out below them under a lovely July morning. She watched his eyes follow the well-worn line of the gallops, then sweep back towards The House.

"Would I have to hold the licence?" he asked.

"Yes!"

"You'd help, though?"

"Try and stop me!"

Giles took great care over his reply. "Because of *me*, I need to think it over. My immediate reaction is, 'Bless you, yes! It's a damned sight better than I deserve.' I need to find out if I've got the bottle to carry it off."

Bess nodded. Giles's return to Cannings Ambo as a passenger on her skirts would not be easy for him. "Let's talk about it next weekend," she suggested.

"Yes, that should give me long enough."

"There's no point in hanging about," Bess said. "You and this place need a son, and I'm thirty-three!"

The reminder that she was three years his senior may have disconcerted Giles: for whatever reason, he took a few steps down the path that led back to Latimer's Barn.

"Hey, where do you think you're going?" Bess asked. Laughing, she pulled him back, heading towards the cover of the trees. There was no time like the present for showing him that it was damned well going to work.

When Giles turned off the main road into the Devizes Lane

on the afternoon of the following Friday, 4 August, he was still undecided and had no idea what he was going to say to Bess. He had two problems.

The first was Janet Foley and what she had provided. His self-disgust at those few weeks was unable to alter the fact that her raw sexuality was firmly and stubbornly implanted in his memory.

The second was fear of what people were going to think of him. All week, he had been trying, with varying degrees of success, to persuade himself that Bess's reputation in the village was unassailable and that she had enough guts for both of them.

His mind was in turmoil. Inasmuch as he was anywhere near a decision, Giles's inclination was to tell Bess that they should leave well alone and stay as they were. Then, totally out of the blue, at the bottom of the drive to Latimer's Barn, everything changed.

A group of about twenty people were blocking the road. Manifestly in celebratory mood, they included Joe Collier and the Reverend Robert Frobisher.

"Hello, what's going on?" Giles asked.

"I'm spreading gossip," Robert Frobisher said. "It's about your niece."

Giles was mystified. Forty-eight hours previously, he had become an uncle when Rebecca gave birth to a daughter, who was, Ann had assured him by telephone, quite the most beautiful baby that anyone had ever seen. What on earth had happened to make the infant so celebrated?

"There's nothing wrong," Robert laughed. "Rebecca and William have decided to call her Leander."

"Leander Flamsteed!" Giles said, smiling happily. "There's a thing."

"Isn't it just! As you can see, the news is going down well."

At The House, Giles found similar excitement in the kitchen, where Ann, Elsie and Liz were at the cooking-sherry. Bess, who had just come in from evening stables and remained in ignorance, looked politely bemused.

"Rebecca's baby is going to be called Leander," Ann said

and Bess nodded approvingly. Catching the mood, she turned to Giles with one eyebrow slightly raised: he knew what she meant.

"Yes!" The loudness and vigour of his utterance was increased by the immediacy of the snap decision. With Ann, Elsie and Liz looking on in astonishment, Bess went to Giles's side. Aware that the move was significant, the onlookers gazed at them, waiting.

"Go on," Bess said to Giles. "Speak!"

He cleared his throat, smiled nervously and said, "Bess and I are going to be married."

Liz let out a whoop and began to dance for joy.

Elsie, after dropping a tray, claimed to have suspected as much for weeks. "Everybody's been saying what a nice couple you make," she claimed.

Dazed, but with tears of happiness in her eyes, Ann hurried to embrace Bess. As they hugged each other, simultaneously laughing and crying, Liz rushed off to spread the word. Once the initial excitement had subsided, Ann and Bess slipped away, unnoticed by Giles and Elsie who had decided that, as prospective son and mother-in-law, they had rather a lot to say to each other.

"This is unbelievable!" Ann said once they had gained the sanctuary of the library. "It changes everything."

"It does indeed," Bess said happily. "We couldn't have arranged *this* to order if our lives had depended on it, yet it all happened very quickly."

"Are you *completely* happy about it?" Ann was concerned.

"Yes." Understanding what was passing through Ann's mind, Bess decided to be frank. "As I told Giles last weekend, I'm very surprised at the way things have turned out – but I love him and I'm going to put him back on his feet."

"You will continue to run the yard?"

"No, Giles must do that," Bess said firmly. "When I'm not making sure that you get some more grandchildren, I'll be out there helping . . . and he'd better listen to me this time!"

"Oh, he will," Ann said. "Don't worry, I'll make sure of it.

Now, while we're here, there's something I want you to do." She pointed to the Big Book on the desk. "I'd like you to take that over."

It was an immense honour, as great as being asked to run the stable, and Bess was unable to find words to express her feelings.

Early in September, during one of Bess's visits to the stud to see Astronomer Royal, Lady Amaryllis wanted to know about the wedding plans.

"Register office on the sixth of October," Bess said. "There's to be a church blessing the day after. Robert Frobisher has promised to make it look as much like a wedding as possible. Honeymoon in Torquay."

"Rebecca can cope while you're away?"

"Oh, yes. There won't be much going on by then. I've nothing for the Dewhurst now that Leslie Giffard's colt has gone wrong." She corrected herself. "Sorry, *we've* nothing for the Dewhurst."

"How's Giles settling in?" Amaryllis asked. Having severed all connections with Bath, Giles had been back in Cannings Ambo for three weeks.

"Very well," Bess replied. "He's still suffering some of the after-effects of that Foley creature, but everyone's treating him like the hero returned and it's done wonders for his confidence. I let him do both lots this morning and he got most of it right!"

"This is miraculous. It's given Ann a new lease of life and even Gideon seems fairly pleased. Our only fly in the ointment is Noel."

"God, is he still dewy-eyed about me?" Bess laughed.

"Most definitely! He's sixteen and you know what *that* means." Amaryllis rolled her eyes eloquently. "I promise to keep him out of the way."

"Thanks." Bess's mood changed. "As a matter of fact, Amaryllis, there's something much more serious you could do for me."

"Yes?"

"I've been wondering what to do about my savings. There's the money Amelia gave me and Leander left me something."

"What's the problem?" Amaryllis asked.

Given a choice between furtiveness and the forthright approach, Bess chose the latter. "I want to keep that money away from the marriage."

"You mean, hide it?"

"Yes."

Amaryllis thought about it. "I think that's a good idea," she replied at last. "Especially in view of what Amelia said in that letter – the rainy day and all that. By the way, do you think Amelia would have approved of you and Giles?"

"No!" Bess said with total confidence. "She'd have tried to make me change my mind."

"Yes, I can imagine it." After a thoughtful silence, Amaryllis was eager to help. "So, what do we do with your money?"

"Will you look after it?" Bess asked. "It's the simplest way . . . we could put it somewhere in your name."

"Of course. That's no problem."

Bess came to the crux of the matter with fading confidence. "Er . . . it's a reasonable amount."

"How much?"

"Two hundred and forty thousand."

"Bloody hell!" Amaryllis looked stunned. "What *have* you been up to?"

"One or two good bets," Bess replied.

"Good! They must have been humdingers!" Back to normal again, Amaryllis frowned. "The only snag is that I wouldn't want to keep that sort of money secret from Gideon," she said. "He's an absolute gem and he would never spy on me, but he *does* have a knack of finding things out. The poor darling might go into a decline if he stumbled across that lot by accident."

"Yes, you'll have to tell him," Bess agreed.

"He'll know how you can get extra interest on it," Amaryllis said. "And don't worry, he won't take risks. He likes people to think that he's a swashbuckler, but he's even more cautious than his father."

452

The assurance was unnecessary. Although Bess was content to remain ignorant of the world beyond Cannings Ambo, she knew that the Timberlake companies were run with great care and probity. Some financial experts thought Gideon rather dull and pedestrian.

After the arrangements for the transfer had been made and Bess was on her way back to Latimer's Barn, Amaryllis thought long and hard about Bess's attitude to her marriage. There was no doubt that she loved Giles, yet her shrewd tactics with her savings indicated reservations. Gideon would be pleased: lacking any vestige of confidence in Giles, his pleasure at the forthcoming marriage had been muted by doubts about Bess's sanity.

Bess treated the register office ceremony, made necessary by Giles's divorced status, as a formality to be shovelled out of the way as quickly as possible. The village agreed with her, turning out in force for the following day's blessing, at which she was dressed as a bride. Everything went perfectly, realising Bess's hope that she could give Giles something to wipe away the memory of the dismal business with Gillian in the same church, six years ago.

At the reception in the large workshop behind Rose House, there were two quietly dissenting voices, neither of which was allowed to cast a shadow over the happy proceedings.

Choosing his moment carefully, so as to catch her when she was briefly alone, Oliver appeared at Bess's side. He had left television and moved to advertising: not particularly interested in what he did, Bess gathered from Ann that it was 'important'.

"Well, Bess, you've made it, at last," he said. Although his manner was perfectly pleasant, there was no mistaking his meaning.

"I did," she agreed. "At least, that's *one* way of looking at it."

He was surprised. "Is there another?"

"There could be, Oliver," Bess said evenly. "If you keep your ears open, you may find that there are some people who think that it's Giles who's made it." She smiled. "I don't agree with them, of course!"

Apparently the very best of friends, they drifted apart to talk to other people.

About an hour later, when Gideon, the master of ceremonies, was preparing to make a short speech designed to terminate the gathering, Bess encountered Rachel. She was clinging to the arm of an unresponsive Leslie Giffard.

"Congratulations, *Mrs Hawksworth*," Rachel said. Her hostility was conveyed in the slight emphasis on Bess's new name.

"Thank you, Your Grace," Bess replied. To the obvious and slightly malicious enjoyment of Leslie Giffard, she bent gracefully to kiss Rachel's cheek.

What Gideon had to say was brief and to the point. He began by praising Ann and expressed the fervent hope that her eldest son's remarriage would bring better times for her. "We wish Bess and Giles every happiness," he went on. "This *is* a great day, though I have to confess to feeling sorry that we are losing a substantial piece of prestige as a result of it." He paused, allowing everyone time to wonder what on earth he was going to say. "I've been ferreting around, and I've discovered that there aren't all that many lady trainers at work anywhere in the world. We, of course, have had the best!" Bess came near to being unsettled by the enthusiastic burst of applause and felt sorry for Giles, at whom Gideon now stared pointedly. "I'm sure we shall be doing *at least* as well in the future!" The cheers and laughter reflected the widespread certainty that the comment was not entirely in jest: Bess and Giles shared the good humour.

They drove to Torquay through a wistfully golden afternoon and occupied the same suite of rooms in which Giles's grandparents and great-grandparents had enjoyed their honeymoons.

Over drinks before dinner, they reviewed the day's events. After they had disposed of all the: "Wasn't so-and-so looking a fright?" and "How about that dress Bill's wife was wearing?" Bess came to a slightly more serious topic.

454

"You and John were having a good chin-wag."

Giles nodded. John Flamsteed had buttonholed him at the reception and kept him talking for nearly fifteen minutes. "He wants to step down as Chairman of the Trustees," he said. "I think the responsibility worries him and he'd like to spend all his time planning the new factory."

Bess understood John's concern. The upsurge of business that Helen was generating for Wm Flamsteed & Sons was straining the cramped capacity in the sheds behind Rose House with the prospect of more pressure to come: Helen had been forced to miss the wedding by a trip to America that promised to yield very large orders. John's scheme for a new factory on or near the Extension was ready to be translated from the drawing board into action.

"And he thinks you should be Chairman?" Bess asked.

"Well . . . yes." Giles was unsure.

"That seems right. The quicker we get back to tradition, the better."

Reassured, Giles said, "I shall get you made a Trustee. It's long overdue."

"No, darling." Bess was adamant. "They've tried already and I don't want to know. There are far more important things for me to do than be messing around with that caper."

"Such as?"

"Rearing your son," Bess replied. "Pretty essential, don't you think?" She edged closer to him on the banquette seat they were sharing. "I'd rather like to be pregnant by the time we leave here," she said softly. "It's nearly eight o'clock, so I don't think we should be too long over this meal."

The two weeks were idyllic. In a moment of brutal honesty, Bess admitted to herself that Giles's love-making was never quite as good as that first night at the end of July: however, he was unfailingly tender and touchingly grateful to be with her. To her surprise, she found that being 'Mrs Hawksworth' was very much to her liking and when they returned to Cannings Ambo, every instinct told her that she was indeed pregnant.

455

Joe, struggling with the embarrassment of being her doctor, subsequently provided confirmation.

Bess experienced a feeling of well-being that did much to soften the disappointment of handing in her licence to the Jockey Club. Nevertheless, it was a far bigger sacrifice than she had envisaged and it left her out of sorts for several days.

CHAPTER 17

1975

'I could see them splitting into two camps'

Bess's son, named Steven months before his arrival, was born on 1 July 1973. The passage of time showed him to be a placid and intelligent child.

Giles, an inordinately proud father, made a point of spending at least an hour a day with him, difficult though this sometimes was. Determined to prove himself, Giles worked hours that even Bess considered excessive: she kept her complaints to a muted minimum and the results spoke for themselves. In 1973, Latimer's Barn sent out seventy-two winners; the following year it was eighty and Giles missed the trainer's championship only by the narrowest of margins. Yet he always found time for Steven, often holding him on his lap while discussing work-plans and race-entries with Bess in the quiet period after evening stables.

At the beginning of June 1975, Alain de Mourville's colt, Renoir, having already won the Two Thousand Guineas, romped home in the Derby to give Giles the ultimate accolade.

A few weeks later, on the evening of Steven's second birthday, Ann received a telephone call from Hubert Prideaux in France with truly wonderful news. Lisette had been safely delivered of a son: both the Duchess and infant Marquess of Glastonbury were thriving.

And Hubert was unstinting in his praise of the part played

by his sister in the accomplishment of what seemed like a miracle.

Early in 1974, a series of meetings involving businessmen from France, Germany and Switzerland took place at Château Mourville. The refurbishment of the vast mansion, eventually completed in 1970, had involved the acquisition of much Flamsteed furniture. It was assembled, put in place, became part of the impressive surroundings and was largely ignored. A visiting industrialist from Frankfurt changed that. As so often, once the interest began, one thing led to another and the European market for such furniture was soon under serious discussion.

John Flamsteed was evasive when Alain contacted him. The new factory on the Extension was working flat out to satisfy American orders: the prospect of at least as much business again for Europe seemed terrifying. Helen was with John when the bombshell burst and she volunteered to go to Fontainebleau to talk to Alain.

"There *must* be something we could do," she insisted. "It's far too good a chance to chuck away."

John smiled quizzically. "Have you ever been there?"

"No." Helen decided to be absolutely frank. "I wasn't allowed to go to Hubert's wedding because of my 'goings-on', and they've been up to their necks since I saw the error of my ways."

John nodded: everyone knew of Lisette's problems. "All right," he said. "It can't do us any harm, I suppose. Go and see what you can do."

Alain and Helen, who had previously met briefly under circumstances that were considerably less than ideal, hit it off tremendously well together. With his beloved Nadia spending most of her time trying to persuade Lisette to resume a normal life, Alain welcomed the company of an attractive woman: in the subtlest way, Helen let him see that a variety of fascinating things might have been possible if their circumstances had been different. Arriving at the château in time for lunch on a Monday, she telephoned John with an answer that same evening.

458

"The stuff can be made over here under licence."

"Are you sure?" John had tremendous faith in Helen, but doubted whether a conclusion reached so quickly could be sound. "What does Alain think?"

"Don't be silly, John!" Helen laughed. "He doesn't know about it yet. It's all my idea."

"Go on," John prompted.

"Two points. Alain's very worried about the village. It's an economic backwater and he's looking for something to liven it up. He can carry on giving hand-outs 'til the cows come home, but he'd prefer that they earned their own keep. The other thing is that there are several beautiful outbuildings going to waste on the estate – they'd make superb workshops."

"Hang on," John said hurriedly. "You can't turn a bunch of French peasants into craftsmen overnight."

"Of course you can't! It would have to be done with new blood, which is exactly what Alain wants. I think it's rather like what your grandfather and Leander did to Cannings Ambo."

They talked for ten minutes, John gradually warming to the idea. "Fair enough, Helen," he said at last. "I'll leave it with you."

She set to. Before the end of the week, John and Alain were arranging talks.

Helen did not seek Lisette out and avoided mentioning her. She had, apparently, shut herself away in a minor wing of the château, shunning contact with everyone except Nadia and the housekeeper, an old friend of the family called Marie-Claire Guillaume.

Developments were rapid after John and Alain had met and produced an agreement in principle, John discovering that he was hungry for all the business he could get. Although always respected, Wm Flamsteed & Sons had frequently been regarded as the Cinderella of Cannings Ambo, only matching Latimer's Barn in prestige and earnings during the Second World War. Now, with Helen's sales, a flood of new ideas from William, and the prospect of expansion into Europe, Rose House was starting to pull its weight.

At Alain's request, Helen was given the task of drawing up

the formal agreement and advising on the conversion of an eighteenth-century dairy into the first workshop. She became a regular passenger on the eight o'clock flight from London to Paris each Monday morning.

It was on her fourth visit that Helen was approached by Marie-Claire while she walked in the gardens on a surprisingly mild February afternoon.

"*Madame la Duchesse* would like you to take tea with her, my lady," was the message, turned into a command by the grave desperation in Marie-Claire's eyes and voice.

Allowing herself to be guided through the labyrinthine corridors of the château, Helen found that she was fearful of what lay in store. Following a total emotional breakdown, Lisette had been refusing to see Hubert since the previous October. Grimly uncommunicative, Hubert had undertaken more work for Stewart's, the bank, and stepped up his attendances at the House of Lords. Since Christmas he had taken to staying in London at weekends.

Lisette, heavily muffled in cardigans and a scarf, was huddled over a fire. She rose at Helen's entry, embraced her, muttered an inaudible greeting and subsided back into the chair. Her gaunt, pale face indicated that she had lost weight and her hair was listless, lacking condition.

Marie-Claire served tea and two plates of assorted cakes. Lisette ate and drank in sporadic bursts of greediness, mostly keeping her eyes fixed on the fire. Helen followed her example of silence. The twenty minutes before Marie-Claire made an inconspicuous gesture indicating that it was time to go were a nerve-racking eternity to Helen.

The pantomime was re-enacted the following day and the day after that. Helen then returned to England and was away for over a week. When Alain collected her at the airport, he seemed to be seeking a conversational opening to make an important point. Sensing his predicament, Helen asked after Lisette.

"Marie-Claire says that she has improved since you sat with her," Alain replied. "Perhaps you would continue?"

There was one more repetition of the frightening silence.

On the following day, after the initial embrace of welcome, Lisette asked: "Helen, how is Hubert?"

"I haven't seen him for several weeks," Helen replied. "I suspect that he is very unhappy and working too hard."

Almost as though she was satisfied with the answer, Lisette sat down and fell silent.

The next day's question was: "Does he love me?"

"Very much," Helen said.

It carried on until the last day of Helen's next visit, two weeks later, when Lisette made a statement instead of asking a question. "Hubert thinks I have let him down."

"He does not!" Helen said firmly, not particularly interested in what Lisette meant.

"He must have a son," Lisette murmured.

"Not necessarily," Helen replied. "Our brother, Edmund, has two perfectly good sons. That's enough." She refrained from pointing out that both Edmund and Judy dreaded the prospect of the dukedom devolving on their part of the family.

"It is still bad for Hubert not to have a son." Lisette showed a flash of petulance.

"Has he ever told you that?" Helen asked. "Well, has he?"

"No," Lisette admitted. "He is always kind . . . very loving."

After that, progress became measurable. At first, the indicator was not what Lisette said so much as what she did. She took more trouble over her appearance, rejecting the cardigans and shapeless skirts in favour of stylish dresses. Even if the talk was only of trivialities, she kept the conversation going rather than lapsing into taciturn silences, and she began to leave her self-imposed prison, at first walking round the château with Helen, pointing out some of the countless striking features of design, and finally venturing into the gardens. It was during a stroll in the park in May, three months after Helen was first summoned to see Lisette, that a dramatic step forward took place.

"You are not happily married," Lisette said, her intense stare at odds with the casualness of her tone. Helen decided that honesty might be a good way to build further confidence between them.

461

"No, I'm not," she replied.

"Why is that?"

"I married the wrong man." Helen made it sound like a minor, largely forgotten irritant.

"You were attracted to him, of course?"

"Yes. We suited each other very well at the time. He was also extremely rich." Helen smiled mockingly. "He still is . . . rich, I mean."

"Have you had lovers?" Lisette asked.

"Several," Helen said. "One of them was good."

"The others?"

"Diversions, I suppose. They weren't nice men."

They walked on in silence, Lisette building up to something. "Will Hubert have another woman?"

"Absolutely and definitely not!" Helen said vehemently. "Never!"

"Are you sure?" Lisette looked puzzled rather than disbelieving. "He is very randy."

As usual, they were conversing in French and Helen had to suppress a smile at Lisette's '*libidineux*', delivered with a perfectly straight face.

"That makes no difference. Hubert is incapable of being unfaithful to you. I'm sure of it!"

When Helen returned to the château two weeks later, Lisette had virtually given up her solitary life and was *en famille* with her parents once more.

"Hubert came to see me last weekend," Helen told Lisette when they were alone. "He's worried and upset that you haven't answered his letters."

Lisette nodded miserably. "I'm ashamed. I have let it go too far and I don't know what to say."

"I can take a message to him," Helen said. "Think about it."

Before dinner the following evening, after a day with the lawyers thrashing out the small print of the licence agreement, Helen found Lisette almost tiresome. Quite suddenly, she seemed to have regained much of her effervescence and was pushing the conversation in a dozen irrelevant directions at once. Calming down at last, she asked, "Do you have a lover *now*, Helen?"

"Yes, as a matter of fact, I do," was the guarded admission.

"Were you with him last night?"

"Er . . . yes."

"I knew it!" Lisette clapped her hands. "I can tell. You are content. There is a bloom." Her face fell. "I miss Hubert very much," she said dolefully.

Scrutinising Lisette, Helen was smitten by the most bizarre idea: it was grotesquely risky, but she did it. In words of brazen, profligate intensity, she described everything that she and her German had done to each other. Lisette was deeply disturbed. For twenty-four hours, Helen thought that she had misjudged matters appallingly, but just before she left for London, Lisette broke down.

"Tell Hubert to come and see me," she said. "As soon as he is able."

There was no question of rushing fences. Throughout Hubert's first visit after the dreadful separation, he made sure that Lisette knew the extent of his feelings without ever looking as though he was going to lay a finger on her. The results were encouraging.

"Progress, I think," he told Helen. "Definite progress. Whatever it is you're doing to her, keep it up!"

"It will be a pleasure," Helen assured him.

From the start of her work on the joint venture, Helen had been given the assistance of Klaus Neumann, one of Alain de Mourville's most senior and trusted lieutenants, who was normally based in Cologne. Klaus was Alain's way of showing that he attached the utmost importance to the regeneration of his village. Helen soon discovered that her comrade-in-arms was incredibly well-qualified: a mechanical, electrical and production engineer, he could hold his own with the lawyers and accountants and was an experienced personnel manager. A big, handsome man of fifty-two, he looked as though he might have been an athlete and remained in formidable condition. He spoke impeccable English and was the most courteous man Helen had ever met outside her family circle.

During their second week of working together, Klaus and Helen forsook the hospitality of the château one evening to drive into Barbizon for dinner. For a while, they talked about the problems they faced in bringing new skills to a village that seemed to have changed little in two hundred years. When the subject had run its course, Klaus set off in a bold new direction.

"Alain tells me that your marriage is unsound," he said.

"He's quite right," Helen replied, not in the least put out at being discussed. "I understand that *you* are a widower."

"For nearly ten years," he replied. He looked at her searchingly. "I have spent much time admiring you," he went on. "You are a most attractive woman, Helen. I think that going to bed with you would be a thrilling experience." He smiled. "I am looking forward to finding out if I am right."

"I see." Helen was non-committal: she did, however, ensure that they lingered not a moment longer than was necessary over their meal.

The accommodation allocated to them in the château, bedroom-suites at either end of a corridor that was discreetly isolated, facilitated the adventure. Helen tossed a coin, called correctly, and took Klaus to her room. He exceeded her expectations by a bountiful margin: very nearly old enough to be her father, Klaus Neumann was a magnificent lover who, in their first sublime hour together, wiped out all her previous experiences.

"Long may our collaboration last," he said before going back to his room to sleep.

"We must make sure that it does," she replied, confident that both John and Alain would welcome her continuing presence in France to drum up sales once the manufacturing capacity was in place.

After Hubert's visit in May, he travelled to Fontainebleau every weekend, courting Lisette as though starting afresh. During the week, Lisette relished the strange game that Helen had started. Without ever asking the identity of her sister-in-law's lover, and pretending that she was incapable of deducing it for herself, the Duchess of Laverstoke was voyeuristic by proxy.

Helen, a willing accomplice, found that the detailed accounts demanded of her produced stimulating anticipation of the next encounter with Klaus. And the beauty of it was, she never had to gild the lily: her powerful lover provided all that was necessary for Lisette's increasingly prurient curiosity.

"Frankly, Lisette, I have no idea how many orgasms I had last night. I gave up counting after eight!"

"What about your man?"

"He came three times." Lisette's frown was disapproving. "He is over fifty, remember," Helen said, explaining her apparent selfishness. "Besides, I want him again tonight, so I had to be careful not to wear him out."

Lisette appreciated that. She was subsequently agog at Helen's description of how the second night of passion began. "We had nearly an hour of *soixante-neuf*! God, it was indescribable."

And so it went on.

The floodgates finally burst open at the end of August. Finding himself dragged into Lisette's bed on the evening of his arrival, Hubert subsequently spent a long time on the telephone rearranging his business appointments for the following week so that his stay could be extended. Lisette went to Eaton Mandeville in October, and it was there that she became pregnant for the third time.

"This is going to be all right," Hubert told Helen. "I know it . . . I can *feel* it. Lisette thinks the same. This is all thanks to you, my dear. You've worked miracles. If you *ever* want help with anything, let me know." He scowled. "How are things with you and Freddie?"

"We're tolerating each other," Helen replied. About to leave for ten days in the Bavarian Alps with Klaus, she refused to become involved in thoughts of her husband.

"Bear it in mind," Hubert said. "You'll get fed up with him one day and I'll be there."

The presentiments were well-founded. Lisette's pregnancy

ran its full term and on 1 July 1975, at Château Mourville, she gave birth to a healthy son. He was baptised Hubert Charles Alain Philippe.

To Rachel's unconcealed disgust, the christening not only took place in France, but made it certain that the tiny Marquess of Glastonbury would be brought up as a Catholic. No one took any notice of Rachel's complaints. She was known to be soured by the departure of Leslie Giffard from her life. He had awarded himself early retirement and gone to live in Switzerland, making it plain that anything more than two very brief visits from Rachel each year would be regarded as a nuisance.

His choice of successor in Mallender and Giffard Foods was Elisabeth, his twenty-five-year-old daughter, appointed in preference to her weak-willed, ineffectual brother. She also took his place as a Trustee at Cannings Ambo.

The July meeting of Trustees was a relaxed, almost euphoric affair. As with so many of the meetings in recent years, Hubert's apology for his absence was recorded and this was followed by a happy, but prolonged discussion of his son's birth. Always inclined to be critical of Giles's chairmanship, Ann felt that he allowed this, together with the continuing back-slapping over Renoir's Derby victory, to go on for too long.

Bess, who had taken Steven to Joe for an injection, was leaving Oak Cottage as the meeting, held in Rose House, broke up. Two of the Trustees, anxious to be away, drove past in their cars. Richard Mallender waved; the other was at pains not to draw attention to herself. Bess was intrigued.

Giles stayed at Rose House for lunch. When he returned, he struck a slightly jarring note. There was nothing specific that Bess could point at, yet she felt ill at ease. In recounting a discussion of a proposal to build more houses in the village, Giles sounded airy-fairy, uncritical of a suggestion that Bess knew was likely to encounter stiff opposition. On an impulse, she decided to talk to Lady Amaryllis.

"It's time I went to see Astronomer Royal," she told Ann. "Will you look after Steven this afternoon?"

Steven and his grandmother were delighted with the arrangement and Bess set off, smiling ironically at her mode of transport. Whereas she would once have gone to Cannings St John on a horse, or in the Projectile, she now used a small, sedate 'family' car.

In her office, Amaryllis was talking to her eldest son, Noel, home for the summer after his first year at Oxford. Seeing Bess, he sprang politely to his feet and said, "Good afternoon, Mrs Hawksworth," ruining everything by blushing.

"Hello, Noel, how are you getting on?" Bess inadvertently made his confusion worse by goggling at him in a blatantly admiring way: he really had grown and filled out most impressively.

"Very well, thank you, Mrs Hawksworth." He turned to Amaryllis. "I'll see you later, Mother," he said and hurried out of the office.

"Quite the young he-man, isn't he?" Amaryllis smiled at Bess. "He's hoping to get himself picked for the boat-race crew next year."

"I can well imagine!" Bess said, her eyes still wide.

"What's this?" Amaryllis asked. "A social call, or is something up?"

"A bit of both," Bess replied, sitting down. "It might be time to broaden my education. Tell me about the Trustees."

"Oho! What's become of the monumental disinterest?" Amaryllis joked.

"Don't worry, it's intact."

"So?"

"I picked up a strange feeling about this morning's meeting," Bess said.

"Did Giles say anything?"

"No, not really. It's this." Bess tapped her nose.

"Actually, it was a complete waste of time," Amaryllis said. "Gideon was furious. There was no preparation and Giles let it degenerate into a talking-shop. It wasn't the first time, either."

"I'd like to know about the individuals involved," Bess said. "There's Ann, Rachel, yourself, Gideon, John and

467

William, Hubert, and Giles. What about the new ones that have appeared since Giles became Chairman?"

"Well, Richard Mallender isn't new, of course," Amaryllis replied. "He took over from his father while you were still running the show."

Bess nodded. "He's all right. How about Helen?"

"What can one say?" Amaryllis spread her hands and smiled expressively. "She's turned from black sheep into blue-eyed girl. I sometimes think that John doesn't know how much furniture she's sold; she was the brains behind the French business, *and* she rescued the Duchess from herself."

"She was elected first and her husband got in as a result?"

"That's about it. Rachel has *always* wanted Freddie to be a Trustee, but John's father wouldn't hear of it."

"He's the estate's banker?" Bess asked.

"Effectively, yes. He's the link between us and the men in Zurich – or wherever."

"And he's unsavoury?"

Again, Amaryllis spread her hands, this time to indicate helpless uncertainty. "I've heard Hubert say that, as a banker, Freddie's bent. There have been some very peculiar stories about his sexual preferences. He and Helen are existing in a state of heavily armed truce."

"Then there's Elisabeth Giffard," Bess prompted.

"Ah, yes, the remarkable Miss Giffard." Amaryllis sucked her pencil and frowned.

"Well?" Bess asked after a long pause.

"According to Gideon, she's wreaking havoc and spilling blood at Mallender and Giffard."

"What's wrong with that outfit?"

"They seem to have grown very big by accident," Amaryllis said. "The turnover last year was close to fifty million, but their organisation is antiquated. Edward and Leslie were always bickering and threatening to split into two separate companies, so they kept opening shops, usually in places that suited their own individual ideas. Meanwhile, nothing was ever done about head office and it turned into a shambles. Elisabeth is 'rationalising' it."

Bess pulled a face. "What's her view on splitting up?"

"She's dead against it. According to her, Mallender and Giffard is like Marks and Spencer – the two halves wouldn't survive without each other."

"And Richard Mallender?"

"I don't think his opinion is important," Amaryllis said. "Brother Adrian runs the show."

"What's he like?"

Amaryllis furrowed her brow. "Not quite as dreadful as his father – although Gideon believes that time will cure that. He married some sort of model after he'd got Helen out of his system. Not a happy union, by all accounts!"

Bess sat and thought. She was fairly certain that Elisabeth Giffard was the girl who, four years ago, when Lindisfarne won the Derby and on numerous other occasions since, was doing her damnedest not to be seen with Richard Mallender. Today, not bothering to stay for the traditional post-meeting lunch, they had driven off together, albeit in different cars. Interesting though it seemed, she decided to say nothing. Instead, she asked about the proposal for new houses.

"Gosh, that *did* upset Gideon!" Amaryllis said. "It cropped up over lunch and only Giles seemed to have received a copy of the briefing paper."

"Whose idea is it?"

"Freddie Christopherson's. He thinks we should build houses to sell to outsiders – people who work in Swindon, for example."

"Good grief!" Bess was shocked. "There's no chance of that getting through, is there?"

"No, especially when Hubert starts taking an interest again – and it had better be soon! Ann was livid. By the way, how did you get to know about it?"

"Giles told me when he came back."

"What did he think of it?"

"He seemed vaguely in favour of it."

"Oh!" Amaryllis was disappointed.

"Exactly," Bess said. "That's how it struck me. I thought I'd better come to see you."

"Er . . . is Giles completely settled?" Amaryllis asked.

"There's no evidence to the contrary," was Bess's strange reply. She hurried on. "At the moment, it's the Trustees that bother me."

"Gideon will be interested to hear that. He talks about it sometimes. What's worrying you?"

"I could see them splitting into two camps." Bess was thoughtful for a moment or two, then she stood up, moved to the side of Amaryllis's desk and reached for pencil and paper. She wrote down six names in a column:

> Ann
> Gideon
> Amaryllis
> Hubert
> John Flamsteed
> William

As an afterthought, she added Giles. Beneath it, she compiled a second list.

> Rachel
> Helen
> Freddie
> Richard Mallender
> Elisabeth Giffard

There was silence as she toyed with the pencil, Amaryllis watching anxiously. Eventually, Bess crossed out Giles in Ann's block and added it to Rachel's.

"You'd put him there?" Amaryllis asked.

"I think so."

"That's very objective of you, Bess."

"Isn't it just!"

Amaryllis looked at Rachel's block. "They're a rum collection," she said thoughtfully.

"I know. This is a guess of what would happen in a real bust-up . . . when the chips are down."

"Six on each side," Amaryllis said. "That's no good." She looked at the list again. "Why have you got Helen voting with Freddie? She wasn't very friendly to him this morning and they have totally different perceptions of Cannings Ambo."

"In the last resort, she'd do what Rachel told her," Bess replied.

"H'm . . . you're probably right. Can I show this to Gideon?"

"By all means."

"You know what he'll say?"

"What?"

"That *you* ought to be a Trustee."

Bess shook her head. "No, it's best for me to stay out of it."

Although they both knew it was unsatisfactory, they left it at that, Bess returning to Latimer's Barn, Amaryllis hoping that Gideon would not be late back from his dash to Bristol after the wasted morning at Rose House.

Bess found Steven contentedly in his element. It was one of the afternoons for Rebecca to be closeted in the office with Giles, so Ann was also looking after Leander. When she put her mind to it, Leander Flamsteed could be a precocious little tyrant, much like her famous namesake at the same age, Rebecca suspected. However, with Steven, she was always charm personified and he, usually the most affectionately gregarious of children, had eyes for no one else when Leander was anywhere near.

On the last Saturday in July, it seemed that most of the village went to Ascot to see Renoir run in the King George VI and Queen Elizabeth Stakes. Alain and Nadia, looking forward to watching their fine colt repeat his Derby performance, were in England for ten days, staying at Eaton Mandeville, where their radiantly happy daughter was now firmly installed as Duchess of Laverstoke. Renoir was favourite and most of the crowd gathered round the paddock saw no reason to disagree. Bess was an exception: she thought he looked below his best.

Entering the home straight, Michael Pilgrim, most definitely in his last season as the Latimer's Barn jockey, pushed Renoir into an effortless-looking lead and it seemed all over bar the shouting. A challenge from Wat Tyler at the furlong distance was bound to peter out; the Newmarket-trained horse had finished fourth at Epsom and was said not to have got the trip. What appeared to be an epic struggle developed, producing great excitement in the crowd. At the end of it, Bess's face was as black as thunder. Everyone was saying how unlucky Renoir had been to lose it: she thought otherwise. Looking around, she saw that Alain and Gideon shared her view. Renoir, unable to find anything extra when it mattered, had stayed woodenly one-paced while Wat Tyler was strengthening with every stride. Another hundred yards and his winning margin would have been four lengths, not the neck that the judge marked in the official record. And if confirmation were needed that he was not right for the race, Renoir was blowing badly when he came back with a grim-looking Michael.

No one said anything to spoil Giles's smiling acceptance of the flood of commiserations on his bad luck, but away from the centre of attraction, Bess and Gideon spoke their minds.

"You haven't been paying enough attention," Gideon said, injecting a trace of humour into the accusation.

"You're right," Bess agreed. "I got carried away with organising the Midsummer Fête."

"That horse was short of work."

"I'd say so, yes."

"Stick to horses, Bess. Anybody can organise a fête."

It proved difficult to persuade Giles to go home. Freddie Christopherson and a group of his friends had decided to have a day out at Ascot, the women crassly unconcerned at having made the mistake of dressing themselves up as if for the Royal Meeting. It was nearly six o'clock before Giles could be prised away from them.

Bess spent half an hour working the conversation round to Renoir on the journey home. Avoiding direct reference to his disappointing performance, she asked: "What are you going to do with him next?"

"I haven't really thought about it," Giles replied. "I wanted to see how he got on today . . . it looks as though he could do with a rest."

With a supreme effort, Bess made no response to his thoroughly unsatisfactory judgement.

Because of the day's disappointment, Bess was keen to make love that evening: she wanted to dispel the suspicion that the relationship that had flowered with Lindisfarne's victory in the King George VI and Queen Elizabeth had come to grief with Renoir's failure in the same race. After Giles had taken the hint of her early departure upstairs for a bath, she tried to ensure that this would be one of his gentler, more controlled displays of passion in which there was some hope for her own satisfaction. Giles had other ideas. Disgruntled to the point where her efforts at participation were minimal, Bess gritted her teeth and willed him to get it over and done with.

Giles's self-centred behaviour, coinciding with a waning of his interest in Steven, had begun about a year ago. The cause was his discovery that attempting to recreate the savagery he had enjoyed with Janet Foley was the only way he could satisfy himself.

CHAPTER 18

1978

'Steven will stay here, of course'

Apart from Giles, no one at Latimer's Barn much cared for Sam Montgomery. Unfortunately, he was necessary.

A boisterously youthful fifty-three, Montgomery was a multi-millionaire who saw no point in being coy about his money. Wealth had come from textiles and mail order, activities that had occupied him for at least fourteen hours a day since he was seventeen. It was said that the death of his wife in 1962 had caused him to disappear for nearly a week, but that apart, he was a workaholic, using an ever-shifting kaleidoscope of charm, pleading and brow-beating to achieve his ends. Then, in 1977, he married a woman only two years older than his daughter, disposed of his business interests to the highest bidder, bought a Georgian mansion near Winchester and set about devoting as much energy to enjoying his money as he had done in making it. Sam Montgomery's chosen hobby was the Turf: he had always wanted to own a racehorse. To make up for lost time, he acquired one hundred and twenty yearlings.

Remarkably, he did it all himself after reading the relevant chapters in a couple of books. He saved over £100,000 in dealer commission and got a collection of animals that would win two hundred and fifty races as two- and three-year-olds. After placing twenty of them in a stable at Newmarket for 1978, he invited himself and his daughter to lunch at Latimer's Barn.

474

For a variety of reasons, some of which troubled Bess, there were fifteen boxes empty: Sam Montgomery solved the problem at a stroke, deeply sorry that Giles could not take more.

"Bit of a nuisance, that is, Mr Hawksworth," he said good-naturedly. "Hardly worth getting off my backside for fifteen. Never mind, every little helps."

"What plans do you have for the others?" Giles asked.

"There's thirty-odd going to three places in Berkshire and I thought I'd get some over to Ireland."

"What about France?" Giles suggested. "We have connections there if it would be any help."

"That's a bloody good idea!" Montgomery said enthusiastically. "Susan will like that, eh, Jane?"

His daughter, who seemed to act as a universal dogsbody, agreed. Susan, Giles presumed, was the new, young wife, who must be considerably more prepossessing than her stepdaughter. Although only twenty-three, Jane Montgomery, skulking behind unsightly horn-rimmed spectacles, and dressed in clothes that could well have come from a charity shop, looked a fright. Bess, hardly giving her a glance, tried to make Giles change his mind.

"Are you sure you want to let *all* fifteen boxes go, darling?" she asked. "Hubert mentioned a friend who might be interested."

"That was three months ago, Bess."

"Even so, I think we ought to give him a little more time."

"No, he's had long enough. Sam's here with his cheque book out, not thinking about it." Giles was so busy playing up to Montgomery that he was unaware of the look Bess gave him.

"Well, what did you think of Latimer's Barn and its denizens?" Montgomery asked Jane as they left Cannings Ambo.

"The place is impressive and I liked Giles Hawksworth." Jane was undergoing a transformation; having discarded the glasses, she was unpinning her tawny hair, hitherto contained in a frumpish bun. "But his wife is poison. She didn't care for you or your money."

"Her prerogative," Sam said. "According to my sources, she's a bloody marvellous trainer."

"That doesn't stop her being a bitch," Jane replied.

"I'd say it helps," Sam chuckled. "Don't underrate her, my love, she's the power behind the throne."

"I don't know about that," Jane said sceptically. "But she's certainly doing her best to keep her husband down."

It was six months before Giles and Jane Montgomery met again on a blustery April afternoon at Newbury.

He had arrived early, invited to lunch with the racecourse management. For the following year, it was planned to introduce a number of new races into Newbury's calendar. One of them, proposed for mid-September, was to be for two-year-old fillies over seven furlongs. The intention was to set the conditions and entry fees such that only high-class entrants would compete; Newbury was looking for an event that attracted Classic prospects and had at least Group Three status. Giles was asked what he thought about the race being called the Leander Hawksworth Stakes.

As the committee had expected, he was very pleased. "I'll put it to my Trustees as soon as possible," he said. "That's purely a formality, of course . . . I can't see them objecting."

The oldest member of the gathering noted the word 'my' in connection with the Trustees: he had been involved in racing for fifty years and had known Leander and Steven reasonably well. With them, it was always 'the' or 'our' Trustees.

"We're looking for sponsorship," said the committee-man responsible for the negotiations.

"That's easy enough," Giles responded. "The Fund will provide whatever you feel you want."

"I think we'd like to avoid that," was the carefully diplomatic reply. "It might be best to steer clear of any suggestions that you are sponsoring your 'own' race. After all, we know what's going to happen, don't we?" The man sent an urbane smile round the table. "Latimer's Barn will provide at least half the winners." Giles joined in the laughter. "No, possibly someone *connected* with you could support the race."

Briefly, Giles was at a loss, then his face lit up. "I know who'd jump at it," he said. "Could I make a phone call?"

By the time that port, brandy and cigars appeared, the matter was well on the way to being settled.

Giles was content to remain in the sanctum of the committee's dining-room until the first race was being run, after which he made a reluctant move. Sam Montgomery had one going in the third and a bit of a show was called for. Some of his horses in other stables had already been out, but the exuberant chestnut colt in the Kingsclere Maiden Stakes was his first runner from Latimer's Barn.

At a distance of fifty yards, Giles assumed that Sam Montgomery was accompanied by his wife: certainly the attractive young woman beside him conformed to the archetypal impression of the sort of second wife a middle-aged millionaire would take. The illusion persisted at close quarters while Giles was shaking Sam's hand. Not until she said, "Hello, Mr Hawksworth, how are you?" did he recognise the voice.

For the next hour, Giles did his best not to peer at her. When, as was bound to happen, she became aware of his bemused scrutiny, she remained impassive, although Giles had the uneasy feeling that Sam wanted to laugh at him. Fortunately, it all came to an abruptly happy end when Sam took his daughter away to help him lead in his first winner.

Afterwards, as Montgomery went off to celebrate with some cronies, Jane guided Giles towards the members' bar.

"I must buy you a drink for that," she said. "You've done wonders for Father. Between you and me he was starting to worry."

"Why?"

"We've had seventeen runners before today and not one of them ever looked like getting anywhere."

"It isn't easy this early in the year," Giles said. "We never do much before the Craven at Newmarket, as a rule. The weather's been worse than ever this time."

"Don't be modest! I knew that things would improve once *you* got going."

Giles felt such an affinity for her that he toyed with the idea of admitting that he had very little to do with training horses these days. She moved the conversation on, however.

"I'm sorry I startled you. It's wrong of me to go from one extreme to the other . . . I usually save that trick for people I can't stand."

It was pointless pretending that he did not know what she was talking about. "Why do you do it?" Giles asked. "It must have taken you hours to make yourself look as awful as you did when you came to Cannings Ambo."

She laughed. "I promise you, it's very easy to achieve that effect! No, seriously, I had to adopt a disguise after I won that gold medal at the Montreal Olympics."

Giles blinked. "I'm afraid I'm dreadfully ignorant. *Which* gold medal?"

"That isn't ignorance, it's a blessed relief. The Press and TV were waiting for me at Heathrow when I got back and they made my life a misery. Hence the disguise. I don't need it these days, thank God, but I do it sometimes when I'm helping Father. It makes people believe that I'm efficient."

"What was the medal for?" Giles asked.

"Fencing. I took it up at college and got quite good at it."

"Obviously," Giles said admiringly. "You've carried on with it, presumably?"

"Yes, nothing like the same standard, though. I belong to a good club in Southampton and I do a bit of coaching. Most of my spare time these days goes on keeping fit." She grinned. "I've turned into a bit of a fanatic!"

It confirmed an idea that had occurred to Giles. Beneath the conventionally stylish clothes that she was wearing today, he had begun to suspect that there was a body that was strong and hard, as well as shapely. He found the idea curiously exciting.

Relaxed and with nothing to prove to each other, they became firm friends in the fifteen minutes that elapsed before Sam Montgomery joined them with more drinks. As was usually the case with Sam, he had a scheme on the boil.

"That jockey of yours, Giles . . . you say this is his first season?"

"Yes, but you don't have to worry. He's been riding since he was about nine. He's good."

"I can see that for myself," Sam replied. "I wouldn't mind having him on all my horses, regardless of who trains 'em. How about it?"

Giles rubbed his chin. "I take your point, Sam, and I'll see what I can do. There are people who might not like it."

Montgomery gave him a long, shrewd look. "I can live with genuine problems," he said. "I *won't* stand for being pissed about by folks that have got nothing better to do than object to everything. You're the gaffer, so see about it!"

"I will," Giles promised.

Bess, Rebecca, Arthur Merriweather and Liz Challoner were running Latimer's Barn, with Giles perilously close to being a figurehead. There had been no spectacular upheaval and the changes, produced by perfectly ordinary circumstances, had been gradual.

The first catalyst had been Giles's laziness. During 1976, it became apparent that he did not like getting up early in the morning after a late-evening journey back from one of the more distant racecourses. Bess, her habit of early rising reinforced by motherhood, began taking out the first lot on those mornings when Giles thought he deserved a lie-in. It started in May, averaging twice a week; by August, Bess was doing it every morning.

In March 1977, Giles was laid low by a severe attack of bronchitis. During his illness, Bess did both lots. When he recovered, she carried on; she did not request his permission and he made no objection. By the middle of the season, an appearance by Giles on the gallops was a noteworthy rarity. At the same time, Liz made it plain that she would prefer to run the administration her way, without interference, and Giles seemed only too glad to oblige. By a circuitous irony, Bess and Giles had reversed the roles they played after Steven's death: she now trained the horses, he took them racing. The result was a steady flow of winners, although there was no Classic victory after Renoir's 1975 Derby.

Rebecca had two more children, both arrivals beautifully timed not to interfere with the work of the racing season. Matthew was born in February 1974, Emma in January 1978. Acting as trainer and assistant, Bess and Rebecca did well together, not particularly caring about the strange situation into which they had drifted; everything worked smoothly, the winners flowed, and that was all that mattered.

When he got back from Newbury, long after Bess had finished evening stables, and at least three hours later than she would have been on the same trip, Giles sensed hostility, both from Bess and Ann. He ignored them, going upstairs to wash and change. Later, over dinner, the mood relaxed when Giles recounted Newbury's plan for the Leander Hawksworth Stakes.

"How wonderful!" Ann said. "Wouldn't she be pleased?"

"We must make sure that we win it at least two years out of three!" Bess declared.

"That's what Johnnie Dawson was afraid of!" Giles laughed. "He didn't think it was quite the thing for us to sponsor it. Never mind, I offered it to Freddie Christopherson and he jumped at the chance."

Immediately, the atmosphere was arctic. Seeing Ann's distress, and knowing that she would not wish to offend Giles, Bess decided that the time had come to put her foot down. "Absolutely not, Giles!" she snapped. "It's entirely inappropriate for that spiv to sponsor Leander's race."

"Here, steady on," Giles protested. "You can't . . ."

"In any case," Bess went on, cutting him off, "he's our banker, for heaven's sake. That hardly makes him disinterested."

"It's been virtually promised to Freddie," Giles said petulantly.

"Then *unpromise* it!" Bess said.

"What the hell am I supposed to say to him?"

"You won't have to," Ann said, intervening in a way that

480

showed how annoyed she was. "I shall raise this at the next Trustees' meeting and it will be turned down flat."

"Honestly, Giles, you are a twerp," Bess said. "It's possible to sponsor a race without too much publicity, so we *can* do it ourselves. It doesn't *have* to be spread all over everywhere . . . have another look at rule thirty-eight."

For the first time, Giles felt deep resentment of Bess: it wasn't a question of having *another* look at the rule. She knew damned well that he didn't realise it existed, let alone what it said. Sheer perversity drove him on to raise the question of Jonathan Pilgrim riding all Sam Montgomery's horses. He knew what the answer would be and Bess did not surprise him.

"Brilliant!" she said sarcastically. "What happens when Montgomery uses Jonathan for some miserable little race at Carlisle while we've got him down for the Derby, or Ascot? How do you fancy him being stuck in the wilds of Ireland when he should be *here* to ride work?"

"All the other top jockeys do it," Giles said.

Bess nodded. "Most of them are chasing money and statistics. Jonathan doesn't want that."

"Possibly not, but we ought to give him the chance to make his own mind up."

"Don't worry," Bess said grimly. "I'll put it to him."

Giles knew what the outcome would be. Believing himself to be in the right, he felt humiliated.

The suggestion that Freddie should sponsor the Leander Hawksworth Stakes in the name of his bank received a comprehensive mauling at the May meeting of Trustees.

After twenty minutes of heated discussion, Rachel forced a vote, despite the strength of the sentiments expressed. She was defeated by eight to three, with Giles abstaining sullenly. Gideon was interested to see that Helen supported Freddie, even though there was evidence to suggest that they had not exchanged a civil word in months. Moreover, before Richard Mallender and Elisabeth Giffard voted against Freddie, they

481

looked at each other inquiringly. Gideon took it as confirmation of Bess's theory of the likely alliances within the group.

Freddie was unconcerned by the snub.

"Your decision has absolutely no validity, or weight, of course," he said, giving everyone who had voted against him a rather nasty look. "What happens in practice is purely a matter between myself and the management of Newbury racecourse."

There was an ominous, tense silence. Although she had given him her vote, it was plain that Helen found Freddie's attitude contemptible. Gideon's response was delivered in quiet, measured tones, making it all the more trenchant.

"If you attempt anything like that, I feel certain that we would wish to withdraw permission for naming the race." Sensing the agreement from Ann, John Flamsteed and Hubert, he underscored the point. "To be sure that our intentions were clear, we might well find it necessary to issue a statement to explain the position."

Freddie Christopherson flushed with the anger of defeat. A public rebuff from one of his bank's most prestigious clients would do incalculable damage in the tightly knit square mile of the City of London. He had no doubt that the loss of the Cannings Ambo account, worth nearly £40,000 a year to him, would follow in short order. There was a need to retreat and apologise; he did it with tolerably good grace.

But Gideon was under no illusions. The seeds of crisis, sown during the affair of the houses for outsiders, were starting to germinate.

Sam Montgomery had to be told that Jonathan Pilgrim would not be available to him for all races, of course, but he also got to hear of the sponsorship fiasco.

"Who wears the trousers at Latimer's Barn?" Jane asked Giles as they celebrated another winner at Bath, ten days after the meeting that had humiliated Freddie.

Giles made a valiant attempt to deflect the question. "Important decisions have to be taken by the Trustees," he said.

She was not satisfied. "Whose name is on the licence? Who answers to the Jockey Club?"

"None of this concerns the Jockey Club," Giles replied. "There's a great deal more to Cannings Ambo than horses, you know. The Trustees have to take the broad view."

"Crap!"

"Jane, I know what you're thinking, and it isn't true. Bess refuses to have anything to do with the Trustees."

"How did you know what I was thinking?" she asked. "It sounds like a very sensitive issue to me, Giles."

"Well, no . . . not really."

"She does all the dirty work out of sight, winking and nudging, pulling strings."

"Don't be silly," Giles said. "You're completely wrong, I promise you, Jane."

But when they parted an hour later, Jane Montgomery knew that Sam's favourite dictum had proved its worth: some of the muck she had slung was sticking.

It never occurred to Giles that Bess would react with strong disapproval when she encountered the 'undisguised', natural Jane. It was at Royal Ascot, the one meeting that Bess insisted on attending. She spotted Jane within minutes of arriving on the first day, recognising her at once.

"What stupid game was she playing when she came to see us last year?" Bess demanded of Giles.

"She doesn't like people to recognise her."

"Why should they do that?"

"The media were difficult when she won a gold medal at the Olympics two years ago."

Bess stared at him as though he was simple-minded. "I've never heard such rot in all my life," she said.

In the paddock before the Coventry Stakes, she seemed to have put hostility behind her, being almost friendly to Jane. Everything went smoothly until the horses came into the ring and Sam produced the inevitable question.

"Well, Giles, what's this nag of mine going to do?"

From where Jane was standing, it was clear that Giles

opened his mouth to speak, but was interrupted by Bess before he could utter a word.

"I don't like predictions, Mr Montgomery, but I *will* say that I think we have a good chance with this one. He's been working very well. He should go close."

She had a soft spot for Vladivostock, a colt by Lindisfarne that Amaryllis had sold to Sam for 20,000 guineas. After being something of an awkward customer, he had come to hand nicely, learned a lot from a race at Salisbury and could, according to both Caesar and Jonathan Pilgrim, prove difficult to beat.

Given a perfect ride by Jonathan, the opposition found him impossible to beat. Before she went to deal with Hubert Prideaux's runner in the following race, Bess permitted herself a rare piece of optimism with Sam. "There's every chance that he'll train on into a very nice horse. We'll do our best." Raking Jane with a look that suddenly showed her hostility, Bess was off.

Jane was given no chance to talk to Giles: Bess took him back to Latimer's Barn while the last race was being run.

"I told you Bess Hawksworth was a bitch," Jane said to Sam when they were home. "The way she talks, you'd think *she* did the bloody training!"

"Steady on, love," Sam said. "From what I hear, she *does*."

"Never!"

"I reckon so." He paused briefly to concentrate on adding ice to a jug of orange squash to quench their thirst caused by the hot afternoon. "I overheard their tame duke and Timberlake talking. She does all the clever stuff with the horses."

"I don't believe it."

"Why not? She was as hot as mustard when she ran the place on her own. According to the Duke of Laverstoke and friend Gideon, Giles is next to useless."

"Rubbish!" Jane was upset.

Sam put an arm round her shoulders, guiding her into the lounge. "You're getting keen on him, aren't you?"

"Well . . . yes."

"If it's any consolation to you, *I* don't think he's useless. He's not doing himself any good where he is, though . . . looks like a case of the square peg in a round hole." Sam's attention wandered to the pool beyond the open French windows. His wife, not a lover of racing, had spent the afternoon sunbathing: now, she was swimming and a brief moment of stillness showed that she was naked. "Your Giles would be very useful indeed in the right job, and I might have an idea about that, so hold on to your patience. I must go and see if Susan wants anything, so you pop off and amuse yourself for an hour."

During the last week in July, the owners and managers of virtually every high-class furniture retailer in France, Belgium, Germany and Switzerland attended one of three open days that were held at Alain de Mourville's château. They saw what forty craftsmen were able to do with the best timber and know-how imported from Wm Flamsteed & Sons. Helen was in charge of the conducted tours, demonstrating a total grasp of the design and manufacturing details. Afterwards, she was busy with her order-book.

Marie-Claire looked after her. Nothing was too much trouble for the English lady who had brought Lisette back from the near-dead, even though Marie-Claire was patently up to her eyes in worry. On the evening of the third day, Helen asked what was wrong.

"It is my son's work, *Madame.*"

"He's with Monsieur de Mourville, isn't he?"

"Not any more. He had to go. For years, he has been speaking of buying a lorry to start his own business, but he stayed with *M'sieur.*" Marie-Claire paused, her face bitter. "To rob him!"

Helen was horrified. "What's going to happen to him?"

"Nothing. *M'sieur* has always been soft on Jacques, for my sake, you understand. It is arranged that Jacques will leave and nothing more will be said. After tomorrow, it will all be over."

"What happens tomorrow?" Helen asked.

"We are going to Paris and I shall sign over my husband's savings to Jacques. Henri said it was for him."

485

"Your husband has been dead a long time?" Helen asked gently.

"Since nineteen forty-four . . . it was the Gestapo. His savings have accumulated tremendously, but I have no need of them here." She waved a hand to signify the goodness and generosity that surrounded her. "My son has promised that I will never see him again. That is good!"

Overcome by the sadness of it all, Helen did not know what to say until Marie-Claire leaned forward with a sparkle in her eyes. "Your friend *Herr* Neumann arrives tomorrow, yes?"

"Yes." Helen smiled. "We are going to the coast in Brittany for a few days."

The following day, Alain's chauffeur drove Marie-Claire to the bank in Paris, picking up Jacques at Créteuil, on the way. He was in a foul, ungrateful mood, causing argument and upset over the perfectly simple matter that had to be transacted. As soon as her part of the bargain was complete, Marie-Claire bade a frosty farewell to her son, leaving him to work out his future while the driver took her back to Fontainebleau as fast as the traffic permitted.

Jacques Guillaume decided to open an account at the bank his father had chosen when he arrived in Paris from Belle Ile in 1933. Later that same day, he deposited the money he had stolen from Alain, the equivalent of nearly £30,000. The assistant manager who dealt with him was glad when he finally left. Henri Guillaume's papers, including the birth certificate of Jacques's grandmother, Maude Flamsteed, lay forgotten in their box in the vaults.

Bess was extremely busy during late summer and early autumn. As a result of brilliant planning, preparation and a good ration of luck, she put Giles into the position where he could take credit for winning all but one of the important series of two-year-old events that were the main feature of racing in September and October. According to the 'experts' of press and TV, Latimer's Barn had the material to win all the 1979 Classics two or three times over.

Steven started school. Although there was no danger of a

child getting lost or facing any form of danger in Cannings Ambo, there was a tradition that mothers always took and collected their offspring during the first year. Bess was reaching the peak of worrying how on earth she was going to fit the morning trip in, when Steven produced the answer.

"I want Leander to look after me," he announced. "She knows *everything*."

Bess accepted that argument was futile. Leander *was* competent to take charge of a new pupil, she passed The House on her journeys to and from school, and the year's difference in their ages caused Steven to regard her as a vastly superior being who must be obeyed. He was also, of course, devoted to her. They were soon a well-known, slightly comical feature of village life as they hurried to and fro. As often as not, Leander would be laying down the law on something, with Steven listening and nodding earnestly.

Watching the performance from an unobtrusive distance one afternoon, Bess and Amaryllis were amused and reminded of the relentless passage of time.

"That pair of comedians didn't exist all that long ago," Amaryllis said. "Leander's already running rings round everybody and I hear she's starting to ride."

"Yes, she is," Bess replied. During the summer, Leander had celebrated her sixth birthday by demanding riding lessons, not from her mother, or anyone else who could spare the time, but from Bess herself. "How are your pair getting on?" Bess asked.

"So-so," Amaryllis replied cheerfully. "Noel's doing his best in London, Desmond's looking very good in Bristol."

Only with an effort did Amaryllis suppress the desire to ask after Giles, who had not been seen much during the past few weeks. That in itself was neither surprising nor worrying; a glance at the newspaper racing pages showed that Latimer's Barn was currently sending out more runners than at any period in its history: Giles was charging all over the country, accompanying them to races.

What worried Amaryllis was the change in Bess since the argument over the Leander Hawksworth Stakes and a rash of other quarrels that were rumoured to have followed it. After achieving considerable success in the role of wife and mother, Bess had reverted to the almost frightening self-sufficiency and competence that had characterised her period in charge of the stable. Ann, also aware of the change, wondered uneasily if Bess had washed her hands of Giles.

In fact, Bess spent that autumn doing Giles an injustice. She was convinced that he was having an affair with Jane Montgomery, who was, she had decided, the sort of woman who might appeal to him.

For all the mysterious absences, largely the result of his tendency to stay far longer than was necessary at a race meeting, Giles did not pay his first visit to Sam Montgomery's house near Winchester until the middle of September and it was another month before he and Jane became lovers.

It was, however, a most spectacular beginning. And the consequences were devastating.

On the day after Vladivostock won the Dewhurst Stakes, Giles went to Winchester to talk to Sam about the plans for the next season. That, at any rate, was what he told Bess and Ann. The reality was that Sam was in Ireland, having flown over that morning with his wife, and that Jane had jumped at Giles's invitation to go out for dinner.

Something was wrong in Ireland, serious enough to have blunted Sam's enjoyment of Vladivostock's runaway Group One victory at Newmarket. It was apparent from the results that Sam's horses in Ireland were not performing anywhere nearly as well as those in England, especially the Latimer's Barn contingent. From Jane's guarded comments, it seemed that the day of reckoning had arrived: Sam was going to 'sort it'. France, also a source of concern, was likely to be next.

Giles had arranged to arrive at six o'clock on what proved to be a miserably wet October day. Finding the atmosphere of The House more than usually oppressive, he made a minor alteration to the story he had concocted and left soon after three o'clock. Following a deliberately leisurely drive, he reached Sam's house at four-fifteen.

As expected, there was no sign of life. Perhaps as a device to give himself and his young wife privacy, Sam had provided completely separate, self-contained accommodation for Jane by converting an old coach-house. Approaching it, Giles saw lights in the windows. The main door was unlocked and he went in. At the end of the entrance hall, a flight of stairs went up to the flat; to the right was the door of the gym that Jane had insisted on when Sam drew up the plans.

Giles was half-way up the stairs when the silence of the building was broken by a burst of metallic noise and resounding thumps from the gym. Retracing his steps, he knocked pointlessly on the door and went in. He had seen the well-equipped, thirty-foot-square room only once, as part of a high-speed tour of inspection conducted by Sam. His memory of it was sketchy. Not that it mattered: Giles found himself confronted by a most thrilling sight.

Jane was sitting astride a bench, raising and lowering a horizontal bar protruding from a structure behind her. A cable and pulley system connected the bar to a stack of weights. Taken aback by his unexpected entry, Jane let the bar go, causing the weights to crash to the floor.

"Giles!" she cried. "Is anything wrong?"

"No. I thought I'd be early."

She stood up, reaching for a towel. After wiping her face and shoulders, she became aware of the way Giles was looking at her.

Wearing only a white leotard, she presented him with a bigger shock than on the afternoon at Newbury when he had failed to recognise her. Jane Montgomery's body, although wondrously shaped, might have been too hard and muscular-looking for some men's tastes, but she was Giles's ideal incarnate.

Their precipitate plunge towards each other brought them into an embrace that began with a collision and a kiss of primitive rapacity.

"This way!" Jane said, pulling him towards a door that, Giles now remembered, led to a sauna, shower

489

and changing-room, in which a cushioned bench offered reasonable comfort.

Giles undressed as quickly as possible, but not quickly enough for Jane. "For God's sake, hurry up," she said as he attempted to hang his suit in a locker. Turning, he found that she was spread out on the bench, the leotard twisted into a skein on the floor.

Discovering that her body felt even better than it looked, Giles went slightly mad once he had entered her and was gripped by the strong legs that were moist with sweat. Powerfully, with animal-like strength and sensuality, Jane Montgomery urged him into carnal turmoil.

It was uncontrollable and rapid. Jane climaxed within thirty seconds, pouring out a stream of ecstatic obscenity that dragged Giles into an ejaculation of blinding ferocity.

"Christ, you were ready for that!" Giles gasped as the shock waves of his orgasm finally died away.

"What about you?" she laughed. "What a state you got yourself into!"

"Well . . ." Giles hesitated, half-afraid of his feelings ". . . it's your body. It's magnificent."

"I've been told I'm a freak . . . often!"

"Rubbish!"

"I suppose I do look rather *masculine*," Jane said.

Giles pulled away to study her. "Only slightly," he replied. "And I like it. To tell you the God's honest truth, Jane, it's what I've been looking for . . . but I didn't know that until a few minutes ago. Do you understand?"

For answer, she drew him back to her.

When they finally went upstairs to the flat after another act of love had served only to sharpen their zest for each other, they decided that going out for a meal would be an unacceptable waste of time. If ever they did feel like food, something quick and convenient from the fridge would do.

In the hours that followed, a surprising and wonderful transformation took place. The wildness of their physical need for each other gradually mellowed into a sense of fellowship that neither of them had ever known before. They exchanged the most secret and intimate confidences, sharing aspirations and fears that had been part of them since childhood, promising infinitely better times in the future.

It was nearly midnight before Giles was able to tear himself away. Jane, wrapped in a bathrobe, and with espadrilles on her feet, went with him to the car. She gazed up at the stars, bright and clear now that the cloud had blown away.

"Is this the real thing?" she asked.

"Oh, yes. Absolutely!" The new Giles was resolutely confident.

"No going back?" Jane was tentative, still not fully prepared to believe what had happened to them.

"No."

"And it's definitely what you want?"

"Yes. How about you?"

"For God's sake, yes!"

The final kiss of the night was tender, enabling Giles to drive back to Latimer's Barn as though there was nothing in the world that could possibly trouble him.

The euphoria of that first night soon evaporated and Giles found the next six weeks a terrible strain. On one pretext or another, he was able to spend three or four afternoons a week with Jane. Her response to their love-making gave him self-respect: no matter how the mood took them, whether their actions were gentle, or savage, Jane's pleasure was deep and genuine.

For a time, that was enough, but he seemed to panic at the end of November. "What am I going to say to Bess?" he asked one afternoon.

Jane took her time responding. "You're frightened of her," she said at last. It was not an accusation, merely a statement of fact.

Giles nodded. "I don't know if 'frightened' is quite the right word . . . I'm certainly in awe of her."

"I used to hate her," Jane said. "Now, I see that she's a very tough woman doing a job."

"And she's damned good at it," Giles insisted. "She's far more of a Hawksworth than me – or Oliver and Rebecca."

"The converts are often the worst," Jane said, smiling wryly. "Do we assume that she'll stay there to run the show?"

"I don't see why not. There's no one else who can do it. But what about me? I've got to have a proper job, Jane. Part of the trouble with Gillian was that I didn't . . . I was only playing at being an estate agent."

"We agreed not to mention her again!" Jane said. "Relax, darling . . . God and Sam will provide."

She was right.

On Giles's next visit, Sam, following his usual habit of keeping his wife in the background, invited himself to tea in Jane's flat and slapped his cards on the table.

"You and Jane want each other, right?"

"Yes, Sam." Giles clutched at Jane's hand as she sat down beside him.

"Right. I reckon I could make good use of you, Giles," Sam said. "My horses aren't being organised properly. It's not too bad here, but things are a mess in Ireland and France. The silly sods are racing my nags against each other!" He paused to glower at the enormity of it. "I need a racing manager to sit on the buggers and make sure they use the sense they were born with. You can live here, or you might like to try Normandy . . . I'm thinking of buying a stud there, by the way. What do you say?"

"It sounds wonderful," Giles replied.

"It's likely to be a big wrench for you," Sam cautioned. "Make sure you think about it!"

"I can give you the answer here and now," Giles said. "Assuming that we can agree terms, I'm yours."

"From when?" The question was sharp. Giles recognised it as a test.

"You'll have to give me time on that one, Sam. I don't want to leave them until someone else – Bess, I expect – is fixed up with a licence." He smiled ruefully. "There's going to be one hell of a row, of course."

"Not very surprising," Sam said. "If I were in their shoes,

I'd kick up a right old stink. What's the best thing to do, dive in now, or wait until after Christmas?"

Giles shrugged. "It doesn't much matter. From their point of view, the sooner they know, the better."

"Mine, too," Sam agreed. "What do you think, Janey?"

"That's a daft question!" she laughed. "I want him here all the time."

"Right, let's talk about money," Sam said.

Giles's original intention was to break the news to Bess on 6 December. There was a Trustees' meeting the following day, at which he envisaged that his final departure from Cannings Ambo could be settled quickly. However, his nerve failed at the last minute. Jane, who was with him when it happened, made no attempt to change his mind or criticise: contrary to a great deal that was to be said about her in the months ahead, she loved Giles dearly. She also understood him far better than anyone else had ever done and knew that driving him into a corner was likely to produce catastrophic results.

"What's the new plan?" she asked.

"The Trustees don't meet again until the eleventh of January," Giles said. "If I wait for a few days, everyone will be preparing for Christmas and my little bit of news will get lost. By January it will be old hat and forgotten."

"All right. When's it to be?"

"Two or three days after this meeting . . . let's say the ninth."

Thinking that he would probably change his mind again, Jane indicated her approval.

By tradition, nothing of any importance was ever discussed at the December meeting of Trustees. Apart from John's mention of a record-breaking year for Wm Flamsteed & Sons, the major topic was Ann's fear that they had not voted enough money for the presents given to every child in the village at Christmas. She was authorised to spend another £1,000 on top of the £5,000 already agreed. Gideon was inclined to issue dark warnings about the

493

waves of industrial unrest that were sweeping the country, but no one was in a mood to listen. Christmas was a great occasion at Cannings Ambo: in any case, it was twenty years since anyone had taken any notice of what the rest of the country was up to.

That afternoon, finding himself alone with Bess and Ann, and with nothing else to do, Giles went off half-cock and blurted out the stark facts. The two women reacted very differently. Bess looked at him as though she had just made a major discovery: she had seen the change in him and had been wondering what lay behind it. Ann, on the other hand, took her son's immense nervous energy to mean that the whole idea was a sudden and momentary aberration.

Deeply shocked, Ann reacted with outrage.

"Really, Giles, you're the absolute limit!" she exploded. "This is another of your wretched infatuations, isn't it?"

He was surprised and offended by the allegation. "No, Mother, it is *not* an infatuation," he retorted angrily.

"It must be! You're obviously one of those men who suffer from it, like a disease. I believe many of them at least have the grace to keep quiet about it and get it out of their systems. *You* want to turn everything upside-down."

"This is not a passing fancy. Jane and I love one another."

"Really? Since when? Last weekend?" Ann's sarcasm was blistering.

"No. It's been developing all year. We became aware of it two months ago."

"*Became aware of it?*" Ann stared at him incredulously. "Giles, what sort of a world are you living in?"

"A very real one!" Giles was badly rattled. He had never seen his mother so angry and feared there was much worse to come.

"What are we supposed to do?" Ann demanded.

"Carry on, of course. This place always has."

"You, meanwhile, will be Sam Montgomery's racing manager and intend marrying his daughter? I suppose it's an improvement on being an estate agent! Is it too

494

much to hope that you bothered to consider the trouble and unhappiness you'll be causing?"

"I've thought of nothing else, Mother. But it's no good, my heart isn't in training and never will be. And let's face facts, shall we? I haven't actually been *allowed* to do any training these last few years!"

"No, because we wanted to keep out of Queer Street!"

"Somebody should have had the guts to tell me!"

"We were too worried and upset, Giles. Since your poor father died, it's been one damned thing after another! We were praying for the best."

Suddenly, as the harsh truth put a stop to the shouting, the small sitting-room was resoundingly quiet. Ashamed of themselves, Ann and Giles remembered that they were not alone. Turning to look at Bess in expectation of an emotional storm, they found her impassive.

"Are you serious about this, Giles?" she asked.

"I'm afraid I am, darling."

"You and the Montgomerys have been into it thoroughly?"

"Yes."

Bess stood up. "Steven will stay here, of course," she said and left the room. Ann, who saw that Bess was deeply hurt beneath the expressionless exterior, drew breath for a verbal onslaught that was to leave Giles reeling.

To all intents and purposes, Giles left Latimer's Barn that evening. Fleeing from Ann's wrath, he grabbed a few clothes and went to Jane, receiving a hero's welcome as he gabbled out the story.

Three days later, he telephoned Bess and asked if he might come to talk to her. She agreed.

They were both strained and tired. Despite all that Jane was doing to help him, Giles was riddled with guilt; Bess had cried herself into a troubled sleep on each of the nights since his departure.

"It's about Steven," Giles began awkwardly. "Ought I to talk to him . . . sort of tell him what's going on?"

"I've done it," Bess said wearily.

"Oh!"

"Don't worry," she said, aggrieved by his suspicious look, "I haven't poisoned his mind."

"No, I'm sure you haven't . . . it's just that you seem to have been awfully quick off the mark."

"What else could I do? I thought I'd better tell him before he started asking questions, or hearing stories."

"How's he taking it?"

"Quite well."

"And you?" Giles regretted the question at once.

"I expect I shall feel better when I've had some sleep," Bess said frostily.

"Yes . . . well . . ." He shifted uncomfortably. "We must come to an arrangement about the licence. It's probably best if I don't hand mine in until you've got yours."

"Why?" She seemed to have no idea what he was getting at.

"Latimer's Barn can't be left without a licence."

"I appreciate your concern," Bess said. "But I'm not sure that I shall be having any say in the matter."

"Why not?" Giles was alarmed.

"It isn't a foregone conclusion that I shall be taking over," Bess told him. "Your mother and I both think that our friend the Dowager Duchess will have a great deal to say about this business."

"Oh, Lord, yes!" Giles took her point. "There's always Gideon and Hubert, though. What do they think?"

"They don't know there's a problem. No one does . . . I haven't talked to my mother or Joseph, yet . . . Steven's promised not to tell Leander."

Giles placed the wrong interpretation on the attempt at secrecy. "Bess, I'm not going to change my mind," he said. "This place has really worn me down and we weren't getting anywhere, were we?"

"I know, Giles. That isn't why we're trying to keep it quiet. Your mother would like a watertight case to put to Gideon and I've got to decide whether I want to stay here."

"You may go?" Giles looked and sounded flabbergasted.

"Why not?" Bess smiled ironically. "I owe an awful lot to Cannings Ambo and some of the people . . . that does *not* mean I admire everything that's happened here. As a matter of fact, Giles, I'm sick to the back teeth with a hell of a lot of it."

"Oh . . . yes, I see." He stared at the floor before asking: "Do you think I could see Steven for a few minutes?"

"He's at Louise House with Leander," Bess replied. "I'd rather not drag him out . . . it might look peculiar."

Dispiritedly, Giles agreed and set about packing clothes to supplement those he had taken in his initial flight.

"We never really got it *all* that right, did we?" he said to Bess as he prepared to leave.

"No." Momentarily, she looked dreadfully sad. "There was that night Lindisfarne won the King George and not much else."

Her assessment of their marriage was even worse than Giles had feared. He was not to know that Bess was laying a great deal of the blame on herself. Deep down, she had always known that it was likely to be a touch-and-go business: why else, for example, had she given Amaryllis her savings?

Helen called at Rose House on 14 December. She was on her way to spend what Hubert had promised would be a good, old-fashioned Christmas at Eaton Mandeville, while Freddie entertained a group of his friends in Surrey. How he was going to insulate his fourteen-year-old son from the more outlandish activities that invariably took place at his house parties, Helen neither knew nor cared. She had two priorities: ahead of her lay a holiday with her two brothers and their families. After that, she was spending New Year with Klaus Neumann at their favourite resort in the Bavarian Alps.

Helen's sole intention in visiting Cannings Ambo was to leave her latest sales report with John. However, at Rose House, she found herself walking into a near-hysterical crisis.

"It's Giles," John explained. "He's leaving to take a job with Sam Montgomery *and* he wants a divorce."

"I don't believe it!" Helen was angry rather than shocked.

497

"I'm afraid it's true." John was at his wits' end. "Apparently, it all blew up a week ago, after our meeting on Thursday, but Ann didn't tell us until this morning."

"Let me guess," Helen said, a cynical edge creeping into her voice. "Giles is involved with Montgomery's daughter?"

"He wants to marry her."

"The bloody fool!"

"Gideon's threatening to strangle him."

"I'll vote for that!" Helen said forcefully. "How's Bess?"

"Pretty livid, according to Ann. She's talking about leaving, too."

"I can't say I blame her," Helen retorted. "She's been messed about and used since Uncle Steven died. That's eleven years ago."

"Even so, what happens if she does clear off?" John asked, appalled at the prospect.

"We'll think of something." Helen indulged in a flash of sardonic humour. "If all else fails, we can do what my *dear* husband almost suggested and turn the gallops into a housing estate. Up-market executive, naturally!" Seeing the look on John's face, she plunged back into seriousness. "Has Hubert been told?"

"I doubt it, although Gideon might have rung him by the time you get there."

"I'll make sure he knows," Helen said.

The consternation in Cannings Ambo was such that no one had thought to convey the news to Eaton Mandeville. Whereas Lisette became emotional over what Helen had to say, Hubert took it all in with impassive gravity. Rachel, who had joined them for tea, seemed scarcely interested: indeed, half an hour later, she had herself driven back to the Dower House.

Hubert was dismayed that his mother had been present to hear the terrible news. Tomorrow, she was due to leave for a three-week holiday with friends in Corfu; it would have been best if she had gone without knowing about Giles's bombshell. Quietly, in his own way and without disturbing Lisette, Hubert worried through a restless night.

He was immensely relieved when Rachel left, as planned, on

the morning of 15 December. Having watched her go, Hubert promptly set off for Latimer's Barn, fearful of what he would find. A long talk with Bess on the telephone had convinced him that things could hardly be worse.

That view was based on ignorance of how Rachel had spent the previous evening after her return to the Dower House.

CHAPTER 19

1979

'. . . *a top-flight medieval despot* . . .'

The Savoy Hotel gave Rachel the biggest problem. Her friends in Corfu accepted the last-minute change of plan without question, and a host of airline booking clerks provided every assistance. But it took a considerable amount of brow-beating before The Savoy surrendered its best suite for three weeks at such short notice.

When she arrived at four-thirty on 15 December, she telephoned Freddie Christopherson from the hotel reception. After his protests had been brushed aside, he cancelled that evening's long-standing engagement and had dinner with Rachel. His bad humour disappeared as soon as she explained the developments at Latimer's Barn.

He was back again for lunch the following day, 16 December. Already, the germ of an idea was on paper, costed and looking feasible. The two men that Freddie brought with him to a late breakfast on Sunday, 17 December, were sufficiently positive to give Rachel the confidence for the next step. On Monday, it was Elisabeth Giffard who obeyed the summons to the Savoy.

After Rachel had set out her stall, Elisabeth gave an immediate commitment to support the scheme.

"And Richard Mallender must be told," Rachel said. "Do you happen to know how I can get hold of him?"

"Don't worry, I'll see to it," Elisabeth replied. After a

moment's thought, she decided to be frank. "Richard and I are very close."

On 19 December, Freddie arrived early to go over what was virtually a complete plan, lacking only a few minor details.

"I'm flying to Corfu this afternoon," Rachel said. "I shall come back a week tomorrow . . . that's the twenty-seventh. On the twenty-eighth, I want Giles here for lunch. Will you arrange that, Freddie?"

"Leave it to me!" It was, he knew, going to be difficult to track Giles down. Making him come to London could be worse. That was of no consequence: what was at stake justified any amount of effort.

Rachel felt elatedly better than at any time for over fifteen years. Passing through Heathrow Airport with a spring in her step, she caught sight of her reflection in the tinted window of a duty-free shop and received corroboration that she looked as good as she felt. Her friends in Corfu commented on her vitality and well-being when they met her, and over dinner at their villa in the hills above Kerkira, the handsome young Greek who doubled as butler and gardener had difficulty in keeping his eyes off her.

"Really, Rachel, I think Apostolos has fallen for you," her hostess said when they were briefly alone together at the end of the meal. "You're honoured."

"How old is he?" Rachel asked, making no secret of the true nature of her interest.

"Twenty-six. He's good! He gave Margot Pemberton a super time when she was over here in the summer."

Later, Rachel made her way to the chalet in which Apostolos Papathemelis lived. She was sixty-four years old, but on that and the following seven nights, the virile young man made her feel thirty. His tireless love-making was better than anything she could remember since Peter Hawksworth. The days after the furious nights were so lazy and idyllic that Rachel almost forgot to send the picture postcards that were so vital to her deception.

Giles divided his Christmas between Jane and Latimer's Barn, pleasing no one.

501

There was a feeling in Cannings Ambo that care had to be taken to stop a very bad situation getting worse. One of the signs of this was that everyone was nervously over-polite to Giles. The exception was Ann, who allowed her feelings to boil over every time she came into contact with her son. In a way, Giles found Ann's virulence comforting, whereas Gideon's frosty reserve was unnerving. John Flamsteed, Rebecca and Hubert made attempts to get Giles to change his mind, but it was brutally clear that Gideon had washed his hands of him.

"*If* we get through this in one piece, we shall be a damned sight better off without him," Gideon told Amaryllis. "Even at his best, a few years ago, Giles never looked convincing."

For Gideon, the major problem was Bess. As the days dragged by, her resolve to have done with it all seemed to harden, raising the spectre of a terrifying possibility.

"If she goes, she'll want to take Steven with her," Amaryllis said to Ann as they raked the matter over yet again on the afternoon of Christmas Eve.

"She can't!" Ann insisted.

"Why not?"

"He's needed here. He belongs to *us*."

Gideon shook his head. "I'm afraid I can't see a court agreeing with that."

"Court?" Ann was mystified. "What on earth do courts have to do with this?"

"Bess could go for legal custody if she had to," Amaryllis said. "The popular press might find that very interesting."

Ann looked appalled as she considered the possibilities. "I'm sure it won't come to that," she said hurriedly. "Bess will stay. Her heart is in this place and she couldn't possibly be so cruel as to drag Steven away." A new thought cheered her up. "In any case, where would she go? What would she live on?"

Amaryllis and Gideon exchanged worried looks. Bess's savings, steadily earning interest, now amounted to over £330,000. "Ann, Bess could get a job with any of Europe's best stables tomorrow," Gideon said. "She is very highly regarded by a lot of influential people. Once this mess becomes common knowledge, she'll be swamped with offers. Believe me, she won't be short of opportunities or money."

"In that case, she simply *must* be persuaded to stay here," Ann said, convincing herself that it was as good as done.

After Ann had left The Hall, Amaryllis sat in silence for a while before she said, "That was pretty noble and clever of you, darling."

"What was?"

"Keeping Bess's secret, but letting Ann know that she wasn't penniless and vulnerable."

"Never mind that," Gideon replied. "You've got to come up with a miracle, my love."

Amaryllis put on a brave face. Because of her closeness to Bess, she had drawn the short straw to become the major negotiator. Progress was non-existent; in fact, over the miserable days of Christmas, there were signs that Bess had made up her mind to go.

On the afternoon of 28 December, Rachel, back in the suite at The Savoy, began to wonder why she was bothering. In the grip of strikes that were now dubbed 'the Winter of Discontent' by the media, England was a shambles. Government indifference to the chaos was producing the stench of political crisis. The darkness of the short days and abysmal weather, together with the loss of Apostolos's youth-giving vigour, made her feel wretchedly old. To cap it all, Giles was being difficult.

Having located Giles at Sam Montgomery's house, twisted his arm into meeting Rachel, and ensured that he kept the appointment, Freddie Christopherson found himself instructed to stay. Rachel's idea was that the presence of someone he liked and respected would help Giles to reach the decision she wanted. His reaction to the explanation of the plan was not encouraging, however.

"Isn't all this rather underhand, Aunt Rachel?" he asked.

"Of course it is!" Rachel snapped. "How else is one supposed to deal with those people?"

"I hope you're not including Mother in that," Giles said stiffly.

"She's a victim of the system," Rachel replied. "As were my mother and Julia Flamsteed. The whole basis of the way Cannings Ambo is run is a total absurdity. Do you know how much is in the Fund?" Giles shook his head. "Go on, Freddie."

"Nine million," Freddie murmured.

Rachel pressed on, taking full advantage of Giles's shock. "My mother lived for nearly fifty years in genteel penury, Giles. Your father was the same. What about you? How much are you worth?"

"Only a few thousand," Giles admitted.

"Most people wouldn't believe it, would they?" Rachel saw that she was making progress at last. "What must outsiders think when they look at Latimer's Barn, or see you with a winner at Ascot? They imagine you're rolling in it, instead of which, you're no better off than the woman who works in the office. Meanwhile, there's *nine* million in the bank, doing nothing but grow, protected by dozens of stupid laws to say that no one is allowed to touch it. Where's it going to end, eh? Freddie has calculated that there could be over twenty million by nineteen-ninety. What will you be doing then, Giles?"

"Working for Sam Montgomery, I suppose."

"You may not be," Rachel said bluntly. "What if there's a repetition of that business with the Foleys and you're slung out with nothing? Oughtn't you to have your own money?"

"How much are you thinking of?" Giles asked.

"Half a million."

"Each?"

"Yes."

Giles held out his glass for a refill from the whisky bottle that Freddie was holding up suggestively. "I can't deny that it's attractive," he said. "But stopping training is awfully drastic, Aunt Rachel. What about Bess?"

"Your precious wife is thinking of leaving and taking Steven with her!"

"Are you sure? I know she wasn't very pleased, but I assumed she'd get over it." Giles was suspicious.

"Tell him, Freddie," Rachel commanded.

"I had a long chat with Helen yesterday afternoon." Freddie smiled at Giles's expression and hastened to explain. "We like to keep in touch occasionally. She's down at Eaton Mandeville and didn't want to tell me all that much, but I got the main points out of her. Bess *is* expected to leave."

"What are they going to do?" Giles asked.

"Someone has suggested that they contact Ian Eaglestone."

"You mean Bernard Dalrymple's assistant?" Giles asked.

"That's the chap."

"Bloody hell!" To Rachel's immense satisfaction, Giles was annoyed.

Bernard Dalrymple's Tewkesbury Lodge stables were one of the biggest and most successful yards in Newmarket. In the past ten years, Dalrymple had been champion trainer four times, eclipsing Latimer's Barn to a certain extent. There were, however, constant rumours about friction between Bernard Dalrymple and his assistant.

"That's the worst thing they could possibly do," Giles stormed.

"Oh?" Rachel looked at him keenly, waiting for an explanation.

"Dalrymple would put the flags out if Eaglestone left him, *especially* to go to Latimer's Barn," Giles said. "He's wanted Bess for years."

"Has he, indeed?" Rachel smiled at Freddie. "And what does she think of his set-up?"

"She's always had a great deal of respect for him," Giles replied, not without resentment. "Under these conditions, she'd go like a flash." His indignation was mounting. "They're idiots! Talking to Eaglestone is a way of making sure that Bess *does* leave."

"I see." Rachel squared up to what she was sure would be the end of the argument. "There are two points I wish to make, Giles. You said, 'Under these conditions'. *You* created them.

505

This shambles is your fault. And I am not simply talking about current problems. This all started with Gillian Foley."

"You encouraged that!" Giles shouted.

"I didn't encourage you to make such a complete fool of yourself, and I most certainly did not encourage you to marry Bess Collier."

"The cook's daughter!" Giles muttered bitterly.

"Precisely! The other thing I want you to grasp is what they will have to offer Eaglestone. Is *he* going to be satisfied with a free house and a few pounds a week for pocket-money?"

Giles gave in. "Very well, Aunt Rachel, what do you want me to do?"

She could see that he was defeated rather than convinced, but that was an incidental nicety: in a hectoring manner, the Dowager Duchess of Laverstoke informed her nephew what was expected of him.

Ian Eaglestone paid his first visit to Cannings Ambo on 2 January. Both Bess and Rebecca refused to have anything to do with him, so it fell to Ann to show him round the yards, assisted by Hubert, who had made a special journey from Eaton Mandeville. Gideon Timberlake, totally unimpressed by what he knew of Eaglestone, made a point of being away on business; Lady Amaryllis was in London, shopping.

Alone in The House, Bess used her bedside telephone to contact Bernard Dalrymple.

"Bess! Happy New Year," he said, delighted to hear from her.

"And to you, with knobs on," she replied cheerfully. "Your man Eaglestone has arrived."

"Oh, dear! That means his wheels didn't turn square and drop off."

"Is that what you were hoping for?" Bess asked.

"That was the least of my prayers," Dalrymple chuckled. "Anyway, never mind him, what about you? Are you any nearer a decision?"

"Not really, Bernard."

"I'm living in hope, Bess."

"You keep doing that! Sending for the foul Eaglestone hasn't increased my confidence in 'the management'."

He laughed sympathetically. "I imagine it's the headless-chicken syndrome. Keep in touch, won't you?"

"Constantly," she assured him.

Richard Mallender and Elisabeth Giffard drove to their remote cottage near Clun in the Welsh borderlands on the afternoon of 5 January, the first Friday of the year. Before leaving London, they spent an hour with Rachel. It was to be the last time they saw each other before the following Thursday's Trustees' meeting, so final plans were agreed.

"I suppose Her Ladyship knows what she's doing?" Elisabeth asked when the fires were lit and they were settling in.

Richard thought about it. "What's bothering you?"

"The *best* she can hope for is to split the vote equally. Let's assume she does that. What happens then?"

"She's counting on surprise and shock," Richard replied. "The closeness of the vote, together with the fact that it happened at all, is likely to demoralise the old guard." Elisabeth accepted the point. "There's a reasonable chance that they might give in there and then. Failing that, Rachel will win one of them over and force another vote."

"And William Flamsteed is the likely sucker?"

"He's a good prospect. With the stable out of the way, furniture would be king. Christopherson's plan calls for over a million pounds-worth of investment and William would gain tremendously."

"And to guarantee future harmony, Rachel wants four million out of the Fund," Elisabeth said. "Afterwards, we each get five hundred thousand as a 'thank you'."

"Correct."

"And that's enough for us to make life downright impossible for your beloved brother?"

"I think so. In any case, we get two bites at the cherry."

Rachel had never doubted their support because she knew of the strains beneath the outwardly placid surface

507

of Mallender and Giffard Foods. While claiming to want the company to remain intact, Elisabeth and Richard were planning the downfall of Adrian Mallender. Three years ago, the company had been forced to raise money by means of a Stock Exchange flotation. Adrian and Elisabeth each had twenty per cent of the equity; a further fifteen per cent was held by friends of Adrian; the other forty-five per cent was public property.

With one million pounds between them, Richard and Elisabeth would be able to make significant inroads into the forty-five per cent. Attractive though this prospect was, Elisabeth favoured the other option, which had her retired father's approval: she could sell her holding. Leslie Giffard had exhibited vindictive glee at the prospect of twenty per cent going *en bloc* to Freddie Christopherson, especially since Freddie's offer was above the current market price. Elisabeth agreed with her father: Adrian and Freddie, forced into bed together, would make a marvellous job of cutting each other's throats.

"*However*," Elisabeth said, "can Her Ladyship split the vote? What about Helen?"

"Yes, I've been thinking about her," Richard said. "I know that Helen is sanctified these days, but her record isn't good."

"Father swears that she's a grade-A bitch," Elisabeth said.

"We could argue the pros and cons all day," Richard said. "My gut feeling is that for half a million, Helen will do as Mummy says."

Elisabeth was deep in thought for a few moments. "I wonder why Rachel is doing this?" she mused.

"Her ideas make quite a lot of commercial sense," Richard replied. "Still more so if you accept that we're going to get a change of Government soon."

"H'm!" Elisabeth was plainly dubious. "What's *really* motivating her?"

Richard grinned. "She loathes Bess."

"She's supposed to be clearing off."

"Maybe," Richard said. "I can't help feeling that particular piece of scaremongering has been beefed up to sway Giles. My impression of Bess is that she rather enjoyed running Latimer's Barn."

Helen returned to Eaton Mandeville from Germany in time for lunch on Sunday. To Hubert's surprise, she was curious about their father's war-time activities.

"Haven't I heard something about him working in military intelligence?" she asked.

"Yes, he did." Hubert peered at her. "Why the interest?"

Helen was uncharacteristically bashful. "It's my friend, Klaus Neumann," she said. "As a matter of fact, I've been with him during the past few days."

Hubert's surprise was multiplied tenfold by Lisette's matter-of-fact statement. "Helen and Klaus have been lovers for about five years, *chéri*. It was they who brought us back together."

Having nearly choked over a mouthful of food, Helen gave Lisette an 'I'll-talk-to-you-later' look. "I found out that Klaus was in intelligence," she said. "The *Wehrmacht*," she added hurriedly, "not Gestapo or SS."

"We're gratified to hear it," Hubert replied with due solemnity.

"Anyway, that set me thinking about Father," Helen said. "Do we know what he got up to?"

"I'm afraid not," Hubert replied. "I believe he was a big-shot. Beyond that, it's a mystery."

"What a shame. Never mind, it wasn't important."

They were finishing the meal when Hubert had a sudden thought. "Do you know, Helen, I've an idea that there's a great wad of Father's papers from the War. They must be somewhere in the study."

"Could we look?" Helen asked eagerly.

"Surely." Hubert was on his feet.

"Don't be long," Lisette warned. "We promised to go over to Malmesbury to see the Drax-Templetons."

"Oh, yes!" Hubert knew that he must not evade the visit to the Earl of Milton, Lady Amaryllis Timberlake's brother, and led the way up to the first floor at a trot. Once inside his study, he gazed around blankly. "Where did I shove them?" he muttered.

Eventually, Helen was about to suggest that they forget all about it when her brother uttered a cry of triumph as he delved into the bottom drawer of a battered old filing-cabinet.

"I'm sure this is the stuff," he said, dumping two discoloured manila folders on the desk. "Yes!" He examined the few sheets of paper that had spilled out. "Don't expect anything earth-shattering. The guv'nor wasn't the sort of chap to make off with state secrets. Look, do you mind if I leave you to it? You heard Lisette give me the gypsy's warning."

"I'll be all right." Helen was already sitting down, ready to search.

It soon emerged that Hubert's theory was probably right. The two folders were packed with a charming, albeit almost incomprehensible, collection of memorabilia. There were reminders that Charles Prideaux had written to himself: "Contact GOC 3rd & 5th Divs re 34/A/Q." There were notes from colleagues about things that had happened while he was away: "Tom B rang. Higgins *didn't* know about Jefferson." Several much-altered drafts for complicated memoranda ran to a dozen or more large sheets of paper: they were mixed up with mess bills, concert programmes, bus tickets, receipts for uniform cleaning and a host of similar trivia, all of which had meant something for a moment or two in the dark days of nearly forty years ago. It took Helen half an hour to realise that the four blue exercise-books were a terse diary, extending from the autumn of 1939 to VE Day in 1945. She set them to one side, intending to take them away to study at length.

Last of all, when she had given up hope of finding anything of significance, was a buff-coloured card that seemed to summarise her father's military career. She smiled at the entry for rank and name: "Colonel Charles Prideaux (Duke of Laverstoke)". As well as a record of his service, with brief details of two commendations, everything about the physical man was listed, including height, weight, colour of eyes and hair.

And his blood group was O.

As a consequence of the birth of her son, Helen knew that her blood group was AB. Overhearing a nurse mentioning the fact, Rachel had said that she, too, was AB.

Helen frowned as a moribund fragment of knowledge flickered at the back of her mind. It refused to come to life. Turning round, she saw a shelf containing Hubert's new *Encyclopaedia Britannica*: she looked up 'Blood Groups'. There was a table listing all parental pairings with the possible and impossible blood groups of a child. AB and O in combination could produce A or B, but not O or AB. On this evidence, the man named on Helen's birth certificate could not possibly be her father.

Icy calm, Helen turned to the diaries. An hour passed before she felt confident that she understood the abbreviations that were used, then she began to scavenge, jotting down notes as she went.

She concentrated first on June 1941, the time nine months before she was born. Charles's remarks about not being able to see Rachel reflected his great disappointment. On two of the weekends he was stuck in London, tied to his desk at the War Office; on the other two, he visited friends in Surrey because Rachel was too busy to see him. Helen turned back to May, finding an identical picture.

By the middle of July, the laconic: "R too busy – again!!" showed bitterness. Then, at the end of the month, Charles took two weeks' leave in Cannings Ambo. The diary probably stayed in London, for there was no entry between 30 July and 15 August. However, the elation of: "R says she can't wait!" was painfully evident, as was the exhausted happiness of 15 August: "Wonderful time. R too much for me. Thank God for a rest!"

On 2 March 1942, Charles recorded his joy at the birth of his daughter. There could be no doubting the depth of his feelings and the words were backed up by Helen's vivid memories of how very much he had loved her. There was no mention that the birth was two months premature, nor had Charles Prideaux ever suspected it, but of one thing Helen

511

was now absolutely certain: the eighth Duke of Laverstoke had not been her father.

Later, when Hubert and Lisette came back from Malmesbury, Helen was perfectly normal as she joined them for drinks before dinner. She joked about the mass of worthless information she had discovered in her father's papers. "And there was this incredible record card from the Army," she concluded. "The only thing missing was his inside leg measurement. It even had his blood group!"

"Very important in a war," Hubert pointed out. "Father was keen on that sort of thing . . . do you know, he marched Edmund and me off for blood tests when I was ten or eleven."

"Whatever for?" Lisette asked.

"In case we got half-killed and needed transfusions," Hubert replied. "Male heirs to the title and all that. Useful, of course, but it put the wind up us, I don't mind telling you." He smiled fondly. "Anyway, it was all right. I was group A, as befitted the senior chap, and Edmund was B. It took him ages to get over that!"

As they laughed over Edmund's needless sense of inferiority, Helen reflected that it was all for the best that girls were of no account in the aristocratic scheme of things: Charles Prideaux had gone to his early grave in ignorance of his wife's infidelity.

After a good night's sleep, Helen was still her normal self when she obeyed the summons to go to the Dower House an hour after Rachel's return from holiday.

Arrogantly certain of Helen's support, Rachel did not waste time in dressing her plan up. Helen came close to grudging admiration of her mother's effrontery: beginning with a frank statement of how she had deceived everyone over her holiday, Rachel set out the scheme as though no one in their right mind could possibly have any objection to it.

As she listened, Helen was struck by two points. The part played by Freddie and his cronies was sickening, and, much more importantly, Helen felt guilty. If she had kept her mouth shut on 14 December, Rachel would have cleared off to Corfu knowing nothing and in no position to organise this piece of chicanery.

"Well, what do you think?" Rachel had finished her exposition and was seeking approval.

"Mother, you leave me speechless with admiration," Helen said. "It's a *marvellous* idea!"

"I can rely on you, then?"

"Absolutely!" Helen made a self-mocking face and gesture. "You know me . . . for half a million pounds, I'd do anything!"

"Excellent, darling." Rachel smiled. "It really is the best way. It's quite lunatic to have all that money doing nothing – I'm certain it isn't what Leander's father had in mind when he started it all off."

"I shall be well-placed with all the investment in William Flamsteed and Sons," Helen said. "Do you want me to have a word with William, by the way?"

"No, we must keep very, very quiet about this," Rachel said. "Please don't say *anything* to Hubert."

"Of course not, Mother."

"And I suggest we avoid each other until the meeting on Thursday. We daren't give anyone the slightest grounds for suspicion."

Helen agreed wholeheartedly. She certainly saw no point in throwing Hubert into a panic over nothing.

Late on Wednesday afternoon, Ann and Gideon sat in the library at The House, silent and totally dejected. Fifteen minutes previously, Ian Eaglestone had set off back to Newmarket after his second visit.

Eaglestone wanted to be the trainer at Latimer's Barn: vividly aware of the status it would confer on him, he wanted it very badly indeed. But that did not mean he was prepared to make concessions in the demands he was making for giving Cannings Ambo the privilege of his presence. A basic salary of £20,000, a £1,000 bonus for every Pattern winner, and a ten per cent share in all stallions that went

513

to the stud were by no means the total of his requirements.

Eventually, Ann broke the silence. "Are we really in such a mess that we have to consider turning to people like him?"

"Over my dead body," Gideon growled. "The man's a self-opinionated charlatan!"

"So, what do we do?" Ann asked.

"There *must* be someone we could put in," Gideon said.

They talked for ten minutes, with Gideon making a strong case for Arthur Merriweather. Ann, unhappy with that idea, was glad to be interrupted by a knock at the door. It was Bess.

"I thought you'd like to know that I've decided to stay," she said. "If you want me, that is."

Gideon's answer was unequivocal. Leaping to his feet, he folded Bess in a crushing embrace and kissed her, rather spoiling it by apologising. Glancing at Ann over his shoulder, Bess saw that she was weeping with gratitude.

"I do think that there will have to be some changes, though," Bess said.

"So do I!" Gideon agreed, guiding her to a chair. "Tell us about them."

The discussion lasted well over an hour, producing total agreement. Soon after six o'clock, there was a flurry of near-panic when Rebecca looked in to tell them that William had been rushed to hospital, suffering from acute appendicitis.

"It's perfectly all right," Rebecca assured them. "He's had the operation and they're very pleased. I'm on my way to watch him come round."

"What about the children?" Ann asked, worrying most about baby Emma.

"Liz Challoner's with them," Rebecca replied.

"Give William our love," Ann said. "I'll go and see him tomorrow evening."

It occurred to no one that William's absence from tomorrow's meeting might be catastrophic.

It was the turn of Latimer's Barn to be the venue for the

meeting and Rachel was the first to arrive, sweeping into The House with a distinctly proprietorial air. Ann, who took it upon herself to provide her sister-in-law with coffee and biscuits, was moved to tell Rachel how good she was looking.

"Thank you," Rachel said. "Corfu agrees with me. I recommend it, especially at this time of year."

Soon after Rachel's appearance, Gideon took up an unobtrusively watchful position in Liz's office. When Giles, the last to arrive, turned up, Gideon took him aside to give him his instructions.

"For the sake of form, you must take the chair," Gideon said. "State your intentions and resign. Once we have an official record of that, you can clear off and we'll elect another Chairman."

Giles, who knew that Rachel had no intention of allowing that to happen, nodded obediently. "Has Bess made up her mind?" he asked.

"No," Gideon replied curtly and marched off towards the dining-room.

Hubert Prideaux, already seated at the table that was covered by a huge sheet of royal-blue baize, saw the first signs of danger as the other Trustees filed in. Freddie Christopherson looked smug; Elisabeth Giffard seemed positively furtive; Richard Mallender was evasive when greeted by Lady Amaryllis and John Flamsteed.

"Where's William?" Rachel asked.

Ann, who had already explained his absence over coffee, was taken aback. "He was taken to hospital yesterday," Gideon said. "Appendicitis. The operation was a complete success and he's very comfortable."

Amid the murmurs of mingled sympathy and relief, Rachel fired a look of sheer jubilation at Freddie: with a majority of six to five, they were going to prevail at the first attempt. Hubert saw the look and exchanged an apprehensive glance with Gideon.

The room was still in that moment when everyone expects the Chairman to call the meeting to order. Giles was bracing

515

himself for the task when Rachel began to speak: her tone was harsh.

"I understand that we are faced with an extremely grave situation. Giles is leaving Cannings Ambo to take up a position with Mr Montgomery. This has been known since the fourteenth of December, possibly even earlier. It is absolutely deplorable that those Trustees who are in day-to-day contact with the affairs of the stable should not have notified this serious matter to those of us who do not have the good fortune to live here, but *are* deeply concerned about the estate's well-being. I find it difficult to overlook the possibility of a conspiracy of silence."

It was a brutally successful pre-emptive strike. Pausing, both for effect and to remove a sheaf of papers from a document case, Rachel was assured of silence. Not even Gideon was able to find words to rebut the charge she had made. Rachel spread her papers out, glared round the table and continued.

"Since my brother died nearly twelve years ago, Latimer's Barn seems to have staggered from one crisis to another." Ann wanted to point out that the period under Bess had been successful and secure, but Rachel, reading her mind, quelled her with a look. "I am heartily sick of it. We seem to be involved in a complicated, risky business simply to build up the Fund. Having said that, the stable's contribution has slumped badly in the last two years. In the twelve months to October, Latimer's Barn made one hundred and four thousand pounds after tax, while the furniture business turned in nearly twice that amount."

"We had a very exceptional year," John protested. "It's got nothing to do with the stable slipping back!"

"You may be right," Rachel said with a regal smile. "However, a mere hundred thousand is a very poor return on a capital asset worth at least four million. If your friends in Switzerland did no better than that we should soon take our custom elsewhere."

"Where does the figure of four million come from?" Gideon demanded.

"That's a realistic valuation of the stable and gallops."

"By whom?"

"Two experts that Freddie has consulted."

Gideon leaned back in his chair to stare hard at Rachel. "Do you have a suggestion to make, Lady Laverstoke?" he asked.

Even Rachel was slightly fazed by his hostile formality before she rallied. "Yes, I most certainly do! I propose that we turn this crisis to our advantage and give up the idea of training horses."

"That's rather outlandish, isn't it, Mother?" said Hubert, the only one of the Latimer's Barn loyalists who was not stunned into silence by the idea. "I *don't* agree with your view that things have been a mess since Uncle Steven's death, and we have a very substantial tradition to consider."

"I don't need lectures on that score, thank you, Hubert. *I* trained a Derby winner!"

"What are your ideas for the stud?" Amaryllis asked.

"It's very profitable. It should carry on." Rachel sounded quite grand about it.

"Where do we get the new stallions from when the ones we've got wear out?"

Animated by the battle, Rachel failed to notice the sarcastic insolence behind Amaryllis's question.

"Buy them!" Rachel said. "It's what most studs do – in fact, I don't know of any other that is attached to a specific racing stable. There's plenty of money. At today's interest rates, the Fund is earning over eight hundred thousand a year. I have a proposal for that, too, I might add."

"What do you intend doing with Latimer's Barn and the gallops?" Ann asked.

"A great deal of the stable premises could be used by an expanded William Flamsteed and Sons," Rachel replied. "The gallops would make an excellent housing development – very much at the top of the market, of course. Freddie has drafted a number of schemes."

On cue, Freddie produced several drawings. Having spread

517

them carefully on the table, he found that no one was interested in them.

"Mother, are we meant to take this seriously?" Hubert asked.

"I'm putting it forward as a formal motion," Rachel replied.

"I second it," Freddie Christopherson added.

"You're suggesting that we wind up Latimer's Barn?" Gideon was dazed, apparently with no fight in him.

Rachel did not bother answering. While Gideon, Hubert and John whispered among themselves in a distraught sort of way, it was Ann who said, "We can't possibly consider that."

"Why not?" Rachel asked.

"William isn't here," Ann said desperately.

"That is unfortunate." Rachel was smoothly unsympathetic. "It is, however, no reason why we should not conduct business as normal."

"This isn't normal business," Ann said angrily. "You can't have motions that would stop us training horses." She looked to Gideon for support: grimly, he shook his head.

"There is nothing in the estate's articles of constitution to prevent it," Rachel said. "In order to ensure fair play, may I have a show of hands of those in favour of treating this scheme as a formal motion?"

She and five others, including Helen, raised their hands.

"A majority," Rachel purred.

"Giles has no right to be voting," Gideon protested.

"He has not yet resigned," Rachel countered.

The room fell silent. Giles squirmed under a withering scowl from Gideon; Helen was unsure whether Hubert was staring at her in sorrow, or anger; Richard Mallender and Elisabeth Giffard did their utmost to appear defiant.

"I think we should vote on it," Freddie said.

"What about time to consider?" Gideon asked.

"What is there to consider?" Freddie asked contemptuously. "Our scheme will provide income of at least three million over the next ten years."

518

"*Our* scheme?" Gideon echoed. Very late in the game, the full enormity of the conspiracy began to dawn on him and he felt a fool. Ann and John Flamsteed were quick to share his sense of defeat.

"May we vote?" Rachel said briskly. "The proposal is that the Cannings Ambo Estate gives up the training of racehorses and puts the buildings and land thus released to more profitable uses. Those in favour."

The hands went up.

Rachel, her left arm in the air, was busy writing and did not bother looking at the others. When Amaryllis said, "That's only five," in a wondering voice, Rachel jerked back to attention. Helen, her hands clasped together on the table, stared at her stonily. Slowly, Rachel's arm came down: embarrassed and fearful, the other four did the same.

"Those against!" Amaryllis said. Helen's was the first hand to shoot up.

"That's six," Gideon announced unnecessarily. "The motion is defeated by six votes to five."

Everyone held their breath.

"What happens now?" Rachel's knuckles were white, but it seemed she was going to retain her self-control.

Gideon looked at Hubert and Ann; they both nodded. "I think we should tell you what *we* intend doing," he said, not bothering to keep the triumph from his voice. "I'm very, very pleased to be able to tell you all that Bess has agreed to carry on at Latimer's Barn. Her application for a licence went in this morning." He gave himself time to savour the reactions. Of those who had not known already, only Helen and Hubert, smiling fondly at each other, were pleased. Rachel and Freddie Christopherson were clearly livid; Giles was aghast; Richard Mallender and Elisabeth Giffard wanted the ground to open and swallow them.

"Actually, that isn't strictly true," Gideon went on. "Bess *will* take over, but only if we meet the conditions she has laid down."

"What are they?" Rachel asked, her voice harsh.

"I think she would like to tell you herself," Gideon said.

Ann rose and went to the door. After she had called Bess, there were footsteps in the corridor; her strong, confident gait sounded more self-assured than ever. There was a pause as Ann gave her a résumé of what had been happening, then, with a brisk, "Good morning, everyone," she strode in.

She was wearing an immaculate dark-grey suit beneath which was a white blouse with a high mandarin collar; her stockings were white, the black patent shoes had gold buckles on the insteps. Giles, who had never seen her dressed in such a way, goggled. When she sat down at the opposite end of the table, he saw that her wedding ring was gone.

"I have three conditions that must be met in full before I agree to take on the responsibility of this place," she said. Not one of those listening doubted her determination. "The first concerns Giles. I will not have him going away from here without anything to show for it. This whole wretched business came about largely because he was virtually penniless when his first wife decided she'd had enough of him. Frankly, I don't give much for his chances with Sam Montgomery and his daughter, but I hope I'm wrong. Whatever happens, Giles must be independent, able to show off a bit of status. I want him to have half a million pounds from the Fund."

There was a stir as surprise turned into vague approval.

"Does anyone here disagree with that?" Bess asked. Getting no response, she turned to John. "I want that officially recorded as a unanimous decision, please. Payment to be made within the month." She shifted her attention to Giles. "I assume that's acceptable to you?"

"Well . . . yes . . . of course. It's generous." For an awful moment, she thought he was going to break down. "It's bloody good of you, Bess."

"Go to the office," she told him. "Liz has a letter of resignation for you to sign and there's a cheque that should keep you going for a few weeks." He nodded, but made no attempt to move. "Now, Giles," Bess said sharply. As he made his way unsteadily to the door, she spoke to him again, this time in tones of affectionate friendship. "Wait for me. You can take me out to lunch when I've finished."

In the expectant silence that followed Giles's departure, Bess walked the length of one of the longest tables ever made by Wm Flamsteed & Sons. Slowly, she sat down in the chair left vacant. Rachel, who had made a point of taking the seat immediately to the right, looked on in outraged disbelief.

"This is my second condition," Bess said. "I don't know how many invitations to become a Trustee I've turned down, but it's time to change my mind. You lot haven't made all that good a job over the last few years, so I shall be Chairman."

Rachel exploded. She was confused. Was this all a pre-arranged plan, or were Helen's betrayal and Bess's ruthless assurance merely a coincidence?

"That is absolutely out of the question!" Rachel shouted. "This has been your game all along, hasn't it, *Mrs Hawksworth*? You wormed your way into my grandmother's affections thirty years ago and you've been trying to gain control ever since. Well, it won't wash, do you hear me?" Beside herself, Rachel was banging the table. "You should never have come here in the first place. My mother-in-law made the mistake of picking you out of the gutter . . . I'm going to make sure that . . ."

She stopped dead as Helen took a piece of paper from her handbag and thrust it at her. When she unfolded it, all the colour drained from Rachel's face and she trembled. Bess was not alone in thinking that she was going to keel over and die. It was sheer hatred that drove her to a far quicker recovery than anyone thought possible.

Unconcerned by the malevolence being directed at her, Helen addressed the meeting. "I am sorry to have to say that I consider my mother, Lady Laverstoke, to be an unfit person to hold Trusteeship," she said. "Apart from what we have seen here today, she spent the Christmas period plotting against Bess and the estate. This was in a London hotel, by the way, *not* Corfu."

Hubert jumped in to support his sister. "I agree, you *are* unsuitable, Mother," he said, addressing Rachel directly. "It would save a vote and a great deal of unpleasantness if you were to resign at once."

Rachel toyed with the idea of a last fight, then gave in,

521

flouncing out of the room with an attempt at dignity, giving Bess and Helen a last look of detestation.

"That brings me to my last condition," Bess said, her calmness earning an admiring glance from Gideon. "I want drastic changes in the group round this table. It's an absolute disgrace that John's wife isn't a Trustee. The same is true of Rebecca. But before we appoint them, there are three more resignations required. I will not work with anyone who supported Lady Laverstoke."

Richard Mallender grunted agreement. "Yes, I can appreciate that. We're very sorry." He and Elisabeth stood up together. "We were promised five hundred thousand pounds each if we voted with Lady Laverstoke."

"Where was she going to get that from?" Amaryllis asked.

"Out of the Fund," Elisabeth replied. "That was going to be the next item on the agenda." She smiled ruefully. "We only wanted the money to foul Adrian up."

Gideon chuckled. "You can do that by selling your shares," he said. "I could be interested."

"Really?"

"Definitely! My boy, Desmond, is looking for directorships. Don't rush off, we can discuss it over lunch."

"I take it that Miss Challenor has letters for us to sign?" Richard said to Bess.

"Yes, she has. Don't forget Lindisfarne, Richard. He'll keep both of you in style for a few years yet."

"Can I carry on sending you horses to train?" Richard asked.

"It will be a pleasure," Bess smiled.

After Richard and Elisabeth had gone, Bess sat back, gazing blandly at Freddie Christopherson.

"I don't intend resigning," he said.

Bess shrugged. "We'll vote you out."

"I'll sue!" Freddie snapped.

"What on earth for?" Gideon laughed. "It goes without saying that we shan't be using your financial services in the future. We're moving to Hubert's bank."

"That deserves a few bucketfuls of dirt!" Freddie replied.

522

"Dirt?" Gideon seemed baffled. "Dirt? My dear chap, what do you mean by *dirt*? Surely you're not thinking about the sort of thing that you and your friends Sibley and Copthorne get up to with Pamela Atkinson?"

Freddie froze, the smirk congealing on his face.

"Hey, that's pretty good," Helen said to Gideon. "You're a little bit out-of-date, but I can tell you about the current merry band of perverts. By the way, Hubert, I think the time has come for that divorce."

"We can start this afternoon, my dear," Hubert said.

Freddie tried to assume an air of Olympian detachment. "So, we all keep our secrets to ourselves, eh?"

"I think so, don't you?" Gideon asked urbanely. "Please say if you're not satisfied. We might be able to think of something else."

Freddie eyed him craftily. "You wouldn't dare go public," he said.

"The thought never entered my mind," Gideon said. "I tell you what, though: neither Cameron Carlyle nor Sven Sigurdson would be impressed."

Mention of his two biggest and most confidential clients, both of whom were notorious puritans, finished Freddie. He walked out with Bess's: "See Miss Challoner!" taunting him. His plans to turn the gallops into a housing development lay abandoned on the table.

No one dared to speak. Ann, on the verge of tears, edged her chair towards Amaryllis to lean on her: Gideon and Hubert opened their mouths several times, but thought better of it; Helen, shaking now that it was over, found Bess's rock-solid composure comforting.

When speech did seem both possible and desirable, there was uproar as everyone began at the same time.

"Stop!" Gideon bellowed. "Can we try to keep calm and sane?"

Ann was bursting to ask a question. "Helen, what was on that piece of paper you gave your mother?"

"I'm dying to know, too," Amaryllis said. "By God, it stopped her!"

"It's something I have to talk to Hubert about first," Helen replied. "I'm afraid that he will probably agree with me that it must be kept private. It's a family thing, you see."

"Spoil-sport!" Amaryllis grinned.

Fearing degeneration into hysteria after the dreadful tension, Gideon became businesslike. "John, produce an official record of Bess's election and installation as Chairman and arrange for her to sign the necessary documents. Hubert, you and I have to fix up the transfer of the Fund. I rather think that Bess feels it should be brought back from Switzerland."

Bess, on her way to the office to check with Liz that the five resignations had been properly completed, called out, "Definitely!" and was gone.

After Hubert and Gideon had compared diaries and arranged to meet at Stewart's in London the following Wednesday, Helen took Hubert to the library to explain to him why the note she had passed to Rachel had said:

Who is my father?

Over lunch in a pub high on the Marlborough Downs, Giles was still in a state of shock. What put the morning's events completely beyond his comprehension was Bess's statement that she and her supporters had known nothing of Rachel's plan.

"I was terrified because I was convinced you'd know," he said. "Hubert or Gideon were bound to get wind of a thing like that."

"I'm sure they would have done, as a rule," Bess said. "But things haven't exactly been normal for the last few weeks. I didn't decide to stay until yesterday afternoon."

"What made you?"

"This and that," Bess said vaguely. "For one thing, I don't like Newmarket."

"*Was* Bernard Dalrymple a possibility?"

"Very much so."

"And what about Helen?" Giles asked.

"She did awfully well." Bess paused to consider the likely

524

sequence of events. "She led Rachel right up the garden path, waited until she saw the whites of her eyes, and – bang!"

"And the note," Giles said. "I heard about that. I wonder what it said."

"Helen wouldn't let on and I don't think she ever will. It must have been something pretty lethal."

Giles shook his head and seemed to wander off into a reverie. Perfectly at ease, Bess carried on eating shepherd's pie.

"Richard Mallender and Elisabeth didn't seem too upset," Giles said at last. "I think they're having lunch with Gideon."

"They were led astray by your aunt," Bess said, smiling at how quaint it sounded.

"Freddie took it badly," Giles said. "He was fuming when you'd finished with him."

"He tried to be difficult and clever, so Gideon had to beat him over the head with his private life," Bess said.

"Oh!"

Bess had the impression that Giles knew a great deal about Christopherson's habits, but decided not to pursue the matter. In any case, Giles's next statement aroused her curiosity.

"This must have been like the good old days."

"What do you mean?"

"When Leander used to sort things out. Some of the stories would make your hair curl."

Bess looked pained. "I'm no Leander, Giles."

"That isn't what they're saying."

"Well, *they* are wrong!" she said, forcefully enough to startle the landlord, who was immersed in a newspaper, looking for winners at the afternoon's two National Hunt meetings. "For one thing, I don't imagine that Leander ever had anything as downright bloody bad as this lot to cope with. Whatever else happened, the Trustees were always on her side, but that mob . . . faugh!" She waved a hand dismissively.

525

As they left the pub and strolled towards the car, Giles was suddenly on the verge of emotional breakdown again.

"I can't tell you how grateful I am for that money, Bess. Actually, I have the feeling that things will work out well with Jane . . . but it's nice to know that if they don't . . . well, you know what I mean."

She decided to make light of it. "That was all ulterior motive, my lad! With a good slice of capital behind you, I'm hoping you'll stay out of my hair and let me get on with running a stable." She kissed him, happy to linger over a last display of affection, sad that it had come to this. "Look after yourself," she said, serious now.

"What about you?" Giles asked. "Will you marry again?"

"With what I'm going to have on my plate?" She laughed. "There won't be time!"

When they reached the front of The House, Bess leaned across to peck her husband on the cheek. "Go on, clear off," she ordered.

She waved and was on her way into the office before Giles had finished turning the car.

"Where are we up to?" she asked Liz.

"I think Richard and Elisabeth are still at The Hall with the Timberlakes," Liz replied. "Mrs Hawksworth, His Grace and Lady Helen are hatching something in the library, and Mr Flamsteed is coming to see you at five o'clock with papers to be signed."

"Right! Give me five minutes to get changed and we'll do some *real* work. I fancy having a go at the plan for two-year-olds."

"Are you going to throw that suit away?" Liz asked.

"Why, do you want it?"

"It would have to be altered," Liz said doubtfully. "I'm not quite as sylph-like as you. Maybe you ought to keep it."

"What for?"

"You never know when you'll want to put the frighteners on another gang of shysters."

"You reckon it's good for that?"

"Isn't that why you bought it?" Liz asked innocently.

Chuckling, Bess dashed off.

Hubert was aghast at what Helen told him. The evidence that they did not share the same father, that she was his half-sister, not sister, seemed incontrovertible. Lunch was taken into the library for them as they raked the problem over without getting anywhere.

"I wonder if it might not be best to let sleeping dogs lie," Hubert said. "Mother is going to be enough of a problem without stirring this hornet's nest up."

"I agree," Helen said. "Nevertheless, I'd like to know who my father was."

"Would you? You're sure?" Hubert was terribly earnest.

"Yes. We must be discreet, of course."

One thing emerged from the rambling discussion that followed: the probability was that Helen's father had lived in, or very near, Cannings Ambo.

"My God, he might still be here!" Helen said, not sure whether the thought pleased or horrified her.

"I doubt that," Hubert replied. "Not even Mother has the nerve to have kept coming back if he were around. I can't help, of course . . . I was four at the time. I can remember nearly everything about Grandmother Emma, but not much else."

"Could Ann help?" Helen asked.

"You don't mind telling her?"

"Do you know of anyone more trustworthy?"

Asked to join them, Ann gaped as Helen told the story. At the end, she made a simple point that had eluded Helen and Hubert. "Your idea must be right, Helen, otherwise your mother would have reacted very differently when you gave her the note."

Helen nodded. "Of course!" She and Hubert exchanged looks. "Can you tell me anything, Aunt Ann? Who was mother's lover?"

"I married Steven in November nineteen forty-one," Ann said. "By that time, you were well on the way. I didn't come here very much before we married because Steven was away at sea all the time."

527

"Oh, well, never mind." Helen tried to hide her disappointment.

"It will be very difficult to find out what was going on behind the scenes, anyway," Ann said. "That was the year of Peter Hawksworth, George's terrible son."

"Yes, the German spy!" Hubert said. "Silas Timberlake had to kill him after he took a shot at Leander."

While Helen boggled at mention of a story of which she knew nothing, Ann, a deeply thoughtful look on her face, pulled the Big Book towards her. After leafing through it for nearly a minute, she sniffed and said, "I see!" as though she understood everything.

"What is it?" Hubert asked.

"Two pages have been removed," Ann said. "Look, you can see the edges – and the numbers, as well. That will be Leander . . . I remember Steven telling me that she was completely taken in by Peter."

Guided by Helen's curiosity, Ann told all she knew about Peter, the way that Silas had become suspicious and tracked him down, the wounding of Leander, and his spectacular death. While Ann did her best with Helen's questions, Hubert was silent, an increasingly intense expression stealing over his face.

"I'm starting to remember this chap," he said. "He and Mother were great friends . . . kindred spirits, you might say. She was very cheerful when he was around . . . rather wild and irresponsible, I suppose."

Ann gazed at him speculatively. "This blood group business," she said to Helen. "Can two ABs produce an AB?"

Helen consulted the small notebook into which she had copied the table from the encyclopaedia. "Yes," she said.

"It's very funny," Ann said hesitantly.

"But?" Helen urged.

"Steven was AB," Ann said. "So are Giles and Oliver. Leander was, too . . . and Amelia . . . she was a regular donor."

"You think AB is a Hawksworth feature?" Helen asked.

"We must *not* jump to conclusions," Hubert said quietly.

528

They talked all afternoon. Although there was every chance that Elsie might have been able to help them, Ann baulked at involving her. Instead, Hubert said he would make inquiries about the inquest that must have followed Peter Hawksworth's death.

News of Giles's departure from Latimer's Barn spread through the racing fraternity and the country houses of southern England like wildfire. Tongues, some of them vicious, were busy. Curiously enough, it was Giles who received the sympathy, allied to an expectation that he would prosper, whereas Latimer's Barn was deemed to be on the way to ruin. Indifferent to the criticism of her that was implied in the stories, Bess shared Gideon's view that they stemmed from rumours that some of the Trustees had been treated shabbily. From mid-April when the first runner went out, Bess set about demolishing the gossip and conjecture.

Long before the end of the season, when her tally of one hundred and forty-four winners was the highest attained by an English trainer since the vastly different days of the 1840s, Bess's detractors had been rendered speechless. Included in her all-conquering progress were successes that gave Giles a flying start to his career as Sam Montgomery's racing manager. Vladivostock, the 1978 Dewhurst Stakes winner, did the business in both the Two Thousand Guineas and the Derby, while two more of Sam's Latimer's Barn horses took good races at Royal Ascot.

"This is terrific stuff for the scandal-mongers," Gideon told Bess. "I wonder what they'll make of it?"

"Do not tempt me into a frank suggestion!" Bess glowered.

There was no shortage of incident and spectacle to keep the tongues wagging. To make up for the horses that a furious Freddie Christopherson had removed from the stable, Bess took ten more of Sam Montgomery's. As if to dance on the grave of whispers about savage disagreements, Bess and Giles were frequently seen chatting together at race meetings. Moreover, when Jane was present, she and Bess were obviously warming to each other: there was little chance of the two women becoming true friends, but they learned to enjoy each other's company.

Most fascinating of all, however, were the things that happened away from public scrutiny.

On the evening of the dramatic January meeting, Bess told Gideon that she intended making Latimer's Barn the most famous racing stable in the world.

"Isn't it that already?" he asked, pretending surprise.

"It's had its moments, but the game's changing and we need to go with it," Bess replied. "British racing has been wrapped in cotton-wool for too long . . . international competition is coming."

"And what are you going to do about it?" Gideon asked.

"Beat the buggers on their own ground!" Bess grinned.

The number of horses that went to race in France was stepped up sharply. Ireland became a regular destination, and, at the age of sixty, Jimmy Farrant found his way to Italy, returning from his first trip to Milan with a Group One scalp on his belt.

Bess's methods were straightforward and intensely demanding: she worked a fourteen-hour day, running everyone ragged while she was about it. The Fund was called on for substantial investment, providing two new horse transporters, a swimming-pool for the horses and structural changes to the yards to make work in them easier. John Flamsteed, the long-suffering Treasurer, felt light-headed when he saw how much five furlongs of all-weather gallop was going to cost, and had to sit down for a few minutes at the discovery that Bess wanted *two* of them.

It was all done with tremendous vigour and panache, providing great entertainment for Gideon.

"Do you know, I'll bet that this is how a top-flight medieval despot used to operate," he said to Amaryllis one day as they watched Bess setting yet another part of the world to rights. "Pretty impressive, isn't it?"

"Oh, yes," Amaryllis replied. "She's changed."

It was perfectly true. During her earlier period in charge

of Latimer's Barn, Bess was always forceful and demanding as far as the work of the stable was concerned, but expected nothing for herself. Now, she made it plain that her life was to be conducted with considerable style.

Elsie's retirement gave the first indication of the way ahead. She decided that it was time to put her feet up when she discovered that Bess had radical ideas on the way The House should be run.

"I know you, my girl," Elsie said. "I've seen this coming for ages. It's going to be all hours that God sends and you're going to want fancy stuff. Me and Stan's going to pack it in!" Immensely proud of Bess, she was perfectly good-natured about it.

"You've earned it," Bess said. "You'll both be entitled to good pensions."

In fact, when Elsie discovered what forty years of working in Cannings Ambo had earned her, she was at a loss for words.

"We shan't know what to do with it all," she gasped.

"Don't get any ideas about spending it on Steven," Bess said sternly. "He's coming along quite well and I'm not having you spoiling him."

Apprehensive at the prospect of Polly Izzard feeling offended at not being offered Elsie's job, Bess discovered that she was to have an unexpectedly free hand. Although only fifty-six, Polly asked about early retirement.

"I've always wanted to see a bit of the world," she told Bess. "They say Cornwall is very nice. If I could take my pension now, I've a mind to start travelling."

The search for a new cook was over before Bess had begun to wonder how to tackle it.

The Duke of Laverstoke was in the process of making Eaton Mandeville earn more money. Horrified by the thought of opening the house and park to the public, he had been smitten with an idea from Edmund's wife, Judy.

"Why not host business conferences and seminars?" she suggested. "Big companies would pay the earth to be here for a few days and the west wing wouldn't want much doing to it."

The decision was soon taken, with Hubert and Lisette engaged in a frenzy of activity, including the search for the necessary staff. Valerie Pepperdine, a rosy-cheeked, softly spoken woman, was too late for a job at Eaton Mandeville, but when Hubert recommended that Bess should talk to her, the matter was settled in a very short time. Valerie had a cordon bleu cookery diploma and was ready to move in as soon as a room could be prepared for her. Aged about thirty, she hinted at a miserable love-affair that was now over, and, like so many before her, went ga-ga over Cannings Ambo, even in its winter drabness. Valerie wanted nothing more than to lose herself in the village and was clearly destined to be a great asset.

Henrietta Corbishley, on the other hand, might well have landed from another planet.

"Nothing would please me more than to find her something to do," Hubert said on the telephone. "I think she'd make things go with a real bang. The trouble is, Lisette would sulk for months if I so much as thought of setting her on."

"Why?" Bess asked.

"You'll know when you see her."

"Oh! *Am* I seeing her?"

"Would you, Bess? The thing is, you see, I mentioned that you might be interested, whereupon she went crackers. Apparently one of her ambitions is to work for you."

"God, she must be insane. What am I supposed to do with her, Hubert?"

"I'm sure you'll think of something."

Two days later, Henrietta Corbishley burst into the office like a hurricane. Her opening greeting of: "Hello, Bess, I've always wanted to meet you!" left its recipient open-mouthed. As Bess held out her hand, Henrietta stopped bouncing around for long enough to show that as well as the phenomenal blonde hair and beautiful bone structure, she had astonishingly blue eyes.

"Er . . . perhaps you'd better come into the library," Bess said, acutely conscious of Liz's amusement.

On the way, Henrietta stared round with wide-eyed awe, as though equating her surroundings to the Sistine Chapel.

"Tell me about yourself," Bess said when they were safely away from spectators.

She was twenty-two. Her father, a colonel in the Brigade of Guards, was on secondment to NATO in Brussels; her mother, once an acclaimed Shakespearian actress, had built a second career as the author of detective novels; the elder of her two brothers, a Royal Navy Commander, was an equerry in the Royal Household; the other was at the Foreign Office. After an education that struck Bess as exotic, Henrietta had worked as a personal assistant to the managing director of a public relations company until, much to everyone's surprise, it had gone bankrupt at half past eleven one morning.

"And the police came to take my boss away!" Henrietta said, much aggrieved.

"When was that?" Bess asked.

"Three weeks ago."

"I have to confess that I don't quite see how you could fit in here," Bess said.

"There must be something I could do . . . I know! You're desperate for a social secretary!"

Bess smiled. "That would keep you going for an hour a week."

"Well, it's a start, isn't it? Now, let's see . . . how about a general factotum . . . someone to fetch and carry, shift the dirty knickers out of the way, press your breeches, clean boots, and give the old heave-ho to discarded lovers?"

Bess laughed. "You mean a lady's maid?"

"Exactly. Just the ticket!"

Thinking about it, Bess found that she liked the idea, liked it very much, in fact. "Would *you* be happy with that?" she asked.

"Would I!" Henrietta was rubbing her hands. "Go on, Bess, give it a try, eh?"

"All right. When can you start?"

"Day after tomorrow? Sorry about the delay, but there's an awful lot to sort out."

"I don't think *I* can be ready that quickly," Bess laughed. "Make it a week on Monday."

"You're not trying to put me off?"

"No, Henrietta, I'm not! To be perfectly honest, now you've given me the idea, I'm looking forward to being pampered."

"Marvellous! My friends call me 'Henry', by the way."

They agreed a salary that would have raised John Flamsteed's eyebrows had Bess not intended paying it out of her own pocket, and Henrietta shot off back to London to prepare for what she thought of as a terrific whizz.

Bess set on two girls from the village as maids, one to help Valerie in the kitchen, the other to keep the house clean and look after Ann. She also brought in a second travelling head lad: he was needed to look after English racing when Jimmy Farrant was busy in Europe.

In 1949, Mr and Mrs Howard Steele of Walthamstow had proudly named their first son Winston Spencer. Thirty years later, the mature man was very happy to be known by the nickname of 'Stainless', first given to him when he began his apprenticeship at the Newmarket stable from which Bess poached him. Even his wife, Mary, always called him Stainless. As a teacher, she too was invaluable, and was soon helping Eileen at the school.

For over two months, The House was in chaos and uproar as builders, plumbers and decorators roamed all over it. The kitchen was gutted and re-equipped to the standard hesitantly suggested by Valerie Pepperdine; a new central-heating system was fitted; Valerie was given a self-contained flat on the ground floor, while mayhem reigned upstairs as a palatial maze of interconnecting rooms was created for Bess, Steven and Henrietta. Pride of place went to a walk-in wardrobe nearly twenty-feet square, the door of which was directly opposite Bess's new bathroom.

"There you are," Bess said to Henrietta when all the hanging rails and shelves were in place. "Get cracking on that."

"Mistress of the wardrobe," Henrietta chortled. "What a hoot!"

534

She had already established the principle that there was no limit to her duties. Given a vague idea of what was wanted, she went to Farquharson's of Bath to buy Bess's clothes. She looked after Steven as though he were a cherished younger brother. When Bess gave a special lunch- or dinner-party, Henrietta waited on table, serving Valerie's delicious offerings with a gusto that invariably produced bemused admiration from the guests. And, having seen Steven off to school, she rode out with the second lot each morning, keeping an eye on Bess. Henrietta's talents were endless: the harsh regime that Bess imposed on herself often gave rise to aches and pains. Using an embrocation invented by her Uncle Grosvenor, with the odour of French polish and aviation spirit, Henrietta massaged the offending twinges away in minutes.

She also spent much of May scouring Wiltshire and adjoining counties in search of the present Bess had decided to buy herself for her fortieth birthday on 1 June. For what she referred to as her 'official duties', she had already acquired a dark-blue Daimler Sovereign motor car. Now, after a long period of silent craving, Bess was going to have a Jaguar XJ-S. It had to be finished in classic British racing green and have beige upholstery. And she was not keen on being part of a waiting-list; it must be available on 31 May so that she could drive it on her birthday.

After several false starts, Henrietta found a dealer in Bristol who was an ardent follower of racing and had friends in high places in the Jaguar plant at Coventry. For Bess Hawksworth of Latimer's Barn, anything was possible, and the glorious machine was delivered to The House on the appointed day.

"That's something else she's got right," Gideon said approvingly as he and Henrietta watched Bess set off on the maiden voyage, accompanied by Amaryllis. "That is most definitely her to a T."

"She's usually pretty good at these things," Henrietta replied, sounding for all the world as though her experience extended over many years, rather than a few months.

A week after the racing season ended, with Bess as champion

535

trainer, the village put on a great show of bringing a happy, much-welcomed surprise to fruition.

Although no one ever went so far as to express open criticism, the persistent bachelordom of the Reverend Robert Frobisher did cause concern. Ann, Julia Flamsteed and Eileen Collier were the leaders of a group who thought there was something wilful in Robert's single state. Then, towards the end of the summer, he presented his fiancée to Cannings Ambo.

Caroline Turnbull had returned to England only a few weeks before, after working for six years with Christian Aid in Zaire and the Central African Republic. Based in Salisbury and seconded to a diocesan committee on which Robert also served, she found herself proposed to a fortnight after their first meeting. The third time that Robert popped the question, five weeks later, she accepted him. At twenty-eight, she was seventeen years younger than her delighted husband-to-be.

An old friend from Robert's college days, now an arch-deacon at York, came to perform the marriage in Robert's own church on a pleasant Saturday in November. Afterwards, the couple were afforded the honour of a reception in one of Wm Flamsteed & Sons' workshops.

"I'm not entirely certain, my darling," Robert whispered to Caroline, "but I think this is the first time it's ever been done for anyone outside the family."

"I shall do my best to show appreciation," Caroline said, determined not to be overawed.

Ann, entranced by the occasion, was more relaxed than she had been for most of the year as Bess gave her a lift back to The House in the Jaguar when it was all over. After making a few complimentary remarks about Caroline and Robert, she said, "Isn't it a relief that Giles is doing so well?"

"Very good," Bess agreed.

"I believe the divorce is settled?" Ann asked tentatively.

"Yes, all wrapped up."

"Giles and Jane plan to marry in January, I think," Ann said.

536

"I know. The idiots have invited me!" Bess thought it very droll.

When Bess drew up at the side door of The House, Ann looked at her, clearly wanting to ask a question. Bess smiled and nodded encouragement.

"There's been something puzzling me since January," Ann said.

"Go on."

"What made you change your mind about staying here? Until the day before that dreadful meeting, we were all sure that you were determined to go."

"I was!" Bess stared fixedly ahead, her fingertips resting on the steering wheel. "It was Steven and Leander," she said.

"What happened?" Ann sounded excited, half-expecting a great revelation.

"Nothing. I watched them together when they came home from school. That's all."

And with that, mystifying though it was, Ann knew she had to be content.

CHAPTER 20

1980

'Do you know why we had to take it in turns?'

After being virtually a recluse in the Dower House at Eaton Mandeville for nearly twelve months, Rachel left on 4 January to live in the Channel Islands. Even while Hubert was raking together the £400,000 necessary to buy her a decent house and provide an income for life, she remained taciturn and ill-humoured.

When Hubert left her at Bristol airport, he forced her to answer the question.

"Yes," she said with a flourish of defiance. "Peter was Helen's father. I loved him!"

In the days that followed, the housekeeper and handyman who had gone into exile with her realised that they were going to be coping with a cantankerous, embittered old woman.

In 1980, both Hubert and Richard Mallender reduced the number of horses they had in training. Hubert, dangerously stretched after financing his mother's move to Jersey, decided that two years of prudence were necessary. Richard had simply forgotten. At the time when he should have been concerning himself with yearlings, he was on a three-month cruise round the world with Elisabeth. After selling her shares to Gideon for a very substantial sum, they had soon grown tired of watching Adrian Mallender squirm. They married and were making a serious professional job of enjoying themselves.

538

The question of the empty boxes was solved at once by Giles, who was always willing to grab extra space at Sam Montgomery's favourite stable. Superficially, there was nothing wrong with having nearly forty of Sam's horses, especially since most of them were good sorts who won more races than Bess demanded as the standard. Even so, she was uneasy: having a third of the yard devoted to a single owner was dangerously close to putting too many eggs in one basket.

At the end of May, as Sam's filly, Horninglow, winner of the One Thousand Guineas, was receiving her final preparations for the Oaks, Bess received an amazing letter from the president of a bank in Zurich. Couched in language that was almost certainly a pedantically accurate translation from a German or French draft, it begged to have the honour of inquiring whether Mrs Hawksworth would be prepared to undertake the training of horses for an Arab prince.

She telephoned Hubert. "I've had a letter from an organisation calling itself Fraunhofer and Pichet Frères," she said.

"Have you, by God!" He was obviously impressed.

"Are they all right?" Bess asked.

"The very best."

"And quite sane?"

"Good gracious, yes! Why?"

"They're asking if I'll train horses for some tin-pot Arab potentate."

"Is this letter from a chap called Hans Eberhard?"

"It is. Tell me all."

"Among other things, Fraunhofer and Pichet specialise in looking after Middle-Eastern gentlemen who want to hide vast quantities of petro-dollars. Some of these people prefer to remain as invisible and anonymous as possible, so Fraunhofer and Pichet offer the complete nursemaid service, usually handled by old Eberhard himself. It's rather like the old-fashioned man of affairs who dealt with everything from the laundry bills and servants' wages to outraged fathers. Presumably he doesn't mention his client's name?"

"Oh, no, it's all wonderfully vague. What should I do?"

"If you want the man's custom, write back and say so. The Arabs are supposed to be good chaps. Sheikh Thingey is very highly regarded at Newmarket."

Bess and Liz, egged on by Henrietta, concocted a suitable reply to Herr Eberhard.

Although things moved fairly quickly, it seemed that a great deal had to happen, not least of which was an assessment of Latimer's Barn and the village by two security consultants. They were the toughest pair Bess had ever seen, and she was happy to leave them to Henrietta, who was unashamedly enthralled by them.

"They were head-bangers!" Bess exclaimed, greeting Henrietta with relief when she returned after six hours with the two men.

"One of them was," Henrietta agreed. "He was the dark one . . . ex-SAS and not a bit nice. The other was ordinary Army and quite sweet."

"What the hell were they looking for?" Bess asked.

"Deciding how easy it would be for someone to do the Prince a mischief while he was here. It seems that at least three lots of tearaways want his head on a plate."

"I see." Bess sank into a chair. "And what conclusion did they reach?"

"We're not at all bad," Henrietta replied brightly. "Our Prince will only need two guards when he condescends to visit."

"Do you know, Henry, I'm bloody glad about that!" Bess said with wasted irony.

But Bess's intelligence service proved fairly effective, too. By the time His Royal Highness Prince Omar bin Khalid al-Melhem turned up at Latimer's Barn for lunch on a quiet Thursday near the end of June, Hubert and Gideon had unearthed a great deal about him.

The youngest of four sons of a desert kingdom, he was allegedly on permanently bad terms with his father. Whereas King Abdul Aziz found both pleasure and profit in playing America off against anyone who was fool enough to join in the game, an Oxford education had made Prince Omar a vociferously enthusiastic Anglophile. His two years as a member of the ruling body of OPEC was ruinous to his father's devious foreign policy: there was no question of allowing him home, nor did he want to return, finding the way his family behaved in their own country tyrannical and hypocritical. When a vacancy was created for him with the United Nations Disaster Relief Organisation in Geneva, everyone was delighted. Prince Omar had lived in Switzerland for five years, never going home, not even for his family's annual visit to Mecca during Ramadan. He was thirty.

He was also, Bess discovered as she waited for him to get out of the Mercedes, tall, strong and devilishly handsome. His voice came as a total surprise. "Good morning, Mrs Hawksworth, it is very good of you to allow me to visit you," was delivered in the flawless tone of an Oxford senior common room.

"Good morning, Your Royal Highness," Bess said confidently, glancing less happily at the two men remaining in the car. The driver was an Arab who was clearly not to be argued with, the other was Henrietta's 'ordinary Army' man.

"Perhaps they could look round until they have lunch with your servants," Prince Omar suggested. Bess agreed, leaving one of the maids to deal with the bodyguards while she showed the Prince into The House.

He stopped to examine and admire the gallery of photographs along the main corridor, smiling at a group from the early years of the century. "Ah, the great Leander Hawksworth!" he said.

"Your Royal Highness is very well-informed," Bess replied.

"I have to be, Mrs Hawksworth, otherwise I would probably not have lived this long. And please call me 'Omar'. We are going to be friends."

Gazing into his dark eyes, Bess felt light-headed.

She introduced Henrietta to Prince Omar and it was plain that they were very much taken with one another. Recovering from the mild disappointment of finding him wearing a five-hundred-pound suit instead of keffiyeh and flowing robes, Henrietta made no bones about being entranced by the Arab. For his part, Prince Omar was mentally stripping Henrietta: Bess found that she was jealous.

As they ate, the conversation remained superficial until they were well into Valerie Pepperdine's superb main course and Omar yielded to Henrietta's offer of wine.

"You don't observe your country's customs?" Bess asked.

"Few of my sort do when they are outside it," he replied.

"And you never go inside?"

"Correct." He smiled. "Everyone is very happy with this, especially my brothers. It leaves them free to plot against my father without worrying about me."

"Isn't your part of the world rather unstable?" Bess asked bluntly.

He nodded. "Totally! Weakness and greed are the dominant factors. Think of all that oil and you understand the stakes."

"Presumably Ayatollah Khomeini doesn't help?"

"Far from it! There is, of course, going to be a war. Iraq is spoiling for it . . . they will trump up an excuse connected with the Shatt-al-Arab waterway. The reality is that Saddam Hussein can't bear the thought of Khomeini being on top of the dunghill. My country will remain neutral and increase its output of oil."

After that, their talk became inconsequential again until, to Henrietta's chagrin, they retreated to the library for coffee. Bess decided that the time had come for business.

"Do you own any horses already, Omar?"

"No."

"Why do you want me to train for you?"

"I would like to win the Derby. My spies tell me that you are the person to do it."

She laughed. "I must warn you that it can be an expensive game. I'm sure you . . ."

"Please!" He took a sheet of paper from an inside pocket. "Read this."

The note, dated three days previously, was from Hans Eberhard of Fraunhofer and Pichet Frères. Addressed to her personally, it was an assurance that Prince Omar was good for two hundred million US dollars.

"Good grief!" Bess whispered. "I'm sorry, Omar, I should have realised."

"Think nothing of it. As you can see, Mrs Hawksworth, I have been quite ruthless in feathering my own nest."

Bess pulled herself together. "I'll start you off next year," she said. "I can offer you facilities for twenty horses if you want them."

"Thank you, Mrs Hawksworth. I shall give that very careful consideration."

Bess had to make do with that.

Horninglow made a splendid job of winning the Oaks on a fine afternoon when Giles and Jane looked very happy together.

"Doesn't that get up your nose?" Sam Montgomery asked Bess as they looked on from a distance that put them out of earshot.

"No!" she replied firmly.

"Not even a little bit?" Sam teased.

"Not even a little bit," she told him. "The stable and I couldn't do anything for him, why shouldn't someone else succeed? Good luck to them."

"You're a remarkable woman, Bess. If it weren't for my dear wife, I'd . . ." Seeing the look in her eye, he changed tack abruptly. "Have we got anything good for Ascot?"

"There's a couple of yours that *might* turn up trumps," she said with her customary caution.

They, together with a filly belonging to Alain de Mourville and two of Gideon's colts, duly did. Liz had been rooting around for months, compiling an archive of every winner ever produced; she was certain that somewhere among the batch of successes was the five-hundredth winner that Latimer's Barn had sent to Royal Ascot. Bess was inordinately proud of the fact, making sure that it came across in a television interview she gave on the last day of the meeting: it was something to stop her worrying about what Prince Omar was up to.

He telephoned one evening at the end of June. After fifteen minutes of hearing what a marvellous time he was having in Geneva, Bess was spitting and remained in a bad mood for days. When, a month later, he rang up again, she was ready to bite his head off, only to be disarmed immediately. If Bess would let him stay at Latimer's Barn on the night of 6 August, he would watch the horses work the following morning and make his final decision.

He arrived at the appointed time of six o'clock in the evening. Although Henrietta was able to give him the full benefit of her undivided attention from the instant he got out of the car and smiled at her, Bess was preoccupied with something else.

Seven hours earlier, Oliver had turned up, completely out of the blue, without any advance notice. From the very start, Ann was annoyed by his attitude.

It began badly. Seeing his intention to stay for at least one night, Ann told him that he would have to sleep somewhere else.

"We can't have you here," she said, agitation making her brusque. "We've got an Arab prince coming and he's manic about security."

"I won't hurt him, Mother," Oliver laughed. "I've resigned from all the terrorist groups, honestly!"

"Don't be silly!" Ann snapped. "Let me think . . . I know . . . Rebecca and William can have you at Louise House."

As luck would have it, Rebecca was in the office and the matter was resolved at once.

"Apart from that, are you glad to see me, Mother?" Oliver asked, still treating the whole thing as a joke.

"Of course. Why can't you warn people you're coming?"

Oliver ignored the complaint. "What's the Sheikh of Araby doing here?"

"He wants Bess to train some horses for him."

Bess did not appear for lunch. After the second lot, she

dashed upstairs, showered and changed into the clothes Henrietta had waiting. Then she tore off to Bath for the two o'clock and two-thirty races. Never keen on Oliver after his remarks at her wedding, she rebuffed his attempt to be friendly with a very curt greeting. Rebecca, eager for any news Oliver might have, joined him and Ann for a meal.

In general, he was expansive about his work and life-style. As a partner in a leading advertising agency, he worked hard, reaped rich rewards, and enjoyed them to the full. At first, his description of the firm sounded glowing; gradually, however, Ann's attention was drawn to the disparagement that began to show through. There were hints about lost chances, creative cowardice, administrative bungling; and it seemed that some people thought Oliver should strike out on his own.

Rebecca's customary question about the possibility of marriage received the standard reply.

"There's plenty of time for that!"

"Don't you believe it," she replied. "You're thirty-four. You'll be fifty before you know where you are. What happened to that girl from Eastbourne? She was jolly nice."

"She was," Oliver agreed warmly. "A friend of mine noticed it, too, and bundled her off to the altar."

"There you are," Rebecca laughed. "You're an idiot!"

As brother and sister indulged in friendly abuse, Ann watched her son closely. Unable to make up her mind, she decided to ask.

"To what do we owe the pleasure of this visit, Oliver?"

There was a noticeable pause before he answered. "Giles was up in town a couple of weeks ago. We had dinner together."

"I see." Ann's tone was suspicious.

"Look, Mother, there's no point in beating about the bush," Oliver said. "He told me that he'd had money out of the Fund."

"Oh, dear." Ann looked resigned. "That was silly of him."

545

"Half a million," Oliver said.

"It was to cover quite extraordinary circumstances," Ann said.

"Meaning that it will never happen again?"

"Exactly."

"That doesn't seem right," Oliver said, attempting to sound reasonable. "Much as I like Giles, he does get himself into some awful scrapes. Paying out under those conditions seems wrong."

"As a matter of fact, Oliver, I agree with you," Ann replied. "If you must know, it was done at Bess's insistence. She made it a condition of staying on here."

Oliver leaned forward earnestly. "Mother, if I can raise two hundred thousand, I have a marvellous chance to start my own agency."

"No, Oliver!" Ann said resolutely. "I won't even *think* of talking to the Trustees about it."

Never quite catching fire, the argument rumbled on until nearly five o'clock when Rebecca put her foot down, made Oliver shut up and took him to Louise House, scolding him as they went. Although slightly peevish, he remained good-natured; it was Ann who had come close to losing her temper.

When Bess returned from Bath at four o'clock, Ann's annoyance was all too evident in her account of the purpose behind Oliver's visit.

"Out of the question!" was Bess's verdict before she hurried away to be ready for Prince Omar's arrival. After the initial formalities, he seemed content to be left with Henrietta, so Bess took the opportunity to join Rebecca, who was officiating at evening stables. She, too, mentioned Oliver, only to receive shorter shrift than Ann.

"Ridiculous!" Bess retorted and strode off to the next box.

Going back to The House shortly after seven, Bess found it quiet apart from Valerie, busy preparing dinner in her superb new kitchen. Ann was spending the night at Louise House, presumably to talk sense into Oliver. Henrietta, waiting with the bath already half-full, had a belligerent finger wagged at her.

"Do not, under any circumstances whatsoever, mention Oliver Hawksworth," Bess ordered.

Henrietta assumed an expression of total incomprehension. "I've never heard of him," she said. As Bess went into the bathroom and began flinging her clothes off, Henrietta followed her, first to add more water, then to pick up widely scattered garments. She disappeared briefly, returning with a tumbler containing a whisky and soda. Bess grabbed at it eagerly.

"How's HRH?" she asked.

"Even more magnificent than last time," Henrietta said. "He's wearing a dinner-jacket, so I'm giving you a long dress – the ice-blue."

"That makes me look like a bloody vestal autocrat!" Bess protested.

"It suits you perfectly," Henrietta laughed, leaping out of the way of a scrubbing brush hurled with deadly intent.

Bess's dinner with Prince Omar was a strangely unsatisfactory experience. They were all dressed up with nowhere to go and nothing to talk about. Omar was intent on a recitation of the social and political intrigues involved in the United Nations circuit in Geneva, all of which seemed deadly dull to Bess. Henrietta, constantly flitting in and out of the dining-room to serve them, came to the conclusion that Bess's boredom was exacerbated by tiredness after a more than usually hectic day.

"Are you sure you want coffee?" Henrietta asked at the end of the meal. "I think you need an early night and this stuff isn't good for you."

Omar laughed at the expression on Bess's face. "Don't worry, Mrs Hawksworth, I have also had an exhausting day," he said. "And at what unearthly hour do I have to be up in the morning?"

"If you want to see *everything*, we should be outside at six o'clock," Bess replied.

"In that case, we both need to get some rest."

Looking into Bess's room at ten-fifteen, Henrietta found her fast asleep. After returning the discarded evening dress to the huge, walk-in wardrobe, she popped her head round Steven's door. Satisfied, Henrietta went to the bathroom to check her hair and make-up: she had already undressed and was naked beneath the silk wrap. She slipped out of the main door of the suite and padded along the corridor to Prince Omar's room at the other end of The House. Confidently, not bothering to knock, she went in.

Woken as usual at five-fifteen by Henrietta with a cup of tea, Bess was refreshed and full of beans.

"Today is most definitely *the* day," she said. "Our desert prince will make his mind up, or I'll know the reason why."

"Hazarding a rough guess, purely off the top of my head, I'd say that you'll find him completely amenable," Henrietta said. It was a cryptic clue to her return to their suite only ten minutes before it was time to wake Bess.

Prince Omar was waiting downstairs in the hall. "Good morning, Omar," Bess said. "My word, you do look the part." His riding clothes must have cost a fortune, she thought.

They found the yards coming to life, although some of the lads and horses looked bleary-eyed. After introducing a sense of purpose with a few pithy words, Bess took the Prince to the 1840 ten-box stable-block to supervise his choice of hack. He rode well, if slightly rigidly, not quite trusting the strange horse.

He watched intently, saving his comments until they were having breakfast after the first lot. "I'm impressed, Mrs Hawksworth. You make it seem so easy. There aren't many people who can control sixty highly strung animals like that."

"Perhaps I have a knack," she said flippantly.

"There's a substantial body of opinion that agrees with that proposition," he said with tongue-in-cheek gravitas.

Included in the second lot were eighteen two-year-olds who had yet to race. Once they were out on the wide spaces of

Cannings Down, Bess detached them from the main group and instructed them to trot and canter as far as the stud, then walk back along the Devizes Lane. Stainless Steele was in charge of them and Leander, revelling in the school holidays, was up on a nice-looking chestnut filly.

"What's special about them?" Prince Omar asked.

"They're the ones that are timid and have been slow to learn," Bess replied.

"Timid?" His eyebrows rose.

"Horses are exactly the same as us, Omar. Some animals find it all a bit too much: they'd much rather stay in a nice paddock with their friends, so we have to treat them tenderly. They'll all be racing within the next six weeks, never fear!"

"Mrs Hawksworth, with you around, I feel no inclination whatsoever to fear!"

All thirty horses that were left after the detachment of the two-year-olds had worked hard the previous day, so Bess gave them nothing more strenuous than a few furlongs of light cantering. By eleven-fifteen, they were back in the yard, Bess was satisfied that everything was to her liking and she began to stroll back to The House with Prince Omar. They followed the Roadway, Omar paying careful attention as Bess elaborated on her ideas for bringing on a shy horse. When they reached the gravel turning-circle in front of The House, Bess halted.

"Oh dear!" she muttered.

Ann and Oliver were standing by his car, engaged in heated argument. Ominously, John Flamsteed was with them. Bess assumed, correctly, that he had been brought in as Treasurer of the Fund to reiterate the impossibility of Oliver's demands. It looked bad. Having slept on it, Oliver had woken in a foul temper and renewed his claim with virulent energy.

"A family row," Bess told Prince Omar.

"It looks very tame compared to my lot," he replied, tactfully turning his back on the scene.

Bess was about to guide the Prince towards the side entrance of The House when Oliver exploded into a final tirade of abuse. Telling his mother and John to go to hell, he flung himself into his car, starting the engine as he slammed

549

the door. It was a powerful, high-performance BMW; under the influence of Oliver's fury, it made a spectacular start, spraying gravel as the wheels spun.

"Ah . . . that seems to be the end of that," Omar said.

"Yes, thank God!"

In an horrific fraction of a second, Bess's relief vanished. Before the noise of the abused BMW had blotted everything else out, she had heard horses in the drive: the two-year-olds were coming back from Cannings St John, invisible behind the screen of poplars in full leaf. And they had sounded close. Trying to head Oliver off, Bess ran towards the car, waving her arms and shouting. In the frenzied heat of the moment, Oliver somehow found time to stick two fingers up at her.

Bess followed him. Ann, John and Prince Omar looked on in amazement, Omar full of admiration for her fitness. They only heard what happened: Bess saw it.

The horses, in pairs, were twenty yards from the point at which Oliver emerged, travelling at forty miles an hour. He had no chance of stopping. Thinking about it afterwards, Bess deduced that blind panic probably delayed his attempts to do so.

Both the leading horses were killed at once. Miraculously, one of the following pair shied away through the poplars with the lad still more or less in control. The other was knocked sideways by a glancing blow from the left-hand side of the car. The next pair escaped, both throwing their riders and barging into trees in the process. Terror had now spread all along the line. Riders were on the ground, rearing animals were kicking each other. Before the BMW finally swerved into a poplar tree, three more horses had been brought down.

Astoundingly, Prince Omar's bodyguards were first on the scene. It was as if they had dropped out of the trees. The Arab was carrying Leander, who was in a dead faint, to safety; the other had got hold of two horses, both of whom looked to be sound.

Ann, John and Prince Omar were horrified at what they found. None of the horses were still mounted; eight lay on the ground, all but the two that were already dead showing terrible signs of distress; three had bolted, seven were being restrained with varying degrees of success. In addition to Leander, eight lads were down and hurt, the others dazed. Stainless, back on his feet, was running to the yards for help.

Seeing that Oliver was still in the car, apparently slumped over the steering wheel, Ann broke into hysterical sobbing. She stopped, whimpering with joy as he shook himself and climbed out. Dashing to him with open arms in the automatic reaction of a mother, Ann halted in her tracks when she saw the look on Bess's face.

"Get him out of my sight before I kill the bastard!" Bess said, her voice quivering with a wrath that sounded truly murderous.

As Prince Omar helped Ann lead Oliver back towards The House, Bess fell to her knees beside a colt called Saint Aidan. Gideon had named him after the man who founded the monastery on Lindisfarne: the Derby winner of that name was his sire. He had needed a great deal of special attention, largely because of his fear of starting stalls. Bess and Arthur Merriweather had spent hours with him and he was very nearly ready. Believing him to be the best of all the juveniles, Bess had entered him for the Royal Lodge Stakes at Ascot and the Dewhurst. But all that was gone now: the blood pumping from the poor creature's nose could only be stemming from the most grievous internal injuries.

For a while, tears and a jangling cacophony in her ears isolated Bess from her surroundings. She was unaware that her brother, Joe, was hurrying up the drive with his black bag, that the thirty lads not involved in the disaster were on their way, or that Henrietta had arrived, pointlessly but bravely clutching the first-aid box from the bathroom cabinet.

Not until Eleanor came did Bess return to something like normal. Assisted by Stainless, Eleanor had brought the grimmest tools of her trade as well as the beautiful oak medicine chest made for her by two apprentices at Wm Flamsteed & Sons.

Nearly six hours later, Henrietta guided Bess into the kitchen and forced her gently into a chair. Valerie Pepperdine, grimly silent, placed a huge mug of tea in front of her: after Henrietta had laced it with whisky from a hip-flask, Bess drank with greedy desperation. Her face streaked with sweat and dirt, her cream breeches irredeemably stained, she looked at the end of her tether.

Ann could not have chosen a more inopportune moment to make the worst error of judgement of her life.

Aware that Bess had come in, she persuaded Oliver that he should attempt to apologise. When they entered the kitchen from the library, Bess gave them both a baleful stare.

"Bess, you mustn't be too hard on Oliver," Ann said. "It *was* an accident, you know."

There was a moment's silence that made Valerie catch her breath in fear: then Bess erupted into incandescent anger.

"Ann, your blasted son has killed nine horses. Yes, *nine*!" She studied the looks on their faces: they had been expecting far fewer. "Nine!" she repeated. "He made a good clean job of two . . . they couldn't have felt very much at all. Eleanor and I had to put the other seven down. Do you know why we had to take it in turns? Because it was too upsetting, even for hard bitches like us! One of them was in Amos Atkins's back garden down in Church Marks . . . he'd smashed both front legs. And that's not the end of it. Leander has a broken arm. She's being bloody brave about it but Steven is on the verge of a breakdown. Caesar and Finbar O'Flanagan are in hospital with concussion, Spider Mackay's got a broken leg and . . ." her voice rose to a terrifying crescendo ". . . Michael Pilgrim's lost two fingers. Remember Michael, do you? He used to ride all our winners. He helps me out three mornings a week and he's been wonderful with a couple of nervous fillies. And what happens?" She glared pure venom at Oliver. "Death and injury because poor little Oliver has a tantrum. The nasty people wouldn't give him two hundred grand when he wants it and he drives off like a maniac. Don't you *ever* try to tell me that was an accident!"

Oliver, unable to face any more, left the kitchen. Without

any idea of what to do, Ann stayed. She took the full force of the next blast.

"That was the most dreadful and *wicked* thing, Ann. Don't be surprised if it's done for me . . . I can tell you here and now, I've more than half a mind to clear off and leave you to it." She paused, looking at the clock: the time was five-thirty. "Why aren't Gideon and Amaryllis here? Haven't they been told yet?"

"No," Ann said wretchedly.

"I suggest you attend to it," Bess said. "Your version of the story might be easier to stomach than mine." She gulped the last of the tea down. "If you'll excuse me, I'll go back to see how the knacker's men are getting on."

Half-way to the door, she stopped, blinked rapidly and shook her head. "I've only just remembered," she said, quiet and detached now. "What happened to Prince Omar?"

"He had a bit of lunch and left," Henrietta replied. "He felt you had more than enough on your hands without bothering about him."

Bess's overwrought mind latched on to a minor detail. "How did he get out?" The drive had, of course, been blocked all afternoon.

"They went across the field to the Extension," Henrietta said.

"I don't suppose he said anything?"

"No."

Bess shrugged. "Too polite, of course. No one with any sense would send horses here . . . look what happens to them." With a last look at Ann, she was gone.

By half past six, the drive was clear, but for Oliver's car. Alone together after the knacker's van had gone on its last trip, Bess and Arthur Merriweather studied it.

The front of the vehicle was badly damaged by the final impact with the poplar tree, much of the bodywork was battered and dented.

"I reckon that's a write-off," Arthur said.

Bess made no comment.

553

They walked to the yards where normal evening stables activity had been suspended in favour of getting the horses settled: Bess could sense the unrest among them. They knew that something totally dreadful had happened.

The nine survivors of the string mown down by Oliver had been moved to a corner of the 1933 yard. After half an hour with them, Bess and Arthur came to the conclusion that they were as well as could be expected.

"Most of the lads have volunteered for night duty," Arthur said. "It'll help if there's someone near them."

"That's very decent of them," Bess replied. "Let them know how much I appreciate it. I don't think you'll see me again today, Arthur."

"If you don't mind me saying so, ma'am, you look fit to drop," Arthur said.

"I feel it." She paused. "How the hell are we supposed to get over a thing like this, Arthur?"

He shook his head. "I'll let you know if I ever find out."

After leaving him, Bess made her way to Louise House where Rebecca and William, greeting her sombrely, refrained from commenting on her condition.

"How are they?" Bess asked.

"Not too bad, *now*. Go and see for yourself."

Bess went upstairs and into Leander's bedroom. Leander herself was propped up in bed, possibly, Bess thought, rather proud of her plastered left arm.

"Hello, you two," Bess said with a cheerfulness that she knew must have sounded forced. "How are things?"

"Not bad, thank you, Aunt Bess," Leander said. Steven nodded agreement.

"How's the arm?" Bess asked.

"A bit painful, but Doctor Joe has made a very good job of fixing it," Leander said, dreadfully serious. "He showed me the X-rays, you know."

"You'll be better tomorrow," Bess promised.

"Yes, the shock will have worn off by then. What's going to happen to Uncle Oliver?"

"I haven't had time to think about it yet, darling," Bess said, smiling wearily.

"I hope it's something very, very bad," Leander said.

They talked for a long time, Bess grateful that Leander had the sense not to ask what the final tally of death and damage was. When Rebecca came up to suggest that they should be thinking of rest, Steven told Bess of his plans.

"I'm staying here until Lea's better," he said. He pronounced the shortened version of her name, which he alone was allowed to use, as the distinctly two-syllable 'Le-ah'. No one knew it, but that was what the first William Flamsteed had always called his sister.

Bess saw the camp bed in the corner and the bag of clothes that she presumed Henrietta had brought across. "He won't be a nuisance, will he?" Bess asked Rebecca.

"Of course not," was the smiling response.

Bess kissed the children and went back downstairs. Realising that she did not want to stay, Rebecca opened the front door, saying: "Business as usual tomorrow?"

"We'll have a go," Bess replied.

The following morning, the mauling that Bess gave Oliver during the rest-break between first and second lots was common knowledge ten minutes after it happened. Half the lads, queuing up outside the office for their pay-packets, heard it: some of them actually saw Bess soon after she had finished and swore that she looked fit to kill.

What it boiled down to was that she had no intention of making a claim on the stable's insurance for the value of the dead horses. Nor, if they were guided by her, would owners expect their own individual policies to pay up. Instead, she intended to sue Oliver for a sum rumoured to be a quarter of a million pounds.

The story was not in the least far-fetched. That afternoon, Bess was seen marching into a solicitor's office in Marlborough: while she was away, the Trustees were in a huddle at Rose House. To cap it all, there was the widespread belief that Oliver could afford it.

At four o'clock, after Bess had paid a flying visit to Rose House, Oliver was driven to Swindon to catch a London train. Soon afterwards, a scrap-merchant removed Oliver's car from the drive with distinct lack of respect: he let it be known that he was acting on Bess's instructions, not those of the owner.

Helen, who was staying overnight at Rose House, went to The House to see Bess at about seven o'clock.

"Hubert would prefer that you backed off," Helen said. "He thinks that the newspapers have got more than enough to keep them going without making them a gift of the dirty washing. Besides, he doesn't see any point in ruining Oliver and turning him into a potential enemy."

"What about Gideon?" Bess asked.

"He's eating fire! He thinks you're right. To be frank, Bess, I offered to have a go at negotiating a compromise."

They talked round the issue for ten minutes, Bess appearing to pay lip-service to Hubert's view while making it plain that she had no intention of reducing her demands.

"Think about it some more," Helen urged. "I'm on your side, but I can see what Hubert means. We were lucky to avoid a damned great scandal over that stunt Mother and Freddie tried to pull last year." After a pause, she added, "Bloody Hawksworths!"

Bess looked at her intently. Although that final remark had been delivered with considerable anger, Helen was deeply upset, possibly on the brink of tears.

"What's wrong, Helen?" Bess asked. "Come on, tell me."

For a moment, Helen had the look of a cornered animal: Bess half-expected her to leap up and dash from the room.

"You mustn't let anyone know I've told you," she said. "Hubert wants it kept *completely* secret."

Bess was careful to conceal the upsurge in her curiosity. "I won't breathe a word," she promised.

"What about your maid?" Helen asked, looking in the direction of the noises coming from the small kitchen.

"Henry's trustworthy, otherwise she wouldn't be here,"

Bess said. To reassure Helen, she closed the sitting-room door.

Stumbling over the sequence in which she presented the facts, Helen related the process by which she had discovered that Peter Hawksworth was her father. Bess sat silent and still, dumbfounded.

"So you see," Helen concluded. "I'm more Hawksworth than any of them . . . *and* I've got bad blood! Everyone knows about Peter, spying for the Nazis and all that, and his father was an utter rogue, as well. Grandmother Clem always thought he was behind the nineteen-o-nine doping scandal." She laughed bitterly. "Actually, she *wasn't* my grandmother, was she? Now we've got Oliver . . . look at him!"

Bess was busy thinking it over. She recalled that Elsie had sometimes hinted at 'goings-on' between Rachel and her cousin Peter: come to think of it, Solstice had dropped one or two hints in the days when they were always travelling to racecourses together.

Unnerved by Bess's silence, Helen seemed to go to pieces. "So you see, for all their achievements, there's a curse on the Hawksworths and I must have more than a fair share of it."

"That's nonsense, Helen," Bess said gently. "You sound as though you've been watching too many bad films."

"I have a good friend in Germany who says the same," Helen replied. "That doesn't stop it preying on my mind, Bess."

"Yes, I can imagine what it must be like. If there ever was anything for you to worry about, don't you think you worked it out of your system a long time ago?"

The delicate reference to her past brought a wan smile to Helen's face. "I'd almost persuaded myself of that," she said. "The thing is, Bess, I'm terrified that it will all come out if you go ahead with this case against Oliver."

There was no reason why it should. However, knowing that this would be no comfort to Helen, Bess refrained from saying so. "I'll think about it carefully," she promised.

Looking at her watch, Helen found it was time she was back at Rose House. After making Bess renew her promise not to reveal anything of their conversation, she fled.

"Lady H looks to be in something of a state," Henrietta said, sauntering into the sitting-room shortly after her departure.

"She has cause to be," Bess replied.

"They're all in a terrific panic over your scheme to castrate Oliver," Henrietta said. "I've been sniffing round." When she continued, she was cautious. "You're not seriously thinking of leaving . . . are you?"

"No, Henry, I'm not. It doesn't fit in with the long-term plan."

"Oh! What plan is this?"

"Mind your own business!" Bess retorted cheerfully. "One thing . . . if I ever did have to leave, I'd take you with me."

"Goodie!" Henrietta rubbed her hands. "Are you eating here, or downstairs?"

"We'll leave the buggers to sweat, Henry. Let's have beans on toast."

Two days later, Bess was working hard at banishing all thoughts of Prince Omar bin Khalid al-Melhem. The idea of training for him had appealed very strongly, but she had to face up to the disappointment of failure.

However, on Sunday afternoon, the most unlikely of times, the surprise arrived.

Bess and Henrietta had been for a walk to Cannings St John and were admiring the flower-beds at the front of The House when they heard a car coming up the drive. Turning, they saw that it was the Mercedes used by Omar on both of his visits, but the only occupant was the Arab bodyguard.

After getting out of the car, he bowed to Bess and presented her with a Perspex case containing fifty orchids. "With the compliments of His Royal Highness," he said. "There is also a letter." After handing it over, he turned to Henrietta with a small, beautifully gift-wrapped package. "Prince Omar wishes you to have a memento of his last visit, Miss Corbishley. He hopes to see you again, soon."

"Er . . . thank you very much." Henrietta blushed and shuffled.

Bess, flabbergasted by the orchids, managed to summon enough presence of mind to ask: "Won't you come inside for some tea?"

"You are kind, madam, but I have many other things to do for His Royal Highness, so I must return to London."

And, without further ado, he did.

"Here, grab these," Bess said, thrusting the Perspex box at Henrietta. "Let's find out what he's got to say for himself."

She wrecked the thick, embossed envelope, then seemed dazed by its contents. Henrietta's impatience was on the point of boiling over before Bess said, "He's sending me twenty horses next season!" No sooner had she spoken than she laid a hand on Henrietta's arm to restrain her. "We're keeping quiet about this," she said. "I don't want anyone to start thinking that Oliver might be *slightly* off the hook. Let's creep upstairs without being seen."

When they were inside their suite of rooms, Henrietta asked to see the letter. As she had expected, Omar made no mention of the accident: he simply waded straight in with an announcement that he intended placing horses at Latimer's Barn. "I like this bit," Henrietta said. " 'I expect you will want me to buy yearlings from your own excellent stud and I am prepared to do that, provided you let me bring in some new blood from Kentucky.' Cheeky, eh?"

"I don't mind," Bess said. "I doubt very much whether we shall have anything like twenty yearlings to sell him . . . I'll have a crafty word with Amaryllis. What do we do with orchids?"

"Put them in water like any other flowers?" Henrietta suggested. "Heaven knows what we use for vases, though. These would look good floating in a soup tureen."

After she had been experimenting in the kitchen for ten minutes, Bess drifted in to inspect progress and ask an innocent-sounding question. "What was your present from HRH?"

"I haven't looked yet. I don't expect it's very much."

There was something hurried and evasive about the reply that alerted Bess. "Come on, let's have a look."

"I'm trying to do something with these orchids," Henrietta complained.

"Never mind that, I want to see what you've got."

Putting a brave face on it, Henrietta produced the small package. Removal of the wrapping-paper revealed a tooled leather case; a complicated emblem was embossed in gold on the lid.

"Open up!" Bess ordered.

Henrietta did so, gaping at what she discovered. Nestling in a bed of satin was a diamond pin.

"Well . . ." Bess was at a loss for a moment or two. "That puts my orchids in their place, doesn't it?"

"Frightful extravagance!" Henrietta muttered. "The silly man's got more money than sense."

"It's nice," Bess said. "Very nice indeed." Taking the pin from its case, she held it up to the light, rotating it so that the jewel caught fire. "That is definitely the genuine article." She fixed it to Henrietta's blouse and stepped back to admire the result. "Yes!"

"I expect I can learn to live with it," Henrietta said bravely. To her great discomfort, she found that Bess was examining her with a searching, speculative look.

"Whatever made him give you that?" Bess asked.

"He's showing off . . . throwing his money around . . . it's his way of tipping the servants."

Bess continued her disconcerting scrutiny. "First thing last Thursday morning, you were confident that Omar would send me some horses," she said.

"That was pure guesswork," Henrietta replied. "I made that perfectly plain at the time."

"Yes, you did. You also bundled me off to bed on Wednesday night . . . all right, I was tired. When you brought my tea on Thursday morning, you weren't dressed." She thought about it. "Henry, you are *always* dressed when you wake me . . . it's part of your 'setting a good example' policy. I think there's something you ought to tell me."

560

Henrietta agreed: the future would be a good deal easier if Bess knew. There were, however, difficulties. "I don't think this comes under the heading of setting a good example," she said in a small voice.

"I'll be the judge of that," Bess said sternly.

"Well . . . the fact is . . . I spent the night with him."

Bess accepted the revelation equably. "How was it arranged? Was it spontaneous combustion or did you fix it up after you'd got rid of me?"

"Neither. It was just after he arrived – while you were doing evening stables with Rebecca."

"What happened?"

"He asked me."

"Just like that?"

"Well . . . yes."

Bess was momentarily nonplussed. "What did he say, exactly?" she wanted to know.

"He told me that he wanted to spend all night making love to me and promised that I would enjoy it," Henrietta said, in a rush of bravado.

"*Bloody* hell!"

Henrietta hastened to clarify a point she thought important. "I did it because I *wanted* to, not to influence him about the horses."

Bess nodded. "And it was a success?"

"Brilliant!" Henrietta grinned. "He's good!"

"Will you be repeating it?"

"I hope so." Misinterpreting the look on Bess's face, Henrietta asked: "Are you cross?"

"No, Henry, not cross . . . flaming jealous, though. I could use a night or two like that!"

Long after Steven returned to The House following Leander's recovery, Bess continued to have nightmares about the events of 7 August. She wrote a pitilessly detailed account of the disaster in the Big Book, hoping that it might bring exorcism. Aware of Bess's disturbed nights, Henrietta realised that the

561

continuing torment played a major part in the treatment Oliver received.

On her own admission, Bess was intransigent. Her starting position was the issue of a writ against Oliver. As the go-between, Helen was told that the sum required to keep it out of court was £400,000: the cost of the horses was increased by £150,000 to cover compensation for injuries, the major share of which was to go to Michael Pilgrim.

Ann, with the nerve-racking task of living under the same roof as Bess, begged for a more lenient line, all to no avail. Happily, the deep bonds of their long-standing alliance reasserted themselves once the bad temper of the immediate aftermath had faded. Although there were times when outsiders might have believed that Ann and Bess were at daggers drawn, they remained good friends, united in their desire to do the best for Latimer's Barn.

Giles had the good sense to keep out of it. In connection with Sam Montgomery's horses, he and Bess spoke to each other several times a week by telephone. Since two of Sam's animals had been among the dead, Giles became one of the first to know of the tragedy. He made sympathetic references to it, but stayed resolutely uninvolved.

It was a difficult time. Bess suffered every bit as much as those on the receiving end of her obdurate stance. Henrietta saw signs of exceptional strain during a three-day visit that Prince Omar made in order to attend to the details of buying yearlings and becoming a registered owner. She correctly attributed Bess's heightened bad temper to frustration at the thought of the excitingly eventful nights that she and Omar were spending together.

At last, as the dismal murk of December closed in, Helen brought good news.

"Hubert is lending Oliver the money," she told Bess. "At least, Stewart's, the bank he works for, is."

"Four hundred thousand?" Bess asked, incredulous.

"I understand that it's secured," Helen said.

"What's he got that's worth four hundred grand?" Bess demanded.

"I think his house is involved," Helen replied.

"Plus a good deal else, I should think," Bess muttered.

As a partner in the firm for which he worked, Oliver had a substantial number of shares. At current market values, they were worth £280,000: Hubert was lending £180,000 against them and £220,000 against the houses that Oliver owned in south London. Purchased in 1974 for a song as flats with sitting tenants, the three properties were now worth about £100,000 each. Had he succeeded in obtaining what he wanted from the Fund, Oliver would have been a wealthy man.

"What must he be earning to service a loan like that?" Helen wondered.

"Quite a lot," Bess said. "It proves I was right to get after him." She sighed wearily, thoroughly fed-up with the whole business. "So long as he pays up and keeps out of my way, I don't give a damn what he earns or does!"

CHAPTER 21

1981

'You're getting famous, Aunt Bess'

February began badly.

"I didn't even know you did the pools!" Bess shouted at Liz when the news broke.

"How can you say that? When we shared the Bungalow, you helped me celebrate that third dividend," Liz bawled, determined not to be intimidated.

Sensing a serious row, Arthur Merriweather sidled out of the office.

Bess did not let a fleeting memory of fifty-two pounds some years ago deter her. "All right, all right . . . but why clear off? Why do I have to suffer just because you've won a bit of money?"

After taking a deep breath, Liz said, "Bess, I've won over *six hundred thousand*," for the umpteenth time.

Bess collapsed into a chair, deflated. "Why go away?" she asked. "There's no need, you know."

"I'm going because I want to live in the sun, in Spain. I happen to believe that this country is going down the pan."

"Spain isn't any better!" Bess said. "The Costas are supposed to be frightful."

"They are," Liz agreed. "And a few miles inland, it's bloody paradise."

"What about your gentleman friend?" Bess asked.

"He's coming with me!"

"Well . . ." Bess spread her hands in a gesture of hopelessness.

"I'm sorry, Bess," Liz said. "I really am. I shall miss this place, but I'd be a fool not to go."

Bess nodded. She agreed. The fury went out of the argument. "Don't mind me, Liz, I'm being selfish. How the hell do I replace you?"

"That's easy," Liz said brightly. "You've got somebody begging for the job."

"Who?" Bess looked startled.

"Noel Timberlake."

"Oh. Has he finally packed it in with the family business?"

Liz looked exasperated. "You don't know any of the important things, do you? It happened a week ago. Lady Amaryllis asked me to put in a good word for him."

Bess did not seem inclined to be impressed by the idea. "He *might* do," she said grudgingly.

"I think he'd be good," Liz said. "He's got an air about him . . . he'd add extra class to the place. And he knows far more about horses than me."

To herself, at any rate, Bess admitted that this was true. Talking to him a few days before Christmas, she had been struck by his knowledge, presumably acquired from his parents. "I'm not short of experts," she said. "How would he cope with answering the phone and typing?"

"He wouldn't," Liz said bluntly. "You'd have to get a girl to do that."

"Wonderful!" Bess scoffed. "This is going to cost me three times what I pay you and the job won't be done anywhere near as well!"

"Calm down and listen," Liz commanded. "You may not realise it, but you still get mixed up in an awful lot of administration. You won't trust me with ordering feed because you know I'd make a mess of it, and you do most of the donkey work to set up the foreign trips. Noel could handle all that."

"What about the girl?" Bess asked. "How do I get her?"

"You don't have to look any further than Cathy Jones," Liz said.

"Ah . . . she's had enough, has she?" Bess asked, the near-inevitability of it not lessening her sense of defeat.

Cathy was a pretty girl from Bristol who had come to work at Latimer's Barn three years ago, when she was sixteen. One of a growing number of female lads, she had taken to it like a duck to water, well able to look after herself in the rough-and-tumble of stable life. But she had been involved in the disaster caused by Oliver. Badly thrown by her terrified horse, she had escaped serious injury, although she had remained black and blue for nearly two weeks. Afterwards, there were increasing signs that her nerve had gone.

"She came to tell me all about it," Liz said. "The poor kid broke down. The last thing she wants is to leave here, but she isn't going to be any use to you in the yard."

"Can she be taught to type?" Bess asked, not knowing the first thing about what was involved.

"Any fool can," Liz grinned. "That's what men have been saying for years, so it must be true."

"You're not going to change your mind?" Bess asked, making one last attempt.

"Sorry, no!"

"In that case, I'll have to think about what you said." Making it plain that she was a long way from being overjoyed, Bess stumped off.

Invited to polite Sunday-afternoon tea at The Hall three days later, Bess decided not to waste time. Comfortable in the sitting-room with Gideon and Amaryllis, she asked, "Is Noel about?"

"He's mooching around Savernake Forest," Amaryllis replied.

"What for?"

"He's looking for somewhere to live."

"In the forest?" Bess was bemused.

"The family owns properties up there," Gideon explained.

566

"My great-grandfather bought a ramshackle estate with bits and pieces dotted all over the place."

Bess sat back thoughtfully. "This rings bells," she said. "Don't love-nests come into it?"

While Gideon affected deafness, Amaryllis gave a gleeful gurgle. "We never talk about things like that, my dear."

"I see. So, what Liz tells me is right, then? Noel has packed it in and wants to move back here?"

"I'm afraid so," Gideon said. "We knew it was more or less bound to happen, and I suppose I admire his guts: at a pinch, he could have carried on, picking up the money and saying nothing."

Amaryllis flashed him a look that was sceptical of such tolerance on his part.

"With Liz deserting, I've got a job going," Bess said. "Do you think Noel might be interested?"

"I think he'd probably give his right arm for it," Amaryllis replied.

Gideon added a touch of paternal cynicism. "He's bound to want a fancy title and more money than any right-thinking person would dream of paying him."

"Give the poor wretch a chance," Amaryllis said. "Now, Bess, what about all that loot Liz has won!"

Noel arrived as Bess was leaving nearly an hour later. After they had eyed each other with a strange mixture of wariness and speculation, Bess took the plunge. "Are you doing anything tomorrow morning?" she asked.

"Nothing that can't be cancelled," Noel said.

"Come and see me at ten o'clock."

"Yes, Mrs Hawksworth."

At least, Bess thought as she drove home, he had got out of the habit of behaving like a goggling idiot in her company.

He was able to keep up the air of confidence during their two-hour chat the following morning. Impressively well-prepared, he produced a number of suggestions for improving efficiency that Bess recognised as potentially helpful.

"Well?" Liz said, after Noel had gone back to The Hall

and Bess emerged from the library where the meeting had taken place.

"He's starting tomorrow," Bess said, trying to be offhand about it. "You can teach him the basics."

"It will be a pleasure!" Liz rolled her eyes suggestively. "Anything for a gorgeous specimen like him . . . God, if I were ten years younger!" She pulled herself together. "What about Cathy Jones?"

"I'm seeing her this afternoon." Bess allowed herself the luxury of an acid comment. "Are you sure I need to bother? Wouldn't you rather stay here and have young Mr Timberlake all to yourself?"

"I won't deny it's tempting," Liz said. "However, the lure of the hacienda and my trusty hidalgo must take precedence."

After a farewell party that ended up being rather tearful, Liz left Cannings Ambo at the end of February. By that time, Noel Timberlake was well into his stride, already relieving Bess of duties that she suddenly appreciated had always been irksome. Cathy, with a secretarial course behind her, was tackling the new job with great enthusiasm. Her life had been further transformed by a move from the hostel to live with Robert and Caroline Frobisher at the Rectory. Expecting her first child at the ripe old age of twenty-nine, Caroline was pleased to have Cathy's help around the rambling house.

During the first week of March, Bess returned from working the second lot in a snowstorm to find Helen waiting for her in the office.

"Can we talk?" Helen asked.

"Of course. Come upstairs. Henry will find us something to eat while I thaw out. This is the time of year that makes me wonder if I shouldn't have been a rich man's plaything . . . the horses aren't too keen on it, either!"

Inside her suite of rooms, Bess collapsed into a chair so that Henrietta could pull her boots off.

"Tomato soup and bacon sandwiches all right?" Henrietta asked. "If not, I'll nip down and see what Valerie's got on the go."

"Soup and sandwiches will be lovely," Helen said and followed Bess into the sitting-room.

"Now then, what's up?" Bess asked, rubbing life into her hands.

"I'm looking for somewhere to live," Helen said. "I'm of 'no fixed abode' since I divorced Freddie."

"And Eaton Mandeville's too big?" Bess asked.

"It is. It's also crowded. This business conference centre seems to be going with a bang. You can't move for 'dynamic' young men."

"Yuk!" Bess said, pulling a gruesome face.

"And I can do without reminders of Mother," Helen added bleakly.

"How about coming to live in the village?" Bess asked. "You'd be handy for the office and workshops."

"That would be ideal," Helen said. "Do you have any plans for the Bungalow now that Liz Challoner's gone?"

"No, nor has anyone else, as far as I know. It's yours if you want it." Bess's face clouded as a thought struck her. "What about your mother? Doesn't this place have even worse associations than Eaton Mandeville?"

"Oddly enough, no," Helen said. "I might have been conceived not far from where we're sitting." She was reflective for a moment. "I feel happy to belong here."

"How long are you staying this time?" Bess asked.

"I'm at Rose House tonight and off to France in the morning."

"I should be able to get you fixed up this afternoon," Bess said. She smiled at Henrietta who had brought the soup in. "I'll get cracking after we've eaten."

"You're sure no one else wants the Bungalow?" Helen asked. "What about young Timberlake?"

"No, he's having some fearful ruin in Savernake Forest done up so that he can get away from it all. I think it's the lodge that Silas had before he moved into Louise House with Dame Amelia."

"It could probably tell a few stories," Helen said.

There was silence as they coped with the scalding soup.

Rather charily, Helen edged into a topic that she knew was risky. "I had dinner with Oliver last Wednesday evening."

Bess made a great effort not to react. The £400,000 had been paid and distributed: she would have been happy never to hear his name mentioned again.

"I was at a loose end in London and he offered to entertain me," Helen said, anxious not to be seen as part of a conspiracy. "He's *very* sorry, Bess." Confronted with stony silence, Helen struggled on. "He told me a fair bit about himself. There was a girl who meant a great deal to him . . . she was killed, in a car crash, of all things!"

"Very sad!" Bess said unsympathetically.

"I felt sorry for him," Helen said. "I'm not suggesting it's any sort of excuse for what he did . . ."

"Good!"

". . . but the girl was killed only a few weeks before he came here, you know."

The look on Bess's face was a clear indication that neither that, nor anything else Helen might discover about Oliver, made the blindest bit of difference.

It was the end of April before the Bungalow had been fitted with a new heating system and redecorated. Helen moved in on the day that Gideon's colt, Athelstan, a handsome chestnut by Astronomer Royal, won the Two Thousand Guineas, setting the seal on a brilliant two weeks: Bess's twenty-five winners before May was the best start to a season Latimer's Barn had ever known.

Eight days later, a rumpus that was to bring home to Bess the fact that she was a celebrity got underway. Hindsight showed that only Piers Clarendon could have perpetrated it.

Clarendon rented a twenty-box yard on the Downs to the north of Marlborough. It was a firmly held belief in racing circles that he was stark-raving mad. "Look out, here's Piers," his cronies would say. "Keep your eyes peeled for the men in white coats – they never let him out of their sight."

Two years previously, one of his fillies had created pandemonium while on the way to the start of the Queen Mary

Stakes at Royal Ascot. One instant she was bowling along like a sewing-machine, the next she had unshipped her jockey and was making wild charges at her opponents as though to scare them into the next county. Eventually, the race was abandoned and Piers was arraigned before the Stewards.

"Well, Major Clarendon, what have you got to say about this?" the senior member barked.

"Sheep, sir," Piers said, assuming a pained expression. "Those sheep spooked her."

"Sheep?" There was a frantic exchange of baffled looks among the Stewards. "What sheep?"

"About a hundred of them, sir. They came dashing off the Old Mile, straight at my filly. Frightened her witless."

"*Sheep*, you say?"

"Sheep, sir. I'd say you need to see to the fencing in Swinley Bottom."

They argued the toss for nearly an hour. Afterwards, the Stewards admitted that none of them had the guts to tell Clarendon he was talking rubbish, for fear that he might turn violent.

Bess, who had a soft spot for Piers, knew that he was incapable of violence. She could understand how some people found his habit of singing operatic arias as he rode out off-putting, and she herself was sometimes irritated by the need to give his horses lifts back from Newbury, Bath and Salisbury after his decrepit old van had given up the ghost yet again. He was not, however, vicious.

Getting on for fifty, though still remarkably young-looking, he had mislaid his wife at some point during the past fifteen years and was slightly in love with Bess. She never objected to his inept fondling and frantically improper suggestions, accusing him of bestowing his true affections on Lady Josephine Wilcox, the wife of one of his owners.

Lady Josephine it was who inspired Piers to make a complete fool of himself. After considering the matter for well over a year, she decided to give him the chance to show what he could do: he was bound to be better than Lord Wilcox, a fearsome man in a boardroom, but useless in bed. The tryst took place at a London hotel and staggered the participants. Over a late breakfast, they reviewed the night's escapades in terms of gloating mutual admiration, promised themselves a repeat performance very soon, and parted. Instead of having the sense to go quietly back to Wiltshire, Piers Clarendon visited his tailor and barber.

He was in a dangerously euphoric mood long before he arrived at his favourite pub. Three double gins made him king of creation. When a group of racing journalists came in, they spotted him at once. Piers was popular with the Press: if things were dull, he could always be relied on to provide some sort of story.

"You're looking bloody chuffed," one of the journalists said to Piers as he paid for a round of drinks. "What's up? Have you just bought next year's Derby winner for a thousand quid?"

"Let us not be silly, Jeff," a colleague said. "Everybody knows they cost five thousand!" The man studied Clarendon closely. "No, I'll tell you what it is . . . you've worked the oracle, haven't you, my old cock? You're getting your leg across the delectable Bess Hawksworth."

For some reason that he was never able to understand, Piers grabbed at the suggestion: it gave him the opportunity to boast about his recent prowess without dropping the real object of his affections in the mire.

"Mind you," he added after a rhapsodic few minutes that stunned his listeners, "Bess and me have been good mates for a long time. We *arrange* things."

Piers found himself piloted into a quiet corner: several drinks materialised in front of him.

"What do you mean, 'arrange things'?" a beguiling voice asked.

"If we each have a horse in the same race, we sometimes like to see the one with the best odds win," Piers said, trotting out a fantasy that had exercised his mind for several years. "It makes sense, doesn't it? Good God, we've got a living to earn!"

The notebooks were out. Dimly conscious of an attentive audience, Piers Clarendon spouted the most unmitigated load of rubbish that even he had ever concocted. Unfortunately, he did so with all the sober conviction that only an intoxicated madman could produce. Not until he discovered that he was alone did Piers shut up. Puzzled, and with the unsettling idea that something out of the ordinary had occurred, he set about making his way home.

Two of the editors spiked the story the moment they heard about it: the third hesitated. The journalist's copy was in limbo for a week until, purely by accident, the pictures editor turned up a photograph of Bess, glamorously self-assured as she led in a big-race winner. "Isn't this the woman Jeff was going on about?" and: "She's a hell of a looker!" set off the process that ended in publication.

Part of Noel Timberlake's morning routine was to scan every national newspaper. There was no missing *The Globe*'s scurrilous effort. The picture of Bess was given eye-catching prominence.

While Cathy Jones gazed at the story in horror, Noel set to work. First he telephoned his mother, then he attempted to contact Piers Clarendon. The girl to whom he spoke sounded utterly distraught: it was now eleven o'clock and Latimer's Barn must have been the last place to discover the article. The girl confessed that Piers had disappeared soon after the first batch of calls at seven-fifteen.

"Would you make sure that Mr Clarendon gets in touch with us if and when he comes back," Noel said with smooth firmness.

Immediately, without pausing to think, he contacted the Jockey Club, leaving a message for the chairman of the Disciplinary Committee. "Mrs Hawksworth rejects the suggestions made in today's *Globe* newspaper that she had an arrangement with Piers Clarendon whereby her horses do not always race on their merits. I'm certain that she will wish to speak to Sir Lionel this afternoon."

Then, under the admiring gaze of Cathy, he sat back to await Bess's return from the second lot.

Her reaction was one of hilarity. "Piers has flipped his lid at last," she said after scanning the piece. "I suppose I'd better talk to the mad bugger."

"He's in hiding, Mrs Hawksworth," Noel told her, going on to explain what else he had done. Her eyebrows rose at his final statement. "The irony is that we own *The Globe* — well, fifty-two per cent of it, anyway."

"We?" Bess asked.

"Timberlake Holdings. There's going to be murder. I think Father's been looking for an excuse to hang the editor."

"I don't want anyone to lose their job on my account," Bess said. "No one will take this rubbish seriously."

"We can't be too careful, Mrs Hawksworth. Your integrity is one of the stable's greatest assets and muck does have a nasty habit of sticking."

Touched by his concern for her, Bess wandered into the kitchen to have lunch with Ann. They were barely settled when Piers Clarendon rushed in, very much the man on the run.

"Piers, you idiot, what *have* you been doing?" Bess laughed.

"I don't know!" he said miserably. "I can remember blundering into the muck-rakers in a pub. After that . . ." He waved a hand to indicate loss of memory.

"You were taken suddenly drunk?"

"Must have been. I was up on cloud nine before I started on the juice." He leaned forward, trying to exclude Ann from the revelation. "I'd spent the night with Josephine Wilcox . . . we had a *frightfully* good time."

"I wonder what Josephine will think of you and me," Bess said, giving him a huge wink.

Piers's face turned ashen. "She was on the blower at seven!" He was struck by a new thought. "Fancy her reading a rag like that with her tea and toast! Damn it, I thought she had taste."

Bess decided not to pursue the point. Instead, as gently as possible, she said, "I presume you'll hand in your licence before *they* tear it up?"

He nodded. "Quite honestly, Bess, it'll be a relief. I've never really looked like doing any good, have I?"

An hour later, Bess decided that it was time to talk to Sir Lionel Warren-Strode at the Jockey Club. She hauled Piers to the telephone in the library and made him speak first. He duly made abject apology and promised to hand in his licence as soon as he had made all the necessary arrangements for his horses and staff.

"You seem to be well on the way to sorting everything out, Mrs Hawksworth," Sir Lionel said when it was her turn.

"I didn't want you losing sleep over me," Bess said, conscious of the need to treat the whole thing as a joke. "Even in these days, you must have enough villainy without wondering if people like me are turning crooked."

"Good Lord, Mrs Hawksworth, the thought would never have crossed our minds. It's a long time since you had a bet."

"Do you people know *everything*?" Bess asked after a pause that was barely perceptible.

Sir Lionel laughed. "Would that we did, Mrs Hawksworth! We rumbled you purely by accident, I might say. One of our investigators was working on something else when he came across your man Jackson piling money on Lindisfarne for the Derby."

"Oh, I see!" Bess was relieved to learn that it was the last of her big bets that had been discovered.

"We assumed it was for you."

"You were right, Sir Lionel."

"Well, no one can accuse you of jiggery-pokery with that one. And what a hammering you gave the bookies, eh? Tell me, have you decided what to do about these bastards at *The Globe*?"

"That will be taken care of," Bess assured him.

She spent the rest of the afternoon knocking sense into Piers Clarendon and looking for ways to help him.

The apology printed by *The Globe* the very next morning was fulsome and much more prominently displayed than was the custom. Noel obviously knew of the havoc Gideon had created within the offices of the newspaper, but refused to reveal details.

Steven's reaction to the affair was originally one of revulsion, made worse by the letters. A van came out from Marlborough with a special delivery of over five hundred, all from total strangers. A retired policeman from Lowestoft said that he was sure everything *The Globe* had said was untrue. "I saw you at Newmarket with Astronomer Royal for the Guineas in 1960," he wrote. "I have been a great admirer of yours ever since. Keep up the good work!" Happily, that was typical of the majority.

A woman who refused to give her address set out the opposite point of view. "It's obscene that somebody as rich as you must be stoops to dishonesty. I've seen you on TV and you obviously spend more on dress in a month than most folk round here have to live on for a year. On top of everything else, you had sex with your accomplice. Disgusting! Well, he's shopped you now and it serves you right!"

Leander came out with a fundamental truth the moment she saw the stack of letters.

"You're getting famous, Aunt Bess. I think it's a good thing."

While Steven, as he invariably did, was adapting to her point of view, Bess realised it was something that she herself had failed to grasp. In all probability, *The Globe* had printed the ludicrous story because she, Bess Hawksworth, was deemed to be 'newsworthy'. If it stayed within reasonable bounds, it might be pleasant to be a minor celebrity.

It was very much in evidence at Epsom two weeks later. After Athelstan had made a thorough job of winning the Derby, Bess was interviewed by Wesley Davies, the self-appointed doyen of TV racing commentators. There was, of course, nothing remotely resembling a mention of poor old Piers: Wesley stuck to Athelstan, the plans for his future, and Bess's prospects for Royal Ascot. Nevertheless, she felt that her appearance before the cameras was drawn out for several minutes longer than usual.

During the following days, requests for interviews flooded in. Three were granted, the rest turned down in a manner calculated to ensure that those concerned never bothered again. Bess featured in a Sunday newspaper's *Day in the life of . . .* series, while Valerie Pepperdine described her kitchen and the food that came out of it for an up-market women's magazine. Henrietta was the principal subject of the final article, a glossy, ten-page spread about Bess's clothes that made much of the walk-in wardrobe and did Farquharson's of Bath no harm at all.

Bess enjoyed the modest fame, amused and touched by the women who wrote for recipes, dress hints and advice on how to be more positive towards their careers. She spent considerable time composing replies to the eleven men who sent proposals of marriage, at least two of which Henrietta considered worthy of investigation. Apart from an outbreak of coughing among the horses in the 1933 yard towards the end of July, Noel's attitude was the only thing that worried Bess.

"Do you know what's wrong with him?" she finally asked Henrietta.

"Nothing, as far as I know."

"Then why is he being so starchy with me?"

"Ah, that's his way of showing disapproval."

"Disapproval!" Bess shouted. "Why does the arrogant young toad think he can disapprove of me?"

"*The Globe* was so busy grovelling about you and Mr Clarendon *not* fixing races that they forgot to mention that you weren't having it off with him, either."

"Everybody knows I wasn't!"

"Noel doesn't," Henrietta said.

"In that case, he's an idiot. And it's none of his business, anyway!"

Yet, as the days passed, Bess was surprised to discover that she wanted Noel to think well of her. When she went into the office one lunch-time to find that Cathy was away, stocking up on stamps, she took the opportunity to sit down in front of Noel's desk, ostensibly to talk about the autumn campaign she was formulating for Prince Omar's horses.

"By the way," she said casually, "I'm going to give your father a flea in his ear when I see him on Saturday."

"Why, what's wrong?" Noel was worried.

"With all the hectic goings-on at the time, I hadn't spotted that his blasted newspaper didn't print a fully comprehensive apology over that business with me and Clarendon."

"Oh?" Noel cocked his head inquisitively.

"The only sort of relationship between us was friendship," Bess said. "I liked him . . . I still do. But that was as far as it went." She paused to fix Noel with a resolute look. "We weren't lovers."

"Well . . . I . . . er . . ." Noel was not quite successful in masking his reaction to the news. "I'm sure Father would be only too pleased to do something. Would you like me to mention it?"

"No, it's far too late. In any case, I suspect I've caused more than enough bloodshed." She switched to her most persuasive tone. "Would you like to tell me what happened at *The Globe*?"

"Oh, no, Mrs Hawksworth, that's a secret." Showing signs of his susceptibility to her, he felt the need to change the subject. "What's going to become of Mr Clarendon's yard?"

"His head lad's taking it over under permit." Bess decided to tackle something that had irritated her since Noel had come to Latimer's Barn. "You're doing a first-class job," she said. "But there is one improvement I'd like to see you make."

"Yes, Mrs Hawksworth?" He was so desperately eager to please, she almost lost the courage to tell him.

"Do you think you could stop this 'Mrs Hawksworth' nonsense? It makes me feel ancient and everyone else calls me 'Bess'."

"Er . . . yes . . . of course." He nerved himself to try it out. "I'll have a go . . . Bess!" Very happy with the result, he smiled self-consciously.

Dismayed by the strong desire to give him a congratulatory kiss, Bess made a flippant remark about him finding it much easier with practice and hurried out of the office.

Helen travelled to Fontainebleau at the end of September in a state of joyous expectation. Due to their divergent business demands, she had not seen Klaus Neumann for nearly two months. After the market strategy meeting called by Alain de Mourville, they were planning a long weekend in Brittany.

There was much to look forward to. Alain's lieutenants from all over Europe were attending the meeting and there was a strong belief that he was proposing to announce an important new role for his son, Laurent, as a prelude to his own retirement. Although she was not directly connected with Alain's business, the invitation extended to Helen suggested that John Flamsteed's hunch about an opening for their furniture to be manufactured in Italy was to become reality. Finally, of course, there was Klaus, now sixty-one, but as youthfully virile and magnificent as ever.

Arriving at the château early in the afternoon, Helen found that she had to be patient. Klaus, who had an important meeting in Frankfurt that was expected to last all day, was booked on the seven o'clock flight to Paris. After kicking her heels for several hours, Helen asked to be excused from the dinner that Alain and Nadia were giving to welcome their guests. She borrowed a car and drove to the airport to meet Klaus.

The aircraft landed, but there was no sign of him. Helen went to the Lufthansa desk to make inquiries. They knew nothing beyond the fact that *Herr* Neumann had failed to check in at Frankfurt. There was one more flight, but it did not arrive until midnight. Rather than wait for nearly four hours, Helen drove back to Château de Mourville. While she was on the way, the message from Alain's representative in Frankfurt came through.

Klaus had died on the bus taking him to the airport. He had left the meeting in the very best of spirits and health: forty minutes later, a massive heart attack killed him.

Helen discovered that she was tough. She dissuaded Alain from postponing the conference, telling him that the best mark of respect for Klaus would be to carry on as normal. However, Marie-Claire, watching over her closely, was conscious of a powerful sense of fatalism enveloping Helen. The only comment that she made on Klaus's shockingly sudden death, although enigmatic, seemed to confirm this.

"How awful to go like that . . . surrounded by strangers. He deserved much better. That's what being mixed up with me does for you!"

Her true feelings surfaced after the funeral in the pretty Bavarian village near Rosenheim. Klaus's sister, Hannelore, his only living relative, had made all the arrangements. Back at the beautiful house in which she and her husband had lived for thirty years, she took Helen to a small room, away from the other mourners.

"I am sorry we never met before this," Hannelore said. "Klaus always spoke of you when he came to see us. You made him very happy."

Helen shook her head. "No, *he* made *me* happy. He was the most wonderful man I ever knew."

Then the tears came.

Helen stayed with Hannelore and her husband for three days. When she travelled back to England, she was purged of grief and certain that something irreplaceable had gone from her life.

John Flamsteed had heard of Neumann's death from Alain. Not entirely sure of the relationship between the dead man and Helen, he asked no questions. There was no one else in Cannings Ambo she felt inclined to confide in, not even Bess.

Soon after, however, she told Oliver, the man whom she increasingly regarded as her companion in misfortune on the dark side of the Hawksworth firmament.

Bess's campaigns with two-year-olds in the autumn were becoming a bookmaker's nightmare. Never less than a very good trainer, she was brilliant with juveniles at the back end. In September and October, she sent four horses out to Pattern races and they all did the business. This was not sufficient reason to stop moaning about missing the Dewhurst Stakes after her current pride and joy went lame three days before it was run, but she was quietly pleased, especially since two of the Group winners belonged to Prince Omar Khalid al-Melhem, putting him on the map in his first season as an owner.

His telephone call to express his thanks, following the delivery of what looked like half a ton of flowers, was long and fulsome. Eventually, when the praise was exhausted, he asked if he might speak to Henrietta. Bess made herself scarce, only to be dug out of her bedroom almost immediately.

"Do you think I could have a week's holiday?" Henrietta asked, as though expecting the roof to cave in.

"Of course. When?"

"The day after tomorrow, I think. Hang on, let's find out exactly what HRH wants."

It emerged that Henrietta was to have a holiday in the Dolomites: not surprisingly, Prince Omar was to join her.

Bess found that being cheerful during the thirty-six hours leading up to Henrietta's departure was difficult. Maintaining the act on her radiantly satisfied return was impossible.

"How involved are you with Omar?" Bess asked after Henrietta had done most of her unpacking and Steven was in bed.

"Emotionally, you mean?"

"Yes."

"Not at all. There's no point, is there? He'd no more think of marrying me than fly to the moon. I'm just one of his amusements. It suits me. Marriage doesn't appeal and he's a terrific stud."

"Hah!" Bess snorted.

Conscious of the threat of sour grapes, Henrietta attempted to move away at a tangent. "Did Piers get off all right?"

During her absence, Clarendon had finally left the area. Promising to do his utmost to make a go of it, he was taking a job as an estate manager to a titled family in the far north of Scotland. "There's hardly anybody there for most of the year," he told Bess over the farewell dinner she bought him. "Even I can't make a mess of it."

Bess's smile indicated that she would not risk a bet.

"Yes, he's gone," she said to Henrietta. Something was bothering her. "He annoyed me."

"How?"

"After making up a pack of lies for *The Globe*, don't you

581

think he should have had the grace to ask me to go to bed with him?"

"What would you have done if he had?" Henrietta asked.

Bess glowered. "You never know, Henry, you never know!"

Helen threw herself into work with a fury that worried John Flamsteed. The factory on the Extension, enlarged during the year, was able to cope with the orders she was bound to bring in; his concern was for her health as she exhibited signs of strain.

She saw more of Oliver. By the end of November, their regular Thursday-night dinner in London had been supplemented by a meeting on Monday. As so often happens with lonely, unhappy people, the approach of Christmas posed a threat.

"What have you got planned?" Oliver asked one evening.

"Nothing. I expect I shall end up shuttling backwards and forwards between Eaton Mandeville and Cannings Ambo." The prospect clearly held no attractions for her. "What about you?"

"I shall go to the cottage."

"What cottage?"

"Oh . . . haven't I told you? It's a Victorian sort of place on the Downs in Berkshire. I bought it a couple of months ago. It's a bit run down, but it's peaceful."

"Would it suit me?" Helen asked.

"Come and have a look on Saturday."

The cottage proved to be a large, five-bedroom house that was still a long way from being completely furnished. Oliver explained that he had sold the flats in London to clear a substantial part of the loan organised by Hubert, but had used part of the capital released to buy this once-elegant house.

"It night be an investment," he said. "To be honest, I couldn't care less . . . the solitude is worth a fortune."

Helen agreed. The nearest building, a farm, was nearly a mile away; the twenty square miles of which Oliver's house was the centre, had no more than three hundred inhabitants.

582

"It's perfect," Helen said. "Could I come and share it with you for part of this blasted holiday?"

Oliver considered it carefully. "I think we should hit it off," he said at last. "Yes, I'd be glad of the company."

They met at the house on the day before Christmas Eve. Taking both cars, they went into Oxford and did enough shopping to withstand a siege. When they returned, Helen put up a few decorations and was busy with a vacuum cleaner, while Oliver stowed away their provisions and lit fires with fuel from the vast supplies of logs and coal he had organised.

On Boxing Day, Helen went to Eaton Mandeville to have lunch with Hubert, Lisette, Edmund, Judy, and their children. Everyone assumed she had come over from Cannings Ambo: Bess and her other friends in the village believed that she was dividing her time between London and Eaton Mandeville.

During the hours of daylight, Helen and Oliver lived private, almost separate lives, walking, reading and dividing domestic chores by unspoken agreement. They came together at dusk each evening, to cook a substantial meal and listen to the radio, talking about everything in general and nothing in particular. Helen's favourite theme was the solace she was deriving from the total isolation of the house.

It was very pleasant and soothing. Speaking with warm praise of their remoteness, Helen was not to know that she was unwittingly adding to a plan that was, as yet, nothing more than a nebulous notion at the back of Oliver's increasingly vindictive mind.

CHAPTER 22

1984

'. . . it's a luxury I might allow myself'

At Easter, Bess reminded Steven that he was due to leave the village school in September to embark on a much more demanding programme of education.

"You're going to a private school," she said.

"Super!" he replied. "There's a good one at Salisbury."

"There's one a mile down the road that's even better," Bess said. Behind the scenes, the plans to send Steven to Marlborough College as a day-boy were well-advanced. "That means you won't have to leave home . . . or Henry." These were meant to be powerful inducements.

"Salisbury's *nicer*," Steven insisted. Although he was perfectly pleasant about it, Bess saw that he was preparing to dig his heels in.

The root of the trouble was Leander, of course. She had been packed off to the Godolphin School in Salisbury in the autumn of the previous year. During the months preceding her departure, Rebecca and William had teetered permanently on the brink of surrender, but Leander's grandmothers had decided that, for once, she would toe the line.

Leander's protests took place against a background of upheaval that increased the difficulties of her long-suffering parents. At the age of sixty-two, John Flamsteed decided to retire, leaving William a free hand with the business. Moreover, John insisted, he and William should swap homes:

everyone would appreciate having a William Flamsteed in charge again at Rose House. Besides, John and Julia wanted to take up gardening in a big way and the somewhat neglected three acres surrounding Louise House was a temptation too good to resist.

During the chaotic three days of house-moving, Leander raised her anti-Salisbury campaign to new heights, choosing the tactics with care. A posh boarding-school would, she claimed, accentuate her natural arrogance; the syllabus was far too élitist for someone who was pretty thick; she would lose touch with the stable; horror of horrors, she might even forget how to ride!

"Give her full marks for low animal cunning," William said to Rebecca as they gritted their teeth and did their best to weather the storm. "She hasn't mentioned the real reason . . . not once!"

"Steven?" Rebecca asked.

"She hates the thought of leaving him."

Soon afterwards, Ann and Julia made a concerted assault on Leander along "Now look here, young lady" lines and she shut up. She went to Salisbury, and, to everyone's surprised relief, got on with the job in hand without attempting to run away. In a delightfully old-fashioned way, Leander and Steven wrote long letters to each other several times a week. Both Bess and Rebecca fished repeatedly to discover at least a flavour of the prolific correspondence, but were told to mind their own business.

For six months everything had appeared to be under control. Now, at the end of April, Steven was threatening another crisis.

"You want to go to school in Salisbury?" Bess asked.

"Yes, please!"

"Have you talked to Leander about it?"

"Why should I? It's got nothing to do with her." His airy denial was almost convincing.

"She isn't allowed out of school on her own. Were you assuming that she was?" Steven said nothing. "You'd be the same. These places have to be jolly careful. Most kids aren't as sensible as you and Leander and they simply aren't fit to be let out. Imagine the stink if they got into trouble."

"Perhaps I'll think about it," Steven said.

"That's a good idea," Bess advised. "I reckon it's like being in prison, you wouldn't have Henry and I'll bet the food's rotten – nothing like the stuff Valerie does for you."

Ten days passed. With a supreme effort, Bess remained silent, assuming that the matter was under debate in the letters that flew back and forth. At last, Steven broached the subject as he and Bess rode across the gallops on a beautiful Saturday afternoon in May.

"I think it would be best if I *did* stay here," he said. "I would miss Henry."

"She'll be pleased," Bess said in a deliberately neutral voice. There had always been an understanding between Steven and Bess that they would never make a fuss about their deep love for each other.

They were silent as their hacks walked a dozen paces.

"Are you working Bathsheba Everdene next Wednesday?" Steven asked.

"Yes. It's her last one before the Derby."

"Will she be in the first lot?"

"No . . . but I'll have a word with Aunt Eileen."

From time to time, when a truly outstanding horse was doing a vital piece of work, Steven was allowed to miss most of the morning's lessons so that he could watch. Bathsheba Everdene was undoubtedly exceptional: defying anyone to contradict her, Bess had proclaimed that she was the best filly Latimer's Barn had ever seen.

As a two-year-old in 1983, Bathsheba Everdene had won all her four races. Her final victory, in the Prix Marcel Boussac at Longchamp, was one of the most impressive performances seen on any European racecourse that year. Bess's pleasure at the filly's exploits was marred by the disappointment of a strained tendon that kept her out of the Leander Hawksworth Stakes at Newbury: following a succession of disappointments in the race, Bathsheba Everdene had been

586

a total certainty to bring the prize back to Latimer's Barn for the first time.

After a winter during which her only enemy was boredom, Bathsheba Everdene set about her 1984 work programme with a zest that raised even Arthur Merriweather's sceptical eyebrows. Rather than bother with a prep race, Bess let her go straight into the One Thousand Guineas.

The way she won it gave rise to several days of excited debate. As Europe's top-rated two-year-old filly of 1983, she was expected to have at least a length in hand over her nearest rivals: in the event, she made them look flat-footed over the Rowley Mile. Not only was her winning margin of eight lengths the greatest in the race since 1859, it was apparent that she would have no difficulty with an extra half-mile. The Oaks was hers for the asking.

But Bess had a much more daring plan in mind. Calling the filly's owner, Gideon Timberlake, and Jonathan Pilgrim into the library for a conference, she told them that she wanted to run Bathsheba Everdene in the Derby.

"My only concern is that she's *too* brave," Gideon said. "I don't want her crocked up trying the impossible. Aren't some of this year's colts very good?"

Bess knew that he had a good point: a very hard race could ruin a horse as effectively as any permanent injury. Jonathan said his piece.

"I won't let her. We'll take it nice and easy."

That was the end of it: Gideon trusted him completely.

The announcement that the filly would take her chance in the Derby gave Bess further proof that she was a celebrity. Journalists fought to interview her, asking increasingly ridiculous questions. An odiously pushy young woman, who had no idea where Epsom was, finally took the biscuit with: "Mrs Hawksworth, is running a filly in the Derby your expression of women's rights?" After that, the Press were kept at arm's length.

On the other hand, Bess enjoyed the public attention that greeted her on the day of the race. As she approached the course in her precious Jaguar, hundreds of total strangers waved and shouted good wishes. In the paddock during the preliminaries to the Derby, there was an assurance about Bess that other trainers found intensely depressing. Partly it was due to her faith in Bathsheba Everdene, partly to the knowledge that she had celebrated her forty-fifth birthday a few days ago and looked better than ever.

There were several moments of deep anxiety during the race. As the seventeen runners swept round Tattenham Corner, Jonathan, after a bumpy ride for the first mile, found himself boxed in by half a dozen no-hopers in the middle of the pack. Two French-trained colts, both of whom were supposed to be good, had first run at the home straight. For a while, it looked bad, if not downright impossible. Then, one of the horses impeding Bathsheba Everdene reacted to the pressure by veering towards the rails and the filly was through the gap like greased lightning. The leaders had a fight on their hands.

She hated the idea of being beaten. With the vast crowd cheering her every inch of the way, Bathsheba Everdene closed with the leading French contender, fighting it out shoulder to shoulder for well over a furlong. At the line, she had it by a neck and, true to his word, Jonathan never laid a finger on her.

Back at Latimer's Barn, Henrietta and Steven watched television as Gideon led his champion in. She was the first filly to win the Derby for nearly fifty years, the last being Leander's own Hyperborean.

"I say, Bess looks pleased with herself," Henrietta chortled.

"I should jolly well think so!" Steven replied. "Do you think she's going to be interviewed, Henry?"

"I'd like to see anyone try to stop her!"

The year had seen the spread of sponsorship to the Classics and one company had gained the privilege of having its name associated with both the Derby and the Oaks. On the Saturday evening at the end of Epsom week, they gave a dinner in London. Asked to be a guest of honour and speaker, Bess jumped at the chance of a platform for the expression of views that were intended to ruffle complacent feathers. Declining the sponsor's offer of luxurious hotel accommodation, she was driven to and from London by Solstice in the Daimler, arriving back home at one o'clock on Sunday morning.

"How was it?" Henrietta asked, helping Bess out of the long evening gown.

"So-so. *Some* of the company wasn't bad. My speech sorted them out. The food was mediocre."

"Let me guess – you'd like a cup of tea?"

"Absolutely! Is Steven all right?"

"Yes. I let him watch the goggle-box until half-ten and he went off like a lamb. He's trying to pretend that he isn't looking forward to tomorrow." Henrietta looked at a clock and corrected herself. "Today."

Rebecca and William were going to Salisbury to spend the day with Leander. Steven had agreed to the suggestion that he might like to accompany them and his cousins, Matthew and Emma.

After making the tea, Henrietta found Bess stretched out in the bath, scowling morosely in the general direction of her feet.

"What's wrong?" Henrietta asked.

"Oh, the usual," Bess replied. "I was up to my armpits in propositions again. Do you know, that idiot Nigel Powycke was doing his damnedest to grope me while I was talking to Lord Beauchamp!"

"So?" Henrietta was not in the least surprised that Powycke, a notorious lecher with a declared penchant for Bess, should be undeterred by the presence of the Jockey Club's Senior Steward. "It's your own fault. You ought to do something about it."

"Such as?" Bess looked forbiddingly suspicious.

"Get yourself a man, for God's sake! If you're known to be involved with someone, most of this nonsense will stop." Henrietta spoke forcefully, expecting a robust reply: instead, Bess mulled it over, nodding her head several times.

"I suppose it's a luxury I might allow myself," she said.

"Why shouldn't you?" Henrietta urged. "This place is

under control and you're secure. In any case, there's more to it than keeping menaces away . . . you *need* a man. You've been lonely for too long."

Bess returned Henrietta's challenging stare. "I'm not going to argue with that, Henry," she said. "How do I find him?"

"You don't have to. For pity's sake, Bess, he's right under your nose, worshipping the ground you walk on!"

Silence fell. Bess sipped from the teacup, taking an excessive interest in her toes. "What about the difference in ages?" she asked.

"It doesn't mean a thing. Have you *noticed* yourself lately? You look a treat. Most women haven't got a body that good when they're half your age!" Henrietta paused, struck by a terrible thought. "You don't object to Noel, do you?"

The biggest and brightest of Bess's smiles lit up her face. "I think he's bloody gorgeous!" she said.

"There you are, then. What are you waiting for?"

After sleeping soundly for eight hours, Bess's mind was made up. She saw Steven off to Salisbury, shut herself in the library, where she could make the call without risk of being overheard, and dialled the number of Noel's forest lodge. She was about to give up in despair, cursing the futility of her crossed fingers, when he answered.

"Noel, hello. It's Bess."

"Oh, hello." He was surprised. "Is something wrong?"

It was a reasonable assumption at ten o'clock on a Sunday morning, especially since she never telephoned him at home for anything other than the solution to a problem. "No, everything's fine," she replied, praying that he could not sense her sudden nervousness. "Do you have any plans for today?"

"Er . . . no . . . I'm trying to do something with the garden."

"How about lunch with me?"

There was a noticeable pause as Noel came to terms with the suggestion. "I'd like that very much," he said.

"I'll be with you at twelve," Bess said, banging down the receiver before he had time to think of arguing.

She tore upstairs, hardly seeing Ann in the corridor at the top, and frightening Henrietta half out of her skin with her precipitate arrival in their suite.

"Where's the fire?" Henrietta asked.

"Quick . . . I'm having lunch with Noel," Bess gasped. "What shall I wear?"

"Where were you thinking of going?"

"How about The Plough at Hatchetts Green?" Bess suggested.

Henrietta wrinkled her nose. "No, that's no good . . . I'll think of something much better while you get dressed up. Follow me!"

Bemused, Bess found herself hauled into Henrietta's bedroom. Wardrobe doors and drawers came open, Henrietta muttering to herself as she tried to make up her mind. Finally, she settled for a white T-shirt and a pair of bright yellow track-suit trousers.

"Henry, have you gone *totally* mad?" Bess pleaded.

"Not in the least. Make sure you wear a really stunning bra and knickers . . . the white silk with pink thingeys would be ideal. Get on with it!"

Returning fifteen minutes later, Henrietta clapped her hands gleefully and Bess, who had helped herself to a pair of tennis shoes, was desperately anxious to agree with her, although she felt bound to make a point.

"I don't look very much like *me*."

"Exactly!" Henrietta crowed. "This is the message we want to give the dear boy . . . the new Bess Hawksworth, just for him. Let me show you what I've been up to."

Valerie Pepperdine always had Sunday off, so Henrietta had been able to run riot in the kitchen. She pointed proudly to the hamper on the table.

"It's a lovely day and you're going to have a picnic . . . *in the forest*." She peered closely at Bess, making sure that she understood what was expected of her. "All right?"

"Yes." The weak smile did not belong to the same Bess Hawksworth who had occupied the winner's enclosure at Epsom only four days ago.

And once on the way, Bess experienced a surge of panic with the realisation that she had no more than a sketchy idea of how to find Noel's remote cottage. She had been there only once before, giving him a lift when his car had broken down eighteen months ago. Miraculously, despite the sudden loss of her confidence, she found it without difficulty, tucked away in the south-western corner of the forest, about two hundred yards along a bumpy track that was a spur of one of the eight radial roads. Hearing the Jaguar arrive, Noel hurried out. Wearing a lightweight suit that was ideal for a summer-Sunday lunch in a good-class hotel, he stopped dead when he saw how Bess was dressed.

"I thought we'd have a picnic," she said, opening the car boot to show him the hamper. He took it to the back of the lodge where there was a large lawn in the shade of the great elm trees that surrounded the property. After a moment's indecision, Noel hurried indoors, returning with a rug and table-cloth. Dropping them alongside the hamper, he said, "I shan't be a minute," and went inside again.

By the time he returned in shirt, jeans and sandals, and carrying a jug of orange juice, Bess had all that was needed for the meal spread out on the cloth.

"That's very inviting," Noel said, sitting down beside her. "I'm going to have avocado pear *and* smoked salmon to start. Is all this Valerie's handiwork?"

"Yes – but she doesn't know how grateful we are! It's her day off, so Henry ransacked the fridges."

"How was the do in London?" he asked. "*Did* you make the speech you were threatening?"

"I did!" Bess replied proudly.

"And?"

"A few people aged by twenty years," she chuckled. "Lord Saxmundham actually gave me a ticking off afterwards."

"He's got a nerve!" Noel said angrily. "Father's told me all about him."

"Such as?" Bess made it plain that, for once, she was eager for gossip.

"He used to have horses with a bloke called Rigby at Newmarket . . . a complete lunatic and bent as hell."

"Was this the one they called 'Blood and stomach pills'?" Bess asked, delving into racing folklore. "Used to lose horses in the fog on the Limekilns?"

Noel grinned. "That's right! The lucky ones stayed lost and ended up in other stables. Anyway, Rigby had a very young wife and Saxmundham took a fancy to her. He decided to teach her how to play billiards."

Bess snorted with mirth and listened avidly as Noel told the scurrilous tale. He was more at ease than she had ever seen him before, and his mood affected her. She became carefree. The responsibilities of Latimer's Barn melted away and she felt total affinity with the young man who was seventeen years her junior. Emboldened by her obvious enjoyment of his anecdote, Noel went on to disclose some of the outrageous things he had learned about the world of business during his time with Timberlake Holdings.

When they had eaten their fill, Bess took the remainder of the food into the lodge's tiny kitchen to put it in a cool place. She thought that Noel intended staying in the garden, but as she turned from the larder, she found him in the doorway. The sun was behind him, lighting up his fair hair and preventing her from seeing the expression on his face until he moved into the shadow of the small room. His look was almost one of fear and pain. Bess was alarmed until she realised that he was suffering untold agony as he summoned courage. Going to his aid, she placed her hands on his shoulders.

Although Noel had intended the kiss to be a chaste, understated display of his feelings, Bess caught fire, burying herself in his arms with a fervour that surprised him before he shared in it. When it was over, he was unsure: he wanted to escape from the incongruous confines of the kitchen, but was unwilling to let go of her. Bess took the moment by the scruff of its neck.

"We need your bedroom," she said, very quiet, very sure. "Does that seem a good idea?"

He could only nod. Checking repeatedly to ensure that

593

this was not a dream, that she was following, he led the way. Apart from the kitchen, the ground-floor was taken up by a comfortable sitting-room and a cubby-hole of a study. Upstairs, the landing had only two doors.

"There!" Noel pointed to the open door of the bedroom and disappeared into the bathroom. Understanding his nervousness, Bess wanted it to be short-lived.

The bedroom was strongly evocative of Lady Amaryllis who had helped Noel settle into the lodge. The decor, carpet and curtains might have belonged to The Hall. Pretty and elegant, the room had surely been waiting for a woman: Bess prayed for success in it. After undressing completely, she drew back the bedclothes and lay down, deliberately leaving herself uncovered.

To her relief, Noel appeared almost at once, still dressed, halting in mid-stride as he crossed the threshold. Bess smiled at his entranced incredulity.

"I'm feasting my eyes," he explained.

"So I see. Don't be all day about it."

Moving to the side of the bed, he knelt down. Slowly and carefully, he leaned forward to pass the tip of his tongue across each of her nipples in turn. Bess showed that she enjoyed it.

"Well, Mr Timberlake," she said when he raised his head and their eyes met.

"Well, Mrs Hawksworth!"

"Here we are."

"Yes." He shook his head. "I don't believe it."

Grasping one of his wrists, she guided his hand between her legs. His eyes opened wide at the discovery that she was ready for him. "Do you believe *that*?" she asked.

He went to the foot of the bed to strip. With his shirt gone, Bess saw the breadth of his shoulders and admired the way his torso tapered to a narrow waist. Removal of the jeans revealed a splendid pair of thighs. Finally, Noel seemed to be having some difficulty getting rid of his briefs. When he turned to face her, the reason was spectacularly obvious: not only was he powerfully erect, he was huge. David Brandon, with whom

Bess had spent three weeks on the cruise in 1968, had been by far the best endowed of the three men she had known, but Noel's massive penis completely surpassed him.

Noel misinterpreted the look of admiration and sharpening desire that flooded Bess's face. "I'm sorry," he said. "As a matter of fact, this damned thing has been known to cause trouble."

"Not here!" Bess told him with confident relish. "Definitely not here!" She stretched out her arms to him and he abandoned his embarrassed immobility, shuddering when he was close enough for her to grasp him. "That is *magnificent*," Bess murmured. "I think all our problems are over. Come along, my boy."

He swung himself into position above her, the power of his strong arms and shoulders raising her craving for him. Very gently, Noel began to penetrate her, producing a cavalcade of sensations for both of them. As she felt herself filling, a combination of reflex action and an irresistible desire to display humorous appreciation of his immensity made Bess go cross-eyed.

"What's wrong?" Noel asked, paralysed with fear.

"Nothing, you fool!" she laughed. "It feels bloody marvellous."

"Are you sure?"

"Yes, Noel, I'm positively, certainly, sure!"

He gave a final thrust and she flushed with the glorious knowledge that she had absorbed him entirely.

Bess reached up to run her fingers through his hair. "Does that feel good for you?" she whispered.

He nodded, not willing to trust words. He was, she saw, savouring her and the circumstances. She allowed him thirty seconds, then her years of agonising loneliness boiled over. "Go on," she ordered, a wild edge on her voice. "Fuck me!"

For one harrowing instant, she thought she had made a terrible mistake. Poised over her, Noel seemed to be deeply offended by the eruption of coarseness. In reality, he was coming to terms with the most electrifyingly wonderful thing ever said to him. He did so rapidly and their world exploded.

Even in the frenzy that followed, Bess had a clear picture of everything that happened. First, she was clutching his muscular thighs, spurring them into more powerful lunges. Then, she flung her legs up to grasp his waist, riding his sturdy bucking with the same innate skills that she used on a horse. The oblivion of her climax was pierced by the desperate noises Noel made as he reared up, his whole body racked by the violence of his orgasm.

Afterwards, she floated, fascinated by the patterns the sun made through the forest foliage on the ceiling. A sudden anthem of bird-song, unusual in the drowsy warmth of early afternoon, strengthened her belief in the total rightness of what she had done.

Turning slightly, she saw tears in Noel's eyes. Knowing what was in his mind, she was untroubled.

"I always imagined it would be good," he said. "But that . . ."

Happiness made him sound almost heartbroken. Bess drew his head to her breasts to comfort both of them. She said, "I love you." There was no need for him to respond.

With all their instincts telling them that they were embarking on a deep and lasting friendship as well as an erotic odyssey, Bess and Noel spent the afternoon and early evening celebrating and venerating each other. Now that the woman he had loved and desired for so long was available to him and demonstrating a profligate willingness to make love, Noel ran riot. Bess, thrilled by her young lover's physical perfection, kindness, and stamina, outpaced him in audacity.

Finally, he fell back exhausted, declaring himself done for.

"That's a good thing, actually," Bess said. "I must go home and talk to Steven."

"About us?"

"Yes."

"Does that mean we might have a future?"

Bess sat up to stare at him. "Let me tell you *exactly* what I think," she said with quiet intensity. "Being here, like this, with you, is going to be the most fabulous thing I've ever known. It's going to make me forget all the bad things that have happened." Her face clouded. "The way Steven Hawksworth wasted away with that vile disease . . . do you remember his funeral, when you came to stand with me? Dame Amelia . . . she died in my arms, you know. Bloody Oliver and those poor horses . . . and strictly between ourselves, Noel, the appalling mess my ex-husband made of things, including our marriage!" She nodded at his look of surprise. "That's right, I'm tough, and people expect me not to care . . . I'm even supposed to shrug it off when folks go round saying that I only married Giles to get into the family. Imagine having to ignore that!" The vehemence ebbed from her. "Do we have a future? I tell you, Noel Timberlake, there'll be hell to pay if we don't."

"What about the difference in our ages?" he asked anxiously.

"Does it bother you?"

He laughed. "After what we've been doing? I mean, look at you!" He stroked a hand inside her thighs. "What legs!" He plunged into seriousness. "What about when the novelty wears off . . . will you still want me?"

She went into his arms. "I shall always want you, sweetheart," she murmured. "*Always*."

For ten minutes she nestled against his strong body, learning more about the feel and smell of him. With a supreme effort, she made herself go to the bathroom to shower. Noel watched as she dressed, entranced as she wriggled into her briefs, bemused by the T-shirt and track-suit trousers. To her amazement, he followed her downstairs and out through the front door without bothering to put on a stitch of clothing.

"Is that why you wanted to live out here?" she asked.

"Definitely!" he said, straight-faced. "Communing with nature stark-naked has always been my top priority."

He stood, waving, as she eased the Jaguar up the track towards the metalled lane. Before a bend removed Noel from view, she stopped, leaned out of the window, and returned the wave. He was like a mythical forest god, made real especially for her.

Back from his trip to Salisbury, Steven was preparing for bed when Bess arrived.

"Was it a good day?" she asked.

"Not bad, thanks."

"How's Leander?"

"Oh, bearing up, you know. Doing her best." Bess found it difficult not to smile. "She thinks I'm not getting enough riding practice."

It was, Bess admitted to herself, true. Not yet able to take charge of a racehorse, Steven tended to be ignored and left to his own devices on a hack. "What does she expect me to do about it?" she asked.

"Nothing. She knows you're busy, so she's going to sort me out in the holidays."

"Good for her! She won't have all that much time, though. Aunt Rebecca and Uncle William are off to France for nearly three weeks."

Steven shook his head. "Leander isn't going with them. She said so today."

"I see. And who's going to look after her?" Bess asked, conscious that it was probably a silly question.

"She'll stay here with us, of course." Steven was far too polite to show the irritation he must have felt. "What have you been doing with yourself?"

"Something rather important," Bess said. "I've been with Noel Timberlake."

"Oh?" To Bess's surprise, Steven looked cheerfully expectant. "Are you and he going to be good friends?"

"Er . . . yes, I think we are." Bess was uneasily conscious that he was ahead of her.

598

"That's good. He's very fond of you, and it's time you had a friend." To make sure that he was making himself plain, he added, "I mean a boyfriend."

Momentarily dumbfounded, Bess struggled to ask: "How do you make that out?"

"I didn't," Steven admitted. "It was Leander."

"And she'll be pleased to know that we're getting on with it?" The gentle sarcasm was ignored, of course.

"Definitely! So am I. Mind you . . ." he became frighteningly earnest ". . . it probably isn't a good idea to marry him."

"I don't think that's on the cards," Bess replied.

"Well, that's all right, then."

To her surprise, the episode gave Bess a belated new insight into her ex-husband. Compared with most of the Hawkesworths and Flamsteeds, Giles was quite an ordinary sort of person. She now saw that Steven and the astounding Leander, neither of whom ever displayed the slightest interest in the things that seemed to obsess most youngsters, if TV and the newspapers were anything to go by, were probably much more typical of the people who had made Cannings Ambo.

Having said goodnight to Steven, Bess went to the sitting-room where Henrietta was making a very poor job of displaying calm disinterest.

"Henry, you look like a bloody great question mark," Bess chuckled as she sat down, stretching out in a gesture of luxurious hedonism.

"What do you expect? I'm agog. How did you get on?"

Bess thought about it, coming to the conclusion that the truth was unbeatable. "We spent a stupendous five hours in bed."

Henrietta was impressed. "Is he good?"

"Magnificent," Bess said with her broadest grin. "Absolutely magnificent. I feel marvellous."

"Actually, you look it."

"Thank you, Henry! I take it you approve?"

"Of course I do! It was my idea."

"Was it? Oh, yes! Well done, Henry!"

No one failed to notice Bess's mood on Monday morning. She was in the yard ten minutes earlier than usual, here, there and everywhere at once, cajoling, chivvying, praising and lambasting, and all in the most lustrous good humour that anyone could remember. Rebecca and Arthur Merriweather exchanged looks and braced themselves for a morning and a half.

While the fun and games on the gallops was in progress, Henrietta waltzed into Noel's office, relieved to find that Cathy Jones was out on an errand.

"Hello, maestro, I need to get into your cottage," she said, enjoying the effect the statement had on him.

"Any particular reason?" he asked mildly.

"The memsahib has instructed me to ensure that you stock a useful range of her clothes," Henrietta replied with mock-grandeur. "She can't be worrying about frocks and clean knickers all the time."

"Blimey!" He was visibly shaken.

"Yes, indeed! You've really been and gorn and done it."

"How about this evening?" Noel suggested weakly.

"That's the spirit! I hope you've got plenty of wardrobe-space."

"I have."

"Expect me at seven. One other thing: does this flea-pit of yours have such a thing as a freezer?"

"Yes, a big one . . . in the outhouse. Why?"

"You are to be stocked up with gourmet goodies from Valerie's kitchen," Henrietta explained. "You need good grub to keep your strength up. Right, see you this evening." In the midst of dashing off, she changed her mind, swooping to place a kiss on his forehead. "Who's a clever boy, then?" she said, laughing at the dazed look on his face.

After lunch, Bess took a pre-emptive strike against gossip: she went round telling people about herself and Noel.

Amaryllis was poleaxed, but could think of only one objection when she recovered. "He's not too young for you?"

"No!" Bess declared.

"I wonder what Gideon will make of this?" Amaryllis sounded uncertain.

"Don't let him come the heavy hand," Bess warned. "If he does, I shall take Noel away to a desert island."

Elsie and Boggysevick approved at once. "I don't know why it's taken you so long," Elsie said. "There's one thing I forgot to hammer into you, my girl: you pass this way but once, so you'd better enjoy yourself."

Boggysevick confirmed the sentiment with a wink. "Your Mr Timberlake is a very *strong* man, I think," he said.

"Yes, Dad," Bess smiled. "Very strong indeed."

At Oak Cottage, Eileen went into hysterics. Joe glanced at her over the top of his glasses. "I suppose you know what you're doing, Bessie?" he said.

"I most certainly do, Joseph!"

"I thought you might."

Finally, Bess told Ann, approaching the matter with some trepidation over dinner while Henrietta was ferrying clothes to Savernake Forest.

"That seems a reasonable arrangement," Ann said. "Noel has adored you for years. I've often felt sorry for him. And there's good historical precedent, of course," Ann smiled. "Hawksworth women have always turned to the Timberlakes for consolation! I sometimes thought it was a pity that Gideon was so happily married when I needed it."

The confession, a reminder of Steven's untimely death, left Bess open-mouthed.

It was a hectic week and Bess was unable to go to Noel's lodge until Saturday. Having been delayed at Lingfield racecourse, and by traffic on the way back, it was nearly eight o'clock when she arrived. After a scorchingly hot day, the evening remained warm and sticky.

"What shall we do for food?" Noel asked, thinking that she would be starving.

"That can wait," she replied. "I want a shower and you!"

Noel insisted on joining her in the bathroom, forcing their

need for each other to breaking point. What followed on the floor was an act of furious necessity, haunted by a doubt that was quickly resolved by Bess's cataclysmic orgasm.

"Thank God!" she gasped. "I *didn't* imagine last Sunday!"

"I was worried about that, too," Noel confessed.

Half an hour later, over one of Valerie's pre-cooked meals from the freezer, Noel told her of the problems their frequent encounters in the office and yard caused him. "I don't know how I've kept my hands off you," he said, trying to make a joke of it. "Wednesday was the worst – those maroon breeches! Couldn't you wear dungarees three sizes too big?"

"What about you on Thursday?" Bess retorted. "Why were you flaunting yourself in those jeans? Cathy nearly passed out when you fetched those invoices from the filing cabinet."

They were eating in the garden and were both naked, enjoying the sybaritic feeling of the evening breeze and the sight of each other's bodies.

"By the way, how did you get on at Lingfield?" Noel asked as an eventual afterthought.

"They both won," Bess said.

"That's nine this week."

"I say!" Bess remembered something. "I bumped into a chap called Penrose . . . he said he was a friend of your father's."

"That's right . . . Cyril Penrose. He's a nice chap."

"He wants me to take his horses."

"Another one!" Noel pulled a face. "At this rate, we could use an extra sixty boxes next year."

"I'm going to talk to the Trustees about it," Bess said. "I fancy going the whole hog and having a hundred."

"That's an awful lot of building."

"Not if we go for one of those big sheds the Americans use," Bess said. "They're relatively cheap and a doddle to work – everything's under cover, you see."

They carried on talking about a massively enlarged Latimer's Barn as they tidied away after the meal and wandered back into the garden where Bess lay down on a gentle slope that was velvet-smooth with moss and lush grass.

"I wonder when I'll start believing that this is real," Noel said, kneeling down beside her.

Bess smiled affectionately. "I'd hate to think I've been telling everyone about a daydream," she replied.

"Yes, I heard about that." He was still unsure what to make of her proclamation.

"It did for the rumour-mongers before they had a chance to get going," Bess said happily.

"Don't you dare tell her I said so, but Mother thought you were doing a bit of boasting as well."

"Of course I was! Any reaction from your father yet?"

Noel laughed. "From what I can gather, he's pleased I've found something useful to do at last. He believes that whatever makes you happy is to be encouraged."

Bess imagined how Gideon would have expressed himself. Stretching out on the cool earth, she experienced pure contentment. Soon, desire would overcome them: until then, she wanted to enjoy a tranquillity that had always eluded her.

Noel woke at six-thirty on Sunday morning to find that he was engaged in love-making. He was, of course, the passive partner: while he lay sprawled on his back, Bess was astride him. She pretended disappointment when his eyes fluttered open to stare up at her with what seemed to be affronted disbelief.

"You are a spoil-sport," she complained. "I was hoping to make you come while you were still asleep."

"I was having a marvellous dream," he grumbled.

"I'm not surprised with what I was doing to you!" She frowned at him. "This is a bit of a let-down, is it?" Leaning forward slightly, she caressed the entire length of his penis with a ripple of her vaginal muscles.

Writhing with pleasure, Noel shook his head. "No. I couldn't honestly call this a let-down."

"Oh, good!" She demonstrated what she could do with her thighs, giving him further ecstatic torture. "I think I'm beginning to get the hang of this."

"You're well on the way," he agreed. "What bothers me is that you weren't satisfied with that set-to in the garden."

"I was *very* satisfied," Bess said. "But it was seven hours ago . . . I want more!" She laughed at him. "That's right, my boy, you're stuck with a middle-aged nymphomaniac. What do you think of that, eh?"

Using his considerable strength to devastating effect, Noel toppled her from her dominant position.

"That's not fair!" she moaned. "I wanted to be on top . . . I can get even more of you that way."

"Later!" he snapped, his voice hardened by urgent desire. "This is what *I* want!"

Bess surrendered joyously, delighted by the discovery that Noel was no longer in awe of her.

The day that followed set the seal on their relationship and the way it was to evolve. Both in the lodge and outside in the forest, they made love almost incessantly. In the cool of the evening, Noel carried out his promise of the early morning; lying back on the grassy bank that had given Bess so much excitement, he let her straddle him, content that she should regulate their pleasure. As she did so, a luminous smile spread across her face.

"Tell me," he said.

"It was something Leander said to me just before she died," Bess murmured. "She thought that the people who followed her were in for a good time. 'Heirs to adventure' she called them."

"That's a nice idea," Noel said reflectively.

They were silent for a while, enjoying the gentle, loving reaction of their bodies. Inasmuch as she was able to display any emotion other than rapture, Bess seemed puzzled.

"What is it?" Noel asked.

"It's taken me a long time to get there," Bess replied. "But, by God, you watch me enjoy it and hang on to it!"

Rebecca and William, together with Matthew and Emma, duly went to France and Leander moved into the house, quickly establishing a formidable routine. After going out with

604

both lots every morning, she attended to Steven's equestrian education in the afternoons, then prepared two horses for evening stables. She also devoted time to marking Steven's card in preparation for his first term at Marlborough College. The fragments that Bess overheard were typically anarchic.

"Latin's a pain in the bum . . . Maths isn't *too* bad, but don't take any notice of Algebra . . . I think they ought to do something about the man who invented Physics . . . we need French for when we go to Longchamp . . . History's interesting, especially the Peasants' Revolt, but ignore all those kings!"

Steven, dreadfully earnest, took it all in.

Bess needed very little persuading by Gideon to send Bathsheba Everdene to Doncaster for the St Leger, and decided that the time had come to unveil Noel to the public.

They travelled to a lavish hotel in the depths of Lincolnshire on Friday, leaving them an easy twenty-five-mile drive to the course on the morning of the race. Bess made a gesture that convinced Noel she must love him dearly: she sat back while he drove. After a week of enforced celibacy, she was desperate for Noel when they reached the hotel. The fierceness of their union was exultant, yet it did not eclipse the honour of being allowed to take charge of her precious Jaguar for nearly two hundred miles.

Arriving at the Town Moor racecourse two hours before the St Leger, Bess and Noel attracted considerable attention. As a result of a morning in the hotel swimming-pool and sauna, during which they had made reckless love in a changing-room, they had an aura of harmony and physical well-being that was striking. Nigel Powycke, the biggest nuisance among Bess's unwelcome admirers, put two and two together and was livid.

Sam Montgomery turned up to watch one of his Newmarket-trained horses run in the St Leger. He was accompanied by Giles, who now spent most of his time in France.

"Where's Jane?" Bess asked as they greeted each other with the affectionate kiss that was the hallmark of this last and most satisfactory stage of their relationship.

"At home," Giles replied. "She's eight months pregnant."
Bess had forgotten that their second child was almost due.

"I suppose you're going to win?" Sam said to Bess.

"It's difficult to see any of this bunch beating my filly," Bess replied with a disdainful look round the paddock.

Sam pulled a face at Giles. "Such confidence!" he said.

"I think she's right," Giles said. "It will be one of the upsets of the century if Bathsheba Everdene doesn't walk all over them."

After the horses had left the paddock, Giles fell in beside Bess as they walked to the grandstand to watch the race.

"How's Steven?" he asked.

"Very well. He's starting at Marlborough on Monday."

"Yes, he told me in his last letter. He sounded pretty pleased about it."

"He is. Are you going to have time to see him while you're over here?"

Giles squirmed. "Not really . . . I'm going back on Wednesday and Sam wants to go to Ireland on Monday." Acutely conscious that he was making excuses yet again, Giles grasped the nettle. "He's not *all* that bothered about seeing me, is he?"

"He likes your letters," Bess said. "And you must make the effort to take him to London before Christmas. You promised."

"I'll do my best."

Bess believed that he would, but it was destined to be a nerve-racking affair, especially if Leander were on holiday and insisted on going with them. She frightened Giles at the best of times: her latest fixation was to discover why her wretched uncle had found it necessary to marry three women before finding the right one.

The St Leger proved to be one of those races in which no one was willing to make the running. After two furlongs of funereal progress, Jonathan Pilgrim decided to jettison his instructions in favour of escape from the close-knit group the twelve runners had formed with its inevitable jostling. When asked to do so, Bathsheba Everdene picked her way out of the bunch and went into a two-length lead. At first, Jonathan settled her at the pace of the rest, but after six furlongs, he let her begin the gradual acceleration that she seemed to want. The opposition were deceived; not until the turn for home was it apparent that Bathsheba Everdene was bowling along at little more than a canter, while the rest were off the bit and struggling. Sam Montgomery and the other owners were only interested in the competition for second and third places. At the line, Bathsheba Everdene was seven lengths clear and Jonathan knew that Gideon would be very pleased: the whip had remained a passive ornament.

The filly was the ninth Derby winner that Latimer's Barn had sent to Doncaster over the years, something for which the Yorkshire crowd were grateful. Bess, accompanied by Gideon and Jonathan, lined up for the sponsor's presentations and were interviewed for TV. When they separated afterwards and Bess was on her way to the stables, she encountered Nigel Powycke, obviously lying in wait for her.

"Congratulations, Bess," he said. "Any chance of your people considering an offer for that filly?"

"Sorry, Nigel, the money hasn't been minted that could buy her."

"Oh, well, no harm in asking. Er . . . young Timberlake . . . he's your administration manager, isn't he?"

"And a very good one."

"I don't remember seeing him at a meeting before."

"It's a special treat," Bess said, totally serious. "He's earned it. You see, Nigel, he's my lover, and I've been giving him a *very* hard time of it."

Noel, who saw the encounter from a distance of fifty yards, commented on Powycke's flabbergasted air of defeat. "What did you say to him?" he asked when they were together afterwards.

"Nothing much," Bess said casually. "To stop him pestering me, I mentioned that I was spoken for. He didn't seem all that pleased, did he?"

There were some who thought Bess was losing her grip. Her

apparent acceptance of Oliver's return to the village drew much comment in The George.

It was Helen's idea.

She and Oliver had remained friends after their solitary Christmas together, although she never went back to the remote house in Berkshire. Oliver was firmly attached to it and drove down most weekends, probably with a woman, Helen thought.

Difficulties at Wm Flamsteed & Sons offered Oliver the chance of partial rehabilitation in Cannings Ambo. A trade fair in Chicago, at which a range of new designs was exhibited, yielded very disappointing results. The orders directly attributable to the venture failed to recover its costs. Helen, who had been involved in setting up and running the Flamsteed stand at the fair, told Oliver of its almost certain failure soon after she returned from America.

"That's bad!" he said. "There's nothing wrong with the product. What was your promotion like?"

"We took a full page in the trade press and had tons of brochures on the stand," Helen replied.

"I'd like to see what you did."

A few days later, he threw up his hands in dismay after inspecting what she had brought. "This is awful, Helen! With stuff like this, you were lucky to get *any* interest. Who handles your advertising?"

It was something Helen had felt uneasy about for some time. "It's mostly our own efforts," she said. "There's a bright girl at the printer's who makes good suggestions."

"That won't do, Helen, not for today, and definitely not for the States."

"Secretly, I agree with you," she said. "The snag is, there's a cultural tradition of Flamsteed's *not* to pay the exorbitant fees that folks like you charge."

Oliver made no immediate response: the idea that occurred to him needed thinking through and discussion with his colleagues. A week later, however, he was able to tell Helen the details.

"I'll *give* you two days a month of my time and a top-flight copy-writer," he said. "We'll do artwork at cost and advise you of the best placings."

"That's very good of you," Helen said. "I'll pass it on to William."

At first, William did not know what to think. Tempted, he felt bound to ask: "Would that mean Oliver coming here?"

"If he doesn't, you'll have to go to him," Helen replied. "That's time and money."

"Bess won't like that!" William said.

"I have every sympathy with her point of view," Helen replied. "But if Oliver keeps well away from Latimer's Barn, I can't see a problem. I'll speak to her about it."

After consulting Rebecca and his father, William decided to accept Oliver's offer. As well as the potential business advantages, Rebecca expressed a strong desire to be able to see her brother without the need to travel, usually at awkward times. The same, she hinted strongly, was true of Ann.

Oliver paid his first visit to Rose House in June, at about the time that Bess and Noel were discovering each other. A start was made on dreaming up a new corporate image for Wm Flamsteed & Sons and Ann was present at the special lunch Rebecca laid on. More by design than accident, Helen had forgotten to mention it to Bess.

It was left to Ann to break the news and she waited until the middle of October. By that time, Bess was very nearly finished with another racing season and heavily preoccupied with thoughts of what she and Noel could make of her additional free time.

She took it well. "He can do what he likes so long as he stays away from my horses," Bess said. "Is he any good at this advertising business?"

"Very good, I understand," Ann replied.

"Well, you never know, he might even be useful!"

Ann refrained from saying so, but Oliver had already proved invaluable: a trial circulation of his ideas in Detroit and Pittsburgh had more than made good the losses of the Chicago fair.

*　　*　　*

609

In November, Noel's younger brother, Desmond, married Antonia Chadburn whom he had known since they came across each other at Oxford in 1978. It was an open secret that Gideon had told them to get on with it: he needed grandsons for dynastic purposes and it was very clear that Noel, pledged to Bess for life, would be unable to provide them.

The social occasion afforded by the wedding was the first opportunity Neil Walker was given of seeing Cannings Ambo in full flight. He had arrived only a month before, brought in by William to look after the small computer that was now vital to Wm Flamsteed & Sons. No one knew much about him because he was renting a house in Marlborough until suitable accommodation could be found in the village.

Neil Walker was a personable, intelligent individual who had yet to make a final decision about Cannings Ambo. Its setting in the Downs, the sheer attractiveness of the village, and the open-handed friendliness of the close-knit community were a pleasant change from the cities in which all his life had been spent. What appeared to lie beneath the surface, however, was less to his taste. Like so many of his background and type, Neil Walker had no objection to a meritocracy wielding almost absolute power so long as he was a leading member of the governing body. After a week of watching how the village worked, he deduced that the chances of him ever being granted such a status were negligible.

But the day of the wedding brought two unexpected and very pleasant surprises. Walker found himself being introduced to the chairman of Timberlake Holdings. Better still, Gideon gave the impression that he would welcome access to a computer expert. Without giving anything away, he indicated that one of his group's subsidiaries needed help. At the least, a lucrative consultancy assignment seemed a definite prospect.

Shortly after Gideon had returned to the more important wedding guests, Henrietta bounced into Neil Walker's life, introducing herself and firing off a barrage of questions. After he had answered them, Henrietta explained her presence by telling him that she belonged to Bess Hawksworth.

Walker was intrigued. He had not met Bess, but was sick of hearing about her and had come to the conclusion that she was the focal point of the autocratic power that, as an outsider, he despised so heartily. It was essential not to say so, however, for whatever else Henrietta was doing as she chatted away, she was signalling her availability.

Prince Omar had not visited Latimer's Barn, or requested her company elsewhere for over eighteen months. Henrietta was looking for an attachment.

CHAPTER 23

1988

'She's going to be something!'

Neil Walker began looking for another job the day after he discovered that Gideon did not intend giving him work.

When he went back to London in August, after only ten months with Wm Flamsteed & Sons, Henrietta was not completely sure that she was pregnant. Joe had to face up to telling her two weeks later: as things were to turn out, Neil Walker, busily carving a niche in an organisation that was much more to his taste than Cannings Ambo, never did learn that he was to be a father.

"What are we going to do about this, then?" Bess asked when she was told.

Henrietta noticed the 'we' and was profoundly grateful.

"I'm going to have the child," she said.

"Good!" It was obvious from Bess's attitude that the other possibility was unthinkable.

"Beyond that, I don't know," Henrietta admitted.

"Adoption?" Bess said tentatively.

"I think I'd hate that."

"In that case, you and the baby must stay here," Bess said firmly. "I'm dead against losing you, Henry, so there'll be a home for you both for as long as you want." She cut short Henrietta's gratitude with an order. "I suggest you take a long weekend to tell your parents about it. And don't look like that. They won't eat you!"

Despite Henrietta's obvious qualms, Bess was certain that Colonel and Mrs Corbishley would be delighted to be grandparents, despite the slightly difficult circumstances. Sure enough, her confidence in them, derived from several encounters over the years, proved well-founded.

The child, a boy, was born on 26 February 1986. With Bess and Noel standing as godparents, he was christened Simon Corbishley. Leander invented the roles of god-sister and brother for herself and Steven. Henrietta's parents, guests at Latimer's Barn for a week, realised that their grandson would lack for nothing, especially love. Not only was Henrietta destined to be a far better mother than they had ever imagined, young Simon won a special place in Bess's heart.

During the winter of 1987–88 Latimer's Barn underwent its biggest expansion ever. The centre-piece of the two-million-pounds investment was a vast shed to provide opulent accommodation for one hundred horses. Nearly two hundred yards long and eighty wide, it lay along a north-south line between the Roadway and an extension of the Back Stretch.

At each end of the shed, massive sliding doors were big enough to allow the largest of the three transporter vans to be driven into the broad central aisle. Much of the routine chores of mucking-out and providing fresh bedding were mechanised with conveyor belts. Alarm systems for unauthorised entry and smoke detection were controlled by a small computer; in an annex at the southern end, there was a 'health club' in which tired horses could receive sun-lamp and jacuzzi treatment.

The designers were Bess, Steven and Leander. After months of scouring books and specialist magazines, Steven drew the final plans. These, along with Leander's voluminous specification, were given to the contractor: Harry Irons, whose family had spent very nearly one hundred and fifty years building Latimer's Barn, said he'd never seen anything like it. Noel stood back in wonder, astounded at the trust Bess placed in Steven and Leander.

The press coverage of the project was extensive. Throughout the winter, a time when flat racing was normally out of the public eye, hardly a day passed without some journalist attempting to find a new angle. On the whole, Bess was pleased, although some of the language used earned her displeasure. Early on, an imbecile on one of the tabloids produced the headline: 'The Hi-Tech Stable' and it stuck. Largely as a consequence, the telephone never stopped ringing.

The major justification for the massive expansion was that Bess had finally agreed to take seven new patrons, all of them well-established in racing. But the 'Hi-Tech' nonsense produced a plague of unsuitable people who wanted to become owners: they were dealt with briskly, especially since Bess intended having only fifty horses in the shed for 1988 in order to allow time for the settling-down process.

Infinitely more welcome were the calls from lads looking for a job. For them, the attraction of working for Bess Hawksworth at Latimer's Barn was increased by stories of the splendid new hostel and houses under construction. Over three hundred experienced lads applied. Bess spoke to fifty of them and set twenty on. The other five vacancies in the first batch went to youngsters from Marlborough who wanted to start at the bottom and learn.

Everything was ready for the end of February 1988 and Bess set about proving that it could all be made to work. The first time she took a string of eighty horses on to Cannings Down, she was half-afraid that she had bitten off more than she could chew.

"Ye Gods, what's it going to be like next year with over a hundred in each lot?" she asked Rebecca and Arthur Merriweather.

Rebecca was inclined to share in the misgivings, but Arthur was having none of it. "It's nothing like as bad as it looks," he said. "We'll soon get the hang of it."

He was right, of course.

There was usually one incident or topic that set the lads speculating with the approach of a new season. This time, all the talk concerned a two-year-old chestnut colt. Never had there been such a divergent crop of rumours. The owner, Gideon Timberlake no less, thought he was destined to be useless and wanted him sent to the sales.

The other side of the argument provided compelling evidence to the contrary. Bess and Miss Leander had broken and schooled him, never letting anyone else near; he had been allocated to Caesar, always a sign of high expectations; and, instead of going into the pampered luxury of the new shed, his box was on the south-facing side of the 1874 yard. As Jimmy Farrant, the stable's statistician, pointed out, Latimer's Barn had won ninety-eight Classic races so far and seventy-three of those victories had come from horses in that line of fifteen boxes.

The colt's name was The Yeoman.

After her 1984 St Leger victory, Bathsheba Everdene was retired to stud at Cannings St John. By late spring of the following year, she was confirmed in foal to Athelstan. Well in advance of the birth, Gideon said that with both sire and dam as Derby winners, and Astronomer Royal as paternal grandsire, the result had to be either a world-beater or a wash-out.

The colt, born at a few minutes to midnight on the same day that saw Simon Corbishley's entry into the world, was perfectly sound and healthy. But he was a chestnut. Gideon, his owner by virtue of his rights to Bathsheba Everdene, was a firm believer in the theory that chestnuts always suffered from lack of courage, poor wind, defective eyesight and downright stupidity. Worse was to come: as the colt began to grow and develop, it became obvious that he was to have a flaxen mane and tail. He was going to be the prettiest horse that anyone had ever seen and was, therefore, doomed to failure.

Leander fell in love with him on sight and the feeling was lavishly mutual. She did much more than drool over him, however: from the day she watched his first attempts to emulate his mother's twice-daily gallops round their paddock, Leander insisted that he was destined to be a superb natural athlete and Bess found no reason to disagree. Unmoved by their opinions, Gideon wanted the colt entered for the Newmarket October sales.

Strangely, it was an offer to buy that changed his mind. In August 1986, Alain de Mourville spent a week at Latimer's Barn, visiting the stud several times: he took one look at the chestnut and offered Lady Amaryllis £300,000 for him. When told, Gideon was badly shaken. A great respecter of Alain's judgement, he decided to hang on to the colt. He was registered as The Yeoman and seemed glad of the chance to show what he could do in the Timberlake colours.

When he finally moved into his new home in the 1874 yard, two things were immediately apparent. He *did* have the makings of a very good horse. To set against this, there was the growing certainty that he only exerted himself when he could see Leander, or knew that she was not far away. Rather like the relationship between Bess and Apollinaire in 1951, it was very noticeable in the middle of April when Leander was back in Salisbury after the Easter holidays. During the three weeks that she had danced attendance on him, The Yeoman had looked like ten million pounds-worth on the gallops; the day after she returned to the Godolphin School, he was mediocre.

Rebecca commented on it at once.

Bess was thoughtful. "We have to assume that Steven will tell Leander," she said.

"Don't worry, I know what's coming," Rebecca sighed. "She'd better leave school this summer."

"Do you want her to carry on?" Bess asked.

"Yes, but I haven't got the vaguest idea how I could justify it. I can't say, 'Look, please spend two years in the sixth form, darling. It won't do *you* any good, but it would make me happy.' In any case, I'm pretty sure William will support her. He thinks she deserves a medal for getting this far."

"Don't give in too easily," Bess advised. "Make the little beast sweat it out."

"I'll try," Rebecca said doubtfully. "You definitely want her for The Yeoman, though?"

"No question about it," Bess replied. "Without her, we may as well forget him."

Purely for something to do, and to find out how he reacted to horses he did not know, Bess gave The Yeoman a run at Newbury in May. Against opposition that was far from outstanding, he finished a disappointing third, although he did nothing wrong.

"He wasn't terribly interested, was he?" Bess asked Jonathan Pilgrim, who had obeyed his instructions to the letter and not forced the colt.

"I think it's something else," Jonathan replied.

"What?"

"I've got a hunch that five furlongs is too sharp for him."

"Will six be any better?" Bess asked.

"I doubt it. I reckon you're looking for at least a mile."

Bess smiled ironically. "We have a problem, don't we?"

Only in the last two months of the season were two-year-olds allowed to race over distances greater than six furlongs.

That evening, she stayed with Noel at his lodge, and even as she lay in his arms, he could see that she was deep in thought.

"What's worrying you?" he asked.

"The Yeoman is proving awkward."

"Tell me about it."

She did, stressing her wish to do well with the colt if only because of Gideon's original misgivings.

"It's annoying," Noel agreed. "By no means uncommon, though. There are lots of great horses who've been no good over the sprint distances as two-year-olds."

"Such as?" Bess asked sceptically.

"Allez-France, Sea-Bird, poor old Shergar," Noel said unhesitatingly. "Nijinsky was hard pressed to get six furlongs . . . and what about Lindisfarne?"

"Do you know, I'd forgotten that," Bess said. "Thank you!"

"There you are," Noel said. "I'm not just a pretty face. You could find all sorts of uses for me."

"There's one I'm particularly interested in at the moment."

"Oh Lord, here we go again!" he moaned.

Although Bess knew that he was joking, her response was fearsomely serious. "Don't run away with the idea that I think life's easy," she said. "I could *scream* at half the things that happen . . . look at yesterday morning, for Christ's sake!" A filly belonging to one of the new owners had pulled up, apparently lame, while exercising. There had been no obvious mishap, but she was in great distress. Eleanor Davidson had rushed out to examine her, only to find that the filly had broken a cannon bone: there was no alternative to putting her down. "That was the worst for a while," Bess went on. "But there's something two or three times a week that makes me wonder whether it's all worth it. And do you know what I always think of when things get bad? I look forward to the next time you can make love to me."

No longer flippant, Noel took powerful possession of her.

Before Leander was able to launch her campaign to escape from school, there was intervention on her behalf from an unexpected quarter. Attending a parents' day in early June, Rebecca found herself tactfully shepherded into the headmistress's study on the pretext of tea and biscuits. Once the door was shut, the severely attractive Miss Buchan got down to brass tacks.

"What are your plans for Leander's future, Mrs Flamsteed?" Seeing Rebecca's speechless quandary, she smiled sympathetically. "It's probably more useful to consider *Leander's* plans for her future."

"Yes, that might be best," Rebecca agreed.

"As I understand it, she will be joining what one might call 'the family business'?"

Despite her nervousness, Rebecca smiled at Miss Buchan's deliberately quaint description of Latimer's Barn. "Most definitely!" she said.

"Leander seems very firmly of the opinion that she should start full-time work this summer."

"Yes." Rebecca decided to put her cards on the table.

618

"The fact is, Miss Buchan, I would like her to stay on for two more years. I know there's no question of her going to university, but I do feel she would benefit . . . after all, I'm an old girl myself."

"Quite." Miss Buchan smiled encouragingly.

"On the other hand, Leander would be useful to us in the stable," Rebecca admitted. "We have a potentially brilliant horse who's as good as useless when she isn't around. Mrs Hawksworth wants her as soon as possible."

"I recommend that you follow Mrs Hawksworth's wishes," Miss Buchan said with quiet firmness.

"Oh!" Rebecca was crestfallen.

"You see, Mrs Flamsteed, I believe that if we attempt to keep Leander here, she will become a disruptive influence. She's been very good and put up with a great deal because she's known that she's *had* to. Her legal obligation to submit to education is over and I think she will object very strongly to being made to stay here. Actually, to be frank with you, I don't imagine for a moment that we *could* keep her here."

Rebecca bowed to the inevitable. "Very well, Miss Buchan. I suppose it's for the best."

"It is, believe me. Perhaps you'd like to give her the good news, Mrs Flamsteed."

Rebecca found Leander with a group of her friends at the tennis courts. Approaching them, she received something of a shock. They were all aged sixteen or thereabouts, but whereas the others were clearly schoolgirls, albeit mature and sophisticated, Leander was a young woman. The others giggled, she smiled; they were unsure what to do with themselves, she was proud and ramrod straight; Leander's hair was a stylishly cut golden mane in superb condition, her companions looked a bit of a mess.

Leander saw Rebecca and hurried to meet her. "Are you all right, Mother?" she asked anxiously. "Betty Cavendish said you'd been captured and dragged off to the dragon's lair."

"Miss Buchan is a very nice woman," Rebecca said, attempting a rebuke. "And *I* asked to see *her*, as a matter of fact."

619

"Oh, I see." Leander looked slightly puzzled, taken in by the white lie that Rebecca had decided to employ.

"Yes. I'm afraid I wanted to tell her that your father and I don't see any point in throwing good money after bad to get you educated. You'll jolly well have to leave at the end of term."

"Crikey! I'll bet she was livid," Leander said.

"I don't think she was all that pleased," Rebecca replied. "If I were you, I'd keep well out of the way until it's time to come home."

"I will. I'm sorry I haven't been any good at learning things," Leander said contritely. "I *have* tried, honestly!"

"I expect your Aunt Bess will be able to fix you up with a job," Rebecca said, knowing full well that Leander had acquired more than enough learning. "You realise that The Yeoman won't settle without you?"

Leander nodded sagely. "I'll do what I can, but it's a big responsibility."

"Do your best, my dear, do your best," Rebecca murmured, finding the strain of keeping a straight face becoming intolerable.

Leander had no such difficulty. Over tea and cream cakes in the marquee, she was a model of obedient solemnity. Not until Rebecca was on her way back to Latimer's Barn did young Miss Flamsteed let rip. Among those parents who were staying on for an evening madrigal concert were fathers who were often rather too eager to visit their daughters' school. They were forced to profess indifference as quite the best-looking girl most of them had ever seen performed a series of astoundingly proficient cartwheels across the main lawn, displaying splendid legs and a pair of decidedly non-regulation knickers.

Steven received the news at seven o'clock that evening while he was immersed in a nasty piece of Physics homework. He looked up briefly, said, "That's good," and returned to the struggle with Newton's laws.

Leander came back to Cannings Ambo on 30 June. Her sole

concession to her emotions was an unequivocal statement that she would never leave again, apart from overnight absences demanded by racing and holidays. The latter, she implied, would be rare. During the afternoon, she haggled ruthlessly with Bess over wages. Having graciously settled for sixty pounds a week, Leander started work in the yard at six-thirty the following morning. Caesar bowed to the inevitable at once. "There you are, Miss Leander," he said, pointing towards The Yeoman's box. "He's all yours!"

It took the colt a few days to become accustomed to his good fortune, then he began to work with a vengeance. On the morning he did his first serious gallop, all activity ceased as everyone gaped, not only at the colt's zest and superb action, but at the fluent concord between him and his exciting rider.

"Will you look at that!" an awed Arthur Merriweather muttered.

"Brilliant," Rebecca agreed.

"I'd say it was eighty years since there's been anything as good," Bess said. She was plucking a figure out of the air: those gathered round her knew what she meant and nodded agreement.

When she was not performing on the gallops or working in the yard, Leander was impatient to begin dressing in a style that enhanced her looks and projected the image she wished to cultivate. Quite simply, that meant copying Bess. On an afternoon when Bess was free, they went into Bath and Farquharson's gained a new customer.

Largely because she was nervous of inactivity, Bess gave The Yeoman a race at the end of August. Over seven furlongs at Newbury, he finished second after being allowed to make his own way. This time, it was clear what had happened: for the first five furlongs, the natural sprinters had made The Yeoman look distinctly pedestrian. Then, as they began to run out of steam, he had passed all but one of them.

"The winning post came too soon," Jonathan said and Bess believed him. She made up her mind about the colt's future on the spot and turned her attention to the next race in which one of Alain de Mourville's horses was attempting a come-back.

Rouget de Lisle was a four-year-old who had missed the previous season through a series of mishaps and illnesses, most of them minor. Among his litany of misfortunes, he went lame on the way to the start in the Two Thousand Guineas, developed a mysterious fever on the day before the Derby, failed abysmally and inexplicably in the Eclipse Stakes, and put himself out of action for a month by banging a knee on a stable door. Now, at long last, he was sound and in good spirits. Bess gave Jonathan a leg up, stood back and crossed her fingers.

For every one of her horses that went on to a racecourse and did exactly what was expected, there were at least five big disappointments. Bess often felt that if she had been given ten pounds for every one of the unfathomable flops she had watched over the years, the total would double her massive, ever-accumulating savings. There were occasions, however, when wildest dreams became reality; they were very, very rare, but that afternoon was one of them. When the starter released them from the stalls, Rouget de Lisle came out like a rocket and set off in a fashion that made Bess absolutely certain that the other eight runners were going to see nothing but his backside for the entire mile and a half. As the race progressed and his lead increased to the final twenty-five lengths, the greatest winning margin ever achieved by one of her horses, Bess's smile broadened until Leander dug her in the ribs and told her to stop the Cheshire-cat act.

An hour later, when they were on their way back home, Leander broke the silence in which Bess liked to extract maximum enjoyment from driving the Jaguar.

"You'll be sending The Yeoman to Ascot and Rouget to Longchamp," she said.

Bess inclined her head in a gesture of affirmation and respect. Leander may not have proved very bright academically, but her grasp of racing strategy was already impressive.

* * *

Steven began the school year in September with a new method of transport. At a cost of over a month's wages, Leander had bought him a racing-type bicycle, something he had always wanted. He set out on it each morning at eight o'clock, while the first lot were going through their paces and there was no one but Henrietta to see him off. But his return soon acquired a distinctive ceremonial.

By ten past four, Leander was waiting at the bottom of the drive. Steven was never more than a few minutes late. When he arrived, Leander kissed him, taking great care over it, embracing him with firm warmth. That completed, Steven dismounted from his cycle and Leander climbed on. Sitting upright, an arm round his shoulders, she chatted and laughed as Steven walked them both up the drive.

They were devoted to Ann and usually went straight to the small sitting-room to have tea and biscuits with her. Ann loved all her grandchildren dearly, but this pair were special: she cherished them as one of the most precious gifts of her life, yet had no idea what to make of them for much of the time. She often thought it might be easier for her if they were more like other teenagers, with short-lived fads, a boisterous disrespect for anything and anyone older than them, and an engaging lack of interest in 'useful' or 'adult' things.

There were times when the other-worldly maturity of Leander and Steven was unnerving. Ann would pull herself together, reminding herself that she was seventy-two and drifting out of touch. Come to think of it, had she ever been *in* touch with the more extraordinary facets of the family into which she had married? Twenty-one years after the death of her beloved Steven, his steely determination was largely forgotten in favour of abiding memories of the loving and gentle side of his nature.

Of one thing Ann was certain: the future of Latimer's Barn lay with these two phenomenal youngsters. It was becoming apparent that both of them would prove capable of holding the licence, a hitherto unknown luxury of choice. Presumably the final decision would be governed by what Leander and Steven wanted to do and their choice of marriage partners.

Ann agreed with Rebecca that talk of them marrying each other was wishful thinking from the village. Certainly they were close, but they had a lot of growing up to do, a process that was bound to be hastened when they met new people.

One afternoon when Steven had disappeared to make an early start on his homework, Ann asked Leander, "Tell me, my dear, how many boys do you know?"

"Apart from Steven and the lads?" Leander asked.

"Yes."

"None."

Ann looked smug, unaware that her granddaughter was wondering what on earth she hoped to make of that totally useless piece of information.

On the last Saturday in September, the clearest possible indication was given of things to come.

Walking The Yeoman round the paddock before the Royal Lodge Stakes at Ascot, Leander attracted admiring glances and comment; she wore navy-blue slacks and a matching roll-neck sweater. At the nape of her neck, a scarlet bow held her golden hair in place. A buzz went through the crowd as her identity was guessed.

"That must be Leander Flamsteed."

"She's going to be something!"

"She is already!"

Seeing the interest, Gideon whispered to Bess, "Don't you think you're overdoing it?"

"Are you going soft?" she demanded. "We *are* the best, why shouldn't we show it?"

Not to be outshone by his companion, The Yeoman looked magnificent, but drew little support from punters, most of whom thought he was way out of his class. Against his modest form, his seven opponents had won eighteen races between them, eleven of Pattern status. Strolling along the line of bookies in the Silver Ring, Solstice had a hundred pounds on at ten to one without creating any interest.

The Yeoman's easy elegance as he set off for the start caused some expert eyes to narrow, but the reservations about his colour, coupled with dire misgivings about his flaxen mane and tail, offset the favourable comments on his action.

From the outset, the race was run at a cracking pace. The Yeoman ambled along at the back, taking his time to settle and looking only mildly interested in the proceedings. Jonathan Pilgrim, also relaxed, was watchful. After four furlongs, the half-way point, he reached his decision. The pair at the front had no hope of maintaining their speed and two of the pursuers were short of stamina.

Bess and Leander, watching through binoculars, saw Jonathan go to work.

"I wonder if that isn't a shade too early," Bess said.

"No, I'd say that was bang on," Leander replied.

"He's going nicely."

"There!" Leander said with quiet satisfaction. "He's changed his legs. Now we shall see."

Standing between them, Gideon marvelled at their cool objectivity: they both seemed to be commenting on something that had nothing whatsoever to do with them. The excitement did not appear for another two furlongs, by which time The Yeoman had wiped the floor with everything in sight and was having a go at the course record.

"There you are, look. What did I tell you?" Leander crowed. "Whoopee!"

"Hush, child," Bess said, the binoculars still glued to her eyes. "Let's have some decorum . . . we have standards to think of. Remember that you're supposed to collect him . . . assuming that Jonathan can stop him, which looks unlikely at the moment!"

Leander dashed off to attend to her duties with The Yeoman and Bess turned to Gideon. "Well?" she smiled.

"I was wrong," he said manfully. "He's a good horse."

"He's a *very* good horse," Bess said. Moving closer and lowering her voice, she added, "For what it's worth, I think he may turn out to be the best horse that Latimer's Barn has ever had."

Gideon stepped back in amazement. "Better than Astronomer Royal?" he asked.

"Yes!" Bess was adamant.

She sang a very different tune when she was grabbed for an interview by Wesley Davies. Yes, The Yeoman had come on well and *might* be a decent horse in the making. No, there weren't any definite plans for him at the moment, it was a question of seeing how he was after his efforts this afternoon. It was, of course, far too early to start speculating about the 1989 Classics.

For the Prix de l'Arc de Triomphe, Bess embarked on a blatant combination of business and pleasure, claiming that it was Alain and Nadia's idea. She and Noel travelled to Fontainebleau five days before the race, leaving Rebecca and Arthur Merriweather to look after Latimer's Barn, while Rouget de Lisle and his party flew over on the morning of the event.

Bess and Noel joined a large group of guests who had come to the château from all over Europe to celebrate Alain's seventieth birthday on Saturday, the eve of the Arc. Always popular and often in the news, Alain had both endured and enjoyed a summer of attention from press and television. Much had been made of his businesses, which now employed over thirty thousand people, his work for charity, and, although he would have preferred to forget it, his war-time escapades with the *Résistance*. Once his birthday was out of the way, he was looking forward to peace and quiet and two weeks with his favourite grandson, the Marquess of Glastonbury, at the château with his parents for an extended holiday.

After lunch on their second day, as Noel allowed himself to be inveigled into playing tennis with Lisette, Bess accepted Hubert's invitation to stroll through the gardens.

"It's ages since we had a good chat," Bess said. "And it isn't all my fault. What have you been doing?"

"Working like stink," Hubert replied. "I've been clearing debts."

"Your mother?" Bess asked.

"Yes. It cost even more than I imagined to get her settled."

"How is she?" Bess felt duty-bound to ask.

"I don't have all that much to do with her," Hubert said. "I went to see her in June and she was pretty vile." He paused, nerving himself to say something that had been on his mind for weeks. "I may not bother going again."

Bess saw the need to change the subject. "When are you going to send me some horses?"

"Next year," Hubert said brightly. "Everything is paid off and there should be money in the kitty before too long. I say, I hear that Gideon's got a good one."

"What, Saxon Prince?"

He laughed at her evasion. "You don't even have to think about it, do you? Perfidy and deception come naturally! Actually, as you well know, I was thinking of The Yeoman . . . I watched him win the Royal Lodge on telly."

"That was a bit of a fluke," Bess said. "He's never up to much at home."

"Oh!" Hubert was perplexed. "That just goes to show how little I know about it," he said sadly. "Because he spread a bunch of decent horses all over the shop, won by half a street and knocked the course record for six, I ran away with the silly idea that he was useful."

"He's not bad," Bess said grudgingly.

"And that caper at Doncaster was another fluke, I suppose?" Hubert suggested.

"Wait and see," Bess said. "Let me get him through the winter before you start counting chickens."

They walked a long way in companionable silence until Bess said, "Aren't you going to ask me about my young man . . ." she grinned mischievously ". . . my toy boy?"

Hubert did something she had always wanted to see. He spluttered with acute embarrassment. "Well, it's none of my business, is it? However . . ." He paused, gathering his resources. "He's obviously doing you a power of good. You look wonderful. Lisette remarked on it the moment you arrived."

"I *feel* wonderful, Hubert," Bess replied. "Half an hour with Noel takes years off me."

627

"If I may say so, my dear, he must have been very active last night!" Hubert said, displaying a flash of ribald daring that took him by surprise and shut him up.

When they reached the tennis courts thirty minutes later, there was no sign of Lisette and Noel, so they went indoors and parted. Bess found Noel in the huge sunken bath that was one of several ostentatiously luxurious features of their suite. He looked so smug that she burst out laughing.

"What did you get up to with the Duchess?" she demanded.

"Absolutely nothing. She's a lovely lady, of course, but not my type."

"I believe you," Bess said grandly. "So, why are you looking so pleased with yourself?"

"I was sketching out a plan of action for you."

"Really?" Bess knelt down beside the bath, plunging a hand into the foam-covered water. Her eyes widened as she encountered his erection. "Bloody hell, Noel," she muttered. "That feels bigger than ever!"

He lifted himself clear of the foam to demonstrate how right she was. "All your fault," he announced. "I was lying here, without a care in the world and I started thinking about you."

"And got in that state?"

"Absolutely!"

"Then it's up to me to do something about it." Bess was taking her clothes off, piling them neatly on a cork-topped stool. "I don't want to be one of those women who starts things she can't finish."

"No one could accuse you of that," Noel smiled as she slid into the bath beside him.

Although their love-making did not need a boost, the short holiday in unfamiliar and glamorous surroundings encouraged them to new heights of activity and satisfaction. On Sunday, Bess arrived at Longchamp glowing after a night that should have left her exhausted: instead, her lustre turned heads. *Parisiennes*, all *très chic*, surveyed Bess with a mixture of envy and baffled resentment. For half an hour before she was needed for the preliminaries to the afternoon's main race, she strolled round the club enclosure on Noel's arm, basking in the curiosity they attracted, conscious that her escort was experiencing difficulty in maintaining a straight face.

"Do you see the way some of these women are looking at me?" Noel whispered. "I feel *naked*!"

"Be grateful they don't know about your vitals," Bess told him. "What about the looks *I'm* getting?"

"I've seen at least ten ladies who want to scratch your eyes out," Noel chuckled.

Rouget de Lisle had travelled well and looked ready for anything. Stainless, still fragile after a bout of air-sickness, reported that the colt had enjoyed the bumpy flight.

"The bugger thought it was entertainment, ma'am, laid on specially for him," Stainless told Bess, who was looking round, half-expecting a familiar head of golden hair to pop up.

"Did Miss Leander try to sneak a trip over?" she asked.

"No, ma'am. She said you'd have enough on your plate without her getting in the way."

Another sign of that exceptional maturity, Bess thought.

When it was time to put Jonathan up on Rouget de Lisle, Bess confessed herself at a loss for instructions. "I can't say anything, apart from, 'Do your best'," she smiled. "There are some pretty tough customers in this one."

"We'll see," Jonathan said noncommittally.

During the closing stages of a scrappy, bad-tempered race that had never settled into a steady tempo, Bess feared that Jonathan might have allowed over-confidence to get the better of him. Once the final tussle took shape, she was certain that their hopes of getting a place in the first four were doomed. But Rouget de Lisle, as if determined to make up for his hitherto disappointing career, had even more pluck and stamina than he had been given credit for: he went at them like a whirlwind in the last hundred yards, snatching victory by a head.

Bess's joy was principally for Alain, who was as excited as a twenty-year-old by his famous victory. He and Bess faced the newspapers and TV together, unable to obtain a quiet moment to themselves until well after the next race had been run.

"Thank you, Bess!" Alain said, kissing her hand gallantly. "A marvellous present for my birthday. Now for some retirement."

Bess, embracing him warmly, scoffed at the idea. "You're full of life. Put your feet up by all means, but I'll be doing my best to get you plenty more days like this."

"Oh, I don't mind that!" he smiled. "So long as God protects me from the ballyhoo, everything is very good."

"Except Marie-Claire," Bess said sombrely.

"Ah!" Alain threw up his hands in despair.

The one unhappiness that Bess was taking away with her concerned the health of her dear old friend Marie-Claire. "I don't think she's very well," she said.

"It's cancer. Not as terrible as my poor friend Steven, but she is dying." Alain softened the stark finality of the statement with a hopeful smile. "She is ready for it. You see, Bess, she believes that she will be with her husband again."

"Is that what *you* think?" Bess was moved to ask.

"All that I know is that each and every one of us has to find his own way out of this life. No one can help with that . . . so, if she thinks she is going to Henri . . ." He shrugged.

Bess was subdued and silent on the journey home, for which she and Noel joined Rouget de Lisle, Stainless and the others on the charter flight to Southampton. Alain's words had been a powerful reminder of the first Leander and her manner of leaving the world she loved so much.

CHAPTER 24

1989

'A complete and utter wrong 'un!'

Bess was in a quandary as to how to get The Yeoman going for 1989 and admitted as much to anyone who might be able to make a useful suggestion.

Ascot's Royal Lodge Stakes had not been the end of his 1988 efforts. Much as she would have liked to win it, Bess did not run the colt in the Dewhurst Stakes, fearing that the seven furlongs would be too short for him. However, on the last Saturday of October, two weeks later than any Latimer's Barn horse had ever been known to set foot on a racecourse, The Yeoman went to Doncaster. It was a dark, murky afternoon of drizzle, low cloud and drifting mist. The visibility was so atrocious that all but the last furlong of the mile-long Futurity Stakes was invisible from the grandstand. The public-address announcer received an electronic signal that they were on their way, but after that, there was nothing: Bess, Leander and Stainless twiddled their thumbs helplessly through an interminable seventy seconds.

When The Yeoman emerged from the gloom, he was out on his own, the Group One prize already safe. Jonathan Pilgrim, joined by the jockeys of the horses who had finished second and third, eight lengths behind him, told the Press what had happened in the fog. Jonathan's contribution, which had Leander in fits, was very simple: "We'd gone about three furlongs and none of the others seemed interested, so I gave my horse his head and he won it."

The Yeoman passed a trouble-free winter. Leander rode him every day and supplemented his feed with raw eggs, malt extract, and brown ale. By March, he was fully grown, adding a superb physique to his film-star looks: he was in need of a race to toughen him up and dispel boredom.

Bess's concern was to find a prep race for what she was sure would be The Yeoman's most difficult assignment, the Two Thousand Guineas: there was every chance that his development over the winter would mean that the mile over which the Guineas was run would now be too short for him. What was to be done?

Subsequent legend had it that Leander came up with the idea that *any* race would do: furthermore, while they were about it, they may as well try him at a mile and a half. Ann and Rebecca were always convinced that it was Steven who had thought of the plan. Ann's comment: "Leander would never have suggested a daft thing like that!" had a ring of truth for many people.

Ann missed a very important point. It didn't matter which of the inseparable pair was responsible: the idea was there and Bess grabbed it. On 10 April, The Yeoman went to Wolverhampton to see what he could do with a race worth £3,000, well under five per cent of what he had won at Doncaster. The move threw the 'experts' into confusion and the sparse Monday-afternoon crowd on the Midland course were, in Leander's words, "Definitely bewizzled."

Told to ride the race in whatever way seemed best, Jonathan Pilgrim dawdled along at a canter for the first four furlongs, then stirred The Yeoman up to produce the most sensational mile that most of the thousand-odd spectators had ever witnessed. Six months later, fortified with the invaluable gift of hindsight, they would be boring people rigid with what they saw that day.

For the Two Thousand Guineas, Leander felt that Jonathan must be given positive instructions. After interminable study of the opposition and much soul-searching, the agreed policy was

632

that The Yeoman should be kept covered up for six furlongs, then unleashed. It worked beautifully. Two French colts and an Irish challenger, all well-known speed-merchants, tried to take the race by storm. After three-quarters of a mile, it seemed certain that one of them was going to get it, but they were all tiring and unable to do anything about the devastating run that Jonathan launched from thirty lengths behind them. It was The Yeoman's best effort yet and he was full of running as he stormed over the line.

The following day, while talking to Alain on the telephone, Bess learned that Marie-Claire had died at about the time that Leander Flamsteed was in the winner's enclosure with her first Classic winner.

In Marie-Claire's address-book, Alain found no less than nine telephone numbers at which her son, Jacques, might be contacted. Extending from his base near Calais to Milan, they were consistent with the area a self-employed lorry driver would cover. On the fourth attempt, a woman in Strasbourg, who appeared to combine the activities of freight agent with running a lodging-house, said that she was expecting Guillaume that evening. He duly rang and Alain told him of his mother's death.

"You are fixing the funeral?" Guillaume asked.

"Of course! It's on Thursday."

"I am invited?" The tone seemed mocking.

"Certainly."

"Then I will come."

Nadia was annoyed by Alain's desire to have done with the conversation as quickly as possible. "You should have asked him if he is bringing *that* woman," she said.

"What does it matter? I expect we shall hardly see him."

He was right. Guillaume appeared in the church at Mourville only minutes before the requiem mass began. He was alone and made no attempt to be sociable. At his mother's grave, he appeared upset for a few moments, then displayed indecent haste to be away. Alain had to hurry after him on a matter of business.

"Your mother made a will. I am her executor and you are the sole beneficiary. She told me that there was about two hundred thousand francs."

"Oh! I see."

That was more like it, Alain thought, watching the cautious hostility of Guillaume's face light up with avarice. "I have already put matters in hand," he said with formal politeness. "The money should be yours in a month or so. I need your address."

Jacques Guillaume fumbled in his wallet, finding that he had only three business cards left. He gave the least battered one to Alain, who put it into a pocket without bothering to look at it. Ready to part, Alain gave him a searching look and was surprised. At forty, when everything was too easy for him, Jacques Guillaume had been overweight and going to seed: seven years later, hard work seemed to be agreeing with him. He was lean and sharp. Alain found something obscurely familiar about Guillaume's eyes and the way he moved his head: it was illusory and the moment was shortened by his overwhelming desire to be away.

After the Two Thousand Guineas, The Yeoman became firm favourite for the Derby, despite his colour and the bizarre goings-on at Wolverhampton.

His trip to Lingfield for the Derby Trial was seen as a piece of training that, really and truly, had nothing to do with the public. The twisting, undulating course in Surrey had always been regarded as a good prelude to Epsom by the people who ran Latimer's Barn, so it was assumed that Bess was simply checking that her colt would handle the bends and hills. The on-course bookies marked The Yeoman up at ten to one *on*, mainly, it was suggested by a wag, because they wanted half an hour off from serious work. Certainly, precious little money changed hands on the race which the chestnut colt won by nine lengths.

On Derby Day, 7 June, the tens of thousands who were on Epsom Downs by nine o'clock were given a treat. The Yeoman, who had realised that something serious was afoot when he was removed from his box at the unearthly hour of five o'clock, was cantered over the entire mile and a half by Leander. And, to provide a surfeit of riches, Bess was with her, riding the five-year-old gelding with whom The Yeoman always preferred to work.

Especially after a well-informed bright-spark began spreading the word that Bess had passed her fiftieth birthday six days ago, their progress was accompanied by a great deal of comment, much of it devoted to admiration of Bess's appearance, *vis-à-vis* her age. It was audible to the two horsewomen.

"This is probably a bit much for you, Aunt Bess," Leander said.

"What is?" Bess asked.

"Fancy becoming the object of men's base desires at your age!"

"Don't be ridiculous, child!"

"You should have brought your ear-trumpet with you," Leander laughed. "It's a pity you can't hear the *incredible* things they're saying about your backside."

Bess, whose ears were functioning perfectly, decided that any show of displeasure would be the most awful hypocrisy and kept quiet.

Even with the calming influence of Lady Amaryllis and Noel, Gideon was a bundle of nerves over lunch in the members' dining-room.

"You'd better hide, or put your head in a bag," Bess told him. "I certainly shan't let you anywhere near the horse unless you improve. He's perfectly calm and he's going to stay that way."

"I'm sorry," Gideon said, painfully aware that he was a liability. "I really would like to win this one."

"So would I, Gideon," Bess replied, fiercely intense. "So would I!"

In fact, by the time the horses were parading in the paddock, Bess deemed that The Yeoman's owner was in a fit state to accompany her. This was largely due to a wine consumption that was vastly in excess of Gideon's normal quota, but no one

635

minded, and the soothing effects of alcohol stood him in good stead during the more than usually extended preliminaries.

"This is a total pain," Bess said to Amaryllis when Gideon was out of the way, watching the horses show themselves off in front of the grandstand. "The only thing right about this place is the course. Everything else is a shambles. It wouldn't be tolerated at Longchamp or Chantilly."

"Our horse is taking it well," Amaryllis said.

"Look at that pair, though," Bess retorted. The two animals following The Yeoman were lathered in sweat and starting to prance agitatedly.

"What are our tactics today?" Amaryllis asked.

"I'm not entirely sure," was Bess's surprising remark. "Leander and Jonathan are sorting it out. My guess is that he'll be held up."

So it proved. At the end of Tattenham Corner, The Yeoman had ten horses in front of him and as many lengths to make up. To the dismay of an ashen-faced Gideon, Jonathan Pilgrim seemed in no hurry to get on with the job.

"He's left himself far too much to do," Gideon moaned.

"Don't worry," Leander said soothingly. "The others will start going backwards in approximately five seconds!"

It was an impressively accurate prediction, based on the three-furlong marker, the point at which The Yeoman was let down and told to get on with it. Bess thought that he probably responded to the roar of the vast crowd: they had put well over two million pounds-worth of bets on him and wanted a good run for their money. They got it: the chestnut colt with the much-maligned flaxen trimmings produced a turn of foot that made people gasp, shout and wave their arms. Steadfastly straight along the centre of the track, The Yeoman tore through the opposition, turning them into seaside donkeys. A furlong from home, Jonathan became involved in some very serious riding, guarding against the infinitely remote possibility that one of the others would come back at him.

"There you are, folks," Leander said. "Pilgrim's progress!"

As everyone laughed and groaned, she fluttered her eyelashes in mock-innocence. "Excuse me," she said demurely.

"I have a horse to collect." As she disappeared into the crowd, one of the truly great Derby winners bounded up the final hill as though he had springs attached to his feet.

"Do you still wish you'd sold him?" Bess asked Gideon as they stood in the winner's enclosure.

He shuddered at the memory. "I've just been offered five million for him," he said cheerfully.

"Who the hell by?" Bess was outraged.

"'Face-ache' Dalgleish."

"Ah, yes!" Bess smiled as all was made clear. The Earl was notorious for his attempts to strike ludicrously hard bargains. "I trust you told him what to do?"

"I mentioned that I thought ten million might be nearer the mark," Gideon replied. "He turned green."

Bess shook her head disapprovingly. "That's still very much on the low side," she said. "I keep telling you, Gideon, I hope he'll turn into a good horse!"

Wesley Davies and his cameraman were hovering: with a broad grin, Bess surrendered to his beckoning and went to be interviewed.

"Well, Bess, this is an historic occasion," he began, showing off his research assistant's efforts.

"It is, Wesley. That was the one hundredth Classic winner from Latimer's Barn."

"And how many of those were Derby winners?"

"That boy was the twenty-second," Bess replied and prepared to give Wesley Davies, and the viewers, the benefit of something his record books wouldn't have told him. "The Yeoman is our second Derby winner to be done by a sixteen-year-old girl called Leander Flamsteed – the first was Bellerophon in eighteen-seventy-six, of course."

"Amazing!" Wesley Davies said.

"It is. Amazing and absolutely marvellous."

"And what are your plans for The Yeoman, Bess?"

"I shall have to see how he is," she replied. "But I'll tell you what I might do."

"Yes?" He was agog.

"If you and your newspaper colleagues don't stop asking

637

me downright silly questions about him, I'll send him back
to Wolverhampton!"

Throughout the next week, Bess received a steady stream
of letters to tell her how much pleasure the look on Wesley
Davies's face had given.

Jacques Guillaume lived in the village of Ailly-le-Comte,
twenty miles south-east of Calais. Ailly, with a population
of less than two hundred, was strung out over a mile-long
lane that was a spur to the main road from Arras to Calais.

His property, a small farm that had bankrupted its previous
owner, was ideal, with almost complete privacy and a barn
to act as a garage for the big articulated lorry. Parts of the
rambling house were uninhabitable, but that was a matter
of no consequence. The property and the Volvo lorry had
cost one and a half million francs, leaving 250,000 francs for
emergencies.

There had been far too many of them. At the root of
all Jacques Guillaume's troubles was the fact that he was
a one-man operation. At any given time, he could either
be driving, or organising the next load, but not both. His
calculation that he could earn good money on twelve days
a month was rarely translated into practice. When Ghislaine
Chaladon had entered his life two years ago, he hoped that
she would be able to help: all that was required was for her to
take telephone calls, be pleasant to would-be customers and
look after a diary. She was, however, completely disinterested.
In any case, her sudden, unexplained absences made the idea
impractical.

Now, at long last, things were looking up. Marie-Claire's
money, though only a modest amount, would be useful, and
an extra source of income was making itself felt. A week
before Christmas, a Dutchman had offered Guillaume 2,000
US dollars to deliver a package to a launderette in north
London. He knew that the parcel, labelled as spare parts
for washing-machines, contained five kilograms of cocaine.

Jacques Guillaume realised that the best hiding-place for
the package was to put it on open display in the cab of his

lorry. The customs officer at Dover hardly bothered to look at it. While his main cargo of building materials was being unloaded, Guillaume completed the mission in a taxi, making no attempt at concealment.

Although the next consignment did not appear until the end of March, Guillaume was not worried. A long-term contract to haul cement from Rotterdam to London put him in frequent touch with the European master of the drug operation. Sure enough on 8 June, he was entrusted with two deliveries.

It was nearly midnight on 10 June when he arrived back at Ailly-le-Comte. He threw a scratch supper together, studying his mail as he ate. Among the bills and circulars was a letter from the bank, a curious piece of work that began with profound apologies. While clearing up his mother's affairs, the manager explained, they had come across some papers belonging to his father, lodged with them in 1933. The bank was at a loss to know how they could possibly have been over-looked during the forty-four years since Henri Guillaume's death and offered abject regrets. When Monsieur next visited them, they would be pleased to hand over the documents.

Jacques was naturally intrigued. Thinking about it, he came to the conclusion that the papers were probably interesting, but useless. He remembered his mother talking about the café they had owned in Paris until 1944 or '45: it could be something to do with that. Still, there was no harm in finding out and he had to visit the bank to deposit the 4,000 dollars that two packets of cocaine had earned him.

Disliking Paris traffic, Guillaume drove to Abbeville and caught a train. At the Gare du Nord, he toyed with the idea of telephoning Heloise Dufresne on the off-chance that her afternoon was free, but decided that business must come first.

The bank was anxious to be rid of their mistake as quickly as possible. A cashier took the hundred-dollar bills without question, gave him a printed slip to record the transaction and exchange rate, and directed him to an inquiry desk at the end of the counter. Here, a hard-faced woman exam-ined the letter, disappeared into a back room and returned almost immediately with an envelope of old-fashioned linen-reinforced paper. The two seals, clearly stamped with a date in October 1933, were intact. The woman pushed a slip of paper at him, Guillaume signed it, and the packet was his.

It was not quite eleven o'clock, early enough to find a corner table in a half-empty café. By the time the girl brought his coffee, Guillaume had discovered that he needed assistance to open the tough old envelope. Smiling, the girl fetched a pair of kitchen scissors.

When he tipped the contents on to the table, the most obvious thing was the prayer book. Opening it revealed the inscription on the flyleaf: it had been presented to Maude Flamsteed on the occasion of her confirmation in 1896, at which time she had been eight. Between the pages of the book, Guillaume found six snapshot photographs, all but one of which featured the same little girl, either alone or with adults. The exception was a picture of a striking-looking woman in her thirties. The eyes commanded his attention: the strength of character behind them was indomitable, even after ninety years as nothing more than a fading image on a piece of paper.

Guillaume was both startled and baffled. The name Flamsteed was very familiar to him: it was the same as those people who had brought the manufacture of furniture to Château de Mourville. Could it be the same family? If so, how had his father come by this strange memento of 1896?

Opening out a carefully folded sheet of newsprint that had fallen underneath the prayer book, Guillaume received a shock that affected his breathing. It was from an English newspaper. The one good thing that had come out of the special school he had attended was an interest in languages, making him fluent in German and English. The long article presented no difficulties. Not that it was necessary to read very much of it: the subject was a racing stable called Latimer's Barn near Marlborough in Wiltshire.

This, of course, was the place that Monsieur de Mourville used; they had produced Rouget de Lisle to crown his seventieth birthday last October. But the connection had not been established until after the War, whereas the date on the newspaper was 1929.

There was a photograph. The woman with the eyes, older, but still beautiful, was arm-in-arm with a man. The text revealed that they were brother and sister. She was Leander Hawksworth, chatelaine of Latimer's Barn, he was William Flamsteed, the man who had founded the furniture business, but who, in 1929, was acting as a racehorse trainer. From comparison with the snapshots from the prayer book, it seemed likely that he was Maude Flamsteed's father.

Nonplussed, at a loss to understand what, if anything, he had learned, Guillaume ordered more coffee and a large cognac. Several minutes passed before he became aware of the three folded documents that had also come out of the envelope. Idly, half-afraid of further mystery, he reached for the biggest of the three.

It was a certificate of the marriage of Maude Flamsteed to Achille Guillaume at Belle Ile in March 1916.

Trembling, he grabbed at the other two. They were both birth certificates, Maude's and his father's.

He caught the one o'clock train back to Abbeville, abandoning his thoughts of Heloise Dufresne: in his agitated state he would have had difficulty enjoying her and she *was* hideously expensive. Passing through Ile-de-France and into Picardie, Jacques Guillaume struggled with the revelation that he was the grandson of a famous and undoubtedly wealthy family.

Winning the Derby had taken almost nothing out of The Yeoman. Allowed to make a leisurely start on the morning after the race, he was full of beans by ten o'clock and cantered six furlongs with the second lot. In response to Leander's question, Bess said that his next target was the Eclipse Stakes at Sandown Park on 8 July.

"Oh!" Leander was surprised. "That's never been a race we've bothered with much."

"That's one of the reasons why I'm sending him," Bess

replied. "We won the first one with Parallelogram back in eighteen-eighty-six, and your Grandfather Steven won it with Redgauntlet in nineteen-fifty. It's time we had another go!"

"In that case, he wants an easy ten days, then bringing back up again, right?" Leander said.

"Exactly!"

Leaving The Yeoman in Leander's care, Bess set about putting the finishing touches to the horses that were going to Royal Ascot, and worrying about her son's future. She was strongly inclined to pursue a course that aroused Noel's disapproval.

"I think Steven should stay at school till he's eighteen," Noel said, careful not to appear to be making an issue of it.

"All right, tell me why," Bess said. They were in his forest lodge, relaxed after love-making. "I need all the help I can get."

"Well . . . it's a question of education, in the broadest sense of the word. The more there is, the better it will be for him."

"It's a good theory," Bess agreed. "What about the one that says his education – and his future – is in the stable?"

"Very difficult to argue against!" Noel smiled.

"And what will Leander have to say if I make him stay on?"

"What it boils down to is, how much are you prepared to give in?" Noel said.

"It's not a question of 'giving in'," Bess said, forcefulness breaking through her languor. "It's what's best for Steven and Latimer's Barn."

"In which order?"

"Probably the other way round, actually. Latimer's Barn comes first. And *don't* look like that, sweetheart! There was a time when that rule went out of the window and we all know where things damned nearly ended up." She was thoughtful for a few moments. "I know what I'll do," she said, clearly happy with the decision. "I'll ask Steven."

Twenty-four hours later, Steven listened attentively as Bess laid out the problem.

"I think it's best if I leave this summer," he said.

"Why?"

"I've no idea what subjects to study in the sixth form and there's an awful lot to learn about horses."

"You don't want anything but the stable?" Bess asked.

"Certainly not!" He was offended by the suggestion. "I think school's dangerous after sixteen."

"How do you make that out?" Bess asked, trying not to laugh.

"It's what started the rot with Father," Steven declared confidently. "And university finished him off. He should have been *here*, not swanning around with fancy ideas."

Bess came close to choking. "Where did you get that idea from?"

"Lea and me worked it out between us," Steven replied.

"I see." Bess thought it wise to say nothing. "So, you're leaving school?"

"It's much the best way, Mother."

Solemnly, they shook hands on it. Then, grinning with relief, they hugged each other.

On 24 July, a Monday, Jacques Guillaume reached London early and settled down to wait for his lorry to be unloaded. He went to one of the cafeterias that served the needs of the men who were transforming the once derelict dockland. Over a fried breakfast, he looked at *The Sporting Life*, a paper he had started buying whenever he was in England.

There was one story dominating all else.

YEOMAN MARCHES ON

was the big headline across the front page. The report was about the King George VI and Queen Elizabeth Stakes, run at Ascot on Saturday.

In four successive Group One victories, The Yeoman had won over £770,000 in prize-money, it was reported, and his trainer said there was more to come. "He's a good, strong horse who loves racing. I'm giving him a rest for ten days and we'll think of something else for him to do."

Guillaume studied the picture of her. The air of slightly arrogant assurance was consistent with privilege. Above all else, however, it was the money that fascinated him. That £770,000 might be exceptional, but observation of the powerful and wealthy made him believe that it was no fluke. Horses like The Yeoman and Rouget de Lisle did not come from nowhere: there were real and substantial riches in Cannings Ambo.

But what, in God's name, had Maude Flamsteed been doing in France in the middle of a terrible war? Had she been cut off and trapped in August 1914? That seemed a poor explanation: her presence in such a remote place as Belle Ile betokened freedom of will, as did her marriage to a man of sixty-two when she was twenty-eight. Guillaume's researches had also uncovered such facts as were known about Maude's death: sixty years on, the assumption that she had met her end accidentally seemed dubious, to say the least.

When his lorry was unloaded, he drove to Dover for an afternoon ferry. Arriving at Ailly-le-Comte shortly before six o'clock, he found that Ghislaine Chaladon had returned.

He had come across her near Bar-le-Duc on a June evening in 1987. On his way back from Interlaken, the woman at the roadside in search of a lift was an obvious lure. Perhaps in her early thirties, she was dressed in anorak and jeans, and carried a rucksack. Taciturn to the point of rudeness, she appeared indifferent as to her destination. After a meal at a bistro north of Verdun, she pointed to a track that disappeared into dense woodland shortly after the resumption of the journey.

"Down there!" she ordered. "I'm horny." To make sure that Guillaume understood her, she scrambled into the compartment at the back of the cab that served as a miniature bedroom on long trips and began to undress.

The coupling, a brutish union between two strangers who had not even exchanged names, was unforgettable. When the astounding woman with the hard, demanding body said that she may as well spend a few days with him, Guillaume was delighted.

Throughout the next day, the most prominent news item concerned a bank robbery in Nancy that involved ten million francs and the deaths of three people who had tried to foil the raid. There were, the police thought, many indicators that the operation had been carried out by a terrorist organisation to obtain funds. Guillaume had picked up the woman he now knew as Ghislaine Chaladon five hours after, and sixty kilometres away from the robbery. When it was announced that one of the gang was believed to be a woman, instinct told him what he was harbouring.

Perversely, the almost certain knowledge that Chaladon was dangerous solved a problem that had caused Guillaume chagrin and distress for nearly twenty years. Even with the superbly talented Heloise Dufresne, he frequently found it impossible to achieve an erection, but with Ghislaine, his virility was guaranteed.

The first few days stretched to ten weeks. Eventually, she began to receive letters, always from Hamburg. Guillaume never saw her write replies, but she could easily have done so while he was away at work. When they began, her departures seemed to be spur-of-the moment decisions, although he soon came to suspect that they were carefully planned.

At first, it was impossible to relate her trips to anything for the simple reason that Guillaume looked no further than events inside France. Broadening the scope produced an amazing observation: while Ghislaine Chaladon was away from Ailly-le-Comte, there was always a terrorist outrage somewhere in Europe or the Middle East. It was absurd. In the two years of their relationship, eleven incidents that could be linked to her had been attributed to no less than five, totally disparate organisations. The thought that his mistress was a member of some élite band of anarchists, whose dreadful skills enabled them to cross national and ideological boundaries, acted as a powerful erotic stimulant on Jacques Guillaume.

On that late-July evening in 1989, Guillaume's contemplation of last week's bombing of a government office in Madrid was cut short by the demands of her taut, combative body.

*　　*　　*

After the St Leger, when The Yeoman joined Agamemnon and Astronomer Royal in the exclusive ranks of Triple Crown winners, Gideon was far from happy about falling in with the final part of Bess's plan.

"Don't you think that the Arc is asking a bit much after what he's done for us this year?" he asked.

"I know the risks," Bess replied. "Believe me, I've given it a lot of thought. I believe he's up to it."

"Nijinsky couldn't do it," Gideon reminded her.

"He'd gone wrong by October," Bess said. "In any case, our horse is better."

The Yeoman duly went to Longchamp on the first Sunday of October to give, most people agreed, the finest performance seen in the Bois de Boulogne since Mill Reef's victory in the race, eighteen years earlier. He won the Prix de l'Arc de Triomphe in exactly the way that Leander and Steven had predicted, by never allowing any of the other nineteen runners a snowball's chance in hell from start to finish. Taking a two-length lead in the first half furlong, The Yeoman extended it to four lengths at the winning post.

"*Now* he's turned into a good horse," Bess said, perfectly straight-faced, leaving Gideon speechless.

Jacques Guillaume watched the televison coverage. The statistics provided by the commentators spoke for themselves. This was The Yeoman's sixth successive Group One victory, bringing his seasonal winnings to over fourteen million francs – or £1,400,000. It was assumed that the colt would now be retired to stud where his earning potential would be well in excess of twenty million francs a year.

There was, Guillaume decided, only one thing to be done.

It took over three weeks to organise, with most of the delay caused by the wait for Ghislaine Chaladon to disappear on one of her mysterious trips. Eventually, he arrived at Rose House at ten-thirty on the morning of 26 October, having crossed the Channel the previous morning and spent the night at a hotel in Marlborough.

It was Rebecca who answered the summons of the doorbell.

"Good morning, *Madame*," he said. "My name is Jacques Guillaume. I have come from France."

"Good morning, Mr . . . er . . . Monsieur Guillaume." Rebecca's initial reaction was to find him rather attractive. She was impressed by his grey suit and colourful silk tie, unaware that they had been bought specially for this moment. "I'm Rebecca Flamsteed. What can I do for you?" She produced a broad smile to illuminate the features that were suggestive of faces he had seen in photographs. "Is it furniture, or horses?"

"Neither, I'm afraid," he said, returning the smile. "I am the son of Marie-Claire Guillaume who was with Monsieur de Mourville for so many years."

"I wondered why the name was familiar," Rebecca said. "Please, come in. It *is* good of you to look us up. This way."

She took him into the huge sitting-room and dining-room combined that occupied half of Rose House's substantial ground floor. Accepting Rebecca's invitation to make himself comfortable, Guillaume held up the packet that he had been concealing.

"I have something here which is interesting," he said, deliberately flattening the statement: the last thing he wanted was drama, or alarm. Carefully, he extracted the prayer book and handed it to Rebecca.

She was puzzled. "I'm sorry. What's this?" she said.

"Inside, *Madame*," he prompted.

Rebecca opened the book. She read the inscription. "Good God!" she said softly, sitting down abruptly. "How did you get hold of this?"

"My father put it in a safe deposit in his bank in nineteen-thirty-three." He explained the circumstances of Henri's death at the age of only twenty-eight and the long delay caused by the bank's carelessness.

"Yes, but how did your father come to have it?" Rebecca asked.

Guillaume delved into the envelope for the marriage and

647

birth certificates. "My father was Maude Flamsteed's son," he said.

The documents were spread out. Rebecca studied them excitedly. "So," she said at last. "You are Maude's grandson?"

"It would seem so."

"Amazing!" She shook her head, smiling. There was no sign of anything untoward; on the contrary, she seemed very pleased. "Excuse me for a moment," Rebecca said. "My husband will want to hear about this."

Although William was close at hand, in the office at the back of the house, it was some time before he appeared. Guillaume waited calmly, imagining the conversation that was likely to be taking place. Predictably, both astonishment and wariness could be seen in William when he entered the spacious room.

"Hello, Mr Guillaume, I'm William Flamsteed." They shook hands. "This is a bolt from the blue, and no mistake. I knew your mother, of course – I was sorry to hear of her death." His look became keen. "I don't think I ever saw you at Mourville."

"No, you were never there when I visited Mother. I am near Calais, you see. I have my own transport company. Before that, I worked for Monsieur de Mourville for twenty years." William was satisfied. They sat down.

Guillaume added the photographs from the prayer book and the 1929 newspaper page to what Rebecca had seen. While William was taking it all in, Rebecca brought coffee and biscuits. Soon after she had left them, there was the noise of a car starting. As expected, she was going to spread the news: Guillaume was gratified by the relaxed state of his nerves.

At Louise House, John and Julia were stunned.

"Is he genuine, do you think?" John asked.

"Looks like it," Rebecca replied. "William's investigating . . . you know what *that* means!"

Julia grinned. Her son's painstakingly conscientious way with difficulties was a by-word.

648

John was uneasy.

"This doesn't seem right to me," he grumbled. "When did Maude clear off?"

"Seventy years ago?" Julia suggested.

"It was more than that . . . it was before the First War. H'm. It's a rum do."

"I think it's exciting," Julia said. "We're going to solve the last great family mystery."

"Absolutely!" Rebecca agreed. "Are you going to sit there looking miserable all day, John, or will you come and meet him? He's dishy and very *French*."

Responding to his daughter-in-law's enthusiasm, John obeyed Julia's instructions to change into something more presentable than his gardening clothes. He insisted on calling at The House first, ostensibly to tell Ann: in reality, he wanted to delve into the Big Book for facts about Maude.

"Well?" Julia asked after John had spent several minutes turning pages and muttering. "What have you found?"

"Nothing. There was obviously a dust-up in nineteen-o-eight when she cleared off to London, and another over the French escapade, but Leander glossed over it."

Ann's intuition put her on John's side. "I don't like the sound of this at all," she said. "Skeletons are best left in cupboards. Remember the other 'long-lost' grandson who appeared from nowhere."

"That was completely different," Rebecca said. "The wretch had always known we were his relatives . . . this chap has only just found out."

"All right, let's get on with it," Julia said. "Are you coming with us, Ann?"

"No, it's best not to." She thought of a good excuse. "We don't want to overwhelm the poor man, do we?"

As they were leaving, Rebecca experienced a curious shiver of disquiet. For no apparent reason, her children were suddenly desperately important. "Do you know where Leander is?" she asked Ann. When racing stopped for the winter, there was little for Rebecca to do around the stable and she tended to lose touch with what was happening.

649

"She's gone to the stud with Bess," Ann replied. "I expect poor Amaryllis is being told how to treat The Yeoman."

Rebecca smiled, well able to envisage the scene. Matthew, who wanted a formal business qualification before starting work at Wm Flamsteed & Sons, was at a boarding-school of his own choice in Bristol; Emma, horse-mad and destined for Latimer's Barn, was at the Godolphin School in Salisbury. Everyone was safe.

After John had been introduced to Jacques Guillaume, he looked at the inscription in the prayer book and his eyebrows rose. "That's my Grandmother Ruth's writing," he said. Guillaume saw that he was sure of the authenticity, but distrustful of the circumstances.

"Jacques and I have been trying to piece a few things together," William said. With everyone paying the closest attention, he outlined what had come to light about Maude and her son, the *Résistance* hero, Henri.

"There are two mysteries," William concluded. "We have no idea how, or why, Maude ended up on an island in the Atlantic, where, incidentally, the Guillaume family had been farming for generations. Jacques has discovered that they're still there, although they're a pretty peculiar lot, by all accounts." Guillaume pulled a face and tapped his forehead eloquently. "The other thing is the question of her death. The inquest verdict was misadventure, but Jacques doesn't like that."

"Do you think she might have committed suicide?" Julia asked.

"Or murder, *Madame*."

"Heavens!"

"One very interesting thing," William said. "She died soon after this newspaper article appeared . . . and how she got hold of that in a remote part of France is anyone's guess."

John rubbed his chin. "Maude was my aunt," he said. "There was never much talk of her, but I remember Father saying that she went off to Paris with a frightful individual

650

called Emmerson . . . I've an idea he was some sort of artist."

"Ah!" Guillaume's exclamation made him the centre of attraction. He had learned something new: for a few moments, he lapsed into sincerity, rather than the calculated front he had been presenting so far. "Now, I think we have it . . . my grandfather had two sons by his first wife. One of them, Pierre, was a painter – quite famous in his time. *That* must be the connection."

John looked dubious. Seeing that Julia was starting to pick up his mood, Rebecca suggested lunch.

While they ate, Guillaume parried several questions about his own life and work. It was, he discovered, fairly easy to be evasive since the inquiries were nothing more than a show of polite interest. Even William, the most openly friendly of the four, was not particularly concerned about his new-found relative.

Towards the end of the meal, Julia said, "You must see our famous stable while you're here, Jacques." She looked at Rebecca. "I suppose that could be organised this afternoon?"

"Oh, yes!"

On the surface it was all very friendly: in reality, they were keeping him at arm's length and preparing to get rid of him.

When Rebecca slipped into the office to telephone Bess, she discovered that Henrietta had been busy, passing on what Ann had told her.

"This is Marie-Claire's son?" Bess asked.

"Yes! Isn't it astounding?" Rebecca was so enthused that she failed to notice Bess's tone.

"What's he like?"

"Very nice," Rebecca replied. "There's quite a strong family likeness when you come to look at him closely." Bess had already realised that she had found the solution to a long-standing puzzle. "Is it all right to bring him up?"

"Certainly," Bess replied. "I'm not doing anything for the next hour."

When Rebecca introduced Guillaume to Bess ten minutes later, there was no sign of recognition between them: he had obviously forgotten the day of Hubert's wedding, and it suited her not to remind him.

"You and your stable are very famous, Mrs Hawksworth," Guillaume said.

"Are you interested in racing?" Bess asked.

"Only a very little," he admitted. "I watched TV when The Yeoman was at Longchamp."

"I'll bet you did!" Bess thought to herself. Aloud, she said, "Come along, let me give you the quick tour." She frowned at the light rain that was starting to fall. "I think we'll confine ourselves to the shed to keep out of this weather."

Walking along the Roadway with Guillaume and Rebecca, Bess was conscious of his sidelong appraisal of her. Inasmuch as she was every bit as arrogant as he had imagined, Guillaume found Bess unsurprising: what he had not been prepared for was her potent sexuality. Unaware that this was due entirely to the attentions of a lover seventeen years her junior, he found himself torn between loathing and desire for her, an uncomfortable combination.

"This is our latest addition," Bess said as they entered the shed. "We have a hundred horses in here during the season, but we're down to seventy at the moment." Her pride in the place was manifest.

Powerful lights gave a golden, sun-like radiance to the huge interior, and the hum of machinery hovered tactfully in the background.

"Is this where The Yeoman lived?" Guillaume asked.

"No, he was in one of the old yards," Bess replied, somehow giving the impression that she thought the question was silly. "If you'd like to come to the far end, you'll be able to see some of the new yearlings we're taking in for next year."

They were on the way down the long aisle of the shed when Leander bobbed out of one of the boxes. "This is my niece," Bess said. "Leander, this is Monsieur Guillaume who appears to be a relative of some sort."

She was beautiful, Guillaume decided, very beautiful indeed. But as she stared at him, making no attempt to shake his hand, he saw the uncanny similarity between her and the woman in the 1929 newspaper photograph. It was especially noticeable in the eyes, eyes that seemed to be looking straight through him, deciphering his thoughts and motives. Uncomfortably, he walked on, catching up with Bess and Rebecca.

While he looked at twenty yearlings, pretending to be interested, Bess pointed out three that belonged to Alain de Mourville.

"Will they be racing in France?" Guillaume asked.

"It's extremely likely," Bess replied. "Quite a lot of my horses will." She smiled and, for an instant, he caught a glimpse of a much warmer woman with a mischievous sense of humour. "There are some good races in France, Monsieur Guillaume, with excellent prize-money. I want some of it!"

"Perhaps I could help you," he said.

"You?" The humour was gone and she was looking at him in haughty disbelief. Rebecca edged away, embarrassed at what she sensed was coming. "What could you do for me?"

Guillaume spread his hands in an expansive gesture. "I have many contacts, Mrs Hawksworth. I could arrange all sorts of things."

"Allow me to assure you that I *do* know my way around your country, Monsieur Guillaume," Bess said with a tolerance that was deliberately laboured. "So far, we've won over a hundred races there. I think we know what we're doing."

"I thought I should offer," he said, inwardly seething.

Bess gave him a look like a skewer. "A strange thought has occurred to me. Do you think that you should have some sort of job because you are 'one of the family' as it were?"

He smiled sardonically. "The thought had crossed my mind," he said.

"Forget it!" she said. "You don't remember me, do you?" All pretence at civility was gone.

"Er . . . should I?" He was badly off-balance.

"I saw you at the wedding of the Duke and Duchess of Laverstoke," Bess said. "I was with your mother a great deal. She was always a good friend to me." She paused, enjoying his discomfort. "She told me a lot. So, I might add, did Monsieur de Mourville." Bess turned on her heel, neither requiring nor expecting a response.

They rejoined Rebecca and went back to her car, parked at the front of The House. After she had said goodbye to Guillaume, Bess drew Rebecca aside.

"He's up to no good," Bess said. "Get rid of him!"

"Oh. Do you think he's making it all up?" Rebecca asked.

"No, he's Marie-Claire's son, all right. He's also a rogue."

"Are you sure, Bess?"

"Positive! His mother told me so."

Bess waved to Guillaume as Rebecca drove off. In the late-autumn dusk, her smile appeared genuine.

Helen and Oliver had spent most of the afternoon in one of the workshops behind Rose House, examining the mock-up of a new design. At four o'clock they went to give William their first impressions and learned that Maude's grandson was at Latimer's Barn.

With Rebecca determined to carry out Bess's instructions, the meeting took place outside Rose House. It was a confused business: Guillaume was gratified by the warmth of Oliver's greeting, but chary of Helen when he realised that she, too, had been a friend of his mother's. Sure enough, after a few minutes of stiffly polite conversation, Helen wanted to be on her way, anxious to get back to the Bungalow for a bath before dinner with Gideon and Amaryllis at The Hall.

Oliver laughed at the look on Guillaume's face as she drove off. "I'll bet you're getting used to that," he said.

"Everyone has been very nice," Guillaume replied diplomatically.

"So, what do you do now?" Oliver asked. "Back to France?"

"Tomorrow. I have a hotel for tonight."

"Where? Marlborough?"

"Yes."

Half-conscious that he was doing something momentous, Oliver made a decision. "I'm going back to London eventually . . . let's have a drink first, eh?"

Steven, who had spent most of the day in the 1874 yard with Eleanor Davidson to improve his veterinary knowledge, was one of the last to hear about Jacques Guillaume.

"Did you see him, Lea?" Steven asked, interrupting the catechism she was conducting on what he had learned from Eleanor.

"Yes!" She pulled a vile face.

"No good?"

"A complete and utter wrong 'un!"

"You're right," Steven said. "Mother's been on the phone to Monsieur de Mourville about him. Apparently he's a shocking individual."

"That was obvious!" Leander said dismissively. "Stop trying to change the subject . . . we were talking about the causes of lameness."

When they were settled in a secluded corner of the bar in Guillaume's hotel, Oliver told the Frenchman what legend and hearsay thought about his grandmother, Maude.

"Reading between the lines, I'd say she was a misfit. She had a cousin called George Hawksworth who was the same. He was shipped off to South Africa at about the time that Maude went to live in London."

"What was the problem?" Guillaume asked.

"My guess would be that your grandmother believed there was life outside Cannings Ambo," Oliver said. "That's still regarded as heresy today . . . a hundred years ago it was probably a flogging matter."

Guillaume's appraisal of Oliver became calculating. "You sound bitter," he said.

Oliver explained how he had built his own career without

help from the family. Accidentally, it seemed, he agreed to have dinner with Guillaume. Once they were in the dining-room, the question of the Fund and its Trustees arose.

"And you are not one of these people?" Guillaume asked.

"Good God, no!" Oliver found the idea laughable. "I was never in the running."

"Tell me . . . how much money is in this Fund?"

"Ah, I know about that," Oliver replied smugly. "My friend Lady Helen *is* a Trustee and she keeps me informed." He paused for effect. "In round figures, fifteen million."

Guillaume gaped at him. "You mean sterling?"

"Oh, yes. And they spent three million not so long back. Did you expect them to be fairly well-off?"

"I did." Guillaume shook his head. "Not to that extent, though."

"They don't know what to do with the stuff," Oliver said. "I say, you didn't come here looking for a handout, did you?"

"Yes, I was hoping there might be something."

Oliver chuckled. "I could have saved you the trouble. They wouldn't give me anything, and my father ran the place for thirty years. There are one or two who might like to oblige, but they're under Bess's thumb . . . I suppose you came across *her?*"

Guillaume smiled ruefully. "I did. She's hard."

"She's a bitch!" Oliver was suddenly angry. He gave Guillaume a scathingly prejudiced account of Bess's progress from stable-hand to mistress of all she surveyed, hinting that she had done him down badly, but avoiding any mention of the reason. "Oh, no, my friend," he concluded, "don't expect anything! The only way you'd ever get money out of that lot is at the point of a gun."

A moment or two later, Oliver became aware that Guillaume was looking at him in a very strange way: at one and the same time, his expression was wild and chillingly calm. "I think that might be arranged," Guillaume said.

Oliver blinked. "Are you serious?"

"Yes."

They stared at each other. Oliver put down his knife and

fork, leaning forward eagerly. "Look here, I want to get square with the bastards. Could you help me?"

"It would cost a lot of money."

"Of course!"

"A great deal of money," Guillaume insisted.

"I understand that."

"Then I can help."

Oliver began to outline the plan that had been festering at the back of his mind for eight years. It was incomplete because he had never been able to see where the necessary help would come from. Jacques Guillaume was soon filling in the blanks.

CHAPTER 25

1990

'I say, something isn't half up!'

In June, Latimer's Barn broke yet more new ground by
sending out two Derby winners in the space of ten days.
The Duke of Laverstoke's Parabola won the Epsom Classic,
Prince Omar's Prospero triumphed in the French Derby, the
Prix du Jockey Club at Chantilly. Prospero, slightly the more
impressive of the two, was Bess's favourite. Omar, bowled
over by his success, broke a long-standing habit and gave a
number of interviews in which he talked openly about himself
and his work.

Five days later, there was a bomb explosion at the United
Nations offices in Geneva. Bess and Henrietta watched in
horror as an evening television news bulletin reported the
incident, showing film of the badly damaged building with
the emergency services at work. It was known that at least
four people had been killed, among them, Prince Omar bin
Khalid al-Melhem. Police were pursuing the theory that the
outrage had been carried out by one of the Middle-Eastern
terrorist groups, with Prince Omar as a specific target; the
other casualties probably had nothing to do with the obscure
dispute behind the atrocity.

Jacques Guillaume returned to Ailly-le-Comte in time to read
of the Geneva bombing in the following day's newspapers.
Ghislaine Chaladon was, of course, away. He noted that one

of her latest victims was involved with Latimer's Barn, but it was nothing more than a passing thought in the face of his own problems.

Oliver and Guillaume had been meeting at weekly intervals for six months. To preserve the secrecy of their association, Oliver went to elaborate lengths to arrange clandestine venues. Guillaume played along with the game, recognising that a major object of the exercise was to leave him with no idea where Oliver lived, worked, or had social contacts in London. Their latest encounter had been in a run-down public house near Dover docks.

The plan was perfected and should have been put into operation at Easter: that, at least, was what Oliver thought, and the continuing prevarication made him bad-tempered.

"It will soon be time for the summer holidays," he said. "We've *got* to do it then. Are you going to be ready?"

"Yes."

"How?" Oliver demanded. "There's a lot to do at my end and I need to be sure."

"I shall think of something," Guillaume said.

"You said that in April and what happened?" Oliver retorted. There was a hiatus while they glared at each other. Oliver went on, struggling to be reasonable. "Look, we agreed that you need help, and it's best if we have a woman. You said you knew of one who would be ideal. Do you?"

"Well . . . yes . . . more or less."

Oliver decided to ignore the hedging. "So, what's the trouble?"

"I haven't had a chance to discuss it with her yet," Guillaume said lamely.

"Jacques, we are talking about two million pounds," Oliver said, the strain of patience showing. "You're in for half . . . that's ten million francs. *Ten million*! Isn't that enough to get you off your backside?"

Guillaume closed his eyes to dwell on the figure. Perhaps Oliver was right; he had been a good deal less than positive. He sat up straight and alert, as though something vital within him had snapped into life.

659

"I will telephone you within a week," he said.

"I'll believe it when it happens," Oliver replied, wearily cynical.

"It will happen!"

Now that he had finally taken the decision to involve Ghislaine Chaladon, Guillaume felt elated, contemptuous of his earlier reluctance to consider her. He had thought her too dangerous for the simple job they were planning: with ten million francs at stake, who could be interested in such finesse?

She returned two days after the Geneva bombing. That in itself was aberrant: normally, at least a week went by before she turned up. Although not exactly nervous, she was unusually tense and energetic. The moment she was inside the house, she was washing the clothes she had worn during the trip; a pair of jeans and a blouse were condemned to the incinerator. After making sure of their destruction, Ghislaine Chaladon was ready for sexual gratification. When her craving had been satisfied, she fell asleep, leaving Guillaume to fetch food and organise a meal.

The night was a disjointed parade of lust and fitful rest. By morning, she had changed again, displaying a tenderness quite unlike anything Guillaume had seen in her before. While she nestled in his arms, he told her of the relatives he had discovered in England and the plan that would bring ten million francs. She listened to it calmly, without interruption, making him wonder whether she was so exhausted that she was about to doze off again.

"That's a great deal of money," she said when he had finished. "It would enable us to disappear."

"Together?"

"Of course." Ghislaine frowned thoughtfully. "This job . . . we would have to go to England and stay there for a time?"

"I'm afraid so," Guillaume said, expecting objections.

"No, no! That is a good thing. We'll do it."

"You like the idea?"

"That money is as good as ours!"

660

It was, Guillaume suspected, an expert criminal opinion.

He telephoned Oliver that evening. As he repeated the assurances that he really did mean business, Guillaume was bemused by the transformation in Ghislaine and asked himself what had gone wrong in Geneva. Whatever it was, the consequences were going to be wonderful.

Ten days after Prince Omar's assassination, both Bess and Henrietta received letters from Hans Eberhard of Fraunhofer and Pichet Frères in Zurich. The opening paragraph of each letter was the same, stating that they were beneficiaries under the Prince's will, made in 1982.

Bess became the owner of any horses that Prince Omar had at Latimer's Barn at the time of his death: there were forty-five, including the French Derby winner and twelve others who had won Pattern races. Bess was free to sell the horses, or race them under her own name. Moreover, if she chose to keep the animals, their training fees were to be paid by money from Prince Omar's estate until 31 December in the year following his death. It was currently costing £16,000 a year to keep a horse in the stable, so over one million pounds was involved, on top of the value of the bloodstock.

The bequest to Henrietta was very straightforward: she received half a million pounds.

It was a long time before they were coherent.

"Do you think he expected to die suddenly and nastily?" Henrietta asked.

"He must have done," Bess replied. "We always thought he was nutty about security, didn't we?" She smiled sadly. "You knew him much better than I did."

"It was never mentioned," Henrietta said. "Actually, now I come to think about it, all we ever talked about was each other . . . as though we were the only two people in the world."

Close to tears, Bess nodded understandingly: rather late in her life, she had found the same unity with Noel.

By the end of the second week in July, Oliver had visited Ailly-le-Comte, and Guillaume and Ghislaine Chaladon had spent two days in England, inspecting his house on the Berkshire Downs. They planned to leave Ailly for good on 31 July or 1 August. Then, on 19 July, Ghislaine received a letter. Its message was clearly serious.

"What's wrong?" Guillaume asked, uneasy at her thoughtful silence.

"Nothing! I'm borrowing your car."

"Where are you going?"

"Never mind. Talk to Hawksworth. We need to go to England as soon as possible . . . tomorrow is good!" This was the Ghislaine Chaladon of old, ruthless, defying him to ask questions.

She was away for nine hours, having travelled, he deduced from the odometer, well over seven hundred kilometres. Not until they were loading up for the journey to England did he discover the suitcase that she had acquired during the mysterious dash. It was a strange shape, long and flat, like an oversized briefcase. And it was very heavy.

"You're taking this?" Guillaume asked.

"Yes!" She glared at him. He sensed trouble, bad trouble, but shrugged his acceptance.

By the time Guillaume drove off the ferry at Dover, he felt they were on holiday. Customs gave no trouble and the young off-duty policeman, waiting for his girlfriend to return from a camping holiday in France, was inconspicuous.

Detective Constable Michael Proctor was almost certain that he recognised the woman in the blue Peugeot. The wig and clever use of cosmetics could not conceal the very distinctive line of the jaw, very similar to that of the young woman he was waiting for. He remembered it from an idle browse through a rogues' gallery six months ago. He made a note of Guillaume's car registration number.

It took time to convince his superiors that Caitlin O'Mara, believed to have strong links with the IRA, had emerged from a cross-Channel ferry. By then, the blue Peugeot was hidden in a shed at the back of Oliver's house, while an English-registered Ford, hired on the way through Guildford, stood at the front.

*   *   *

During the morning of 22 July, forty-eight hours after Jacques Guillaume and his mistress had left Ailly-le-Comte, the police descended on the village. They were not ordinary *gendarmes*, but members of the GIGN, the special élite force for tackling the most serious crime. The officer in charge of the operation had a photograph of Ghislaine Chaladon which Madame Bosson, a spiteful old crone who acted as the village spy, immediately identified as the woman who lived with Guillaume the haulier. They were, she said, away on holiday: Spain, she had been told. Equipped with every authority under the sun, the GIGN smashed their way into Guillaume's house. Three hours later, they left without telling Madam Bosson whether they had found anything significant.

Unaware of what his careless boasting to another lorry driver had done, Guillaume found Oliver's house unnervingly boring. The isolation was tedious, then eerie. Ghislaine was perfectly content. She studied the road that passed within twenty yards of the house. With the aid of an Ordnance Survey map, she saw that it was arrow-straight for well over a mile. Overall, it was falling gently from east to west, but two hundred yards to the west of the cottage there was a hollow deep enough to lose a car for several seconds. That, and the two-acre copse on the eastern flank of the cottage were minor weaknesses: the rest was perfect.

The road, nothing more than a lane connecting two B-class routes, carried very little traffic, most of it to an unvarying timetable. At six-thirty in the morning, a young man drove from west to east, very fast, in a sports car. Twelve hours later, he returned. Between these two landmarks, a school bus, the post-office van, a courier service, and three tractors appeared with a regularity that Guillaume, a stranger with no knowledge of how the area worked, found maddening.

On their third day, Oliver came to discuss the fine detail of the plan. Guillaume received a precise summary of what would be required of him, complete except for the date on which they would act: that, Oliver explained, was still an unknown. At Ghislaine's insistence, they thrashed out the financial arrangements and exchanged ideas for the safe disposal of a great deal of money in low-denomination banknotes.

After that, Guillaume was able to go out in the hired Ford. Indolently at ease, Ghislaine refused to accompany him, laughing at his eagerness to learn the geography and work out intricate tactics. He combined sight-seeing with finding out the lie of the land and twice drove past Latimer's Barn along the Devizes Lane. On the second occasion, at about ten-thirty in the morning, a hundred horses were at work on Cannings Down. Even to his cynical eyes, they made a stirringly beautiful sight and he was tempted to stop until he reminded himself of the dire consequences of being recognised.

Late on the afternoon of the seventh day, Guillaume returned to the remote house to find that Oliver had turned up during his absence. The atmosphere was charged: looking at Ghislaine's conceited smile and Oliver's sheepishness, Guillaume was sure they had been to bed together. They chatted uneasily until five o'clock when Oliver announced that he was going to Cannings Ambo.

"Are you coming back here afterwards?" Guillaume asked anxiously.

"Give me a couple of hours and I should know a thing or two," Oliver replied.

After he had gone, Ghislaine took Guillaume to task over the state of his nerves. "Look at you," she said scornfully. "What are you going to be like once we get started?"

"I shall be all right," he snapped. "It's this hanging about I can't stand. Why did we have to come here so soon? What went wrong, eh? I have a right to know."

"Shut up!" Ghislaine said.

Brooding silence enveloped them for a few minutes. "Have you been screwing Hawksworth?" he asked sulkily.

"Yes." She smiled. "He was nervous, but he taught me a trick I didn't know. I liked it!"

"What was it?" Guillaume asked, his face registering a mixture of disapproval and prurient curiosity.

She looked at him calculatingly. "Are you going to get a grip on yourself?" she demanded.

"Yes. I promise!"

"So!" She stood up. "Come with me and I'll show you."

They were still upstairs when Oliver returned three hours later. He was excited enough to ignore their dishevelled condition: it was all arranged for 2 August, the day after tomorrow.

At the age of twelve, Emma Flamsteed was obviously a product of what someone once called 'the aristocracy of Cannings Ambo'. She was a smaller version of the sister she worshipped; some said she might even turn out to be better looking than Leander. Although she had the same single-mindedness, Emma's first year at the Godolphin School had shown her to be susceptible to outside influences. On the whole, William and Rebecca were glad of this, even though it had brought Craig Skye into their lives.

Skye was an Australian teenager who had rocketed to prominence as a pop-star during the previous six months. His almost outlandish physical beauty was producing sensational effects among girls in the twelve to fourteen age-group and Emma was not immune. In addition to his records, she fought for posters, lapel badges and copies of the monthly magazine that was devoted to him, his younger brother, pet dog, and, when all else failed, his parents.

Everyone knew that he was in England for the summer: his face, accompanied by stories of unmitigated banality, was never out of the popular press. Prepared to kill for a ticket to one of his concerts, Emma was unable to believe her luck when she discovered what was available to her as a free alternative. On 2 August, Craig Skye was making a video of his new record, scheduled to be a number-one hit when it was released at the end of September. For some reason known only to those responsible for creativity, it was being filmed at a country house in Gloucestershire, with a new advertising agency playing a prominent part. That agency, appointed to counteract a slight fall in the popularity of Skye's last record, was the one with which Oliver was a senior partner.

Emma's discovery that her uncle was not personally involved

gave rise to a difficult few moments. However, when told that, yes, he *could* take her to watch and arrange for her to have lunch with her idol, she was ecstatic. After spending the previous night at Rose House, Oliver was ready to set out at the appointed time of eight o'clock. Emma, who seemed not to have been to bed, was sick with excitement.

Rebecca and Leander, out with the first lot on the gallops, were not present for the departure. Matthew, who was using his summer holiday to work alongside the apprentices at Wm Flamsteed & Sons, waved solemnly, managing to avoid giving the impression that the little sister whom he adored could be a bit of a pain when she put her mind to it.

Out of respect for Emma's nerves, Oliver kept quiet once they were underway, heading through Marlborough and towards Swindon. As they climbed the hill up to the Downs, an unmarked green van appeared behind them, moving in until it was dangerously near.

"Who's that idiot?" Oliver muttered, scowling into the mirror.

Emma turned to see for herself. The van was certainly close. The driver, a woman wearing dark glasses, was alone in the vehicle. After half a mile she turned off to the left.

"Thank you!" Oliver said. "Women drivers!" He grinned at Emma. "I'll have to stop for petrol," he explained. "I forgot to fill up last night." When they reached the garage, another mile or so along the road, he promised not to be long. "We've plenty of time," he said reassuringly.

"Don't worry, Uncle Oliver," Emma said, producing the latest issue of the Craig Skye magazine from her bag. "Do you think I could have a bar of chocolate, please?"

"Feeling better?" he asked.

"Much, thank you."

Oliver helped himself to petrol before strolling to the shop and cash-desk. As on the rehearsal, the distance from the furthest of the six pumps was fifty-eight paces. There was a bonus: Oliver found himself stuck behind a self-opinionated man, who, having made a mess of writing a cheque, was blaming the girl on the till for his own incompetence.

Studiously turning his back on the view outside, Oliver exchanged an understanding look with the girl.

Her reaction was almost precisely what he had hoped for. Having persuaded the man to start again, she looked up, closed her eyes in exasperation, then glanced briefly across the forecourt. She returned her attention to the awkward customer, not realising or believing what she had seen. When she looked up again, her face was sharp with alarm.

"Hey!" She jumped from her stool, grabbing Oliver's arm. "Look! Isn't that your little girl?"

Whirling round, Oliver saw that the green van was alongside his car. Two people, both wearing hoods, were in the final stages of dragging Emma from the car and bundling her into the van. Emma was screaming.

Oliver knocked over a rack of motor accessories as he dashed outside. Emma had disappeared into the back of the van, the shorter of her two assailants, dressed in combat fatigues, diving after her. Oliver got to the driver's door of the van as it began to move. A glancing blow through the open window sent him sprawling. With protesting tyres, the van was on its way.

"Are you all right?" The girl was bending over Oliver, helping him up. "You're one of the Hawksworths from Cannings Ambo, aren't you?"

"Yes . . . that was Emma Flamsteed they've taken. Quickly, we must ring the police . . . and my brother-in-law!"

Emma did her best to put up a fight, but she was no match for the woman who knelt astride her to put sticking plaster over her mouth. Another sort of adhesive tape was used to secure her wrists and ankles.

Once they were away from the petrol station without sign of immediate pursuit, the van slowed down to a steady fifty miles an hour. Ten minutes later, it turned right on to a minor road. Another mile and there was a left turn into a lane. The speed dropped to a crawl, they lurched over a bumpy surface and the sun was blotted out by trees.

667

The woman was out of the back door in a flash. Turning her head, Emma saw that there was a car within feet of her. The woman lifted her bodily, dumping her on the floor between front and back seats, throwing a rug over her. With the woman in the back seat and the man driving, they reversed out of the wood.

Emma was snatched at 8.27 a.m. The first police car arrived at 8.41; William reached the petrol station three minutes later in his own car.

Between them, Oliver and the girl from the cash-desk remembered the registration number of the van. While one officer was transmitting that to the control room, two others began to take statements.

When she had recounted all that she had seen, William drew the girl to one side.

"Look, I'd very much appreciate it if you could do us a favour," he said.

"Yes, of course!" Like many people for miles around, she had the highest respect for the Hawksworths and Flamsteeds.

"This is obviously a very bad business. I'm going to ask the police if they will keep the Press and TV out of it. Will you help us with that, please?"

"Oh, yes, Mr Flamsteed."

"Thank you . . . we shall make it worth your while."

"There's no need to go to any trouble," the girl said.

"We will," was the firm reply.

To Oliver, who had always regarded his brother-in-law as an amiable nonentity, William's behaviour during the critical hours that followed came as a revelation. He went to Latimer's Barn, where breakfast was being taken between lots, spoke to Rebecca, and brought her home without revealing the true nature of the crisis until they reached Rose House.

"We must *not* panic," William concluded. "And I think it's important that we don't have the media involved, so we shall have to do our best to keep quiet about it."

"Even here, in the village?" Rebecca asked shakily.

"Yes . . . if we can."

"What about the police all over the place?"

"They'll be clearing off soon. After that, we sit and wait."

"What for?" Rebecca was fearful.

"Presumably, the kidnappers will make contact with us."

Rebecca was silent for a few moments. "We shall have to let the family know," she said.

"I don't see how we can avoid *that*," William agreed.

Matthew was brought in from the workshop to be told. He took it calmly, reaching the same conclusion as William: if they kept their heads, Emma would be recovered unharmed. Oliver saw that Rebecca was experiencing difficulty accepting this, but she was still able to join William and Matthew in expressing misplaced sympathy.

"What a beastly thing to get mixed up in, Oliver. Are you sure you won't have a drink? You look awful, my dear."

Prepared for recriminations for not taking sufficient care of Emma, Oliver was acutely embarrassed. Ironically, this lent credibility to his demeanour.

They reached Oliver's house at 9.20 a.m.

Emma was carted indoors with the rug covering her head. Still unable to see, she was slung over a shoulder and carried up a flight of stairs. After she was put on a bed, there was a delay, during which she could hear two people moving about. When the rug was finally removed, there was only the woman. She used scissors to cut the tapes on Emma's wrists and ankles, indicating that she herself should remove the plaster from her mouth.

Making no attempt to move, Emma stared unblinkingly at Ghislaine Chaladon, taking in every feature of the hard face.

"Are you expecting to ransom me?" Emma asked.

"Yes. You will not be hurt."

Emma noted the accent, but made no comment on it.

It took a long silence to make Ghislaine realise that Emma did not intend to say anything else. Piqued, she stood up and left the room, locking the door on the outside.

* * *

Curious to know why her mother had disappeared, Leander abandoned her usual practice of taking lunch at Latimer's Barn and went to Rose House on Steven's bicycle. While Rebecca was telling her of Emma's kidnap, Matthew called out that William was wanted on the telephone.

"The police have found the van," William reported when he came back. "Abandoned in a spinney at Winterbourne Pypard. Stolen from Reading last night, apparently."

"What time did they find it?" Leander asked.

"Not all that long ago," William said ruefully.

There was no need for comment. The senior police officer conveying the news to William had admitted that it was not a good start.

Throughout her lunch-time stay, Leander sat beside Rebecca, holding her hand. Much to Oliver's discomfort, she ignored him. He steeled himself to stay at Rose House until at least the following morning: it had seemed such an undemanding task when the plan was drawn up.

Jacques Guillaume, initially elated by the smooth success of the kidnap, became fretful as the morning progressed. After locking Emma up, Ghislaine barely spoke, exacerbating the long wait for the one o'clock news on television. When the bulletin passed without mention of their crime, Guillaume was irritable.

"Be quiet!" Ghislaine ordered. "It's too soon."

She left him and went to the kitchen, where a salad for Emma's lunch was already prepared.

An armchair was one of the items that had been moved into the large bedroom for Emma's comfort; Ghislaine found her sitting in it, absorbed in a book. Seeing the meal, she moved to the table, her face expressionless as she studied the food.

"Is that all right for you?" Ghislaine asked. "Is there anything else you would like?"

Emma shook her head and placed the book so that she could read it while she ate. Feeling rather as if she had been sent packing, Ghislaine went away, locking the door.

670

The examination of her prison conducted by Emma during the morning revealed the extent of the preparations made for her. Only one of the two doors in the room was locked: the other led into a bathroom, big and old-fashioned. There was another door, next to the bath, but that was locked, and the window, like the one in the bedroom, was boarded up. An ample supply of towels was supplemented by toiletries, and a refrigerator contained cans of soft drinks.

In the wardrobe, there were brand-new blouses, skirts and jeans that looked to be about the right size. A small chest of drawers was filled with pyjamas, underwear and socks.

Finally, there were the books, twenty of them, all new. Only two were not to her taste. The accuracy of the selection was never far from Emma's thoughts as she settled down to while away the afternoon.

That evening, Bess and Henrietta dined alone, with only young Simon for company: everyone else was at Rose House.

Henrietta had been with Rebecca for most of the afternoon and thus knew everything there was to be known, including the complete lack of police progress. After transferring from the green van, Emma and her captors had disappeared.

"She's not showing it all that much, but Leander's pretty upset," Henrietta said.

"I know," Bess replied. "For once, you can *see* her leaning on Steven. She does it all the time, but it's normally hidden."

There was a pause. "What do you think of this business?" Henrietta asked nervously.

Bess took a long time to answer. "Do you *really* want to know?" she asked.

"Yes!"

"Well, Henry, it strikes me as utterly and totally remarkable that two thugs in a stolen van should be on hand the minute Oliver sets off on a trip with Emma." Bess paused to allow time for the full implication of what she was saying to sink in.

"And the coincidence is even more amazing than that. These thugs, who *happen* to stumble across a little girl whom they instantly recognise as being worth kidnapping, have another car waiting for them in the middle of nowhere *and* a place to hide Emma."

Henrietta gazed at her in shocked disbelief. "You're surely not suggesting . . ." She lacked the courage to finish.

"Of course I am!" Bess was annoyed that anyone should be capable of imagining any other explanation. "And if the same thought hasn't occurred to the police, they're morons!"

At eight-thirty, Ghislaine went to see if there was anything Emma needed before she settled down for the night. Already in bed, her golden hair gleaming after a vigorous brushing, Emma greeted the question with a curt shake of the head. In what she subsequently cursed as a moment of weakness, Ghislaine stood, looking at Emma, receiving a hard stare in return.

"You're French, aren't you?" Emma said, investing the simple statement of the obvious with a meaning that seemed strangely alarming.

When she returned to Guillaume, waiting anxiously for the nine o'clock news, Ghislaine said: "Who are these people this girl belongs to? Are they tough?"

He laughed derisively. "Of course not! They've lived in the lap of luxury for too long. They're as soft as grease."

"Their daughter isn't!" Ghislaine retorted. "She's hard."

"And you know, I suppose? You're the expert on hardness." There was a sneer in his voice.

They sat through the nine o'clock news, Guillaume becoming more unsettled with every minute that passed without mention of Emma.

For nearly an hour, Guillaume and Ghislaine grumbled and argued, never quite reaching open hostility. When they went to bed after listening at Emma's door, Ghislaine was voraciously lustful. Humiliatingly, Guillaume's state of mind left him without the ability to achieve an erection.

"Look at you!" Ghislaine spat when she finally gave up her efforts to arouse him. "Nobody could call you an expert on hardness, eh?" Grabbing him round the neck, she forced his face between her thighs. "Go on, do *something* useful!" she ordered.

The police returned Oliver's car the following morning, grudgingly admitting that neither it nor the green van had yielded any worthwhile evidence. Ann, who had arrived at Rose House early, saw that it was going to be a difficult day.

Guillaume had a dreadful morning. Delivering Emma's breakfast, Ghislaine had been asked: "Why is the man with you keeping out of my way?" When planning the crime, Oliver had established that Emma had never seen Guillaume. But she would, Ghislaine reasoned, have heard about his futile visit to Cannings Ambo the previous autumn and must not be allowed to see him. Emma's question led to a train of thought that upset Ghislaine, and she made sure her companion suffered with her.

"Why don't you go out?" she asked Guillaume when she finally tired of baiting him.

"I don't trust you with the girl," he replied.

She smiled mockingly. "You'll have to on Monday."

Guillaume was to drive to Bristol to post a letter to William and Rebecca. The delay of five days between Emma's abduction and the arrival of the demand was meant to produce maximum stress at Rose House, followed by overwhelming relief at learning how to secure her release within forty-eight hours. The letter had been produced on a computer-driven laser printer in Oliver's office and was as untraceable as any message made up of words cut from a newspaper.

Oliver took Ann out to lunch in Marlborough. On the way, they passed Helen. Her flight from America, which should have reached London at 7.00 a.m., had been delayed in Boston for over two hours with an engine fault. Calling in at Rose House to drop off a report on her trip, she learned of Emma's kidnap.

Had William and Rebecca not been so preoccupied, they might have noticed the haste of Helen's departure and her frame of mind. Helen was appalled, more by the conclusion to which she had jumped, than by the news itself.

Bess was outside The House talking to Arthur Merriweather, but Helen's hectic arrival and the look on her face caused Arthur to make himself scarce.

"You've obviously heard about Emma," Bess said.

"Yes." Helen paused before it came out in a rush. "Look, Bess, I know this might sound ridiculous, but I think Oliver's involved."

"So do I! This is his way of getting money from the Fund."

"There's a chance that I know where she is."

"Where?" Bess took the astounding disclosure in her stride.

"Oliver has – or had, at any rate – a house up near Kingston Lisle. It's on the Downs, very lonely."

Bess looked at her intently. "You must be the only person round here who knows that," she said quietly.

"I spent Christmas with him when we were both fed-up a few years back," Helen said. "This is pure speculation, of course."

"I know. My instinct tells me that it's right, though."

"So, what do we do?" Helen asked. "Tell the police?"

Bess shook her head. "Not until we've had a look at it. Come on, my car!"

Hurrying out of the side door to tell Bess that she was wanted on the telephone, Noel was in time to see the tail of the XJ-S disappearing into the drive. It was Leander, on her way back from the 1933 yard with Steven, who pointed out that the engine of Helen's car was still running.

"I say, something isn't half up!" she said.

Bess covered the twenty-one miles in eighteen minutes. She drew up on the side of the road, three-quarters of a mile to the east of the house, reaching for her binoculars.

"I can't see a damned thing for those trees," she complained. The spinney made the outbuildings and all but the front of the house invisible. "I'll have to get closer."

"Drive past it and let me have a look," Helen suggested. Bess did so, keeping to a sedate thirty miles an hour.

"Well?" she asked, reversing into a gateway at the end of the long straight.

"The curtains are the same," Helen said. "And I'm fairly sure I recognised a bookcase in one of the downstairs rooms."

"But no sign of life?"

"No."

Bess finished turning and headed back. Neither of them spoke.

Jacques Guillaume, messing about at the back of the house, had watched them go down the lane. The unusual event, especially involving such a magnificent car, relieved some of the morning's boredom and tension. Seeing the vehicle stop, turn round and then begin to return, he assumed that the driver was lost. He made his way to the front of the house, intending to get a closer look at a marque that was rarely seen on French roads.

The Jaguar came out of the dip very slowly. More surprisingly, it stopped about one hundred and fifty yards from him. He frowned. Both the driver and passenger had sun visors obscuring their faces.

"It *is* him, isn't it?" Helen said.

"Definitely. We were right."

"What do we do now?"

"This!" Selecting reverse, Bess stamped on the accelerator.

Guillaume felt unease as the car hurtled backwards. Although it disappeared from view in the dip, he heard the furious three-point turn, followed immediately by a blast of engine noise. When the Jaguar reappeared, it was being pushed to the limit of its performance as it sped away.

It was bizarre and menacing. He wondered whether to tell Ghislaine, but decided against it. As a reflex action, he glanced at his watch: it was seven minutes past one.

Bess and Helen reached Marlborough police station at 1.28 p.m. They arrived at a bad time; everyone connected with Emma's case was either at lunch or attending some sort of conference and were not to be disturbed. Sergeant Hardisty, an old friend of Bess's, tried to make notes and find people to help, but it was painfully obvious that they were getting nowhere and Bess's temper was shortening. After fifteen minutes, the Sergeant was still struggling with fundamentals.

"Now, Mrs Hawksworth, how do you spell this Frenchman's name?"

"Guillaume," Bess said, her teeth gritted. "G, U, I, L, L, A, U, M, E."

An attractive woman Detective Sergeant, passing through the reception area at that moment, turned abruptly towards Bess.

"Excuse me, madam, did I hear you say 'Guillaume'?" she asked.

"Yes!"

The woman's face registered something close to alarm. "Do you know this man?"

Bess told the story again, this time in no doubt that it was being absorbed. "Would you wait for a few minutes, please," the Detective Sergeant said and hurried away to an office.

When she returned, she was holding two sheets of computer print-out. Sergeant Hardisty sneaked a look at the first few lines and blenched.

"Well?" Bess asked. "What the devil's going on?"

"Chief Superintendent Bradford will tell you, madam," the Detective Sergeant replied. "He's on his way back from Swindon now. Would you like to come to a waiting-room? I'll arrange some tea."

By the time the Chief Superintendent arrived at 2.15, there were several dozen sheets of print-out for his attention. Sergeant Hardisty had whispered to Bess that he had never seen anything like it; they had even received a message from the Ministry of Defence.

At 2.45, Bess and Helen set off back to Cannings Ambo in company with two police cars full of men.

At Rose House, Ann and Oliver, not long back from a leisurely lunch, were sharing a pot of coffee with William and Rebecca. There was a faint suggestion of relaxation in the air, but Chief Superintendent Bradford was in no position to respect it.

"Mr Hawksworth, are you the owner of a property known as 'Greywall' near Kingston Lisle?" he asked.

Ann, Rebecca and William were surprised by the question and the tone in which it was posed. Then they saw Oliver's reaction: every drop of colour drained from his face.

"That's a damned silly thing to be asking at a time like this," he blustered.

"Yes, or no, Mr Hawksworth?" Bradford said implacably.

"Yes," Oliver muttered.

"Are you aware that a person called Jacques Guillaume appears to be living there?" the Chief Superintendent asked.

Ann, Rebecca and William looked thunderstruck. Oliver had nothing to say.

"What's he doing, Mr Hawksworth?" Bradford went on. "Is he holding your niece, Emma?"

There was an unbearable silence. Of all the eyes on him, Oliver was most aware of Bess's pitiless glare. Eventually, his head bowed, he said, "Yes." It came out as an unreal croak.

Not sure of what she was doing, Ann stood up. On the point of making an angry lunge towards Oliver, her legs buckled and she fainted. Two women police officers knelt to attend to her; Rebecca turned away and wept; William was stupefied, incapable of speech or movement.

Oliver was taken away: Bess thought he looked almost relieved. Bradford drew Rebecca and William together and sat them down in a corner. "Lady Helen and Mrs Hawksworth tell me that Guillaume is a relative of yours," he said, his tone was conversational, as though they were chatting over a garden fence.

677

"Yes." William collected his thoughts. "His grandmother was my great-grandfather's sister. She was rather wild and notorious."

Bradford nodded sympathetically. "This fellow Guillaume entered the country on or around the twentieth of July. Soon afterwards, the French and German police began sending messages all over the place . . . it wasn't him they were interested in . . . it's the woman he's believed to be travelling with." He paused. "*If* all the assumptions are correct, she's one of the most wanted terrorists in the world. She's alleged to be a 'consultant' to at least six major groups of villains."

Rebecca and William gazed at him in horror. "What in the name of God is she doing with Jacques Guillaume?" Rebecca asked.

"No one's sure," Bradford replied. "He seems to be an insignificant sort of bloke, so she could be using him as a cover for a normal life. It looks as though your brother may be able to throw some light on that, Mrs Flamsteed."

Ann, regaining consciousness, was sobbing. After whispered exchanges, Bess agreed to take her back to Latimer's Barn. Alerted to the possibility of crisis by tales of the police presence at Rose House, Henrietta had been like a cat on hot bricks and took charge of Ann, guiding her upstairs.

"She looks dreadful," Noel said. "What's happened?"

At that moment, Leander and Steven came into the office, their faces expectant and fearful. They remained silent both during and after Bess's account of events.

"What do we do?" Noel asked.

"All sorts of things," Bess replied, the briskness of her manner concealing her uncertainty about the immediate future. "Ann needs Giles: Noel, will you find out where he is and tell him to get here *at once*? Leander, you should be with your parents. Steven, upstairs and help Henry with your grandmother."

They all did as they were told and Bess ran through the orchard to Louise House. She made John and Julia sit still while she explained the position.

"We'll stay put for a while," John said. "William and Rebecca must be up to their ears."

"Give them an hour," Bess suggested.

"If Emma *is* in that house, what are they going to do about it?" Julia asked.

"Get her out as soon as possible," Bess replied.

At Rose House, Chief Superintendent Bradford was outlining his plans to William and Rebecca. He was unaware that the Chief Constable, placed under considerable pressure from London, was handing the operation over to others.

Commander Andrew Stapleton of the Anti-Terrorist Squad, accompanied by an Army officer and followed by a detachment of ten men, reached Wiltshire at 4.45 p.m. He established a control room in a trailer midway between Swindon and Oliver's house.

Commander Stapleton had a passing interest in the wishes of the French and German police; he recognised that the Swiss and Belgian authorities also had claims, but he doubted very much whether they would get what they wanted. Ghislaine Chaladon, Caitlin O'Mara, Kirsti Gerhardssen, or anything else she chose to call herself, had been responsible for the deaths of three Metropolitan Police officers in 1987. *That* was top of Stapleton's agenda: the foreigners could form a queue for any left-overs.

He was, of course, aware of the problems posed by Emma. When questioned by the Chief Constable, he gave the impression that he was deeply concerned about her. The Chief Constable, secretly glad to be rid of the responsibility, persuaded himself that a long period of siege and negotiation lay ahead.

By 5.15, Commander Stapleton was issuing a stream of orders. When Chief Superintendent Bradford found himself subordinated to Stapleton as little more than a traffic controller, he made no attempt to conceal his resentment.

After the green Jaguar's strange performance, Jacques Guillaume watched the afternoon return to normal. At 4.10, the school bus went past with nine children, as usual; at 5.35, more or less on time, the smaller of the three tractors chugged towards Lisle Maybourne, a village about three miles away.

The first signs of trouble were ambiguous non-events: the post van did not appear at six o'clock; the milk lorry was missing; although he had gone to work that morning, the young businessman failed to show up on his way home. And there was nothing to replace them. After 5.35, there was no traffic on the lane.

On a still summer's evening, the helicopter was audible when it was no more than a speck in the south-western sky. Going into the kitchen, Guillaume found that Ghislaine had stopped work to watch it. Without any attempt to conceal its purpose, it flew straight at them, dropping down to roof-top height for the last few hundred yards. The noise faded, leaving a silence that was oppressive.

"They've done well," Ghislaine said, a resentful smile of admiration changing her face briefly.

"That bastard Hawksworth must have given in and talked!" Guillaume raved. He stared round wildly, expecting salvation or inspiration. "Look, we don't have to stay here . . . there's nothing in it for us . . . we can leave the girl and go."

"Go? How?"

"There are two cars out there!"

She smiled at him pityingly. "Why has all the traffic stopped?"

"Ah . . . you've noticed that, too? You think they have road-blocks?"

"Certainly."

"All right, we'll go across country."

Her laugh was mocking. "What would you use for cover? Look at it!" She pointed through the window. "How far is the horizon . . . four kilometres? Five? And there isn't a blade of grass more than half a centimetre high. The helicopter would have you in minutes."

Guillaume's face sagged. "We're done for, then?"

"Cretin!" Ghislaine snapped. "We shall leave after dark. Get to the nearest village and take a car. Easy!"

For nearly an hour, he believed her. Then, at ten minutes to eight, the helicopter came back.

Ghislaine was upstairs with Emma, Guillaume was watching television. This time, the machine hovered between the house and outbuildings. The noise was unbearable. Dashing to a back window, Guillaume saw that a spiral of dust was being sucked up by the rotors. Unbelievably, a voice, grotesquely amplified hundreds of times, bellowed through the din. "O'Mara! Chaladon! Gerhardssen! This is Commander Stapleton. I missed you by thirty seconds in Southwark three years ago. I shall make up for that before too long. I hope you understand!"

The helicopter roared off. After wasting time watching the dust settle, Guillaume pounded upstairs. Ghislaine was emerging from Emma's room.

"What the hell is going on?" he gasped, semi-hysterical. "Who is this man Stapleton?"

Badly flustered, Ghislaine brushed past him, making for their bedroom. When he grabbed her arm, she whirled round to deliver a violent blow across the bridge of his nose. Reeling back, dazed and with streaming eyes, it was nearly a minute before he could follow. By the time he reached the room, she had dragged the unusual, flat suitcase from under the bed and was assembling a Kalashnikov rifle. Still in the case, nestling in tissue paper, were two hand-guns and clips of ammunition.

"People will do what I want," she said grimly. "Keep your head, my friend, and there will be no difficulty. Panic and you are dead!"

The final proof that his companion *was* as dangerous as he had supposed brought repugnance.

"They're looking for *you*, aren't they?" Guillaume said. "They aren't interested in me . . ." He stopped, glaring at her. She read the desperate thoughts passing through his mind and was amused. He was edging towards the bed, the suitcase and the pistols. With loving care, she placed the mouth of the rifle against his heart.

"Those guns aren't loaded," she whispered, her voice as silky as her inner thighs. "But *this* is! If you become stupid, I

681

shall put bullets in your knees. You understand? Good. Now, turn around."

Emma heard them go downstairs. She, too, had been unnerved by the din of the helicopter and the terrifying voice. Her meal was untouched and she was forcing herself to sit still by counting up to a thousand. It was going to be ages and ages before she felt that it was safe to check, but she was almost certain that the woman had forgotten to lock the door when she dashed out.

By 8.30 p.m., Ann was asleep, knocked out by the sedatives Joe had insisted on. Steven was doing the last rounds of the yards and the shed with Arthur Merriweather and Stainless, making everything secure for the night. Bess and Helen were in the library, debating whether Hubert and Alain should be informed of Emma's abduction.

There was an especially strong case for telling Alain because of Guillaume's involvement, and Bess had reached the stage of believing that Hubert ought to know. In the end, it was Helen who decided against it. "It would only cause unnecessary worry," she said. "There's nothing they can do, and it's probably going to be days before they can get Emma out."

"I don't see this taking very long," Bess said. Under Helen's searching look, she felt bound to offer an explanation. "These Anti-Terrorist people from London won't waste time. They want the woman badly . . . and Stapleton is a hard man, by all accounts. He sorted out that IRA unit in Watford."

Helen, who remembered the incident, and knew that Bess had spent twenty minutes alone with Chief Superintendent Bradford, took this to be official and was worried. Another thought was bothering her. "Shouldn't *we* be doing something?" she asked. "Surely, we ought to be near Emma."

At Rose House, the same conclusion was dawning on William. Starting to think straight again after the shock of the afternoon, he put it to Bradford, who had looked in with the latest news before returning to the vicinity of Oliver's house for what he feared was going to be a tedious night.

"Look here, Chief Superintendent, my wife and I want to

be near this place in case anything happens," William said. "Emma may need us."

This aspect of the problem had been overlooked at the planning meeting, hurriedly convened and dominated by Stapleton's views and requirements. On top of everything else, the Chief Constable had cleared off to a County Council dinner in Trowbridge, leaving Bradford to resolve a dispute over petty bureaucracy. The western end of the lane past Oliver's house lay in Wiltshire, the eastern end in Berkshire. When the road-blocks were instituted at five-thirty, Bradford's men dealt with both ends of the lane. An hour later, the Berkshire force discovered that its territorial rights were being infringed and all hell was let loose. Sorting the mess out had left an already disenchanted Bradford a good deal less sharp than he might have been: in any case, William's question was valid.

"I suggest you join my men, Mr Flamsteed," Bradford said. "Look, let me show you." He marked the site of his road-block on William's map. "If anything develops, we shall be able to get you up to the house fast enough."

"You'll be there, Mr Bradford?" Rebecca asked nervously.

"All night, Mrs Flamsteed. I'm on my way now."

After the Chief Superintendent had gone, Rebecca became more edgy. "Do you think Bess would come with us?" she asked. "I'd feel much better if she did."

"We can but ask," William said, reaching for the telephone.

Bess, pleased to be involved, agreed at once. Helen was desperately keen to go with her. At a little before ten o'clock, two cars left Cannings Ambo, Bess leading the way in the XJ-S.

An hour earlier, when dusk began to close in, Stapleton had put the helicopter into the air again, instructing the pilot that he was to make repeated low-level passes over the house, using a siren and searchlight to add to the morale-sapping process. The ease with which the night-flying operation was carried out caused Ghislaine Chaladon great concern: it suggested

683

an impressive range of technological aids. Given that infra-red imaging equipment might be one of them, their escape across country was going to be a chancy business. She attempted to think of a solution as she sat watching the news with Guillaume, the rifle on her lap.

Under cover of the racket from the helicopter and television, Emma tiptoed to the door of her room, grasped the handle and turned. As she had suspected, it was unlocked. She slid the key gently from the lock. Closing the door, but leaving it unlocked, she hurried to the wardrobe, crept inside and shut herself in, nestling comfortably on the pile of towels she had prepared earlier.

Twenty minutes of near peace and quiet followed, but Guillaume's nerves were worsening. The return of the helicopter reduced him to a terrible state: that, Ghislaine knew, was the main purpose of the exercise. This man Stapleton was no fool.

"Don't move!" she told Guillaume as she stood up.

"Where are you going?" he asked frantically.

"To fix that chopper," she replied.

She stood at the back door as the helicopter came at her from the south-west. At the appropriate moment, she discharged the entire contents of the Kalashnikov's magazine at it. One of the first shots destroyed the searchlight: although she was to be deprived of the satisfaction of knowing it, another left the pilot barely able to land the machine.

Her deadly prowess struck terror into Guillaume, who had crept up behind her to watch. The fearsome noise of the gun, only feet below her, frightened Emma for the first time since her ordeal began. Lying low in the copse with his men, Stapleton nodded to himself. "Right, you mad bitch," he said quietly. "We can play that game, too!"

But first, he had to go through the motions of allowing a negotiator to make an attempt to end it peacefully.

When William, Rebecca, Bess and Helen arrived at the road-block, they found that something akin to a convivial atmosphere enveloped the gathering. It was a balmy night and a mess-van was providing tea and sandwiches: only the intermittent chatter of radios seemed to prevent it being a bizarre social occasion.

"Has anything been happening?" Bess asked the Chief Superintendent.

"No, not really." Bradford had no intention of telling her about the disabling of the helicopter and its pilot. "They'll be having a go at talking them out soon."

They were standing far enough away from William and Rebecca for Bess to ask a frank question. "Is there any chance of success?"

Bradford rubbed his chin. "Could be. The experts have got a theory that Guillaume had no idea what this woman was when he got mixed up with her. He could crack easily."

Bess nodded and strolled back to the Jaguar to ask Helen, who had insisted on remaining in the car, if she wanted tea.

"No thanks, I'll stay here," Helen said. "Go and look after Rebecca."

"All right, but don't get yourself upset," Bess warned. "Forget all this nonsense about 'bad blood'." She knew that the outrage perpetrated by Oliver and Maude's grandson had rekindled Helen's tortured misgivings about her own parentage. But Helen had no intention of being upset; her nod concealed a sense of destiny that was tantamount to elation.

She waited with composed patience. The mess-van was fifty yards away, with her view of it restricted by William's car. That meant that no one could see her properly. After ten minutes, when they must have been immersed in speculation about Emma, Helen judged the moment to be right. Slipping from the Jaguar, she crawled on all-fours to the hedge. Wriggling through it, she found that it was bramble and congratulated herself on the choice of old jeans and sweater. After moving on hands and knees for several minutes, Helen stood up to assess her position. No one had seen her go and only a thousand yards of downland lay between her and Oliver's house. It was an easy walk. With the lane some twenty yards to her left, she set out.

* * *

There were two negotiators, a woman and a man, both of whom could, if need be, speak perfect French. They were installed in an outbuilding at the back of the house with Stapleton and five of his men. The other five marksmen had worked their way behind the wall on the northern side of the lane to cover the front of the house.

The woman, a Metropolitan Police Inspector, began with an appeal to Guillaume, the soft target. Using a loudhailer, she spoke in English, her tone level and matter-of-fact.

"Jacques Guillaume, don't you think you should give yourself up before you get in any deeper? We don't think you intended to get mixed up in anything *this* nasty."

Ghislaine Chaladon was in a front bedroom, straining her eyes against the darkness. She was certain that she had seen some of Stapleton's men getting into position behind the wall across the lane and was wondering if she could reach them with one of the two hand-grenades that had been hidden in the flat suitcase.

After making rapid progress, Helen was trudging up the hill out of the dip, knowing that she would soon have to proceed more carefully. She could hear the blare of the loudhailer, but was unable to distinguish what was being said. Back at the road-block, Bess and William had their hands full with Rebecca, who had broken down after learning of Oliver's admissions under cross-examination.

Eventually, after deciding that there was nothing she could do about the men at the front, Ghislaine moved to a back bedroom: the woman with the loudhailer was becoming annoying.

". . . so you see, Oliver Hawksworth has told us a great deal. He believes that you didn't know much about your companion. To be honest, he's blaming himself for forcing you into this."

Guillaume, beguiled by the voice, heard Ghislaine's movements upstairs and assumed that her activities left him free to do as he pleased.

Emerging from the dip, Helen crouched low. The night was lit by the tenuous glow of a waning moon, a thin crescent on its back. Now that her eyes were accustomed, she could see a great deal. She assumed that the house must be surrounded, yet there was no evidence of any obstruction between her and the western wall, blind except for a small, unlit window at the end of the landing. She moved forward stealthily and waited, expecting to be challenged. Nothing happened. She advanced again. Still nothing: it was as though the attention of the entire world was fixed on that soothing voice from the loudhailer. Standing up, Helen ran as fast as she could. She swerved wildly to avoid a bed of rose bushes and nearly tripped over an abandoned lawn-mower before reaching the wall and falling in a heap to recover her breath.

Jacques Guillaume was in the passage that ran from the front door to the kitchen, listening for any sign that Ghislaine had heard him leave the lounge.

"We would like you to come out," the hypnotic voice went on. "It will make things very much easier for everyone if you do. You have nothing to gain by staying in there with that woman. Come out, please, Monsieur Guillaume."

He strode through the kitchen resolutely, not even noticing the two hand-guns that Ghislaine had left on the table in readiness for a last desperate bid for freedom. Unbolting the door, he walked out with his hands high in the air.

He found himself dazzled by lights. After the initial shock, he set out towards them.

The unnatural silence was shattered by the sound of breaking glass as Ghislaine wrecked the window with the butt of the Kalashnikov. Her aim was quick and deadly: all four shots struck Guillaume. Maude Flamsteed's grandson was dead when he hit the ground. To Ghislaine's astonishment, someone was firing back at her. Two bullets screamed into the window-frame, spraying her with splinters: they obviously cared nothing for Emma. Contemptuously, Ghislaine tossed a hand-grenade towards the outbuildings.

Helen, peering round the corner of the house, saw it all.

"The bastards won't be expecting *that*!" Ghislaine had thought as she threw the grenade. She was right. The explosion, and the devastation it caused among the rickety

687

outbuildings, wrought mayhem, killing two of Stapleton's men outright, leaving the others momentarily numbed and incapable. Helen, however, was untouched by the havoc and had a vividly clear idea of what she must do. With debris still clattering down, she raced to the door that Guillaume had left open.

It was as she was hurrying to a front bedroom, expecting an attack from that direction, that Ghislaine noticed that the key was missing from the door to Emma's prison. Frowning, rifle at the ready, she turned the handle, stood back and kicked the door open. The empty room came as an unpleasant shock. When she went into the bathroom, Ghislaine knew she would not find Emma. Kneeling, she was about to look under the bed when a gunshot rang out. It came from inside the house, probably the kitchen.

Helen had spotted the weapons on the table the instant she was inside. Not stopping to think after what she had seen happen to Guillaume, she picked one up, surprised at its weight. She was concerned at her ignorance of firearms. Pointing the gun at the window, she tried to fire a test shot, only to find that the trigger refused to budge. Locating the safety-catch, she moved it through ninety degrees and tried again, producing the noise that added to Ghislaine's presentiment that finally, after all her terrible adventures, she was trapped.

Helen was at the foot of the stairs when Ghislaine appeared on the landing. Instinctively, and without fear, Helen copied the stance she had seen so many times on television, feet apart with legs braced, the gun held in both hands with arms fully extended so that she was looking along the barrel. Ghislaine was casual, the rifle in one hand at her side.

The two women, one full of a dreadful tension and purpose, the other almost lackadaisical, remained motionless.

For five seconds, they remained staring at each other.

The unbearable silence was broken in the worst possible way. Emma, having decided that the single shot downstairs meant that it was safe to come out, opened the bedroom door. She saw only one person.

"Aunt Helen!" she screamed.

Ghislaine Chaladon turned, a look of cruel satisfaction spreading across her face. Although there was no doubting her intention, the way she pointed the Kalashnikov at Emma was almost offhand. Somehow, it emphasised her chilling brutality.

Unflinching, Helen fired. The bullet entered Ghislaine's chest high up, just below her right shoulder: it felled her and she was crippled with severe pain, but she remained conscious. She was face down on the landing with the rifle in an ideal position for firing. Hit in the stomach, Helen spun across the hall to land in the doorway of the lounge.

It was five minutes past eleven when Bess discovered that Helen was missing. Even as she hurried to inform Chief Superintendent Bradford, a radio message was coming through from Commander Stapleton.

"We've got Emma Flamsteed. You can come and collect her. I doubt you'll get a statement until she's with her parents . . . she's playing merry hell!"

Complete confusion followed the mad dash along the lane. The joy of Emma's reunion with William and Rebecca was short-lived, blighted by the awful wound in Helen's stomach. The stench of chaos and destruction was appalling. When the ambulances arrived, a member of the medical team discovered that Ghislaine Chaladon, ignored since Stapleton's men had burst into the house and disarmed her, had bled to death.

Bess refused to leave Helen, persuading the ambulance crew to let her accompany her grievously ill friend. As they came to a halt at the casualty entrance of the hospital in Swindon and the banshee howl of the siren finally abated, Helen regained consciousness.

"Is Emma all right?" she asked feebly.

"Yes!" Bess grasped the hand that was offered to her.

Helen smiled. Briefly, she looked radiantly beautiful, far younger than her forty-eight years. "There's no need to worry about bad blood any more," she said. "Everyone can relax."

*　　*　　*

Bess did not reach Cannings Ambo until nearly six o'clock, over three hours after Emma, Rebecca and William. She paused at the bottom of the drive to listen to the Jaguar's engine ticking over, certain that the young policeman who had driven it from Oliver's dreadful house to the hospital had somehow managed to upset the timing. There were, of course, other things to worry about: coming over the Downs from Swindon, Bess had been angered by the beauty of the morning. Then she remembered the sublime dawn thirty-five years ago that had followed the death of Leander Hawksworth. God! What would *she* have made of this?

As she let the car drift to a standstill in front of The House, Bess was not unduly surprised to see Hubert hurrying out towards her: Henrietta had doubtless been up all night, organising and informing. Hubert opened the door, sensed Bess's inability to move, and knelt down on the gravel, his face level with hers. He had, she noticed, cut himself shaving, a sign of stress never seen before.

He had a complaint and used it in a way that attempted to inject levity. "Do you know, it's been a shambles . . . no one seemed to know which hospital they'd taken Helen to. Not even Henry could find out."

Bess shook her head. "Things were chaotic," she said. She was silent, struggling for words. "In fact, it was a terrible mess. That woman, Chaladon was . . . well, we can't understand such people, of course." The attempt to formulate coherent thoughts was too much for her. "I know Emma's safe, but . . ." She shrugged helplessly.

Hubert waited. After steeling herself, Bess came out with it. "Helen's dead, Hubert. They did their best, but she went as they were stitching her up after the operation." She fell forward into his arms and wept.

Ten minutes later, when Steven and Leander ventured out, she was pulling herself together. Nevertheless, Leander felt justified in reaching a down-to-earth judgement. "You look done in, Aunt Bess."

"I am!" Bess agreed. "I'm very much afraid that Helen died during surgery."

Briefly, Leander was close to tears. "According to Emma, she was a very brave lady," she said.

"Yes, she was," Bess said, praying that Leander would not cry. "Is Emma still OK?"

"Never better." Leander seized at the opportunity of a joke. "Guess what . . . the little beast is moaning about missing that toad Craig Skye. Yuk! She ought to be grateful." She looked hard at Bess. "You're not fit for much and Mother's up there." She pointed into the air. "Meanwhile, we have two hundred and twenty horses raring to go."

For the first time in her life, Bess looked helpless.

"It's quite easy," Steven said brightly. "Lea's taking them out and I'm going to be her assistant."

Not only did Bess agree at once, Hubert saw that the idea bucked her up. "Take my hack, Leander," she said.

"She's already got him saddled," Steven grinned, skipping out of range of the swipe Leander aimed at him.

After Steven and Leander had disappeared towards the yards, Hubert helped Bess out of her car. "Come inside," he said gently.

"Actually, I'm starving," she admitted, ashamed of herself. "I could eat a horse."

"Not one of mine, I hope," Hubert smiled, relieved to see that Bess found it mildly funny.

The kitchen was full of people. In her determination to get to Valerie Pepperdine and food, Bess ignored most of them. Elsie and Boggysevick, both looking worried and drawn, were given kisses; Amaryllis and Gideon were favoured with a nod, but Bess Hawksworth wanted bacon, egg, sausage, and anything else that was going. Once she was eating, everyone except Ann and Valerie drifted away. Sitting opposite Bess, Ann looked remarkably calm and well.

"Giles should be here by lunch-time," she said. "He was in touch after you left last night. Thank you for arranging that, Bess."

There was no need for a reply: Bess took a swig of tea from a pint mug and attacked two new rashers of bacon that Valerie had deposited on her plate.

691

"I'm so very sorry for the *terrible* things Oliver has done," Ann said. "You were right about him."

Bess took her time. "You mustn't blame yourself," she replied. "It's the system here. Every so often, it's bound to produce a wrong 'un. It's got nothing to do with breeding, or bad blood."

"I often wonder where Steven and I went wrong with our sons," Ann said, a sense of guilt threatening the courage with which she was facing the aftermath of Emma's abduction.

"Don't!" Bess said forcefully. "If you must blame something, try that lot out there." She waved a fork in the direction of the stable. "Your Steven did a magnificent job with it after the War . . . and there'll *never* be another season like nineteen-sixty. He had every right to assume that his sons would respect and follow him, but they had their own silly ideas."

"*Your* Steven doesn't," Ann said, profoundly thankful for the praise given to the husband she still revered after twenty-three years of widowhood.

"Ah . . . well . . ." Bess wiped the back of a hand across her mouth and pushed her empty plate away. "That's because of my secret weapon." She stood up, stretching. "I'm going to have a bath and get into some clean clothes."

At eight o'clock, she shut herself in the library to telephone Alain de Mourville. The House was a hive of activity as people continued to come in from the village to learn the events of the night. Rebecca, who had absorbed and interpreted all that Emma had to say, told Hubert of the part played by Helen: he listened in attentive silence, sadly proud of his half-sister. Amidst the incessant flurry of comings and goings, only Ann realised that Bess spent a very long time talking to Alain: it was over an hour before she emerged to announce that Alain's son, Laurent, was coming over to Cannings Ambo at once to help with any 'French' problems that Guillaume and Chaladon might have left behind. Rebecca said that Chief Superintendent Bradford would be very pleased.

Bess's mood was changing. In the kitchen, crowded again as breakfast was taken after the first lot, she swooped on

Steven and Leander, her head bowed between their shoulders to whisper. The two young people nodded, Bess smiled, kissed them both and beckoned to Hubert who was looking rather lost in the hubbub of life that was forced to carry on as normal.

They stood in the corridor, surrounded by the picture gallery. "Listen, Hubert, I'm clearing off for a couple of days," Bess said. "We must decide about Helen's funeral. Where do you think she should be buried?"

"Could it be here, in Cannings Ambo?" he asked hopefully.

"Absolutely! I think that's exactly right. I'll speak to Robert Frobisher before I go. What's wrong?" Hubert, very badly upset by Helen's death, suddenly looked annoyed.

"I wonder if I ought to invite that awful son of hers?" he muttered.

Bess had all but forgotten Miles Christopherson. "I suppose you ought to tell him," she said. "How old is he?"

"About twenty-five, I think." Hubert did not relish the prospect. However, his face brightened as he noticed the picture by which they were standing. It was Leander's eightieth birthday photograph, taken on 1 June 1940. Cradled in her arms she had Bess, whose first birthday had fallen that same day.

"What a long way it's been for you," Hubert said.

"And it isn't quite over yet," Bess replied. She kissed him. "I must get cracking, my dear. I'll talk to you the day after tomorrow."

Leaving Hubert pondering the possible significance of that word 'quite', she hurried to the office to find that Noel had finally turned up.

"Where have you been?" Bess demanded.

"Er . . . I'm sorry," he said, far from sure how to react to her strange mood. "Father called me out to help Henry and I didn't get away until three o'clock."

"You've had some sleep?" Bess inquired.

"Yes."

She seemed pleased. "Right. Give me ten minutes. Sit

down and behave yourself, but *don't* get involved in anything. Let Cathy and Henry do it all." With an encouraging smile, she dashed off to telephone Robert Frobisher and collect a few items from upstairs.

When she returned, a sports-bag over her shoulder, she clasped Noel's hand, obviously intent on taking him away. "Mr Timberlake is going to be missing for two days," she told Henrietta and Cathy, both of whom were gaping at her open-mouthed. "If you run into problems, Steven and Leander are in charge."

And, with that astounding statement, she dragged Noel outside.

"Leave your car here," Bess said firmly. "You won't need it."

"Where are we going?" he asked lamely.

Her look told him that, yes, it was a stupid question. "Your cottage, you fool!" she said. "It's time for a rest." Reconsidering this, she smiled. "At least, *I'm* going to have a rest . . . you're going to be working bloody hard!"

There was one more surprise. At the bottom of the drive, she turned right, not left, and dawdled along the Devizes Lane for half a mile, stopping at a point that had a good view of the gallops.

The second lot were coming out. Half-way down the line of one hundred and ten horses, Leander and Steven were riding together, deep in conversation. Suddenly, Leander urged her hack into a canter. As she passed the string, Steven fell back to the rear to join Arthur Merriweather. Orders were being given. Standing in the stirrups, Leander was chivvying lads and horses. As they all began to trot, the ragged casualness disappeared, replaced by order and discipline. Wheeling towards the lane to move them into a big circle, Leander must have seen the distinctive green Jaguar and realised she was being observed: she carried on as though she and the hundred-odd thoroughbreds were the only creatures in existence.

"A lovely sight," Noel said quietly.

"Yes." Bess took a last look. "She's not bad for an eighteen-year-old."

Bess Hawksworth and Noel Timberlake set off for Savernake Forest. There, he made love to her until she was forgetting the horror of the night and starting to believe that nothing as bad could ever happen again.

As sleep was claiming her, he saw a flicker of resolve cross her face.

"You've made up your mind?" Noel asked.

"I have."

"When?"

"It will be four years."

"That's a long time." Noel was sounding a note of caution, implying that things might go wrong.

Bess shook her head. "No, not really. And there'll be lots of good things to enjoy. You'll see . . . everything will work out."

As if to demonstrate her confidence, Bess fell asleep.

ENVOI

15 October 1994

'We tossed a coin for it'

The people of Cannings Ambo had always been part of Bess's good fortune and she admired them greatly. Yet, much to her amusement, they proved singularly lacking in discernment when it came to spotting what was there for all to see, as plain as a pikestaff, simple, and very beautiful.

In all fairness, there were excuses. Oliver's instigation of Emma's kidnap had given rise to powerful feelings of shame and anger. Although such sentiments were muted out of respect for Ann, most people felt that the eight-year prison sentence imposed on Oliver was on the lenient side. The stench of disgrace was slow to clear and folk were wary, looking over their shoulders for another dreadful event. As the unexceptional months passed, the absence of trouble generated relief: grateful for small mercies, Cannings Ambo did not expect a miracle.

Even the climate joined the conspiracy to conceal the facts. Spring, arriving early, was the most exciting seasonal rebirth for thirty years. Day after day of mild weather had the gallops riding to perfection in early March. The wiseacres of Church Green said it could never last, but it did, without a suggestion of night frost to dim the glory of the blossom in the orchard. By mid May, with the hedgerows a fragrant riot of wild flowers and the village street a green tunnel of lush foliage, Cannings Ambo seemed the most beautiful place on earth. It was a sumptuous, beguiling distraction from what appeared to be no more than the continuation of an alliance that had been going on for at least ten years.

A select few did have an idea. Amaryllis, Eileen Collier and Caroline Frobisher were convinced that there was definitely something in it. But the only person they felt able to talk to was Ann, and she stuck to the theory that had always obsessed her, investing it with a misleading authority.

"No, I'm sorry, that's pie in the sky," she said categorically. "Frankly, I wish it *could* be true, but it isn't, and there's no point in building up false hopes."

To their subsequent disgust, Amaryllis, Eileen and Caroline allowed themselves to be convinced.

The 1991 season was very average for Latimer's Barn, mainly because of a virulent bug that affected every horse, preventing any attempt to race in June and July. To make up for it, Bess was champion trainer in 1992 and 1993. During both years, no one was ever certain who was acting as her assistant. Wanting more time with her family, Rebecca slipped into obscurity, leaving Steven and Leander in the front line. However, to the outsider, there was never any clear idea of who was doing what. One day, Steven would be with Bess on the gallops while Leander took horses racing; the day after, Leander did both lots on her own, Steven went to the races, and Bess appeared to do nothing.

Bess finally let Ann into the secret on the evening of 30 June 1994, the day before Steven's twenty-first birthday.

"Steven and Leander are announcing their engagement tomorrow," Bess said over dinner in her upstairs suite. "It's going to be in all the posh papers."

Ann opened and closed her mouth several times without succeeding in making any sort of noise.

"There you are," Bess grinned. "That will teach you to ignore the glaringly obvious."

Ann seemed to be looking for an objection. "They're awfully young," was her ultimate, rather half-hearted offering.

"Only according to their birth certificates," Bess answered.

"Up here . . ." she tapped her forehead ". . . they're as old as the hills."

"Neither of them has ever looked at anyone else," Ann said, unsure of whether she was complaining, or commenting on something wonderful.

"There was no need," Bess replied. "They were made for each other. The absolutely marvellous thing is that they had the sense to realise it from the start – about fifteen years ago at a rough guess. *That's* how they showed the greatest maturity."

Ann stared at Bess shrewdly. "You've known this all along," she said. It was an affectionate accusation.

"Yes, guilty, I'm afraid."

"It's why you stayed after Giles left, isn't it?" Ann went on. "I remember you said something about watching them together."

"That *was* my main purpose at the time," Bess conceded. "Parting them would have been criminal." She smiled. "Of course, I'm glad I stayed for lots of other reasons."

"Tell me . . ." An amusing thought occurred to Ann. "Do Rebecca and William know about this?"

"Not yet." Bess glanced at her watch. "Leander and Steven will be breaking the news in half an hour."

"And Giles?" Ann asked.

"I'll ring him later."

"This is like a well-planned military operation," Ann said.

"It is, rather." Bess paused, gathering her thoughts. "The wedding will be on the fifteenth of October – that's the day after the Dewhurst and the end of our season. The honeymoon will be at Torquay, and they'll be taking charge of Latimer's Barn immediately afterwards. I shall be out of their way and gone before Christmas."

"Gone?" Ann straightened up, surprised and alarmed. "Gone? What do you mean?"

"I'm moving to another stable. At Chantilly."

"I see." Ann nodded as she considered it. "So, you've finally got fed up with us?"

"I deserve a change," Bess replied carefully. "And the very last thing that Steven and Leander will want is me looking over their shoulders all the time." Ann was content to accept what she knew was, at best, a half-truth. "This started four years ago with Laurent de Mourville," Bess explained. "He and some of his friends want me to look after about seventy horses."

"Where is this place?"

"It's Pierre Chapelon's old yard on the road to Senlis . . . you may have been past it."

Ann nodded, dim recollections of holidays with Steven in the 1950s and '60s stirring. "What are the arrangements?"

"I've bought it," Bess said.

"Good gracious!" Ann blinked. "Have you done *that* well out of Prospero?"

The French Derby winner left to Bess by Prince Omar had proved a popular stallion at Alain's stud near Deauville. "I had to add some of my savings," Bess smiled. "Henry chipped in, too. She's coming with me, by the way, and young Simon is going to be a trainer when he grows up."

"And Noel will be with you?"

"Definitely!"

Ann shook her head, bemused, still struggling to take it all in. "Shall you be competing against us?" she asked.

"Good God, yes!"

Ann was lost in thought for a long time. "Do you know, Bess, you've done something that no one in this family has ever managed in over a hundred and thirty years . . . you've given us *two* splendid young people who are capable of running the place."

"And the opposition won't see them for smoke once they get going," Bess said.

News of the engagement took the village by storm the following day. By lunch-time, it was being hailed as the event of the century, a resonant echo of that legendary 1881 marriage: nothing but good could come of it.

Even so, there was an element of something akin to dismay

699

at Bess's impending departure. Despite the bountiful gift of having a Leander and Steven Hawksworth in charge of the stable and village again, the evacuee from the East End of London, who had made good her promise to turn Latimer's Barn into the world's most famous racing stable, would be sorely missed.

Once the initial shock had been assimilated, however, Bess found that many of the staff wanted to go with her: they had no qualms about the future of Latimer's Barn, it was simply that their loyalty to her was so great. Because the stable at Chantilly had been allowed to run down since Pierre Chapelon left at the end of 1993, Bess was starting from scratch, but was reluctant to rob Steven and Leander of good hands. Not that there was any need; once the racing press had printed the story, there was a flood of telephone calls and letters from stable-lads who, for a variety of outlandish and disreputable reasons, fancied their chances in France. After careful discussion with her son and future daughter-in-law, Bess elected to take five of her existing crew to form the nucleus of whatever collection of misfits she eventually chose to forge into a team. The list was headed by Caesar, now in his mid-forties, and happily married with two young daughters. He was to be head lad in the new regime.

Amidst all the excitement, there was sadness. Elsie, widowed by Boggysevick's death in 1992, declined to be uprooted.

"No, love, I'm staying here," she said. "This place has been good to me and it's where I belong. Besides, I can't leave Stan . . . he's waiting for me in the bone-yard."

And dear old Solstice, the man who had taught Bess to ride and guarded her every move, was another who had to refuse.

"You've left it too late for me, ma'am," he said sorrowfully. "I'm seventy-four, and I'd best stay here where I'm known." His eyes misted over. "Twenty and thirty years ago, when you were tousling the bookies, I always thought you were after your own place. I'd have been with you in a flash. But now . . ." he summoned a sparkle of wry humour ". . . you can't expect me to cope with foreigners *and* funny food at my age!"

700

In response, Bess did something that he'd often day-dreamed about long ago, when they used to travel thousands of miles together: she kissed him. Ancient though he felt, Solstice Jackson discovered why she was able to command the attentions of young Noel Timberlake.

The wedding-day, Saturday 15 October, dawned grey and foggy, but by nine o'clock, the sun had broken through. An hour later, it was one of those golden autumn days on which the village looked absolutely perfect.

Robert Frobisher, up since well before six to worry about the most momentous event in his career as Rector of Cannings Ambo, was in the church while the mist still clung to the water-meadows along the River Kennet. A dozen ladies were putting the finishing touches to a lorry-load of flowers that had taken most of the previous afternoon to bring in and arrange.

Robert knew that he wasn't a particle of use. He was getting in the way and deserving the looks of irritation. Event-ually, after tripping over the chancel steps, upsetting a floral masterpiece in the process, he went home to try Caroline's patience. As he did so, Amaryllis waved from the lane. Her early-morning constitutional had already detected signs of hectic activity at both Latimer's Barn and Rose House.

The first of the guests, those who had travelled long distances and stayed in the area overnight, began to trickle into church at ten-fifteen. The ushers, formidably led by Leander's brother, Matthew, set to with a will.

By quarter to eleven, with the locals arriving *en masse*, it was apparent that there would soon be standing-room only. At ten minutes to, Steven, together with his best man, young Hubert Prideaux, slipped into the front pews. Bess squeezed her son's hand, almost pleased to see that, for once, his nonchalance had deserted him.

Imperceptibly, the great congregation of over five hundred fell silent. At one minute to eleven, the hush was unbearable. People seemed to have stopped breathing, no one dared look round.

The clock in the tower sounded the first stroke and the longest sixty seconds in Cannings Ambo's history ended as Leander's grandfather, John, a doughty organist, launched into the Bridal March to announce her prompt arrival.

Especially in the shaft of sunlight that slanted through the south windows to greet her, she looked breathtaking. Only the most attractive of women with a perfect figure could have got away with such a simple dress that was, in the words of one slightly disappointed matron, "Pretty much straight up and down and hardly a train to speak of." As with her namesake in 1881, Leander Flamsteed had her face uncovered, and the lace head-dress was held in place by a wreath of wild flowers. Her bridesmaids were Emma and three pretty little girls whose fathers worked at Latimer's Barn. To her left, William looked so pleased with himself that Rebecca thought he was in danger of exploding.

Steven and Hubert, visibly moved, rose to meet her. Everyone took their positions. Robert Frobisher, in his most mellifluous and resonant voice, began the service, the good, old-fashioned version of 1662.

Steven's nervousness soon left him, although he was unable to enjoy the rich cadences of the liturgy with quite the same relish as his bride. Her declaration: "I, Leander, take thee, Steven, to my wedded husband, to have and to hold from this day forward, for better for worse, for richer for poorer, in sickness and in health, to love, cherish and obey, till death us do part, according to God's holy ordinance; and thereto I give thee my troth," was delivered with great gusto. She added a little something to 'troth', leaving no one in any doubt that she understood the full meaning of the lovely old word and set great store by it.

Robert pronounced them man and wife and there was a rousing attack on the hymn, 'For all the Saints, who from their labours rest'. At the line: 'But lo! there breaks a yet more glorious day', Leander turned to look at Bess. The two women, both Hawksworths by marriage, exchanged glowing smiles.

After they had been to the vestry to sign the register, Leander stepped aside from her grandfather's rumbustious efforts with Mendelssohn's Wedding March to go first to her parents, then to Steven's. Each received a kiss and a whisper. When it came to Giles's turn, he was relieved to see that his daughter-in-law appeared to have forgotten that she had once considered him an idiot.

"Bless you for coming, Uncle Giles," she murmured.

"My dear, it's a very great pleasure," he replied.

Radiating happiness and sheer high spirits, Leander Hawksworth set sail down the aisle on the arm of a young man who was so full of pride that he looked close to tears.

The bun-fight in the big workshop behind Rose House was a constant stream of delights. Both Bess and Ann were glad to see that Giles, accompanied by Jane, the wife with whom he had indeed found permanent contentment, was given warm acceptance as a true scion of the village. Oliver had created a vacuum that needed to be filled and Giles was, of course, the groom's father, a matter on which the newest Mrs Hawksworth was given opportunity to comment.

"Well, at least you approve of my son," Giles said as they laughed together in a family group.

Leander regarded him with the utmost seriousness. "You're like a lot of horses," she said. "Hopeless on the racecourse, amazingly good at stud."

Waiting for the uproar of mirth to die down, Giles added a postscript. "If I'd been a racehorse, I'd never have been allowed within miles of such high-class fillies as Bess and Jane."

When all the speechifying and toasting was finished, Leander and Steven moved round to make their farewells: two o'clock, the time they had stipulated for their escape, was approaching. Gideon had an important question, one that everyone was dying to ask: "Which of you is going to hold the licence?"

Steven looked at him soulfully, waiting for the silence

that enveloped the workshop to deepen until a pin might be heard. "My wife will," he said. "We tossed a coin for it. I lost!"

In the applause and laughter, nobody really believed him. Of all the descendants of Giles Flamsteed, the Greenwich wine-merchant, none would require less prompting than this couple as to what was meet and proper. At long last, Latimer's Barn was to be openly and officially under the control of a beautiful, self-possessed young woman called Leander Hawksworth. It was planned that in three or four years when the children began to arrive, Steven would take over, but that was something that the spectators to the joys of 15 October did not need to worry about.

At eight o'clock that evening, Bess was in the library, preparing to carry out one of her last major duties at Latimer's Barn. Before handing the Big Book over to Steven and Leander, she had to record their marriage. After nearly an hour of jottings on scraps of paper, she was ready to start. She began a new page, number 603 of the 960, making the tome good for at least another fifty years. She wrote the date at the top and underlined it. A final fidget with the blotting-paper, and she was off.

The true Heirs to Adventure, Leander Flamsteed and Steven Hawksworth, were married at 11 o'clock this morning in the Church of St Luke and St John, Cannings Ambo. The Reverend Robert Frobisher performed the ceremony before a very large congregation of family and friends. The bride was given in marriage by her father, William Flamsteed, of Rose House. The best man was Lord Hubert Prideaux, Marquess of Glastonbury. The bridesmaids were Emma Flamsteed, Lucy Middleton, Elisabeth Farrant and Joanna Pilgrim. Afterwards, a reception was held . . .

When it was finished, Bess went outside and savoured the wistful scents of the still, autumn evening. She had devoted nearly thirty years to Latimer's Barn, sharing every one of its triumphs, disappointments, and catastrophes. Most people

704

said that she had saved the place, unaware of the million to one chance that had brought it about. If the Duchess of Laverstoke had found someone else on Chippenham railway station that day in 1939 . . .

DEREK NICHOLLS

THE BLUE RIBAND

From Ireland to the rolling Berkshire downs and the blue-grass country of Kentucky, from sleepy country courses to the dazzle of Ascot and finally Epsom, winning the Derby had been his grandfather's unfulfilled dream.

When Edward Manning takes over the old man's racing stables in Ireland, he realises that the dream has become his own. But it could only ever be made to come true with the help of women – especially the beautiful Caroline.

'Horse racing's *Gone With The Wind*'

Newcastle Evening Chronicle

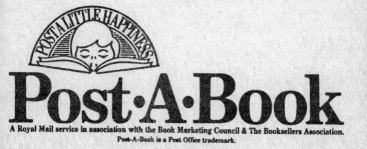

Post·A·Book

A Royal Mail service in association with the Book Marketing Council & The Booksellers Association.

Post-A-Book is a Post Office trademark.

DEREK NICHOLLS

WITH MAGIC IN HER EYES

"Derek Nicholls writes with style and wit and his characters are wonderful. I love them all."
ANN VICTORIA ROBERTS author of *Louisa Elliott*

As a girl, she was a rebel. As a woman, she was a leader, a lover, a mother. But always, she was a fighter.

Leander Flamsteed was destined to rule the great racing stables built up by her father and to become the central figure in an unforgettable family.

Through the pomp and circumstance of the Victorian era to the tragedy of the Great War and on into the middle of our century, *With Magic in her Eyes* is the enchanting story of a vibrant heroine and her times.

HODDER AND STOUGHTON PAPERBACKS